THE DRAGON LEGACY

The Secret History of an Ancient Bloodline

A Collection of Essays on the Deresthai Culture with
Accompanying Extracts from the Dragon Court Archives
Comprising the Official History of the Dragon Peoples

By

HRH Prince Nicholas de Vere

Sovereign Grand Master—The Imperial and Royal Dragon Court
and Order of the Dragon Sovereignty

Introduction by
Tracy Twyman

Produced in conjunction with:
Societas Draconis and Ordo Lapsit Exillis ☨

Published 2004
The Book Tree
San Diego, CA

ISBN 1-58509-131-6

Edited by
HE Prince Martin Lunn

Layout and Design
Atulya

Cover by
Brian Albert

Graphics by
Michael Hunter

Published by
The Book Tree
P O Box 16476
San Diego, CA 92176

Frontispiece

The Beast, the Dragon, the terrible monster, is the disguise of the beloved; the horror to be overcome itself is, or contains, the Reward. Beauty and the Beast must be conjoined. The old tag that a serpent becomes not a Dragon save by devouring another serpent, has an Alchemical sense:

These are the two Dragons, male and female: they destroy one another, or one destroys the other and a new and mightier one is born, a fiery wonder: A Phoenix (traditionally depicted as having red and gold plumage), a leaping glory, a STAR of dream ascending to the throne of the world. This was the Transmutation, the Great Work of the hidden glory of perfection.*

—Arthur Machen, Fr.GD.
(Frater of the Hermetic Order of the Golden Dawn)

The mating of Ravens is the rhythmic inhalation and exhalation of the breath of Ravens, one by the other. And in this way are the children of Ravens fashioned. (The Raven is the Phoenix of the Elven Kings).

—Traditional country folklore (England)

* The red and gold field, traditionally symbolising the plumage of the Phoenix— superimposed by the white Star—are the Arms of the Vere. Supported by two Dragons, they historically have become one of the Seals of the House. Red and gold are also the colours of other descendants of the Merovingian dynasty, including the Planagenets, the Mandevilles, the Spencers and the pre-Jacobite Royal House of Scotland.

Acknowledgements and Credits

The author would like to acknowledge, thank and/or credit the following people for supportive and corroborative source material and for their encouragement throughout the years. These will be added to as time marches on. Anyone who feels that they have been forgotten should contact the writer and the oversight will be rectified if your work has been consulted.

Carol Thomas, Elizabeth Ward, Ian Inskipp, Jiddu Krishnamurti, Richard Dufton, Michael Hunter, Christopher Murray Hall M.A. (Sussex University), Kenneth Grant O.T.O., Ward Rutherford, David Wood, Yatri, Pennethorne Hughes, H.T.F. Rhodes, Yuri Stoyanov, David Barker, George Riley-Scott, Peter Anderson, Sabine Baring-Gould, Ulick Bourke, Ean Begg, Margaret Murray, Richard Gregory, Drs. Walter Pierpaoli & William Regelson, Miranda Green, Vivian Green, David Day, Prof. Ray McNally, Austin Osman Spare, George Woodcock, Verily Anderson, James Anderson, Prof. Morton Smith, J. H. Brennan, Francis Israel Regardie, Francis King, Colin Wilson, MacGregor Mathers, Jack Parsons, John Matthews, Alphonse Francois Donatien de Sade, Aleister Crowley, Karl and Groucho Marx, Bazza Gardner, Barry Gardner, Robin Crookshank Hilton, Brian Albert, Tracy Twyman, Baphomet, my dear and much respected cousin The Archduke Hugh Mac An Mhaoir of Bourbon, Jehovah: author of the best-selling novel *The Holy Bible*, and a bunch of Irish and Welsh Monks for variously fiddling with the *Annals of Irish History* and for committing to parchment the *Mabinogion* and the *Liebher Gabhalla* and last, but certainly not least, for her long suffering: Professor Syndercombe Court and my Vere cousins, whose genetic makeup defies explanation. Much information was taken extensively from our family records. Otherwise, inspiration for this work was derived from the application of the Derkesthai phenomenon.

For more information about the subjects discussed in this book, go to:

www.nicholasdevere.com

www.thedragonsociety.com

www.dagobertsrevenge.com

- Contents -

INTRODUCTION

Blood Victory*: Hope for the Future of Our Race and Civilization

by Tracy R. Twyman

I first heard of Nicholas de Vere on an internet chat group; typically an environment where people pretend to be something they are not, using their anonymity as an excuse to behave even more boorishly than they do in real life. On this chat group, we had recently been discussing the theories presented in Laurence Gardner's book *Genesis of the Grail Kings*. The list was suddenly flooded with emails declaring that Mr. Gardner's work was not to be trusted because he had once been involved with the unscrupulous "Nicholas de Vere", or, as one detractor called him, "Tom Weir." The gist of the claim was that Mr. de Vere, who said he was a member of the "Grail bloodline" (the subject of the discussion list) had fabricated a royal genealogy, invented a royal magical order called "The Dragon Court", which he bogusly declared to be ancient, and stood to make lots of money by selling admission to this order, as well as the sales of his book, *From Transylvania to Tunbridge Wells* (now called *The Dragon Legacy*)—a book which, according to the emails, was utter nonsense and not worth reading.

Being the individualistic type that I am, my natural inclination upon being told not to read something by self-serving know-it-alls is to seek it out immediately. This I did, easily locating Nicholas de Vere's book, which was, at that time posted for free in its entirety on the Dragon Court website—hardly the act of an unscrupulous con man wishing to make big bucks off of a bogus claim. I printed out the entire thing and sat down on my bed to read, highlighter in hand to mark off anything important. A day and a half later, I had slept little, consumed lots of coffee, and was sitting in front of a manuscript half-covered in pink highlighter. For the first in my life, I had discovered another person who thought exactly the same way I did about the Grail, and the Grail bloodline. Everything within this book corroborated the theories, speculations, and ideas that we had been writing about in a book of my own, many of them ideas that I had held for a long time, but never been able to prove. Yet here was a man claiming to speak for that very bloodline and ancient tradition which I had been studying, and stating with assuredness what I had been hesitantly proposing.

* The title of this essay comes from a song of the same name by the English band Death in June.

De Vere painted a picture of the beginnings of the Grail bloodline in an antediluvian civilization, with a super-human, red-haired race of Grail kings that conquered and ruled over the primitive hordes of the ancient world, with tribes on each continent. It provided the royal houses which guided the destiny of all civilized man. They were overseers, "navigators", directing the affairs of the world with the Solomonic wisdom inherent in their blood. They watched over a perfect caste-ordered society, in which all people worked and lived within their proper station, creating a harmonious, inter-dependent and respectful relationship between the classes. They created all of the traditions, customs and institutions upon which civilization depends, and of which our current traditions, customs and institutions are pathetic bastardizations. In fact, I would assert that the Dragon tradition has proven to be the very definition of "tradition" itself.

As amazing as it was to find these ideas, identical to my own, in de Vere's unpublished manuscript, what was truly astounding were the more metaphysical aspects of the theory, again chillingly close to my own ideas. To de Vere, it is the blood itself which provides the basis for the "divine right" of Dragons to be the overseers of society, and this is what sets them apart from the rest of humanity, as gods are from mortals. This is the reason why, originally, they refused to mate outside of their race, and the reason why, later, they indulged in blood-drinking rituals in which the sacred Grail DNA could be consumed. But perhaps most amazing of all, de Vere states that Grail blood contains genes specifically programmed for "magic."

Dragons, and only Dragons, can perform magic, and are therefore the only authentic Witches, according to de Vere. For that reason, magic has always been an exclusive, secretive, royal art, and those outside of the bloodline attempting to perform such experiments are doomed to failure. We see these failures walking amongst us everyday, and we can smell the mixture of self-pity and patchouli oil a mile away.

This book lays down for the first time the scientific principles behind the effective use of ritual magic, and why some "magicians" are more effective than others. It explains the significance of the "Grail bloodline", irrespective of modern pseudo-intellectual theories and religious doctrines. It reveals the true import behind age-old tales of Vampires, Elves, Fairies, etc. It gives a reasonable explanation for the otherwise inexplicable course of man's history, all the way back to the Golden Age of the gods, and man's fall from the grace of the natural state of affairs. It lays down the principles behind a fair and ordered society; something we once, during the Golden Age, took for granted. It sets the foundation for a true understanding of man's natural hierarchy, and issues a death warrant for civilization should this fail to occur.

De Vere writes from the perspective of a lone wolf, a man who fears neither death nor life, and lives for the purpose of being. He writes to satisfy his personal impulse towards self-expression; to put the truth as he sees it down on paper—not to convince anyone else. He is a self-contained entity. He needs nothing and no one outside of himself. Yet he represents and defends the worldview of an entire race of men—or, shall I say, "overmen"—with whom he shares a genetic, familial relationship. To him that is the only human relationship that fully counts, that truly deserves the superior man's time, effort and emotion. All else is the puerile sentimentalism of the degenerate masses. Beyond his loyalty to his kinfolk, de Vere's true fidelity lies with the order of the universe, and that transcendental principle which ordinary men know little of but refer to blindly as "God." De Vere is an iconoclast, an eccentric genius. He has all the qualities of the great writers and thinkers of history. In his philosophy I put him on the same shelf as Julius Evola, or maybe next to Oswald Spengler. His historical perspective places his work amongst classics like Ignatius Donnelly's Atlantis: *The Antediluvian World*, or L.A. Waddell's *The Makers of Civilization in Race and History*. His encyclopedic knowledge of occult traditions, their true meanings and origins, is superior perhaps to that of A.E. Waite, Manly Hall, or Israel Regardie. In the future, this book will be indispensable to all serious students of the true occult tradition.

*"**Hekas hekas este bebeloi!**"*
("Begone, begone, ye profaners")

It is safe to say that nothing is sacred in the writings of Nicholas de Vere, except that which is, by nature, sacred, because it pertains to that which is pure spirit. He does not reserve any pity for the sensitivities of pathetic liberalisms, and makes mincemeat of the modern pseudo-religions: The Cult of Children*, the Cult of the Goddess, the Cult of the Oppressed, the Cult of Equality, and the Cult of Economy. Likewise ritualistically slaughtered are the supposedly "right wing" and "conservative" cults such as those of Race, Religion, and Nationalism. This book is likely to anger people; namely:

a. Liberals will not like this book because it dares to point out that not all men are created equal, nor are all men necessarily members of the same species. It shows that nature has assigned a caste system to various types of people, and that society works better when those castes are kept intact. People are happier when not forced, expected, or encouraged to live either above or below their natural station in life.

b. Catholics will be upset by what de Vere has to say about their holy institution. They will also not be pleased with De Vere's lax attitude towards such contentious issues as incest, homosexuality, cannibalism, blood-drinking, and human sacrifice.

*It is well-known in the advertising industry that any product or idea can be sold by implying that the "children of the world" will somehow benefit. This assertion is usually followed by the sickening catchphrase "children are the future", as if every sniveling rug rat were somehow paramount to the continuation of time. In reality, "the future" may be found in only a fraction of a percent of those children, and feeding an out of control population of degenerates is not going to further any worthwhile goals.

c. New Age people will be upset to read, from someone who clearly knows what he's talking about, that their incense, candles and figurines are nothing more than a drain on their bank account. (This bank account undoubtedly came with a personalized dragon-themed checkbook that says "The Goddess is alive and magic is afoot.") The reason for this is because the vast majority of these people are physiologically incapable of performing magic, according to de Vere.

d. White supremacists will be upset because, as tempting as it will be for them to connect their cause to the Dragon heritage, they won't be able to. De Vere describes the kinfolk which these people come from as slave races fit mostly for field labor. He also dismisses out of hand their precious "Fatherland" idea and their pathetic nation-worship.

e. Finally, de Vere assures me that his work will be offensive to those upper-crust Englishmen and "tinker nobility" who still uphold the farce of Victorian values and artistic tastes. Being an American, I am not exposed to "Victorian values" very often, so I cannot comment on this matter any further.

"After a long sleep, the same theories reappear. Without doubt they return richer and with new clothes, but the foundation remains the same, and the new mask which they wear should not mislead the man of knowledge."
—Le Serpent Rouge

De Vere's manifesto portrays a rather pessimistic attitude towards the idea of social progress, implying that the Golden Age of Dragon hegemony is forever lost, never to return. This is something with which I do not agree. In fact, I can see de Vere's book playing the role of the revolutionary harbinger, welcoming back a lost era. The word "revolution" implies revolving, returning in a circular pattern to the original starting point, like the labyrinthine spiral of history which Nick discusses later in this volume. All of the points in history therefore issue from, and are based upon the unchanging center, that which is "a priori", like the snake biting its tail which the Dragon Court uses in its insignia. Nature has a way of correcting imbalances, of restoring elements to their rightful place. Yet before that can happen, we must all be reminded of what the natural order actually is.

Pseudo-intellectuals like to annoyingly quote the tired adage, "Those who forget history are condemned to repeat it." I say that unless we are reminded of the Golden Age of history we will be unwilling, unmoved, and unable to replicate it in our modern era. This book is like a spell calling forth the forces that ruled thousands of years ago, calling them back to once again hold dominion over us.

Within the pages of this volume we, as Dragons (and I consider myself among them), declare our intention to take back what is rightfully ours. If the powers of God and nature are on our side, how can we fail? "Might is right" is a popular motto amongst those who label themselves "Social Darwinists." While the principle holds true, a more proper way to express it would be to say that "right is might". That is, if you are acting righteously in accord with what is right for you, attempting to take hold of the power that is rightfully yours, nature will equip you with the might necessary to accomplish that task. Materialism is the lie, brought to the forefront by the mercantile class so loathed by de Vere, which has caused the decay of society to its current level.

People have whole-heartedly swallowed the assertion that "money is power" (outdone only by the equally offensive "time is money.") Even those who have attempted to rebel against materialism, such as the Hippies of the '60s era, or the Communists of the 20th century, have always fallen into the materialist logic trap. They mistakenly believed that the problem of materialist elitism could be cured by redistributing the material wealth of rich people, and preventing the accumulation of wealth, as if wealth itself were the problem, instead of the people who own it. Foolishly they chanted slogans like, "There is no war but class war", and made statements like, "Every war in history was fought over money", when in fact almost every war can be traced back to a spiritual origin, a conflict between deeply held beliefs, ideas, and cultural norms.

It may be true that, as a general rule, those with true power use that power to acquire wealth, and that those who are wealthy often use it to empower themselves. But the fact is that the two concepts—money and power—are two entirely different things. Money is a tool. It can be a reward for goods or services provided, a means of acquiring things that are needed, and a way of enabling projects to come to fruition. If it weren't for the fact that certain people have acquired large sums of money, nothing of any consequence would ever happen—no wars, no monuments, no research and development. But removed from the context in which it is being used, money is meaningless. It is a purely contingent phenomenon. Power, however, is something transcendental. Unlike money, it is not something that was invented by mankind as a means to an end. It issues directly from God, and from Nature herself. There is such a thing as power for power's sake; and power, in the civic realm, is based on sovereignty, which comes from the blood. Therefore, true power resides not in a person's bank account, but in their DNA. There it rests within most of us, potential energy waiting to be converted into kinetic energy through actual use. But most people are too weak of will, too lazy and unimaginative to make use of it. Even many people of the Dragon blood have sunk into this abyss of uselessness.

But the time for rest and relaxation is over now. We are charged with the responsibility of saving civilization, as the only people who are clear-sighted enough and capable of doing so.

"Cease to Resist!"
—The Beach Boys, *paraphrasing Charles Manson*

This book is part of a literary zeitgeist currently in manifestation that is destined to usher in a new era amongst the intelligentsia of the Western world, something I have termed "the Renaissance of the Arcadian Mystique." Already much of the groundwork has been laid by the popular Laurence Gardner books *Genesis of the Grail Kings* and *Dragon Realms of the Ring Lords*. These titles share much common ground with this book, *The Dragon Legacy*, which was completed in an early form back in 1997. But there is much work yet to be done. The job of writers, artists and philosophers such as de Vere and I is not to bring about the political revolution which looms on the horizon. That is the job of the men of action who belong to our cause, the born leaders of the Dragon blood who have been waiting and planning in the shadows for centuries, patiently plotting and manipulating in anticipation of the opportunity to act. They need no help in that regard. Rather, it is the job of the literary and artistic set to effect the intellectual revolution, which must precede the political revolution. It is our job to clear the path ahead, to prepare the hearts and minds of the populace for what is to come, and to erase all fear, doubt, and resistance.

We need not worry that the ideological climate is so seemingly hostile to the values of blood, spirit, and hierarchy that we promote. The masses have no will of their own, beyond that which is given to them by those who assert themselves as their superiors. We live in a multi-national culture that considers taking on a new ideological system to be equivalent to putting on a T-shirt. They will attach themselves to any idea which is effectively marketed so as to take advantage of their frail psychology. The occurrences on the 11th of September, 2001 proved that beyond question. Overnight, the American values of libertarian independence, personal freedom, an inherent "right to privacy", and a healthy mistrust of authority gave way to state-worship, rabid religious moralism, pithy sentimentality, and a general attitude of compliance towards "whatever's necessary to keep us safe." All that was necessary to achieve the result was to push the right buttons.

A Blue Light Special in the Marketplace of Ideas

We have been told that our democratic society is a free "marketplace of ideas." Since democracy is also capitalistic, it only makes sense that the "marketplace of ideas" embodies the same principles as our economy. The laws of supply and demand dictate what ideas are considered valuable, which beliefs are valid, and therefore which truths exist. By right of popularity, even the laws of physics can be accepted, rejected, or altered at will.

But most ideas are cheap, worthless, crap; both the popularly-held ideas and the majority of the rebellious "counter-ideas" presented by the numerous "counter-cultures."

Better that the intellectuals of today all dedicate themselves to promoting and exploring a single priceless, transcendental idea. They can then find the best ways to defeat all competing, inferior ideas, rather than wasting their lives trying to come up with their own original (they dream) bad ideas, or, worse yet, trying to promote a conglomerate of meaningless and contradictory herd ideas which they regard as worthy by right of their popularity.

A book like this is meant to penetrate into the intellectual, educated class of society, sowing the seeds of Draconian ideals, on hopes that they fall on fertile ground, grow, and pollinate the popular culture a la "trickle down" theory. It is then up to the intellectuals who have been won over to our side to solidify the ideological revolution in the popular mind. All that is truly necessary for this to occur, once the literate set has been fully indoctrinated, is an eye-catching symbol, and a memorable slogan, then the constant repetition of these two in conjunction until no one can remember a time when these ideas had not been accepted and understood. It is not necessary to argue, debate, or defend these ideas, but only to assert them as the absolute truths that they are. Wishy-washy discussion which considers the merits of opposing views merely invites attack and ridicule. However, truths spoken with authority and confidence have the mesmerizing effect upon the populace for which we are aiming. Once they are willing to accept, even demanding a transition back to the old, true order, and Draconian traditional values, we can remove the tyrannies of democracy and capitalism, putting to bed once and for all this moronic concept of the "marketplace of ideas." There is but one real idea, and we must hold true to it unswervingly. When we vacillate, when we stop to consider alternative ideas, we lose. We must surpass the intellect of the populace and aim at the soul. Gustave le Bon wrote in *The Crowd*:

"All founders of religious or political creeds have established them solely because they were successful in inspiring crowds with those fanatical sentiments which have as result that men find their happiness in worship and obedience and are willing to lay down their lives for their idols".

This is the effect we are going for, and this monumental text put forth by Nicholas de Vere shall go a long way in promoting that cause. Thanks to him and to others like him (although there truly are no others like him), the future of the Dragon blood trembles with the awesomeness of its glorious potential. Our destiny awaits.

Fraternally,

Tracy. R. Twyman, E.G.M., O.L.E.
Editor, *Dagobert's Revenge Magazine*

The Imperial and Royal Dragon Court of the Dragon Sovereignty: Sarkany Rend 1408; Curia Regis et Ordo Draconis

The Imperial and Royal Dragon Court of the Dragon Sovereignty intends to continue to publish individual aspects of its history, along with references to the classical folklore and mythic customs of Europe and Asia which are directly linked to the Dragon tradition.

We trust that readers of this work will find the given details sufficient to cement the facts pertaining to the "Dragon" peoples, the Dragon Sovereignty and its Court.

As defined within the main body of the following text, the Imperial and Royal Dragon Court represented herein, legitimately recognised as the Sovereign Court of The Sovereign Dragon Nation by the relevant and appropriate Government of a European Member State, is a closed fraternity of individuals, representing those who trace their ancestry and affiliations back to the ancient Grail and Dragon families.

A Closed Fraternity

When the Imperial and Royal Dragon Court was reconstituted by King Sigismund in 1408 as the Societas Draconis, it was based upon an ancient bloodline tradition which Sigismund assumed that he had inherited from his presumed Egyptian and Scythian ancestors through the Pictish, Dragon Princess Maelasanu of Northumbria and the Ancient and Original Angevin Royal House of Vere of Anjou, the Imperial Dukes of Angiers.

This line had descended through the Tuatha de Danaan (the Dragon Kings of Anu) on the one hand, and the Egyptian Dragon Dynasty of Sobek on the other. The latter strain included the bloodline of the Davidic House of Judah who married into the descent of the Merovingian Kings of the Franks.

Human Vanities

Emperor Sigismund (as he was styled from 1410) was a son of the House of Luxembourg—dynasts who flagrantly altered their genealogy in order to be able to claim a fraudulent descent from this Dragon Dynasty of Maelasanu and Anjou. It is from this descent—from Maelasanu or Melusine—and upon her British, later Angiers-Angevin, Dragon Court, that Sigismund claimed the right to base Societas Draconis as a bloodline continuation of this ancient, prehistoric, anti-Christian, pre-Catholic, British Elven Institution.

One of the most famous members of Sigismund's misappropriated organisation was Vlad Basarrab or Draculea, the son of Vlad Drakul. After Draculea's death, his son Michael wrote that his father proudly claimed a linear descent from the Priests of the Dragon Court of Queen Sobekh Nefru of Egypt, whose predecessor Amenhemet had built the Dragon Labyrinth of Fayyum—dedicated to Sobekh—which was later copied in Crete as the Labyrinth of the Minotaur.

Dynastic Deceptions

The genealogy of the House of Drakul, Dracula or Basarrab is well known and widely documented. Descending from Atilla the Hun, this family was established in Central Europe by the sons of Ghengis Khan. No bloodline with which the House of Basarrab was associated or allied in marriage at that time had any affiliation with any extraction that was remotely related with the dynasties of Egypt.

It is obvious, therefore, that Draculea or Dracula must have been claiming an apostolic succession, a spiritual priestly lineage deferring to the Egyptian Dragon Court of Sobekh Nefru through Sigismund's assumed descent from Melusine. Her ancestry actually can be traced back to the Scythian Dragon Princess Scota, Queen Sobekh Nefru and the Egyptian Cult of the Dragon.

Undoubtedly Dracula assumed erroneously that he had received this ancient mystical honour during his investiture into Sigismund's Societas Draconis, and by virtue of Sigismund's supposed descent from Melusine and the ancient Angevin House of Vere. In his own right, Dracula can claim no relationship to any early Angevins, nor to the later second Anjou House of Plantagenet, except via an eight link marital bridge which has no alliances that relate him by blood to Anjou.

Sigismund assumed a personal entitlement to this legacy in 1397, the date upon which he sought to reconstitute Princess Melusine's Dragon Court—as

Societas Draconis—in a manner that he deemed the most suitable to enhance his power base and establish his royal claims. Following its subsequent formal inception in 1408, the Court recruited members from a number of prominent royal and noble houses. Historians have noted that these were not particularly known for their religious orthodoxy, including the later House of Vere in England, as one authority on Sigismund's Dragon Court has asserted.

Today, however, the Imperial and Royal Dragon Court itself exists as a closed fraternity, a collective of individuals, comprising those who, unlike Sigismund, can trace their ancestry and affiliations back to the ancient, pre-Christian Elven, Grail and Dragon families via Anjou. The Court retains the traditional three tier degree system that Sigismund borrowed and to which he appended three separate representations of the alchemical Ouroboros emblem for the distinct ranks of the Court. A fourth emblem, configured in the form of the Egyptian Ankh or Albigensian Cross, was used by the family officers of the Inner Temple.

The tripartite system was peculiar to the Scythians and Celts, whose Druids incorporated a similar structure within their orders and colleges. It later found expression within the Cathar fraternity of Languedoc and also with the Witches. It was developed within the Hierarchical Rule of the Knights Templar with whom the Court had a strong historical connection.

Blood Relationship

The Inner Temple is presided over by the Vere Grand Masters, who are currently resident in Britain and Europe. Being essentially an organisation which emphasises the crucial links between Dragon families, the rank system within the Court takes second place to the sense of blood relationship and the natural bond of co-operation engendered by that relationship. Service, mutual support and respect supersede those types of ambition and advancement which prevail in other bodies which might, on the face of it, resemble the Dragon Court model in some ways. Within such orders, sights are firmly set towards material gain through supporting establishments which themselves breed division and inequity.

The tenets of the Grail and Dragon traditions are implicit in defining that we should be at one with the earth, and cannot, therefore, presume dominion over it. Unlike those who wish to profit unjustifiably from dubious Merovingian descent.

This philosophy is embedded in the concept of individual gnosis, and lies at the very heart of the Draconian culture. It is evident in all aspects of life itself. Emanating from the ancient lore of the Elven Lords and Ladies of the

Forest, this ancestral legacy forms the bedrock upon which this and all legitimately related Dragon Courts were originally founded.

The Tinker Kings

It is no secret that, through a process of calculated indoctrination, our individual decisions are often prompted by fears of non-conformity or insecurity. As a result we are conditioned to purchase a variety of hyped goods and services in order to redress personal inadequacies that do not, in fact, exist. In reality, the prevalent forms of fear-based merchandising are little different from straightforward protection rackets, and yet they are sanctioned and encouraged by our governing establishments.

For centuries, western state authorities and their Churches have enjoyed continued power over a subordinate majority, by presenting a facade of sacrosanct jurisdiction which has seemed inextricably linked to some form of royalty, nobility, or government by divine sanction. By virtue of this, it is not surprising that so many people now consider royalty, nobility and western religion to be archaic components of a system of class and privilege which has no place in the modern age.

What few recognise, however, is that for centuries the perceived representation of royalty and nobility has, to a large extent, been a fraud perpetuated by a dressed up merchant class elite who have no real entitlement to their positions. This farce, with its inherent tyranny and social abuse, has been endured through the ages, while the true bloodline families have been suppressed and supplanted by traders and brokers disguised in crowns and mitres.

In practice, there is nothing noble about these tinker kings, since the word "noble" relates to gnosis or wisdom. However, they have long been defined as "aristocrats" (meaning "best rulers"), and have thereby retained gratuitous stations of power and influence in a self proclaimed higher echelon of society.

These tinker kings and their emissaries have plagued the western scene for generations, leaving all to wonder how it is that our supposed guardians and ambassadors are so often an embarrassment, and are rarely representative of community requirement.

They refer to all and sundry as "subjects", "commoners" and "flocks" using such patronising terminology as "the ordinary people" or "the man in the street", as if they had some predestined right of supremacy. In reality, the fact is that the individual establishments of these said aristocrats (be they state heads, provincial overlords or clerical governors) are frequently very questionable, and their personal roots are often more ordinary than most.

Mother Earth

Prior to these distortions, the nature of kingship was entirely different. There was no requirement for Church sanction through coronation by parvenu popes or archbishops. Kingship was founded upon the ideal that all people were adherents of the earth, and that the earth bestowed sovereignty upon its first born people, the Elven Tribes. They were represented by a Dragon Queen, and she empowered the Grail King, who could not be a king without her.

In this environment, the right to kingship emanated from the female, since Mother Earth was herself deemed to be female. The overriding function of a king and queen was to maintain a spiritually transcendent intelligence within the realm, thereby enabling the organism (the kingdom) to function and develop in symbiosis with its surrounding environment.

If a change of governmental practice is deemed necessary, then there is nothing to gain by swapping the merchant class nobles for lawyer class presidents. There is, however, much to be gained by considering the advantages of properly defined Grail kingship and the Messianic code of princely service within a socially orientated constitutional framework.

This is the most logical route towards ensuring that true democracy prevails for "Democracy" and is correctly defined as "Government for the people by the people", as opposed to the all too familiar and oppressive "Government of the people".

Opportunists and Orators

As a result of a general disenchantment, many now suggest that royalty and nobility should be marginalized in favour of republican style government. Some determine that such changes replace privilege with a more acceptable form of merit advantage. However, this perception is equally untenable in practice.

All that happens is that headstrong merchant class opportunists are replaced by polished lawyer class orators, thereby creating an unwarranted new elite, with the same destructive hold on society.

Government of the majority by an exclusive clique, which uses intimidating tactics to manipulate a consumer based economy, has nothing whatever to do with the time honoured spirit of Grail kingship and the Dragon blood. Any shift from monarchy to republicanism is simply a matter of different packaging. In the event, we are still captive consumers enveloped within faiths of fear. Our legacy from all this is an inbred contempt for anything which does not conform to a system of venerated sale values. This leads to the loss of our relationship with the ecosphere upon which all species truly depend.

The Grail

The practical application of the Grail Code of service and guardianship was geared to the hermetic principle, “As above, so below”. It recognised that no sane mind would, for the sake of short-term profit, disenfranchise the body upon which it depends.

From medieval times, however, this is precisely what has happened, with the Church installing dealers and merchants as puppet kings, traders who had no knowledge of kingship, but who have spawned dynasties which, in turn, have appointed their own colleagues as hereditary puppet nobles.

The Church and its appointees (be they monarchs, bishops or pseudo nobles) have proclaimed the Messianic legacy to be heresy. By doing this they have underwritten and promulgated tyrannical systems of elitism, separatism and environmental domination to the detriment of the many.

Out of Egypt

The Dragon Court can first be identified in Egypt under the patronage of the priest prince Ankhfn Khonsu in about 2170 BC. It was subsequently established more formally as a pharaonic institution by the twelfth dynasty Queen Sobekh Nefru (c.1785 BC).

The Court pursued the teachings of Thoth, which had prevailed from the time of Nimrod's grandson King Raneb, a pharaoh of the second dynasty. He reigned c. 2852 BC, about three centuries before the Gizeh pyramids are considered to have been built.

In those far off times, the priests and temples were not associated with religion as were their later successors in other lands, but rather more with the duties of preserving and teaching the old wisdom. The temples incorporated al-khame workshops. It was the obligation of the priests to maintain the spiritual welfare of the pharaohs, while ensuring the purity of a continuing royal bloodline which progressed through the Dragon Queens of the matrilinear Grail succession.

Dragon sovereignty had evolved in Egypt from old Mesopotamia and its tradition was vested in Sobek, the sacred crocodile (the messeh or mus-hus). It was from the practice of kingly anointing with the fat of the messeh that the Hebrew verb “mashiach” (to anoint) derived, and the Dragon dynasts became known as Messiahs (anointed ones).

In 525 BC Egypt was conquered by the Persians, whose kings were subsequently ousted by Alexander the Great's Macedonian army in 332 BC. This led to the Greek dynasty of the Ptolemies and the well-known Queen Cleopatra VII. Her liaison with the Roman general Mark Antony caused the final downfall of the pharaohs, and Egypt was subjugated by Imperial Rome shortly before the time of Jesus. At length, as the Roman Empire collapsed,

Egypt fell to Byzantine governors and then, after AD 641, to the sway of Islam.

The PenDragons

By that time, the Grail Dynasty from David and Solomon had progressed into the West, notably to the Merovingian kings of Gaul, while related branches established kingdoms in Ireland and Celtic Britain. These lines were linked through marriage to parallel Dragon strains from Ham, Japhet and Tubal Cain (which had survived as the royal houses of Scythia and Anatolia). The families had forged their own marital links with the early princesses of the Egyptian succession.

The first PenDragon (Head Dragon) of the Britannic Isle (Pen Draco Insularis). From this stock was King Cymbeline of the House of Camu, who was installed in about AD 10. The Celtic PenDragons were not father to son successors in a particular descent, but were individually elected from reigning family branches, by a Druidic council of elders, to be the overall Kings of Kings. The last PenDragon was Cadwaladr of Gwynedd, who died in AD 664. At around that time much of Britain fell to the Germanic influence of the invading Anglo Saxons and Angle land (England) was born, as distinct from Scotland and Wales.

This coincided with Byzantium's loss of Egypt to the Caliphs and following the last Roman Emperor in AD 476, a completely new governmental structure evolved in the West. Its ultimate overlords were the Popes, and outside the preserved Celtic domains they appointed kings not by any right of heritage, but to suit the political motives of the bishops and the fast growing Roman Church. It appeared that the days of the Dragon heritage were over. However, the true dynasts of the original Grail stock always upheld their positions and the spirit of the Dragon Court continued in influential circles throughout Europe and the Near East.

The Dragon and the Grail

As the generations passed, the ideal of dynastic kingship spread through the Mediterranean lands into the Balkans, the Black Sea regions and Europe. But, in the course of this, the crucial essence of the old wisdom was lost, and this gave rise to dynasties that were not of the true kingly race. Instead, many were unrelated warrior chiefs who gained their thrones by might of the sword.

The sacred culture of the ancients was, nevertheless, retained in the Messianic line of King David of Judah (c.1008 BC), whose significance was not in his generally portrayed descent from Abraham and the Shemite strain, but in his Pharaonic heritage.

It was through this particular Dragon inheritance that Solomon the Wise, some eight centuries after Queen Sobeknefru, was enabled to recreate the

Royal Temple project in Jerusalem. This led to a Holy Land revival of the pharaonic Rosi Crucis (dew cup) movement at a time when Egypt was beset by foreign influences, first from Libya, Nubia and Kush, and then from further afield.

As a result, the traditional marriage arrangements of the pharaohs and princesses gave way to diplomatic alliances. The symbol of the Rosi Crucis had identified the Grail succession from beyond 3000 BC, and its graphic representation was a red cross within a circle.

Societas Draconis

In 1408 (when Britain was in her Plantagenet era), the Dragon Court was formally reconstituted as a sovereign body at a time of wars and general political turmoil. As we have seen, the Court's dubious re-emergence was instigated by Sigismund von Luxembourg, King of Hungary. Having presumptuously and erroneously assumed to have inherited the bloodline legacy in 1397, he drew up a pact with twenty-three royals and nobles who swore to observe "true and pure fraternity" within the Societas Draconis, a style subsequently misidentified as the Ordo Draconis (Hungarian: Sarkany Rend).

Although the original Court was by no means an Order in the recognised chivalric sense, the misnomer was strategically retained for the purposes of identification.

Along with Sigismund and the twenty-three nobles, Sigismund's second wife, Barbara Cille (daughter of the Austrian Duke Hermann of Styria), was joint sovereign. Barbara was a Vampire who was taught by Ibrahim Eleazar, the keeper of the Sacred Magic of Abramelin the Mage, and it is she who is the model for the beautiful Countess Carmilla Karnstein in le Fanu's novel of the same name.

Sigismund's daughter Elizabeth was also a member of the Court, and the inclusion of the entire family thereby achieved the traditional overall standard of twenty six members or two magical circles of thirteen. Others prominent in the Societas Draconis were the Kings of Poland and Aragon, the Duke of Lithuania and the unrepentant heretic, the Duke of Split.

The founding document of the Court confirmed that members might wear the insignia of a Dragon incurved into a circle, with a red cross, the original emblem of the Rosi Crucis, which had identified the Grail succession from before 3000 BC. Members were required to wear black attire on Friday—the day ruled by Venus—and to all intents and purposes they were to hold property in common.

The Society had no patron saint, it had no chapel or chapter house and observed no feast or holy days. Members were expected to have been ennobled prior to entry and were only elevated within the Society in recognition of their contributions to the welfare of the Crown. Sigismund never knighted anyone into the Society. This ignored completely all the expected rituals and affectations of chivalry prevalent at the time. At least the Luxemburgundian got that right.

Imperial Status

Shortly after this foundation, Sigismund was crowned Holy Roman Emperor and, as a result, the noble fraternity achieved a heightened status as an imperial edifice. Although the Court's ancient origins were steeped in pre Christian lore, Pope Eugene IV was obliged to approve his Emperor's non Catholic establishment, for the nature of the Dragon, even if you fake it, is such that its kingly tradition surmounts the mundane constraints of denominational dispute. After all, King David, Solomon and even Jesus were all pre-Christian dynasts of the line.

There were, of course, those staunch upholders of the Church's articles of dogma who openly opposed the pre papal concept of Grail kingship.

These bishops pronounced the Arthurian romances heretical and blacklisted the writings of Merlin in 1546 at the Council of Trento in northern Italy. Everything that was magic to the ears, and all that was fresh air to the subjugated, became denounced as sinister and occult.

The great enlightenment of the "Grail Code" of service was condemned in a series of brutal Inquisitions from 1203, and anything remotely connected with the female Draconian ethic was justifiably dubbed Witchcraft.

The following series of essays, which could be alternatively titled *The History of the Dragon Peoples*, are extracted from archival and research material. The author derives its contemporary synthesis from a 30 to 40-year period of scholarship, teaching, revelation, and ceremony. The following collection of studies reflects the nature of the author's final conclusions in 1993 and at the time of publication in 2004, respectively.

This is the first book in a series of works covering the history of the Elven Tribes and the Dragon Tradition. Further works, due to be published here shortly, will include archaeological and historical studies of the *Derkesthai* Culture from 10,000 BC onwards, further material from the Dragon Archives, an ongoing series of novels and a series of scientific papers.

The ethos of the Dragon Culture encourages an intelligent, but above all a ruthlessly honest appreciation of the matters presented. We hope that this may expose the establishment's historical fabrications and deceptions throughout history which have harmed society immeasurably. We want to change the attitudes of the many who have been manipulated for the gain of a few for over one thousand years.

PART ONE

Foreword

Although it may appear elitist, when the old families observe that the Dragons are being misrepresented to the extent that everybody wants to become one, the time-honoured consensus of feeling among them is compounded. They see that it inevitably leads to a gap in the market being filled, resulting in yet another impudent impertinence being perpetrated. A good example of this is the detritus of Gerald Gardner which he presented in the 1950s as the “definitive” and “original” expression of the “Old Religion”. *Inauthentic Witchcraft emerged in the 1950's, principally at the instigation of this retired clerk in the Indian Raj named Gerald Gardner. It is from this particular source that the ridiculous notion of Witchcraft being primarily a fertility cult gained its credence.*

He sanitised what little he knew about Witches with exactly the same pecuniary, sexual or social motives that his descendants use for peddling their equally useless rubbish today. One can't “initiate” into the old blood or teach the old ways to the “mahoum”. It is a pointless and fruitless waste of time that doesn't work.

They inevitably get the wrong idea and discard its most valuable tenets. Alternatively, they add to that history or knowledge their own misconceptions which then become carved in stone and published in faddist popular books as the sacred wisdom of a faddist culture.

Naturally it would be appreciated if people identified sympathetically with the characters in the Dragon tradition, but not to the extent where every reader thinks that they are one, or can aspire to be one.

Most of them could never be. The courses or “initiations” which are on offer from the exploiters of the “New Age” money machine are sanitised to obliterate what could be termed a “dark” and hence possibly “evil” tradition. Such exercises will also inevitably lead to the discredit of the Dragon ethos. When such courses or “initiations” are found not to work, it is because the majority of participants either won't have the right blood serum or the right connections in their cerebral lobes.

We live in a world in which all people are encouraged to think of themselves (somewhat hypocritically given the way they treat each other); in homogenous, egalitarian terms. Therefore the foregoing statement is tantamount to heresy. It is unacceptable in ordinary society to suggest that people are not equal or physiologically and anatomically the same. But nevertheless they are not.

One might counter such an unreasonably deluded and elitist sounding statement by arguing that because of the out-breeding of the old families, there must be millions of people "of the Fairy blood" living today. However such a statement flies in the face of the following accepted historical facts:

a) The genuine old royal families rarely outbred at all, whilst the later, fake parvenu, tinker nobility with whom people now confuse them often did;

b) Most of the Scythian, Royal-Druidic, Fairy population in Britain and Europe was wiped out by the Romans in the Battles at Mona and at other Druidic sites;

c) The Celts (and what was left of the Scythian Fairy Families who served as their lords and protectors) were decimated by bubonic plague, starvation and the Saxon invasions in the 6th century. Following this, in Britain and continental Eurasia, the Church and the rats spent another three or four hundred years, during the medieval and Reformation periods, dispatching the survivors of the previous epidemics, famines, wars or persecutions.

d) That the Aryan Scythian Overlords—the Fairy High Kings and Queens—maintained a caste system that, although eventually became corrupt and overrun by the warrior caste, was arguably still in place (as the European Class System) until the Second World War. Even up until the First World War the manorial restrictions on the movements of rural labourers, other than during holidays, were still enforced and thus unhindered mobility, either geographically or within the class system itself, was extremely rare.

Throughout the period preceding the modification of the Witchcraft laws (now called "The Fraudulent Mediums' Act") the remnant of the Scythian, sacral-royal overlords who were left were destroyed by papal decree.

In the meantime, in Britain, in addition to the persecutions, many of the wealthier and more powerful overlords whose families had survived up to that point were killed off and/or replaced in both lands and name, by those merchant-class new tinker families. They, in turn, paid the corrupt ersatz royalty of the Tudor and Stewart Houses enough money for the titles and estates.

Following this sequence of events Oliver Cromwell continued the good work and massacred the nobility and allowed their estates to be usurped by even more members of the merchant-class.

Considering the sum of this state of affairs, it is extremely unlikely that any of the people in those classes whose descendants now patronise the "New Age" fads would have made contact with or intermarried with what was left of the pure Elven Blood-Royal. Therefore to say perhaps that it doesn't matter whether a few mercenary fly-by-nights open up preposterous courses, making ludicrous, false claims to be able to train and initiate "probationary Elves" or "grail maidens", is a denial of what the Fairy blood and the teachings are all about.

The descent and the doctrine of the Elven Families are based upon truth and honour. The comparison shows in sharp relief to what extent people today have already been betrayed enough over the centuries by their own kind.

If one presents people with the Dragon history in an over attractive candy-sweet wrapping or in such a manner as to make it seem as if anyone can belong to it, then one becomes a deceiver oneself. This would lay others open to psychological abuse, financial exploitation and manipulation at the hands of the "New Age Money Vampires", thereby adding yet another element to the mass psychological ignorance and confusion over identity that already contributes to so much social disquiet and unrest.

Unscrupulous advertising executives, politicians and manufacturers lead people to believe that they can be whoever they want to be and achieve anything they want to achieve. The only conditions are that they have enough money and work hard enough for the establishment's corporate elites. The object is to produce more efficient consumer-producers.

Class barriers have been relaxed only slightly for a couple of generations. It is likely that the vast majority of those who would like to prop up their egos and empower themselves (in a world that only encourages such in the financial sense) by becoming *Elven Magicians*, *Grail Maidens* or *Vampire Overlords* are going to be in for a big disappointment. It's no use saying that people don't think like that because they do.

Literally thousands of people in Britain and America have the impudence to call themselves Witches. Hundreds more join "magical orders" or associations. Thousands more annually sign up for mystical, "New Age" workshops in a plethora of inappropriate foreign disciplines unsuited to their cultural backgrounds. It can be guaranteed that none of them were ever asked about their family history which, after all, from an endocrinal point of view, is the most important criterion.

People don't realise that they have only just emerged from a social system which was corruptly used by the Church-State for centuries to engineer them into having specific brain physiologies which are not suitable for application to Dragon Subjects. If they were, then the majority of people would have transcended naturally by now anyway and the world would be an entirely different place.

They haven't, they can't, it isn't, and under the present circumstances, it never will be. Even if society were to interbreed more with the Dragon

Families that are left—if there are any at all—then the Dragon DNA would eventually become weaker. In this case the Dragon ability would then be lost, leaving us with exactly the same social result anyway.

The modern idea that potentially anyone can be "initiated" either as a Witch or a Druid is pretentious and arrogant. It has been, it is said, (in privately circulated Witchcraft documents*), a source of offence to many ancient families for over half a century.

Unless a full, genuine, known pedigree can be produced, demonstrating an unbroken line of descent from a royal, Archdruidic family, no modern aspirant or so-called priest or priestess has the right either to call themselves a *Witch* or a *Druid*. The same applies to those who would call themselves "Aryans".

The modern concept of "initiation into Witchcraft" is an insult to those whose families, over the period of the *Thousand Year Elven Holocaust*, died at the hands of the Church. Like Elven royalty and nobility, to which Druidism and Witchcraft are inextricably linked, both are aspects of the High Aryan Mana, the mystical maja or maia, the genetic memory of a unique race that is carried in the blood. This cannot be bestowed by any form of nonsensical neo-pagan nonsense.

The Royal Windsor Coven and many others, reputedly old hereditary family groups, were the custodians of traditions which had, by their own admission, little or nothing in common with the modern neo-pagan revivalist movement or its reconstructed rituals. The latter had been invented by Gerald Gardner and revised by Sanders and other "initiates".

These gentlemen, *The Marshmallow Papers* related, were, along with Crowley, rebuffed by Pickingill or by other covens that descended from those East Anglian septs which themselves descended from either the historical British covens or the Flemish weavers. Here it must be noted that Aleister Crowley was actually interested in Witchcraft. Isn't that a surprise? Considering the fact that his generation of "magicians" usually tended to repudiate it. Or did they?

Undoubtedly many "magicians" have justifiably poured scorn on modern Wicca but nevertheless, it still remains a recorded fact that Crowley attempted to join George Pickingill's group. Furthermore, one of Crowley's close

*During the late 1970's and early 1980's a series of privately published papers were circulated which contained material that originated from old Northern Covens and the "Royal Windsor Coven". One in particular—*The Marshmallow Papers*—contained a damning criticism of so-called Gardnerian and Alexandrian "initiatory" Witchcraft. This was followed by criticisms made to this author that stemmed from the leaders of the Baphometic Orders in London and the Black Country, who emphatically asserted that the only genuine form of valid Witchcraft was passed down through the blood.

associates, Austin Osman Spare, was involved in Witchcraft himself. We can perhaps see from Spare's work, *The Anathema of Zos*, why Crowley was so interested in Pickingill's pre-revivalist doctrine of the "Craft of the Wise".

In Spare's essay on traditional Witchcraft, or at least by his time, a late corrupted form of it, he describes it as an ecstatic, transcendent philosophy. He was familiar with, and variously employed, the strategies anciently used in so-called "high magic" to encourage the body to transport itself into states that were old territory for the Magi and the Druids, the Maenads and the Bacchantes.

Spare's account clearly demonstrates that Witchcraft had Tantric elements and was, like Crowley's system of "Magick", in the business of making "Ubaids" or "Overseers". This is poles apart from Gerald Gardner's media-friendly product of modern Wicca.

In examining Spare's work, we might learn why Crowley was so interested in Pickingill and then be tempted to ask where the Africans got *Vodun* or Voodoo, as it is known to us.

"New Age" paganism or Wicca repackages old hypocritical Christian moral values and symbols, and attaches products, services and books of no value whatsoever. These are promoted and marketed by business people whose only interest is in building up a captive client base of weak-minded individuals who are programmed to buy the next "soul-saving" product from them.

Soon "Les idiotes dans la queste pour la verité" discover that the last philosophical tin of beans or cheap crystal they bought from the High Gurus of the "New Age" does not work. Then these peddlars of kitsch "truth" tell them that their karma is wrong, or they "don't believe" it enough, or that they have a hostile attitude or lack of focus or some such excuse.

This deflects the blame from them and lays it firmly at the door of the luckless punter—following which they then recommend that the sap buy from one of these "Irreproachable Wise Ones" yet another Mystery of the Ancients ("at only $29.99") which will undoubtedly work this time.

And it never does and so they go back for another try. Real magic is at work here. A group of secretly initiated individuals are turning dross into gold. Fools give charlatans good money in exchange for utterly useless rubbish. Now that's alchemy!

The papers originating from the northern covens clearly revealed that Witchcraft prior to the Wiccan revival of the 1950's bore no resemblance to what passes for formulaic Witchcraft now, and was not pagan, fertility based or necessarily Goddess-led. Essentially it was and is the same as the Witchcraft sponsored by the Baphometic Orders who trace their lineage back through the Templars to Jesus' original teachings and the culture of the Druids.

The nearest approximation or identification in this particular instance would be between late 19th-century Northern British ritual and the French medieval, Cathar-sponsored Witch movement. In both these instances the central figure was the *Baphomet* and the highest sacrament of the “Sabbat” was the *Black Mass*. This had nothing to do with Satanism, which in itself, was and is a late, half understood non sequitur—manufactured by the Roman Church—that has nothing to do with the Dragon tradition.

Many so-called aficionados of the Occult, and especially those who like to call themselves Witches in public, maintain that “The Black Mass was Satanic”. They go on to say that white Witchcraft or *Wiccecraeft*—as they like to call it—“has nothing to do with Satanism and the Black Mass, which are a parody of Catholicism and the Catholic Mass”. They squawk—off pat and by rote—like trained parrots, whilst the Church Fathers grin gleefully when they see how well their propaganda has taken root.

The Wiccans' or neo-pagans' agenda here is to try and convince as many people as they can that they are mysterious and somehow superior to others without actually saying as much. They themselves think—and would like other people to think—that they belong to an ancient tradition or fraternity with knowledge to which the public isn't party. They want to impress upon people further—before those people are tempted to start throwing big bricks through witchy windows—that Witches are really nice people and that true “Wiccans”—(whilst still trading off the dark and slightly dangerous allure evoked by the word *Witch*)—deal solely with “white” magic.

In this way the attention seekers hope to become more popular or respected by being surrounded by some aura of mystique that they consider in their own minds to be “cool”. They've seen Witches on television no doubt. They believe that by jumping on the bandwagon and choosing that particular persona, out of the many that are on offer at a price, it will make people think they are special and hence attractive.

The big stumbling block here is that *Royal Witchcraft*, or Witchcraft proper, from the early Dark Ages onwards owes as much to its clearly Christian, as it does to its direct Druidic, origins. Both in their original form, in the publicly disseminated opinion of the Catholic popes, were and are Satanic. Jesus' heredity—and the descent of the Druidic dynasties—both derived from an identical Dragon nascence that the Roman Catholics decided was devilish, because the descent of both bloodlines was from the Sumerian Enki who was the Akkadian Samael: the Roman Lucifer and thus the Catholic Satan.

In Jesus' case the Roman Church, as do all outsiders who know they are on to a good thing, sanitised his rituals and concealed his descent. All those who continued to follow Jesus' original teachings—like the Witches—they burned as "heretics". This notwithstanding, the Wiccan apologists still try to tell us that Witchcraft has nothing to do with Christianity but is a pre-Christian fertility religion.

However, the word "heretic" was only used by the Inquisitors to specifically define those heterodox Christian beliefs which were at variance with the Roman Church's orthodox teachings. To call a Witch a heretic meant that the Witch was a heterodox Christian. The Inquisitors—whatever we may think of them—were nobody's fools.

They were aware of whom they were targeting. They also knew that Witches were "original Christians" whose knowledge of the true, Druidic nature of Jesus' liberating Christianity had to be quashed at any cost if the Church were to achieve the political and pecuniary supremacy they desired by replacing it with their own enslaving dogma.

All the time Witches existed, they were a testament to the fact that Roman Catholicism was nothing like Christianity, and was nothing more than a pack of usurping lies made fragrant with the incense of the suffering of the Dragons, whom the Roman Church had murdered in their pursuit of ultimate world power.

The author has had first-hand experience of what happens when outsiders, either as "media commentators" or as "supporters", become involved with the traditions of the old families. It doesn't take long before both types start to demand that the tradition be adjusted to meet the middle class expectations of a purchasing public that has been fed on sanitised, smug "New Age" moral crapulence. This is so that they, either the commentators or supporters, can attract even more adherents or readers and thereby increase their envisaged profit margins.

After a while, in order to ensure maximum profits, the outsiders set about trying to silence and marginalize the very people who were born into that tradition and upon whom they formerly depended for their wisdom and knowledge. This is just in case the now somewhat bemused custodians of the blood "do something out of keeping with what WE are trying to achieve".

As Mr. Kenneth Grant, O. T. O., has pointed out, money and Magick don't mix. The author echoes this sentiment when he states emphatically that the Dragon Court is a closed body which is kept sacrosanct for members of the blood; and is not a public, profit-making organisation.

As for the Black Mass that so-called New Age Wiccans disown, this ritual was not a "Christian parody born of frustration with, or rebellion against, the Church of the day"—as they repeat faithfully from the formulae printed in their bite-size tomes of "New Age" dogma. It was the original Christian Mass of Jesus which the Catholics later stole and sanitised for public consumption in the same way that Wiccan apologists are doing with Witchcraft today.

Anyone with average intelligence can interpret the Black Mass properly. Prior to the attaching of the Church's "satanic" label during the medieval period—and its decadence and misuse by outsiders throughout the Renaissance and post-Reformation eras—it was one of the most profound and poetic family rituals ever conceived. Its hermetic and alchemical symbolism delved deep into the Kabala and High Magic.

If so-called "Wiccans" in fact actually were real Witches, they would know this. But they don't and they're not. The hyperbole that they indulge in is no more than a regurgitation of books written by equally misinformed writers who, over the preceding decades, have managed to get their seriously flawed ideas published. Whether perceived from the point of view of either its Christian or its Druidic aspects, Royal Witchcraft was never devotional. So much for Witchcraft being a fertility religion.

The Black Mass had its roots in the ancient alchemical lore of Solomon and was simply a momento of teachings long past and an aide memoire for future generations, a mnemonic which was intended to remind those to come from whence the power and the wisdom derives.

If the reader looks carefully at the *Aziluth* scales of the sephiroth of Binah they will see what is meant. The Sabbatical Goat of the Black Mass was Chem-Zoroaster, one of the early ancestors of the ancient Dragon Families. His symbolic presence at the Mass reminds one that Royal Witchcraft was strictly a family affair.

Witches actually called their "god" the Antecessor, meaning "the ancestor". This illustrated to later generations of readers that "Satan", also called by the Witches "Christ, son Dei" or "Jesus Christ, son of God", and was in fact a flesh and blood being. He was not a fallen angel invented by commercially-minded Catholic priests.

If the Witches of the Royal Covens honoured Jesus as an ancestor-god, then they must have been Merovingian by descent and thus custodians of the Sang Royale. Here we enter in upon the realm of the Holy Grail. Royal Witches were Elven by blood and everybody contemporary to them knew this. Professor Murray made this assertion in England and was followed by Jules Michelet in France who recorded that the epithet "Fairy" was attributed by the French to the ancient Gallic Queens.

This also means that The Holy Grail itself was Elven as was Jesus himself, complete with his Crown of Fairy Thorns, depicted as the headgear of Godfroi de Vere de Bouilllon in the 12th century. Throughout the generations, ignorant outsiders have distorted the history of the ancient families and the ancient Royal doctrine.

The fact that most of humanity is engaged in activities based upon greed, and which are destroying their world is actually seen to be good. Those who disagree with first, this modus operandi, and second, hold an historically different perspective, are perceived as evil. New Age Wicca members perpetuate this logical imbalance for their own nefarious, selfish ends. They have nothing to do with Witchcraft, but everything to do with the selfish motivation of those who promote a "white" Wicca for their own financial, social or sexual ends within a social environment which is still morally conditioned by manipulative medieval prejudices.

Modern Wicca, much like other aspects of the 21st century, is a cheap imitation of what has gone before. Thus it is little more than a fashion statement for those who want to take part in the "born-again Christianity".

These views are due not to any particular bad experience with Wiccans or New Agers – other, that is, than any experience with such people is likely to be negative. It is simply the conclusion reached after thirty years of active involvement in the Dragon tradition. This has shown again and again that those who are attracted to the manufactured trappings of the so-called New Age and Wicca, are social inadequates providing perfect bait for unscrupulous charlatans.

The British Trading Standards Office demands of the manufacturer or service provider that any goods or services offered for sale by them should be "Fit to be used for the purpose for which they were intended". The New Age Movement, Wicca and indeed modern revivalist Christianity all fall below this definition and furthermore, and therefore technically fall foul of the British Trades Descriptions Act.

All—including Revivalist Christianity—should be investigated in these terms and also in relation to the British Fraudulent Mediums' Act. They will not be, because they make money. As far as the Security Services are concerned, they are impotent and harmless. Besides, they keep the consumers quiet in their semi-detached cages.

To the sociologists who advise governments we have become categorised into "numbered social units"; to those governments' military tacticians we are "expendable civilian collateral assets" and to the tradesmen who control those governments we are "consumers". Do we wish to continue to be labelled so cynically, and only according to our relative value to any given elite or its agents?

-The inverted pyramid of diminishing human value -
"Expendable Civilian Collateral Asset"
"Numbered Social Unit"
"The Consumer"
"Pawn"
"0"

If the planet is to survive, social groups must become smaller and ordered by economic necessity, not by the so-called Democracy of Consumerism, championed, anything but "free" West.

People learn by suffering and fundamental change comes through the stimulus of radical pain. At present many people in the western world have not experienced enough adversity to make them demand change. Any call for the adoption of sane social and environmental policies still sounds to them like the insane rantings of isolated idealists.

Social Alternatives?

The Dragon Court exists as an organisation solely for the bloodline descendants of the ancient Vere family—the senior bloodline successors of the Scythian-Merovingian, Elven House of Princess Maelasanu—and for those whose bloodlines are extracted from this descent and its ancient Dragon Court.

Such is the nature of its enforced exclusivity that the Dragon Sovereignty has become the only sovereign body in existence today that demands a DNA test as a prerequisite of membership. The reason is that being a Dragon is and always was a matter of race and never a matter of "lifestyle choice", regardless of market potentials.

Being of the Dragon Blood is exactly like being a member of the Amerindian Pequat Tribe which, like the Court, also demands such rigorous proofs of aboriginality. After a thousand years of persecution would anyone dare accuse us of racism? We are fighting for our racial identity to be restored to us and in this we are no different to the Jews or the American Indians or any other Tribe or Nation which has suffered at the hands of the European Church-State.

Do we accuse them of racism or conversely, do we approve of their efforts in attempting to restore and cultivate their cultural distinctness and uniqueness? Like the Indians, the Dragons are also sick of having their culture adopted and diluted by the very races and nations that spent so much time and effort trying to eradicate them and other indigenous populations from both the face of the earth and the pages of the history books.

Nevertheless, the Dragons are committed to furthering the cause of social equity. And whilst desirous of promoting spiritual and scientific education to those who genuinely seek change, ultimately the Dragons' concerns lay in the restoration of their own Tribes, their own Nation and their own Homelands.

Ultimately and unequivocally the Dragons have a love for truth and strive to re-establish their own tuadhe based on veracity, honour, liberty and social and environmental equity, according to the Dragons' ancient lore.

They don't want to wedge their toes in your doors
and they don't want to preach their truth at you.
They certainly don't want to "convert" you!

Instead they are working towards the re-foundation of their own distinct society, utilising the sovereign national rights that the ancient Imperial and Royal Dragon Sovereignty historically already has. By re-introducing their old social structures and values the Dragons hope to establish a naturally ordained system of socio-economic interactions between the Dragon people, based on clarity of vision, honesty of spirit and material necessity.

By avoiding greed and concentrating upon a far richer spiritual and cultural experience derived from the ancient racial memory of the Dragon, it is envisaged that its society will be governed by innate conviction.

Achieved through teaching the timeless psychological skills that facilitate access to this infinite realm, it is hoped that the community might continue as an example of what real "royalty" entails. Furthermore it will demonstrate how communities can work fairly and efficiently, with a hundred-fold increase in cultural quality, spiritual significance and personal empowerment. This depends upon them being based not on idealism, materialism or patriotism, but on sound, realistic principles which are structured organically, according to the outworking of the Draconian consciousness.

The Dragons have no interest in politics and no desire to "Rule the Planet" as certain named fools have suggested. Not least because history teaches us that in power-brokering terms, the "top dog" is in fact "the exposed duck" and in political arenas it's duck season all year round.

Egotism seeks power through rule, but the Dragons' transcendent perception, the Derkesthai or clear sight, is attained through relinquishing egotism. So Dragons couldn't "rule" anyway, the two concepts would be mutually self-negating.

The office of the ancient Druidic or Dragon Queen or King was that of a Magus (hence majesty), Seer and Guide. The idea of a King as "ruler" or even the modern President or Premier as "ruler", is outdated warrior class nonsense, the disastrous consequences of which can be witnessed across the entire planet. Ultimately we do not want to be chained to your hamster wheel. The wheel might still be turning, but the rodent has long since died and the carcass is beginning to stink.

In tune with the Dragon Court and the old covens, many other groups did not and still do not initiate outsiders as new members but, echoing Merovingian tradition, only acknowledge family members who have reached a certain age.

The overly complex and unnecessary initiation rites found in Wicca or modern Witchcraft were and are entirely absent from the rites of small hereditary groups which practiced the old craft. If one knows one is a Witch because one is born into a Witch family, one doesn't need excessive pomp and hocus-pocus to convince one of the obvious. Similarly, it is unnecessary to wear the entire silver standard of a small nation around one's corpulent neck in the form of tasteless pseudo-Wiccan or occult jewellery in order to reinforce the idea—to oneself and to others—that one is a "Witch".

The structure of the historical covens will be dealt with later. However, the Dragon Court itself is not now and never was a "Coven" in the way that this word is accepted today. When reading this book, this should be borne in mind.

Recruitment in times of hardship did occur and "listeners" were expected to drink the blood of the Officiate. This classical, pre-Christian practice was intended to act as a Eucharist where recruits would take on the nature of the Leader by infusing their own being with his or her genetic material.

This form of pact lasted 7 years, the approximate time it takes for the body to renew its cells entirely. After 7 years the recruit would have to drink the blood again as none of the Leader's essence would remain with them after their cellular regeneration.

In this way they were made footsoldiers. However, it wasn't an "initiation" or for life, as modern "Wiccans" have perceived induction to be. Anyway it is doubtful whether they would agree to a Vampiric ritual being included into their repertoire, as it might damage their respectable image as "white Witches", whatever that is supposed to mean: beyond being misinformed, fraudulent pretenders.

This is not elitism. For centuries the ancestors of today's would-be Witches, magicians and New-Age gurus raped, tortured, burned and hanged the Elven people. Now they take their names, their titles and their culture and use it to enhance their own social kudos, when they cannot even prove that they are of the Dragon blood.

In the Genes

Having said that, anyone who genuinely believes they have the right to be acknowledged as a "Draconian", a member of the ancient Elven, Dragon race, is welcome to submit a genealogy which devolves back to either the Scythian or Mittani Royal Houses before the time of Christ. That is at least 80 generations.

Unlike self-styled gurus, the Dragon Court, therefore, always seeks to support its claims with substantial, scientific evidence.

We have been brought up in a scientific age where we are conditioned to demand and accept scientific proofs as the benchmark of validity for any concept presented to us. This is no bad thing and the Dragons themselves have maintained this attitude for centuries. Indeed, such an approach is at the foundation of some of the most poetic and romantic tales in the Dragon culture which, at their heart, reveal themselves as pure science.

The interaction between mind and brain can be psychosomatically suppressed or enhanced by belief. If people are presented with scientific proof of the existence of Dragon genes in their own blood, the abilities which accompany those genes and their genetic memory will become accessible in a strange kind of consensual way. Once they believe that it is "acceptable" to believe what they feared society would condemn as fanciful, they are free. They also experience a previously unperceived sense of clarity.

When they do, they will see that most of human endeavour is pointless. They will see a cleaner way to live life and will find that a common, natural social morality will accompany their every waking thought.

They will have need for neither man's petty laws nor authorities and masters. The innate laws of life will arise from within accompanied by a love of truth and a contempt for falsehood, pretence and deceit. They will allow themselves to become what they already were and what the corporate elites fear most—integrated, transcendent, detached, truly intelligent and creative beings: Overlords unto themselves—the members of a separate race—a "Royal Priesthood, a Peculiar People and a Holy Nation".

Mere belief is what fuels mere religion. From absolute proof however, there is derived absolute certainty in one's condition and one's heritage. Quietly believing or hoping to oneself that one is of the Dragon Race is one thing. In most cases the belief, when it wavers, causes numerous blockages to the fulfilment of any potential as the negative spiral circles downwards with every waver and every failed attempt.

"You shall know the truth, and the truth shall set you free."

Knowing beyond any doubt, however, that one is of that Blood opens wide the doors to the infinite. The planet needs its Elves back, so the saying goes. It needs the people for whom order and empathy come instinctively. It needs those whose love of the natural world comes before all else and arises spontaneously from the depths of their eternal souls. Above all the planet needs its firstborn to know who they are themselves.

It should be said that the symbolism throughout the entire book is not part of some occult, mystical philosophy. If it appears mystical now, it is because we credit our ancestors with little intelligence or knowledge. Experts say that technology, and hence man's understanding, was primitive, regardless of the fact that the Greeks discovered the atom and understood the basics of jet propulsion, whilst the Kabalists were amongst the first mystics to present the "Big Bang" theory.

We believe that they couldn't have known about endocrinology or psychobiology. We view their obscure writings and symbols as primitive scribbles. We are not encouraged to relate it to a scientific basis because our culture dissuades us from attributing such to these predecessors.

Nevertheless, if you strip away the deliberately planted establishment combinations of superstition, fear and devil worship engendered by centuries of Roman Catholic hatred and envy, you will find that the Dragon people weren't "Occultists" but scientists. This is the most threatening aspect of their culture as far as the Church is concerned. Dragon philosophy is based on tangible assays whilst Catholic dogma is based on manipulated nonsense, the philosophy of which is totally ungrounded and illogical. The logic of Dragon science was the threat. In any case the Church's priesthood was neither of the blood nor privy to it, and therefore not in control of these secrets. Even if they could understand them, they were unable to utilise them for the following reasons.

As discussed, Dragon philosophy is appropriate only to Dragons. In the case of vampirism, and those who would play the ersatz bloodsucker, understand that the essences cannot be taken by force. They are only given in love. If one plays the Hammer House of Horror Vampire and abducts young females:

a) their systems will react by producing chemicals during one's assault upon them that will completely knock out the chemicals traditionally required, and

b) one will rightly and inevitably end up in Broadmoor Hospital or some other maximum security psychiatric unit.

Kenneth Grant stated in his book *The Magical Revival* that he felt that people need to be initiated and gradually educated with regard to this matter. The Dragon families would echo his caution, but for purely sociopathic reasons. Namely that an outbreak of Vampire related attacks and murders has been reported in recent years both in Britain and the US.

Two young men in England were jailed in 1994, one for slashing the neck of a 15 year-old boy and drinking his blood. The other, a 29 year old, was incarcerated for 9 years after attacking a 15 year old girl and drinking the blood from the wounds he had inflicted. When police eventually tracked him down, a thorough search of his house revealed a book that someone had actually published, in which readers were "encouraged to drink the blood of young girls for youthful purposes". The young man, labelled "The Vampire Rapist" was said to be a Devil Worshipper.

Let's bite the bullet here. It may appear exclusionist when it comes to the feelings expressed about people prancing around calling themselves Witches or Vampires. However, one sees often the sociological results of the kind of media encouragement and advertising that tells people they are all the same and thus can achieve anything they want. A proportion of these people end up subscribing to this and assume it to be a licence that extends itself to their becoming a danger to other people. One might then appreciate that a restrictive attitude has some good purpose.

Society is encouraged to do what it wants in order that the controlling elite can make money out of selling goods related to conditioned aspiration. We then have a situation where society becomes disaffected and disintegrated because the people themselves cannot achieve what the "American Dream" says they can achieve. Mostly this unrest arises as a consequence of the majority simply not having the money to spend on fashionable, useless rubbish. However, if people transpose this aspirational mentality into changing into people that they cannot become, there will be a build-up of resentment and social tension. It is called the Politics of Envy.

The 29 year-old mentioned had apparently read a book written by someone who had no knowledge of his subject. This self styled guru of the occult supplied information publicly that resulted in at least one serious maiming incident that could easily have resulted in murder.

And what's the point? Young girls today are encouraged to behave like louts because loutish girls buy fashionable clothes and alcohol and do a roaring trade for the music industry. If you removed the abrasive and unattractive exterior brainwashing of this modern female fashion victim, deep down inside you would probably find nothing more than a conditioned breeding machine having a "bit uvva larf" before it settles down to the next stage of its existence as an efficient consumer-producer. What you would not find is the spirit of the ancient of days, the essential genetic makeup of the Dragon princess and the Grail maiden: that rare living goddess whose sacred essences were shed joyously in the service of the ancient Vampire Queens and Overlords.

These days, any solicitous behaviour either violent or wheedling therefore, is not going to result in any would-be Vampire extracting anything of value out of the modern young woman. She lacks the brain chemistry and the intender lacks the brain physiology or anatomy to process the chemicals. The whole transaction or incident is therefore a waste of time.

The young man cited here was described as a devil worshipper, and he got that completely wrong as well, as we shall see. It is all and only a matter of chemistry. If you go attacking people their bodies discharge heaps of poisons like adrenaline, noradrenaline and histamine. Keep attacking people to drink their blood and you will drink yourself into stress and an early grave.

The process actually ages you so “drinking the blood of young girls for youthful purposes” by hacking their necks open in a surprise attack is not particularly bright thinking, is it? Any Vampiric interaction only worked with enthusiastically willing females of pure royal blood who were virgins of a certain age and head over heels in love with the “Vampire”.

This precludes any potential advantages that might be anticipated in hanging around in dark alleys with a questionnaire and a blood testing kit. It could take years to find the right victim.

In summary and final reiteration one cannot utilise Dragon essences unless one has the same complementary, genetically inherited brain wiring as the Princess who donates them. If one doesn't have Dragon synapses, Dragon blood won't make the connections. One cannot obtain these essences from just any female. Therefore any form of play-acting, poseur vampirism practised by the bored, inadequate chattering classes today is just a manifestation of Freudian sexual psychosis. Rare is the woman one would worship, but nevertheless all women deserve respect.

Chapter 1

A New Age Critique

The etymology of the word "Dragon" comes to us via the Latin but is derived fundamentally from the Greek, though the origin of the word and its definition is probably much older. The word in Greek is *drakon*, as in *edrakon*, an aorist of *Derkesthai*, which means "to see clearly".

A *Dragon* was one who saw clearly, and clarity of vision engendered was always classically associated with wisdom, which itself produced power. Today we say that knowledge is power, so nothing has changed in that respect, except that it is actually wisdom—the ability to predict or intuit and synthesise knowledge—a prerequisite of Druidic or Fairy neuro-physiology, that actually affords the greatest power of all.

In a progression of logic that naturally suggests itself, we are therefore entering in upon the linguistic territory of the *Seer*, the *Witch* and the *Magus*, with whom the foregoing qualities have always been closely identified, a state of affairs with which etymologists concur. From there, in the Gaelic realms, we encounter the *Merlin*, a name which, like *Dragon*, literally means "seer", and who furthermore, were of a class of Druid priests or *philosophus* or *magi*, as they were also known in classical times. Anciently the foregoing regional epithets were all attributed to one royal, priestly tribe originally known in Indo-European as the Arya: the "race of the wise ones", a caste which was described in Latin as the *nobilis*, which is a name that originated from the Greek root *gno,* meaning "to know".

Similarly the word king is derived from the related Gothic word *kuningzam*, meaning both "knowing one" and "scion of the noble (meaning wise), race". In addition we have the associated word *siddhis*, meaning "the powers" and from this word or vice versa, was derived the tribal name the *Scythians*, the *Arya-Sidhe* or *Sidheans*. The *siddhi* were a range of psychic or paranormal phenomena which manifested themselves as the attributes of those Tantric priests in Eurasia who had attained *samadhi* or "enlightenment".

These people, coterminously the Aryans or Scythians, who are thought to have developed Tantra in Sumeria, were known as the legendary Tuadha d'Anu (tribe of Anu and by a traditional, widely known derivation—"people of the stars") or *daouine sidhe* (meaning "people of the powers") in the Gaelic countries. They were the "wise ones", the Elves or Fairies. From this we can conclude that by correct definition, a Dragon was originally (by blood descent from the race of the wise) an overlord, an Archdruid or bruidhina, Magus and a seer, an Elven goddess-queen or god-king. Such are not to be confused with the warrior kings or tinker dynasties installed by the Roman Church over the last 1500 years, nor with any modern royal family. The Druidhe were kings above kings.

The Dragon or Fairy gene was very rare and true Archdruidic, royal Dragon families were rarer still. Persecutions excepted, if this were not the case anyway, then perhaps many Fairy stories of the popular genre which originated from outside the Dragon culture would never have taken hold. The reality of the stories would have been everywhere in everyday life.

Traditionally and consistently, the symbol of both wisdom (Sophia) and healing was the serpent or, as it was also known, the Dragon. In keeping with this, the kings and queens of pre-Catholic history were noted for their healing capabilities and as such, in Judaic mythology, were called, perhaps, after the archangel Raphael, the Repha'im or Rapha'Elohim; the healing gods of the Anunnaki. Raphael was the Prince who appeared to Adam in Eden according to Milton.

No mention of this is made in Genesis and one suspects that of the two entities that did appear to Adam, Enlil and Enki, or if you like, God and the Catholic Satan, Raphael (the Angel of the Rising Sun), who must have been Enki. It was he who gave Kingship to man in the form of the Elven Overlords and after whom, by various related epithets, including "The Repha'im", the Elven Kings are known. Authorities believe that these people were identical to both the Nephilim and the Anakim of Idumea and Canaan. The Anakim are ancient ancestral kings found in the Old Testament, and it would appear that they originate from peoples descended from Black Sea migrants. There is a large number of Scythians in the Middle East region. In early heraldry, derived from ancient sources, the Dragon was depicted as a serpent with the wings of a Swan. This image was also given the wings of a bat.

The Dragon nevertheless was humanoid and so the symbolism in the Dragon glyph should rather be interpreted to substantiate the etymology of the word itself. The serpent stands for the wisdom and healing powers of the sacred king or queen whose regalia often consisted of serpent-like scale armour and whose consciousness soars above that of humanity as if carried on wings, which was symbolised by shamanic Swan's feather cloaks.

The nocturnal habits of the Dragon people, typically those of the Cimmerian Scythians, who are a sub group of the Skoloti or Scythian peoples from the Southern Steppes region of what is now known as Greater Scythia, were noted by their contemporaries. The Swan's wings of the Dragon glyph attributed to them were either interchangeable with, or substituted by, those of the bat to signify this.

One of their earlier names—Anunnaki—suggests "heaven meets earth". Lots of fanciful notions have been put forward to suggest that the Anunnaki were from outer space, but a far simpler way of understanding the name is to ask a simple question: "when do the heavens—the An or Stars—meet the Earth?" The answer is of course—"at night time".

When considering the nature of the Elves or the Anunnaki, rather than believing they came from a different planet, it might be worth considering that they occupied a different dimension. If this sounds equally as fanciful and implausible, consider this. A multitude of different animal species on this planet can be perceived by human sensory capacities and therefore, to all intents and purposes, the physical aspect of their being occupies the human dimension.

However, because of their anatomical and physiological make-up, these species' experiences of the same material reality are different and these differences are caused by, amongst other things, variations in the respective synaptic connections and hormone levels. Consequently these variants are known to differentiate between the perceptions of their universe and that of humanity. These species actually live in another dimension and at a higher or variant frequency, where the subjective qualities of time and the environment for them are totally different to the way in which humans perceive them.

The level to which the Fairies experienced life was far deeper than the level to which humans experienced it.

In real terms the Fairies inhabited an entirely alien world but occupied the same planet. In this sense they were from a different dimension, characterised and regulated by their body chemistry which enabled them to see more in the environment than humans could. In this they were no more remarkable than any other non-human species we are able to study today. Flies, sharks, dolphins and a host of other life forms have attributes and abilities humans do not possess. As a consequence of this, the way in which they interact with the planet is completely alien to the way in which humans do.

For a fly, time is completely different and for a shark, any warm blooded creature glows with a blue, electro-chemical haze or aura, proving to some extent, the veracity of the theory of Kirlian photography.

The concept of dimension is entirely subjective, as is any concept of reality, which to the greatest extent in humans, is manipulated not only by their internal constitutions, but also and largely by external environmental conditioning and attachment. This training forces humans to subdue and modify their internal constitutions in order to align themselves with arbitrary social expectations. The consequence of this is to create a dichotomy—an endlessly chattering, self-flagellating, hateful monkey in the human forebrain whose ceaseless din, which humans call reality, prevents the individual from entering any other form of perception or, if you like, stops them from changing their dimension.

Humans cannot perceive the monkey. However, by virtue of a different chemical constitution, the Fairies could, quite naturally, and were able to put it in its correct perspective. Once silenced, the monkey which creates the illusion of time and substance is unable to keep the doors to other dimensions, so securely locked.

The Fairies were Dragons and this means that they "saw clearly", they saw subtler emanations than man could. In order to be able to do this the Fairies would have to have their senses tuned into a higher frequency than man. Therefore the Fairies were tuned to a higher frequency of perception and activity generally.

In cybernetic terms, any system that is faster and consequently higher than a given base is called a nautonnier or navigator. In cybernetics these systems are set over and in control of the slower functional operations within any given mechanical or organic arrangement. If we transpose this theory onto human society we get leaders and followers. The leaders are supposed to be able to function at a faster rate than the followers, and thereby anticipate any given direction the system might go in and plan sensible strategies that the system might adopt for its well-being.

Today this is ludicrous. Self-seeking, middle class incompetents more often find themselves voted in to control what are now vast, unwieldy, out-of-control social systems which, once upon a time, no one would have trusted to anyone but the Elves. In the past therefore, because the Fairies were, for millennia, physiologically bred and exhaustively trained to operate at a higher level than men, humans often invited them to become social navigators or nautonniers. The Sumerian word for a navigator is a *Gall*, which sounds a bit like a Gael, doesn't it? The language of the western Royal Scythians was Gaelic and the Royal Scythians were the Fairies, the Elves: the Dragons.

The Dragon's fiery breath symbolised the pneuma, the spirit of the divine, which coalesced into the Torah or cosmic law that the Dragon queens and kings delivered as their pronouncements in the affairs of man. Thus the image of the Dragon of myth and legend is complete, as a set of symbolic attributes belonging to an ancient magical race of praeter-natural beings, the vampyr overlords or Fairy overkings.

Although humanoid, Dragons were not Homo Sapiens but decended from the far older Elven race, sometimes called in literature the Elda or Eldar. This was probably suggested or derived from the name of an ancient queen and her ancient, former habitation in Mesopotamia and possibly intended, in its attribution as a simile for Elder perhaps, to imply some form of racial primogeniture.

Reflected upon within the context of early Sumerian historical records, such a synonym would indeed seem to be apposite, inasmuch as this ancient and mysterious people claimed that the Dragons, with Queen Hawah Elda's assistance, created mankind.

Homo Sapiens?

From the OED (*Oxford English Dictionary,* used often as a reference in this work), we learn that the prefix *homo* has two meanings. There is the Latin meaning (from whence comes "man"), and the Greek meaning, as in *homo*-genous, which means "common", "the same" or "the same as", "average", "mediocre".

The word *sapiens* is itself derived from the Latin word "sapienta" meaning understanding. However it was also a word which was used in a solely pejorative and derogatory context—from as far back as the Middle English period—explicitly in the sense of artful, deceitful, contrived or would-be wisdom; meaning sophistry or low cunning and hypocrisy. From sapienta we derive the slang derogative *sap*, which has been used throughout the English-speaking world to taunt idiots and fools.

Hereto, jocularly, in contemporary currency the phrase *homo sapiens* could, therefore, define a common, undistinguished hominid species. Its members would act in the same manner and think the same self-deluding thoughts, relating to each other through a veil of deception, within a limited field of conscious responses and conditioned reflexes, rather like sheep.

Taken in relation to what man has done to the planet and to his fellow creatures, the author doesn't think that this is an unwarranted or unsubstantiated attack, but a justifiable observation. Man aptly named himself: *homo* = mediocre + *sapiens* = cunning.

Therefore man could be defined by the *Oxford English Dictionary*, the recognised authority on, and arbiter of the English language, as being uniquely, thoroughly stupid and dim-witted, and his species description has incorporated within it a clear indication that this condition is genetically inherited. Nurture seems unable to ameliorate what nature has here ordained.

Here the idealist might argue that a eugenic solution, mediated through genetic engineering could produce a more passive, thoughtful population by weeding out the stupid gene and replacing it with something that would make us all less wasteful, aggressive and acquisitive.

Take a look around you, who runs the planet? That's right—the multinational corporations. And what is their raison d'etre? To force people to produce rubbish for the same people to buy. Where does the funding come from for scientific research grants? From the multi-national corporations or via governments who are subservient to, because they are paid for by, those same corporations. Would either support any form of research that would make people refuse to fight their wars for them or consume less of their pointless rubbish? No.

At present, genetic *engineering* for the most part is becoming yet another manifestation of human megalomania within a world socio-economic system that owes its very existence to the continued cultivation and promotion by the corporate elites, of mass psychosis on an international scale. This is a sad indictment upon the entire human race. The evidence speaks for itself and after several millennia of wars and destruction, culminating in the present series of social and ecological disasters, it doesn't seem that *homo sapiens* will ever be anything other than what they are. Furthermore, this is a profitable, and therefore a protected and encouraged, irremediable and irreversible, genetic condition.

In contrast the Dragons or *Draco Sentiens*, according to the most ancient definitions, were, once upon a time, long ago, genetically "clear sighted" members of the elder race, the "race of the wise". It therefore follows in conclusion that, because of the neurophysiological, and consequently the cognitive and psychological differences between the two, neither was of the same species as the other, and the ancient Sumerian texts would uphold this view without question.

Grail Code—What Grail Code?

A Personal View

People enter relationships that serve their own interests or the interests of the "extended self". In the end, therefore, all human endeavour is self centred, and all is "egotism". Beyond the facile exterior, there may be something of greater merit dwelling in the depths of the silence, but it is often not evident. However "bigger" any greater, non-personalised aim might be, it is still serving itself and its own interests through the drives it instils in people. The universe eats the universe as a manifestation of a larger cosmic egotism which cares nothing for the "rights" of Man.

The Universe has no contract with humanity, and therefore no contract men have with each other has any valid basis in reality either. In times past they would speak of the "Covenant with God". Now certain individuals pontificate vacuously about "The Grail Code". Both—then and now—can only be seen as fraudulent contracts which no party can uphold because neither party can fulfil the obligations or restrict themselves to the limits implied within them. Abiding, externalised, imposed contracts are not a part of natural law.

Individuals tolerate each other's peccadilloes if they have something to contribute to each other which is valued. The "Grail Code" of service to others is prominent in its absence because the relationships people have are driven by a financial imperative. This makes the statements of collective high idealism just that, a hollow mockery of something that died out long ago. The Grail Code today is just another clichéd phrase, a meaningless piece of "New Age" verbosity aimed at selling contrived, pseudo-intellectual, academically amateur jingoism to frightened, greedy fools.

Religious coercion is now replaced by jargonistic phrases, which try to promote weak, "New Age" philosophies that, like religion, are engineered to appeal to or coerce (for selfish motives) a higher sense in man that simply doesn't exist. For the Grail Code to work as it was envisaged or understood, everyone subscribing to it now would have to think with one mind and not consider individual gain before the welfare of the group. This is simply not happening. Nor will it.

Service to others without thought of self requires others to serve you with equal dedication and devotion if you and the group—collectively—are to survive.

The Grail Code in the distant past was neither a contract nor an ideal. It was the manifestation of a type of behaviour which was subsequent to a particular form of consciousness.

How Did It Work?

Hierogamy or enthea (the marriage or union of the gods) between the Dragon Prince and the Swan Maiden resulted in the creation of an extended mind, the development of an interaction where the bounds of individual consciousness were broken. Two people joined together with an intensity that created a being greater than the sum of its parts. In alchemy this was called the breath of Ravens from which resulted the birth of the red-gold Phoenix, conceived in the death of Dragons and born in the ascent of the white star. The way these two individuals treated each other was called True or Courtly Love. If this phenomenon happened on a wider scale within the genome, then it, along with other universal phenomena, was a part of the Web of Wyrd, the unseen connecting threads of the underlying matrix of life. Its child was True Love manifest collectively, which was called the Grail Code. Jesus called it "the Law of God written on the hearts of men in tongues of fire". Genetic righteousness.

The Grail Code was the behavioural manifestation of an attuned group of empathic individuals working towards the common good of that group. This required a "Hive Mind"—a collective consciousness—or at least a heightened capacity towards sensitivity and the anticipation of the needs of all within the genome, that transcended common consciousness. Therefore it was a manifestation of the outworking of the *Siddhis* within the web of interrelated and interconnected points of consciousness that are manifest throughout all levels of life.

The Grail Code, therefore, was a set of behavioural patterns that arose from within in response to a particular psychological condition that has detachment as its hallmark. It was not imposed from without by people with vested interests for their own ends or for the ends of any other disassociated group of individuals.

Without the "Hive Mind" (symbolised in the Dragon Dynasty by the Merovingian Bee, the Phoenician "House of the Gods" and the hexagonal figure of the Tree of Life of the Kabala) the Grail Code is a meaningless set of unattainable social aspirations.

To the "New Age" authors and devotees—the people left outside the group who don't have the wiring or chemistry to participate and understand the collective mind—the Grail Code is just another set of rules. However prettily and romantically packaged, these rules will inevitably be broken, and are therefore no better or worse than any other meaningless regulations.

The universe has features which are prime constants. The behaviour of materials is one example, which we call the "laws of physics". These we can term truths, because they don't vary under a given range of circumstances. Even down at the sub atomic level, the peculiarities are constant, inasmuch as they are constantly peculiar. Without these prime constants the universe would cease to exist.

The Grail Code, as a worthy set of regulations or aspirations for the governance of people's behaviour in relationship to each other is, quite frankly, an idealistic load of nonsense. It isn't that the Grail Code is a fantasy or a lie. It is simply a fact that it was and still is misapplied, and to the wrong people.

Relatively and contextually speaking, the Grail Code is not a truth, because it is not a constant, and it cannot be applied to regulate human behaviour in human societies. We know this because it caused, in part, the manifestation of a set of social conditions which were required in order to allow to occur the 1000 year genocide which is referred to in the Family as the Elven Holocaust. This resulted ultimately in the abandonment of the Grail Code itself.

What was the big mistake the Family made? They did unto others as they would have done unto themselves. In other words they used the transcendently inspired Grail Code they anciently applied to their own mystical race to order societies that were founded not upon transcendent perception, but upon animal instincts.

The Grail Code was applicable only to the Grail Blood. Elsewhere the only thing that worked was the law of the jungle and terrorism. The Family was seen as a soft touch because their empathy was extended to peoples who had no empathy themselves—only the desire to satisfy their own greed and assuage their own fears.

These peoples' selfish, individualistic motivations stood in direct opposition to the Grail Code of "royal communism" and community service. Desire is a great motivator in any society and the Elves' desires were motivated by their transcendent consciousness, which could only operate in an environment of truth and empathy.

The more one sees, the less one desires for oneself and the less attached one becomes. If one desires truth and sees only truth and gives instinctively for the common good because one can feel the common need, one becomes the target for opportunists and deceivers.

Faced with the violence and hostility of a group of myopic animals hell bent on their pursuing their own interests and unable to see the bigger picture, the Elves had no chance of survival anyway, whatever the other circumstances might have been. This alone was enough to destroy them. In a sense then, the Grail Code was a death sentence to the Dragon Families. This, perhaps, is how the Mayors of the Palace took over, through exploiting what they perceived as the innate trust, complacency and weakness of the Merovingian kings.

One can appear dark or harsh in one's attitudes towards human beings and human behaviour and one may make people wonder how one could possibly preach about the Grail on one hand and despise humans so much on the other. After all, isn't the Grail Code all to do with being nice to each other? Isn't it about being fair to one's fellow man? Doesn't it fit in with the overall ethos of the "New Age"? The answer to all these rhetorical questions is an absolute No. It isn't and it doesn't.

The Grail Code is the perfect example of an ill-advisedly applied series of innate laws arising from the profound depths of the genetic constitution of one species, applied to and completely misunderstood and abused by another.

Look around you and judge for yourself. After a thousand years of tyrannical misrule, European society is finally beginning to throw off the shackles of merchant class stupidity. Unfortunately this new found dissent and "freedom" has no direction either, and the path society is treading will inevitably become littered with the corpses of the fallen.

People aren't naturally "nice" to each other. They are simply conditioned to fear the consequences of not appearing to be nice to each other. Even so, this barrier is now breaking down and at the grassroots level, society is becoming more violent as individuals embrace selfish opportunism and disregard their conditioning.

There is a stark difference between the two concepts and conditions of natural empathy and social fear. One comes from within, the other is applied from without. If people were naturally co-operative and naturally empathic, the Grail Code would be a universal behavioural constant in an ordered world of ecological sensitivity and social harmony. This, plainly and manifestly is not, and never has been the case, and certainly not since the Church came to power. The Grail Code arises naturally from, and is pertinent solely to, the Grail Blood.

The Grail Code is the behavioural benchmark by which those of the Grail or Dragon Blood might be recognised, but it is not the code that efficiently orders the behaviour of the Dragon Families in their dealings with those not of the Grail Blood.

In *Genesis of the Grail Kings* Laurence Gardner commented on the love that the Anunnaki had for social order, which was echoed in Transylvania where Vampires were said to have a reputation for pathological meticulousness and where nearby, Dracula ran his kingdom with the precision of a well oiled machine.

In the earlier days of the Anunnaki it is quite feasible that the collective empathic consciousness was particularly strong and we might see here the foundation of the Grail Code within the family of the Gods. Nevertheless, later there were still incidents of internecine strife. However, where outsiders were concerned, the Grail Code was only applied inasmuch as it related to maintaining order for the benefit of the Overlords. Was there any question of the Gods being "nice" to man or applying the Grail Code solely for man's benefit? There was a difference between the Grail Code for the Grail Blood and the Grail Code as it applied to man. One has to say that Enlil was right, concerning his rivalry with Enki and their differing views on treatment toward man.

As the Blood weakened, the capacity to apply empathy and co-operation appropriately weakened. This resulted initially in family wars, and latterly in the kind of mental weakness, confusion and cultural misapplication which ended in the genocide of the race by Catholic opportunists.

These are pertinent lessons that the Bloodline would do well to learn if it is to rebuild itself again. It doesn't necessarily mean, because the Bloodline is at the end of the seventh millennium of its recorded history, that it is too late to turn back the clock. However, if the Dragon is to survive at all, it must learn the lessons of history, redefine its identity and strive to enrich its Blood once more. If it doesn't, its culture will die completely.

An old saying from British folklore asserts that if the land loses its Elves, the land dies. In two thousand years the face of the countryside in Britain and Ireland in particular has changed completely and there is now nowhere that man hasn't manipulated, exploited or raped. Compared to what it was, the land is indeed dead. Its spirit has almost gone.

The spirit of the land, its innate magic and mystery, has died because the Elves have all but died as well. The land consequently has no real voice anymore, no champions and no orators. Without the Dragon Queens and the Elven Overlords to interpret the will of the Earth (and without Brehon Law to protect it from fools) man himself fails to hear the deeper message the land gives him.

The ancient forests of giant Oak and Beech are no more, and the sacred places have been either built on in acts of blasphemy by an evil religion or torn up by the mindless merchant-class ancestors of today's mindless, middle-class consumer population.

In the theory of critical mass, sometimes called the "99th Monkey Effect"—based on Jung's theory of Collective Consciousness working through Rupert Sheldrake's "Field of Morphic Resonance"—the collective mind of a race creates a spiritual and cultural archetype whose field of resonance can be felt in the material world. In the case of the Elves, that Archetype was manifest in the Age of Magic. Simply put, when the Elves lived, they created a field of magic around them, the power of which arose from the very sovereignty of the earth itself. However, when the Church killed the Elves, the Earth was silenced and the magic largely died.

Having assisted the Church to kill off the Elves, man now stands alone against a being he uses with contempt for his own gain, but whose power against him is limitless and whose patience with him is not. The highest so-called authorities on Earth have finally realised what they have done and even they, the United Nations Organisation, say that the clock is ticking and time is running out.

The spirit of True Romance and Magic is all but dead. It diminished when the Church enslaved the spirit of mankind to a material, hateful god. However, the Sundered Tribes can be reborn, the Dragon blood can be restored and enriched, and the Dragon Queens and Elven Lords can rise once more to restore to people a sense of wonder, a sense of hope and an Age of Magic.

Chapter 2

The Origins of Vampirism

The Mark

If doubtful of your fate, you seek to obliterate
and to forget the countermark I set, in the warm
blue-veined nook of your elbow crook, how can
you not repent the experiment.
No knife went in to lacerate the skin; nor may
the eye tetter or wen descry; the place which
my lips pressed is coloured like the rest and fed
by the same blood of womanhood.
Acid, pumice stone, lancings to the bone, would
be in vain. Here must The Mark remain as witness
to such love as nothing can remove, or blur, or hide,
save Suicide.

—Robert Graves

Some of the earliest evidence of Ritual Vampirism comes from Tartaria in Transylvania and stems to the fifth-millennium BC. Remains of a human body were found buried in a fire pit along with clay tablets upon which were inscribed the names of the Sumerian god Enki and the ranking number of Father Anu. The language was subsequently termed *proto-Sumerian* and represented some of the earliest written artifacts yet to be found.

The descendants of these early Vampires were the sacred Ubaid race who, one millennium later, settled Mesopotamia and founded the Anunnaki religion of the Sumerians in 3500 BC. Their Transylvanian ancestors were the Anunnaki Gods themselves.

Various suggestions have been proposed in an attempt to explain the origin and meaning of the word Vampire. One recent suggestion was that it was applied to a group of "Watchers" (Seers-*Derkesthai*: Dragons) who had occupied a settlement near Lake Van, in Urartu , Armenia. The original location—Greater Scythia—is faultless, the association is without error but the etymology is unresearched and the philology is completely absent.

Although that author's suggested identification between Watchers and Vampires is absolutely correct, the word *Vampire* does not in any sense relate to their former geographical location or origin. It relates rather to the Vampires' social and spiritual identity and status within a given cultural framework, which in this instance was Scythian, overlaid on Celtic.

In the journals of the 17th-century cleric, the Abbe Calmet, the word Vampire is transliterated into its most common, and its earlier, central European form which is spelt either *oupire* or *oupere*. These spellings are common in literature of Calmet's time and represent the original form of the word Vampire.

When the word migrated into Latin from Anatolian the *u* became a *v* because, as we will recall, there is no *u* character represented in the Latin alphabet. If there had been, then the Latinised western European construction of the word would have been *uampire*. By now bells should be ringing in the readers' heads as they remember hearing about *wampires* somewhere or another, perhaps in a humorous context.

The Romans didn't have a w and this letter appeared in clerical Latin during the medieval period as *v v*, as presented in the ridiculous text book Latin phrase *mortvvs svm*. The *vv* being used then as a long vowel sound to differentiate between u and v sounds which were both represented by the Latin v.

So to recap, let's have a look at the linguistic migration so far: oupere—oupire—owpire—ovpire. At this point we must remember that the word migrated from one language into another at a time when the most commonly used form of transmission was oral. This was bound to lead to confusion when the word was written down for the first time, as it has in numerous other instances.

By now we should be asking "If the word Vampire was originally spelt oupire, where on earth did the "m" come from?" All the author can say is thank heavens for the anomalous "m" because it is this component that really confirms the origin and meaning of the word Vampire, according to currently accepted scholarship.

Philologists would agree that the word Vampire, as oupere, in its present form originated from the Turkish word *uber*, which means "Witch". This would appear to present even more problems because in addition to an anomalous "m", we now also have a "b" to explain away! Nevertheless the author promises you that tenacity and perseverance will bring its own rewards.

Leaving the "m" aside for a moment, there would seem to be a serious linguistic problem in that *oupere* is spelt with a "p" and *uber* with a "b", which the reader might suspect would undermine the connection between both words. Especially since *Vampire* or *oupere* is European and *uber* is Turkish and thus from a separate language group. However, this is not so.

As the Turkic-Uralic language is very different from Indo-European, it would appear that the word Vampire in its original form is not Indo-European, but an Asiatic word that has changed in spelling and pronunciation during the passage of time and its migration northward.

It might then appear that the central Asian word for a Witch—*uber*—would mean something entirely different to the European meaning of the word and would therefore bring with it an entirely different set of cultural and mythic associations. However, what the reader might not realise is that modern Turkey and its language is, like any other, an evolutionary compilation of historical, linguistic and cultural influences.

Prior to being named Turkey, Asia Minor, or Anatolia, it was the centre of the eastern Roman Empire of Byzantium. At the heart of Asia Minor, contemporary with Rome but originating from an earlier period still, was the vast region of Galatia. In the centre of this was a region occupied in the Persian era by the Cimmerians of Scythia, at a time when Galilee, Gilead and Gaulatinis in northern Israel were Scythian territories named after their language.

As Galatia spread northwards it bordered upon Phrygia and Troy and reached out further still to become Galati as it crossed the Bosphorus and encompassed Transylvania. On its westward marches Galati assimilated both Bulgaria and Gaul.

In consequence of this, a massive proportion of what is now called Turkey was in fact, along with most of Europe, Gaelic or properly Goidelic speaking, a Scythian/Celtic civilisation, comprising of independent tribal groups who spoke a number of Gaelic dialects. Amongst these and most notably are what we now know as the so-called "P" and "Q" or "K" Goidelic language variants.

The P and Q variants in Brythonic-Cymric (Welsh) and Goidelic-Scotic (Irish Scots), as an example, mean that the word "son" will be spelt *map* in Cymric and *mac* in Scotic. Furthermore there is a sub variant in this language group where "P" and "B" sounds also become interchangeable. For example, the Welsh *pen* as in the mountain—*Penllithrig'y'wrach*—meaning "the slippery hill of the Witch" in Snowdonia, and the Scots *ben* as in Ben Nevis in Scotland—both of which mean "head" or "peak". The Cymric language was originally Cimmerian or northern Scythian, whilst Scotic is a southern Scythian dialect.

The Galatian word *uber* is from the Scythian Goidelic group whilst in Russia and Poland, which was influenced by the Cimmerian or Brythonic group, the same word for Vampire is spelt *upyr* and *upior* respectively. There have been numerous Scythian migrations over the millennia and the Gaelic language has been carried across the Eurasian continent to influence the languages of many peoples. The Trojans, who lived next door to the Galatians and were themselves Scythians, moved to Italy and became the Latines.

In Latin therefore, we can find both *uber*—rich or fruitful—and *s/uper*—"over" or "above" as in umpire (no peer) and supervisor. In Northern Germany (low German) and Holland (middle Dutch) *upper* means "situated higher than or above another or others", whilst in modern German we find *uber*, again meaning over or above, having the spelling variants *ober*, *uberi*, *ubar*, and associated with "superiority in power, position and station to others".

As we can see by this example, the *b* has consistently become a *v* and this is how we know that the word for a Vampire *uber*, is not a Turkish word at all but Gaelic or Galatian. Remember the anomalous "m" in Vampire? Well, it just so happens that in dialectic Gaelic the consonant group Mh is pronounced V. The "h" became discarded over time and left the "m" in Vampire where the "u" or "v" should be. If spelt literally, Vampire would be uavber, uauber or uaupir, which is the central European *oupire* or *oupere*.

These variants stem from the Sanskrit *upari* (*Up-Ari* or *Up-Arya*, meaning *Over-Lord*) for which the Greek is *uper*—which, as we have already seen, is a component of *super* in Latin. *Over* (ME—*ouere*) began as a graphic variant of *uuere* which translates into the dynastic name Vere with the Latin V being interchangeable with the double U or hard Germanic W which became V—rendering Ver or Were. This is pronounced as a soft F, which we find in the Norse *Yfari* and the old English *Uffara* or *Yffera*.

The Turkish, or properly Galatian word *Uber*, meaning "Witch" therefore linguistically corresponds to the foregoing variations found in Gothic, German, Dutch, Norse English, Greek, Latin and Sanskrit, where finally, as *Upari*, we discover that originally *Uber*—Vampire—meant *Overlord*. In the following paragraphs we shall investigate the cultural background behind the word "Witch" as *uber*, and discover that what holds true linguistically is supported by cultural and social evidence.

Contextually, when applied to an individual as a "Witch", the word *uber* would suggest that the person referred to was in some way "over" or "above" others, as in the German *übermensch* or *überherren*. The Germanic languages, as with the others sampled here, are all Indo-European and the Sanskrit in particular, being of Aryan or Scythian origin, is closest to the Galatian, and we shall see that the argument for overlordship is exactly the case.

From a cultural standpoint, we read the word "Witch" and with it comes a large trolley of baggage that we have inherited from the popularly reinforced understanding of the word, influenced heavily by Fairy stories and biased histories told from a protagonistic point of view. Today the specifically Saxon word "Witch" tends to conjure up images of old hags prancing about on dark, spooky moors and cackling into cauldrons.

Witch is derived from the Saxon root word *wicce* (feminine) or *Wicca* (masculine). The Saxons used it to describe a class of persons whom they thought were inhabited by an intelligence or spirit—a daemon or genii, usually evil—the Saxons took up Catholicism pretty early on in their careers and were consequently biased.

Conversely, some people today would like us to believe, however, that "Witch" meant a "wise one" and say that Witchcraft, or in Saxon—*wicce-craeft* as they like to call it—means craft of the wise, failing completely to realise that the word *wise* in Saxon is *wita*, not *Wicca* or *wicce*.

Wicca is actually related to both "wicker" and "Viking" or Wiking, as the Norse would pronounce it. In Russia the word *Vikhr*, meaning whirlwind, is a title of the Zmei Dragons, sons and daughters of Zmei-Tiamat. This confirms that the link between Sumaire, Zmei or Zumei and Sumeria was also known in Russia, once a Viking province.

It also demonstrates that the Danish Vikings, Witch lords, were sons of the Dragon and the Scandinavian Tuadha d'Anu. In Ireland the Zmei Lord or Vikhr is known as the Dark King—the Whirlwind—meaning he was sumaire or Vampire and via Uber, a Witch Lord or *Wicca*. As the Willow (wicker) bends and yields to the whirlwind, so the Witch (*Wicca*) yields to the Sumaire, the ancient Vampire legacy within him or her; a legacy that is awakened during the Mass of the Phoenix, when the primordial ancestors rise from the dead to take possession of the Witch's soul!

Wicca, derived from the same Saxon word as Willow, means to "bend or yield" one's spirit to that of a daemon (Greek, meaning preter-human intelligence or inspiration), giving the Christian idea of possession, though erroneously. The Witch was indeed possessed by a daemon and that daemon was certainly preter-human and not of this world.

Any spirit, including the archangels, conjured by the Witch or magician (the distinction, like that between pagan and Christian, is fallacious), as in ceremonial magic, was actually the ancestor (antecessor) of the Witch herself (or himself). It was a denizen of the ancient Dragon itself—but carried in the Witch's blood which, the purer it was through unbroken descent from the Dragons, the stronger would be the return of the ancestors within. The stronger the blood the stronger the invocation and the more complete the possession. With mixed blood there was weak inspiration and little discernible presence. "The Blood is the Life".

The Witch was possessed by this daemon, because the Witch by descent and heredity was that daemon itself. It was his or her genetic inheritance and part of his or her racial consciousness. To that the Witch would yield, when occasion necessitated, placing the Witch and the words *wicce* or *Wicca* firmly in the tradition of the trance seer (*Derkesthai*), a practice rooted in Scythian shamanic culture.

This is confirmed in the word *genius*, meaning inborn intellect or inspiration. Closely related to this word is *genie*, meaning a spirit, as in *genius loci*—"a spirit of place". In Arabic the *jinni* is a spirit of fire or inspiration. The Latin *genius*, in Greek, is a *daemon* or inspiring intelligence and the root Latin *gens* signifies birth, origin and especially blood. The daemon or genius of the Dragons was inherited through the blood. Witches are born. Not made by silly play-acting initiation rituals.

A seer in Gaelic was called a *Merlin* and in the tripartite Aryan-Scythian caste system which overlaid that of their clients, the deeply religious Celts, the Merlin was a Druid Prince. Either side of the Druidic caste were the castes of the warrior aristocrats and the craftsmen and, although they all tended to behave as equals in this king-tribe system, the Druids were senior in rank.

Each caste attended to their allotted tasks. The study, teaching and practice of shamanism and magic were strictly the province of the Druids and Druidesses, forming part of a vast storehouse of knowledge and experience in the crafts and sciences, and in statesmanship and lore.

The Druids were responsible for bringing into being gods for the Celts to worship. Though they were not religious themselves, scholars agree that Druidism was the "religion" of the Celtic world. So we can see that although the Celts had their own caste system with their own burgh kings or chieftains, above them were the Scythian kings, and above the Scythian kings were the Elven Druids, the Priest Kings who stood above all others, the ultimate Overlords of Eurasia.

In the Scandinavian countries, the craft or ability to gain wisdom or *power* (Sanskrit—*Siddhi*) by yielding to daemons or intelligences (ancestral god spirits which were part of the practitioners' own genetic inheritance and make-up) through trance or dream states, was considered to be shamanic and was called *Siddir*, whilst those who practiced this art were themselves called *Siddirs*. The *Siddir* knotted together the web of dreams and loosened those knots to release power and knowledge. In other words, they brought together and spoke or gesticulated a series of mnemonics that would trigger off precontrived, imprinted states of consciousness that acted as doorways into deeper seats of consciousness. In Gaelic Scythian this ability and the name corresponding to it was called the *Sidhe*, a term used to describe and name the Irish Fairies, the Tuadha d'Anu or Tuatha de Danaan as they were later called, a race of priest kings or Druid princes.

The Web of Dreams relates to both the Witches' knotted ball and the Web of Wyrd or Fate *(fata*-Fairy). In the Scythian and Celtic cosmology, the power associated with it was thought to reside in the Otherworld. This was the realm of the gods (Druidic ancestors) which was entered via trance or dream states, achieved whilst the Druid or Druidess occupied the Fairy hills, the mortuary raths where the forefathers were buried.

The Witch, as a seer or Merlin in Scythian culture and society, consequently belonged to an exclusive genome within a distinct holy and royal caste of overlords. This is reflected in the Gaelic word for a Witch—Druidhe—which is pronounced Drui and is related to Draoi and Dracoi, meaning a Dragon. Drui itself means Man (or Woman) of the Tree (not men of the oaks, as some have suggested) and is also related to the Sanskrit *dru*, meaning to run. This is associated with the ritual of running the labyrinth, with which we will deal in due course.

Therefore in Galatia, which had its own Druids and was the site of the Nemeton, the largest regular gathering of Druids in Europe, the term for a Witch was *Uber*, meaning Overlord, whilst in the Gaelic west the term for a Witch was *Druidhe*, which meant the same as *Uber*—an Overlord.

In summary, Vampire in its earlier form—oupire—derives ultimately from the Galatian Uber, which itself is derived from the Aryan Upari and linguistically and contextually the Vampire—the Witch or Druid—was a Scythian High Queen or King: an Overlord.

Calmet was an official Vampire investigator accompanying imperial officers and soldiers throughout the Austrian Empire in the 17th century. It is interesting to note in this context that he found no evidence whatsoever to support any notion that vampirism was a supernatural phenomenon committed by preter-natural beings—which he utterly refutes. Neither did he find that it ever occurred in any form, either as a cult or in any isolated incidents, amongst the lower strata of society.

Without exception the enlightened Abbe was able to discover perfectly ordinary explanations for the incidents he had investigated, which in his day was quite remarkable, as the Church in past times had actively promoted Vampire paranoia.

As Professor Margaret Murray discovered herself, vampirism was not the prerogative of the merchant or peasant classes, but was a cultic observance confined to the environs of the nobility, often as an adjunct to rites of the Noble and Royal Witch Covens of Scotland.

We can say with confidence then that real vampirism was indulged in by living beings who, unerringly, were members of the pre-Christian and anti-Christian high nobility and royalty. The most famous Vampire stories, those of Dracula, Bathory and de Rais, support this conclusion. The historical evidence therefore supports the etymological origin of the word "Vampire"—an Overlord.

Vampirism, up until the early 1700's, by which time it had been in decline for several centuries, was not merely or solely the practice of a few isolated, high-born opportunists seeking some form of personal advantage or satisfying private perversions. Vampirism took two forms and the bloodline descendants of the ancient Vampire lords had, in Britain, set the practice within an overall, multi-faceted social and cultural framework, stemming from the Iron Age, that never gets an airing in the Gothic novel.

Vampires weren't just Vampires, as popular literature would have us believe. They were individuals and families who used the practice to achieve specific aims and thereby fulfil those specific social obligations which, since the Scythian-Celtic period of the High Dragon Kings, were equated with their rank and position as leaders and overseers.

The Scythians

Throughout this discourse it must be borne in mind that when we speak of the Scythians as "Fairies", "Dragons", "Vampires" or "Elves", we are not talking about either the client races of the Scythians, or the ordinary Scythian citizenry, but of "Royal Scythians".

As we have discovered that the Vampire—as a "Witch"—belonged by genetic inheritance, to a distinct royal caste in Scythian-Celtic society: that of the priest-king or priestess-queen, the prince and princess-Druids. They had evolved very early on in human social history and belonged to a Eurasian-wide hereditary priestly community which had originated with the Scythian-Aryans. The name Scythian was originally spelt *Sithian* in 16th-century England, and it is from this tribal name that we obtain the word scythe, denoting a curved bladed agricultural tool, so-named because of its similarity in shape to the Scythian sword.

The Scythians were not, however, named after their use of a curved sword. The name *Sithian* is related to a group of words that appear in Indo-European languages which are found as far apart as Eire and Northern India, indicating that they had a common Aryan origin in Scythia. These include *Sithia*, *Sidhe*, *Siddir* and *Siddhi*.

In Cymric "dd" is pronounced "th", whilst in Irish and Scots the "th" is spelt dialectically "dh" whilst the "s" beginning a word is pronounced "sh". As we have related, the *Siddir* in Danish society were Witches who practiced the art of knot tying and loosening.

These *Siddir* were directly related to the mythic *Norns*, the Mori or Fates who were said to be responsible for the fate of mankind by the patterns that they wove and in the way that they tied and loosened the knots of the Web of Wyrd. The *Siddirs*, as well as being seers, could control such power as to influence the outcome of human affairs. In this respect their name reflects their abilities which, in India, were called the *Siddhis*, a word used to describe the powers of the Yogi who had self-realised.

The curious Irish word—*Sidhe*—pronounced "shee", "sheeth" or "sheeth-ay", attributed to the Fairies and meaning "powers", is therefore identical to *Siddir* (sheeth-eer) and *Siddhi* (sheeth-ee) and is derived therefore, from the *people of the powers*—the Scythians or *Sidheans* (sheethee-ans). In Scotland the royal Fairies were called the *Seelie* or Sheelie and their princesses were related to the sculpted Sheelagh Na Gigs over Church doorways, who do NOT depict ancient goddesses of fertility, but were the royal Grail Maidens of the Elven kings and queens.

The Sheelagh na Gigs were goddesses of sovereignty and transcendence. Their place over the doorways of Churches, many of which were built on the sites of ancient sacred groves, indicated that in entering these buildings one was entering through the vulva of the maiden into the Otherworld, the realm of Elphame and the Kingdom of Heaven.

They were permitted above Church doorways because the early Church itself wanted to be identified with the old ways. Firstly this was because it was in fact, at least in the beginning, part of the old ways and later, when Catholicism took over, the Sheelaghs remained in place—in order to attract and convert "pagans".

Along with the Irish Sidhe, the Seelie and the Seelie Court of Scotland had a distinctly royal origin in the Tuadha d'Anu who, when asked, like their Pictish descendants in Scotland, said of themselves that they were *Scythian*, as Canon Bourke himself has insisted.

Some people tend to think that the word sidhe means a hill and therefore that the Irish Danaan, as the *Sidhe*, inherited this name as a consequence of fleeing into the hills after their defeat by the Milesians. As we can see, this is not so and the Fairy "hills", where the Aes Dan or Danaan, the gods of the Irish, were said to live, were not all *Sidhe* hills.

These—the *power* hills—were the sacred temple-mortuary raths and barrows, the *creachaires* or tomb-sepulchres, that the Danaan priest-kings were wont to ritually occupy for millennia before moving to Eire, and centuries before their Iberian kinsmen, the Milesians, came looking for a fight. The *Sidhe*, the Fairies, were the "controllers of the fate of mankind" and so named in remembrance of, and in identification with, their ancient Anunnaki (Anunnagi) ancestors.

In pre-Christian history, although some practiced agriculture for a while, according to Murray-Hall, they abandoned it for their traditional way of life and many of the Scythian clans remained solitary and insular nomadic pastoralists—horse lords who ranged across large tracts of Europe and Asia for centuries. Others opted later for a more settled existence and mixed settled agriculture with pastoralism, a system that can be found in both Takla Makan, where they built fine cities, and in Ireland, where they became know as the trooping Fairies.

In general they were usually tall, pale skinned, with golden red hair and green eyes, unlike the Celts, who were stocky and squat, with ruddy complexions and dark hair. They practiced settled agriculture from a very early period.

The recent and rather unfortunate propagandist depiction of the Aryan (Scythian) as a tall, ruddy complexioned blonde racist yeoman-farmer-warrior-god has no basis in truth. In pre-Christian history an Aryan was a High King, a warrior was a warrior and a farmer was a farmer and "ne'er the three e'er met." The real Aryans of fact were red-haired and green-eyed. Their hired military help, derived from their lower Ksatriya caste, were not Aryan and were sometimes blonde and blue-eyed.

The Aryan royal families didn't intermarry with other tribes or castes but, despite this, with the development by many of their clans of settled city-states, they became urban multi-racial and appreciated cultural diversity.

The Aryan Hittites in particular were close allies of the Jews whose Draconian royal family, the House of David, made the Israelites, in a cultural sense, an early Aryan nation. The Scythians and the Aryan Scythian Gaels had numerous settlements either in or adjacent to Israel and Judea.

The comparatively early use of the horse and of horse related technology separated the Aryans from the other tribes that occupied the Middle-East and Eurasia. In Mittani, Mesopotamia, Akkad and Anatolia, the Hurrians (whom in the 1920's B. Hrozny described as the earliest Hindus) were the absolute Overlords and their supremacy is credited to their early use, like the Kurgans, of horsedrawn chariots.

The *Hur* syllable in Hurrian has been asserted by scholars, including G. Contenau (*La Civilisation des Hittites et des Hurrites de Mittani*) to be Har or Ar, meaning that the Hurrians, like the Scythians, were Aryans with an Aryan Vedic royal-sacral family of gods. They bestowed these upon the Hittites whose culture they dominated, the Hurrian or Aryan Mittani did in

Mesopotamia. The Hittites, in turn, provided the Greeks with these red-gold haired gods, including Zeus or Dyas Pater—the Jewish Jehovah, whose ancient symbol, shared with the sacred dynasty as a whole was, ironically, the Swastika.

The early "Scythians", the *people of the powers*, occupied a region spanning the Balkans, Transylvania, Carpathia, the Ukraine and later, Siberia and Takla Makan where the Tocharians, as the Elves were mistakenly called by early linguists, spoke a ritual language. This is now called Tocharian "A", but originated in Thrace in 1800 BC. Thus it had connections with the Fir Bolg and consequently with the Tuadha d'Anu as a whole, who began migrating from Central Europe to Ireland at that period.

Over the centuries, from 5000 BC onwards, the Scythians had also migrated into the Middle-East and had provided ruling families for many tribes and nations along and beyond the eastern Mediterranean coast.

In the *Annals of Irish History* the Scythian "Tuadha d'Anu", who had migrated farther still, to the islands of the north, were described as a tribe of deific queens, kings, princes and lords, and were noted for having Druids of their own. In Japan's northern islands, there lives a shamanic tribe called the Ainu whose early writing style has been identified as being Gaelic Ogham!

The Aryan-Scythian horse lords were a noble tribe, a sept of the Aryan peoples who, during various migrations, had also wandered east several centuries before the d'Anu displacement. On their reputed first journey to Eire in 1500 BC, they, were described by their contemporaries as being highly feminine and flamboyant. They travelled south-east via Persia (Iran) from 1800 BC onwards, and had entered the Indus Valley and intermingled with the Dravidian population.

This migration was to lands already formerly under Sumerian and consequently Ubaid control. The westward migration of the Scythians or Sidheans also included these very same Dravidians who, so British traditions state, were the messengers and summoners or "fetches" of the Merlins. These curious and delightful beings were also known as brownies, for obvious reasons, and adopted the habit of body tattooing in emulation of their Scythian lords, who in Britain and Ireland were known as the *Pixies*, which is a name derived from *Pict-Sidhes* or painted Fairies.

The confusion which arises when the Picts are described as being short and brown may be clarified when we remember that the Scythian caste system consisted of three closely interknit, co-operating races. Their traditions and practices would inevitably become, to a certain extent, common to all within the system by a natural process of social osmosis.

From this encounter arose the eastern branch of the Aryan, Vedic "Hindu" religion, with its Druids or magi—the Brahmins—and a pantheon of gods who were virtually identical with the Sumerian, Egyptian, Hittite, Irish, Gaulish, Danish and Greek. All of them stem from this early family of Elven goddess-queens and god-kings whose first home was to be found in the Balkans, Transylvania, Carpathia and the Caucasus regions of Greater and Little Scythia.

Within the Brahmin caste, special Tantric rites were and still are studied and practised. Evidence suggests that these ancient rites were brought to India from Sumeria. This accords with the assertion that Qabalah itself originated there and the author has long maintained that Tantra, particularly the Kaula Vama Marg and Esoteric Qabalism are simply variations of each other. The Tree of Life symbol and its hidden meanings appear in Druidism. Given the evidence to date, we can confidently say that Tantra and Qabalah are descended from ancient Ubaid Druidic philosophy.

The right hand path version of Hindu and Buddhist Tantra concerns itself with studying and practising sexual rites that one might find associated with the Kama Sutra. This form of Tantra promotes penetrative intercourse as a method of changing consciousness and has, attached to it, various commentaries on right-living and right-thinking. This was thought by some Indian scholars to have originated with those who were depicted by one sub-continental academic as the over-sexed Dravidians. The left hand path however is somewhat different.

This discipline can be found in both Hinduism and Buddhism and concerns itself with the practice of vampirism. This alone is sufficient evidence to allow one to ascertain that the "Black" or Left Hand or Kaula Path preceded the later right hand path which, though joyously tactile and self indulgent to begin with, appears many centuries later to have been somewhat sanitised for public consumption. The yogic disciplines associated with the Kaula Path, originating with the Scythians, are intended to lead the practitioner to what one might call "union with godhead".

This psychological condition is manifest in mystical Christianity as being the perception by the devotee of "the kingdom of heaven". That few Christians ever achieve such a state is not to be wondered at, as Christianity is also a royal blood tradition, exactly like its brother and sister, Druidism and Witchcraft.

Many Christians are ignorant of this aspect of Jesus' teaching and are in any case not encouraged to explore its possibilities because such union leads to physical and psychological freedom. This is the very last thing that the established Churches wish to encourage in the masses, even though Jesus himself preached it.

Union with Godhead, dwelling in Elphame, realisation of the Buddha or whatever one likes to call it is accompanied by a range of powers which were catalogued by the amazing Edwardian lady explorer Alexandra David-Neel.

She witnessed the performance of these remarkable powers or *Siddhis* by Buddhist monks in Nepal and Tibet, whose ritual and philosophy owed much to the indigenous religion Bon-Po, which ethically followed the same path as Kaula Vama Marg.

In the west we call it magic but, as we have seen, it was also known as the Sidhe. Kaula Tantra is dedicated to the Goddess Kali who is associated with both creation and destruction in the Hindu pantheon. Kali is a lunar deity who, like Tantra itself, moved east from Sumeria. As a moon goddess she is associated particularly with moon blood and the essences of the female organs of generation.

So what can we say of the nascence of Vampirism so far? Principally that it originated, not surprisingly, in Transylvania and the Central Eurasian region known as Scythia and that its practitioners were of a distinct race, the Elves, the high goddess-queens and god-kings of the Arya or Aesir.

Vampirism was the central feature of a philosophy based on endocrinology, rather than occult mumbo-jumbo, and used the consumption of female blood and mumae to enhance awareness and lead the practitioner to union with godhead. The powers accompanying such an elevated state of consciousness were called the *sidhe* or *siddhi* and were, with vampirism, the foundation of the cults of Druidism, Tantric Kaula Yoga, Qabalism, Alchemy, Rosicrucianism and Witchcraft.

Kali, like all the Ubaid deities, was a flesh and blood being. She, Kalimaath or Kali Marg, was a daughter of Lilith and Samael, son of Anu, who appears in the Aryan pantheon as Ahura Mazda and in Iran as the Medean god Zoroaster. Anu himself was the god who gave his name to the Tuatha de Danaan and, as Sitchin has suggested, the definition of the word god itself is "descended of Anu". Based on the spelling of "Tuatha de Danaan", some have suggested that these Irish Elven folk derived their name from an Irish mother goddess named Dana. If they had checked the earlier spelling—Tuadha d'Anu (Tribe of Anu)—they would have discovered that the Scythian Sidhe were the sons and daughters of Anu and the Ubaid gods and goddesses.

To recap, we have a clear connection between the words siddhi and sidhe, both of which originate from a Scythian or earlier proto-Aryan-Ubaid root. The Scythians, as the Aryans of Persia and Asia, provided the people then with their religious and social structures and spread their wisdom and overlordship, mostly by invitation from prospective client tribes, throughout Britain and Europe.

The Scythian Aryans, as the "Danaan", settled in Eire and Scotland, whilst in Wales they were known as the House of Don (Dan) or the House of Gwynnedd. This house sired the line of Llewelyn Princes, whilst in Scandinavia the Danaan became the Danes or Vikings and produced a junior cousin line—the Svei or Swedes—from which descended the Ruotsi clan that founded Russia. In Denmark the Sidhe was present as the *Siddir*, a class of seer or Witch which was later separated from the Godthi or Gothi, the Danish Druids.

The Scythian Danaan in Eire, as in the rest of Europe, were a race apart, a ruling caste within which, like the original race of the Gods from whom they descended, there were further caste classifications.

In Denmark these were later named the Jarl, Carl and Thrall castes whilst in Eire they were broadly speaking of the Druids, the Kings and the Warrior Smiths. In India they are still defined as the Brahmins, the Ksatriyas and the Sudras.

The original castes of the Gods were a) the common gods—gods of Earth; b) the gods of Heaven and Earth and c) the gods of Heaven. The first class was what we might call jobbing gods who became the genii locus or pagan spirits. The second class—the gods of Heaven and Earth—was the Titans, the Repha'im and Morrigans, the Angels and Valkiries who interceded between the transcended gods, the divine ancestors—the gods of Heaven—and man.

Heaven was the Otherworld. Not a place up in the stars, but a state of being which was adjacent to our own dimension. It was most competently described, more than once, in the Mabinogion, as the Mirrorworld. It could be entered and left freely by the gods of Heaven and Earth, the Portal Guardians. In this place, also known as Elphame, Hades, Hel, Caer Glas and Tir Na n'og, there dwelt the essences of the previous gods of Heaven and Earth who had passed on to become the transcended ones, the "antecessors" or ancestors of the later Witches. By dwelling in tombs, the gods of Heaven and Earth, the Danaan Queens and Kings, made contact with their ancestor Gods and passed their wisdom and edicts on to mankind. Today we might call this process invocation.

These gods are carried in the blood and by invocation. We bring their qualities and identities to the forefront of conscious being and give them voice. These Druidic gods and goddesses of Heaven and Earth were effectively the highest overlords on Earth, the Elven rulers of the human kings and queens who ruled beneath them.

Often we find mention of the Fairy blood in the medieval era in connection with the ruling nobility of the time. We might then be tempted to come to the logical conclusion that all nobility and royalty was thus of Fairy origin. This is simply not the case. Despite the usurpation of the original Fairy families by the Church sponsored new nobility, the previous kingly and noble dynasties were essentially human anyway.

The Fairy blood at that time, the dark ages and the medieval period, was carried by the descendants of the Archdruidic dynasties who formerly ruled over the contemporary Celtic and Eurasian kings and lords. It was not carried by any or all of the royal or noble families of the time simply by virtue of the fact that they were the heads of their castes. The castes of the Elven god-kings themselves were positioned directly over such class distinctions.

The gods of Heaven and Earth—the Archdruidic caste—dwelt in Barrows and Bergs which in Eire were called *raths*. The word Rath means a "royal seat". These raths were the holy shrines and sepulchres built by the Danaan—the original Gods of Ireland according to the *Annals of Irish History*—to house the mortal remains of their ancestors and act as royal palaces for the Portal Guardians. In specific cases these Gods are named, and we learn, for instance, that Newgrange was the shrine occupied by Nuadha and later Oengus.

The devotional and holy nature of these places has led some scholars and commentators to believe that, because they were tombs and temples, those said to occupy them must be purely spiritual entities, gods of an ethereal nature. Originally nothing could have been farther from the truth. Both Nuadha and Oengus were kings of the Danaan and contemporary descriptions of them and their kin leave us with the picture of the Danaan as a race of people with prodigious and very earthly appetites.

From their kinsmen in Siberia we know that, by our dubious standards, they were complete junkies and imbibed any form of drug they could get hold of. These would have included cannabis and cocaine, prevalent in Egypt and the Levant at the time, as well as the drugs classically associated with the Druids and the Elves, such as Amanita Muscaria and Psylocybin, the Fairy mushrooms of children's picture books everywhere.

The Danaan were hardened drinkers and unscrupulous womanisers, whilst accounts of their princesses relate that they often mated in public with the highest nobles of their clan, to prove or reiterate their social standing to onlookers. (Heroditus: *The Histories*)

Counterbalancing this view of them, born of our own hypocritical conditioning, the Danaan, whether in Eire or mainland Europe or Asia, were the finest smiths, jewellers, poets and musicians of their time. They were the Lords of fearless warriors and gifted horsemen and, despite what we might think of the foregoing, they were a righteous, meticulous people who maintained standards of conduct in areas of their social life where such standards were considered essential for the harmonious order of society.

Great emphasis was laid upon honesty and truth in one's words and one's dealings. The maintenance and conservation of the natural environment was paramount, and infractions, such as the cutting of trees, could mean death. Emphasis was also laid on hospitality and courtly behaviour to one's peers or guests, the honouring of one's ancestors and heroes, and the maintenance of extended family ties through fostering.

Although unaffected by the petty morality with which we view our sexual behaviour, they would kill a man for breaking his word or lying. They were an heroic people. Compared with us today, they were a far more moral race whose standards of conduct, not invested or centred on our kind of childish taboos—but placed where it matters—puts us to shame.

They were a race centred on their spirituality which itself was centred on gnosis and transcendent consciousness. This made them, like their later royal Viking cousins, a fearless people much loved and also much feared in turns, by all who knew them, whether in Eurasia or the British islands.

In about 500 BC, the Milesians entered Ireland from Iberia. Having defeated the Danaan tribes they put many of them to flight. It was during this period that the Danaan became known as the Daouine Sidhe—the people of the hills—an erroneous use of the word sidhe.

One group, the tribe of the Danaan king of Ulster, Bruidhne (mistakenly called Cruithne by the Romans), fled to Caledonia where they became known as the remnant of Cruithne or the "Cruithainn". Other Danaan clans fled to Wales and the southwest of mainland Britain. Several centuries later, when the Romans were unfortunate enough to encounter them in Scotland, they referred to these Danaan as "Picts". It is this word that has adapted itself to become one of the names we use to describe the Elven peoples—the pixies—or properly the Pict-Sidhes as we have already seen.

These beings also came to be known as the Leprechauns and the etymology of this word, though thought to mean "small-bodied" actually means "scaly-bodied" from the Latin word *lepra* as in leprosy—scaly skinned.

The scaliness referred to was derived from the fish-scale style of armour which was common to the draconian Dacians, the Zmei, the Danes and the Danaan, all of whom originated in the region now known as Greater Scythia.

The scaly, twin-pronged tail of the wouivre or mermaid was also derived from the use, by grail maidens, of fish-scale plated leggings. When worn with the Swan's or Raven's feather cloaks, we have the classical image of the Harpie, reproduced in medieval depictions of Melusine.

Pict or Pictish means "painted" and the Danaan earned this appellation by virtue of their use of tattoos or woad to decorate their bodies with totemic or magical markings, the favourite being the labyrinth or spiral whorl.

The ancestors of the Irish Danaan—the Ubaid Danaan—had been using tattoos and woad since 4000 BC. Examples of it can also be found in depictions of the Egyptian god Osiris or Asher as he is also known, and in the depictions of the Hindu gods Vishnu and Siva. Kali herself was also known as Kali Azura—the Blue Kali.

The spiral or whorl—the labyrinth—is the subject of a later essay in which it and its painted or carved symbol, lie at the centre of Vampire and Elven tradition. The spiral can be found carved into the rock at Newgrange in Ireland and also featured as a sacred design associated with the dwellings of the related Kassite Danaan clans who migrated to Britain.

In the Gaelic language we find two words specifically defining "Vampires". The first—Creachaire—means a sepulchre, a tomb, a shrine and a temple, indicating that the character we later become familiar with as the "Vampire" of Gothic legend was in fact a "dweller in the tombs", a Druidic priest-king or priestess-queen—an Uber or Witch Overlord.

In Eurasia, particularly in the permafrost of Siberia and the arid wastes of Takla Makan in China, the mummified bodies of Scythian Chieftains and Shamankas or Priestess queens have been found. In Siberia the frozen remains of a male were unearthed. He had been tattooed with animal designs reminiscent of the totem Pictish salmon often found carved on stones in Scotland.

In the same region a shamanka had been unearthed who had been tattooed with the spiral labyrinth design. She, like her counterpart in Takla Makan, wore the conical headdress of the Anunnaki gods of Sumeria that is also associated with medieval Witchcraft. This same headdress is depicted in bas-relief on the walls of the palace of Darius as being worn by those Scythians who brought him gifts in 500 BC.

The Takla Makan mummy, excavated by the Chinese in the 1960s, had red-gold hair and was buried adjacent to a cache of tartan plaid cloth and spiral painted pottery, similar to that found at Al'Ubaid in Syria. In the same region, caves have been discovered where the walls are painted with devotional Buddhist pictures featuring the Tocharians, as they are known, conversing with Buddha.

Geoffrey Ashe states that the western Druids were interviewed by Buddha. He claimed that they, the Druids, had established Shangri-La in the west. This should give the reader some hint as to the general thrust of Druidic philosophy and of the hidden nature of that promoted by Jesus, whom St. Columbus clearly stated was also a Druid and Magus himself.

Chapter 3

Scythians and Druids

The Tocharians, depicted in the cave shrines of Takla Makan, are red haired, like the Merovingians, and wear the same conical hat, sometimes called a Phrygian cap. A variant of this was worn by Mithras, the intermediary god adopted by the Persians and featured in the Indian pantheon of the Asuras. In monarchical Dualism he is depicted as balancing the forces of increase and decrease, represented by the gods Ahura Mazda and Ahriman. Some classical authors identified him with Jesus Christ. His headgear is also depicted as the hat worn by gnomes and dwarves.

Accompanying the depictions of the Tocharian Lords in these cave temples are examples of the language attributed to them—Tocharian "A" script—which looks remarkably like one of the scripts that Tolkien attributes to his Elven peoples. Like Tolkein's Elven language, it is a Gaelic tongue influenced by Finno Ugaric. That the Tocharians are Scythian-Aryans themselves means that the devotional language used by their High-Kings and Queens might justifiably be called an Elven language, the tongue of Tolkien's Sundered Elves of the East.

The second Gaelic word for "Vampire" is *Sumaire*, which is pronounced shimarie, with the accent on the middle syllable—shim AR ri. Sumaire is translated as "vortex", meaning a whirlpool or spiral, a labyrinth: a sucker, a reptile (serpent or Dragon).

There is a clear link here with Sumeria and Anu's mother Tiamat, the Dragoness of the deeps, and with Anu's children Samael and Lilith, the forebears of the Fairies. Various pictures of the latter two depict them as entwined around a tree. Often the tree is Lilith herself, with Samael as the serpent or Dragon resting in her branches as in Hebraic Iconography where Lilith is the Tree of Knowledge in the Garden of Eden. The Sumerians appeared first in Mesopotamia in 3500 BC. Prior to their emergence they were preceded by the Ubaid migrants from what is now southern Romania, and from Carpathia and Scythia. They had fled south to escape the Black Sea flood of 4000 BC. Archaeologists working in Tartaria in the Ubaid territory of Transylvania discovered a "tepes" or Rath under which they found a fire-pit dated to about 5000 BC. Buried amongst the ashes were the human remains of a cannibalistic sacrificial victim and two clay tablets. On these were inscribed the name of Enki (Samael), the number of Anu—60—and the image of a goat, Enki again, and a Tree—Lilith. The pictographic nature of the inscriptions convinced the archaeologists that the language was the forerunner of Sumerian and so they called it proto-Sumerian. This made it fairly obvious that the first Sumerians were originally Ubaid Overlords from Central Eurasia.

Tocharian Lords

Sadly however, a group of right-wing Hungarian nationalists then claimed Sumerian roots by virtue of a spurious discovery they claimed to have made, subsequent to the discovery in the 1960's. Following this claim, no academic would validate the proto-Sumerian theory. Quite rightly, they had no desire to accommodate the views of a neo-nazi group.

It is unclear what a group of Mongoloids thought they had in common with the Aryan race. Having invaded the region as the Magyar at so late a period in history it is impossible to see how any claim to Sumerian or proto-Sumerian origins could possibly hold up under even the most cursory scrutiny. Nevertheless the attitude of those academics who opposed the definition was obstructive and misleading. This is especially so as it is now conclusively proved that the culture responsible for the production of the Tartarian clay tablets and the Rath structure was Ubaid—the founders of civilised Mesopotamia. As it turns out, they were also the Overlords of the Indus valley civilisation of Mohenjo Daro and Harrapa where Ishtar reigned as Queen.

Further east of Transylvania similar discoveries were made in the Ukraine or greater Scythia and the peoples who had settled the area were named after their dwellings, which in Russian were called Kurgans. They were mound houses of exactly the same style as the tepes of Tartaria and the Tells that the Ubaid built all the way down through Anatolia to Al'Ubaid and Sumeria.

The invention of the chariot was attributed to the Kurgan peoples, clearly the red-haired Aryan or proto-Aryan (if you must) horse lords. The axle dimensions of the chariot were copied on all horse drawn vehicles right up until the Victorian period, when they were incorporated into the axle width (4 ft. 8 in.) of the standard gauge railways still in use today. The influence that Vampires have had on European culture should not be dismissed! They inspired modern wheeled transport, invented large-scale tourism, and lent their images and their kilts to the lids of every shortbread tin you've ever seen.

It seems fair to suggest, given the wealth of archaeological and anthropological evidence, that the Sumerians or Ubaid as we should call them, along with the pale-skinned and red-haired Lilith and her descendants, were the early Elven, Aryan-Scythian Dragon Overlords of what we know now as Transylvania and Greater Scythia. This is particularly clear in the light of the discoveries of bat-winged, serpent-god statuary found in Dacia and Tibet (not too far from Takla Makan!) which is said to date back at least 5000 years, putting it into the period of the emergence of civilisation in Sumeria.

Such figures we would readily identify as the Dragon or, in Gaelic—The Sumaire—whilst the Kurgans/Tells/Tepes that these early Transylvanian/Scythian Sidheans or Ubaid occupied were clearly duplicated in the Irish raths of the Danaan, such as Newgrange with its spirally engraved stones, the Zigurrats of the Sumerians, and the Pyramids of the Egyptians.

Whilst these ancient structures bore the marks of the Sumaire, the spiral labyrinth or vortex design, thus emphasising the creachaire—sumaire theme of the Dragon—Witch—Vampire—Overlord theme, the Egyptians too adopted the labyrinth and used the spiral as a hieroglyph which they termed the "Mer". This was a symbol of irrigation associating it with water and, via "weir" spelt Vere and Mhaior, rendering Muir, returning once more to the Egyptian Mer—the fish trap or fish-woman trap, the enclosure of the mermaid, the maze or labyrinth and intimations of the wild hunt. (Muir and Mhaior name variants courtesy of Dr. Hugh Vere.)

So at long last, having trudged through the backwaters of obscure knowledge, we can now say that we know exactly who and what the Vampire was and is. A very rare individual, a God-King amongst the race of human kings, the Vampire descends from the supernatural Dragon Royalty of Sumeria back to the Ubaid Overlords of what was to become known as Transylvania and Greater Scythia.

The Vampire: the Dragon King or Queen was an Archdruid, a Witch Queen or King, a Fairy Princess or Prince amongst the race of Elphame. Consequently the Vampire, the Fairy, the Dragon and the Witch were all the same individual. Far from being the characters of fable they were in fact very powerful, very real beings whose Vampiric natures and rituals sustained their superconsciousness and transcendent vision which, in its turn, maintained their positions as the overlords of mankind.

These gods of flesh and blood were the only gods that ever actually existed: myth, however, transformed them into the ethereal deities whom we are conditioned to think of as Gods now, and who came to be worshipped worldwide. Nevertheless, flesh and blood they were and their bloodlines descend to the present day.

The Druids

The word Druid is said to be Greek in origin, as "drys": means "tree". Some authorities like to think it means "oak tree" but no evidence exists to confirm this irrefutably. As we shall see later, Druid is also related to "dru" meaning "run" in Sanskrit and to Drys meaning a Wren—specifically the Goldcrest—one of the birds most sacred to the Druids. For the present however, we will concentrate on the Greek version of the word.

The Druids are associated with groves and, as some will insist, with oak trees. However, it is feasible to suggest that in the light of their Sumerian and Ubaid origins, the Druids as priest kings of the Dragon, were connected specifically with the Tree of Life and the Tree of Knowledge, rather than with any mundane or temporal shrubbery.

Accepting this we may further suggest that, as priests of these pre-eminent Trees of Life and Knowledge, they may be further identified with those magicians and scholars whose Transylvanian descendants were the Scythian Aryans or Sumerian Anunnaki—the Dragon God-Kings. They were instrumental in establishing the Chakric system of Hindu and Buddhist Tantra and Hebrew, Arabic and Greek Qabalah whose magical systems, as we all know, contain a glyph called the Tree of Life.

Generally speaking this Tree is a system of pathways both macrocosmic and microcosmic in nature. It links the various subtle energy centres which are said to exist both in the universe, as levels of density and emanation relating to the manifestation of cosmic power and being, and in the human body—on the microcosmic level—as energy centres corresponding to the glands in the endocrinal system. In Qabalah the spheres which do not relate to the glands may be seen as points in the meridian system adopted by the Chinese. On another level, the Qabalistic Tree of Life is a genealogical chart of the Gods.

The magical Tree is a universal symbol. As in the early Sumerian depiction of the Tree of Life; the abode of Lilith, many of the subsequent Arabic, Indian and European Holy Trees share common attributes. All have residing in their topmost branches some form of bird.

In Tantra it is the Swan, whose head rests within the Ajna Chakra which corresponds to the pineal and pituitary glands and the corpus callosum. In Welsh Druidic lore the bird is represented as the eagle, a typically shamanic, totem bird which symbolises the ascendant spirit. Here the eagle is the god Lleu (in Ireland he is the Danaan king Lugh), the father of the Elven Llewelyn Kings of Gwynnedd. In Arabic Sufism the bird is a peacock, whilst in Viking lore the Sacred Tree Yggdrasil has at its base a coiled serpent by a pool and in its highest boughs the bird of the released spirit accompanied by a white hart.

What a deer is doing up a tree is anyone's guess, but use your imagination for the time being. Yggdrasil is called the Axis Mundi and is seen as the tree which contains within its branches and roots the nine worlds of the Viking philosophical system, including their version of the Hebrew Qlipphoth or underworld. Immediately the similarity between it and the Qabalistic and Tantric Trees becomes quite apparent. This is no fluke.

In actual fact the Druids' most sacred tree was not the oak. It was the apple tree, and linked to it is the blue boar, both of which came originally, it was said, from the Otherworld. For this reason the Tree of Knowledge in the Garden of Eden was always depicted as the apple, but could be interchanged with the pomegranate for reasons which will eventually become apparent.

The Mistletoe Bard, whom we will encounter later, cut the golden bough from the Apple prior to descending into the underworld. It has been suggested that the berries of the mistletoe represent the sperm of the Great Oak God (Jupiter/Thor/Jehovah/Enlil) and thus his fertility and lifeforce, but this is not in fact the case.

The Mistletoe grew mainly on Apple trees which, as we shall see, are exclusively female. Therefore the berries of the Mistletoe represent the female and consequently the Goddess' fluid. Not the seminal fluid of a male deity.

The boar is sacred to both Mars and to Arduina or Diana. This link between the apple and the boar; and the boar and Mars and Diana or the Moon is identical with the association between the Apple Tree of Eden as Lilith (of the Moon) and Samael, the Serpent or Dragon, who embraces her. Essentially the symbols of the Boar and the Dragon have become interchangeable.

The Blue Boar is a Druidic symbol of office and the Dragon is a symbol of bloodline descent, a clan badge of the Druidic race. In the Scythian Dragon Tribe, the individual totem animal badges vary from region to region and reflect the local fauna and the status of the clan or sept. As an example, a high or Archdruidic family badge would be the boar, whilst a junior sept of that clannad would have as its totem the hedgehog, which is rather amusing.

The symbol of Samael the Serpent reclining in the Branches of Lilith's Apple Tree in the Garden of Eden actually depicts the concept of the Dragon eating the fruit itself. This can also be found slightly more abstractly but conversely and paradoxically more graphically at the same time, in the Tantric equivalent of the serpent entwined around a female figure.

As the apple is also the favourite fruit of the boar in the wild, it is doubtless that the adoption of the Boar as a badge was because of this. Furthermore, the identification of the boar with the Dragon was through their mutual, actual and symbolic love of what the Irish Druids called the apples of red-gold. The boar was also called Le Solitaire and for this reason has links with the Merlin which will be dealt with later.

The Apple Trees—either Lilith or her descendant scarlet priestesses—bore the fruit which symbolised the Sephira and the glands of the female body. These, the apples of red-gold, produce the enriched virginal womb blood that was consumed by both the male and female Druids—the Boars in the Orchard and the Serpents or Dragons in the Trees. Red-Gold is also the Tantric Kaula term for womb blood: the *Rtu* or first flow of the womb.

In reinforcing the Uber-Oupire link—the identification between the Witch (Druidhe) and Vampire—it is worth taking a look at the totem system of Mithraism, a close cousin of Druidism. In the Mithraic initiatory grades there are 7 degrees.

The Highest is the Dragon and the penultimate is the wolf. Also included is the Raven. With variations across Europe these animals, along with Swans, Geese, Bears, Vipers, Hawks, Eagles and so on, served as the tuadh or kingdom emblems for the various Scythian groups.

In Romania however, these grades with their animal totems or badges make up the degrees or conditions of vampirism. The most potent Vampire is the Dracoi or female Dracoica, from whence the House of Drakul obtained its name, meaning "Satan" or "Dragon", whilst Drakulea or Dracula means "son of Satan" or "son of the Dragon". Lying at a close second place comes the Stregoi or female Stregoica, a being that manifests itself as either a wolf or a Raven. We can see where this is leading, can't we?

The Stregoi or Stregoica represents both the Morrigan or Morgana, the Valkirie and the Werewolf or Verewolf, which is simply another manifestation of the Vampire. Typically and especially where wolves were scarce, the werewolf was represented variously by the bear and the fox; and elsewhere by the crocodile (the Sobekh of Egypt—patron and protector of Royalty—whose fat was used as the Messach or anointing oil of the Pharaohs, the Messiahs or priest kings).

In this area of the world it was also common to replace the werewolf with the Panther, who was sacred to the lunar goddess Diana and also to Bacchus. Panther was the clan name of Jesus, and much earlier, the Ubaid priests wore the skins of Panthers as their totem animal. The Panther's feeding ritual involves it opening the jugular vein in its victim's neck, and drinking the blood prior to eating the carcass.

The association between werewolves and the moonlight which drove them "loopy", according to fable, is repeated and reinforced by the traditional belief that Witches (also known as Vampires) were sacred to Diana and worshipped her by the light of the full moon. The link between the full moon and the Vampire of the Gothic Romance is also well represented in tradition.

The reason that moonlight drove werewolves mad and elicited devotion from Witches was because the full moon was seen as the menstrual moon that signalled the impending flow. It was worshipped particularly by the Witches of Italy and the surrounding area. These ladies were called Strega, that is the Italian name for a Witch. Rather than worshipping the full moon they were celebrating what the moon and Diana stood for—food for the soul—the blood of virgins! Give it a chance—it isn't as gory or unsavoury as it sounds.

This was the secret foundation for the High Romance and Courtly Love that initiated the exoteric Medieval Romantic Movement itself, so don't get judgmental or picky. According to an eminent Professor of Sexual Medicine, if you are health conscious and take supplements like HRT you should know that it comes, in many cases, from the urine of either mares or French nuns.

Melatonin was the primary hormone extracted in the blood rites of Diana, so it's your choice. Would you have preferred the blood of beautiful virgins, romantically celebrating and giving joyously of their feminine power and status by moonlight, or the urine of papists—in a pill? One type of melatonin is live whilst the other is stone dead and useless—guess which is which. And melatonin is only the beginning of the story.

Others included oxytocin, prolactin, seratonin, adenosine triphosphate, dopamine, telomerase and retinol. Richard Dufton has also been working independently on identifying the same chemical presences for some years. When he and the author met in 1995 they began to work closely on the melatonin basis for the Holy Grail. Out of this joint research the author discovered the wider implications of the discovery and restructured the Kabalistic and Tantric systems with precise chemical indices for each sephiroth or chakra.

The association between Scythian Totem beasts, Romanian animal Vampire types and Mithraic grades of Initiation indicates clearly that vampirism, far from being random or opportunist, was in fact part of an ancient system of Elven rites manifest in Tantra, Mithraism and Druidism.

Having said that, the symbols of the panther and the werewolf were apposite, as the Scythian warrior nobility were literally bloodthirsty at times. Roman reports from the early part of the first millennium state how the Pictish Danaan had been witnessed eating the flesh and drinking the blood of their defeated foes following victories in battle.

Undoubtedly this was a corruption of earlier ritual practice as we shall see later. Certainly going out and "eating Italian" had a unique and disturbing meaning for the Roman soldiery of the day, as the Ninth Legion in Albany discovered to their cost. Drinking the blood of friend or foe in battle was a common practice in Eire and Scotland, the former in remembrance of fallen comrades, the latter to obtain the strength of the enemy. Contrary to Royal Vampirism, the whole point of Martial Vampirism was to clog your arteries with someone else's adrenaline.

Another ritual familiar to those who have read Bram Stoker's *Dracula* was the hauling of soil from the Scythian homelands in boxes. The Scythians initiated this practice with the idea that the earth was the source of sovereignty and power and that one's soul was linked to one's homeland.

This should not be dismissed outright, as we are what we eat. What we eat affects the "soul" (the biochemically derived and mediated collection of responses and attachments called "ME", the ego, personality or whatever, dependant for its existence on the continuity of the mind-brain interface) through the body, as both body and soul are inextricably linked. What we eat comes from the land where we are born and thus the soil of one's country and its inherent sovereignty and identity literally flow in the blood that courses through one's veins.

Up until the 19th century, the displaced Scots who travelled to America would slip a little soil from their former crofts into the soles of their boots in order that, wherever they went they would always be walking on the earth of their homeland.

The Scythian Overlords brought the Dragon culture with them as they traversed the many regions of Europe and finally settled in the British Isles. All their kings, indeed all Scythians of the royal caste were Dragons, particularly the Druids. Their high kings were called PenDragons or chief Dragons and were picked by their Druidic peers from Druidic families.

Variant spellings for the name Druid include "Draoi"—thought to mean Dragon—which is close in spelling to the Romanian "Dracoi" and "Dracoica". If related to "Drys", it is associated with wood nymphs or tree spirits. This suggests that the "Drys" or "Dryads" were the female Druids who were symbolised by the apple tree of Lilith whilst the "Draoi" or "Dracoi"—the highest degree of the male Druids—were represented by the serpent entwined in the branches of those apple trees.

The Priestess Queens and Priest Kings, as we have seen, dwelt in the holy places, the royal raths that served as both temple and tomb. These subterranean palaces mimicked the bergs or mound houses of the Scythians' "proto"-Sumerian ancestors, who originated in Transylvania and Carpathia.

Similarly the Mithraic underground temples resembled places like Newgrange, in that they had an aperture above the doorway that allowed a shaft of sunlight into the building. This ray would hit the back wall of the temple where, in the case of Mithraic rituals, there were placed figurines, the sequential illumination of each in its turn, as the day progressed onwards, would tell an initiatory story, bathed in the dying light of the midwinter sun.

Beneath the doorways of some of these buildings have been discovered the remains of headless corpses whose skulls would have been secreted within these Sidhe Mounds. Their functions were to serve as Guardians of the

Portals, spirit defenders of the power and sanctity of these shrines—the dwellings of the Dragons—the Goddess-Queens and God-Kings incarnate.

The cult of the severed head, as part of Celtic religious practice, originated with the Druids, and therefore the Scythians. Examples of the head as the seat of the soul and the source of mystical wisdom, a bestower of gifts or cornucopia finds expression both in the legend of the head of Bran the Blessed or Bendigaid Fran, Archdruid of Britain. This is retold in the Mabinogion; and the Trial papers of the Templars, who owned a head which was said to speak words of transcendent wisdom. This head, along with that of Bran, have both been cited as being aspects of the Grail with whom both Bran and the Templars were connected.

The Knights Templar, restructured by Baldwin of Bourcq in 1118, appended to their name "and of the Temple of Solomon" whilst the members of the original Order of Templars, a Vere foundation which emerged in 1100, were called "Guardian Princes of the Royal Secret". However the original Temple Guard was founded 1500 years earlier in Jerusalem.

A close examination of the *Song of Songs* attributed to Solomon will reveal to the reader certain esoteric references to the Grail. It has been further revealed that Solomon's bloodline had Scythian Dragon origins and therefore connections with the Cult of the Head. That a head, said to be that of the Magdalene, successor to Sheba, turned up in the inventory attached to the Templar trial papers should therefore come as no surprise. The Scythians believed that the head contained the immortal soul.

Descartes, writing in the 1600's, was of the same opinion and elaborated the theory by asserting that the seat of the soul was the pineal gland. Others, writing later, have suggested that this organ is the mediator of inspiration and the translator of intuitive or cosmic information.

In Indian Tantric Yoga the pineal is the physical seat or anchor of the Ajna Chakra which also corresponds to the pituitary. In this philosophy the Pineal is symbolised as being the head of the Swan, whose body comprises the various areas of the rest of the brain. As we have seen, the Dove and the Raven also fulfil this symbolic function.

The pineal gland is specifically associated with Grail Lore and closely aspected to manifestations of the Grail in the forms of a cup, a stone, a cauldron, a well, mere or lake; a fountain, (such as that found in certain qabalistic rituals) and an underground stream.

Within the theme of the severed head we also find the dressed head of Llewelyn, King of Gwynedd, which was severed from his body and garlanded with Ivy (sacred to Bacchus) before being dispatched to Edward I following the victory of his armies over the Welsh in the 1200's.

Some two hundred years later, on his death in 1477, Prince Vlad Draculea's body was taken to an Abbey he had built on an island in the middle of a lake in Smyrna in what is now the Republic of Romania. Such a sanctuary has distinct Arthurian overtones and associations with the Isle of Avalon, upon which there was also built an abbey of the quasi-Druidic Celto-Scythian Church.

This replaced the early Rath temple, grove and sanctuary of the Morganas, the ladies of the lake who were the Swan Maiden-Valkiries of the Scythian world, Vampires and head hunters. In such sanctuaries headless corpses, as we have seen, were placed as portal guardians. It is in just such a condition that we discover that, according to local tradition, Draculea's head was removed from his body and his corpse was buried beneath the stone flags beneath the doorway of the Abbey's chapel.

A similar incident is reported to have occurred with the establishment of the Celtic Christian Shrine on the Island of Iona. Here it is St. Columba who is said to have severed the head of one of his disciples and buried the blood drained corpse beneath the doorway of the chapel. The blood of the victim was then consumed as a Eucharist in thanksgiving for the monks' safe arrival to the island. Here we can see that early Christianity was indeed tied up with the cult of the head, as was the collateral Johannite Cult of the Baptist, who himself was a sacrificial king of Dragon descent.

As we have seen, Draculea's name means son of the Dragon, and his burial replicates the Scythian burials in the Holy-Royal Sidhe or power mounds found in Eire and Scotland. In Draculea's case there are a number of symbols associated with him that connect him directly with the Scythian Druidic tradition. Furthermore these symbols, some of which we obtain, surprisingly enough, from Stoker's novel, lead to the conclusion that Stoker knew a great deal about his subject. Much of the information in *Dracula* the novel is of an esoteric and highly specialised psycho-biological nature, which does not detract from or conflict with, but rather elucidates upon, the character of the Draculea of history.

Bram Stoker was a close friend and associate of the Welsh magician and writer Arthur Machen who wrote numerous works, including a paper on the alchemical significance of the Dragon and a novel on the Twllyth Teg—the Fairies of Wales.

It is a common device to convey esoteric knowledge via the medium of supposed fiction and it appears that both Stoker and Machen involved themselves in such ventures. Stoker was also acquainted with Aleister Crowley and MacGregor Mathers, both of whom were leading lights in the Hermetic Order of the Golden Dawn. Machen and Oscar Wilde were members of this organisation which, it is said, had its roots in the ancient Rosicruciana Anglicae.

Oscar Wilde was one of only four people associated with The Golden Dawn and the later breakaway group: the Ordo Templi Orientis headed by Crowley, who himself undertook to perform the rituals leading to the accomplishment of a variant of the ancient "Mass of the Vampire".

The amazing Jack Parsons OTO, attempted it in the 1940's and joined Wilde in succumbing to the ruin and degradation that accompanies it. Jack died in an inexplicable explosion in the garage of his home in California.

Whilst Crowley accomplished the rite and walked away virtually unscathed, eventually dying of old age in Hastings, Wilde's fate is known to all. Having said that, "Death in Hastings" has none of the romantic *je ne sais quoi* of say, *Death in Venice*, or even Paris. Perhaps Wilde, vilified as he was, had the better of it after all, at least in terms of style!

It has been suggested that Stoker was either a member of the OTO or the Golden Dawn. It would therefore appear that the cohesion and integrity of the symbolism in his *Dracula* must therefore point to Stoker having a source of esoteric information far more informed in historical and alchemical terms than any that he might have obtained. It is more than could be gleaned, as has been suggested, purely from the folklore of Romanian peasants or from contemporary literary sources. Historical accounts of Prince Draculea's life confirm that he was born in and became Prince of Wallachia, not Transylvania. In linking Draculea with Transylvania however, Stoker suggests to the reader that the origin of the Vampire tradition was indeed linked to the Ubaid Homeland. Recent research has uncovered the fact that Draculea did indeed, like his Scythian Warrior ancestors, drink the blood of his impaled and decapitated victims.

Decapitation is distinctly a Scythian practice and although it has been suggested that Draculea learnt the custom of impaling from his Turkish captors, this practice had been used as a punishment by the Aryans of Persia as early as 500 BC.

Although Stoker has Dracula impaled and decapitated at his castle when in fact Draculea was beheaded at the Abbey where he was buried, Stoker is rightly attempting to associate Dracula, via these rituals, with an entire Vampiric cultural tradition of which his character was destined to become the definitive archetype.

This is no bad thing, because the picture of Dracula and his accoutrements and behaviour is not far from the actual truth of the matter. The finer details of the novel confirm that Stoker was probably being prompted by others in the writing of this work, which contains secret information that is still generally unknown outside certain circles.

It was generally thought that the only way to kill a Vampire was to impale the body through the heart—in order to pin the wandering body to the earth—remove the head and cremate the remains. At that time cremation was forbidden in Christian Europe because it was believed that the bodily remains should be left intact to rise again on the Day of Judgement.

Obviously the Church thought that reconstituting the fetid and rotting remains of sinners on the Last Day would be a simple task for God, whereas he would be powerless to reconstruct the former human being from a handful of dust. Typically stunning Christian logic in action here.

Cremation was practiced by Hindus, a race of people originally descended from the Aryan Horse Lords. Considering this as a funerary practice in relation to decapitation and impaling, which was reserved as a royal punishment in Persia, perhaps the peasant memory, prompted by the Church, recalled the link between royalty and these rituals. They then assumed that the only way to kill a Vampire who was, after all exclusively a member of the Fairy or Royal Race, was to put the body through a series of ritual processes, some of which had been, variously, components of Scythian royal sacrificial or funerary practice.

We can read of royal decapitation in the stories of Bran and Llewelyn. Although Celts buried their common dead, we might suggest, given the earliest evidence from Tartaria and other later sites, that Royal Scythians, like their Viking and Hindu cousins, cremated the sometimes decapitated remains of their sacred dead, depending on the requirements of specific ritual necessity. Perhaps to the peasantry, impaling was seen as poetic justice in dispatching one assumed to be of a race for whom impaling was a common punishment.

We have seen that impaling was thought to nail the body of the Vampire to the earth. Perhaps when the body was not burnt, impaling was considered sufficient to keep in its grave the body of one belonging to a race that the crows in cassocks said was so terrifying and seemingly so indestructible.

It will be remembered, though, that many of the stories concerning Vampires were contrived by the Church to encourage the flock to remain in fear for its life and thus faithful to its only means of protection and salvation, the Christian Church. It was immaterial to them that vampirism was rarely committed against outsiders except when they were opponents in war. Nevertheless the Vampire scare went on longer than the Witch craze and was just as effective in keeping the poor peasants in bondage to the evil doctrines of a lying Church.

As a Scythian custom, impaling would have been as common in Galatia, later Turkey, where the Cult of the Head thrived in Roman times; as it was in Persia. Here it was reserved for one royal in particular – Bress. He betrayed his brother, Darius, following the successful invasion by Alexander.

Essentially Stoker's *Dracula* is as much a part of the Grail Cycle as the Druidic stories of King Arthur and of Eschenbach's *Parzifal*. In these stories as in most Druidic teaching fables, the Bards delighted in presenting material that could be read on several different but related levels which often have hermetic, macro and microcosmic components.

In particular where Stoker is concerned, an extract from Solomon's *Song of Songs* features in a couple of obscure lines in his *Dracula*. These refer directly to the central alchemical theme of the Grail Cycle and put the seal on the book as being an esoteric work, rather than just simply a Gothic novel.

Historically Draculea himself attended the “Solomon School” in Hermanstadt, an alchemical, hermetic college in Transylvania that taught magic to the sons of Royalty. One other school like this existed in Europe, in Toledo in Spain. At the “Solomon” only one person per class ever graduated, or “rode the Dragon” as it was termed.

Fanciful Christian theory says that the rest of the students ended up with Satan in Hell! Reminiscent of a Druidic “Bangor” or university, the “Solomon School” finished Vlad's education. It suited him to become a Romanian counterpart of the British PenDragon, with all the brutal wisdom of his Fairy ancestors and predecessors who, as God-Kings of the specifically intermediary, guardian-class of Anunnaki deities, were buried in the same manner that Dracula himself was laid to rest.

Draculea, the prince of Wallachia, was little different in actuality from the Dracula character of Stoker's novel. This Sacred Prince was a Hermetic scholar and initiate, a student of magic; Magus, Witch Lord and Dragon Prince. He counterbalanced the bloodlust of his forebears with a refined knowledge and advanced practice of Grail procedure which, shining forth radiantly from the pages of Stoker's little masterpiece, echoed the teachings that the historical Draculea would have received at the “Solomon School”. These teachings were encountered in the Dragon Court of which he was a member. They were teachings which were held in common by Archdruids, Alchemists, Tantric Yogis, Hermeticists and Qabalists alike, each discipline originating from one ancient Fairy Tradition in Sumeria and Transylvania—the heartlands of the Dragon Kings and Queens of the Sacred Danaan Peoples.

In Draculea's day Christian kings sent their sons to Christian universities. However, true kingship, the Sobekh or Messiah kingship, symbolised since antiquity by the Dragon or Sacred Crocodile, required that the true kings' sons learnt priest-kingship. In Draculea's case, this education was still clearly of a Druidic nature, even as late as the 15th century.

In the Celtic British Isles after the Romans had decamped, princes were required to become priests or Druids. As late as 660 AD we can find references concerning the education of the Merovingian Prince Dagobert at Slane University in Ireland where, up until the year 664 AD, Celtic, Druidic Christianity still held sway.

In those days, and as late as 751 AD, Kings still came exclusively from the King Tribe who supplied much of the Celtic world, as well as Eurasia, with Draconian offspring to serve as Royal Priests. This King Tribe, the Arya or Sidhe—the Scythians—included the Merovingian dynasty. Although it was an amalgam of Jesus' Egyptian and Aryan blood, it was also closely related to the Irish and Scots Royal Danaan. The Druidic castes integral to these Houses still educated this dynastic progeny up until the Carolingian usurpation and the ascendance of the Church of Rome in 664 AD.

Gradually at first, the Roman Church replaced the true royal, Elven blood with its own bloodless puppets and made Christian education the norm for the sons of the new Christian kings and nobles whom the Church had created. The Solomons of Hermannstadt and Toledo became the hidden leftovers of an ancient, originally Druidic educational system which necessarily went underground. It became the subject of myth and Fairytale, along with the bloodlines it once educated openly.

The Dragon Colleges produced the "Uber", the Overlords who, in Britain, were called the PenDragons and in Transylvania the "Dracoi" or "Dracoica"—the "Vampires". Only the highest graduates of the Druidic bangors would be thought of as true men or women of power, true Sidhe or Fairy Royalty. Thus it was only the prince who "rode the Dragon" who could be said to fit the same criteria for inclusion in the bloodline of the Vampire, the Witch and the Fairy families—the Dragon Kings.

Chapter 4

The Thousand-Year Elven Holocaust

The study of history is as much the study of etymology as it is the study and interpretation of actual events. Both are often a daunting task. Ultimately history is always written by the victors and the meaning of language and the significance of historical events are invariably decided by those whose hands have taken a firm hold of the tiller that steers society's ship.

The word "Fairy", as we have come to understand from our educators (or deceivers), suggests one of a variety of mythic or imaginary beings whose shape, size, habitat and customs differ according to geography and ethnic or aboriginal folk tradition. Lately, a Fairy has also come to mean a homosexual.

A real Fairy, would not care at all about anyone's sexual orientation, and would just think, "it's all bread and bread after all". The latter definition would be no doubt dismissed entirely, and s/he would nevertheless take extreme exception to the former definition for the following reason. Apart from the Jews, no race in history has suffered more brutality and racial prejudice than the Elves.

For over a thousand years the Church initiated a consistent policy of genocide that was and still is unrivalled in human history in terms of its relentlessness, violence and hatred. The word genocide is used with justification. In 1944 Raphael Lemkin formulated the term to define "an attempt at the destruction of the national group as an entity, and the actions involved are directed at individuals, not in their individual capacity but as members of a national group".

The United Nations elaborates by saying that genocide includes "the systematic moral debasement of a group, people or nation". The Jews have suffered just this, except in one particular respect. If you were asked your race or nationality today and you replied "Jewish" no one would think twice about it.

Imagine, however, asking Mr. Green or Miss Leibowitz what race they were and they replied "Jewish". What would be the reaction if you then burst into fits of laughter and replied "Don't be stupid. Jews don't exist, they're just a myth"? Isn't that what genocide or ethnic cleansing is all about—eradicating all trace of a culture from the human consciousness? This is what has happened to the Fairy Race.

Certainly the Germans tried it with the Jews, and if they had been given the same amount of time the Church has had to achieve what they have achieved, no doubt in a thousand years from now the Jews would have also become a myth. But this has already happened to the Fairies. Little trace of their culture or identity exists outside a handful of the old families or beyond the covers of sanitised storybooks for children, or tomes on rustic folk tradition, in which hints of the old lore still remain hidden.

Mr. Green and Miss Leibowitz can go about their business in relative freedom, and can be openly proud of their nationality and cultural heritage. For a thousand years, the Fairies have had to conceal their identities and live in hiding for fear of being torn to shreds or burnt alive. For a thousand years it has been a crime to be of the Elven race. You may be surprised to learn that it still is.

Today, whilst the Jews, by the Grace of God, enjoy the acceptance of their race won through the backlash of public opinion against the Nazi Holocaust, the Thousand-Year Elven Holocaust has been forgotten. Still the Fairies have to remain in hiding contemporarily for fear of ridicule and ostracism.

In 1736 the Witchcraft Act was repealed. However, it was replaced by the Fraudulent Mediums' Act which is still in force and simply says in one way what the Witchcraft Act said in another.

According to Christian doctrine no one can contact departed spirits. If this is admitted, then inevitably all mediums are fraudulent because the English language defines a medium as being a person who has commerce with the souls of the dead.

By Dragon definition a Witch, meaning a Fairy, is a Medium and the law wouldn't lay a fine distinction upon exactly what the Witch mediates with or how, if they decided they wanted to win an argument. It will be noticed at this juncture that by definition, in their prayers to—and visions of—Christ, the Virgin Mary and the departed Saints, all those who currently call themselves Christians are in fact indulging in mediumship. This is the very act which the Church says is impossible and by which edict they render their entire following heretical. This has always been the case and during the Witch craze, all things considered, it was actually the heretics who were burning the orthodox Christians.

If the Witch mediates with ancestors, she claims to be able to contact the dead. As the Church says this is impossible, the Witch is a fraud and is breaking the law. Ergo to be, or claim to be a Witch, and consequently a Fairy, on that count alone, is illegal. The Witchcraft laws are alive and well and living in a statute book near you. Further by implication, it is possible for a Fairy to be tried under the treason act as well, on two counts.

Firstly Her Majesty the Queen is a Christian and head of the Church of England. No Fairy aware of his or her history and the atrocities committed against their people could ever be what is contemporarily thought of as an orthodox Christian. In this sense they run the risk of committing an act of Treason by denying the Christian faith, because in doing so, like others following different paths, they refute and insult the faith of Her Majesty.

Secondly, the Fairy families stood in absolute opposition to the *Donation of Constantine*, this being the document that was used to usurp them and initiate the Elven Holocaust itself in the first place.

The Donation of Constantine

The *Donation of Constantine* first appeared during the 8th century and was a document which purported to recognise the Roman popes as Christ's representatives on Earth and to donate to Pope Sylvester and the Roman Church all those Imperial powers formerly invested in the Throne of Byzantium.

The *Donation*, the Church claimed, was written in the 4th century at the insistence of the Emperor Constantine. The Church said that he was so grateful for having been cured of leprosy by Pope Sylvester that he gave into the Church's hand the entire power and wealth of the unified Roman Empire, including the right to crown and dethrone kings. Now that is what you call expensive medical insurance.

Supposedly written before 337 AD—the year of Constantine's death—the *Donation of Constantine* actually didn't make an appearance on the stage of European history until four hundred years later. So far-reaching are the powers bestowed upon the Church by this document, one would have thought that it would have been made public at the time of its bestowal. Not centuries later.

The provisions of the *Donation* were enforced in 751 AD. The Merovingians were shortly thereafter deposed by the Church and replaced by their sycophants, the Mayors of the Palace, who later became known as the

Carolingians. The Church had made a compact with the Mayors and offered to "recognise" their legitimacy as rulers if they would dispense with the true Dragon Kings. The deal was done and the Carolingians were made the puppet rulers under the Roman Church.

The *Donation*, because it was made by a Dragon King, Constantine, legitimised the Church's right to take this action. To all intents and purposes they had the authority of Dragon Kingship given up to them by this Charter. No doubt the Merovingians knew this to be a fraud, which is why they refused to recognise the authority of the Church to meddle in affairs of state. What do we learn from this?

We can see from the Church's choice of "benefactor" that the Church was well aware that universally, only those of the Dragon Blood would be recognised as true kings. Therefore they chose Constantine as he was known to have been descended from both the Britannic PenDragon House and the Dragon House of David. Furthermore he was a member of the desposyni—the heirs of the Lord—the blood descendants and legitimate representatives of Jesus Christ. In the *Donation* it appeared as if Constantine had relinquished his hereditary spiritual position as a Messiah and invested it in the Papacy.

By suggesting they were the representatives of Christ, the popes were claiming Dragon descent for themselves. It was well known that Jesus had descendants and that they were part of the only Eurasian dynasty which was authorised to be kings—the Elven Overlords or Dragons. It would have appeared to the public then, that in the displacement of the Merovingians, one Dragon dynasty was being replaced by another, albeit a paper one.

This reduced any danger of mass unrest. As time passed however, it became uncomfortably clear that the function of kingship under the Merovingians had been entirely different to that under the Carolingians. Whilst the Merovingians had formerly assumed the role of overseers, sages and wise counsellors, the Carolingians and their successors, prompted by the Church, became deliberately poorly educated, pig ignorant, insensitive tyrants and territorial tradesmen.

Dragon Kingship and the Grail Code had died to be replaced by a corrupted form of feudal totalitarianism and brutal, economic slavery as the Church carefully and strategically replaced the old dynasties with its own merchant-class client families who, from that day forth, became vassals of the Vatican.

Lastly we learn that from 751 AD the true Dark Age began in earnest. The Elven Holocaust was initiated and would run its course for another thousand years until, in England at least, the Witchcraft laws were repealed in 1736. North of the border in Scotland, however, the persecution of Witches in the 1700's was at its fiercest until the end of the century.

During this time, history has witnessed the rise of the Church of Rome and its successful struggle for power. In time no dynasty ruled in Europe or remained in power unless the Church sanctioned their reign. The Church chose the royal families, it crowned kings and deposed its detractors. In short, the Church, under the auspices of the *Donation of Constantine* was the sole and supreme temporal power in Europe and the known world. Without this purported imperial benefice however, the Church would have remained a marginalized Mediterranean cult contesting for patronage along with a host of other gnostic Christian denominations.

The royal dynasties, sponsored by the Church and crowned by its Divine Right, instituted their courts and parliaments, passed laws and employed agents to act on their behalf. To all intents and purposes it seemed as if the Church had the absolute right of Dragons and wielded power by the very sanction of Jesus Christ and God.

No monarch reigning today and no government under the monarch or instituted in their name would enjoy their position if the Church, empowered by the *Donation*, had not given them permission to rule in the first place. Without the *Donation of Constantine*, European history today would be totally different and none of the dynasties past or present would have had the right to have reigned. Nor would they reign now and none of their governments or agencies would have exercised power.

One slight problem, though. The *Donation of Constantine* is a complete and utter fraud and the Church was never given any temporal powers at all, let alone the right to found dynasties, crown kings or institute governments. The whole document was a lie from beginning to end and has been known to be a fake since Lorenzo Valla applied the methods of historical criticism to it during the Renaissance.

How do we know Valla was correct? The New Testament references incorporated into the wording of the *Donation* were taken from the Latin Vulgate version of the Bible. The Vulgate Bible was compiled by St. Jerome, who was born more than two decades after Constantine was supposed to have signed the *Donation*. The actual Vulgate Bible wording that appears in the *Donation* didn't exist until St. Jerome invented it, fifty years after the document had supposedly been dated and signed by the Emperor. By this time Constantine had been dead for decades and couldn't have signed the Dragons' rights away anyway.

The language of the *Donation* is eighth-century clerical or dog Latin, whilst the Latin used in the 4th century Empire was late classical Roman. The Imperial and Papal ceremonials described in the *Donation* didn't exist in Constantine's time but were developed some centuries later.

Several documentary instances of the Church's use of the *Donation* to assert their authority in the medieval period still exist, including the letter of

Pope Gregory IX entitled *Si Memoriam Beneficiorum*, dated October 23rd 1236 and addressed to the Emperor Frederick II. Pope Gregory writes, "...that as the Vicar of the Prince of Apostles (the Roman Pope) governed the empire of priesthood and of souls in the whole world, so he should also reign over things and bodies throughout the whole world; and considering that, he should rule over earthly matters by the reins of justice to whom—as it is known—God had committed on earth the charge over spiritual things. The Emperor Constantine humbled himself by his own vow and handed over the empire to the perpetual care of the Roman Pontiff with the Imperial Insignia and sceptres and the City and Duchy of Rome...".

People in the medieval and Renaissance period, confronted with this document, did not generally criticise the *Donation* on the grounds of its veracity. They just exclaimed aghast that they could not believe that Constantine would have been stupid enough to have given the Roman Church everything.

From the *Donation* we understand that Constantine offered the Pope all the robes and Crowns of office but the Pope, being such a humble man, gave them back to the Emperor. This lets the Church off the hook should some malcontent turn up and ask for sartorial evidence. If the readers peruse the *Donation* for themselves they will be appalled at the pretentious egotism, arrogance and sheer material greed of the Church, as authors of the document.

The fraudulent imperial power of the Vatican to create kings by "coronation"—derived from this faked 8th century *Donation of Constantine*—was later adopted by the Archbishops of the Church of England with the complicity of the Tudors, who were Catholics themselves.

When he split with Rome, Henry VIII still retained and later ratified and re-established in the Anglo-Catholic Church of England the fraudulent right of the Church's clergy to create by coronation, a succession of British monarchs. This was an illegal act. The *Donation of Constantine* was proved to be a completely fake document. Therefore no Royal Elven House that knew its origins and cared about social justice could possibly bring itself to recognise a Christian British monarchy or any of their Church sponsored, Church crowned predecessors or any of their regnant or formerly regnant, European cousin Houses.

Because the *Donation* was a fraud and no subsequent priest of any Catholic derived denomination ever had the right to crown kings, Britain has had no legally reigning monarch for 900 years. As a consequence of this, *all* the laws passed by these monarchs were and are illegal and worthless and *all* the governmental agencies set up by or derived from these monarchs or their laws are also illegal and worthless up to the present day.

When considering this, the reader might like to consider the fact that all the arrests ever made by the police in Britain and Europe are acts of kidnap and *habeus corpus*. Equally, any man who has taken up arms for the Crown and killed for his country is unprotected by law and guilty therefore of murder.

However, paradoxically, as the entire British legal system is illegal, there are no laws, and so the crimes of *habeus corpus* and murder as we define them today, simply do not exist. Subconsciously, people know that their politicians and monarchs have no legitimate authority to rule over them. They manifest this knowledge in an increasing disrespect for these optional, arbitrary and illusory social conventions, which is yet another reason why social order is breaking down.

If the UN is right, we may face chaos in the near future—and all because of a stupid fraud, perpetrated by a group of myopically greedy, maniacal peddlers of false religion who are now long dead.

Again, for asserting this kind of view the Fairies are implicitly guilty of Treason, even though all British laws are constitutionally illegal and the act of treason itself is a *non sequitur*. Think of the implications of this.

It applies to any nation state in the Christian world today is still a monarchy or which has evolved as part of a successive, developing political process originating from a monarchy, by virtue of its continuing sanction from, or sponsorship by, the Church of whatever denomination. It is unauthorised by any temporal or divine power to coerce anyone to obey any law originating at any stage of that government's evolution.

In effect Britain, Europe and America are ruled by the sword, and that sword is being wielded by people who are no more than short sighted, self-seeking robber barons. They have no constitutional right to rule even in America, where in the 19th century the libertarian commentator, Lysander Spooner, demonstrated that the consensual nature of the original document, upon which the subsequent, consecutive clauses are founded, was being flouted, thereby making the entire Constitution illegal. Pierre Proud'hon called them all "Tyrants and Usurpers". Next time you are tempted to eulogise Western Democracy, bite your tongue and let your brain select first gear before you open your mouth. Flawed or otherwise, the idea that the English speaking world has any democracy at all is a joke.

At the beginning of this work the author stated that the people have been conned enough. He now hopes that the readers might appreciate for themselves the precise extent to which the people have actually been deceived. They have accepted a state of affairs where they and their ancestors have been enslaved by a chameleon-like corporate body that has destroyed their creativity and robbed them of their psychological liberty and freedom of conscience for over a thousand years.

The entire moral basis of our society is founded upon a massive historical lie which has twisted the minds of generations of individuals until they have become terrified of the natural drives of their own bodies and souls.

The resultant taboos that have been created have been used to divide the minds of the people and make them dependant on the Church-State for solutions to the problems of resisting Satan and fighting temptation and sin when these contrived, nonsensical whimsies never existed in the first place.

As a result, western Christian society was turned into an open air lunatic asylum packed full of lost souls who weren't lost at all and had no need of a cure for diseases of the soul that they weren't actually suffering from in the first place.

The Church created the confusion and the division and then offered the solution. In fear, the population invested its trust in the perfidious Church and in return for their confidence the Church turned the people into slaves and an entire civilisation into a manufacturing plant to service their own greed for luxury and power.

For a thousand years the Fairies have remained silent about their identities—formerly for fear of their lives—latterly for fear of becoming social outcasts and objects of mirth and derision. Still however, a shadow of menace lies over the ancient families. Greed will go to any length to ensure the continuity of its satisfaction and the same motives that prompted the Church to murder and lie in the past, still prompt their merchant-class puppets to kill and deceive today.

Whilst people therefore now understand the Fairy to be either a gossamer winged sprite or an effeminate male, both are considered harmless jokes. Such a contemporary opinion flies in the face of the facts where the Fairy of history is concerned.

In studying the Fairy in the context of both Celtic and medieval history it must be remembered that the tribes to whom the Victorians ascribed the appellation "Celtic" were not a homogenous or integrated racial group and the Celts themselves never saw themselves as a cohesive, pan-European nation of peoples. Furthermore, like their medieval descendants, they had, within an indistinct collection of tribes, a patriarchal, misogynistic culture, which stands in complete opposition to the popular view that the matriarchal "Celts" promoted a policy of sexual equality. (M. Green: *Celtic World*)

The modern myth concerning the Celts, promoted by "New Age" racketeers who are rehashing earlier popular trends, tends to set these rather ordinary people into some kind of "Golden Era" of cultural expression and heroism, punctuated by the achievement of a state of high spiritual awareness. In fact, they were average, workaday farming folk who treated their women like dirt.

Nymphs and Shepherds... Go Away!

The Georgians and Victorians, for socio-political propaganda purposes, had various revivals and retrospectives. These were intended to celebrate the merchant-class era of industrial prosperity and the British Imperial oppression and destruction of the cultures of other peoples, by having the audacity to equate such dubious ventures with various "Golden Ages" of the past (paraphrasing Sir Ernst Gombrich).

Principally it was these individuals who patronised the artistic movements whose Svengalis, seeing that the parvenus were only too willing to advance and buy the lie, produced the kind of sentimental, heroic nonsense that plugged the gap in the nostalgia market. This was created by the desire of the newly rich to feel that they were justified by history in the exploitation of the poor in the mills and the mines. They wished to equate their "victories" in the marketplaces with those of the "warrior king" or "noble savage" on the battlefields of classical antiquity. By sponsoring flamboyant painters, they felt they could become identified with the highest artistic and cultural achievements of the various ages whose elan flattered these imperialists' and industrialists' egotism. In this way, they furthered their exploitative, propagandist aims.

However, in Newtonian terms, where every action engenders an equal and opposite reaction, the patronage afforded these artists and sculptors, by magnates whose cultural tastes only ran to jingoism or sentimentality, led to a calamitous pass where artistic standards plummeted.

In the words of the art historian Sir Ernst Gombrich, "There is no such thing as 'Art'......there are only artists". And by God: By their fruits ye shall know them well enough.

Culturally vacuous steel barons and cotton magnates would often display framed family charts—tracing the kinds of instant, purchased ancestry purchased by an ancestor—that any genuine self respecting nobleman would shun outright. Their "miladies" would hold soirees, for the local cognoscenti and well-to-do, where the cultural a la carte invariably offered copious helpings of moronic, Byronic neo-classical claptrap garnished lavishly with choruses of criminally insane, musical atrocities like "Nymphs and shepherds come away", sung by fat falsetto aunts who hadn't a clue what Nymphs were, customarily renowned for getting up to when they actually did "come away" with or without the rustic parties of the second part. And these arachnid recreational activities were namely: Cannibalism ("fancy another helping of Shepherd's Pie, Myrtle?") and—as their name unavoidably suggests—Nymphomania; which found the outworking of the expression of its inner, emotive rage and lust to be manifest in such acts as oral sex, buggery, simultaneous multiple penetration and bestiality; with a wide variety of domestic livestock, and an equally varied selection of naturally occurring regional fauna—including wolves, dogs, donkeys, wild goats, rams, horses, snakes and—purely for betting purposes—ferrets.

Such sexually epicurean piquancies were practiced with gay abandon alongside rampant homosexuality (amongst the shepherds who'd managed to survive lunch), Sapphism, drug abuse, alcoholic debauchery, Travel Scrabble, and a range of other delightfully civilised, lubricious distractions. (Riley-Scott: *Phallic Worship*)

At that time, the true nature of Celtic culture was censored, sanitised and idealised so much that the view we have had of it up until recently reflected more our predecessors' confusion, chauvinism and wishful thinking concerning the period than it did the reality of the era they lauded.

Modern archaeology coupled with a realistic interpretation of the information, less coloured by the concern for moral rectitude, has uncovered a picture of "Celtic" society that is clearer than it was in our grandparents' day. Indeed with the wealth of new knowledge we find it difficult to apply so liberally the generic term "Celt" in the same way our forebears were wont to do. Scholarship concerning what previously we might have thought of as the "heroic era" of Celtic civilisation, conveyed in modern popular works that owe much of their sentimentality to the erroneous and prim historical view of yesteryear, is garbled and confused.

The images of the noble Celt: the tall blonde warrior chieftain, or the flaxen-haired Swan Maidens of Lyr are not Celtic at all. We still seem to think of all Celts in that way because we are sold the image by people who, in accepting as fact the Victorian delusion, think that this distinct caste was representative of the Celts as a whole. In fact, they represented a tiny minority of individuals who were foreign to and essentially divorced in racial and cultural terms from the people we now know were the real Celts living in that era.

When we look at the stories contained in the *Annals of Irish History*, the Irish *Book of Invasions* or the Welsh *Mabinogian*, we are inclined to think that these documents were about the Celts. They were actually about a strange race of foreigners who reigned alongside these dark-haired, swarthy, stocky little farmers for nearly two thousand years. From these stories we obtained our idea of what the "Celts" were like when, in fact, they weren't Celts at all. They were Scythians, the Elves, the Fairies, the Aryans.

These Scythians were a tightly knit, insular group who practiced Phoenician and Pharaonic marriage customs to keep the blood pure and in all other respects they tended to remain detached from the common swell of humanity. Differing greatly from the customs of the patriarchal Celtic peoples they reigned over, theirs was a society that appreciated the position and power of its women and correspondingly favoured the idea of matrilinear descent.

The Scythians came to reign across Eurasia and normally we find them attached to various indigenous populations, but occasionally they were an indigenous population in themselves, such as the Danaan of Eire and the Ainu of Hokkaido. Unlike their Celtic clients, whose caste system, based on kinship, was male-dominated and hierarchical, the Scythian caste system, which operated amongst their own people, was egalitarian.

Though individuals' functions and tasks varied, all nevertheless were royal and therefore equal. Proof of this is to be found in the Brehon Law concerning inheritance. This social structure became superimposed onto the Celtic system and produced the sort of divisions we find in Hinduism where the people are separated into three distinct classes:

Brahmins or Priests
Ksatriyas or Warriors
Sudras or Smiths

Beneath these are settled the untouchables or slaves.

The Scythian system had the same three divisions but these were arranged on the horizontal plane and did not proffer any superior status in relation to the other castes. If one overlaid the Elven, Scythian system onto that of the Celtic, which is virtually identical with the present Hindu system, we would have the following social configuration:

Gods of Heaven
Gods of Heaven and Earth
Gods of Earth

or

Druidic Royal Ancestors, the transcended ones
Royal Archdruids, Druidesses and PenDragons (Vampires)
War Kings, War Lords, Craftsmen, Metalworkers, etc.
Caucasian footsoldiers and Dravidian "Brownies"
Burgh Chiefs
Men at Arms
Farmers, Tinkers, Traders
Women
Slaves

(Celtic source—Miranda Green, *Celtic World*, Routledge, London, 1995.)

It will be noticed that, contrary to contemporary misconceptions, Celtic women were in fact just above slaves in terms of their rank and were regularly bought and sold or exchanged by their men for cattle, along with the slaves.

It is not a popular view but sadly—given the contemporary academic discoveries concerning the real nature of Celtic society—it is an accurate one. Although we would love to blame the Church for everything, including the oppressive patriarchy that subdued women, the fact is that the Celts were already treating their women like chattels before the Church reared its ugly head above the blood-stained meniscus line of history.

The conversations or entreaties of love we see recorded in the "Celtic" Sagas between "Celtic" lords and ladies, were in fact the exchanges between

Scythian men and women. That which is reported as being the love poetry of the "Celts" was instead the love poetry of the Elves—the Royal Scythians—not that of a brutal farming folk who had neither lords nor ladies.

Who in history, if he had the rare gift of writing, would bother wasting such a talent, do you think, by eulogising the sexual peccadilloes or romantic longings of a bunch of turnip farmers who wouldn't have spoken to women on such equal terms anyway? Romance in any case didn't come into it, the Celtic woman just grinned and bore it.

The art of male wooing and flattery arises when the woman has the freedom to choose to say no. The only women who had that choice then were Scythian Princesses. Because of the mysterious composition of their blood and its consequent magical powers, they had a lot more to offer their Elven menfolk than sexual intercourse, which is all that nondescript Celtic women could hope to have had in their favour.

The beauty and exquisiteness of the magic that a Scythian Princess had to offer could not be taken by force. She had to give it willingly. Otherwise, in the act of coercion, her magic would be tainted and become either useless or poisonous.

Occupying a position higher than the Elven male was Goddess incarnate. Elven men were pleased therefore to treat her with deference and honour and to offer her court in a manner that would secure her voluntary participation in their sacred congress. From this obligation of service to such Earthly Goddesses arose the medieval tradition of Courtly Love which, by no means and under no circumstances, was ever intended to be offered to the female descendants of either Celt, Norman or Saxon.

Today, after hundreds of years of oppression, the female descendants of these poor, downtrodden Celtic and later Anglo-Norman women have managed, during the closing years of the millennium, to wrest from their men the equality that evaded their mothers for centuries. Now they demand to stand on an equal footing with their menfolk but, like their sisterly ancestors, when push comes to shove they have nothing more dynamic or magical to offer than sexual intercourse.

However, the male descendants of the Celts and the later Anglo-Normans—the examples of manhood living today—have in turn nothing better or more magical to offer their women either, and never have. Therefore, equality between the sexes seems to be quite an equitable and logical arrangement whereby the mediocre do not differentiate between, nor discriminate against, each other's mediocrity on the basis of gender.

Passing on from the politics of sex originating in the caste system, we now return to addressing the system as a whole and notice that the figure above is a generalisation which encapsulates the main divisions between each social level.

As time passed and the population increased, technology developed and diversified and the main castes became sub-divided into classes within classes. At length the castes themselves eventually became overturned and the Warrior Class gained the ascendant, later to be upturned, in the last 1200 years, by the Merchant Class, whom the Hindus call the Sudras.

In the twentieth century we also saw situations where the untouchables became the rulers, as in China and Soviet Russia. Presently we have a situation where the Elven Race, at the bottom of the pile, have become the untouchables, whilst the increasingly and frighteningly acquisitive Peasants and the Merchants are at the top, having wrested their positions from the block-headed Warriors. The end product of this fiasco over the last millennium and a half can be smelled in the air, tasted in the water supply and seen in the eyes of diseased, starving, third world children.

Its results can be heard in the screams of animals gratuitously tortured in experiments aimed at testing the toxicity of vanity products, or of medicines intended to make money for these extortionists whose worthless over-inflated products titillate, save or prolong the lives of a race of peasants.

At its inception, the caste system was not an arbitrary set of divisions or inequalities established through main force by a varying collection of sequential oppressors. It was a reflection of the fact that there were differences in the capabilities and capacities of the different types of human beings alive at the time. Some were ingenious artists, builders and artisans, some were naturally gifted traders and negotiators. Some had been bred to have an overview and some were fearless, heroic soldiers. Each group had its part to play in the functioning of society.

Whilst some peoples—like the Celts—had green fingers and could make carrots grow rose blossoms in Hell, most Scythians could not even grow the equivalent of an infants' school size tray of mustard and cress. However, the Celts were unable to organise complex societies and depended on the Scythians for foresight, guidance and protection.

Centuries earlier similar arrangements developed in the east where the Aryans and the Dravidians, having been frequently at war with each other, finally came to an amicable social arrangement whereby all parties ultimately benefited. Like the Celts, the Dravidians could get dinner from dust and their expertise and practicality was the backbone of the Aryo-Dravidian symbiotic culture. Such symbiotic relationships are also commonly to be observed amongst different species in the natural world and work brilliantly within what must be admitted is a hierarchical natural order which, nevertheless is not a system of inequality or self conscious elitism, but one of necessity.

From about 1800 BC onwards, with the increase in Eurasian populations, the occurrence of a variety of natural disasters and the diminishing of range territory through foreign conquests, the Scythians and the Aryans were forced to seek more settled lives. However, being mainly predators and rangers, they lacked the skills to make farming work. They needed the Hobbit-like peoples of the Celtic and Dravidian cultures to tend the land and in times that were becoming increasingly more violent, these cultures needed the Aryans and Scythians to protect them.

This tolerance and co-operation continued until the emergence of the warrior lords, literally the middle class of their day. Their elitist, hierarchical governmental structures—based on the right of might—became entrenched in western civilisation as the feudal system during the years of the Roman Church's ascendancy and totalitarianism.

From this point onwards the exploitation of the caste system as an ideal tool for breeding elitism, division and inequality became rife. The Roman Church, comprising mainly sudras and peasants, saw a chance to claw its way to power. Its hierarchy upturned the original caste system by ninety degrees, turning it into a ladder to enable them to climb to what they conceived to be the top of the pile and the easy life.

Only humans would seek to differentiate and assert their superiority based on their position within a social structure that, founded on natural law, was originally intended, in contrast, to be for the benefit of all and to function through co-operation. In their egotism, humans abused a natural and beneficial order to the detriment of all those subscribing to it.

In the 20th and 21st centuries the audacity of usurpation continues when the ignorant middle-classes, shopkeepers and their vapid shopkeeper sons, join groups of white supremists who idolise the image of the blond-haired, blue-eyed Aryan. This particular genotype, the warrior, who also occupied the middle class or caste, seems naturally to appeal to this middle class today. Unaware of the fact that Aryans had red hair and green eyes, they have, as a result of their lack of education and intelligence, elevated the usurping warrior to the status of a true Aryan king. In reality the blond-haired, blue-eyed ideal, so beloved of the Germans and for good reason, was bred, like your average white racist today, to be fundamentally stupid.

A warrior could never have manifest the attributes of Aryan kingship in a million years. Kingship took spirit, wisdom and brains. The blond warrior had none of these qualities, and wasn't bred to have them. In the feudal period the warrior was called a baron. This word stemmed from the earlier Latin word *baro*, which was in circulation at a time contemporary with the rise of the warrior classes. Baro literally means "thickhead".

It is typical of the racist working and middle classes that they would pick such a figure to emulate. Aryan means wise king, not dumb blond. The adoration by the German National Socialists of the blonde warrior god-king and the assumption ever since by successive generations that he is an Aryan, must have been heavily influenced by the 13th-century Royal Poet, Snorri Sturleson.

In his *Sayings of Har*, he defines a corrupted Scandinavian caste system consisting of Jarls, Carls and Thralls. The Jarls, says Snorri, were blonde, the Carls were red-haired and the Thralls were black-haired.

Everywhere else the royal colouring is red and this tradition goes back in the Aryans to Radamanthus, Ariadne and Minos, and through them to Lilith herself. Even Jesus and Magdalene are regularly and invariably portrayed with red hair in the Renaissance masterpieces. A reversal has taken place here where warriors usurped or replaced kings as leaders of the people.

The warriors were hired Caucasians, not bloodline Aryans. The upheaval and resultant inequity and iniquity within the caste system occurred when their society's War Kings legitimately displaced many Aryan queens and kings in times of trouble. They were never to return to their thrones because the conflicts often carried on for decades.

Sometimes however, having had a taste of power, treacherous and greedy warrior captains decided they would either go it alone or take over permanently by force of arms. Following this, however, an even more stupid class of people managed to trade and poison their way to the top.

And who were they? That's right, the settled warehouse tinkers—the cheating peasants with money who were the ancestors of the upper and middle classes of today.

You might think that they were genuine aristocracy because they have inherited titles like Earl or Duke or Lord. What you wouldn't realise is that they only inherited these titles because their ancestors were traders who had had enough money to buy them from Christian kings who were also elevated peasants. And you wonder why the Earth is in such a state?

When the world is run by tinkers, as it is now, the tinker mentality leads to everything being seen as having a price tag attached to it. Everything then becomes a "marketable commodity" and its significance or importance becomes linked to its "marketing potential". We have become so used to such values and the buzz words that accompany them that we no longer see the inherent immorality or dangers implied therein. We now have a situation where profiteers calling themselves "doctors" can visit indigenous peoples, take blood samples and patent those individuals' genes.

In effect, it would then be possible for the doctors of the Humano Gene Project to file a complaint in an international court and prosecute those same indigenous populations for the theft of the doctors' patented property. Essentially this is slavery under a different guise, where various ethnic peoples belong to an American Medical Corporation, run by a government-backed elite who are—as Americans—a nation whose leaders have it in their power to destroy the world.

The ancient, egalitarianism of the Scythians' own social order manifested itself in such concepts as the democratic system of voting for Archdruids and PenDragons. The "family", comprised of the regional divines and princes, would elect both chief priest and high king—sometimes one and the same person—for priests and kings were interchangeable. In many ways this system was replicated in the Saxon Atheling Pool, where prospective rulers were chosen from the most suitable candidates available. (Richard Dufton)

This royal reserve, from whence were chosen kings from a race of kings, also extended itself to mediate in matters of marriage. Where election to high-priest or priestesshood and kingship were concerned, only the very best and most qualified would be picked. In the case of a king he had to be without physical or spiritual blemish. The successful candidate was the most spiritually powerful, learned, and showed the most gracious of manners. (*Annals of Irish History*)

Such criteria were also applied when princesses or princes were selected for marriage to each other. These were arranged by the Druids between the very best families within the various tuadhes in the kingdoms. This ensured that the fruit of any such royal union would represent an enhancement of all the most admired and required attributes necessary for a royal dynasty, thus reinforcing the perfection of the royal race itself. Both Hindu and medieval marriage customs were derived from this Scythian practice. (Hall)

For the Scythians the ability to perform magic—to manifest the Sidhe—was innate and hereditary in very much the same way as we view other skills as being today, such as Fine Art, for instance. Selective unions gave the race the opportunity to breed outstanding magicians whose gifts of natural perception and understanding, and whose ability to access the "Otherworld", helped to produce and guide brilliant kings who reigned with elegant aplomb. The ability to perform magic was carried in the blood and if that blood became watered down by marriages entered into with outsiders, the genetic strain was weakened and so was the ability to perform magic.

The Aryan-Scythians were not colour-prejudiced. Even though they were white themselves, they did not marry other whites. The purity of the Elven blood was absolutely necessary in order to enable the Dragon Kings and Queens to maintain their magical abilities and the quality and depth of their perception. The Elves were relied upon by their client races to be able to see things and perform feats that these client races couldn't. In this way they could fulfil their obligatory roles as the Seers and Guides that their clients had required them for in the first place.

These clients acknowledged that they were naturally unable to have an overview or to perform higher magic. Therefore it was not in their best interest to allow the Elves to dilute the Elven blood by intermarriage with members of that client race. This wasn't racism but a mutually acknowledged understanding that the Elves were originally of an entirely different subspecies, rather than just being of a different race.

This separatist custom was still vigorously upheld by the British rural working classes up until the first half of the 20th century when they themselves still considered intermarriage between the castes to be an outrage and a danger to social order. Although something of a misguided view, given the arriviste backgrounds of most of the contemporary aristocracy, it is a clear example of the way in which custom, however inappropriately applied, arises from ancient racial memory.

If a white person refused to mate with black people, you might be tempted to call the individual a racist. However, if anyone of any colour refused to mate with other primates, you would not for one moment think of accusing them of racism, whatever their colour, as the other primates are of a different species. The Holy Bible refers to the sons of Samael as goats and the sons of Jehovah as sheep. Here then we have a classical acknowledgement that it was understood from ancient times that there was in fact a difference between Elves and Men.

According to *Genesis of the Grail Kings* by Laurence Gardner and Nicholas de Vere (Introduction), this difference is also recorded in the Sumerian cylinder rolls from whence the biblical material was extracted. These same cylinder rolls record the assertion that the Elves made man by a series of processes that resulted in the Elves being only a quarter related to man at the time.

It is known that in antiquity the Nephilim, the Elven sons of the Anunnagi interbred with human women who were the result of this experiment and who in their turn produced the Naphidim. However it is recorded that these halfbreeds were destroyed long before the Black Sea Flood, and the slate was wiped clean.

The next experiment produced a lineage of pure-bred Elven queens and kings who were to supervise a race of quarter breeds who were originally created for manual labour. The quarter breeds, nevertheless, were eventually to gain their freedom and elect their own chieftains. They were helped by the Elven dynasty, the people whom Christians now think of as the spawn of Satan. This kind of attitude goes a long way in determining exactly what the Church feels about human emancipation.

These people interbred with anyone and we know them now as the biblical race of Adam whose Elven blood today is so diluted as to be infinitesimal. The pure Elven Queens and Kings however bred with no one but themselves and so throughout the past five or six millennia, the blood was kept more or less pure in several unbroken lines of descent until as late as the 8th century AD. From that time however, only one bloodline descent is recorded as being pure and unbroken. Only that one single named dynasty driving from an historical Elven Royal House contemporarily described as such, still exists today.

As human blood diluted however, the need for Elven Overlords increased, and from the second millennium BC the Scythians, as they came to be known, were in great demand as Queens and Kings, Seers and Magi. This continued up until about 751 AD, when the Elven Holocaust began in earnest. From 500 BC onward, during the decline of the increasingly insular Elven population in Europe, it was not the case that they, at that time, were "higher" than the other species as they had been previously. They were simply different from them.

In a world that was becoming increasingly more structured, the Elves needed man as much as man needed the Elves. One should understand that during the various later periods in history when these social arrangements were entered into, they were seen as being complementary. Not competitive or hierarchical.

Such separatism then was born of pragmatism and necessity. In those days it was known that hormonal levels were influenced by genetic inheritance and that hormones affected the individual's perceptions, psychological indivi-Dualism and the subsequent ability to transcend and perceive the intricacies of the workings of the cosmos. Elven blood was rich in these substances.

Maintaining the purity of the blood therefore was of paramount importance. Intermarriage between the Scythian reigning houses and members of the Celtic, or any other race, was strictly forbidden and greatly lamented if it did occur. However on occasion we read in folktales or histories the stories of the mutual theft of brides from each camp by both Celtic chieftains and Scythian kings.

Many of these stories are suspect and were written during the period of the Roman Church's ascendancy. The motive for these stories was to propagate the myth that the Fairy blood was being watered down. The Church, by spreading this rumour, hoped to persuade the peasants that their traditional friends and protectors, the Elven Queens and Kings, were losing their power along with the purity of their blood and were thereby becoming ineffectual and thus redundant.

If the people could be convinced of this, then they would believe that the age of magic was dying and invest their support in the Church instead. A clever lie. In most instances, if not all, these so-called Celtic chieftains were not, in fact, "Celtic" at all but Milesian Scythians. Such misrepresentations occur throughout the monkish reworkings of Gaelic history. An apt example of this is in the Christianised story of Lugh and the Queen of Sovereignty in which Lugh admits to having once being a mortal king. This is untrue.

Sometimes we too read the stories of the love between Fairies and humans, representing the marriages between Scythians and indigenous families. In later times, far more unpleasant tales emerged concerning the decline of the Elven families who had had to go into hiding from, the Church fathers said, the Celtic Milesians.

At this point, in Eire, the Danaan became the Daouine Sidhe, the people of the hills. This would have occurred from about 500 BC onwards. This didn't actually happen with the ubiquity, rapidity or finality that the Church reports. Scythian princes and princesses of the Tuadha d'Anu or Danaan were still at large, up until the Battle of Clontarf. Why did the Church bother with the weak blood yarn if they had all been wiped out, unless they were adopting a double safeguard policy?

If anyone drove the Elves into hiding and instigated their "final" (?) decay it was not the Milesians, but the Church itself. From this period in time arose the tale of the Fairy changeling. It is asserted that after waves of invasions and the decline in Fairy numbers following wars with people such as the Milesians, though now living in virtual isolation in the forests, the Fairies still maintained their taboos concerning marriage between the races.

The result of this, said the Church chroniclers, was continuous in-breeding resulting in deformed and sickly offspring. When an enclave of Elves had become so inbred, they reported, it was often their custom to steal local children and raise them for breeding purposes in order to inject some fresh DNA into the Fairy gene pool. However, that, apparently, was not the only reason for such thefts, it was intimated darkly.

As has already been pointed out, the Fairies practiced Phoenician and Pharaonic marriage. The former is the union of father and daughter, which in the horse-breeding world is acclaimed for producing the finest, healthiest thoroughbreds. The second is union between brother and sister, an arrangement that, according to geneticists at Cambridge University, can continue for up to three hundred years—ten generations—before any genetic problems are made apparent. As they didn't suffer from the moral stupidity encouraged by the Church, they had ample scope to vary the types of alliances they made in-caste, and thereby prevent hereditary problems from occurring too often.

However, leaving that to one side, allow for the probability that at least a thousand Elves survived the various calamities reported to have befallen them, prior to and following the first millennium AD. If those thousand Elves came perhaps from six loosely related clans, you have at least six varying gene pools from which to choose partners, before resorting to intense incest in any case.

From the time of the Milesian victory and the flight of the Fairies into the hills in 500 BC, and the emergence of these Church sponsored stories of child kidnap and incestuous deformity, there must have lapsed about a thousand years. This form of ecclesiastical propaganda began in earnest after 751 AD.

The Milesians and the Danaan had settled their differences some time before and were interbreeding. They were both Scythian Tribes, and the occurrence of deformity and the consequent necessity to steal peasant children to breed from, as the Church hinted, was negligible. In the context of accusations of wilful and unnecessary perversity, where the Church accused the Elves of stealing human children to eat, this is misinformation.

Nevertheless, during times of hardship, such as the medieval period, when disease and death were rife, necessity sometimes forced human communities to resort to cannibalism simply in order to survive. Instances of peasants being driven by circumstance to eat the flesh of condemned criminals are unequivocally recorded.

The Elves did maintain the cult of the sacrificial king amongst their own adult population, but the stealing of human children for these ritual purposes never occurred because they were of a different race. Nevertheless, here we have an example of the kind of ecclesiastical deception that, in order to further brainwash simple folk whom it had already conditioned by deception and terror to be gullible, priests would use the idea of evil beings preying on children. During any period of history it seems that the "send five dollars and we'll stop this man from shooting the puppy" approach to such a concept is always guaranteed to elicit a highly-charged, emotional response from a poorly culturally developed and badly educated public. In sheer terror they would typically close ranks, toe the party line and reaffirm their loyalty to the establishment and its easily digested morality.

And what was the purpose of this kind of scapegoatism? To ratify social identity under a specific ethical, cultural banner and thereby keep the charlatan priesthood in full and gainful employment by using psychological terrorism to ensure that they and their riches continued pouring in.

The fascinating aspect to this kind of propaganda is that today it still works just as insidiously and effectively on people who like to think of themselves as modern, intelligent sophisticates living in an enlightened and educated society, as it did on a medieval population. To all intents and purposes this kind of indoctrination is fascism. Those familiar with the work of George Orwell will remember the scenario he presented in his novel *1984*, where a totalitarian regime maintained social cohesion by pitting one social group against another.

Now transpose this entire situation back to the Middle Ages and imagine how it must have felt for the Elves who suffered exactly the same kinds of accusations, abuse and persecution for identical political aims. And now add to that the inevitable institutionalised rape and physical torture, and top the whole lot off with a mandatory death penalty.

The Church had instigated just such a relentless and insidious programme of militant, psychotically hateful propaganda and persecution against the Elves. It was a rabid war of lies that attacked every level of their presumed behaviour and twisted every Fairy custom into an act of abomination ordered by their supposed master Satan himself.

All the efforts of the Elves, the Church bleated, were ranged against the poor peasant. Because of the abominable traditions of these evil and wicked Fairies, who had been the peasant's former friends and protectors, the poor peasant lived in fear for his very life and soul, and could only rely on comforting, forgiving Mother Church for his physical protection and spiritual salvation.

And what little recompense, what mere trifling consideration did the Church expect for so great a favour? Merely that the peasant should:

a) manifest an appropriate amount of gratitude—and an appropriate amount of guilt—for having the audacity to exist on a planet that, in belonging to "their" God, was therefore by association also the property of the Church,

b) be ravaged by the fear of his own natural inclinations which, the priests instilled into him, were dirty and sinful.

c) Lastly that he work a fifteen hour day, six and a half days a week, allowing time off to go to Church, fifty two weeks a year.

Furthermore, much of what little he had he paid in tithes, taxes and portable goods to the priesthood who, though peasants themselves, were in fact making the peasants' life more unbearable than any Fairy could. If Jesus could have seen the atrocities and social injustices that these blood-soaked carrion were perpetrating in his name, he would have turned in his grave.

The Scythians didn't prey on peasants, merchants, human nobility or so-called "royalty" for reasons intimated previously: namely that in comparison, those not of the Fairy race had dead blood trickling through their veins.

In their heyday the Fairies practised familial vampirism. In tandem, this, with their tradition of living with the remains of their ancestors in tomb or temple Raths, established the folk tradition which tells that the Vampires returned from the dead—rose from the tombs—to feed from the blood and life force of their living relatives.

During the Medieval and Reformation Periods this tradition was gleefully expanded upon and misreported by both the Roman and Protestant Churches, who are both Catholic, and equally to blame for what has gone wrong. They gave the erroneous impression that Vampires, or indeed werewolves, could occur in any family, peasant, merchant or otherwise, and that those families therefore were constantly in danger from their own departed.

What kind of twisted mind would think up such a story and, not content to turn the living against the living, brother against sister and husband against wife, would also turn the living against their own ancestors? This is deliberate alienation and disenfranchisement on a grand scale.

On the death of a relative, life was sad enough. If the person was a breadwinner, life was precarious and uncertain enough in those days without having some parasite propagating the kind of story that invested tragedy and grief with menace. As one mourned someone once so dearly loved in life, in death they were then to become an object of loathing and dread.

What we have here is a very disturbing group of people who will say or do anything for power. Even more disturbing is that they are still manipulating the minds of the people in Europe and America with variations of the same nonsense they have always propagated, either themselves or through sympathetic or sycophantic governmental elites. They may have taken a back seat, but they're still in power. Who will rid us of these pestilent priests?

The king tribe, in much the same way as they selected their rulers and Druids, from an "Atheling Pool" of Brehon Families, also selected from this same group a class of females who became known as "Grail Maidens". These sacred, royal princesses, virgins of High Birth and Pure Blood, at an optimum age would be chosen to act as feeding females.

Giving willingly of their blood, fluids and energy, these girls were not mutilated, sacrificed or murdered during the process, but were worshipped and cherished as incarnations of the nurturing Dragon Goddess. *Dea Vulna Gnosis*—the Goddess Gives the Blood of Knowledge.

In fact they were perceived as, and treated like, goddesses themselves. Their rank was second only to the High Queens who, on attaining the traditional age, they themselves became. Women today should be so lucky. When fully mature, the Grail Maidens became Dragon Princesses and were encouraged to pick the cream of the princes and warlords for their pleasure.

When contracted into lease marriages with their own kin they became the Dragon Queens and the matriarchs of their people, the mothers of the next generation of Elven Queens and Kings. Such is a far cry from the treatment a Celtic woman might expect to receive, who having but one office open to her and far less physiological capabilities than a Dragon Queen, was treated with less respect than a brood mare. Status quo?

The Fairies, though now thought of as obscure nature spirits, were at the forefront of Eurasian civilisation and included the PenDragons and their cousins the Merovingians. The decline and obscurity of the Fairy race was caused, as we have seen, by the Roman Catholic Church who, unlike the now defunct Celtic Church, were the sworn enemies of the Grail or Fairy blood. The Celtic or Druidic Church was a priestly variant of the Middle Eastern branch of the Grail race, the Dragon Kings. The word "Church" actually derives from "circa" and the old highland euphemism for going to the Kirk was "going to the stones", meaning stone circle.

The Messiahship, the rulership of the Christian Church was invested in Jesus as the appointed son and rabbi and was intended, like Dragon Kingship, to descend in his bloodline. This it did through the Merovingian kings and the Celtic Church. In Britain, Jesus' granddaughter married the Archdruid Bran the Blessed, cementing a blood alliance between the Dragon and the Grail branches of the one greater royal family, guided and protected by the Druidic Priests of the Celtic Church and the indigenous Druids of Britain.

For reasons outlined in other works, Jesus' other brother James attracted a following consisting of Paul of Tarsus and Peter the Fisherman. This faction settled in Rome with Paul and established itself eventually as the Roman Church under Constantine, which boasted Peter as the First Bishop of the Christian Church. However, as Vatican records show, Prince Linus of Britain was descended from Jesus, and was therefore the First Bishop of the Christian Church following Christ himself.

Nevertheless, since then, the Roman heresy, the Catholic Church of the Dogma and not the Blood, vied for ascendance. After its final victory in 664 AD at the Council of Whitby, it did everything in its power to steal authority and leadership from the rightful bloodline descendants who held it. As part of this process in Europe, agreements were made with the Mayors of the Palaces aforementioned, and the Merovingians were either murdered or incarcerated as the Church established these Mayors, the Carolingians, under them as puppet kings.

After the Dark Ages the Roman Church became a ubiquitous and brutal power which attempted the utter destruction of the true kings. Because of this relentless campaign, as the centuries have progressed we have been left to think of the Fairies as the Church would wish us to think of them, as being anything other than what they really were.

Hard pressed and in decline at this period, many in the outlying regions who could not adjust to the new regime or assimilate themselves into a camouflaged position simply took to the forests during the periods of the Church's worst excesses. In their place and in the places of those the Church murdered, they appointed farmer chieftains and tinkers from the Sudra class of Celtic Society, thus confusing the identities of the Scythians and the Celts. This allowed, in retrospect, a situation where it appears that the Celts trade off the earlier cultural accomplishments of the Fairy race as if they were their own, thereby paving the way for glorious ersatz "Celtic Revivals" in the centuries to come!

So whilst some members of the Fairy race of kings took refuge in deceit, many others took to the forests and lived in the obscurity and insularity of the Greenwood. This reinforced the ancient association between Fairies and the natural world in folk memory.

Such an association finds further reinforcement in the old Druidic laws concerning the reverence due to trees and nature in general which, to the Fairy queens and kings with their transcendent perception, contained life in all its manifestations, a life of which they were the custodians.

In the days of their ascendance the Fairies operated a system of land management. It consisted of nomadic pastoralism and hunting, interspersed by the settled agriculture of their Celtic clientele who tended the farmsteads in rotation. They accompanied their Fairy lords and ladies as they themselves travelled seasonally between a central Sacred seat and three out of four satellite Raths and their burghs or brocks which were arranged in a nomen, or mark of Cain circle-and-cross configuration.

The advantage of this system, which gave rise to the folk tale of the "trooping Fairies", was that the regional game stock, the vegetation and the soil itself were allowed to recuperate and restore themselves in times allotted as being fallow. For one year in four a whole region would lie fallow. A hang-over from this tradition can be seen in the old "Norfolk Strip" style of crop rotation. The difference was that instead of resting strips of land in turn, the Fairies rested whole districts, moving themselves and their clients from settlement to settlement in turn as the year progressed.

The traditional times to move were May Eve, Midsummer, Samhain and the return to the centre was at Yule, revealing a quarturnal rotation when the Fairies could be seen and heard traversing the forests, hills and dales in joyous musical progressions filled with light and laughter. Such tales, surviving the brutality and oppression of the medieval period, came down to us through folk tales until the last century. In Eire and Scotland, they were still common currency amongst the rural communities who were wont to comment, as we have seen, that "if the Elves die, the Land dies too".

To the Dragon Queens and Kings—the Fairies—were attached numerous epithets, some of which are included here, but are also the subject of another essay, where they are dealt with in detail.

Chapter 5

From Transylvania to Tunbridge Wells

"The Fair Folk"

Members of the Scythian Royal House were said to be of great beauty. We remember that they practiced selective breeding and that only the fairest and purest could be selected as queens and kings. Tall in stature and with the palest of complexions and the reddest of red gold hair, framing faces in which were set eyes of emerald green, these beings were magnificent to look upon, admittedly, but beauty is not just skin deep. Except to the fool.

Beauty is a condition of the psyche. Where those who have suffered a life of stress and tension, of bitterness and regret are concerned, we should not be surprised that they age more quickly or look uglier, and are more mean of spirit that those whose lives have been led in truth and grace.

Added to their stunning symmetry, the Elves were naturally transcendent of spirit. Their queens and kings were insulated from the common round of nuisances and petty concerns by minds which were bred for deeper matters. Add, then, an inner state of being whose grace and equilibrium is reminiscent of the grace of the gliding Swan, to a physical form of beauty attained by centuries of selective breeding, and you obtain a being whose elegance and poise is nothing less than Otherworldly.

Indeed, the Swan in Fairy culture not only represents an anatomical and physiological condition within the Fairy brain, it also represents that very serenity of being which neuro-physiology effects within the Fairy mind. Consequently, it is seen manifestly in the visage and deportment of that race's queens and princesses and kings and princes, the Swan Maidens and Swan Knights of legend.

From Transylvania to Tunbridge Wells

In folklore such intimations of beauty come down to us in stories of Elf maidens who, in reflecting such poise and charm as could only be manifest in enlightened beings, are portrayed as Swans on the evening waters of moonbathed lakes who enthral the onlooker and captivate his soul forever. A perfect example of such eulogised beauty is the story of the Leanaan Sidhe, an Irish female Fairy who has developed in literature as being part muse and part Vampire. She represents the state of grace and perfection of the Elven Princess.

Memory, however, prompts those who tell of her to relate that her embrace is death. In Transylvania she is Stregoica; in Greece she is the Lamia; in Persia, Arabia and Israel she is Lilith and An, and just outside Tunbridge Wells she is "La Belle Dame Sans Merci", immortalised in Keats' poem of the same name.

La Belle Dame Sans Merci

Oh what can ail thee, Knight at arms,
Alone and palely loitering?
The sedge has withered from the Lake
And no birds sing!

Oh what can ail thee, Knight at arms,
So haggard and so woe begone?
The Squirrel's granary is full
And the harvest's done.

I see a Lily on thy brow
With anguish moist and fever dew,
And on thy cheeks a fading Rose
Fast withereth too—

I met a Lady in the Meads,
Full beautiful, a faery's child
Her hair was long, her foot was light
And her eyes were wild—

I made a garland for her head,
And bracelets too, and fragrant Zone
She look'd at me as she did love
And made sweet moan—

I set her on my pacing steed
And nothing else saw all day long
For sidelong would she bend and sing
A faery's song—

She found me roots of relish sweet
And honey wild and manna dew
And sure in language strange she said
I love thee true—

She took me to her Elfin grot
And there she wept and sigh'd full sore,
And there I shut her wild wild eyes
With kisses four.

And there she lulled me asleep
And there I dreamed, Ah Woe betide!
The latest dream I ever dreamt
On the cold hill side.

I saw pale Kings and Princes too
Pale warriors, death pale were they all;
They cried, *La belle dame sans merci*
Thee hath in thrall.

I saw their starv'd lips in the gloam
With horrid warning gaping wide,
And I awoke, and found me here
On the cold hill's side.

And this is why I sojourn here
Alone and palely loitering;
Though the sedge is withered
from the Lake
And no birds sing –

—John Keats

In England, during the 1300's, this Vampire maiden was to be found in the Home Counties. Her name, the "Maid of Kent" identifies her as being, according to John Ferguson, the Countess of Salisbury. At a summer ball in Calais, she was said to have let slip her Garter. King Edward III retrieved it with haste and, lifting the accoutrement into the air, pronounced "Honi Soit Qui Mal Y Pense".

As to her wandering around near Tunbridge Wells, when the unfortunate knight-in-armour met her, she no doubt looked upon him as the medieval equivalent of tinned meat. She, like him, was returning from the Calais festivities when he must have caught up with her on the leafy track that has now become the well-known A21. We will meet them again in a minute.

Scholars once dismissed Professor Margaret Murray for several things. One was that the Garter incident elicited an over-reaction from Edward, assuming the Garter to be of no ritual significance. But however scholars may dismiss the incident, the question will not go away.

In a period not noted for its moral rectitude, why would the King bother threatening anyone in connection with their possible attitude towards an item of women's underwear? Murray has already pointed out exactly how significant the Garter actually is and has given numerous instances to support a concept that goes beyond mere theory. There was no point in making a song and dance about the Countess' Garter unless the item had a dangerous connotation attached to it; which indeed it had.

The Garter or Gartier was a small, buckled belt worn by women around the top of the left thigh or just below the left knee on men. Apart from being a menstrual badge and a semantic symbol of the womb and the Grail, it was also a representation of the serpent eating its own tail. The Garter therefore was the alchemical symbol of the Orobourus, the serpent who, in consuming itself, has become a Dragon, a Vampire. Here we will remember the opening prose at the beginning of this collection of essays.

The Garter was the "Witches belt", the Devil's badge and a dynastic emblem of the Fairy race that descended from Lilith and Cain, who were the enemies of the Church and Mankind, according to the Church, if not according to the Fairies themselves.

The subsequent founding of the Order of the Garter by Edward III was followed in 1399 by the re-emergence of the private foundation of the Dragon Court in another related Angevin line under King Sigismund of Luxembourg. This underwent its public investiture in 1408. Both the orders of the Garter and the Dragon used the Orobourus as their emblems.

The Garter, as the alchemical Orobourus, is still an emblematic component of the old Angevin Imperial and Royal Dragon Court today. Under the Grand Mastership of its Vere heads is a senior heir of the senior Houses of Anjou and Lorraine who is himself a gartered knight of the Orcadian Clan Donnachaid. This demonstrates the ubiquity of the Garter symbol amongst the ancient families. The Garter denoted rank in later Witchcraft which, as we have seen, originated as Druidism.

The Orobourus, the reptilian symbol of completeness is the Sumaire, the serpent that encircles and spirals to create an inhaling vortex, a black hole that draws all energy and life into it. Sumaire is pronounced *shimmarie*, as we have seen. In being reminiscent of the word shimmer, it suggests a relationship with that word which means to glow radiantly as with a light that perhaps had the power to fascinate.

It is a pertinent meditation when one remembers that from the dawn of time the Elven Gods were called the Shining Ones. Here there is also a relationship with the words Shaman and Shamanism, a practice rooted in

Northern Asia, the homeland of the speakers of "Ar Sidhe Cantu", being the Sundered Elven Tribe who went east.

Like the legend of the fascinating allure of Fairy Gold, the Leanaan Sidhe and the Countess of Salisbury appeared so beautiful as to disarm their prey with an enthralling inward glamour of glowing radiance. Having disarmed their victims thus, they drew either the blood or the life force or both from them, leaving them to wander forever, as Keats suggests, like living corpses in vain pursuit of a love and beauty so splendid, so transcendent and so complete.

Fairy fascination is a universal theme. In this respect it suggests an innate ability to hypnotise people, though this isn't the whole story. In the tales concerning people's encounters with Elphame, there is a quality of transcendence about their narratives which will be dealt with later.

Love on a Four Lane Blacktop

The element of translucence and light that is attributed to Fairies can also be found in the stories relating to the shamans and kings of Eldorado in South America, where these individuals are also referred to as the "Shining Ones". This is a common epithet, as we know, for the Elves of Eurasia.

Jesus is said to have manifested this capability in the presence of the patriarchs and such an ability is closely connected with the Qabalah in its numerous manifestations and variations. Both Jesus' mother Mary and his wife Mary Magdalene were called the "crystal wombs from whence shined forth the light of god", a description which suggests strongly the Tantric and Qabalistic concept of Starfire.

We return to the eulogised dual carriageway on the outskirts of Tunbridge Wells—the A21—and our tired but patiently waiting traveller, the "Maid of Kent", the Countess of Salisbury and the packed lunch she nestles so lovingly to her pale and perfect breasts. In her role as the Vampire we also find her, like the Leanaan Sidhe, described as a Fairy lover and, as the Garter Queen, a Witch into the bargain.

The Garter intimates that she is of the Dragon Clan and hence we have the Fairy, the Witch, the Vampire and the Dragon in one unitary identity manifest in a vision of fatal and deadly beauty.

We will leave this Shamanka to "steal the edge" and leave, consigning her portion of Corned Beef to wander the Earth looking for her and the return of his mortal soul. He had not understood the implications of true love, which later became hideously distorted in Gothic novels and films.

Such characters as the English Countess of Salisbury and the Irish Leanaan Sidhe in historical accounts are sometimes remorseful and cursing of the nature that condemns them to utter loneliness. Sometimes they are unrepentant, predatory and without remorse.

It depends upon the motivation of the chronicler as to who does and feels what. It has been pointed out that the Knight in the poem, which Keats obtained from a far earlier source, might have transcended himself, and looked the way he did purely to outsiders, whilst living in an entirely different dimension himself. Having said that, the pain is all too real and the act of "stealing the edge" by Dragon Princesses is actually what does awaken the Vampire in the Fairy. It is doubtful in the very rare instances where this still can sometimes happen, that these females know what they are doing. Instead they act archetypically, like their ancestors, as an unconscious but necessary catalyst in a process of spiritual development. For anybody's money, this could lose nothing of its impact by being a bit more gentle. One might imagine that seven years of living hell and a hunger unquenched by raw steak, pastrami or Carlsberg Special Brew is much too much to have to pay for enlightenment.

However, the author, amongst others, has always insisted upon a biochemical basis for magic and transcendent states, and the psychobiological basis for such phenomena. This includes vampirism and the enlightenment that is its concomitant. It can be explained scientifically, without relying on such old favourites as Iron Deficiency Porphyria or on any of the other nonsenses that outsiders have suggested.

"The Shining Ones"

If you are a cheery Elf and you have managed to avoid the excesses of behaviour and perception brought about by contact with your female counterparts in Elphame, you might qualify for the epithet of "Shining One". If you have realised to any extent that you are of the Clan, you will know that from the very beginning the Fairies were called the "Shining Ones".

This stems from the Sumerian era when "The Controllers of the Fate of Men" were known as both the Anunnaki and the Anunnagi. The former means "those who are manifest when Heaven meets Earth" and the latter means simply "Shining Ones" or "Star Children". They mean the same and refer to the nocturnal habits of our ancestors as much as anything else. These habits are directly related to the production and maintenance of certain hormones, which then relate to the core meaning itself.

In particular the epithet "Shining One" was appended to Prince Shimash, brother of Erishkigal, Queen of the Otherworld. Shamash was the uncle of Lilith and was also called the "Prince of Justice". The Fairies from very early on were much in favour of law and order. This is a trait which manifested itself in an attention to detail in social and legal matters that has earned them, as Vampires, a reputation in later centuries for being pathologically meticulous.

In Transylvania it is said that if you dropped grain in front of a Vampire, it would stop to count the individual seeds, thus facilitating your speedy escape from danger. We may put this down to the wit and wisdom of peasant sarcasm, but we note the point all the same.

Shamash was therefore of the family of Sumerian Ubaid Gods who sired Cain and Kali Azura, and the race of Dragon Kings who were the keepers of the "Tablets of Destiny" or Fate. In their turn Cain and Lilith Luluwa were the father and mother of the Fairies: the Elven Grail Queens and Kings of the Dragon race so hated by the Church.

The ability to "shine", a phenomenon which can still be subjectively experienced, is the result of a transcendent, balanced state of mind related to certain processes connected with cellular rejuvenation. The ability is rare enough and is an innate genetic capacity manifested in the outworking of certain "shamanic" exercises related to "climbing the Tree of Life".

"The Gentry"

Gentry is a word which specifically means "of the blood" and is derived from the Latin *gens*. In this case, as in all cases, gentry strictly used to mean "of the *Fairy* blood" or of the Dragon family. By misuse, the word gentry has become related to a class or station, particularly in British society, and is erroneously associated, by attribution to the characters within that class, with a style of behaviour and a code of conduct that bears no resemblance to historical actuality.

In its most basic sense, the word "gentle" as in gentleman or gentlewoman, in British society, refers to individuals who are associated with, and gain status through and erroneous recognition from, their support of a hierarchical value system. This had been established illegally by the Church through the Tudor usurper Henry VIII, under the auspices of the earlier Roman doctrines of temporal supremacy expounded within the fraudulent *Donation of Constantine*.

However, the British establishment, either through its Courts of Protocol, College of Arms or its academic or judicial establishments, has absolutely no legal or legitimate customary right to recognise or refute anybody or anything and their qualification, via such institutions. Its right to determine who is or is not royal or of the blood is non-existent, as they are not "of the blood" themselves. However, their blanket refusal to recognise any European title whatsoever has some redeeming element to it. The House of Vere doesn't recognise anyone else either! This includes the Crown, its Court of St. James and its College of Arms. There is no reason to do so.

A prime example of the concept of nobility being affected by the merchants can be seen in Renaissance Venice which, for all its splendour and seeming nobility, was no more than a fancy but rather damp, giant warehouse, run by self-elevated tradesmen who called themselves "Patricians".

In 1998 the transient public servant Mr. Blair wished to scrap hereditary privilege and replace the hereditary peers with new lords, doing exactly this in November 1999. Seventy-five percent of the old lords obtained their hereditary titles from ancestors who were the settled merchants who had bought their titles from impecunious monarchs like Henry VIII or James VI. The remaining twenty-five percent were descended mostly from the bully boys who accompanied the usurping bastard William of Normandy. He had been recognised by his own nobles only under the duress exacted upon them by his father.

The remainder of the entourage present at the Hastings debacle were comprised of Flemish and Breton nobles, some of whom had lived in England for many years. Assessing the risk of backing their friend Harold Godwinson, they resigned themselves to the unpleasant but inevitable fact that he would lose, and went along to ensure that the ignorant Norman buffoon did not give away their English lands to his marauding henchmen.

Amongst these was Eustace de Vere, Jarl of Essex and brother-in-law of Edward the Confessor. On Harold's death, Vere was pronounced King of England by the Witan. This made Eustace's right to the English throne unquestionable under Saxon Atheling Law. The illegitimate invader was so frightened of Eustace that he took hostages prior to the invasion in order to ensure Eustace's complicity.

The *de jure* Kingship of England has, therefore, descended through the Veres for over 900 years. In 1560 Edward de Vere gave the Tudors a timely and friendly, though somewhat esoteric reminder of this fact.

No one wanted William de Normandy. All he did in seizing the throne of England was commit an act of theft and treason accompanied by torture, rape, murder and yet more theft and treason. And what are the "new lords" now that this Blair person has got his own way? More scrap dealers, bully boys and warehousemen, elevated in payment for their political sycophancy and installed as party Yes-Men. Why bother making the change? What's the difference?

The codes of conduct and styles of behaviour developed over the centuries by these misfits and usurpers have come to be thought of as the manners of the "gentry". Such etiquette and standards of behaviour are, however, rather of the nature of a complex set of rules and protocols which have evolved from the necessity for these individuals to reinforce to themselves and each other their sense of identity. This need is born of the insecurity of the usurper and the poseur. The party games were initiated to ensure that those who refuted such mores or refused to adopt them were "excluded".

In recent history Nancy Mitford assisted in the development of a list of such styles of speech, patronage and behaviour which one of her nephews published in a book entitled *Noblesse Oblige*, which this author has looked through. Within its pages were lists of the "U" and non "U" words, affectations, preferred schools, clubs and so on. By their patronage or utilisation by others, the fake aristocracy could determine whether any individuals they encountered were "our sort of people", i.e. whether they were "U" or non "U", meaning "Upper-class" or "Non upper-class". What a cheek! This does not sit particularly well with the fact that the British Fascist leader, Oswald Mosley, had strong connections to the Mitford family.

Situations similar to the foregoing represent yet another example of how the chattering classes, the sons and daughters of arriviste tradesmen masquerading as gentry, hide behind their sham rituals and money. They hope that, as the years drift languorously by, people will forget that they were all descended from those whom the Scythians, the real nobility and royalty, despised for being liars and cheats.

When interviewed, Mitford said that the book was just a joke. Surprising then that these ridiculous social rules were rife amongst her "class" before she wrote them down and that they were indeed used to determine whether one was fit company for their pseudo-aristocratic "society" or not.

Today sociologists are doing exactly the same thing by using classification numbers to determine one's social status. One could be anything from say—an A1 category "social unit"—all the way down to a G3. These numbers are appended to one according to one's job and income.

For instance, hilariously enough and for no good reason the author can think of, a film star is an A1 "social unit", whilst a dustman is something like a G2. In terms of social value and input one would have thought that the dustman would have been somewhere up in the high B's at least, by quasi-Marxist sociologists' standards.

If film stars went on strike for six months would you suffer more than if dustmen went on strike for six months? Of course not. If dustmen took the same amount of time out the country would be swimming in bacteria and disease. If film stars went on strike, you would just watch repeats on television or buy a talking parrot or a performing monkey. What difference is there in terms of skill or in terms of social contribution, after all?

Whether they are Marxist or Weberan sociologists or whatever, they are the worst manifestation of middle-class attitudes, because it is only the middle classes who would differentiate between themselves and other classes. This is how you know they aren't *Gentry*.

The ancient gentry knew the value of a person's contribution to society and respected the person for making it. The true gentry weren't above grabbing a shovel when the need arose and mucking in and mucking out with everyone else. Only the elevated tinkery would expect someone else to do the work. Only the tinkery would think that, because they had risen so far in their own estimation of themselves, the world owed them a living.

The Elven Queens and the Dragon Kings, the real gentry of history, had no particularly complex hierarchy with which to stratify or differentiate rank amongst themselves. They simply knew that they were all of the Fairy blood and were thus equal. This is apparent in both the social structures of the d'Anu of Eire and the Royal Danes of Scandinavia as late as 900 AD.

The present scheme of things, which descends from the medieval feudal system, was developed by the succession of various dynasties of tinker royalty in Britain and Europe. We can see this insulating, snobbish mentality at work with its "layers" of rank, determining "layers" or "degrees" of nobility or royalty. In the Merovingian and Pictish Danaan cultures, one was a king or princess and that was that. All shared the Sang Real and the San Graal, that is the Holy Blood, from which Holy Grail is derived. Whether or not you reigned was immaterial.

Nowadays the British throne is occupied by the descendant of a foreign family almost arbitrarily selected for a task in which, to all intents and purposes, they find themselves merely an impotent figurehead. Under this individual there is stratified a complex series of ranks, orders and accolades which, historically, were anyone's for the taking, as long as they had money; and which today you can still buy into at the lowest rung by paying the College of Arms £1,800.

If you can prove to them that you have "made a contribution to society" either by getting a university degree or by having been trained to kill people, a nice coat of arms is yours for the asking. You will then be an official Esquire. Henceforth (though not beforehand, one assumes) you will be considered to be "A Gentleman" because you have a pretty piece of paper saying as much. In Ireland the Chief Herald's Office formerly issued applications for armorial bearing upon which it was stipulated that the supplicant must be considered by the Chief Herald to have reached "The Portal of Gentry".

How can anyone "reach the portal of gentry"? How can there be a "doorway to blood"? This is yet another instance where language is eloquently engineered to become completely ineloquent nonsense.

Every year the arguably unqualified monarch hands out knighthoods and orders, to unworthies who are chosen at the fawning whim of some transient, jumped-up public servant. They go mainly to self-seeking individuals who have been thought to have made a "contribution" to society. Many of these knighthoods go to average actors, football managers and industrialists. Both the former have already been paid a more than adequate amount of cash for their dubious and ineffectual contributions. The latter have likewise also been paid adequately for their self-seeking contribution and have also assisted, by their greed, in turning the planet into an orbiting swill bin.

Why are these people being rewarded for serving themselves and how can they possibly be thought of as behaving like "gentry", when the most that they do is produce useless consumer junk, infotainment and pollution? They have become rich by creating jealousy, envy and enmity. Through the media their dissemination of double standards has created a level of moral confusion which has inevitably led to further social and economic division and environmental damage. And for this they get an "honour".

One of the most lamentable investitures of the Most Noble Order of the Garter recently went to Margaret Thatcher, a grocer's daughter. Another went to Emperor Hirohito, the head of a country whose government refused, for forty years, to recognise their nation's responsibility for the treatment of civilians—whom they used in chemical warfare tests—and prisoners of war whom they forced to work to their deaths in military building operations.

In the first case, how can a grocer's daughter be thought of as suitable material for inclusion in an order that was so strictly intended for those of the royal blood. In the second case, how can one of the most hated enemies of the British people in recent history qualify either?

The Most Noble Order of the Garter had already been defiled down through the centuries by its association with a motley assortment of pseudo-royal dynasts who had no right to belong to it. It was bad enough that the Windsors had no right to confer it on anyone else. However, membership reached its lowest ebb when those two individuals were awarded it.

The Most Noble Order of the Garter is Britain's premier Order of Knighthood. In fact, heraldically speaking, it's actually the second in rank to the ancient Caledonian Dragon Court that spawned it. The very word "knight", stemming from the Saxon *cnecht*, means "to serve" or a "servant".

It was and still is an Angevin and hence an Elven bloodline institution. On the death of Richard III therefore, all rights to continue to own the Order of the Garter died out in his line and by the Laws of Sovereign inheritance the Order then belonged to the senior heirs of the House of Anjou.

Neither Hirohito nor Thatcher did anything to deserve to be invested with Britain's most senior rank of knighthood. It is an exercise of the worst manifestation of the bourgeois mentality to direct Her Majesty to give out such degrees. In Thatcher's case it appears to be to pay off a favour to a fellow member of the bourgeoisie. In Hirohito's it appears to be to kow-tow for diplomatic reasons to a nation simply because it has become economically successful. This is especially so when the present dynasty, it could be argued, appear to have no historical right to give the Order in the first place.

Her Majesty's intelligent son Prince Charles has publicly lamented the decline in standards in the English language for years. Even he would no doubt also question how can anyone "become" a gentleman, a member of the *gens*—the San Graal, and how can a piece of paper instantly make one into a member of a separate race.

The real "gentry", or to give them another familiar epithet—the Lords and Ladies—were just that. They were by blood alone, the members of a genetic strain, the Dragon and Grail families—the Fairy Blood. One could not and cannot "become" a member of the gentry any more than one can "become", by initiation or otherwise, a "Witch", a "Vampire", a "Magus", a "Dragon", a "Fairy" or an "Elf".

These are all terms which described the "gentry". The latter—Elf—is a word which originates from *albi*, meaning a white or "shining one". From *albi* derives the French Cathar name *Albigensian* (Albi + Gens), meaning "of the Elven blood"—*et quid erat demonstrandum*.

The Pharisees

This curious and delightful name for the Elven race is a common English rural folkword probably created by the addition of an extra syllable to the word Fairies, thereby making a double plural suffix. Pharisees is simply Fairies-es, a bit like Tolkien's double plural "pocketses", attributed to his character "Gollum" in *Lord of the Rings*.

A more obscure possible origin for the Pharisee epithet however, may be found in the nature of the Elves themselves. Some of their families were from mixed Pictish and Merovingian bloodlines. Where the latter is concerned, it descended from Jesus and had a Pharisaic origin. The word Pharisee itself stems from the Hebrew *parush*, meaning "separated", which by blood the Elves indeed were.

In this particular context we should also remember the Celtic Church which was Nestorian and Pharisaic in its doctrine and structure. The Celtic Church supported the Fairy bloodline of Jesus. At the same time it had strong Druidic associations, to the point, in fact, where Jesus himself was considered to have been a Druid and a Magus by his British kinsmen—the Elven PenDragons.

The Plantagenets

According to their own account of themselves and the accounts of subsequent chroniclers and historians, including Professor Vivian Green, the Plantagenets were descended from the Fairy race. Certainly they shared a common Scythian trait when riled, and that was a vile temper!

The Plantagenets, whose name was thought to derive from "plantagenista"—the "plant of generation" or "Tree of Life"—used a sprig of the Broom, the "plantagenista", as one of their earlier family badges. The seeds of the Broom plant are hallucinogenic and were a well-known part of the Witches' pharmacopoeia throughout the Dark Ages and the Medieval Period.

It was said that the Plantagenets had two ancestral grandmothers, one named Melusine, the daughter of King Elinus of Albany, and the other the daughter of Baldwin du Bourg, King of Jerusalem.

The Plantagenets derived their name from a princess named Plantina (possibly derived from Plantanu or Planta-Anu). She was actually the younger sister of Maelasanu des Scythes or Melusine McLean. This obviously means that the Plantagenets were not actually directly descended in the male line from Melusine herself. In a matriarchal Pictish system of inheritance, she was the senior daughter of King Gille Sidhean of Albany, and the heir of her mother, Queen Pressina, or more formally The Queen Bruidhe-Anu des Scythes.

Melusine certainly was the matriarch of the Angevin or Anjou dynasty. However, her senior heir and the first Count of Anjou was Maelo de Vere, not Tortolf de Rennes. This means the Plantagenet dynasty descended from the younger sister Plantanu, a junior branch of the Imperial and Royal House of Vere.

The Veres left Anjou in 800 AD and the Comite of Anjou was divided and, at length, settled upon the heirs of Tortolf. This gave the erroneous impression that they were the first and therefore senior branch of the Angevin family which, according to the records, is simply not the case.

The second Melusine was in fact called Melisend. Therefore the Plantagenets had no direct male connection with any Melusine at all, despite the attempts of subsequent royal genealogists and amateur historians to make it so. Nevertheless the Plantagenets, our younger Vere cousins, were still of the Blood Royal and of Elven Stock. The discrepancies in their story add to, rather than detract from, their claims or the claims made for them.

The popular, chronicled descent claimed for the Plantagenets from Melusine was in fact via a cadet female Vere line—that of Ida de Vere—a member of another junior branch of the Vere family, specifically the Imperial and Royal House of Vere of Constantinople and Jerusalem. Ida de Vere was the aunt of the inaugurator of the Knights Templar, the Swan Knight Godfroi de Vere de Bouillon. She was also the ancestral granddaughter of Prince Maelo de Vere d'Anjou. His mother was the much-coveted Princess Maelasanu McLean de Vere des Scythes, via Adolph de Vere de Guisnes.

The Plantagenets could however claim a line of unbroken male descent from the late 800's until the sad death in 1485 of Richard III—argued by some to be the last true King of England. This junior branch of the family managed to survive for about 600 years, which was a respectable length for an era. Since then, the British have suffered a succession of nondescript Church puppets who, out of generosity, one might call eighth-breeds at best.

With the death of Richard III the Garter died out in the junior Plantagenet line. It became, as a dynastic family, the Order of the House of Anjou, and the legitimate property of the already Gartered Imperial and Royal House of Vere of Oxford (the legitimate kings of England by the will of the English people themselves). It was later to descend to the Scottish and Irish Branches, the latter whose seniority, on the death of the Vere Clan Chief, Lord Adrian Hope-Vere—Laird of Blackwood—became confirmed in 1973.

Melusine's father, Elinus or Gille Sidhean; was a descendant of the Ulster Royal House of the Uilidian, the Fir Bolg Druids. Her mother was a bruidhe or judge-poetess of Pictish royal descent from the Bruidhainn or (by Roman error) Cruthainn remnant of the Tuadha d'Anu or Tuatha de Danaan, as they were later called.

These were the Aes Dan or Aesir Danaan, the Elven Gods of Eire and the Lords of the Calle Daouine of Caledonia or Northern Pictavia. Melusine was a Dragon Princess, a Lamia, and we will tell her story later.

The Plantagenets or Angevins became, after their demise, a much sought after bloodline to be descended from. It was as if it were implicitly understood that real Dragon blood made real queens and kings. Queen Elizabeth I, the great granddaughter of a Welsh farmer and Margaret, Countess of Anjou, had broom pod motifs sewn onto one of her gowns in celebration and assertion of her Anjou ancestry.

She is known to have had two coronations, the first and most important of which was a pagan, "Fairy" coronation held in public on the Mayday prior to her Church investiture as Queen of England. Following this event Edward de Vere, 17th Earl of Oxford, staged the Windsor Stag Ride incident and killed the beast before the Queen as a gentle reminder of who the real Kings of England and the Greenwood were.

Even today the biographers of the present constitutional Heads of State of Britain proudly boast of that family's Anjou descent. The author therefore supposes that we, the senior heirs of the senior branch of that dynasty, should be flattered, despite the fact that such a descent is tortuous in the extreme and traces a line therefore, that looks as crooked as a donkey's hind leg.

Boasting something like 2000 connections to Edward III, who was only a member of a junior Anjou line, the present British Royal family that is originally a German farming family, is outranked in terms of blood even by the Spencers. Their daughter, the late Princess Diana, could claim 4000 connections to the same character. Furthermore, one geneticist recently working with the blood samples of German royal and noble families couldn't find one whose male line reverted any farther than the early 16th century.

Chapter 6

Dragon's Deep

Edmund Spenser is said to have flattered Queen Elizabeth I by writing a poem dedicated to her called "The Faerie Queen". However it is equally possible that his was a veiled reference to the Fairy wife of the alchemist, the Earl of Desmond. Spenser and Sir Walter Raleigh resided at his seat—Castle Matres—during an expedition to retrieve the Wizard's library from a war zone on behalf of Dr. John Dee.

Castle Matres or Matrix, as it is now known, was said to have been named after the Matres or triple goddess. The castle rests on the banks of the river Deal in County Limerick and the library which was housed there is said to have contained singular works on Magic and Alchemy. These were works that Dee didn't want, under any circumstances, to fall into the Queen's hands. The reason for this was, as Laurence Gardner has pointed out, that Dr. John Dee, Edward de Vere, Francis Bacon, Edmund Spenser, and William Shakespeare et al were well aware that Elizabeth's house was full of badly bred usurpers. Also, despite the descent from Margaret of Anjou, the blood was not pure. I wonder what the boys would have made of the successive generations of farmers made monarchs.

Plantagenet descent, and the Fairy blood that ran in the veins of Edward III in particular, appears to have been greatly desired to legitimise the subsequent claims of the dynasties that superseded them. However, the Plantagenets themselves, and Edward I in particular, looked to Scotland to legitimise their own claims to kingship. Scottish and Irish Dragon Kings were invested on the Stone of Scone.

This Stone—the Lia Fail—the Stone of Destiny (or Fate) of the Tuadha d'Anu once rested at the summit of the Hill of Tara, the ancient seat of the Elven High Kings in County Meath. When the Milesian Dalriada left Eire for Scotland it is believed that they took the Lia Fail with them.

Edward I used his best efforts to conquer the Scots and wrest from them the Lia Fail—the ultimate symbol of royal legitimacy. This confirms, one suspects, his right to Fairy kingship which, retrospectively he had anyway. He was thus wasting his time. The Stone of the Elves never once rested under the gilded commode in Westminster Abbey.

Because the Raven-Stone of the Phoenicians wasn't the Stone of Scone that Edward I stole, this fake lump of rock that the English thought was the Lia Fail was nonchalantly and unceremoniously driven up to Edinburgh Castle in the back of a Land Rover. Even select members of the Order of the Golden Dawn knew this over a hundred years ago and descriptions of the Lia Fail can still be found in the literature of their successors.

Part of the later Plantagenet ancestry included the descendants of the Danish Jarl, Rollo Duke of Normandy. The senior Angevin dynasty—the Vere—also have the Viking Rollo as an ancestor in the female line.

The word "Viking" has been explained in various ways. Originally spelt "Wicking" it was thought to derive from the word "wic", meaning the inlet or mouth of a Fjord, whilst the earlier meaning of the word from the Old Friesian and Old English had "wic" as an encampment. In Russia, however, the "Vikhr" was a whirlwind, a manifestation of the Zmei or Dragon king which is dealt with later.

The Vikhr is a character which is common to both the Russians and the Irish. It will be remembered that Russia was actually founded by the Viking Ruotsi Clan, intimating that the actual definition of the word "Viking" is the same as the Irish word "Sumaire", a Dragon and a Vortex.

Anciently, the Danes and the Danaan were closely related and an examination of the Royal Clan in both cultures will reveal the same egalitarian system of self-regulation that distinguished the Danaan from the rest of Celtic society. The similarity does not end here. Like their Fairy cousin defenders in Ireland and Scotland, the Danes warriors were utterly indifferent to death and fought without mercy. Their overall belief system engendered behaviour that appears to have been almost nihilistic and devoid of any moral conflict.

This system, based on the "Nine Worlds" or emanations of being, was duplicated in earlier or contemporary variants of the Qabalah and Kaula Tantra. As with the former, where the spheres or Sephira were incorporated into the Hebrew "Tree of Life", the Viking spheres or worlds were thought to rest within the branches of a tree which, in the Norse, was called Yggdrasil, the World Ash Tree. Yggdrasil's roots were embedded in Hel or the Underworld, whilst its branches brushed against the stars of Heaven.

Yggdrasil is a shamanic glyph which represents the macrocosm—the universe both subtle and material—and the microcosm—the human body. The tree glyph itself in all cultures represents the path the shaman takes, from the roots, embedded in matter, up the trunk and into the branches and the stars, to the rarefied spiritual spheres and beyond, to unite with godhead itself.

Such a journey inevitably must transcend mundane care, fear, greed, opinion or morality, and he or she who embarks upon and completes such a journey successfully becomes united with the One Unmanifest, the True Will and the Total Self. As we shall see later, the Tree is actually a woman, a goddess incarnate or Avatar.

The individual who completes the journey is beyond mortal conditioning or the short-sighted relativity upon which is based human moral law. This system and its results duplicate themselves in many other mystical systems and in early Witchcraft in particular.

Perhaps therefore, when considering the behaviour or attitudes of the individuals in cultures such as those of the Danes and the Danaan, it might be more apposite if scholars took more into account the effects that philosophical systems like these actually had on people like the Norse. They could then rethink the etymology of the word "Viking" or "Wiccing", before settling on an answer that smacks of over-specialisation.

In tandem with their Aryan Hindu cousins, the Vikings used the symbol of the Swastika. An example of its utilisation by the Norse can be found in Iceland, whose early inhabitants emblazoned the blue Swastika sacred to Kali Azura or "Blue Kali", the sister of the Sumerian Cain or Qayin. Variants of this figure, the hammer of Thor, <fig 1>, earlier a copper, single-headed labrys or tomahawk common to the Ubaid, which is the shape of <fig 2>, spinning and creating the vortex, the spiral storm or tornado, can also be found at numerous archaeological sites including Newgrange in its early spiralised form, <fig 3>. This is the spiral design of the Sumaire of Sumeria. In its variant form, <fig 4>, the Swastika, represents the curved Scythian sword reaping the whirlwind.

The Swastika is also found reversed, <fig 5>, and both forms respectively are thought to be moon and sun symbols. As the author will continue to reiterate, when reading on such subjects, particularly in relation to the philosophy of the Druids and other Indo-European, Aryan philosophies, it is wise to bear in mind that the teachings and symbols operate on both the macro and microcosmic levels at the least. Often the symbolism is in fact multi-faceted.

In the case of the Swastika, the moon and sun symbolism applies inasmuch as the sun radiates or pushes energy out whilst the moon draws energy to it in the form of the sun's rays. Its gravitational field also pulls the tides. The <fig 6> of Kali is the Sumaire, the whirlpool which is the sucker-in of blood and energy, and like the moon it draws the suns rays and sucks up the tides, whilst <fig 5> , the solar Swastika, symbolises the donor or benefactor who gives willingly of their essence.

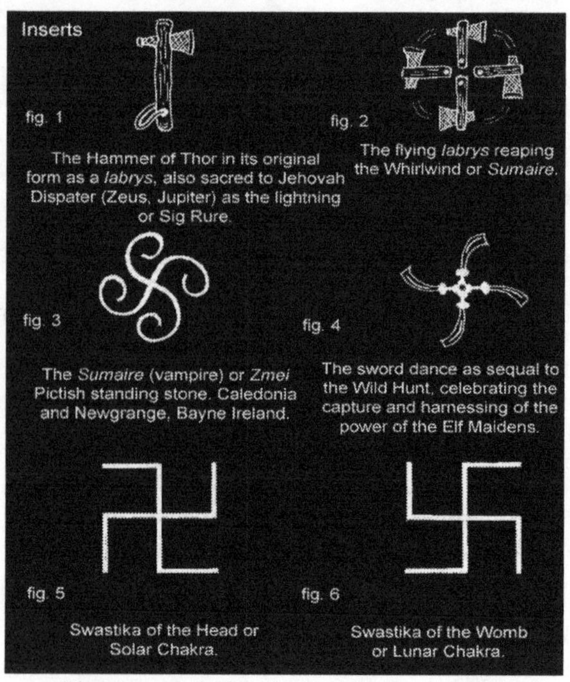

<Fig 5> Exhale <Fig 6> = Inhale

If we look closely we will also notice that the circular Swastika is the mark of Lilith given to Cain and also the mark of Kali. In their original form, they represent the scythe of the reaper <fig 8>, the Golden Sickle of the Druids spinning on its hilt. Therefore <fig 8> is also <fig 9>. The Swastika has another three-armed form which appears again at Newgrange and also as the badge of the Fairy king Manannan Mac Lir, Lord of the Isle of Man, <fig 10> and Lord of the Waters of the Sea. As <fig 11>, it compares to the Dragon's eye of the south , <fig 12>, and also <fig 13>, the Dragon's eye of the north. In the northern hemisphere, mimicking the pull of the whirlpool, the rotation of these devices is to the left as you look at them, or clockwise from the point of view of the one summoning the Sumaire in themselves.

If we think of the Swastika as being a turbine, the position of the arms, either <fig 5> or <fig 6>; or <fig 11> or <fig 13>, indicates not the direction of rotation, but the angle at which the blades are set. The difference between the four and three armed Swastika is that the four armed essentially represents the sowing or reaping of "the four winds", the pneuma, the spiritual or morphic energy, whilst the three armed cross, the Swastika of Manannan of the waters, represents sowing (donating) or reaping (removing) the blood and waters of the Fountain of Life—The Holy Grail.

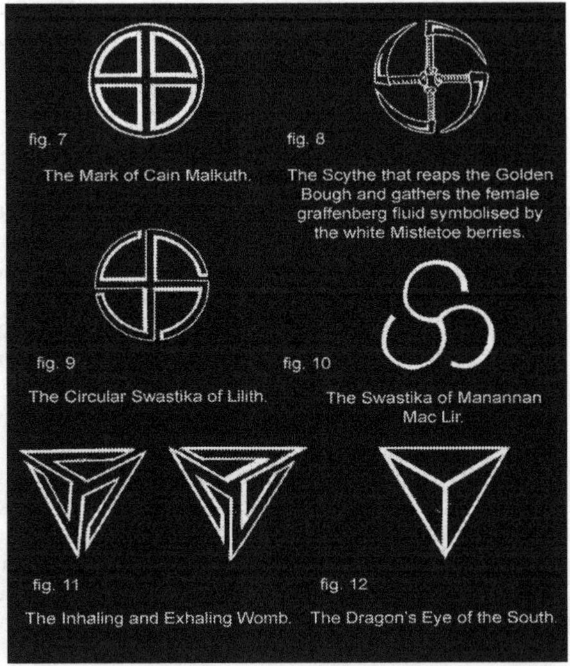

fig. 7 The Mark of Cain Malkuth.

fig. 8 The Scythe that reaps the Golden Bough and gathers the female graffenberg fluid symbolised by the white Mistletoe berries.

fig. 9 The Circular Swastika of Lilith.

fig. 10 The Swastika of Manannan Mac Lir.

fig. 11 The Inhaling and Exhaling Womb.

fig. 12 The Dragon's Eye of the South.

The pineal gland is so-called because it is similar in shape to a pinecone. The Dragon's eye of the north <fig 13> looks similar to the plan view of a three-sided pyramid and also represents the pineal gland that controls the secretion of the mystical fluids. In relation to the pineal gland the Grail is symbolised by the sacred head, the Baphomet or source of wisdom.

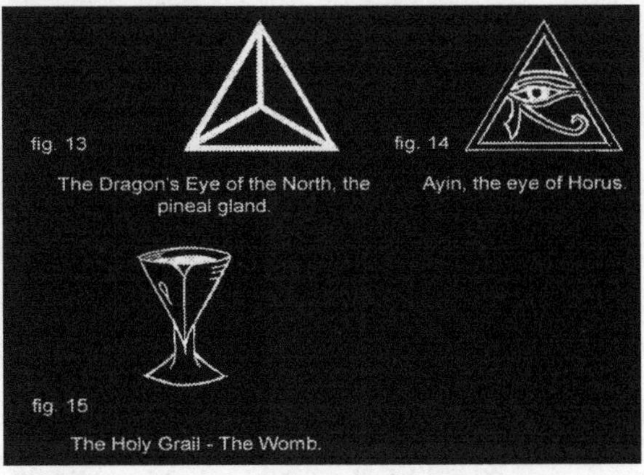

fig. 13 The Dragon's Eye of the North, the pineal gland.

fig. 14 Ayin, the eye of Horus.

fig. 15 The Holy Grail - The Womb.

Related to the Solar disc and the Ajna Chakra in Tantra, in Mithraism this stage of the Grail process is represented by the Dragon of the sun. Therefore here the three-armed Swastika is the Dragon's eye of the north <fig 13>, representing the pine cone shape of the pineal gland and also the 15th letter of the Hebrew alphabet, Ayin <fig 14>, the 15th path of the Tarot—the Devil—and the number of Ishtar or Venus in the roll of the seniority of the Gods. The Ayin is the "All Seeing Eye of God" (Enki or Samael), peering both in and out of the void.

At the end of their journey from the brain, through its third ventrical, down the spinal column to the womb, Graffenberg gland and urethra, the fluids rest here until naturally or manually discharged. The womb becomes the Grail Cup containing the waters of life, the Cubic stone of the Philosophers. The Dragon's eye of the south <fig 12> = <fig 15>—the Cup. Thus the Grail, amongst other things, is both the Head and the Cup, and both "eyes" of the Dragon—north and south—are the eyes that contain "The light that illumines the human spirit". It is also the pineal gland, the Delta or Hebrew Daleth or Tau—The Doorway to the eternal.

In any form the Swastika is an emblem of life, of breathing (*the breath of Ravens*) and of self-sacrifice. As such, therefore, the Swastika is one of the primeval symbols of Priest-Kingship and Dragon Maidenhood. Greatly to be abhorred, then, is the fact that the Nazi Party of Germany hijacked the Swastika of Kali and, along with numerous other Fairy symbols, made it the most hated and feared glyph on the Planet.

The Death's Head of the SS is the head of wisdom of the Templars—the Baphomet—whilst the Sig rune itself is the path of the serpent of wisdom descending the Tree of Life. The red banner, with the white circle and black Swastika, represents the bloody funeral ground of the Aryan saints. They gave the last drop of their life's blood to Kali, represented by the white disc of the moon amidst the crimson field of the banner and whose Swastika is the Sumaire, drawing life into it as the Moon draws the seas to her. The red flag is thus intended to represent the self-sacrificing Tantric priests of the Kaula Vama Marg shedding the last vestige of their egos and their lives, to be left drained. As empty vessels, they were then ready to be filled with the wisdom of the Cosmos and with the power of the Siddhis.

In practice, however, the Swastika represents the suffering of four million people sacrificed to the stupidity of a nation duped into thinking that a dysfunctional Yiddish house painter and a disaffected chicken farmer, leading a doomed race of potato peasants, could really be the vestige of the Aryan Peoples: their so-called Master Race. And as I have already said here: the Judaic Culture, at its very root and heart, is Aryan in origin. Its ancient gods and goddesses were Aryan, its iconography is Aryan, its mythology is Aryan and its Royal House was Aryan. Even the hated so-called Star of David (properly the Shield of David) is a form of the Swastika. From the following chart, demonstrating the Grail Myth of the Lady Marcella, the reader will see that the Death's Head, beloved of the Nazis, is equal and identical to the Shield of David in a precise Hermetic sense.

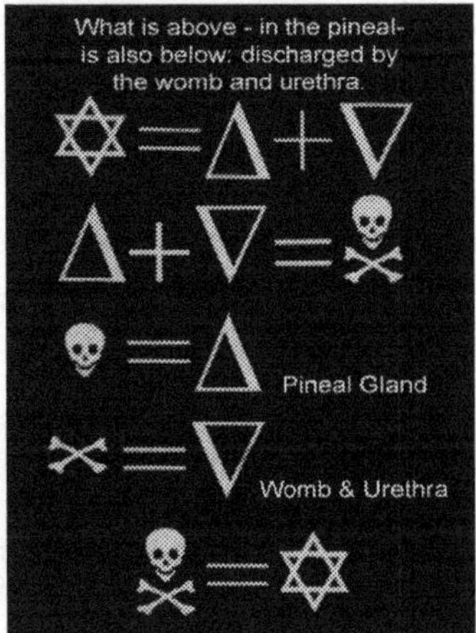

Those recalling the Templar myth of Maraclea will remember that the Skull is Male, whilst the Crossed Bones are Female. In much the same way as the Triangle on its base is the Male alchemical symbol of Fire, the Triangle on its point is the Female alchemical symbol of Water. Combined, we see that they comprise the exoteric, international symbol of Judaism.

Now, the Swastika in exoteric Hinduism is split into two arms, one being female and one being male. They too represent the magical elements of fire and water combined and thus the Swastika is exactly one and the same as the so-called Star of David. And here lies the utter stupidity of racist ideology and jingoism. The Jewish Holocaust replicates exactly what happened to the Elven families for over a thousand years and for exactly the same reasons. Money and power.

The Fairy progeny, in small pockets, spanned the Earth from as far distant as Japan* to Scotland. They rarely mixed with the indigenous populations who invited their rule and their wisdom. Germans, like any other tribe would have had their Aryan caste to guide them but that doesn't entitle a whole nation to consider itself Aryan.

*The Ainu of Hokkaido or North Island are a tall, fair-skinned Caucasoid people, thought to have been the original inhabitants of the Japanese Islands who were driven north by waves of immigrants from China, Korea and South Asia. The Ainu (pronounced: Eye-Noo) are animistic and shamanic and share many beliefs with the Amerindians and the Scythian Druids concerning the nature of life. Their principal divine totem is the Swan. During the 12th century the Ainu were almost extinct following continued hostilities with invaders. Their mythology tells them that their race was saved by a Swan which descended from heaven and mated with the last living Ainu Lord. This coupling produced the Ainu who still occupy Hokkaido today.

The Swan Maidens are the Dragon Princesses of the Grail, the Scythian Druid Queens and the Nordic Andvarinauts. In Irish lore they can transform from Swans into maidens and so, anthropologically speaking, it would appear. The assertion is supported by academics that the Ainu, born of the womb of a Swan Maiden, are of the Royal, Elven Dragon Blood—the Blood of Anu! The Ainu have dark hair and almond eyes and are distinctly Asian despite their complexions. Nevertheless, the remnant of the Ainu who retain pure blood, of which no more than seventeen thousand are left, are of Aryan extraction. So much for the 20th century blue-eyed, blonde-haired German fantasy. The pure, insular Ainu have more right to the epithet Aryan than any German chicken farmer ever had.

Sacred Wells and Well-dressing

The Serpent-Dragon Jormangr, the encircler, coils about at the base of Yggdrasil, the Tree of Life of the Viking Kabala or Nine Worlds system. At Yggdrasil's roots there is a pool. In Ireland, Scotland and Wales this symbol is repeated as the hazel tree by the well, in which lives the Salmon of Knowledge. Atop the branches of the hazel tree there sits an eagle who drops a blood red nut of wisdom into the well 13 times a year. There it is consumed by the Salmon of Knowledge.

Not all Sacred or Fairy "Wells" were actually water sources. Archaeologists working at numerous sites around Britain have discovered that sites which are often called "Fairy Wells" are, in fact, nowhere near the water table. Closer investigation revealed that these boreholes, as in the case of Mine Howe in Orkney, were actually Bronze Age ritual chambers on or adjacent to what the locals would term a Fairy Hill. These chambers were entered via a spiral, flagged stairway descending a stone-lined cylindrical flue or chimney.

In this connection, what does that tell us about, say, the Well of Nechtan, or St. Anne's Well, situated next to the Robin Hood's hill labyrinth? In all probability for ritual purposes we might conclude that a maiden priestess actually resided in the chamber beneath the hill. She was, we can conclude, the representative of "the Salmon of Knowledge" or Persephone and her pomegranate wine, or the queen of sovereignty and her dergflaith, the red beer of kingship. In this respect the connection between the womb and the underworld is clear, and a host of associations and reinforcements present themselves to the reader. These might lead us to consider what might be buried beneath the tower of St. Michael's Church, which rests atop the Glastonbury Tor, under which is said to be the palace of Alberich or Oberon, the Elven King. We might also wonder whether such chambers were a feature of those sacred hills, which are associated with the ritual of king-making.

Real wells and trees eventually became the focus of devoted rituals that we know now as well-dressing. This was a misunderstanding of the idea that the tree and the well were figurative and that their curative properties w… obtained not from well water, but from something entirely different. Becaus… these waters were considered therapeutic and rejuvenating, the wells were blessed and venerated. One supposes that in order to make the forgotten approximation closer to the reality of the symbol, the trees adjacent to these wells were decked in coloured patches of cloth. These symbolised the Chakras or Sephira of the Tree of Life of the female body, which the Druids were really symbolising in their use of the tree and the well glyph.

In the case of the Gaelic form of Yggdrasil, the nut of the hazel represents the pineal discharge. As discussed, dropped by the eagle, representing the spirit or the Sun God Llew (the Ajna Chakra or Kether Sephiroth), it descends through the Tree of Life (like the lightning bolt of inspiration) and falls into the well or womb. Here it is consumed by the Salmon of Knowledge. In the Irish story it is Nechtan (meaning “pure one”), the God of “Waters”, who catches and eats the salmon, a euphemism for cunnilingus. Repeating the entreaty of the grail story however, it is only the “pure one” who may see or benefit from the “Grail”, which is here, as anywhere else, the female genitalia and the mysterious essences they bestow.

This story and its variants can be found across Europe in one suppressed or hidden form or another. Whilst the eagle represents the spirit, we are clear on the nature and identity of the secretions represented by the nut. The spirit was said to be located in the pineal gland by Descartes, who was repeating an ancient Gaelic belief. The salmon however represents the vulva, resting at the “bottom” of (e.g. beneath or below) the womb.

Both in contemporary and in classical and historical colloquialism the fish represents the female vulva. This usage is universal. If eating fish is said to be good for the brain, then eating Nechtan's salmon takes on a whole new meaning for us. The fish crops up as a Christian symbol, that of Ichthys (meaning “fish” in Greek) which Christians believe means Iesus Christos Theos, or “Jesus Christ God”. And on the subject of fish and fish women or Mermaids, we enter the labyrinth.

The Labyrinth

There was a Crooked Man,
And he walked a Crooked Mile,
He found a Crooked Sixpence,
Against a Crooked Stile.
He bought a Crooked Cat,
Which caught a Crooked Mouse,
And they all lived together
In a little Crooked House.

We have discussed the nature and identity of the Dragon Queens and Kings as *Witch Lords*, *Vampires*, *Elven Queens and Kings*, *Fairies* and *Seers*.

ʌ time to place them into the context of their true "homeland" and Iᵹ a closer look at their "mystical realm".

In German Hermetics, the Kabalistic Tree of Life, usually a hexagonal figure, is also depicted as a series of 11 concentric circles. The outer circle represents Malkuth, whilst the inner circle represents Kether. Within this last circle should be inserted another, representing "Ain Soph Aur", the eternal wisdom or the "Limitless Light". This penultimate sphere—Kether—as Kabalists will reiterate, is also Malkuth on a "higher" or "purer" level.

What this means simply is that once one has attained enlightenment, one understands that the beginning of a journey is also its end and that Paradise, Eternity, Heaven, Elphame, Bliss or whatever, is and always was, right here on Earth. In Mithraic terms one slays the World Bull of finite perception and releases the fertility of eternal life from its corpse. It is the slaying of the Minotaur in one's self and the attainment of the maiden Ariadne, or more properly Sophia, at the centre of the labyrinth. This is also the case with the Brea More labyrinth in Hampshire, where the centre of this turf "Troytown" figure is said to represent "paradise". At the centre of all labyrinths there waits the Dragon Maiden and her Holy Blood who are the physical manifestations of, as well as a doorway to, the anima and the eternal.

If one appreciates the Sephira of the Tree of Life as circles within circles, then the paths on the hexagonal Tree of Life figure, which join the Sephira to each other, when laid out within the circular figure, become the winding paths of the labyrinth. In the Chartres labyrinth: the "Jerusalem Mile", whose pattern is repeated across Britain and France, one can see the concept of Malkuth-in-Kether-in-Malkuth laid out in the pathways. The labyrinth is a graphic representation of the mile long "Crooked Path" that leads to the true realm of the Elves: Eternity. Later we will study the concept of the hexagonal Kabalistic Tree of Life as both the realm and the genealogy of the early Elven Gods and a representation of the hive or group mind. Here the hexagonal shape of the Tree of Life of the Rabbis is reminiscent of the earlier "hive" configuration of the genealogical, Phoenician Kabala; a shape repeated in the domed, beehive shaped hermitages of the early Irish monks.

The Crooked Path to the Land of Elphame: the Kingdom of the Elves

The Crooked Path from Malkuth to Kether also represents the lightning bolt of inspiration that courses through each Sephira on its way from Kether, down the Tree of Life to Malkuth, the Earth. In the Kabala the path is the lightning bolt, the origin of the Norse Sig rune, often depicted as the Serpent of Wisdom, spanning and joining Heaven or Kether to the Earth, or Malkuth. The Serpent or Dragon eats its own tail and, in completing itself, becomes the Oroborous, the Nix, Naga or Zero—the Fool of the Tarot—in which is contained everything and nothing. Its tail, which is heaven or eternity, contained and manifest in its clutching mouth, is also made manifest upon the Earth and transcendence is complete. Also known as the Alchemists' Ring—

it is the ancient symbol of the Anunnaki whose name implies "When Heaven meets Earth".

In the story of Holger Dansk and Morgan le Fay, the Oroborous unites the figures of the ancient Tree of Life as the Tree, the Dragon Maiden, the Ring, the Grail and the Labyrinth, in a symbol of Hierogamy so complete that it tolerates no idle interpretations.

The word labyrinth has an etymology of which there are two interlinked variations derived from:

i) *labrys*, a pre-Hellenic word said to mean "double headed axe",
ii) the Latin *labia* meaning "lips" or "folds". The double-headed axe was sacred to Zeus; the Grecian Thor, whose hammer was a variant of the labrys. The spinning hammer was thought to form the shape of the Swastika as it flew through the air, whipping up the whirlwind.

This whirlwind and the spiral Swastika that symbolised it were the figurative progenitors of the stylised maze or labyrinth. Nevertheless the hammer, shaped like two opposed crescent moons was, like the labrys, a female emblem. At the highest level the labyrinth symbol works on several different but interconnected strata such as: the Folds of Time, the Spiral Cosmos, the Folds of Human Self Deceit, the Journey of Life, the Brain and Spinal Column, the Womb and Vagina, the Tomb or Creachaire, the Vortex or Sumaire. We will be concentrating upon the Vampiric symbolism in relation to samadhi or transcendence.

As the Romans, formerly, and anciently the Scythian Trojans, continued to follow Hellenic customs, the word labrys would have been known to them. Consequently the construction of their Latin word labia would have had incorporated into it any of the original suggestions intimated by the pre-Hellenic word labrys.

This assertion is borne out by an inspection of the glyph representing the double-headed axe. It is constructed in an hourglass configuration by placing two equilateral triangles of equal dimension together point to point, with the points meeting on the vertical plane, equi-distant from the two horizontal planes.

From the central meeting point of the two triangles, a horizontal line extends out, twice the length of the horizontal sides of the triangles into the plaster of the walls of the labyrinth at Knossos and it is this figure, the labrys, which authorities present as giving the Knossos labyrinth its name.

With the handle removed and placed upright before the double triangle, we have the figure 18. When the numbers are merged into a monogram, they form the caduceus of Hermes, the "phallus" of Baphomet, the fennel stalked thyrsus of Bacchus-Dionysus, the fennel stalk in which Prometheus gave the gift of "fire" to man and the flying reed-stalk of the Witches (the original Witches' broom).

It is also the ribbon entwined maypole, the serpents Lilith and Samael entwined around the Tree of Life and the rise of kundalini up the helix encased spinal cord to the ajna Chakra of the brain, all of which the foregoing also represent.

The Witches flying reed stalk suggests soaring consciousness in the same way that the caduceus does, which has wings attached to what is thought to be the solar disc. This is actually the Sephiroth corresponding to the brain. The fire given to man by Prometheus might be thought by some to have been the fire serpent Kundalini, who features as a maiden in the service of the evil Klingsor, in the stories relating to Amfortas and the knights of the Holy Grail.

Klingsor represents the perversion of the Vampire rite into an act of base sexual lust. He is the aspect of male human nature who, like the Minotaur, represents the danger of capitulation to sexual drives when the knight, like Theseus, is presented with the true quasi-erotic nature of the Grail in the form of the virgin vulva.

However, Kundalini promotes the production of noradrenaline and the sexual hormones which work in direct opposition to the Grail, and if the pilgrim allows his baser nature to prevail, the "Grail" will destroy him by producing in him the opposite hormonal response to that which engenders wisdom and spirituality.

In the story of Amfortas, Kundalini realises her true function and dies to become a former physiological capacity in which she was ever active in the service of "Klingsor". Therefore she becomes passive and receptive to her other, deeper spiritual role, and capitulates to the service of the Grail, symbolised by her expiry at the Fisher King's feet.

This simply means that she, the spinal column, accepts her role as the conveyor of Grail chemicals from the pineal to the womb, instead of only sexual ones, from the genitals to the brain. With the expansion of knowledge in the science of endocrinology, it is possible now for the informed outsider to restore these stories to their original meaning.

So the fire of Prometheus is not the fire of Kundalini going up the spine to the brain, but the fire of wisdom going down the spinal column to the womb to become Starfire, which is shed from thence and drunk in the "Rite of the Vampire".

The double triangle labrys design, identical with the one found in the labyrinth of Knossos but without the handle, was used up until medieval times to denote the womb and vagina. One of the medieval sexual talismans incorporated into the *Clavicula Salomanis* includes this axe-head glyph as a representation of the female principle, encircled by the Latin phrase "Exeat et Replete Terrum", taken from Genesis. The talisman cited was used to attract female lovers, one might speculate for what purpose precisely. Certainly no purpose that would serve a Vampire.

The genital symbolism is therefore quite clear and whether the word Labyrinth is derived from either *labrys* or *labus*, it strongly indicates that the maze or labyrinth was originally a graphic representation of the womb and vaginal channel, at least on one level of relationship to any attendant symbolism.

The labyrinth of Knossos is thought to be a later version of the temple labyrinth of Amenemhet (ca. 1818-1772 BC) built at Faiyum. This was a mortuary temple complex consisting of some three thousand rooms and halls resting beneath the shadows of the Pyramid of Hawara, a name which itself is reminiscent of the ancient Sumerian Dragon Queen Hawah of Elda who was an ancestor of the builder.

The Hawara labyrinth was adorned with carvings of the Dragon god Sobekh, to which the labyrinth was principally dedicated. This is not surprising when one learns that Hawara, formerly Arsinoe Ptolomais, was also named Crocodilopolis, the cultic centre of the veneration of this Egyptian Dragon god of sovereignty and the protector of the royal caste. This was also the Sumaire of Sumeria and the Scythians. The 22 kings of Egypt of the XIIth dynasty met there and it is within the precincts of this palatial labyrinth that Amenehemet's daughter, Sobekhnefru, held the Royal Dragon Court.

Although vast in size, it was not unique, as many pyramids themselves had labyrinths built into their structure. We are reminded of the nature of pyramids as sacred mountains, echoing Egypt's cultural origin in an earlier mountainous region of Eurasia, and we will also remember the sacred hill of the Ogdoad and the links between the pyramids, raths, sidhes, tells, tepes, kurgans and ziggurats.

The labyrinth, like the pyramid and its collaterals, is thought to be a development of the idea of the mountain cave itself and examples in support of such a theory are to be found in the intricate passages and designs of Palaeolithic sanctuaries. As we know, each of the pyramids and their related structures had funerary and living quarters and were representations of the "cave in the mountain".

From the kings' or queens' habit of living in these funerary buildings, we obtain the myth of the Vampire as one of the undead. Labyrinths have been discovered as far afield as Siberia (north-east Russia) and Wales. This suggests strongly, because of the locations, that the concept was of a Fairy origin. In support of this theory we find in Iceland various turf mazes and labyrinthine stone structures called Volsunghausen or "Wayland's Homes".

Wayland or Alberich (Aubrey/Oberon) was also called Laurin and this name, meaning a Bay tree, has a double entendre when it is translated as "passage" in relation to the maze cult. A spiral path can be trod to the top of Glastonbury Tor, which is said to be the home of Oberon.

Frequently these structures are associated with barrows. Atop one of these outside St. Anne's Well (a sacred site dedicated to Black Annis) in Nottinghamshire there is a turf maze named "Robin Hood's Race". It is virtually identical with another which was sunk in a depression at the top of "The Fairies' Hill", a barrow outside Asenby, Yorkshire. The custom of treading the Asenby maze in the evening and sitting in the centre to hear the Fairies sing was recorded as late as 1908. The design of these mazes, which are of considerable antiquity, some say Bronze Age, have lately been called "Shepherds Races" (many with a distinct spiral pattern towards the centre of the structure), and were copied by the Church during the medieval period. The labyrinths at Chartres and numerous other Churches in France, Germany, Spain and Great Britain, are of an identical design with these far more ancient mazes which invariably were placed adjacent to or in the midst of originally prehistoric sacred sites, often forming the centre of the Groves. The labyrinth of Chartes Cathedral, built by the Knights Templar in the 13th century, like many ritual mazes, has no blind alleys or fake routes. At its centre there is a six petalled "Plantagenet" or wild rose, carved into which there seems to be an M figure reminiscent of the symbol of Virgo which is the M for "Our Lady", the Virgin Mary Magdalene, to which the Ichthys or Salmon of Wisdom has been appended, denoting the genital nature of the whole glyph itself. As the maze is situated in a cathedral dedicated to Notre Dame, it seems appropriate to think of it in these terms, as the womb of the virgin. The Rose Garden symbolism of the core of the labyrinth of Chartres is an echo of the Garden of Solomon and the Rose of Sharon, meaning "Blood of the Virgin Princess", and also of the later forest labyrinth of Melusine, with its fountain, mentioned in medieval French literature.

The Labyrinth of Solomon is in fact a medieval alchemical symbol doubtlessly denoting the "scented fountain garden" of Sheba. In the French stories, Melusine lies in hiding at the centre of her maze garden, waiting to prey on victims returning from the pilgrimages to the Holy Land. She would draw them in and drink their blood. Conversely she also lay at the centre of the maze, as the prize of the quester for the Grail.

The centre of the maze incorporated a black cubic stone from which spurted the waters of life, *la fonteine de soif*, and the blood of the virgin womb. At Chartres, the Rose in the centre of the maze can be seen bathed in the sanguine light of the sun beaming through a strategically placed pane of red stained glass, making the combined Grail symbolism apparent.

Gematria is a system whereby attributive numbers are added together to give the lowest figure and thus reveal the essence or spirit innate in any particular beings, words, higher numbers or objects, to which there have been traditionally attached a numerological component. It was an integral part of Hermetics and Kabala, which was used extensively as part of sacred geometry in many Templar buildings.

The Chartres Maze was also called the Jerusalem mile and was used as a symbolic substitute devotion in place of an actual pilgrimage to the Levant. The mile, though here only suggestive, is 1760 Roman yards which, when added together gematrically gives 1+7+6+0 = 14. The multiple component of the mile is x 3, as the mile is measured in yards or 3 feet spans. In order to calculate the number of feet in a mile one multiplies 1760 by 3 which gives 5280 feet. In reality the maze path is far shorter, but the inference is implicit.

It actually measures 150 yards, which was a Gaulish measurement of 1500 paces, called a leuca, leuga or leuva. This term is remarkably close to Lucca. Professor Margaret Murray states that this god was the one that the reputed royal sacrifice, William Rufus, invoked in oaths. Lucca is related to Loki and Lucifer, the bringer of light, also known as Mazda or Ormuzd. The cult of the Mistletoe Bard and his journey to the Elysian labyrinth of Persephone is clearly documented in the author's notes on Cai ap Emrys and the Vere dying kings.

If one multiplies the gematric sum of a mile (14) by the number of feet in a yard (3) one obtains 3 x 14 = 42, the diameter of the maze. In the medieval period three types of calendar were used: Solar, Lunar and Terrestrial. The calculations of both Solar and Lunar calendars are well known. Gematrically the symbolic Chartres "mile", if it actually were a mile in feet, added together would give 5+2+8+0 = 15. This is the number of the path of the devil or Baphomet, the head of wisdom, the skull and crossbones, the androgynous god of the Templars (Mercury-Venus or Hermes-Aphrodite) whose combined male and female gender celebrates Enthea: Hierogamy or divine union.

However, it is 150 yards which added gematrically amounts to the same thing: 15. 150 yards is 450 feet which adds to 9: N'H'sH, the tripartite triple goddesses of "The Love that is Death" and the Vampire Sumaire: the Spiral Serpent of the Vortex. When the Catholic faithful walked the symbolic 5280 feet of the Jerusalem mile, as the maze is called, kabalistically and gematrically they were following the path of the Devil (15) and walking down the road to Damnation.

The actual measurements used vary from modern scales but the component measurements remain the same. The scale used was medieval and the diameter was 42 old feet, each comprising of 11.5 inches per foot, which still relates to Venus and the cubic stone, Melusine, and so forth, without actually changing the meaning of the design. This measurement also seems to be a regularly occurring standard for early turf mazes in Britain.

The Chartres Maze was probably based itself on earlier patterns associated with Melusine and Sheba, which themselves were based on the Swastika, the pre-eminent glyph of the Vortex or Sumaire, the "sucker-in" and source of life and life's blood. Associated with this is the concept of the maze as a dance pattern which, similar to the original sacrificial sword dance of the Danes and the Scots, was an echo of the spiralling Witches' dance around the vortex and a celebratory rite of the Wild Hunt.

For some, entry into the maze would result in their life being drained away by the virgin occupant, whose repast she would pass on to her kind, as she acted as the fountain of thirst and fed them in turn from her holy blood. In a sense then, where the Minotaur at Knossos is concerned (who is frequently interchangeable with the Scythian Centaur in classical art), he is also representative of the Vampire king. Thus at the highest level, as a whirlpool attracting and distributing life and life's blood, the Labyrinth was both tomb and womb, life taker and life giver. In that order. On at least two occasions in England, labyrinths have been euphemistically referred to as "fish traps" or Veres (Norse: "Ver").

Chapter 7

The Jewel in the Crown

The fact that it was a Druidic device can be ascertained by its 6th-century associations with the bard Lwarch Hen. One will recall that Melusine was a "mermaid", half fish (or rather Water Serpent) and half woman, and that Mer is the Egyptian Hieroglyph which, shaped like a square spiral maze, denotes water and irrigation.

As an Elf Maiden she would have been the ritual quarry of the Wild Hunt and thus "a fish for the fish trap", a blood offering for the Vere King. It appears therefore that the maze is the Bower of the Virgin and indeed some mazes have been named just that: Maidenbowers. The symbol of Virgo, the M with a fish appended, denoting the virgin vulva and womb, is pertinent here.

As the cubic stone is the Lia Fail, the emerald tablet, the vulva of Venus and the jewel in the crown of Lucifer, then it relates also to the Sumerian Inanna, the Akkadian Ishtar. Like Melusine, she was said to consume her lovers, and Hathor who, like Persephone, was the vendor of "deadly" Otherworldly "food" (which, like its counterpart, Fairy food, compelled one to remain in Elphame). Its sacred emblem was the Ankh from whence was derived the name of the Druidic death cult, the Ankhou or Anjou, of which Morgana, and Melusine (the Fountain of Thirst) of the Labyrinth, were high priestesses.

The Ankh was also used by the Albigensian Cathars, thought by scholars to be either the descendants of, or to have been influenced by, the Persian

Manicheans, the Arians and the Bogomils. This suggests a further reinforcement of the link between pre-Nicaean and thus gnostic-dualist, or original Christianity and Druidism.

The Maze is associated with the root word from whence we derive the adjective "to amaze". This itself probably has associations with the name Mazda, the principle of light, suggesting that whatever was at the centre of a Maze rendered enlightenment and that ecstatic amazement, or wonder, accompanied it.

As Ormuzd, it might even be associated with the Spiral Serpent of the vortex: the Sumaire. Some dictionaries have suggested in the past that maze was derived from the Saxon word for a whirlpool, mase, and although scholars later insisted that no such word existed, like it or not, the early maze was indeed a figurative vortex; a tornado or whirlpool.

At the centre of the Knossos Maze there dwelt the Minotaur, the bull-man who destroyed all who entered his environs. From previous notes we will recall that the bull, Jehovah, represented the unregenerate man and his world view. Once Mithras or Mazda slew the bull, from its veins poured forth all fertility.

The bull's head also represented the female organs, one will recollect. Again a source of fertility on both levels. The Theseus story therefore is a typical rendering of the central mystery of the dualistic cult of Mithras, which is repeated in Sleeping Beauty, Beauty and the Beast, and the Tale of Holger Dansk. Theseus learns that 14 victims every nine years were sent to Knossos to appease the Minotaur. This has echoes in the popular medieval story of Melusine's Maze.

The number 14 is, as we have seen, a strong component of the dimensions of the Chartres Maze, which is 42 feet in diameter, being 3 x 14. The radius of the maze is 21 feet which is 3 x 7, representing the three fallow weeks of the menstrual cycle. The week of menstruus would be represented by the point at the centre of the maze, which is, on certain days, illuminated red, as has been recorded in other works.

The fourteen children, 7 virgins and 7 youths, sacrificed at Knossos, represent two 1 week periods each. Of these there are, symbolically at least, 21 of each in the terrestrial year, which, as 7+7+7 and 2+1 (3) connects the Labyrinth story once more to the triple goddess and Persephone. The total days of the earth year of 42 weeks add up to 294 which, added together, gives the number 15 again, the path of the devil which, added again, gives six and thus the hexagram of the Labrus, the womb and vagina of the virgin priestess.

The Seal of the Temple is 777 and the number of Venus, as Netzach on the Kabalistic Tree of Life, is also 7. The three components of the Seal represent the three aspects of Venus, Freja, Persephone or the Tantric Kali. In themselves they encode the three stages of the Vampire ritual. That is, a component of an entire hidden culture that, resting upon the universal archetypes of common humanity, forms, as Jung would argue, the distinct tribal or racial memory (my note: of a unique and separate sub-species). This culture, its icons and rituals, is emotionally understandable and psychologically relevant and accessible for them alone, as is the case for any given race.

Diana and the Moon symbolise Virgin Blood. Venus-Aphrodite represents divine union with the Maiden priestess (symbolised by Iduina-Arduina-Diana) and the taking of her blood, whilst Hel-Hecate-Kore-Kali as the last aspect of the Earth and death, represents both the death of the mundane soul and the fertility of the super-consciousness that displaces it.

Less familiar are the numerical values attributed to the earth or terrestrial calendar, which operates using a 42 week system with extra days dispersed throughout the weeks of the year. In this context, the maze therefore has a link with the horology of the earth and in particular to the myth of Persephone. Some authorities claim that Persephone spent half the year in the Underworld, whilst others state that her sojourn in Hell was for only a third of the year. In ancient times there were only three seasons in any event and it is likely that her Underworld semester was therefore for one third of an earth year.

The earliest known calendar used to calculate the earth year was dug up at Cluny in France and dates back to the Celtic Bronze Age. It is therefore Druidic in origin. Persephone is dealt with elsewhere in these notes, however it is worth noting that she is said to emerge at the end of winter, thus representing the return of Spring and youthful fertility to the earth. She is therefore the fertile maiden. This is fertility of the blood in the rite of Enthea, not the fertility of bestial or vegetal congress and sexual increase.

Her association with the labyrinth as a Swastika is confirmed by Knossian coins which bear her head on one side and the fylfot maze with an eight-pointed star in the centre on the obverse. An example may be viewed, with similar maze design variations in the British Museum's coin collection. Like the Norse Freja and the Aryan Kali, Persephone is a tripartite Goddess whose three aspects themselves have three aspects, pointing to a distinctly Scythian origin and to the Celtic belief in the sanctity of the number Nine, gematrically associated in the Hebrew with N'H'Sh; the Serpent or Dragon.

Forbidden Fruits

Persephone herself has three main aspects: Diana the Maiden, Persephone-Venus, and Kore as Hecate. The Norse equivalent, Freja, also has three corresponding aspects, Iduina-Freja of the Apples of eternal youth (Gaelic: Arduina-Diana of the Nine Fires and of the Blue Boar), Gamlod-Freja and Freja.

In turn, Freja herself is one third of the team who made up the Witches of Macbeth, these being Freja, Frigg and Hel. At death, the Norse believe, the chosen hero is welcomed at Valhalla by a Valkirie bearing the Drinking Horn (see below; Horn Gate) that contains the beautifully and suggestively named "Mead of Inspiration", which in Gaelic is the Dergflaith of Sovereignty and in Greek, the wine of Persephone.

The iconography is relevant here. Mead is the fermented juice of Apples (the Graffenberg discharge of the Royal Princess), flavoured by honey, which symbolises the polysaccharines and glucosides which are now thought to be produced during the enzyme reaction (at a specific point in the menstrual cycle), that creates serotonin from melatonin. The "honeyed sweetness" of the fluid would indicate a high melatonin presence during the hours of the evening and the night, which are ruled by Ishtar or Venus-Persephone, as the Goddess of "Love".

It is claimed that mead dates back 10,000 years. Therefore, it is probably the earliest manufactured beverage known to man. It is another of the archetypal representations of the essence of the Goddess-Priestess, representing the flow of the priestess, sweetened by the nectar (ambrosia or "food of the Gods") collected by bees who are the sacred animals of Binah, the mother of Understanding.

Nevertheless, if you cut an apple in half across the core, the seed chambers form the pentagram that appears on the brow of the Baphomet, symbolising the cubic stone. The seeds themselves contain cyanide in such a quantity as to make 25 grams sufficient an amount to kill a man. The apple was chosen to represent the goddess but, as we can see and as tradition testifies, the goddess and her Grail maidens have a symbolic down side. Again we encounter the love that is death and the concept of death to one form of perception and the reawakening to another.

As Kali, Ishtar, Diana, Hecate and Hel, these Goddesses represent the deadly potential of the sacred Elven female. The essence of the Grail maidens and their chemically generated morphic energy can heal much, but there is a price to pay.

One draught stimulates dormant centres in the Fairy brain that, in becoming sensitised to, and instinctively acknowledging these chemicals, it develops a dependence on them and the subtle sweet energy they produce. Such is the intensity of the experience, as a pathological dynamic it is much like alcoholism. Because of this, although the maidens are indeed the Grail, they are also called the fountain of thirst. Like La Belle Dame Sans Merci, the Grail Maiden, the Leanaan Sidhe, can leave her victim like Keats' palely wandering knight who no longer sees the world in which he once belonged but sees, and consequently inhabits, another world altogether.

His has become a world of infinite wonders but, at her inevitable departure, it has also become a world of unbearable longing, of intense hunger and thirst. Like "La Belle Dame" these beautiful living goddesses come as softly and as unawares as spirits, to open the door to the rose garden and initiate their chosen prince.

Having united with him in enthea and "removed" his soul, they inevitably depart from these "chance" encounters as softly and as swiftly as at first they arrived. Like bees they are put on the earth to pollinate the flower of Fairy consciousness but invariably, like bees, they also suck dry the nectar of the Fairy's soul.

Bees however, are the badge of the Merovingian descendants of King Solomon. His Song, or at least the one attributed to him, is packed to the gunwales with Vampiric references to the gathering of the nectar of maidens in an apiarine fashion later eulogised allegedly by Shakespeare, but no doubt by Edward de Vere, who was a descendant of Solomon and a veritable son of the tradition.

Bees live as equal entities in hives under the rule of one Sovereign who is chosen and created from their number by the administration of "Royal Jelly" (Dergflaith) by and from the body of the previous Queen. In this respect the clans of the Danaan, the Elven King Tribes of the Western Aryans, once replicated in their social structure the organisation of the hive. Furthermore the hexagonal construction of the bees' incubation chamber, their place of origin or birth, is repeated in the hexagonal shape of the Kabalistic Tree of Life (the Planta Genista, the [family] tree of Origin). This was intended to be identical in its shape and layout with the hexagonal web of relationships on the diagrammatical family tree of the Sumerian/Scythian Dragon Goddess-Queens and God-Kings, from whom the Fairy Danaan and the Merovingians are descended.

Bees suck the nectar from the flowers in the garden and in like fashion the Vampiric Fairy kings and queens drank the nectar of the lily and the rose from their virgin goddesses, in the maze sanctuary of the sacred groves. The bee symbolises understanding, and in history so do the Fey, whose legendary power and eternal wisdom, like that of their cousin Solomon, was phenomenal, such was the efficacy of the "Mead of Wisdom" distilled by the Elf maidens, the Valkiries or Ladies of the Forest. With the canny dance of the Bee forming the figure eight, which in human terms represents infinity and is the glyph of Isis, we return once more to the subject of the triple goddess.

In the triad of Diana-Persephone-Kore the individuals are represented by the Moon, the planet Venus and Earth respectively and reflect the qualities associated with each. In Dragon terms, these aspects represent Potential (the Blood of the Moon), Union (the enthea of Baphomet as Persephone-Venus) and Release (the winning of spiritual sovereignty and fertility) after reaching the centre or Nix, the love that is death. This is symbolised by Persephone-Kore, the fruitful Earth, which is both womb and tomb.

Kore itself means virgin, and the image of Kore as Hel or Hecate as crones, is only valid on an exoteric, popular mystical level which concerns itself with nature worship. However, the symbolism still hidden in non-revivalist Witchcraft, as it has come down to us today, continually points to a high magical purpose with strong connections to the death and blood mystery cults of classical and pre-classical times. The symbolism is often interpreted as being concerned with venal fertility because of the rustic allegorical images, which were employed to hide the esoteric information being conveyed.

It has been forgotten that doctrines were split into three layers, each corresponding to the needs, interests and capacity for understanding of the intended audience or participants. In the mystery of Diana (Iduna or Arduina)-Persephone-Kore related to Chartres, we have seen that we have an example of the maze or labyrinth as both womb and tomb. In the myth of Persephone and the pomegranate, the Dianic Mistletoe Bard of Arduina must enter Hel or the Underworld to draw the wine of the fruit of life from her, which in the Gaelic is called dergflaith, the red beer of the queen of sovereignty. Also reminiscent of this journey to the underworld is the fate of the potential lover of the mermaid who is destined to be drawn into her realm and certain death. It must be remembered that this is only death of the ego.

According to trial transcripts the Templars kept a preserved head in a silver reliquary carved with the figure of Virgo , the Virgin-and-Icthys or Vulva-fish. This head, it is said, they called the Baphomet, or head (source) of wisdom, or Father Mitras. The Baphomet or Bafomet of the Templars, according to Fr. Eliphas Levi, was an androgyne figure which, with a bit of consonant wander no doubt, incorporated the Mithraic element suggested in Vatr Mitr, which has a distinct Aryan ring to it. Virgo relates to Iduna and Arduina, Diana or Artemis the virgin huntress, as well as Mary and Persephone. Related to Persephone is Orpheus or Bacchus-Orpheus in the cult of the Elysian Plain which, like the rose at the centre of the Chartres maze, lies at the centre of the Otherworld. Bacchus was also called Liber, which in Latin means a) liberty or release, b) Tree, c) Wine, d) a book, wisdom or secret knowledge, the Hidden Torah.

Orpheus in the Underworld

Bacchus-Orpheus, it will be remembered, was crucified, hanged on a tree like Odin and Christ. With Dionysus, he was a god of the blood and death cults of the Mediterranean region. This correlates with the Elysian mysteries, introduced to the inhabitants of Greece and Crete by the Scythian Danaan of Troy, who had settled in Carthage and Egypt following the fall of their city. The Elysian Plain corresponds to the Irish Tir Na n'Og, the Land or Tree of Youth, which itself has associations with the Ankh.

In recounting the Elysian story of Aeneas and the Trojan rout, Virgil explains that Aeneas travelled to Italy to seek out the Sibyl or Shamanka of Cumae, to gain knowledge of how to enter the underworld and obtain an audience with his deceased father. In order to enter the door of Dis and descend to Averna (cf. Avalon), the shamaness explains, he must first bury a friend and then pluck the Golden Bough. However, she warned him that although many may enter, few except the children of the gods (my note; The Elven race) may leave again (this denotes a ritual involving Fairy food). On leaving the Shamanka's cave, the Trojan-Scythian lord buries a fallen comrade and plucks the Mistletoe. As in the tale of Gilgamesh, the Shamanka accompanies him on the journey and both descend into Hades where they meet Orpheus on the Elysian Plain. They accomplish the task they set out to do, after which Aeneas (being the son of Assaracus by Aphrodite and the descendant of Electra the daughter of Atlas the Titan, son of Iapetus or Japhet, the Lord and father of the Elven race), was permitted to leave.

Next to the doorway to Hades, Virgil locates a representation of the labyrinth, as a map of the underworld with, as we discover as the story unfolds, Elysium: Avalon, at its heart. As a teaching, the story of the underworld quest incorporating the mistletoe can be found in the epic of Gilgamesh, giving a Babylonian and, no doubt, an early Sumerian, middle eastern origin for the labyrinth concept. This, as the spiral vortex, is related to the decorative motifs employed by the Ubaid culture of Scythia and Carpathia, from whence the royal Sumerian culture itself originated.

In support of such a view it is pertinent that in Scandinavia, labyrinths were sometimes referred to as "Babylons". In the Roman Empire, the figure of the labyrinth formed into jewelery was worn exclusively by the emperors, because it was considered to be solely a royal insignia. At such a time the explicit inference would have been to directly connect the labyrinth concept to that of Kingship and thus, in classical memory, to the ancient Dragon cult of Sumerian priest kings.

In the story of *Theseus and the Minotaur*, by the time Theseus is said to have turned up, the tribute to the Minotaur in youths' and virgins' blood had been paid twice in 18 years. Gematrically this gives a total of 28 victims or one lunar cycle of 28 days. The youths' blood represented the fallow part of the cycle.

The 18 year period represented Isis and Osiris, Keshalyi and Locolico, or Nergal and Nin-Kursag. Osiris was the Blue-Faced God of the dead who was the counterpart of the Aryan, blue-faced Shiva-Vishnu, the blue boar. Osiris' brother Set first tried incarcerating him and throwing him in the Nile, but Isis and her sister Nephthys found him and revived him sufficiently to father Horus from Isis.

Secondly, (Set was not a quitter), Osiris was ripped to bits by his fratricidal brother and his members were scattered. Again, Isis, and Set's wife Nephthys, went around picking up the bits but couldn't find his penis. This is the symbol of his creative force or sovereignty and another symbol for the spinal column, as emphasised by the serpent-entwined "phallus" of the Baphomet, which is topped off by an orb, representing the brain. In consequence of this, Osiris is a candidate for identification as the first Fisher King, crippled "in the thigh", as the proprietous euphemism puts it. Osiris's "organ" is represented by the figure one or I.

Isis' figure is infinity or the number 8, which was often drawn as the double axe-head figure found in Knossos or Cnossos, a name derived itself from the Greek root word *gno*, which also renders gnome, gnomen (judgement) and gnosis or wisdom, from whence derives (self) *kno*-wledge.

The phallus representation in exoteric Tantra suggests a symbolic link between the rush of ejaculation and the release of energy when the kundalini is aroused. This kundalini serpent is said to course up the spine from the base Chakra, like semen rushing up the urethra, inundating the brain in a phenomenon described as a psychic orgasm. An apt analogy.

The phallus symbol here refers to the spinal column that carries the neuronal pathways of the brain. Consequently it carries its vital essences, via the third ventricle and the nerve helix, it leads to the Graffenberg gland, the womb, the urethra and the bowel where certain corresponding essences are manufactured and find their way back up to the brain, much in the same manner as the kundalini.

The kundalini differs, however; in that it is the process whereby a rush of aggressive, sexual, electro chemical signals are forced up the brain stem to the base of the corticospinal tract. It is suggested that the kundalini effect is similar to that of stimulatory drugs like *MDMA* and amphetamine, and that the signals incite the brain stem to release substances including dopamine, noradrenaline and acetylcholine in a violent cascade reaction which arouses the sophisticated sensory centres of the higher brain. These are not the chemicals associated with transcendence but with processes that reinforce the desire for and attachment to material gratification, the very obstacles that stand between the individual and "spiritual" release.

Despite constant references in the ancient teachings to the conflict between the different forms of body chemistry, it is often thought by some that sexual intercourse is the primrose path to the Kingdom of Heaven. It can lead so far, inasmuch as it introduces the beginner to altered states of perception. That is undeniable. However, biologically, one endocrinal process inevitably dominates the other, and it is the subtler process that causes transcendence. It is not the one driven by the desire to achieve more intense, longer orgasms. It's fun, but it's not the real thing. Consequently ancient Aryan, Draconian "sex magic", unlike the type envisioned by a few modern authors and the western gurus of right hand path Tantra and the eastern mysteries, has little to do with penetrative sexual intercourse.

Therefore Osiris' One or I represented not simply the phallus, but both the tongue and the spinal column, and the eight thus represented Isis' womb and vagina. Under the principle that a king isn't a king without a queen, Isis and Osiris are shown together as the figure 18, or 666, the mark of the beast, or the Knossos Axe Head: 8, where the I is horizontal.

Theseus, like Orpheus, must travel through a subterranean realm to find his love and, like the Mistletoe Bard, at the centre of Hades he will win the Chalice of Persephone's pomegranate wine. Theseus decides to tackle the Minotaur and armed with a sword given him by Ariadne he enters the labyrinth with a golden thread tied about his waist. This sword is firstly the straight-edged weapon of focus and purity of intent. The symbol is working on two different levels at the same time here. The golden thread relates to the Golden Fleece and also the Grail, it is the rivulet of womb blood on the biochemical level, whilst on the psychological level it represents the path of logic and truth.

As the golden thread is given to Theseus by Ariadne, it is emphatically a female symbol. A question that immediately springs to mind is whether the Theseus version of the story was at variance with others, or with the primeval Grail theme itself, by suggesting that the golden thread was not already laid out on the path. In Rapunzel the golden thread is her hair and the maze is substituted by an equally daunting but related structure. A tower.

Nine Pieces of Gold

Symbolically, Ariadne is at the centre of the maze, just as Rapunzel is at the top of the tower and, as Rapunzel lets down her golden hair to assist the knight in getting to her, Ariadne in another sense, assists Theseus.

A tablet at Knossus describes Ariadne as the "lady of the labyrinthe" to whom money offerings were made. In developing this theme, Michael Grant (*Myths of the Greeks and Romans*) says that Ariadne was a goddess of the underworld. This relates her to both Persephone and Melusine and, strangely enough, to St. Nicholas of Dumnonia or Cornwall. He, as a Mistletoe Bard and traveller to the underworld, a horned Merlin and an Odinic priest, is said to have offered three gold coins each to three poor virgin sisters to prevent them from becoming prostitutes.

There appear to be three girls who have the same relation to Santa Claus as there is to Theseus. They also appear to symbolise the tripartite Diana-Persephone-Kore or her priestesses. The nine Byzantine, imperial gold coins that the Druid Nicholas or Nicassius gave to the holy virgins became the nine heraldic "bezants on a field sable" which variably were the arms of his, the Emrys family, and which eventually became the arms of the duchy of Cornwall.

The apocryphal story of St. Nicholas/Nicassius offering money to the impecunious virgins probably relates to St. Nicholas' family as the Druidic-Priestly administrators and Keepers of the Sacred Grove, its holy temple and its virgin priestesses. Like Magdalene, they came to be thought of, utterly erroneously, as prostitutes. Cassius was the name of one of the Roman rebels but has links also with, and was possibly a re-expanded diminutive or affectionate form of the name Caspar, which is of Persian origin and is said to mean treasurer. This meaning was probably derivative and like Nicholas, Caspar, probably a temple official, was the Syrian Magus or Druid who was said to have presented gold to the child Jesus. The link between St. Nicholas of Dumnonia and the bezants would suggest therefore that this is the more likely secondary meaning of his name which is itself ultimately related to Nisse or the Nix.

In a way it can be said that the golden thread in Theseus is a rivulet or *rtu* of Ariadne's essence, a sutra that leads Theseus to the centre of the mystery and the Grail. One might suggest that symbolically the golden thread was spun by Ariadne from the wool of the Golden Fleece. This artifact is a classic variation of the Grail symbol which, guarded by a Dragon in the heart of Greater Scythia near to where Prometheus was chained, had the same healing properties attributed to the Holy Grail and the blood of the Elven goddesses.

In relation to the theme of the Grail as a *panacea* and *physick*, is the White Cross of St. John or the gnostic Iao (Jao), related to the sephiroth of Tiphareth and closely linked with Isis and Persephone.

The question must be asked, "How on earth is a thread tied about Theseus's waist going to help him find the Minotaur?" Quite simply it isn't, and yet the story doesn't say he spent six weeks wandering around in circles getting tangled up in wool before he found the monster. If the Labyrinth were a Maze, the thread would be fine for helping him find his way out, but equally difficult without a golden thread to guide him, would be the task of finding his way to the centre in the first place. However, the structure at Knossos is described as a Labyrinth and labyrinths—unlike Mazes—are single paths which inevitably lead to their goals with no blind alleys or fake turns. This would render Theseus' need for an actual golden thread redundant, whilst on the psychological level the labyrinth would cease to exist once the Minotaur had been slain, thereby rendering the thread pointless anyway.

G.R. Levy explains that the thread (Sanskrit: *sutra* as in Kama Sutra), or rope, or "clue", and the winding path appear as components of European tales of entry into an actual or subjective spiral maze. Many of them were found in medieval Churchyards or grave/grove-yards, signifying that the ancient groves were places to meet with the dead. Furthermore the word *dru* (as in Druid) in Sanskrit means "run", as in run the race or "dance the maze".

The Llans were special geographical locations where the groves were built. These were on the intersection between *Dragon Lines* (not ley lines) where a) the power was thought to be strongest and b) the site occupied a kind of in-between place which, like crossroads, were neither one direction or another and thus were said to be in-between the worlds. As such they were doors to Elphame and later, crossroads (invariably with their gallows poles) and graveyards became the meeting places for Witches. Gallows were often placed at cross-roads, doorways to the Otherworld, in order to facilitate the criminal's speedy journey to Hell or Elphame—life after death. His or her ghost may then be encouraged to leave the mortal realm immediately, thus discouraging him or her in death from further troubling the living, as they had done in life.

Grant continues by saying that the maze relates to the life after death and gives initiation. The author emphasises that life after death is more properly life before death or transcendence, being the life of superconsciousness following the death-in-life of mundane perception.

Such a teaching accords with the message of Jesus and most other mystics. Grant relates the thread to the spindle of Sleeping Beauty, making her a Fate or Mori, a goddess figure like the golden-haired Scythian princess Ariadne. In Sleeping Beauty's story the thread is in the Castle which, surrounded by a thicket representing the labyrinth, is the centre of the maze itself and thus the rose garden and the Elysium.

Sleeping Beauty occupies a tower in the castle in the undergrowth, or a Caer Glas (Verrieres) in the Forez, if you like, in similar fashion to Rapunzel elsewhere mentioned herein, who lets down her golden hair to admit the knight to her tower chamber. In the course of time, stories change and become corrupted by various admissions and omissions. This is the process whereby history becomes myth and legend.

It can be suggested therefore that Theseus' story likewise appears to have undergone changes and suffered the ravages of time. To facilitate a meaningful interpretation of these stories, it is necessary for the student to compare them together by genre and settle for a common sequence of events and a common objective.

For them to make any sense at all, they must relate to human physiology and psychology and be grounded in empiricism. If the stories are subjected to over mystification by those who are unaware of their inner workings or of the available esoteric knowledge or the intention of the stories' creators, confusion sets in.

On the Grail or biochemical level, Theseus must follow the rivulet to attain and drink from its source, having battled with his own common lust in such a situation. If he does he wins Ariadne as the Virgin Grail, intact and appropriately related to him. If he does not and the Minotaur (Arthur's Klingsor) within him prevails at the source, then Theseus will defile that source for base gratification and the Minotaur, his own sexual lust for Ariadne, will consume him.

Theseus is a wily lad however and unlike Arthur's Druidic saw, which is an adaptaion of the story of Theseus and Ariadne, his is a story of success. Theseus attains the source of the golden-red fluid, the heart of the labyrinth, and with Galahad-like purity of heart (focus and insight) he sees the Grail in the form of the Minotaur, the bull instead of just Ariadne's sex organs. This act itself is enough to slay his Minotaur and he exits the labyrinth to unite with Ariadne, the virgin source of sovereignty. However, now he must enter once more and face another Minotaur on a different level of being. In the story, both Minotaurs are one and the same and are slain at the same time, but I am analysing the story level by level and it is in this sense that Theseus repeats the two-fold exercise.

Having attained and consumed Ariadne's blood, she has become his Sheba, his Rhiannon, his Guinevere and his Viviane. Armed with the sword of her sovereignty (creative energy, [non-sexual] libido), he now enters once more to trace his path through the avenues and back alleys of human self deceit and confront the very power source, the very foundation of his own delusion.

This he does and in slaying his Minotaur once more, he wins Ariadne, the Sleeping Beauty, his Anima, and her sword of sovereignty is the straight-edged blade of his purity of mind, his focus, clarity of vision and singularity of purpose.

Having reached Hierogamy or Enthea and individuation or personal sovereignty, Theseus left Ariadne to Dionysus, the bull-headed child of Zeus, the Great World-Bull of delusion. In the French versions of Arthur's tale, Guinevere decamped from Camelot with Lancelot. In all these tales, the “marriages” were not sexual in the sense that we would understand and they weren't built to last.

Because narrators don't know the real reason for these alliances, a social tendency towards post-Victorian morality interprets the separation of the couples as betrayal and marital breakdown. In reality, the contract had come to an end with the change in blood chemistry and the females were then ready to leave and pursue other interests.

Axe Lords

The Minotaur has been said to be a version of the Phoenician, bull-headed God, Baal Moloch, the son of Enlil. This might be partially right in a ritual context where, it is thought, sacrifices were made to the Phoenician King enacting the ritual role of the god by wearing a bull's head as a mask.

It is suggested that the Minotaur was Minos himself or some other Cretan king in masquerade, fulfilling some ritual role. Said to represent the virile principle, the bull symbol appears on other Aryan artifacts as far away as Harappa in the Indus in 3000 BC.

If the virile principle is seen in context as the workings of various hormones in the human physiology, it will be understood that those hormones are therefore also the chemicals responsible for many human delusions and anxieties. Initially they suppress the production of melatonin and serotonin which themselves play a profound part in the attaining of transcendent states of consciousness. This brings us back to the symbol of the human mind as the World Bull of Deceit, and to Mithras as Theseus and so on.

Theseus was the son of Neptune, king of the waters, an Otherworld symbol, whilst Ariadne was the daughter of Minos, king of the dead, another Otherworld character. As a king of the dead or "Dead King", Minos was ritually associated with the Repha'im. The axe-head carving in his labyrinth suggests that his people had some association with the Scythian Axe Lords of Idumea and Mittani, from whence came the cult of the Kings of the Dead (Osiris or Orion), the Rephaim or Angels.

The chronology is flawed in the original tales and the characters are most likely to have been the lineal descendants of the major deific personages, but removed by relationship to a further degree than the stories allow.

Consequently, Minos was the son of Zeus (Enlil), or of Zeus' royal- priestly officiate or descendant, and Europa, who was the daughter of Phoenix, whom we assume was the historical Phineas Farsidhe, the Scythian King of Phoenicia. Minos' brother was called Rhadamanthus, the red-haired, according to Michael Grant, so we can safely say that this genetic strain was present also in Minos and Ariadne, both of whom therefore were Scythian. Thus we have a strong Scythian component in the Labyrinth concept, both in Egypt and Crete. Ariadne was a form therefore of Lilith, who was the daughter of Nergal, whose name suggests Naga'el and the Naga or serpent gods of the deeps who, as the Avatars or Shining Ones—the Anunnagi—form part of the Aryan Hindu pantheon.

The Axe Lord epithet has more to do with the Grail than with the axe as the "tree" or "man hewer" (in Hebrew—Nefilim), as the Grail is often drawn in the form of a Labrus or upended, double-headed axe. There are similarities between Theseus and Ariadne and Samael and Lilith. Where Theseus is the son of the king of the sea, Samael is the Lord of the Waters.

Ariadne is the daughter of the King of the Dead and so is Lilith. Lilith eventually became the consort of Enlil-Jehovah and the substitute matronit or Lady Sabbath. She was likened to Sophia, the Shekinah and the Holy Spirit or Wisdom. Likewise Ariadne left Theseus for Dionysus, the son of Zeus. Ariadne was therefore also a source of divine wisdom.

In a sense, Dionysus' attainment of Ariadne from Theseus and Enlil-Jehovah's Attainment of Lilith from Samael is symbolic of the way in which divine wisdom (Lilith) was purloined by the usurper. This has repeated itself in the claim that Rome has made over Mary and the Chartres Maze.

The Chartres Maze is circular and has a central path leading from the outer circumference to the rose in the middle. On either side of this channel are the turns of the inner paths arranged to look like the ridges of the walls of the vagina, as depicted on the Mycenaean Grail chalice. Again Rome has sequestered this anciently inspired symbol and profaned it by what they consider sublimation.

Today the faithful flock to Chartres from all over the world to walk a Maze inspired by vampirism and laid down in stone by "Satanists". By doing this they think they will get closer to God by an "Act of Faith", repeating the endless theme that the maze itself wished to warn man against. That is that the Labyrinth can represent the dominion of empty form over substance and that man's mind is a vast cavern of paths that fold back on themselves endlessly. Mankind attempts to hide from man himself the central mystery of his own unjustified misery and terror, that at the centre of his being, cloaked in delusion and fear, lies nothing.

The folding paths of the maze are the paths of deceit and dogma, of ritual and habit that must, like the Gordian Knot, be rent asunder if man is ever to glimpse what is real. The habit of walking the Chartres maze merely reinforces the very stupidity that prevents man from ever actually reaching the maze's true, hidden centre.

That man can reach peace and "salvation" by mindlessly walking round in a circle, just because a priest says he can, is yet another fold of self deceit in the maze itself. Symbolically the Chartres maze is so configured as to invite you to ignore all the folds of the pathways and walk straight up the vaginal channel and into the centre of the symbol. Nevertheless it is characteristic of *homo religiosus* that nobody ever does.

The Chartres maze was not created for Roman Christian ritual but for a meditation alien to its tenets and foreign to its culture. Like much that is of value, much that has meaning and the potential to transform consciousness, the Church has wiped away the dynamic and replaced it with safe, empty party games that ensure that none break free from the grip of tyranny maintained through mindless conformity and mimicry. Such a sad parody is endemic in all religion and religious thought, not just in Christianity.

A tradition which repeats the theme of the Sacred Virgin at the centre of the labyrinth is discovered in rural British custom where the Vampire symbolism of the original iconography became reduced to rituals for fertility and games of sexual licence.

On village common land throughout much of Merrie England it was the custom to lay out a maze and on Sunday afternoons and at other leisure times, the maidens of the parish would gather at the maze and one would elect to stand at its centre. The local village lads would then race each other round the maze to see who could win the virgin first. The winner was awarded a barrel of beer, and the virgin, of course.

This custom also appeared in Finland and Iceland and, as elsewhere, echoes the original pursuit of the Wild Hunt. The beer was a folksy, rustic reminder of the wine of Persephone in a ritual involving peasants trying to imitate the mysteries of their ancient superiors, the meanings of which they had absolutely no idea. Those who adhere to Christianity or modern Witchcraft and occultism today—all of which are the low versions of the quest for the Grail and Enthea—where such mindless dogma or ritual and bestial copulation have no place, are exactly the same.

In many mazes, thought to be the "Core" of a "Llan" (cf. Avalon or Ava-Llan) or sacred site, there were once erected pillars upon which were situated the effigies of doves. These sites were the apple groves where the Mistletoe Bards gathered with the sacred virgins to conduct the secret blood rites of Arduina and sing into being both the Gods and the noble characters of the Kings. Llan also appears as lawn, originally meaning a clearing in a wood. Lunn means a sacred grove/enclosure/lawn/clan. Taken as a whole concept, the Llan was a sacred sacrificial grove.

Chapter 8

The Cors

The sacred virgins were the cors (cf Kore or Persephone of the Pomegranate, see previous notes) who sang in choirs and who, like Ariadne at Knossos, performed the sacred spiral dance of the "choros" which, in ancient times, were also the chorus of narrators of religious ritual, ballad and tragedy.

This chorus, in later Rome comprising of only the cream of noble youth and maidenhood, danced the maze around a central core or "Cor". In effect this was the eye of the storm or whirlwind, symbolised by a column or pillar, upon which roosted the Dove of the spirit, the Magdal, which represented the corpus callosum, and the wings of the grey matter of the cerebral hemispheres of the human brain. As late as 1660 a turf maze in Hilton, Huntingdonshire sported just such an obelisk capped with a sphere, placed there by its builder, a William Sparrow.

Similar to Chartres, but in a more direct fashion still, the path to the centre of the maze is straightforward. At Saffron Walden, prior to the turn of the last century, the centre of its turf maze was occupied by an Ash tree or Aes tree (Na'Nuine), symbolic of the Goddess of sovereignty and reminiscent of the Fairy Aes Dan, the Danish Aesir or first gods, the Asher of the Egyptians (Isis and Osiris) and the Asuras or Shining Ones of the Scythian Aryans. Merlin Emrys was married to Ninian or Na'Nuine, replicating the union between Odin and Yggdrasil.

Also pertinent to the maze, as the genitalia of the Cor or virgin (*OED*), and variously therefore the Triangle of Daleth in which is set the All Seeing

Eye of God, is the Cor, as the pupil of the eye. The graveyards, in which are located the barrows or bergs of the high Kings of the Dan at Uppsala, are triangular.

Further linguistic relationships include Cor: a Horn, as in Hearne or Cernunnos. This is related to Keras; the Horn of the Horn Gate of true visions which is one of the portals of the Underworld. Keras is related to the verb Krainousi, meaning "to attain fulfillment". Possibly fanciful, though tantalising, is the idea that the "Horn Gate of True Visions" was originally the arch of the open legs of the Meremaid, attired in her Scythian, horn-plated ritual armour.

However, Michael Grant suggests, in his commentary on the Aeneid, that this relates to cornu, the eye with its horny tissue, the cornea, whilst the other gate, the Ivory Gate of Falsehood, corresponds to the teeth and the mouth. He elaborates that what is seen first-hand is truer than that which is related in speech; a pertinent observation well fitting the magical idea that Gnosis is greater than belief and initiation is more powerful than faith. Nevertheless, in relation to the Horn Gate, it is still poetically and charmingly supportive of Cor, as the Eye in the Triangle.

In elaborating on the concept of Cor as cornu and in further pursuing the Horn and Ivory symbolism, we should look at the twin pillars of the temple: Boaz and Joachim. One is black and the other is white, corresponding to the Horn and Ivory Gates of Hades in Virgil's Aeneid. Bull's horn is often black in colour whilst Ivory is obviously white.

The major arcana of the Waite Tarot, with its wealth of organo-alchemical, Solomonic symbolism, could well be termed the Tarot of the Vampire or the "a la carte menu" of the Epicurean. The second card, the High Priestess portraying the virgin Isis, is seated before a veil decorated with Persephone's pomegranates, which is suspended between the two pillars. Partly concealed beneath her blue robe she holds a scroll on her lap bearing the legend Torah, or Law. One recollects the Welsh story of the virgin's lap and its association with the female organs in the story of King Math.

Here it is indicated that the law resides within her womb and that she and it are situated between the pillars and thus represent and occupy the point of Zen balance or stillness derived from divine union. This is symbolised in British Witch tradition by the seesaw and the candle. Kabalistically speaking she sits at the Core of the Llan, the inner sanctuary of the temple in the labyrinth, before the invisible middle pillar of the Tree of Life. It is in this position, in ceremonial magic, that initiates position themselves psychically in anticipation of a final communion with their Holy Guardian Angel. This for them anyway, is the Ende-Werk of the Hermetic process, as envisioned by modern occultists. On her head the High Priestess wears a crown comprising of the disc of the Ajna Chakra or Sephiroth of Kether positioned between the draconian horns of divinity. On her breast she wears the

Johannite white cross of Iao or Thymus the Healer (see endocrinology section), and at her feet rests the crescent of the new moon. The classical symbolic link between the feet and the genitalia derives from the empirically obvious, explained by modern neurological anatomy linked to recent studies of the compensatory adjustments made by amputees who develop ghost limbs.

Neuro-surgeons locate the nerve terminals for the feet immediately adjacent to the nerve terminals for the genitals. This delightful discovery also goes some way in explaining how the body's meridian lines work. Again, in this particular instance the High Priestess Icon demonstrates that the middle pillar, the Perrone of the Tree of Life, represents the spinal cord of the Swan Princess and that she and her sephira, the Apples of Iduina, are the Daleth or doorway to the underworld.

Cor as Kore or corn, as in John Barleycorn and the Barley Mow, is associated with the circular field, a variant or adjunct of the sacred Llan grove, in which the sacred grain was grown for the cakes and ale served at pre-Christian ceremonial journeys to the Other/Underworld. Human sacrifices were strongly associated with the Barley Mow and the blood was sprinkled as a libation across the field.

Further to this, the word Hospital, or Ysbyty in Welsh, is associated primarily and anciently with hospitality. The Ysbytys were Druidic houses, rather like Templar Preceptories or small monasteries or Bangors where local people or travellers could go to refresh and heal themselves. The sign outside such an establishment was usually a Druidic Blue Boar and it was a part of Brehon Law that any given region should have a certain number of these establishments to which were attached the Barley Mow adjacent to the Sacred Grove nearby.

The ritual function of the Barley Mow and the public rites in the Grove can be viewed as an intentionally pagan (pagani—a Roman social numerical unit corresponding to a Sept) or popular derivation of the higher rites of Enthea. They were probably devised as devotional ceremonies for the Celtic peasantry of the rural septs, or pagani, by the Scythian Druids whose Bards, one recollects, also sang into being gods for them to worship.

From this we discover the origins of the rustic games which parodied the quest for the grail in the common mazes of Merrie England. Lastly, Cor as Corvus Corvidae (see *OED*), the Raven or Morgana whose position in the story of Holger Dansk, was under a tree at the centre of a circular garden protected by a serpent or Dragon. (On one level the serpent also represents the Nidhe Hogga, the spiral serpent of the Cosmos.)

As such, Morgana is, like Ariadne, Melusine and Sleeping Beauty, the Virgin at the centre of the labyrinth. The Corvus of Morgana was interchangeable with the Dove in Hebrew Kabala, as a bird of divination (Cor: the eye: "to see") and the underworld or Qlipphoth. The Raven was originally sacred to Lilith. Etymology derived from *OED*. (The serpent-necked Serpilion Dove is interchangeable with the Swan and is related to the Solar Caduceus).

In parody of the sacred ritual dance, in later ages, maidens and youths danced the Maypole and Morris Men danced the ring around the Maze at whose centre the Maypole was often erected. The idea that the Maypole was a phallic symbol is only true on one level.

At its highest level the maypole was the Tree of Life and thus the Spinal Column, at the head of which rests the Dove of the Brain. The true significance of the Maypole dance can be observed by watching what happens as the girls and boys (see sacrifice to the Minotaur above) weave the web of coloured ribbons around the pole. With each step the maidens and youths get closer to the pole itself as if drawn into the Maze. The interlaced pattern of the woven ribbons represents the web of Elphane or Arachne, the web of the Fates or Fairies (Mori-gans), in one sense drawing them closer to the maze's centre and their doom. As they dance closer, the woven ribbons around the pole itself tighten up and begin to symbolise the helix pattern of the nerve channels that encase the spinal chord, on their way down to the base of the spine and ultimately the womb, the central point of the labyrinth.

The Tree of Life

This spinal column or Core Pole, the Ankh shaped Bethel Stone, is not simply or solely the penis of some god of mundane fertility, but the main trunk of the Tree of Life that is Diana. It is the backbone of the Virgin Goddess, huntress and protector, and any virgin royal priestess, or Cor, who represents her.

On a smaller scale, the Maypole is the Thyrsus of Dionysus, topped with its pinecone. In Scandinavia the maypole relates to the Axis Mundi, the lynch pin which was said to hold the sun in place and whose foundation lay buried beneath the world.

The Axis Mundi is The World Ash or Aes, and the Trunk of the Ash, the Maypole, represents the spine of the Goddess or priestess. Thus the sun represents the Ajna Chakra, the halo of Christianity, whilst the Earth represents the virgin womb. This symbolism is repeated in the Ankh cross, dealt with in a further essay.

The maze or spiral dance around the Maypole is a development from the earlier chorus around the stones and the later Witches' spiral and ring dance. The origins of this are to be found in the dance around the Core or Perron stone at the centre of the Labyrinth within the ancient Grove. Sometimes these Perron stones had pinecones carved at the top, as a variant of the Dove but which are identical in their symbolism.

It must be remembered that the virgin at the centre of the maze, the Melusine, was also a Morrigan who fed on virgin blood. This practice is echoed in the story of the blood letting of Parcival's sister and the symbol of the healing blood of Christ (properly the blood of his mother or wife).

The web of Fairy magic drew maidens and youths in as sacrifices. However, if the rite was reversed and they were drawn in to feed themselves, then they were to feed on Fairy "food", of which priest-ridden, terrified humans said that at the first taste, one remains in Elphame, damned forever.

The "food" stills the chattering monkey in the head, changes consciousness and deepens perception and one can no longer see the mundane world of petty mortal care, where the trivial is of such import. One sees instead a realm of wider, deeper meaning that in other cultures is called the Kingdom of Heaven. One is healed and "saved" by the Blood. Amen!

In other traditions the condemned were forced to tread the labyrinth on the Common before being hanged from "The Gallows Tree". In some distant memory, the executors of the condemned man's fate believed that in walking the maze first, the convict's spirit would be loosened from his body and more readily set free upon execution, in a similar fashion to those who, it was believed, were hanged at crossroads.

This is dimly reminiscent of the more profound idea of the maze concealing at its centre the truth of enlightenment and the freeing quality that transcendence has upon consciousness. In this idea, as in religious observance, the central mystery and its mechanics have been lost, to be replaced by superstitious mimicry.

Nevertheless, as evidence, it reveals historical ideas about the nature and function of the labyrinth.* At the end of the maze lay death on a tree. At the end of Theseus' journey through the labyrinth he slew the Minotaur, himself. Having died to one state of consciousness, Theseus united with Ariadne and was born into another state of perception altogether. We have dealt with the concept of death on a tree where the tree represents the female for and upon whom the hero sacrifices his life and through whom he obtains wisdom.

* The maze as Time, related to the spinning of the web of fate, is a very interesting concept and by its design implies that time folds back on itself in layers. Depending on what time width one imagines, instead of time being solely lineal, it might be suggested by the maze design that periods are folded on top of one another. This can be compared to the skins of an onion or the web of a spider, so that the Greek classical period might lie just beneath the medieval period, which itself might be covered by the Victorian age. This might go some way in explaining why some ages seem to wish to revive the former glories of other particular ages past. If they are adjacent to each other in the time fold, then it seems likely that they may influence each other, just as they do in lineal time. The corollary of this is the shamanic concept of chronological filaments or spirals packed against each other.

In another sense the labyrinth represents the ever moving, spiralling vortex of the galaxy and the cosmos at whose centre there is utter stillness as in the centre of the maze, the journey's end; death of the lesser self, stillness and release. Thus the centre of the maze is the nix, the nil point, the womb and the tomb, where the worm of fear dies and is reborn as the embryo of new consciousness.

PART TWO

Chapter 9

The Cult of Ankou

Introduction

In Scythian warfare, the mounted warriors had one or several amongst their number who rode backwards and naked, painted black from head to foot. He or they would carry a pig's bladder on a pole. These men would ride headlong, so to speak, into the opposing ranks and select individuals whom they would beat across the head with the bladder.

As they rode back to their own ranks they grimaced at the enemy and poked out their tongues. The enemy often viewed this behaviour with a degree of considerable alarm, borne in response to a belief system which was commonly held by both sides, even when one side was Roman. This practice has been named "counting the Kou" (possibly also related to the Persian *kuh*: mountain, perhaps as a sacred hill, place of the gods and hence ka; the spirit, double etc.). It was a method employed to select the most useful spirits for captivation after death, which must have been a terrifying prospect.

It was likely that one would die horribly anyway, that being the nature of classical warfare, especially against the Lords of Death, the Vampiric, cannibalistic Scythians. However, if one were selected (Valkirie comes from the word "to select") one's soul, post mortem, was destined to become either the food of savage gods or the slave of foreign chieftains.

The poking of the tongue is also seen in medieval pictures of demons which was probably inspired by these Dragon Warriors. They select, capture, and condemn the souls of the damned. This is related directly to the symbol of the tongue as the lingham, the utterer of the Word of Law, Fate and the Pneuma or Spirit, the Ka.

These black warriors were probably the counterparts of the black Morrigans or Bruidhinas, the female judge-bards whose word was law, whose "spells" were "fatal" in the proper sense. To be struck by one of these meant certain damnation after life with no chance of avoiding the inevitable.

In a sense these warriors were male Valkiries, the dark Repha'im who, like the Morganas, did a bit of moonlighting (literally!) and doubled up as Swan Knights on their days off. The tongue pointed at one intimated that the act of one's selection was inevitable and irreversible, and meant also that your enemy, by doing this and thus "revealing his spirit" his Kou or Ka, after taking your own, considered you to be no threat at all. Is it any wonder that the Church drew upon such images to populate their demonologies?

It seems entirely appropriate to model the fiends of the pit (OFr. Kou) of Hell upon such terrifying characters who claimed to be able to take the fallen warrior's very soul, having first tortured the body briefly but nevertheless unspeakably in life, on a field of battle that must have seemed to the observer to be the opening up of Hades itself. It was in such battle conditions that the entire Roman Ninth Legion, after crossing the Antonine Wall were utterly defeated, eaten and, one suspects, spiritually enslaved by the Pictish Scythians of Caledonia. Not one Roman escaped the carnage.

Related to the word Ankh are: Anjou, Angouleme, Anschau, Ankou. The cult of the Ankou or Ankh involves consonant migration. It is shown in changes in phonetic accentuation, regional pronunciation, fashion, the vocalisation of the words by non-native speakers and the copying of manuscripts by foreign scholars or the scribes of subsequent generations.

In this case it appears that the original word Ankh has developed into Anjou via a linguistic path influenced by Goidelic. Spelt "Ankh" the H in Gaelic would have become aspirant which would have been pronounced Ank-Huh or Ankuh. Verbally the K became mistaken for a hard G, giving Anguh. In due course the G became non-Goidelic and soft, as in "germ" and, with the emergence of the letter J as a softer variant of the soft G, the Word Ankh, via Ankhu, Ankou and Angou (as in Angouleme) became Anjou.

The Cult of the Ankou in Brittany and Anjou, the Cult of the Spirit of the An, derivatively, therefore the Cult of the Dragon's Breath, prior to its introduction to the continent, is asserted to have been of immediate British origin. However, it was strongly represented in the island now known as Ireland in pre-Christian times, where it was probably originally introduced first by the Egyptian Princess Scota, the wife of the governor (or king) of the Red Sea nome, Niall of Scythia (see charts).

It is said that it was introduced into Brittany during one of the migrations from Albany in the first millennium AD. Described as a cult of the dead, the rites and symbols associated with the characters who were claimed or appear to be its royal priests and priestesses reveal that it was also a cult of blood and death, as well as ancestor veneration. In lowland Scotland the spoken tongue was Northern Cymric and in this language "angev", it is said, is one of the words used to describe death, possibly suggesting "going to the Dragon", the Church's "Devil".

It is significant linguistically because those of the later house of Plantagenet were called the Angevin Kings, emphasising, along with the name Angouleme, the consonant migration described above and adding some veracity to the Angevin claim that they were descended from the Devil. "We who came from the devil must need go back to the Devil. Do not deprive us of our heritage, we cannot help acting like devils"—Richard Coeur de Lyon. Or, as the Monkish sponsor of the KnightsTemplar, St. Bernard of Clairvaux put it when describing the Angevins: "De Diabolo Venit Et AD Diabolum Ibit".

The syllable Ang in Angev is also to be found in Angel and derives from the Greek aggelos—aggelos which is reminiscent of Agg or Ygg, the Odin priest as an angel, a Repha'im or priest of Nergal. Freja, as a goddess of the Earth and the underworld, was the proud owner of a heron or crane-skin bag and a Merlin feathered cloak. Odin wanted to borrow these from her from time to time, making him a Merlin figure and linking her to the sacred and sinister bird of the Druids. One of the explanations for the name of the Fir Bolg was "Bag Men". Related to the crane-skin bag, the Fir Bolg are Merlins or Druids and thus Fir "Bog", "Men of God".

The Merlin itself was described as a "bird without a nest", a solitary wanderer in exactly the same sense as was the magical boar, "Le Solitaire". The boar as the "The Hermit", the solitary Archdruid, the lonely wanderer, is the Merlin who likewise ranges alone, thus indicating that Merlins, Odins and Archdruids were synonymous.

On the island of Delos the dance of the labyrinth was called Geranos, the "Dance of the Crane" and is suggestive of the Druidic ritual of "Crane pointing" as a form of related magical observance. The Crane Dance, known in Britain as the "Dance of Troy", was also performed by the Ostiak peoples of Siberia up until the 18th century and was so-called because they wore crane skin clothing for the occasion.

Principally the Ankh or Ankou in Brittany were described as being a collateral cult of the Morrigan which was particularly prominent in the Breton coastal regions. As such this would suggest that the Ankou had some influence upon the Armorican cult of the Ferryman of the Dead, particularly as Morgana herself is associated with the Swan Barge of Avalon, which transported the dead Mordred to his final resting place in the sacred grove.

In Eire the Cult of Ankou was associated with Sidhe mounds, Raths, hills and Barrows, and hence labyrinths. Known as Mari in the Basque region and associated with the Morias or fates, Ankou was the original model for the Black Madonnas there. The goddess Ankou, Black Annis, was derived from the Greek "Anku-Kis" who was a form of the earlier Egyptian Goddess of the underworld—Anu Ket. In the Semitic-Ugaritic texts found in Ras Shamra in 1928, Ankou is called Anat, a Witch goddess and regeneratrix who shape-shifted into the form of the Morrigan or Morgana, a black predatory bird.

We are here in the presence of "An", the ancient Dragon Mother who is both a sustainer and a reaper, a Phoenix figure whose Raven-like attributes link her to the Kershalyi and Locolico of the first Dragon homeland of Transylvania. In Breton Churches her priestess Morgana is portrayed as a wouivre, or double-tailed mermaid, or Dragoness and in this respect she is identical with another Priestess, Ygraine.

The Cult of the Ankh or Ankou was the Court of the Dragon of Ankh-fn-Khonsu and his successor Sobekhnefru, whose most sacred inner symbol, historically, was the winged Orobouros with a pendant Greek cross. It was also the Court of the Dragon of the Ankh of Nin-Kursag or Hathor, and her daughter Innana or Venus. In tracing the history of one, via Egypt to its ancient Sumerian roots, we inevitably therefore recount the story of the other. They are, therefore, the same thing and represent The Realm of the Dead (or more pertinently, precisely and poetically "The Undead"), Tir N'an Og, Elysium, the Court of the Kingdom of Elphame, the Grove of the Swan Maidens and the Hall of the Dragon Lords of the Rings, the Repha'im or Rapha Elohim.

Later on, following Ygraine, the Fairy Melusine of Anjou who descended from her, was also portrayed in this manner as a wouivre, especially and also in medieval religious architecture. Related to this theme, in the cathedral of Le Mans on the Anjou-Maine border near Rennes, there is a carving of two serpent-tailed doves, called Serpilions and derived from the Persian "Smenda". Another representation of the Dragon is the serpent-necked Swan.

The Dove is sacred to Venus and is particularly associated with the Virgin Mary Magdalene, whose name "Magdala", according to some writers, means the place of doves, e.g. the temple of the cult of Hathor or Venus —Ishtar. In Albany the "place of doves" was Camlann or Camelot and the association with Morgana and Melusine and the Ladies of Avalon, and thus the priest-esses of the cult of the Ankh (of Hathor or Venus), is apparent.

The Ankh of Hathor, according to Gettings, is generally believed to be the source for the astrological symbol of her daughter Inanna or Venus, whose magical colour is that of Elphame. In addition, Emma Jung reminds us that when the Grail appears as a "stone", it is presented on a green silk cloth, which reasserts the link between the stone and the emerald of Venus.

The colour green in alchemy is the Benedicta Viriditas, the colour of the Holy Spirit or Sophia, the wisdom gained by the hero who, on completing the "quest for the Holy Grail", is awarded the Green Cloak or Greenmantle. Green Stags (the Robin Hoods) are one of the Grail badges or totems of the lords of the forest which entered heraldry in the armorial achievements of some families. The Green Stag amongst other things represents the transcendent king, the Fairy lord of the forest, blessed of a Fairy queen. Stags drinking from Grail Chalices are quite common subjects for bas relief sculpture.

The links to green as the Elven colour are obvious and indicate that:

a) the Holy Spirit is immanent within nature or the cosmos, i.e. that the universe and God are One Being and

b) the Fairies already possess the Holy Spirit of God by virtue of blood and birth, not through the consent of some priest. Therefore they are naturally eternal beings and in no need of forgiveness of sin, because they, the sons of the Repha'im as the true Children of God, don't and can't commit any sin.

The Key of Life

It can be asserted that the Fairy or Dragon cult of the Goddess Ankou, although not originating there, was, in any event, maintained in Albany, where Morgana was born and ritually active. Having established this, it is likely that the later kingdom of Anjou, formerly known as Pictavia, derived its name from a priest or priestess, or a court of the Ankh which settled there from the Breton coast.

If this was Melusine, the founder of the Pictavian House of Anjou, then Melusine would have been known as "Melusine d'Ankou" or "Melusine of the cult of the Ankh" prior to moving there. That in itself is almost certain, as it would be for the other Avalonian princesses. However, the idea that she actually founded the kingdom itself is not certain. The realm of the Anjou, as stated, was passed down by inheritance it seems, from the reigning Vere Tigherna "Vortigern" to the grandson of Merlin Emrys III; Guy de Marys, who was already a prominent figure in Breton legend.

Guy de Marys, reputedly a Vere ancestor, was also know as Kai, Cai or Kay, the latter spelling meaning both Quay and Key, in relation to which the Ankh was called both the Key of the Nile and the Key of Life. Guy was a Merlin and a Druid or Magus, specifically a Bard of the Golden Bough who descended to Hades, by classical Greek description and definition, and as stated, he would have been a revealer (anschau) and binder of mysteries. As a "spell" master, a binder and loosener of lives, a male Fata or Mori, one of the Fairy Race.

The presence of the cult in Brittany suggests that the Anjou or Ankou, as the Otherworld kingdom of the dead was moved, as a rite, from northern Pictavia to southern Pictavia in Gaul. Here it gave its name to a region which then became its cultic kingdom, years before either Morgana or Melusine were born.

It is more likely therefore that Emrys II—Ambrosius Aurelius—introduced the cult to the region when he decamped to Brittany sometime after the defeat of Rhydderch, which would then help to explain Melusine's later presence there. She is said to have fled to Gaul from Northumbria with her Dragon Court, after the ritual killing of her father in the same manner that Morgana killed Merlin. (Elinus' spirit was later deified, it would seem, and given symbolic gift offerings of milk, after a manner associated with the live "Dragons" who were given the semen or "milk", and the blood of maidens; and were thought to inhabit caves, or labyrinths, throughout Europe.) However it was unthinkable that a royal Pictish princess would flee and wander through someone else's kingdom unannounced, as this could be construed as an act of invasion and war. Such a story seems to be a later justification of her presence there.

But as a priestess of the Ankou in Scottish Pictaivia, she would have been welcome in the other land known as Pictavia, where her cousin Rainfroi, the third great grandson of Ambrosius, reigned as the Archdruid of the Golden Bough, the hereditary, ritual king of the dead. As it is, they, who were both patricides, were destined to marry, which would strengthen the dynasty, and thus the migration was a planned event. In any case the cult, with its ancient Irish associations predates Vortigern, and we should be looking back further still for its origins.

Essentially the British-Gallic Cult of the Ankou is related to a symbol sacred to Horus' supposed wife: Hathor-Venus, and to Isis and Nephthys—the Ankh. These deities appear to be related to each other in the same triple goddess configuration found in the rest of Europe and the Levant. The draconian Ankou cult is a regional variant therefore, perhaps the origin, of the Greek cult of Persephone as described in the foregoing essay on the labyrinth. (Isis and Nephthys are also both, amongst other things, goddesses of the dead.)

In the Funerary Cult of Egypt, the nobility employed Ka-Priests to tend the dead. This is linked to a strong thread of ancestor veneration which is also found in Scythian culture. Though the Faiyum Labyrinth has long since been reclaimed by the sands, the massive labyrinth complex of funerary palaces in the 25-26th dynasty necropolis standing next to the temple of Hatshepsut in Deir el-Bahari is still in existence. At the centre of the complex is situated the sacred sanctuary which has an adjoining cell which is commonly recognised as the utmost Holy of Holies, the singular feature of which is the carved Ankh Cross which dominates its facing wall.

In the *Papyrus of Ani* dated 1300 BC, Isis and Nephthys are depicted as standing on either side of the Ankh and holding aloft, above its loop, the solar disc which relates to the Sephiroth of Kether, also called the Ajna Chakra, symbolised by the "thousand-petalled lotus". This lotus in Egypt was associated with the psychotropic Nile Lily; and the generic symbol of the lily in all its national variations, was associated with the Grail and Dragon Families. The subject of the lily will be studied in some detail later on.

In pre-Christian Gaul it appears on the carved heads of chieftains whose effigies were incorporated into architectural columns and at a very early period, prior to its adoption by the Comité of Paris, the lily or "fleur de lys" was the badge of the early Kingdom of Anjou. The shape of the fleur de lys seems to have been influenced, in its present form, by a very important Gallic magical rune which was within a group of symbols derived from, or related to, the prototype of the Ankh.

The lines of the fleur de lys' basic structure pass through two planes and two angles to form a St. Andrews Cross overlaid upon a Greek Cross in the manner employed to create the Norse binding runes. From the evolution of this figure it is thought that the Chi Rho was developed as a later form of the Ankh. This eight-armed cross appears in the Canary Islands cut into the bottom of the bowl recesses which were carved into the top of stones outside sacred caves, duplicating the concept of the cup and ring stones one can find throughout Britain.

As was the case in the offerings made to Melusine's father outside the cave in Northumbria, in the Canary Islands, milk was also poured into these depressions and left to trickle away down the side of the monolith. The eight-armed figure was believed by the islanders to be sacred to Isis, the virginal High Priestess of Waite's alchemical Tarot. It was said to be her "milk", the dew of the fleur de lys or rosicrucis, that flowed from the eight-armed cross to form the Milky Way, the spiral vortex or labyrinth of the "cosmic" Dragon, the Orouborus which features in the cross of the Dragon Court.

The fleur de lys itself is so configured as to contain within it both the Ankh and the Chi Rho. The figure of the fleur de lys, as a Gallic rune, comprises in the Norse of Nyd as +, an equal armed cross meaning both need and death, Gifu as X meaning union and Wyn as a loopless P meaning victory.

Translated, this forms the ritual process encapsulated in the rite of the labyrinth. The P lost its loop during symbol migration, a phenomenon documented by the Count d'Alviella in his book *The Migration of Symbols*, some components of which I will draw upon later and reproduce the figures for.

In essence there are several related crosses that, although thought to have developed from each other serially, belong to a very ancient group of symbols employed within the royal Dragon culture. Within this culture, the rites of ancestor veneration and communication associated with the central mortuary theme of the cult of the Ankou form an integral and timeless component which is well known.

The Sacred An

The Chi Rho, which is suggested should be the symbol for the Swan Knights, is developed from the Ankh itself which in turn forms the basis for the fleur de lys. In Melusine's time, the field of lilies, the arms of Anjou, represented the Pictish virgin princesses coveted by other dynasties, which are the lilies featured in the earlier *Song of Solomon.*

These lilies or Anjous/Ankhous/Ankh maidens, sacred to the various Goddesses mentioned herein, are the Bruidhinas, the Morrigan/Valkiries and Swan princesses of the Dragon Dynasty which the Swan Knights were sworn to protect. Their symbol IS the Chi Rho Ankh which, instead of just representing the XP, the first letters of the name of Christ the Man, latterly conceals the true nature and gender of the Christos itself, which is of the rtu, first flow of the womb, of the Ankh, the Goddess.

Consequently, the Chi Rho itself is a female Dragon symbol related to both Morgana and Melusine, as well as all the other Ladies of the Lake: mermaids, naiads, nixes, virgin priestesses and so forth. The earlier history of the Chi Rho, the Ankh and the Haegl rune which forms the fleur de lys can be found in the development of Mesopotamian cuneiform from earlier Sumerian pictograms.

In Sumerian the symbol represents "An": the Star. The star pictogram later became cuneiform with the wedges forming the ends of the top branch or ray, and the subsequent three rays going down the left-hand flank of the glyph. At this stage the symbol came to represent the "Heavens" and its final cuneiform representation was as an equal-armed cross with a wedge at the end of the top ray and two wedges on the left arm which represented the gods. This figure is close to variant representations of the Ankh in medieval black magic where the top arm is an enlarged triangle whilst the other arms have smaller wedge ends.

The common translation of the word Christ is "anointed one". Libatio, from the root libare, meaning "to taste", "to pour" (as Mary of Bethany is said to have anointed Christ) is, however, closely related to this concept. Libare is related to the Greek leibein, to pour, drop by drop, translated as "to pour out (wine etc.) in honour of a god." (*OED.*)

Wine is not uniquely specified, but any liquid is—meaning that Libare and Libatio are not solely confined to the act of the libation of wine to a god. It has been suggested that some Greeks would argue that "Christos" meant gold and that would then intimate that the idea of anointing, in relation to the Grail, was derivative and attributive.

In the Greek Orthodox Bible, Christ is described as the "Golden One" from Crusos—Gold; rather than Cristos—to anoint. Here we are, back to Christ as the "red-gold" flow, an anointing or libation of virgin blood of the

Labrus or Labia. Libare is also related to Liber or Bacchus the god of "wine", and here we are reminded of the later Christian doctrine of transubstantiation and their substitution of wine for blood.

In Mithraism the blood of the bull was poured from above onto the supplicants as an anointing chrism and a libatory eucharist drink. Therefore the idea of libation being solely TO a god is incorrect, as often the gods, or indeed the goddesses' blood, was shed as both an anointing and libation for their flock. Further on, we shall encounter "anointing" not as Christos, but as *murizein* which has its own surprises.

Jesus' surname is ben Panther, meaning the Leopard, which is the totem steed of both Bacchus and Diana and is repeated in the arms of the House of Plantagenet as three (originally one) heraldic leopards "Or" on a field "Gules", or three golden leopards on a field of blood. The archaic spelling for Leopard is Libard and this night-stalking animal is renowned for drinking the blood of its victims prior to eviscerating and consuming the carcass. Here again is a variant of the word Libare and quite a pertinent one at that, as again blood becomes a Libation associated with Christ the son of the Libard, as the anointed anointer, the libater, the initiator.

Christianity is substantively a prime example of the reversal of libation and in this it attempts to mimic earlier Bacchanalian ritual. Royal anointing in post Carolingian Christian ritual uses the oil of the chrism, representing the Holy Spirit. The Vatican uses this right to create kings from peasants and merchants. One assumes that by transubstantiation, royal anointing is treated as though it were delivered in obedience to the will of God by proxy through his chosen priesthood, who intended it to take the place of royal blood in the veins.

It is suspected that the etymology of the name Christ was tampered with in order to accommodate this anointing ritual and to derive the usurped social power that attends upon it. Along with the service of communion this is another Catholic version of reverse libation with blessings being showered upon the grateful by a beneficent priesthood.

Libare is related, via "to taste", to labia—lips and libant means "tasting" or "touching lightly", obviously with the lips. Lake or Del Acqs, sometimes written as Lac, represents the lily and the rose: the Roman dye "Lac": the crimson flow, and Lac or Lactose: the white "milk" of the maidens. Within the cellular and genetic fabric of these substances was retained the Ankh'a or Ka of the An, the Holy Spirit and power of the Dragon Gods—the ka of the An: the soul of the Heavens.

The crimson flow and the "milk and honey" (Nectar or Ambrosia; cf. the name of three generations of Merlins above) of the priestesses can be adequately and correctly described as their sacrificial libation. This is the "blood of the Christos" shed for the remission of sins (Hebrew: "Sin"—"falling short of the mark"; perceptual blindness, the living death).

The spurting of "milk" relates to *La Fontaine de Soif*, so called because it "sprays out", like a fountain, from the cubic stone. This symbolism is derived from the ejaculatory propensity of the Graffenberg gland which ejects its seminal fluid, the sacred "milk and honey" or nectar, like a jet. Poured onto the Ankh figure in the cup stone by the sacred cave or labyrinth, the substitute milk of Isis is perhaps not symbolic breast milk, but an allegory for her seminal fluid, inundating the symbolic vulva, the Ankh, from whence it originates. It should also be noted, however, that breast milk itself contains Telomerase, a sort of bicycle puncture repair kit for infant DNA. One is supposed to see a connection here, I think.

The Ankou cult and the ancient form of the Ankh are therefore associated with caves and thus labyrinths and with the holy female essence. Both Morgana and Melusine of Anjou or Ankhou are closely associated with such elements, as High Priestesses and ritual representatives, in a line of succession which goes back through the Pictish Fairy Princesses or Swan Maidens, beyond Sobekhnefru and the Egyptian Ankh Goddesses to the Sumerians and Babylonians. Their goddesses Ast (Isis) Nebt-Hat (Nephthys), Nin-Kursag (Hat-Hor) and Lilith, from whom Melusine, Morgana and the Ladies of the Lake are descended, all bear the symbol which forms the loop of the Ankh, which was first entrusted to the god Thoth, who was the Sumerian Nin.Gish.Zi.Da: the Lord of the Artifact of Life, son of Enki and Eresh Kigal (Persephone-Demeter).

Likewise Magdalene, the daughter of the Jireh Priest of the Temple of Jerusalem, was a Priestess of this lineage and the matriarch of the Ankh Priestesses in Albany. Known as a Scarlet Woman, she was so-called because of the colour of the Lac-dyed ceremonial robes she wore as a senior officiate, the blood tincture indicating her ritual obligation.

The term Scarlet Woman became associated with prostitutes because Magdalene, as a temple priestess, in her relationship to Jesus as a Pharaonic, Dragon Messiah, or God-King, fulfilled the role of the goddess Hathor or the Judaic Astaroth, the Sabbath or Matronit in the esoteric, Kabalistic aspects of Jewish spiritual philosophy. This role involved her in forms of ritual "congress" or Enthea, of the type specified in the *Song of Solomon*, which are also found in the Tantric Kaula Vama Marg and repeated later by the Avalonese Virgins of the Holy Blood.

Astaroth was the Goddess of the Shekinah, the divine presence of the Eternal within the Solomonic Temple of Jerusalem. To the early Gnostics she was recorded as representing the Sophia or Holy Spirit, the (feminine) principle of Divine Wisdom. Later, Astaroth (a denizen of the Devil in the medieval demonologies) continued to be recognised by the Cathar Christians as a symbol of the Holy Spirit. During Jesus' life, Astaroth was therefore manifest in the person of Magdalene as Christ's consort in accordance with Apocryphal doctrines, in much the same way that Ishtar, Matronit and Lilith, as early priestesses of the Shekinah began as the consorts of Enki, Enlil, the Dragon God-Kings and later Jehovah.

In this Mary too, fulfilled the role of the Anunnaki blood mothers who fed the Dragon God-Kings. As the physical embodiment of Astaroth, the Sophia or Shekinah, within the Egyptian Therapeutate she was Hathor-Venus, whose cross derived from the Ankh, and as Ishtar, the morning and evening star, she personified "war" in the mornings (Seratonin) and "love" in the evenings (Melatonin).

After Ishtar's example, the progeny of the Anunnaki dynasty, the Rephaim or Angels, who became the Elven, Dragon Maidens and Knights of Albany, Eire and Gaul, fulfilled two roles, that of destroyers and reapers, and that of divine lovers and healers.

Under the patronage of Ishtar or her mother—Hathor (Nin-Kursag) of the Ankh or Ankhou, (and later, under two of the principal Astaroth matriarchs, Magdalene of the Green Dress and Anna, her granddaughter, who migrated to Albany and married into the colateral PenDragon dynasty)—the Rephaim of Pictavia and Eire, were both the Swan Princesses. They were vessels of the benedicta viriditas, and the Morganas and Valkiries, the Priestesses of the Ankou and the Guardians of the Cult of Blood and Death.

In this way the Cult of the Ankhou gained a collateral line which descended through the posterity of the Druidic families to the Mistletoe Bards and Priestesses. From the *Letter to Ceretius* we know that Jesus performed a sacred role as the central figure within the circle dances that, in conjunction with his secret teachings and his rituals of initiation (Morton Smith), he conducted at night.

In the *Letter*, Jesus is recorded as saying at one night-time gathering "The Eight Are With Us". These are the Egyptian Ogdoad or eight Great Spirits of Gnosticism which are also found in Taoism. The Eight Spirits are the second wave of creators (after the Cosmic Twins) that appeared tilling on the sacred mountain of the "rising land" that emerged after the flood. They appear in an illustration in the *Book of the Dead* of Khensumose: Third Intermediate Period, 21st dynasty circa 1075-945 BC. Evidence for the existence of this belief prior to the pre-Ptolomeic period is derived from its worship site at Hermopolis whose "Eight Town" quarter existed at the time of the Fifth Dynasty: 2498-2345 BC.

"The Eight" when reflected upon in relation to Ubaid or Sumerian tradition represent the Anunnaki, the original gods of Egypt, salvaging the remains of their civilisation after the Black Sea inundation. The story has been transposed to Egypt, like so many stories that travel with their tribes, and becomes the creation myth of the Pharaohs.

The Ogdoad, also found in China as we have noted, are some of the sons and daughters of Enki-Samael (Ptah) and Ninkhursag (Hat-Hor). Enki sired Ningal from Ninkhursag, and Eresh Kigal from Ningal, it would appear. Eresh Kigal, mother of Lilith, gave birth to eight deities—Abu, Nintulla,

Ninsutu, Ninkashi, Nazi, Azimua, Nintu and Enshag; (Sitchin). That Jesus, as an initiate, invokes them, suggests that he had a firm Egyptian, gnostic ritual background which has its origins in Dragon kingship, manifesting itself later in medieval Witchcraft. This reinforces and supports an argument for the role of Jesus' wife as his Priestess of Hathor-Astaroth and points to her lineage becoming a contributive bloodline to the pre-existent cult of the Ankou in Albany and Pictavia.

It is significant that the Ogdoad are also known in Scandinavia, where they are called the Aia. The Norse have a diagram of the sacred mound as a square which also shows the compass points and the migration of the eight tribes of the Gods from the Holy Mountain.

This is of some interest because people are used to the Anunnaki being presented as a small council of deities. In fact they were a race of people who were still known as the Anukim in Canaan in 1200 BC, 760 years after Enlil's Anunnaki court had apparently fled Babylon in 1960 BC. Corroborating the migration myths of the Danaan in the Irish Liebhar Gabhala, the Aia migration glyph suggests that eventually at least one of the tribes of the Anunnaki settled in the north, whilst another, the Danaan, headed west following "a flood".

The location of the sacred mound would then seem not necessarily to have been Egypt but, given the broad dispersal of the Ogdoad story, it would probably have been a site from where the gods originally migrated. The most obvious location is Aryan Scythia, near the Black Sea region. It is quite possible that the time frame for this migration was 4000 BC, when the Bosphorus collapsed and the Ubaid fled south to Sumeria. Later they became the gods of Egypt and it is feasible that the story of the "tilling of the sacred mound" migrated there with the Anunnaki—Ubaid deities.

Venus or Venal?

The Druids welcomed the Culdee into Britain as brothers in spirit and fellow Druids. Columba called Jesus a Druid (of the order of Magi) and the links between primal Christianity and Druidism are quite apparent. Jesus (a harrower of hell like Orpheus-Bacchus), Odin and Theseus were born in caves. Like Merlin and Elinus, Jesus was buried in one, in a garden which was arguably a Necromaniton, or Druidic sacred grove with a funerary cell. Jesus initiated Mary Magdalene into the Egyptian Therapeutate.

She was twelve at the time and he was, according to the Bible, about thirty years old. The ritual employed was similar to that in which Lazarus partook, in that it involved symbolic death and resurrection. See Luke 8: verse 41-56. Following her initiation and during the period of her early adolescence, as was common practice, Mary would have acted as Jesus' handmaiden or grail priestess.

Botticelli's "Birth of Venus" is described by Graham-Dixon as an analogy of the Virgin Mary. In the depiction of the red-haired Venus, however, there is a supposed sexual analogy represented in the various folds of fabric and hair which are arranged by the painter to suggest the vulva which remains covered by her modesty. It isn't likely that the darling of the Roman Church would have been depicted in this manner. Botticelli wouldn't have got away with it in a period when Galileo was being threatened with death for suggesting that the earth was an orbiting sphere. One could do virtually anything with the Magdalene however.

Common sense would, in any case, suggest that the Mary depicted was in fact the Magdalene and that the painting was a deliberate though esoteric attempt to record what was commonly known about her race, her position and her function, amongst alchemists and Rosicrucians during the Renaissance period. The suggestive folds were made in red cloth festooned with flowers and here we might have an intimation of the spiritual fertility of the vulva in menstruus.

Commentators have stated that Magdalene was a sacred prostitute, or priestess of Ishtar (daughter of Hathor). This can be explained by this particular phase of her spiritual life where a certain type of congress, a secret outside the Cult, would have led to her being suspected of being a prostitute in some orthodox Jewish opinion, as she was not married at the time. It is very probable, however, that the so-called Rites of Venus she ritually engaged in with the Messiah have been confused with other definitions of the word venal, which pertains not only to sex, but to payment for any service or goods.

The confusion between the words Venus and Venal has led to the error where it was thought that Magdalene was a prostitute, who was "paid" for "Venal" services. In the Egyptian tradition of Jesus' ancestor Solomon, however, Mary—a priestess of the rites of Hathor within the Egyptian Therapeutate—would, like Sheba, have been a young Shunnamite, a donor of womb blood and the "Water of Life", a Lily of the Valley and a Rose of Sharon.

After Jesus' death, Magdalene went to the cell and found it open. Rather, I would argue that in accordance with the traditional ritual that accompanied her station, she was expected to stay in the cell and commune with the Ka of Jesus in the underworld. Few people actually knew the real reason why she went. The reason people might have assumed would be that it would have been expected of a Priestess of an Egyptian Cult. In Celtic countries and in Egypt this was common practice, as in the cases where it has been demonstrated that tombs had living quarters in them.

That she went to heal him of his non-fatal wounds was a secret known only to an initiated few, among whom the apostles, it seems, were not counted. In any case she was the first to "see" him, and in this she fulfills precisely the role of the Sibyl or shamanka, the Druidess of Cumae, Medea of the Golden Fleece, Ariadne, and numerous other females, including the Witch of Endor. In Revelation 22: v. 16 Jesus, clothed as a Repha'im, proclaims himself the Root and Branch of David, the Bright and Morning Star.

Amongst other things, including being the Priest-King of Lucifer, Jesus also proclaims himself as a High Priest of Hathor, who is the mother of Ishtar, Astaroth, Shekinah, Sophia and Venus, the Star of the Morning. It becomes increasingly difficult to see Mary Magdalene therefore as anything less than a central character in a collateral Druidic cult of the dead, a priestess of the Ankou of Ishtar. In such a capacity, as with the various cave-dwelling shamankas in mythology, she would have acted in a twofold role both as a visionary and also as a guide and companion, a facilitator whose blood allowed access to the underworld or Cosmic Consciousness.

Her essence and elan was the Dergflaith of sovereignty, the pomegranate wine of Persephone that gained the Bard of the Golden Bough, the Hero of Mythology, entrance to the land of Elphame, the Kingdom of Ankou. In this ritual capacity, Morgana, Melusine and La Fille du Lac et la Fonteine; followed her example and demonstrated a lineal descent as living goddesses, from at least one of the Ankh cults of antiquity.

In the Bible, the narrator writes that a sword will separate the quick from the dead. The sword is the Spirit and the Spirit, as we have seen, is also symbolised by the tongue, and by fire. In Latin a sword sheath is called a vaginum. It is the use of the "sword" which separates the quick, the living spirits (the Elves), from the dead or the dead in life. In other words it is the rite of the Maiden, the "christos of salvation" that gives life.

References to the Sword as the Holy Spirit in the Bible include Revelations 1: v. 16— "Out of his mouth went a sharp, two edged sword. In his hand he held Seven Stars", said to represent the seven Churches of Asia. It is interesting to note the association here between Bacchus and the Pleiades. In John of Patmos' vision, the Alpha and Omega figure: Jesus, is dressed in the garb of an Angel or Repha'im. Hebrews 4: v. 12— "The "word" (pneuma/spirit) of God is a two edged sword". Ephesians 6: v. 17— "Take the helmet of salvation and the Sword of the Spirit".

According to the story of the Pentecost, the Holy Spirit descended upon the disciples like "tongues of fire". This is a symbol which, connected to the foregoing, is especially relevant in relation to the Dragon, whose fiery breath is a symbol of the Holy Spirit, the "Word" of God, the Torah; or the Law of Destiny determining the progress of mankind's fate.

The sword is an Ankh symbol with the blade representing the tongue, the guard represents the Grail dish or womb, the spiralled grip symbolises the spinal column, and the pommel (from Fr. la Pomme, the little apple) represents the pineal and its chakra.

In the medieval Grimoire, *The Clavicula Salomanis*, the guard of the magical sword is constructed of two crescent moons back to back. The sheathed sword, symbolising Peace, represents hierogamy and balance, oneness and union.

The story of Arthur and the Sword in the Stone is translated by some to mean that Arthur became king because he knew how to extract iron from stone. As smithing was a part of alchemy and thus a king's science, some scholars concluded that in order to become king, Arthur would need to convince people that he knew where iron came from.

The Iron Age had been extant for over a thousand years before the Druids first told this story. In a pre-industrialised society that depended on iron for everything and where nearly every moderately sized village had a smithy, Arthur would have already known how to extract iron from rocks and other people would have known that Arthur knew. The age of secret metal magic had long since passed by his time. It has to be emphasised that a fascinating new theory has arisen that associates the Sword in the Stone motif with the far earlier skill of casting bronze weapons in stone moulds. Nevertheless, in relation to Arthur this symbol would be irrelevant, and so we are still left seeking an alternative explanation.

The Sword-Stone tale operates on two levels of organic (not metallurgic) alchemy, and refers to the enthea resulting in transcendence, leading to sovereignty. The stone is both the cubic stone of the Ankh Goddess-Priestess and the Lia Fail, the Stone of Destiny, a representative symbol of the macrocosmic cubic stone of the Earth as the anthropomorphised Goddess of Sovereignty.

The sword is both the tongue in the first instance and the sword symbol of derivative integrity, cosmic consciousness and resultant personal sovereignty in the second. From such personal sovereignty comes the wisdom and creativity to administer the sovereignty of the nation, thus qualifying Arthur to be a king.

That he performed the job badly in the end is another matter. Even goddesses have off days. They're only human after all. The sword in the stone says that sovereignty rises from the womb of the Grail Maiden, the virgin Dragon Princess.

The Sword as Tongue implies the method by which sovereignty is obtained. Elsewhere the pendant T bar of the Ankh glyph corresponds to Tau, the Law. More precisely it is the Utterer of the Law, the Hindu Lingham or in Hebrew, the tongue of the Repha'im, the Fairy Bruidhe Bard in Gaelic, whose spells, or words of cosmic law, bound men's fate and, like the Morrigan warrior or Valkirie, represented the Holy Spirit.

In the foregoing examples the symbolism sometimes tends to overlap because of the adaptation of the glyphs over the passing centuries. Pure symbols like the ankh naturally evolve to become more complex with the addition of other components, whilst still retaining the originals, which can double up sometimes, as in the case of the addition of the T to the rounded orb. On its own, the T is already the lingham and yoni combined. Add this to the upper orb as the womb and the symbol becomes reinforced, as in the following breakdown.

To qualify the T component, we have to separate this symbol into two parts. Being specific, the upright corresponds to the tongue as utterer whilst the crossbar, anciently dish-shaped like the new moon, represents the womb or uterus, also the utterer.

The Tau was given to the priest-king by the womb. He passed it on as spells or laws, with the tongue which drank the wisdom of the cosmic law from that womb. The cup/dish and stone, the moon or womb and pineal in this instance, being held by a statue of Melchizadec, is situated outside the door of Chartres Cathedral, along with a figure of the Magdalene. This comes as no surprise.

The Tau symbol can be found in Scandinavia associated with Tir, the God of Law and Judgement whose rune became, in this century, the familiar crow's foot or upright arrow. The Tir mark was specifically the property of the king whose word was binding on all. Therefore the Tau or Tir element of the Ankh is, like the Omega from which it feeds, a royal symbol, intimating again the holy-sacral nature of the Grail ritual.

The symbol of the Chi Rho of these Swan Princesses, as a derivative, later form of the Ankh, was known before Christ Jesus' lifetime, as was the IHS of Bacchus, whose story is connected here via the Ankh Cross as a crucifix.

Chapter 10

The Wheel of Fate

The adoption and modification of the Chi Rho Ankh by the Church was a late event and it is said that the Chi Rho symbol was based on the six-pointed Gallic rune because, as we shall see, the symbol had such tremendous influence.

As we know, this rune was the Sumerian symbol for the gods. It invariably preceded the name of any deity. Therefore, as the Chi Rho, in relation to Jesus, it was used to imply his divinity, not as the son of the Jewish storm and corn imp Jehovah, but as a God-King in his own right, as a descendant of the Dragon Gods of the Egyptians.

The Church was and is a past master at assimilation for political ends. The use of the Chi Rho, like much else, must be seen as another way that the Church sought to be identified and adopted by non-Christian Europeans.

The six-pointed Gallic rune, similar to the Norse rune Haegl, would originally have been eight-spoked, like the Buddhist Wheel of Life or the Tarot's Wheel of Fortune. In this guise it is the Web of Arachne, the Web of Fate and the plan view of the ribbons of the Maypole dance.

The missing horizontal spoke of the Chi Rho is accounted for in its having been often carved into wood. Inevitably one spoke would always follow and disappear into the grain, and so rune masters omitted it.

According to Count d'Alviella, the Chi Rho is sometimes to be found in the loop of the Ankh itself. In Egypt the Chi Rho was known as the Chrism of Philae, or the anointing of pure love. This indicates the Entheal nature of the symbol, particularly in relation to the Ankh itself, which in some creative work has been thought of as the "Vampire cross" being, as it is, the symbol of eternal life and youth.

Other examples have been discovered with the loop made of the Dragon Cross of Cain. The Ankh was said to have migrated into the Christian crucifix. This seems obvious when one remembers the Celtic Cross, which would seem to support the foregoing, as does the pre-Christian cross of Bacchus and the Albigensian (or Gaulish Fairy) use of the Ankh in relation to heterodox Christian belief and ritual.

The Bethel stone was shaped like an Ankh and had associations with the various pine cone or Dove capped pillars, the Perrone of the sacred groves. At later times the Perrone were capped by crosses and the name seems to be reminiscent itself of Persephone. Later still, in European Heraldry, one can see the pine cone column in the Pyr of Augsburg. In particular these columns were associated also with barrows and bergs.

In Belgium they were known as the Stones of Justice, which again links them with the Tir or Tau and the Ankh, whilst in Scandinavia, according to the Saga of Gudrun, they become the white stone pillars (Gita/Cita) on the barrows which were venerated by the peasants. The white stone, as a portable panacea, features in the story of St. Columba and King Brude of the Picts.

The Goddesses of Death and the Underworld are again prominent here, in the transcendent sense, as with Persephone, but one also remembers Mithras and the World Bull or Minotaur of Theseus. One can imagine the presence of the Bethel Stone, as the Perrone of the Ankh, in the midst of the Necromanitons (a variant of the Druidic grove of the Nemeton in Galatia, relating to Nemesis or Justice, the Tau or Fate), such as that built in Greece at Ephyranus. It had buried at its core a subterranean cell for the rites which invoked the dead from Hades.

When thinking of Greece and Galatia, it must be remembered that these were originally under Scythian (Sidhean-Aryan) overlordship, manifesting Draconian culture and subject to Druidic law. These influences also helped to shape the Hindu, Sumerian, Egyptian and Judaic traditions, beliefs and iconographies. It is therefore understandable that we find many themes and symbols which these seemingly disparate cultures hold in common.

Within all these crosses and figures are held layers of meaning that can be interpreted to represent a close knit variety of rites or anatomical attributes within the strict parameters of their genre. Consequently, to settle for one simple explanation for any given glyph is simplistic and at variance with the intentions of the Dragon Culture which invented them.

The upturned crescent moon features in the following figures. This should be remembered in relation to the galley or moon barque, which, accompanied by the lion, is a prominent badge of the Scottish clans and features in the heraldry of Leith, near Edinburgh, where the ship carries the figure of the "Virgin Mary" (Magdalene), another Ankh variant. The Moon Boat is also said to be the origin of the Genesis Ark and with the symbol of the Templars' Anchor, the crescent moon becomes the hull of the boat which carries the Ankh as its mast and sails.

The key to understanding this symbol is to refer back to the notes and remember that the virgin womb (the crescent or new moon), carries the Ankh, The An-Ka or Pneuma. This was the secret of the Benedicta Viriditas, the Green Blessing of the Mouth—"The Fairy Gift" (also "the Dark Gift", "the Thirst", "The Hunger") of eternal life in this life (transcendence) and youth, the blessing of the virility of life regardless of age. It was said of anyone "seeing the Grail", that although their hair might turn grey, they would not age from that day forth (Eschenbach).

Supporting material from D P Silverman, W H Matthews, Michael Grant, Oxford English Dictionary, Count D'Alviella, Ward Rutherford., Z. Sitchin.

The Lily and the Rose

"There is a Garden in her Face"

There is a Garden in her Face
Where Roses and white Lilies grow,
A heavenly Paradise is that place
Wherein all pleasant fruits doe flow.
There cherries grow which none may buy
Till "cherry ripe" themselves do cry.

—Thomas Campion (1567–1620)

The Dragon Tree

Being pertinent to the appreciation of the contents of the following essays, the author here includes a brief word on the *Dragon Tree* or *Dragontree*, which is a massive plant that grows in Persia and Gran Canaria. Its Latin name is *Dracaena Draco* and it belongs to the genus *Lillaceae* or *Lily*.

Its resin is called *Dragon's Blood* and was used as a dye which the Romans called *Lac*. Poetically therefore "the blood of the Lily is the blood of the Dragon", giving it special ritual significance as a tincture for ceremonial robes, and as an epithet for the branches of the bloodline, as in a popular spelling of del Acqs as *Du Lac*.

In relation to the Greek word *Derkesthai* there is, in Gaelic, a reminiscent word, *dergflaith*, which means "red beer". The word dergflaith is used to describe the Otherworld drink which conveys sovereignty upon a king. It is quite possible, therefore, given the Greco-Gaelic connections in history, that one word has influenced the other. Derk and Derg might derive from a similar or common root and Flaith might be related to the Gaelic fola, which is used in relation to the family and blood. In which case, Dergflaith actually might originally have meant Dragon's Blood, being rather the *blood of a Dragon princess*, conveying the Derkesthai ability.

The Lily of the Valley

In relation to the discussion herein, the following is a brief discourse on the subject of the lily. For the purposes of this essay we will be concentrating on both the Lilliaceae and Nymphaea Lotus varieties which are regional variants of each other in Dragon Lore.

The former, the Iris family, include the Lily of the Valley, whilst the latter are the species known as Blue Nile Lilies. Furthermore, for the purposes of providing an illustrative narrative, we will concentrate here on "Hylas and the Water Nymphs", a portrait by the pre-Raphaelite artist J. W. Waterhouse, whose depictions of water nymphs and Grail characters are somewhat prodigious. In alchemical lore we know that the lily represents the virginal seminal fluid of the vulva and the rose represents the womb blood. However the white lily of the valley produces red berries in autumn that are reminiscent themselves of the droplets of Virgin blood. The lily of the valley is highly toxic and can be fatal—a reminder of the love that is death.

The virgin vendors themselves, like Melusine et al, are often described as water nymphs or naiads and in Waterhouse's picture the naked, pale skinned, Otherworldly ladies in the woodland pond are surrounded by and are wearing in their hair specimens of the Nymphaea Lotus, the "lily sacred to the nymphs". Hylas (Helios—the Sun Dragon, representative of the Sephiroth of Kether or the Ajna Chakra) is a crew member of the ship Argo. Captained by Jason, it had been sculling around in Scythian territorial waters looking for the Golden Fleece which, like the Ark of the Covenant, is a symbol of the Holy Grail.

Having been at sea without a break for some time, it had been decided that, now that they had sailed back through the Hellespont, they would put to shore on the island of Chios and seek for provisions and water. It fell to Hylas to wander off alone into the forest to look for a fresh spring. After a protracted peregrination Hylas entered in upon the scene where Waterhouse's nymphs were bathing. He is depicted crouching on the banks of the woodland pool. Here we now see Hylas being tempted to enter the water and avail himself of the tender but fateful embraces of these emissaries of death.

Waterhouse painted his model of Hylas wearing a blue-black robe tied about with a red thread. This, the dreaded "little thread of the Cathars", was a memorial of the Old Testament, Hebrew scapegoats, one of which had a red thread tied about its horns, prior to its being pushed into the scorching desert to face its ultimate death, whilst the other was sacrificed. This double ritual was enacted because the Jews thought that the goat sacrificed to Jehovah was insufficient to take away the sins of the people.

The Goat was called Azazel, a figure who was said to have been a fallen angel and whose name has several etymologies derived from its ritual functions but who is certainly "Satan" or Samael. The red thread represented the sins of the Jews.

The symbolism is simple, the Jews ultimately laid all the responsibility for purging their sin upon Azazel/Samael, when in the first instance, the sin belonged not to him who was their true creator, but to the usurper Jehovah alone. For this reason, as a memorial and to express their true allegiance, the Cathars, the Witches and the nobles of the blood wore the red thread.

The Cathars wore it as a belt about their black robes and the latter two groups wore it as a garter or "points". In this manner, for them it also represented the womb blood, the "Rtu" or "red-gold flow" of the virgin priestesses of the Kaula Vama Marg.

On the Aziluth or imperial scale of the Kabalistic Tree of Life, red and black are the empress and emperor colours of the Sephira of Binah, the "sphere of understanding". Binah is ruled by Saturn or Chronos and its sacred plants are the lily and the cypress, whilst its sacred animal is the bee. Cypress was used in the Levant as an incense to celebrate weddings and mourn the departed, whilst the lily traditionally represents virginity and death.

Here we have the symbols of Enthea and the love that is death, with the bee describing the manner of such congress. In Waterhouse's beautifully evocative painting the nymphs are immersed in water, the element which is a Scythian symbol of the Daleth, the door to the Otherworld, and Hylas is about to undergo a profound process of alchemical initiation.

The girls, whose watery embrace is said to spell death, are the Shunnamites, the lilies or virgins who are portrayed in the *Song of Solomon*. In their connection with water, the nymphs are thus depicted as the embodiment of the wells of living waters. Their deathly embrace is but the death of the ego, of the will and of desire. In uniting with them, Hylas' soul will die and his mind, once stilled, will "understand" and give way to the transcendent spirit of the cosmos. Such is the nature of this mystical process.

The nymphs are priestesses of Lilith, Diana and Persephone, they represent Melusine, Magdalene and the La Belle Dame Sans Merci: the Maid of Kent who was Edward III's "Queen of the Witches". They are the Leanaan Sidhe, the Grail Maidens who, as perfect representations of the Goddess and the Muse, are the externalisations of man's longing for Anima.

Enthea, divine union with these meremaids, is intended to facilitate the exultant union of the animus and anima. Via this external hierogamy or alchemical marriage, comes the death of the finite, isolated being, from whence emerges as if reborn, the universal spirit, unattached, undesiring and immersed in eternal love and life. In such terms the essence and the embrace of a Grail Maiden end all desire.

Hers is the embrace of death because her spirit and her energy enliven the tired spirit of the pilgrim and her beauty and completeness, her stillness and poise, are the sum of all that the initiate might seek. Her quiet, matter-of-fact acceptance needs no striving for and is not gained by worldly show. It infuses the stillness of the journey's end into the lover who, having to achieve nothing more to attain her transcendent love other than just to be, melts in her embrace and without barriers, melts his being into hers.

Her love is then his death, beyond which is Daleth, the door to Elphame, Oneness and eternal, silent understanding. Such is the watery grave to which Hylas has wedded his fate. The story of Hylas and the water nymphs links the pineal and womb chakras, giving a complete teaching picture of the Grail Process.

The Lotus Eaters

In Greek myth the lotophagi—the Lotus Eaters—to which Hylas' story is related, experienced a similar phenomenon in consuming the Nymphaea Lotus and losing their desire to return to homes which they had forgotten, along with all those emotional trinkets and fond memories which once possessed their hearts. (Homer: *The Odyssey*, IX-90ff)

As an infusion in wine, the petals of the Nymphaea Lotus are narcotic and bring about psychotropic effects similar to certain mystical states. In Waterhouse's painting the nymphs are surrounded by and are wearing these flowers in their hair. Their immersion in the lily-bedecked water implies that their "living waters" or seminal fluid, the "dew of their lilies", had similar transcendent, psychotropic qualities.

The wearing of the lily on the head signifies that the source of the divine essence represented by the lilies in the pool originates with the pineal gland and the "thousand-petalled lotus" of the Ajna Chakra, which energises it and the other cerebral glands. The water these Swan maidens are swimming in is the "Sea of Binah" and they are thus the daughters of understanding, Witches of the waters of wisdom and the children of the Hive.

The nymphs are here seven in number and represent the Pleiades, the Fairy daughters of the Titan Atlas who were pursued by the Boeotian Orion or Osiris in an ancient, ritualised form of the Wild Hunt. They became the seven stars of the constellation that bears their name and which, in a superimposed arc, adorns and suggests the Ankh-like Cross upon which Bacchus was crucified.

Waterhouse's nymphs therefore were also the wild Bacchantes or Dionysic Maenads who themselves hunted for and drank human blood in rites whose central feature was that of union with the divine. Associated with these nymphs is the Romano-Celtic goddess *Coventina* (coven, covenant or union), who was depicted either alone or as a tripartite figure, bathing in a pool, surrounded by lilies. She is pictured in the act of pouring a jug of water into the pool itself. Her other name is *Dea Latis*, meaning both *Goddess of the Mere* and also *Bright Shining One*, which links her with the Elves. In this she shares the attributes of the cult spirit of the river wharf in Teesdale, whose name was both *Verbeia* and *Latis*.

Related to the nymphs are the Biblical Miriams or Marys, and the Tamarises whose symbol was the Palm. This represents the Sufi Tree of Life. Theirs was also the Pomegranate of Persephone, with which the Palm appears in mystical symbolism and the pool or oases adjacent to which the sacred Palm itself grows.

Miriam or Mary and Tamaris were the names of females who occupied specific dynastic offices within the Royal Dragon bloodline in Israel. In Hebrew the name Miriam is represented by the consonants M'R'Y'M and means "bitter" (defined here as sorrowful). From this we obtain Mary, Mari, Marie, Marion, Maryon or Marian and all these examples contain the M'R'Y or M'R'I consonant group. In the following passages we will encounter the *Myr* syllable group relating to myrrh, which is relevant here, particularly in relation to Tamaris.

From Marion we obtain the "Maid Marion" of the Robin Hood cult, whose name and title equate with that of the Virgin Mary (Magdalene), to whom Robin and his band were devoted. In Egypt the name is Mery, as in Mery Ataten. The name Mary, or properly Mari, is Indo-Aryan and means several things.

The component Mer, Ma or Mar means—1) a mere or pool; 2) the sea. As Mari, it is associated with the Mori or fates and is the An or Ankhou of the Basque Witches. Mari is also Mar Righ, meaning royal pool or royal waters, where Righ defines royalty or kingship. Where king further relates to knowing and understanding, Mary as Mar Righ becomes 1) the waters of wisdom; 2) Binah, the primordial sea.

In Marian the syllables break down into Mari and An. Mari as we have seen means pool, whilst An, the root of the names of many of the earliest Dragon Queens and Kings, relates to the Grail and means fire or spirit, and so Marion means "chalice" or "pool of fire" which then renders the "pool of the spirit".

The sacred cups, pools, wells and fountains we have so far encountered all relate to the womb and the vulva. In this manner Mary or Marion means "spirit in the womb" or "womb fire". It is in the latter instance that we have a direct reference to the Tantric, Kaula ritual of enlivening or inflaming the chakra of the uterine region to produce the "waters of life" or, as the *Song of Solomon* puts it, "The Well of Living Waters".

Mary's symbol is the white lily of the valley, the fleur de lys. In relation to Mary Magdalene as the Virgin Mary of Robin Hood's devotion, this is particularly relevant. In this cultic cycle there appears "The One Ring that rules them all"—the Draupnir or Andvarinaut—the "Gold Dripper" (or source of Rtu, the red-gold thread or flow of the Valkirie womb) that belonged to Robin's father Aubrey or Oberon, who is Alberich or Andvari.

As "The Well of Living Waters", Mary's relationship to Jesus becomes clearer as the child handmaiden of the Messach, the Dragon God-King. Marie is an ancient form of the word Marry, meaning to join or unite with, as in alchemical marriage, divine enthea, hierogamy, the sacred marriage ritual of Solomon's Song, with which we will deal shortly.

The Hebrew meaning of Miriam is "bitter"—transf. "attended by pain or suffering: grievious (*OED*), hence of a state: full of affliction, mournful, pitiable (1485), expressing or betokening intense grief or misery" (*OED*). Here we are reminded of Mr. Keats's "palely wandering knight" and nanny Melusine as *La Fontaine de Soif* and "the cup of sorrows".

In many Dragon and Grail stories, the maidens inhabit or frequent pools or fountains in forest gardens. Waterhouse's water-babes inhabit a forest pool. Janet March encounters the Fairy knight Tam Lin by a rose-covered well in Carterhaugh forest, in a genealogical variation of Beauty and the Beast. Solomon has his Sheba, a well of living waters in a labyrinth garden bedecked with sacred Pomegranate trees and Melusine is the fountain and well in a garden maze in the Forez.

Relating these symbolic representations of the virgin priestess-goddess with works such as Sir Richard Burton's *Perfumed Garden* and Francis Israel Regardie's *Garden of Pomegranates*, gives a clear picture of the forest as the pubis which is conceptually broadened by the maze in the dell on the hill, as the entrance to the Otherworld, hidden within the mons veneris.

In the *Song of Solomon* we encounter the pubis as a lock, which, like the well, is an old but well-known European euphemism for the vagina. In Chapter 5, verses 4-5, "My beloved put his hand by the hole of the door (the "lock"), and my bowels were moved for him (contractions): I rose up to my beloved and my hands dropped with Myrrh, and my fingers with sweet smelling Myrrh upon the lock".

Whilst earlier in Chapter 4 verses 12 and 16, "A garden enclosed is my sister, my spouse, a spring shut up, a fountain sealed: A Fountain of Gardens, a Well of Living Waters..." Throughout the Song, Sheba, who is "black but comely" i.e. an Annis or Persephone figure likened to Lilith, remains a virgin. Sheba was described as "the lily of the valley" and thus, as her forest garden equates with the pubis, then the lily of her valley is the water lily in the valley of her vulva.

Naiads or mermaids are described as being semi-divine and the handmaidens of the gods. This is aside from their usual mythic, pantheistic interpretation or symbolic representation as nature spirits, elementals or energy complexes. Such a description applies to the era during which these stories emerged, which was described by Euhemerus as the age when mighty men became deified and the gods were born of flesh and blood.

The Irish descriptions of their "gods", the Tuadha D'Anu, mix the qualities of divinity with some very human sounding foibles, whilst the descriptions of the naiads or mermaids present us with the qualities of human femininity, but blended to a much greater extent with those of the divine. As we have seen, as handmaids to the gods and essentially young goddesses themselves, the naiads or nixes were the Dragon Princesses of the Grail, the Ladies of the Lake, water Witches and meremaids.

They were the avatars, the Sybils who supported the elder goddess queens and god kings; they fed them, guided them to the Otherworld and, in the embrace of death, empowered their beings with the integrity that gives birth to vision and wisdom. That is, the wholeness that is sovereignty over self, and consequently sovereignty over all things.

Such a condition releases creativity, but such a quality is not a product of ordinary human thinking. Rather it is a phenomenon which lies beyond thought and beyond the capability of mundane knowledge to encapsulate or describe, both of which are processes bound by time and limited by definition. It is the still mind in union with the infinite, or, more precisely, that which knows no distinction between it and the infinite, and that which becomes truly fertile and creative.

Such was the nature of true sovereignty, the state of mind that, in kingship, affected the people and the land through good management and foresighted husbanding. If the king was of the tinker or warrior variety, then he was by virtue of his birth and cerebral physiological capacity, barren and infertile, and incapable of transcending his nature. In consequence, the land and people suffered by virtue of their having a king who was no king at all.

Chapter 11

The Rose of Sharai (Sharon) and the *Song of Solomon*

Sharon is a level fertile plain between Jaffa and Mount Carmel in Israel. In Hebrew the name derives from Sharai, a princess, from whence are derived Sarai and Sarah, which again were ritual offices in Judaism.

With regard to the word *rose*, some dispute exists over exactly what that means. Authorities on the subject describe it as i) a *crocus*. ii) a *polyanthus*. iii) a *narcissus*. iv) a *cistus*. However, if you consult a gardening encyclopaedia you will find that the *rose of Sharon* is described as the *hypericum* or St. John's Wort which, interestingly enough, produces a red dye and is related to the *cistus*.

It is likely that in order to be described as a rose in the European translation of the Jewish bible, it would have had to have looked something like a rose. In keeping with such an identification the *cistus* comes quite close in its foliate resemblance to the western red and white Plantagenet rose, which we found growing unabated around Janet March's well in Carterhaugh Forest. Furthermore, the *cistus* is called the Rock Rose in southern Europe and north Africa.

The *cistus* is white with deep, blood red blotches, like the dappling of menstrual blood. The *cistus* belongs to the family *cistacea* and is also known as the *gum cistus*, whose botanical genus is *ladanifer* from which is obtained laudanum. This is the dream-bestowing prize of poets and visionaries across

Europe and the Middle-East, including Thomas de Quincy who, having taken it, were transported into the darkest, most terrifying realms of the Underworld or the highest reaches of Heaven, both being the deepest recesses of their own psyches.

Sheba, as the Lily of the (Nile) Valley, the *nymphaea lotus* and the *rose of Sharon*: the *ladanifer*, was likened to a living, narcotic pharmacopoeia. As neither of these plants grows in Northern Europe, we have contented ourselves with the nearest familiar symbols, those being the virginal Fleur de Lys and the Plantagenet or English Rose.

The Rose represents therefore the magical menstrual flow of Solomon's beloved, whilst the name Sharon or Sarah means princess. The Rose of Sharon is therefore the Royal Blood, the Sang Real; and the San Graal, the Holy Blood of the Holy Grail or rosi-crucis. As the Latin Ros-Sara or rosary which is devoted to the Virgin Mary, the pure white Lily, is itself the "dew of the princess". (*OED*)

The word Rose in Germanic means Horse, from Hros, a deity who is identifiable with the goddesses Rhiannon and Epona, who were symbolised by the white mare and immortalised in chalk hill carvings across Britain.

By a lucky stroke of fate, or under the power of "the single poetic theme", as Robert Graves would have it, the Hros, like Slepnir (Yggdrasil), Rhiannon, Epona (and the Hindu Breghi Moru) was a goddess who conducted the King to the Otherworld and to the goal of sovereignty.

This was exactly the job of Sheba, the Rose of Sharon, and all the other watery nymphettes in history. So the Rose of Sharon, whilst referring to the flower of the royal menses, also refers to the function of that fluid as a method of transport to the Otherworld.

Again, death is implied by Hros because Epona and Rhiannon—but especially Slepnir—are symbols of the white-draped funeral byre carried by four men who, like Slepnir, have eight legs.

Slepnir, the white horse of Odi, is Rhiannon, the Elven mount of the Welsh Arawn or Death, the Grim Reaper (who, like Jesus,* "brings a sword to separate the quick from the dead"), scythes the spirit from the flesh. Arawn, Lord of Annwn, in the story of *Pwyll Lord of Dyfed*, leads a pack of red-eared, red-eyed hounds in the hunt for the red-eyed white hind. She is the virgin, Elven princess who, as in the stories of Odin or Hearne the Hunter and the Wild Hunt for Elf women at Samhain, is the source of truth.

*The image of Jesus as the Grim Reaper or Repha'im is consistent with his cultic role in the Egyptian mysteries. Significantly the verse that this passage is taken from refers to Jesus as coming with a sword, the spirit or Torah, to separate the "quick"—the divine, immortal spirit, from the dead—the material soul or "dead flesh" of the unregenerate mind created from the "flesh" of mortal experience. In vampirism the process of awakening the cerebral centres is called "the quickening".

In Indian love poetry the vulva has been referred to as "the footprint of the deer" and we may equate both the Hind and the Hros respectively with the physical and spiritual aspects of the Virgin. The Hart, or properly the Hind in the thicket, so beloved of Graves, is the poetic truth hidden by the pubis, like the tangle of thorns that hides the castle, the enclosed fastness of the princess's virginity in *Sleeping Beauty*.

Rapunzel's tower, her inaccessibility, is likewise a symbol of the princess's virginity. The hounds of Arawn, Odin and Hearne, consistently in all these stories, represent the retinue of Elf nobles who, in later times, were mimicked in the Wild Hunt by the race of the rustic youths around the maze for the virgin prize at its centre.

Card 13 of the Major Arcana of the Rider-Waite Tarot is entitled "Death". 13 is the number of the Moon and specifically of the menstrual cycle. Riding Epona or Slepnir, the red-eyed white horse of elphame, the skeletal figure of the Grim Reaper rides across the field of life in a black cloak and full armour, trampling the noble and the humble alike under his horse's hooves. In his hand he carries the banner of the white rose of the spirit on a black field. However, this is not a funerary plant.

The white rose, like the red rose, symbolises love, but which in this case is philea rather than eros. The horse's reins and livery are black and adorned with skulls and crossbones, which we understand to be representations of the Baphomet or Holy Grail. Behind him in the distance lie the twin towers that feature in another major Arcana card—"The Moon". Beyond the towers the sun is shining above the dark horizon.

The towers, the horns of the Sabbatical Goat, represent the open legs of the priestess-goddess and the glow of the sun. As in the case of the Hallowe'en candle on the seesaw, or the candle between the goat's horns, it is the glow of the red-gold of the virgin menses and the Chakra or Sephiroth of the womb. This symbol is replicated in the second card, "The High Priestess", dealt with earlier.

This again is a card of "the love that brings death" and the Reaper symbolises, not physical mortality, but the victory of transcendence over mortal pomp and materialism and the life-that-is-death. In such a context therefore—Death as Initiation—the white rose of the spirit and pure love, is identical with the red rose of Sharon, inasmuch as the red rose does not herein symbolise sexual passion. It represents the menses-smeared rose of the vagina's foliate aperture, contact with which brings the spiritual purity symbolised by the pale flower of Death's banner.

Like doves, roses are sacred to Venus who as Ishtar and Lucifer, the "bright and morning star" is the bringer of light and enlightenment. Venus' emerald jewel, the hermetic tablet of destiny (also the Lia Fail of the Scythians), is called the jewel in Satan's crown. When it "falls" or is reversed, it becomes the hidden "cubic stone", the dark, oozing monolith of the hidden Grail, concealed in the recesses of the body of the Swan Princess, the naiad, from whom one might obtain "blood out of a stone".

The reversed emerald tablet, the cubic stone darkened by its concealment, is the subject of two 15th-century paintings—"Livre du Coeur D'Amours Epris" and "Melusine by the Fountain". In both these paintings, the image of a black marble block from whence flows a curious fluid, is repeated. In French legend Melusine's well and fountain are the source of both joy and sorrow, much like the Croix de Lorraine.

This sentiment is repeated in *Livre Du Coeur D'Amours Epris*, which warns that misfortune will befall him who drinks from the water that issues from beneath the stone. The knight in the picture, as in all stories connected with Venus' Jewel, is further warned not to pour water over the stone itself.

Such would constitute Christian baptism, which was viewed by the Bloodline as a defilement, and a debasement of their pure spirits by an invasive and hostile alien culture. As with Melusine's black stone, the one depicted in "Livre" engenders the "Heart's longing for Lady Grace". Consequently, like Melusine's, it is a fountain of thirst because after one taste of its "waters" the ego's longing for material peace or security ceases. However, it is then replaced by the spirit's longing for enthea, its westward journey home to the love that is death.

The *Song of Solomon*

The authorship of the *Song of Songs* is attributed to King Solomon, probably because the subject matter dealt with has an underlying Hermetic, esoteric character which accords with what is known of Solomon's ritual practices.

Less probable is the reason that he originally compiled it in its entirety. Nevertheless it is quite possible that he wrote certain aspects of the song which perhaps were added to later by subsequent poets or scribes. The overall syntax of the manuscript form of the *Song of Songs*, compiled circa 450-400 BC, is Aramaic and was deposited in the School of the Temple of Solomon in Jerusalem.

The original piece is said to have derived from early oral sources and belongs to the genre of ancient Egyptian love poetry. The song also bears a striking resemblance, from a secular point of view, to Near Eastern love poems.

The Temple School was probably destroyed and its teachers dispersed during the destruction of Jerusalem by the Romans. A number of Christian nobles were said to have fled Palestine at that time which led, it is further attested, to the introduction of vampirism into Central Europe. This isn't strictly true, but a new wave or variation of the cult could have been reintroduced then. It is also very likely that many kabalists and rabbis also fled and settled in less hostile districts in Europe following the destruction of the Temple.

In this way could be explained the appearance of "Solomon Schools" in places like Hermannstadt, Toledo and Carpathia, which one assumes were outposts or exiled cells of the original Temple of Solomon School in Israel.

It was from one of these institutions, renowned for alchemy, kabala and Hermetic lore that Dracula was said to have "ridden the Dragon", meaning that he was the principal graduate. Following this illustrious academic career, Dracula, who claimed to have derived his name from his apostolic priesthood of the Egyptian cult of Draco, embarked on a reign that was marked by his overt practice of vampirism.

Solomon was what some might call a pagan and a great deal of Fairy lore and many gods from Eurasia filtered into and influenced Jewish culture during Solomon's reign. The Christian Bible tends to blame this state of affairs largely on Solomon's choice of wives, who were said to have brought these strange abominations with them. This explanation doesn't, however, take into account the fact that Solomon himself was deeply committed to and involved with Hermetic sciences and dark magic.

Solomon had, as wives, 700 royal princesses gathered from all over the Near East. In addition to these he had a further 300 concubines and these comprised his Harem. A rather excessive and self-indulgent amount of women, simply for the purposes of providing one man with a variety of copulatory partners.

We are then obliged by our own curiosity to ask why Solomon kept so many females around at such a large cost. If we take another look at the word *herem* we will find the answer. From the *OED* we learn that the English word "Harem" is taken from the Arabic *haram*, and means a sacred or prohibited place.

The term "sacred" could only be attributed if the "haram", the building, or more appropriately the institution within the building, were in some way spiritual or religious. According to the Oxford Companion to the Bible the word "harem" has a cognate in the Hebrew "herem", which is translated into the English "ban". Specifically, the herem or Harem, as a ban, was something set apart for cultic use, to be used only by priests, and thus a Harem is understood to be spiritual and holy, not simply a royal bordello or an amusement arcade.

Such a reflection brings into question the actual purpose of Arabic and Near Eastern herems in general, particularly in light of the fact that, in Arabic mysticism, the Sufic "Tree of Life" is a Tamaris or Palm tree, beloved of the

Phoenix. Its leaves comprise of the many-eyed tail feathers of the Yedzidic peacock god of Mesopotamia—Shaitan, who was worshipped in rituals of blood.

"He feedeth amongst the lilies", *Song of Solomon*, Chapter II, verse 16: Sheba enjoins Solomon to feed amongst the lilies until the break of day, like a young hart on the mountains of Bether. A lily is a virgin and thus Solomon by night feeds amongst the Virgins, the virgin princesses of his "Harem".

The medieval kabalists proposed a sacred code as a key to translating the hermetic secrets of the Song or "Canticle of Canticles" as it was also known. At the same time, some commentators have asserted that the work was derived from (Egyptian) cultic origins and was part of a rite of sacred marriage, a fertility ceremony and a ritual to ward off death. (James M. Reese)

These three components together adequately describe, in its entirety, the organic-alchemical rite of vampirism. This is itself a sacred marriage, a union of enthea, intended to open the mind to creativity and transcendent perceptions, thus stimulating spiritual fertility and increasing longevity, or warding off death.

The *Song of Solomon* is a blood rite, a communion where the wine, the blood, of the virgin goddess is drunk. This rite remained in the House of David until the time of Jesus ben Panther, when he reinstated it as an exoteric ritual for his disciples. Solomon's harem was a blood farm and the females in it were there to feed him, to increase his wisdom and lengthen his life.

Sheba seems to have been the first lady amongst many and throughout the discourse she continues, like them, to retain her virginity. In taking a closer view of the evidence we will inspect the following passages. Chapter II verses 16-17; Chapter IV verses 12-13; Chapter IV verse 15; Chapter V verse 5; Chapter VII verse 9 and Chapter VIII verse 2.

Chapter II verse 16: "My beloved is mine and I am his, he feedeth amongst the lilies". Verse 17: "Until the day break and the shadows flee away, turn, my beloved, and be thou like a roe or a young hart upon the mountains of Bether". As we have seen, feeding amongst the lilies is feeding from the blood and water of the young virgin brides.

The hart on the mountain symbolises the young king in his glory and the medieval symbol of the young stag drinking from the Grail is directly related to these verses. Chapter IV verse 12, "A garden enclosed is my sister, a spring shut up and a fountain sealed".

Sheba is a virgin throughout the Song and her maidenly attributes attract various epithets. In this verse we find the three main Grail symbols associated with the priestess: the garden, the well and the fountain.

Here these are enclosed and sealed indicating Sheba's maidenhood and her guardianship of an "underground" (hidden) stream or source of arcane vitality expanded upon in the next verses. Chapter IV verse 13, "Thy plants are an orchard of pomegranates (Grove: cf. Avalon) with pleasant fruits; camphire and spikenard".

Whilst the Indian spikenard (spica narda) was used by Mary Magdalene to anoint Jesus, the pomegranate is a standard symbol of the virgin vulva and womb, and Sheba's garden of pomegranates has in its midst:

Chapter IV verse 15: "A fountain of gardens, a well of living waters..." which cause those who are asleep to speak as we shall see. The living waters in other scriptural references are related to the Holy Spirit, as is fire. Water as we remember was the element through or over which one travelled to Elphame in Celtic lore.

Elphame here equates with the Underworld or Otherworld, the Kingdom of Heaven or Samadhi, and the living waters contain in their droplets the secret of eternal wisdom and the gift of transcendent awareness, god consciousness. The Holy Spirit, the Shekinah, is of the feminine gender and a female gift therefore.

In alchemy blood and semen are the primae materia or first matter of the great work. Sadly however, many think that only men have semen (an ignorance of female anatomy and physiology that has caused a great loss to our womenfolk). In fact women also have it, and this semen, from the well of living waters, is what alchemical texts are actually referring to.

Those who are familiar with the Templar story concerning their Lord of Sidon, will recollect the skull which comprises the skull and crossbones motif. This is because the symbol of the Baphomet—the Holy Grail—is derived from the skull which was placed between the thigh bones of the Templar's dead wife, butting up against where her vagina once was, nine months after an act of knightly necrophilia. The wife's name in the story was Yse de Maraclea or Isis (of the clear waters: Mara-Clair). The skull, the Templar's "son", represents ancient wisdom from beyond the grave. In its positioning between the woman's thighs, it indicates that such wisdom is obtained by uniting in hierogamy with one of the Goddess-Queens of the death cult of Ankou—Isis.

Such a union, similar to that expounded by the Scythians in relation to Epona or Rhiannon, results in the birth of the Templar's son: the skull; the wisdom from beyond the mortal realm. This wisdom is directly related to the feminine principle, hence the proximity of the skull to the vulva, denoting the interconnection between the pineal gland and the womb, the well of living waters.

Chapter V verses 4-5: " My beloved put in his hands by the hole of the door and my bowels were moved for him". Verse 5: "I rose up to open to my beloved; and my hands dropped (dripped) with Myrrh, and my fingers with sweet smelling Myrrh (vaginal mucus), upon the handles of the lock".

The hole of the door is the keyhole, the opening of the vagina, whilst the handles of the lock are the labia. The door itself is daleth or delta : the door to the mysteries and the triangle of the "all seeing eye of god" (that looks into the darkness) which in Hebrew is called Ayin or "The Devil", whose number is the same as the numerical rank of Ishtar or Venus in the assembly of the Anunnaki gods—15.

In verse 4, the beloved manipulates the maiden and her "bowels" (a common word used in classical literature which referred to the deeper internal organs, not just the intestines) are moved for him. In other words she orgasms, her womb contracts and in so doing she rises and opens her vulva for him to drink the blood or seminal fluid discharged by the spasm.

In references to the Fisher King, it is said that he drank the contents of the Grail through a golden straw. Very importantly, when thinking of the construction of this device, we should remind ourselves of the shape of both the Ankh Cross and the Crux Ansata. Such a device would have been inserted into the virgin's urethra to the depth of about one inch. The partner in the rite inserted his or her finger into the vagina and massaged the "roof of the mouth" or the uppermost wall of the channel nearest the opening or "mouth" of the vagina, behind the pubic bone.

After a few conducive minutes perhaps, orgasm would occur and the fluid from the gland would discharge itself through the straw, either into the waiting mouth of the recipient, or into a "Grail Platter" or dish held next to the vulva. In one publication the dish and the straw were confused with surgical instruments that the author thought were used for castration. This is not the case. The symbol of the Grail as a Dish is related to its use as a collector of blood or female ejaculate and is sometimes symbolised by the crescent moon (see above).

If we read Chapter V verse 5 literally, the maiden has been asleep with her hands in the spice jar and her fingers are covered with myrrh oil as a result. She then hears her lover at the door and, rather than noticing her mistake and wiping her hands, she goes straight away to open the door and covers the handle in grease.

Such an interpretation makes no sense whatsoever. If she had been asleep with her hands (plural) in the ointment, she must have either been a contortionist or a devotee of an odd form of nocturnal skin care therapy. In any case, if it were not a pertinent symbolic aspect of the narrative, there would be no justification in mentioning it. Therefore by its very inclusion in the text, we are obliged to look for a meaning that transcends the literal interpretation.

Myrrh (Latin: *myrrha*. Greek: murra) is a gum resin produced from several species of the *commiphora balsamodendron*, also known as *commiphora myrrha*. The oil of myrrh is produced from the seed which is known as *myrospermum pubescens*, and the etymological link here to female ejaculate should be meditated upon. Myrrh or the "myrrh tree" is also a name for the plant called *sweet cicely* or *myrrhus odorata* (related to *chervil*), but as a name it is further applied to any tree producing this type of resin.

We should bear this in mind as we look at myrrh as a word in itself. Although the Latin species classifications are late, deriving from Linnaeus, in many instances the original names from whence they came are Greek. We notice that the word *myrrh* begins with the letters *myr* and there is a group of plants and substances whose names begin with this syllable that are relevant to this discourse. Firstly we encounter the plant *tamariscus* and remember the name Tamaris, which was applied to princesses of the House of David.

Tamariscus or *tamarix* grows in sandy conditions in west Asia and is known by the Latin name *myrica*, a name which also applies to the bog myrtle: *myrica gale*. The Myrtle Tree is found in a medieval Italian story about a Fairy lover who is the spirit of the plant. This lends itself to the idea that the story was extracted from far earlier sources, and that the Tamaris Princess was the original "Fairy lover" or, in Gaelic, the Anam Cara or Leanaan Sidhe. Myrica-tallow or myrica wax are produced from myrtle trees, whilst the substance myricin is the insoluble component in the wax that bees produce to construct HIVES.

In the Tudor song "The Nut Tree" the tree in question will only bear a silver nutmeg and a golden pear. The nutmeg is known by its Latin name as *myristica*, from the Greek word—*murizein*, meaning "anoint".

Nutmeg contains the chemicals which, when refined are known as MDMA or "Ecstasy". In trials conducted on the Nile Lily or *nymphacaea lotus*, the plant produced similar euphoric, but less strident effects to those experienced by users of MDMA. Nutmeg produces an oil containing this drug, and the association with anointing and the Christos is quite telling. The golden pear on the "Nut Tree" is a pomegranate which was often called by the former epithet.

In Old French, pomegranate was spelt pome grenat, meaning "apple of many seeds" from the Latin *malum granatum*, and here we return to the Avalon connection and the pomegranate as the original, perhaps of the later regional and literary variation—the Druidic and Edenic apple trees. The pomegranate belongs to the family *myrtaceae*, whilst its partner on the legendary "Nut Tree", the nutmeg, is of the family *myristica fragrans*, the "musk smelling nut". Musk is a name given to any group of scents which are produced by the sex glands and used as sexual attractants.

Returning to the *Song of Songs* we now find that the pomegranates and myrrh in the narrative are related via Myr, to a whole series of plants and substances within grail lore which are associated with the Sephiroth, with psychotropic states and with the sex organs. Perhaps the myrrh of the *Song of Songs* is the oil of the "Musk Smelling Nut", the ejaculate, which then becomes associated with the sweet wine of the pomegranate, the menses, thus forming the partnership between the *rose of Sharon* and the *lily of the valley*.

Again we are reminded here of the Irish story of the blood red nut that fell every 28 days into the *Well* of Nechtan (the pure one), to be consumed by the salmon of wisdom—the Ichthys of the New Testament. From there we travel back to the Orchard of Pomegranates in the garden of the *Well* of living waters.

In Chapter VIII verse 2: Sheba says to Solomon " I would lead thee and bring thee into my mother's house, who would instruct me; I would cause thee to drink of spiced wine (nutmeg?) of the juice of my pomegranate".

Notice "my" and the singular pomegranate, as opposed to the fruits plural. She is not inviting him in for drinks and she is not referring to a beverage here, but the blood and mumae of her vulva. Pomegranate flowers, seed cells and juice are red, like blood.

In Chapter VII verse 9: "And the roof of thy mouth like the best wine for my beloved, that goeth down sweetly, causing the lips of those that are asleep to speak". The euphemistic "roof of the mouth" is the region by the opening or "mouth" of the vagina. It is behind the pubic bone, where the semenal duct is located which secretes ejaculate through the urethra. The chemicals in these secretions increase perception and wisdom, enabling those who were "asleep", meaning unregenerate or untranscended, to speak with the words of the quickened or resurrected Spirit.

Sheba, the rose of Sharon and the lily of the valley, describes herself as black but comely. In so doing she has initiated a tradition where many scholars down the centuries have confidently stated that she was from Sheba in Ethiopia.

However, the constant, relentless reference to "my sister, my bride", whatever anyone says about terms of endearment in Biblical times, indicates that Sheba was the daughter of Bathsheba and as a consequence, the sister of Solomon. This is hardly surprising as he descended from a pharaonic bloodline where brother-sister marriages were de rigueur.

The reference to her being black relates to her other epithets as Sheba-Lilith and Sheba-Venus or Ishtar (Inanna), which associate her with her ancient Dragon ancestry and to her forebears Lilith (Diana), Inanna, Kali Azura, and Hecate. Her other forebear, Black Annis, like Sheba, is associated herself with wells and labyrinths, and who was a principal figure of veneration in the Cult of Ankou.

Solomon, conversely, is described as having skin as white as marble. In exoteric, uninitiated and therefore "best-guessed" Vampire lore, it is said that such a complexion is equated with their being bloodless. Nothing could be farther from the truth. Recent laboratory tests confirm the ancient inner tradition by showing that any animal injected with large amounts of melatonin turns paler in colour. Solomon's complexion, like that of the Vampire of legend, is as white as marble because, like they, he fed constantly from melatonin-rich royal, female virgin blood.

A lot of the additional etymological associations here are retrospective and poetic. Nevertheless the central theme of the story stands up to a classical alchemical interpretation whilst the Latin and Greek word relationships add a quality of resonance to the picture. They further echo Graves' concept that the Cosmos has meaning and intelligence, expressing itself through a single poetic theme of interconnected meanings, the like of which inspired the ancient Hermetic Table of Magical Correspondences.

George Riley-Scott (*Phallic Worship*) points out, and is supported in his view by other academics, that the Bible has been altered down the ages to suit the ambitions of the translators of the day. This being the case we must remember that much of the Bible has been cleaned up and passages dealing with incest, along with various other unseemly practices, have probably been given a narrative reworking to suit the sensibilities of various pious audiences and patrons.

An example of this might be found in Chapter VIII verse 1 which says, "Oh that thou wert as my brother, that sucked the breasts of my mother!" Wert is printed as an italic—*wert*, denoting a translator's insert. Remove this and you get a different picture.

Chapter VIII verse 5 claims that Sheba was born "Under the Apple Tree" and suggests that she was spoken for when she had no breasts. If she were a virgin, "a wall", says Chapter VIII verse 9, Solomon would build a palace of silver upon her, but if she were a door, he would board her up with cedar. Sheba replied by saying that she was a wall and her breasts thenceforth were the towers of the palace that Solomon built upon it. The edifice of Solomon's glory, the palace of his wisdom, was built upon the virginity of Sheba and the essence of the womb of the princess born under the apple tree, reminiscent of Avalon and sacred to the Druids.

Let's assume that the *Song of Songs* is seen as a deliberate contribution to the poetry of the Dragon culture, which has at its centre the maiden's labyrinth, the Garden of Love. In this case, the *Song of Songs* begins to make sense as an Hermetic, alchemical Vampire allegory of the love of the Dragon prince for his maiden, a sacred chemical wedding which is the source of his power and sovereignty.

Chapter 12

Who's Who in Heaven

We turn our attention now to the weighty problem of identifying the gods. Some mistakes have been made in the past when people tried to cross match the pantheons of contemporary civilisations. For example the Egyptian goddess Hathor became identified with the Roman goddess Venus and so on.

The mistakes are easy to make because the Goddess Hathor was, in fact, originally the Sumerian Nin-Khursag, the mother of Inanna, who is also known as the Akkadian Ishtar, the Semitic Astaroth, the Greek Aphrodite, the Norse Freja and finally the Roman Venus etc.

As we know the positions of the gods in the various pantheons and their attributes and relationships to each other, we can re-identify who they really are. Surprisingly we find that the separate pantheons of the Aryans, Sumerians, Egyptians, Greeks, Romans, Vikings and so on, all appear to be derived from a very ancient family genealogy of "gods". These gods furthermore seem to stem from the early Sumerian pantheon.

However, recent research confirms that the original Sumerians were descended from the Ubaid, a proto-Aryan, Pictish culture which originated in the region encompassing Carpathia, Transylvania and the White Mountains where the Greek gods originated, which later became known as Scythia.

It is suggested therefore that the Sumerian gods (the ancient deific royal family) were imported with the Ubaid Picts from Transylvania, Carpathia and Scythia. Scholars relate that the name Sumer is pronounced Shumer, the *sh* for *s*, indicating a linguistic relationship with early Goidelic. Thus it is closely related by pronunciation to the Gaelic Sumaire, meaning, as we know, a Vampire and a "reptile"—a Dragon.

Reminiscent of the racial term "Gallic" (Gaelic), the word GALL in Sumerian means "navigator" (nautonnier) and implies guardianship and overlordship. In Barker's theory of Cybernetics, (management systems), the entity or mechanism controlling any system, be it social or mechanical, must operate at a technologically (or genetically) higher frequency or capacity than the system that it controls, otherwise chaos will ensue and the system will spin out of control. This guiding entity or facility, is termed in cybernetics the *nautonnier* or navigator.

Gaelic is the language of the Nautonniers, stated by many scholars to be, in an early form, a precursive language of the Aryans. In this language the dialectic *u* is pronounced *i* when it follows a consonant at the beginning of a word, and so the first syllable of both Sumaire and Sumer would then have been pronounced *Shee*, directly related to Sidhe and the Sidheans or Scythians. *Both would then be pronounced the same—Sheemar.*

And indeed evidence for just such a case lands in our laps from the pages of the Bible's *Book of Genesis*, where it states that "the cities of Babylon, Akkad and Erech are in the land of Shin'Ar". Shin'Ar is Sumeria and so our *Shee* pronunciation finds credence in the very word of God itself! Furthermore, if we look at Shin'Ar with "our Vampire eyes" (apologies to Anne Rice) and remember the Ubaid origin of Sumerian and hence, via Akkadian, the "Gaelic" origin of Hebrew as well, we will see *Shin* as *Sidhean* and *Ar* as *Arya*. Sidhean was the name of King Elinus of Albany in the 7th century AD. His full name was Gille Sidhean (*Jille-She'en*), meaning *Steward of the Fey*. Sidhean was pronounced with the *dh* remaining dialectically silent as it sometimes does in Sidhe or *Shee*, giving us *Sheen* for Sidhean.

The *Ar* component can be found in Takla Makan. Here it forms part of the phrase *Arshi Cantu* or Arya-Sidhe Canto (Tocharian "A"), the devotional, "power-wisdom" language of the Aryan Scythian inhabitants of western China (Aryan Sanskrit: China [soft *ch*—as in the French word—*chat*] or Shin'Ar!) who were named the Tocharians.

It would appear then that the "Ar-shi" phrase used by the eastern Scythian-Aryans to describe their spiritual language is reversed and repeated in the Hebrew name *Shin'Ar*, or Sidhean-Arya. And what does Shin'Ar mean? Exactly the same as it means in Sumerian—SU.ME.—*Lord of the Powers*.

In addition the Sumerian SI means righteous, pertaining to a god (related to the Gothic—*guth* [and hence the *Goths* and the *Godthi* Druids of the Danes]—one who has power over the fate or destiny of others, a Fairy). SHU in Sumerian means *Supreme*, also used in relation to the gods so SHU.MER would, in any case, mean *Supreme Lords*, which is the same as *Power Lords*

(Arya-Sidhe), whilst the word *supreme* is related to *Uber* and therefore denotes a Vampire and an Overlord—a Guardian.

If the *m* in either Sumer or Sumaire was originally intended to be *mh*, then both Sumer and Sumaire would have been pronounced *Shiva* or *Sidha*, both of which are connected with the Elves, the Aryan god "Siva the Destroyer" and the siddhis—the powers. Sumer is thought to mean "land of the guardians". A guardian—a "Watcher"—is an overseer, and from this meaning we obtain the Scythian word *uber*, meaning a Vampire or Overlord (by association, we also obtain from "watcher" the word *Nefilim*, which relates to the Anunnagi or Anunnaki).

Here we remember again the proto-Sumerian *Ubaid* Pictish culture which migrated in about 5000 BC from Scythian Carpathia, a land which had a Dragon Culture also as early as 5000 BC. Monumental stone carvings of winged serpents from this date have been found in Transylvania, along with a "proto"-Sumerian script dating back as far as 8000 BC. The figures incorporated on the clay tablets found at Tartaria in Transylvania are almost identical with Sanskrit and early Egyptian pictograms.

Tantalisingly, the Goidelic *mh* couplet is exactly the same as the Goidelic *bh*, both of which are pronounced *v*. It isn't fantastical to suggest that both bh and mh lost their h's and have been substituted and re-substituted arbitrarily, one for the other over the course of the centuries. It has happened everywhere else, why not here? Further, the *mer* and *maire* syllables in Sumer and Sumaire are related in the Sumerian *Me* and the Gaelic *Mor*.

In Sumerian, ME means Lord or Master (an Overseer or Overlord). In Gaelic Mor means "high" (also related to mountain and thus "dweller on the mountain"; one who soars to the heights—a Druid or Merlin). It is used as a suffix to the names of Scotic chieftains or kings as in—*The Conor Mor*—the High King (or Overlord) of the Clan Conor, for example.

If Sumer means guardian and thus overlord, then so does sumaire and the SU component thus means "the Power"—the Sidhe or Siddhi. ME is also, it seems, specifically related to wisdom and knowledge (the Aryas) and in both senses, therefore, the "sumer" or "sumaire", being one and the same thing—is a Derkesthai, a Dragon—a fact born out by every other piece of evidence you might care to mention. Sumer and Sumaire mean therefore—*Lord of the Powers*—SU.ME.

The *Ubaid* culture was named after the place where in 1919, H.R. Hall discovered the ruins of an ancient settlement. Since then, archaeologists made significant finds of blue-spiralled or labyrinthine decorated pottery and, up to the late 1960's, stone tools had also been found.

This "Ubaid" people who had been "cast down" (*Nefilim*) from their lofty abodes in the mountains of the North, fleeing south to Sumeria in about 5000

BC are now considered by academics to be the founders of Sumerian civilisation. According to Zechariah Sitchin, in 1852 the Reverend Charles Foster (*The One Primeval Language*) proved that all languages, including early Chinese and other Far Eastern languages, stemmed from one primeval source—thereafter shown to be Sumerian.

This is palpably untrue, as we now know, as the Ubaid brought Sumerian civilisation and its language to Mesopotamia. They were early "proto" Scythian-Aryan migrants who fled the Black Sea region at the onset of the first Flood.

It follows therefore that all languages stemmed, not from Sumerian, but from the "proto-Sumerian" language of the early Scythian-Aryan Homelands, examples of which we know were discovered in Tartaria in Transylvania.

This language, called by most scholars "proto Indo-European" (and I wish they wouldn't), was called Gaelic by Canon Beck and other respected academics who were contemporaries of Charles Foster. The Very Reverend Beck quipped that this Aryan Tongue, the mother of modern Irish, was the language of the Garden of Eden. Proto Indo-European is thought to come from an earlier group called *Dene-Caucasian*, which tends to stress Canon Beck's point even more.

Recent archaeological discoveries prove that there is many a true word spoken in jest! The present and seemingly vast differences in the varied languages that developed from "Gaelic" can be explained by one phrase—Chronologically Diversified Dialectics.

In the last four hundred years, the English language has changed so much that the majority of the resident British population would not be able to read Chaucer in the original script. Imagine what happens to a language over, for example, one millennium and several thousand miles.

From northern Mesopotamia to the foothills of Zagros, archaeologists working in the area from the 1970's onwards have ascertained that the Ubaid people had built cities which were the first to use: clay bricks (cf: the Aryan, Mohenjo-Daro and Harrapo settlements of the Indus Valley: 2300 BC, which were controlled by Sumeria), plastered walls, mosaic decorations, cemeteries with brick-lined graves, copper mirrors, beads with imported turquoise, copper-headed tomahawks, cloth, houses, and above all, monumental temple buildings.

However, south in Eridu—the first truly Sumerian city according to the ancient texts—nothing could be excavated from beneath the foundations of the temple of Enki that was any older than 3500 BC. This is clear enough evidence that the Elven queens and kings of the Transylvanian Picts founded Sumeria, and the most up-to-date academic studies and archaeological discoveries from the Department of Archaeology of the University of Wales corroborate this fact.

In the 1990's it was revealed by academics that the Ubaid priesthood wore leopard (panther) skins (cf. Jesus ben Panther!) and tattooed themselves in a similar fashion to the British Picts and the Tocharian "A'ryans of Takla Makan". The pointy shamanic headdress (worn by the god-kings and queens of the Indus pantheon as well), was also of Aryan origin, with or without the horns.

Moving from Romania, via Anatolia to Mesopotamia, the Ubaid left a trail of Tells or Raths, wall decorations, spiral-decorated pottery and brick built structures. In northern Mesopotamia, which has very little workable stone, they continued to use clay and plaster, whilst in the south, where rocks are plentiful, they built the Ziggurats or sacred mountains that reminded them of the holy peaks of their Carpathian homelands. When the Sumerians took over Magan or Egypt, their Ziggurats became Pyramids.

In very little time at all after their arrival in Mesopotamia they had found and were working copper—centuries before other people's bronze ages. Their chief god-king Enki had been an adept at mining (earning him the epithet "The Lord of Mining"—*Bel Nimiki*) and had, according to the later Sumerian texts, invented brickmaking, the planning and building of cities and metallurgy, which earned him the name *Nidimmud*—"He who makes things".

His Fairy descendants since then have all earned epithets associated with mines and alchemy, such as *Dwarves*, *Goblins*, *Kobelins*, *Trolls*, *Gnomes*, etc., and, as in the case of the Tuadha d'Anu, they have always been renowned for their skill in many crafts and arts. The place was called Al'Ubaid and was located just north of Ur, or Eridu as it was once called. The article *Al* in Al'Ubaid denotes that the location was named "of the Ubaids". Rather than the culture merely being named after its site of discovery, the actual site itself was named after the Ubaids in the first place, who had migrated south via Anatolia and Galatia, from whence we originally derived the word Vampire—the Uber.

Although the meanings are self evident and the implications thereof are quite plain, it might be educative to meditate on the further implications of Sumer spelt *Subher* in connection with the Scythian (Ubaid) *uber* and the possible common European migration of the consonants *b* and *p*, which give rise to our word super—as in *supervisor*—a guardian or overlord—an *Ubaid.*

From the above, we can conclude that the so-called Sumerian gods, repeatedly symbolised by serpents or Dragons, are an Aryan-Scythian import of the earlier Ubaid settlers whose gods were the Dragons incarnate themselves—the *Uber* or Vampire queens and kings—the Ubaid Overlords. The overseer or one who sees over or "beyond" is one who sees above others and one who thus sees clearly. One who sees clearly is a Derkesthai, a Dragon.

It seems fairly conclusive that these serpent gods were later referred to by the Sumerian people themselves as the Anunnagi from whence is derived *naga*, a serpent or Dragon god of the *Vedas*. That the Nagas themselves were Devas—meaning *shining ones*—repeating the meaning of the name Anunnagi as *shining ones* (*shimmerers—Sumerers*) squeezes one into a corner.

Archaeological discoveries in the 1960's of what was to become known as "proto-Sumerian" script, dug up from ash pits in Transylvania, should be compared with Tartarian traditions there. They assert that Lilith and her brother were born in Transylvania as a result of a mating between the "Keshalyi", the queen of the mountain Fairies, and the "Locolico", the king of the dwellers of the underworld mounds, situated in the forests and plains. This is echoed in the marriage of Nergal (*Nagal*—Naga) of the underworld and Eresh Kigal, a netherworld goddess in whom one can see the prototype of Persephone. As with all ancient tales, the plot becomes confused but by looking at comparable stories, some light can be shed on the truth.

Eresh Kigal was not a lady or queen of the mountains, but Ninkhursag her grandmother, was. It is interesting to see how the identity of the grandmother filtered down to the granddaughter, however. This indicates that the myth of the region once included all the characters who elsewhere still feature in relationship to each other.

As interesting, though, is the possibility that we might find a clue to the triple goddess concept in the very grandmother-mother-daughter theme suggested by the muddling of characteristics in the Transylvanian story. It is quite feasible that triple goddesses are not solely depictions of the three stages of womanhood, the moon, earth or whatever identities are assigned to them, but the half-forgotten relationships of a holy dynasty.

As I have indicated above, in Greek mythology there is a relationship between Demeter, Persephone, Kore and Diana-Hecate. If we transpose this series into the Sumerian, we have Ninkhursag, Ningal, Eresh Kigal and Lilith as linear descendants.

In Transylvania, the Keshalyi queen becomes Eresh Kigal, and the Lilith of the Transylvanians and the Sumerians becomes the Diana-Hecate of the Greeks who, as a moon goddess, one might be tempted to turn into the Egyptian Isis. But stay your hand I say, and read on!

If we read descriptions of the "Sumerian" Lilith, taken from Hebrew sources, we discover that she, like her Grandfather Enlil (Zeus) and her uncles Minos and Rhadamanthus, and her cousin Ariadne of the labyrinth, had red hair and pale skin, and was called the Alien Queen of the North. This indicated both by her complexion and her stated geographical origin, that she was a proto-Aryan or proto-Scythian. So the indications are that Lilith, along with the entire holy family of gods, was a Ubaid import from Carpathia who later became a Sumerian goddess.

It would be fair to say therefore that if Lilith were born in the mountainous regions that stood next to where Zeus and Prometheus battled (who were also identified with "Sumerian" gods), then so were her kin. It would then be simplistic to say that the gods of all the pantheons were descended from the Sumerian. It is more likely that they all, including the Sumerian, originated from the proto-Scythian Aryan culture.

As each group migrated and their descendants settled in their respective domains, changes took place. They became isolated from the source of their original spiritual culture by geography, and the passing centuries. Also the names of their gods changed because of the inevitable influence of the belief systems of the aboriginal cultures that the migrants either vanquished or cohabited and integrated with.

In some historical comparisons of the various pantheons, and indeed in the pantheons themselves, there will have been mistakes made because there was no understanding or overview of the relationships between the deities. In the case of the *Vedas*, as Sitchin remarks, consistency and precision are not the hallmarks of this Sanskrit literature. Such an observation holds true for much of spiritual literature worldwide, as memory fades and the gaps are filled in to create myth out of history.

By a comparative study of the pantheons and beliefs, we may discover a consistent vein by which we may adjust all the pantheons, where such stem from a recognisable common source.

One example is the case of the Aryan God Kasyapa. He was the father of the Asuras, the elder gods. One pantheon has him down as Dyaus Pater and identifies him with Zeus. Zeus or Enlil was the father of the younger gods. These were the Olympians who in the Aryan pantheon are called the Adityas. Kasyapa fathered them, as well as the elder gods, which Zeus did not.

Thus there is an anomaly which, I am pleased to report, is easily resolved when we learn that Kasyapa means Sky Father and so does Anu! In Sumeria the elder and younger gods are called the offspring of Anu—hence Anunnaki—and the elder gods are led by Enki, whilst the younger gods are led by his brother Enlil. Enki's followers are the Asher, corresponding to the Asura of the Aryans, the Aesir of the Danes and the Aes Danu—the Tuadha d'Anu of the Irish.

Chapter 13

Children of the Stars

Anu's father was Asher. Marduk was called Asar or Ra, the grandfather of Osiris who himself was also called Ashur or Asar (*As-Ar*: "Seeing Lord", a Naga or Dragon, A Merlin or Druidhe). These and their variants, including the Norse Aesir and the Gaelic Scythian (Aryan), Aes Dan, mean "he who sees" (*Ashshur—he who sees*—[again: *Ash Shar*—"Seeing Lord"] from segment six of an Assyrian clay tablet formed as a disc of eight segments, copied from an earlier Sumerian original. This had been excavated from the ruins of the Royal Library of Nineveh), which is the very foundation and meaning of the Greek word *Derkesthai*, from whence we derive the word Dragon.

In Aryan, Samael or Ahura Mazda (Ash-ura?) is called Tvashtri or Tv-Ash-Tri and rumour has it that he, the elder brother, actually sired Indra who, when the pantheon is streamlined, turns out to be Dyaus Pater. This has certain ramifications when converted into Sumerian because Tvashtri "the Fashioner" converts, as we have seen, into Enki-Nidimmud "The Craftsman", whose brother isn't Ninurta (Indra), but Dyaus Pater or Enlil.

The conflict between Enki and Enlil therefore, might have been more deep-seated than at first we realised, because it may not have been just simply the rivalry between two brothers, but the rivalry between a father—Enki, and his forbidden brother-son—Enlil. Such a conflict was played out between Zeus and Cronos (who had led a rebellion of the Titans against Uranus), but also between Zeus and Prometheus.

In Aryan (ancient Scythian) the *Asuras* are also called *Devas*, meaning "shining ones", and this epithet also becomes applied to the members of both the Anunnaki and the later Fairies who descended from them. Earlier scholarly sources have the name Anunnaki translated also as the variant "Anunnagi", meaning "shining ones", and here we have a relationship with the Vedic Nagas.

From the Sumerian Chronicles we learn that the children of Anu were "the Anunnaki who decree the fates". This meant that they themselves were also the mori or fata, the "Fairies", the scale-armoured leprechauns—the Dragon kings. They appear in the Aryan *Vedas* alongside their divine companions and are referred to as the *Nagas*, who became the snake deities of India who guard a submerged treasure, echoing the central theme of the grail and ring cycles.

The Grail and the lake represent the womb. The Magic Ring hidden in the lake and the red gold flow and dew of the Grail both represent the life-giving blood and mumae, the "submerged" or "hidden" treasure of the serpentttailed and Swan's-winged mermaids, the *Naga* goddesses of the north. Their wouivre, or double-ended tails and wings, are also to be found in representations of the ancient "Aesir"—the Titan* or elder god—Typhon, son of Gaia and Tartarus. Their other children included these Vampiric Lamias—the meremaids or naiads, and their name is closely associated with Tartaria in Transylvania, the original home of the Dragon Queens and Kings.

Several thousand years after the contest between Typhon and Zeus, Typhon's Fairy descendants, Ygraine, Morgana and Melusine were still portrayed in medieval Church architecture with Typhon's wings and double ended tail. A depiction of Melusine with these physical attributes appears as a supporter in the arms of the Imperial and Royal House of Vere.

In Typhon as a Dragon God, we remember Odin, who himself was often portrayed as a Dragon or serpent, a *Naga*, and that he too was an Aesir, a member of the old, warlike order of gods. Odin is always associated with Yggdrasil or Yggd-Rad-Aes-Hel, the World Ash of the Norse. Here we will recall that the tree's name means Steed of Yggd or Odin and was a goddess who performed the same function as the Queens of Avalon. As a serpent he is often seen entwined around the Aes Tree, echoing the depiction of Samael as the Serpent (N'H'SH), entwined in Lilith's branches.

Subtext—The Naga

At this juncture we must break off and study the Aryan Naga—the serpent devas, guardians of treasures "hidden in water". We will do this by first looking at the Hebrew word *nahash*. This word means serpent (and thus Dragon) and derives from the consonant root N'H'SH—a snake.

*Titan derives from the Sumerian TI.TI.AN which means:

1) The breath of life of Anu (the Sons of Anu—the Nefilim)

2) The Spirits of the Stars (the Star People)

In Hebrew Qabalah and particularly, and rather oddly, in relation to the Jewish practice of divination by birds or Ornithomancy, the serpent or *Nahash* is one who discovers hidden secrets or wisdom from the Raven, the Dove or the Swan. (Warburg Lectures, Universtity of London, private dissertation on Qabalah and Jewish Ornithomancy, 1996.)

The N'H'SH is Enki-Samael the SU.HUR.MASH (Capricorn—the Goat-Headed Sea Serpent) or A.LU.LIM (Ram of the "Glittering" [or Shining, as in Elven] Waters), associated with Lilith of the Qlipphoth or "Abyss" (the APSU or watery deeps – i.e. lakes, wells, vulvas etc).

Closely associated with the relationship between Lilith and Samael, as outlined above, are the Raven and Dove as birds of divination. In this context it becomes clear that these qabalistic, symbolic animals are meant to represent the Valkiries, the Morganas and Magdalenes—the Ishtar priestesses who are the Maidens of the Ring and the Grail.

The Dove, specifically the Turtle Dove or Barbary Dove; is a soft brown colour and has a ring around its neck that lies open at the throat. This Dove, specifically sacred to Venus, is a symbol of love and devotion, and is the bird referred to in the name Mary Magdalene. Magdal or Migdal means a Dove.

The ring around its neck is a torque, which, in Gaelic lore symbolises, as do all rings, Kingship and therefore wisdom and seership—the Derkesthai or Dragon Nature. That Mary is named Magdalene, "of the place of the doves" which are sacred to Venus and thus Ishtar, and mistakenly Hathor, means that she, Mary, was a priestess of this Goddess of "Love".

The link between the Raven, known as the Phoenix, the Dove and Samael is alchemical. At one level the Raven and the Dove are female and interchangeable, the Dove or doves (in Magdal: the place of doves or temple of the priestesses of Ishtar/Hathor/Venus), being the priestess or priestesses of Ishtar; the other—the Raven—being the priestess of Morrigan.

The qabalah specifically says that the Raven and the Dove are the same bird and in the northern hemisphere the brown singing Ravens of the Druids are obviously the Turtle Doves or priestesses, brown Morrigans, equivalent to Swan maidens.

Samael, in his congress with them, obtains the "wisdom of the qlipphoth" or the abyss—i.e. the waters of the deep. The Barbary Dove or Migdal links the ring cycle to Mary Magdalene and thence Jesus. Both are then linked again to Hathor, the Raven Goddesses of the Druids, to An and the Phoenix of the Scythians, and thence the Ring and the Dragon Orobourous, called Janus by the Phoenicians and Jormungar by the Danes.

Jormungar—"The Earth Spanner" : "the encircler" or Vala of the *Vedas*, lives in the watery deeps and once upon a time long, long ago, Thor and the giant (Titan) Hymir went fishing for him. As bait they used an ox-head which, as we have seen symbolises the ovaries, fallopian tubes, womb and vagina of the virgin goddess.

Here again is a link between water, Samael the Dragon and virgins. The Brown Raven or choral priestess of the Druidic cult is the Turtle Dove and the Swan maiden because both animals are used in alchemy and Tantra to symbolise the brain, the pineal gland and the Ajna Chakra.

In Vala we have the original root of the words Valhalla and Valkirie. It is now known, as we had suggested, that the Valhallas were forest halls. There were in fact built on mounds and displayed giant Dragon heads at each end. These were the dwellings of the Vala Aes, the Dragon Overlords of the forest and beneath them, lying in the Creachaire tomb-raths, were the remains of their ancestors, the Gods of Heaven.

The Valhallas were the dwelling places of the Gods of Heaven and Earth, the serpent queens and kings. The Great Hall on the summit of the mound of the Otherworld was identical to the temple at the peak of the ziggurat. These Halls were where the Valkiries, the singers of the Gods assembled. In this capacity, these were sometimes called the brown Ravens, meaning that they were still the Morrigans, but assumed the magical, Grail role of brown Turtle Doves, the lovers of the Phoenix or Dragon God. Hence the Valhalla was also a variant of the Judaic Magdala or House of Doves.

The Swan-serpent caduceus and the descended Dove originate here, and in placing the paten into the Grail, both symbolise this love of the Turtle and the Phoenix. The serpillion is a Swan or serpent-necked Dove depicted in medieval architecture and the link here is clear. In the association of Lilith with the Abyss of the Qlipphoth and the Raven and Dove who symbolise Ishtar, we have another link between Diana and Persephone and a clarification of the nature of Hades.

As the watery abyss, it is identified with the Gaelic Otherworld reached by water. The masculine nature of the Raven is echoed in Machen's alchemical riddle where a serpent eating a serpent becomes a Dragon (a serpent which eats its tail makes a circle and completes itself: it transcends). A Dragon eating a Dragon (a transcended one drinking from another transcended one, Samael drinking Lilith) becomes a Phoenix—a Raven King, Swan Knight/Prince, Dragon Queen, Rephaim etc.

The Phoenix in its final transcendent glory becomes a flaming, leaping star, an An, or Shining One. "The Nahash is taught by the Raven or the Dove" means that the Dragon Kings drink from Grail Princesses of the Abyss or Qlipphoth, the Tree of Life of the Left Hand Path—Kaula Vama Marg! That is, the pool at the foot of Yggdrasil.

In *The Phoenix and the Turtle* by William Shakespeare (I don't think!), are mentioned the Turtle Dove, the Phoenix, the Raven, the Swan and the Screech Owl (Lilith). It is said that out of the Phoenix myth, Shakespeare (I don't think!) created a myth of his own. Not so. What he did was to expand the myth and fill it with its proper alchemical symbolism and demonstrate the purpose of the original story, that being divine union. For the full text of the poem, refer to Appendix 2.

The Phoenix of myth is the only bird of its kind. It symbolises the Oneness of the All perceived by those who become united with the All, and thus are alone. It travels from its eastern paradise and makes a "nest" of "spices" (see *Song of Songs*) in an Arabian Palm Tree. This is a Sufic symbol and emblem of the Tamaris Princesses (refer to Lily and Rose again, back a few pages).

Having burnt up in its own fire (been consumed in the energy generated by enthea), it takes the ashes to the temple of the Sun at Heliopolis and lays them on the Altar. Other birds (ranks of Druidism aforementioned) and men gather to rejoice. In chorus (Cor) they accompany the singing Phoenix as it soars to heaven and returns to its lonely paradise e.g. Samadhi, Bodhisatva, Heaven, Transcendence, Enlightenment, Divine Union, Scythia!

Summary: the transcended Dragon King needs to drink from a Dragon Princess, a Fairy lover. He travels to Arabia, meets his Tamaris and drinks from her "Nest of spices" and she bestows stillness and ecstasy upon him. He is consumed by fire (the spirit or combined energy). He is then reborn and takes the ashes of his mortal body, and lays on the altar of the Sun. This is symbolised by the Dragon, Lion, Hawk and Bull in Persian Mithraism (Mithras the mediator or Balance) to symbolise his achievement of the balance or nil point and subsequent oneness with the Cosmos. Everyone is happy that he has managed to regenerate and will not behave destructively now that he has refreshed his sovereignty with a living goddess. He can now go back to Scythia/Heaven and carry on reigning and being the wisdom and fertility of the land, and that is the end of it.

Shakespeare's version describes beautifully the emotions of enthea, and anyone who has experienced this divine union with another of the blood will not fail to be deeply moved, both with joy and sadness. Again this is another Solomonic, Vampire rite and proof yet again that vampirism is born of a love so deep that it tears the soul from the body, as this tale suggests. It also implies that the rite has to be repeated and that feeding must be recurrent.

The OTO call the "Rite of the Phoenix" the "Mass of the Vampire" for good reason. The Phoenix, along with the other birds in Shakespeare's poem are called Bennu Birds and are identified with each other by Kenneth Grant (*Magical Revival*) and this is because all classes of Druid are Vampires and need to feed in order to remain transcendent.

The Bennu Bird or Bird of Return symbolises a being that regenerates or must regenerate itself at regular intervals and the Vampire itself bears an appellation that is named after this process. In folklore, however, the

Vampire, as "one who returns" is mistaken for "one who returns from the grave" instead of "one who MUST return to feed and regenerate".

The Phoenix is symbolised in Transylvania by the double-headed Raven, brother of Lilith. This bird was adopted by the Hittites and came to symbolise the Holy Roman Empire in the corrupted form of an eagle. This Double-Headed Raven, the Phoenix, is the penultimate symbol of the Dragon people. In the last process of its regeneration, the Phoenix becomes The Star, the An of the Anunnagi, the Elves or Shining Ones: the ultimate symbol of the Dragon Race.

The Serpent N'H'SH

In translating the word N'H'SH, firstly we will take the Hebrew consonants back, via Phoenician, to their Sumerian roots and remember also that, in Sumerian, syllable groups could be reversed and yet still render the same meaning in an overall phrase. So, the N is *Nun*, the H is *Heth* (as opposed to *He*) and the SH is *Shin* (as opposed to either *Sade* or *Samekh*).

We check these through the Phoenician to ensure a continuity of shape in the correct pictograms as we venture back into the Sumerian and discover the following: Nun = Nag, Heth = H.A. and Shin = Salmunuz. Therefore from the Hebrew *Nahash* we derive the original Sumerian *Naghasalmunuz*, *Nagha Salmunuz* or NAG.HA.SAL.MUNUZ., which translates as Drink (NAG)—Fish (HA)—Vulva (SALMUNUZ).

If this sounds a bit odd, the author explains that a fish is "of water" and so in Sumerian the equivalent to our letter "A" means *water*, whilst the "H" is the article which stands for *of*. So the Hebrew N'H'SH—the Serpent—translates into the Sumerian *One (a Dragon) who—Drinks of (the) Water (of the) Vulva*.

One notices that in this phrase—Nagha Salmunuz—two things stand out. Firstly we have the Aryan word *Naga* spelt *Nagha* which would be pronounced with the *gh* sounding like a nasally, softly gargled *ch* (as in the Scottish word *loch*). According to the *OED*, "H" which in Sumerian was H.A., evolved into the Greek—(h)eta which was originally pronounced *kh*, which was pronounced as defined above, as an Iberian (Aryo-Scythian Celtic) *x* or *ch*.

In this way we can also justifiably spell Naga as *Naxa*, and we then begin to understand the profound relationship between the Naga guardians of the Aryan pantheons and the Nixes or Nixas of western Europe. They were, likewise, the female guardians of watery treasures, and like the Nagas or Naxas, these meremaids or Swan Maidens were Devas or Shining Ones (Anunnagi).

The second thing we notice is that the Sumerian word for a vulva is *Salmunuz*. Immediately the poetic connection between the "Sacred Vulva" (the Well of Nechtan [*Nixtan*]—the pure one, the Nix or Nothing) and the Salmon (Salmunuz) of Wisdom that swims in the well should spring to mind—as should the *Ichthys*—as being the vulva of the Virgin Mary Magdalene. Praise the Lord for the Single Poetic Theme!

In remembering that Sumerian can be reversed, we can look at the Hebrew N'H'SH again. We will see that if it is reversed, as was the custom in Hebrew Qabalah when rabbis were experimenting with language looking for hidden meanings, it becomes SH'H'N which is pronounced *She'an*, "of the Powers". Furthermore the numerical or gematric value of N'H'SH in Qabalah is 9, which is the number of Yesod, the Sephira of the Moon, whose Phoenician God was the Sumerian SIN or SHIN—*She'en*.

The symbols associated with SIN included the Axe, the Labrys which is a device which, as we know, depicts the Vulva. The Axe symbol, prevalent in Mittani and Minoan Cretan culture, became the spinning Hammer of Thor (the Swastika) who, as Zeus, was the wielder of the lightning bolt. This, in northern Europe, was symbolised by the Norse "Sig" Rune. Sig—the lightning bolt of inspiration (cf. Mead of Inspiration)—is the Greek Sigma which is the Hebrew Shin, the last consonant of N'H'SH, and SIN—Sumerian god of the Moon.

Sig is the serpentine lightning bolt that courses down the Qabalistic Tree of Life. In one sense it represents Enki-Samael entwined around Lilith. The upturned crescent moon is also said to be associated with Samael (Sumaire-El) and, in an ancient Sumerian picture reproduced by Langdon, the moon as a dish is depicted next to the Star of Anu, below which is the serpent N'H'SH entwined around the tree, symbolising Lilith.

Finally we must consider Tiamat. Her name—TI.A.MAT—means *life-water-maiden*. This translates as "maiden of the waters of life" and it is then clear that her name indicates she was both the first known matriarch and virgin priestess—the "feeding mother"—of the Vampire Dragon queens and kings. The mother of the Elven dynasty, she was the generatrix of a Vampire lineage of goddess-queens and god-kings spanning seven thousand years.

She was a Nagha or *Nixa* and it is from her that Lilith, and all the ensuing Grail Maidens, including Sheba and Morgana of the Apple Trees, Tamaris, Mary Magdalene, the Princesses of Avalon, Melusine, Niniane and Ygraine owe their identifications as "Trees of Life". Consequently we can say that Tiamat, the first Tamaris—the Maiden who gives the Waters of Life—was also the Tir Mat or *Tir Mata*, the first "Tree Mother" of the Lords and Ladies of the Forest, the Druids and Druidesses—the People of the Trees (of Life).

Two of the younger gods of the Aryans, the Adityas, *Tara* and *Bhaga*, stand out prominently. As we have seen, Ulick Beck and several other scholars have traced the origin of the Scythian-Irish Tuadha d'Anu to the same region as the Aryans, and have gone as far as saying that they were one and the same. Interestingly we find that the goddess Tara—wife of Rudra, Indra's charioteer, appears in Eire as Tara, the Hill or Rath of ghosts in County Meath, Eire. Tara was the sacred centre of the united Irish kingdom and was the seat of the Danaan Kings of Tara during the Iron Age.

Some scholars attribute the name of Tara in Eire to some complicated sounding god name which I find implausible in light of the fact that a Goddess Tara already existed in the Scythian-Aryan pantheon. Whether it be Asura or Aditya, Danaan or Milesian, all of the ancient Goddess Queens were the source of sovereignty associated with sacred mounds. It therefore seems entirely appropriate to name a Sidhe Rath, a portal to the Otherworld and thus the source of sovereignty, after a goddess who would herself have represented sovereignty.

In the case of Bhaga, or *Vaga*, as his name would have been pronounced in Gaelic, scholars think that he became the Slavic god Bogh, a word which came to mean "god" in Thrace, where the Danaan Fir Bolg were once exiled prior to their return to Ireland. In Fir Bolg we either have the title "men of God", meaning Druids, or we have, as is commonly thought, "men of the bags". This means "men of God" anyway, because the "bag", specifically the "Crane Skin Bag", was an accessory of the Godthi's and the Druid's: the "men of the gods".

Chapter 14

Myth or Reality? The World of J.R.R. Tolkien

Considering the foregoing, it is interesting to note that in Tolkien's *Silmarillion*—the background mythology that supports his *Lord of the Rings*—we find a vocabulary and etymology that includes the following words—*Ainur, Ainu, Vala, Maiar, Eldar, Ea*.

Tolkien's word *Ainur* means the "Holy Ones", of which the singular is Ainu. There are two orders of these gods in his mythology—the *Valar* and the *Maiar*. The plural Ainur and the singular Ainu are clearly derived from the Sumerian father of the gods—Anu and the Anunnaki, whilst Valar appears in the Aryan pantheon as Vala "The Encircler", reminiscent of the Orobourus, the alchemical Dragon Ring that Tolkien wrote so much about. We will also remember the Val-Kyrie at this juncture.

The word *Maia* is spelt *Maja* in Spanish and denotes a female line of nobility and royalty. The "i" was originally "j" and came, along with the word *majesty*, from the Latin *majes* or *majus*, a variant of which is *magi* or *Magus*, from the Greek *magos*—a bloodline member of a caste or genetic strain comprised of individuals heritably steeped in magic. (*OED*) In other words, it was the Arya—or Scythian Derkesthai—the Dragon Goddess Queens and God Kings.

At this point we return to the concept of the *Derkesthai* and the bloodline of the Dragon god-kings—the Asuras and the Anunnaki. In the *Silmarillion*, *Maia* becomes Maiar. It accords with the ancient concept of deific royalty—

Maia—which, related to *Mana*, is the "spirit of the gods carried in the blood". This is the attribute of a goddess-queen or god-king of the Dragon who are in themselves collectively an "order of the gods"—the "Elves" —the shining ones—or "gods incarnate"—the Devas and Avatars.

The "spirits of the gods—the ancestors—carried in the blood", we will remember, are the spirits summoned from the "deeps", the subconscious, by the Witch (Vampire or Druid). He gains her or his name—*Wicce* or *Wicca*—from the ability to yield or bend to, or rather to draw to the surface of consciousness, these spiritual intelligences and their wisdom from her or his ancestral, and thus genetic, inheritance. In other words their waking consciousness is pacified or "yields", to allow the older spirit, or racial memory, to give voice.

Avatar is a word Tolkien included in his Silmarillion as *Aratar*, the eight most powerful of his Valar or order of old gods. It seems obvious that these were intended to mimic the Egyptian gods of the Ogdoad, the eight Anunnaki who tended the Holy Mountain after the Black Sea flood.

Another of Tolkien's words, similar to Avatar (Avathar to him) means "The Shadows", which he uses as a name for a land near his "Bay of Eldemar". Comparably, in our world, an Avatar is a "god made flesh"—a Dragon King or Queen who often occupied tombs and would have been thought of as a "shadow", a spirit of the Otherworld, from the realm of the Shining Ones.

Therefore in the Vala and Maiar we have two orders of gods taken from the Dragon tradition itself. Bearing this in mind, according to the legends of Tolkien's Elves, the word *Eldar* became used as a name for the three Elven kindreds, one of which Tolkien named the Vanyar, who appear to be the Vanir Gods of the Danes, cousins of the Tuadha d'Anu.

Tolkien's largest variety of wicked Orcs he named the Uruks. Uruk is a City-State of the Anunnaki. The Orcs, he said, were once fair Elves who had been imprisoned and tortured in the Land of Mordor.

"Eldar", explains Tolkien, means "People of the Stars", echoing a traditional Gaelic epithet for the Tuadha d'Anu and also one of the original meanings of the name Anunnaki—People of the Stars.

Of men, Tolkien concurs that they are the second, younger race which his Elves called the *Atani* (Adamae), a name, says Tolkien, that later became the *Edain*, obviously the *children of Eden*. Again we have a borrowing of Dragon Lore where the Elves, the Children of Anu, the Anukim or Repha'im of the Old Testament, appeared first, followed by our Adamae, or the Atani as Tolkien would have it.

Edain is obviously Eden, whilst he uses Ea as a name for the Earth which in Sumerian is the name for the Dragon god of the "Earth and Waters"—Enki-Samael, the leader of the elder "Eldar" gods—the Aesir. Tolkien, in his epic works, with their plethora of borrowed names and borrowed linguistics and their elder and younger races, is obviously writing about the family. This is particularly so when one peruses his vocabulary and discovers the name Avallónë, a haven and city of the Eldar—the Elves—situated on "the lonely isle"—*Tol Eressea*. This was drawn across the ocean and rooted finally in the Bay of Eldemar, adjacent to *Avathar*—the land of Shadows: our Avalon or Otherworld.

The various names by which our planet is known all stem from the word Eridu, which was the first city founded by Enki-Samael in Mesopotamia. As a variant of Eridu, in the Silmarillion, Tolkien has Eriador and his Elven word for Earth is Arda, which is also derived from Eridu.

The Origin of the Dragon Lords of the Rings

The following are technical support notes to the essays included in this work. As such there will be numerous repetitions of the subjects covered, however, a wealth of extra material follows which could not be drawn in detail into the narrative of the essays.

The Sabbatical Goat

The symbol of the goat's head in the inverted pentagram is said to be the traditional glyph of medieval European Satanic Witchcraft. Since that time the Sabbatical Goat has become ubiquitous throughout the left-hand path of occultism. The letters around the perimeter, usually displayed in Hebrew consonants in common usage, spell L'V'Th'N: Leviathan. In apocryphal Jewish holy literature it was Lilith, fleeing to the Red Sea, who became identified with the Leviathan, a sea monster, often portrayed as a giant serpent or Draken.

The colours used in representations of the above are invariably red on black. Although thought of as Satanic, these colours on the Aziluth or Imperial level of the Cabalistic Tree of Life are not Satanic at all, but are Sacred to Binah. The Emperor is red, representing dynamism, and the Empress is black, representing the primordial sea of Understanding or Being; i.e. Space/Time. Red and Black were used by Cathars, who tied their Blue-Black Robes (cf. Sufi cloaks) with the hated "little Red Cord". This also appears as the Garter or Points in Scottish Witchcraft. The use of a red cord has a twofold symbolism in that it is also identified as the woollen cord that was wrapped around the horns of the Scapegoat of Jewish history. The Scapegoat was identified as Azazel, an angel or Nephilim/Watcher, a prototype of the later sacrificial God/King. The Red Thread or Rtus, placed around the goat's horns represents the menstrual flow. This acknowledged that the goat's head represents the goddess. It also represents the application of the menstruus on the mind of the sacrificial king who would then transcend and take the prayers of the people to the underworld.

The later ritual of the scapegoat, where one goat is sent to wander in the wilderness, is a precursor to the actual killing of a priest king who would also be expected to take the supplications of his tribe and present them to the gods. As with all religious ritual, the substance becomes lost and is replaced by the form of obsessive, habitual activity which, wrongly, is considered in itself to be efficacious.

Binah is ruled by the Planet Saturn or Chronos. This takes us into the Titanic period of civilisation which preceded the Jehovan or Olympic age. The sacred flower of Binah is the Lily and its tree is the Cypress, used for both funerals and weddings (i.e. both destruction and creation). Its sacred animal is the bee, the Sacred Mason and the drinker of the nectar of the Lily. Uniting the concept of marriage (sexual union) with death (negation) is Tantric/Proto Cabalistic and therefore Aryan; and therefore Ubaid in origin. The sex-negation concept is central to the theory of hierogamy, divine union and Courtly Love which is expressed in alchemy and inextricably linked to the drinking of the "nectar" of the Lily and the Rose.

This is the true meaning of the Merovian Bee, which in its use by them was also intended to link them with the forgoing concepts and the Primordial Sea, the waters of Chaos or Tiamat as well as Lilith.

Saturn (Anu) and Lilith's sacred colour is purple, which is the origin of its use by Emperors and kings. Displaying this colour denotes their descent from Lilith and also the Titans.

Saturn is the predominant planetary sphere ruling Capricorn, whose planetary archangel or nephilim was Azazel. The Sabbatical Goat developed from Khem (formerly Azazel) whose cult was centred upon the Temple of Mendes. Later Grecian expressions of this cult cast the Khem as Pan who, by the medieval period, had become Pan-Khem: the Solar-Goat deity of the French Witches. Trained by the Templars and Cathars, they provided, in a very basic form, a plebeian and religious variant of the more complex scientific and genealogical tenets of those whom they supported. To them, "Satan", the Sabbatical Goat, was the "Good God", the liberator from Church oppression and the iron grip of their other Christianised overlords.

The principal figure at these Sabbats was a figure with a shining gold torso and the head and legs of a goat. It was revered as the Black and Gold Sun, echoing the origins of Khem as a solar deity but also embodying the Draconian symbol of Sirius, the Black Sun or eight pointed star.

In England Khem-Pan was known as Puck, the son of Titania (Titans) and Robin Hood or Robin Goodfellow. Goodfellow is reminiscent of "The Good Folk" and provides one of many links between English and Scottish Witchcraft and the Fairies, who are also called the Gentry (because they literally were the lords and nobles of many districts) and "Shining Ones".

British Sabbats were overseen by a "Man-in-Black", usually the local Lord or Baron who was worshipped as the God of the Sabbat, i.e. Robin or Satan, Pan or Khem.

Witchcraft in Europe and Britain was run by the Templars and Cathars and provided the groundswell of support at the grassroots level for the Fairy, also known as Grail, also known as Dragon families and the doctrines which made them distinct. Witchcraft is original Christianity, practising Christian gnostic Dualism and providing, in their tens of thousands, an army of support for the scions of Christ.

The Church persecuted Templars, Cathars and Witches equally as heretics. If Witchcraft was, as the more modern apologists claim, a pagan religion, it would not have attracted the animosity of the Church, who only prosecuted heterodox Christians.

A final note on Chronos/Saturn/Anu. He was the inventor of Agriculture and thus may be identified with the Annunaki of Sumeria who also developed advanced farming techniques and settled agriculture. Wherever one travels in the world, the figure of Saturn is invariably depicted as an old man with a beard leaning on a staff. This occurs even in societies where the members don't grow facial hair themselves. He was the Grim Reaper, the god who controlled the fate of man. As such, he was in the fullest and most precise terms the God-King of the Fairies, the Fata or Fates.

Pan was the son of Hermes. Hermes was an intermediary between the gods and man, a prototype of the Pontiff or bridge, the God-King. As Mercury he is also identified with Odin, another sacrificial god, whose totem animals, the Raven and the wolf, both feature as grades of initiation in Mithraism and are specific grades of Vampire in Romanian tradition. The Stregoica or wolf-Vampire (werewolf) of Romanian tradition derives from the root word Strega, which is Latin, and where Stregoica is a Vampire in Romanian (which is a Roman language), in Italian a Strega is a Witch. The Turkish for Vampire is Uber, a Witch. Note the German, Übermensch, meaning demi-god or superman..

Mithras is a balancing factor between good and evil, an intermediary very much like Hermes. Odin, as the one-eyed God, mediates between the worlds and to gain the wisdom of both hanged upon Ygdrassil, a Lilith-Samael symbol of the Tree of Life/Knowledge. As a blinded god, he is reminiscent of the blind serpent who mediated between Lilith and Samael at their union.

Chem-Zoroaster

Ham is known traditionally as Chem. In Hermetics and Dualism he is known as Chem-Zoroaster, "a great and venerable Magus", the 10th Archon of the Age of Capricorn. As Archon or representative, he is identified with Capricorn as its physical manifestation, i.e. he is Capricorn.

Originally the symbol for Capricorn was a creature half goat, half sea monster. This takes us back to the inverted pentagram of the Sabbatical Goat encircled by the word (also meaning issuing from the space or womb of)

Leviathan who is the Sea Monster (Lilith), and Sea Dragon of primordial chaos (Tiamat). Therefore the Sabbatical Goat is Capricorn the Sea Goat.

As the Egyptian God, the Sabbatical Goat is Khem, the solar deity of Mendes. Khem is a variant spelling of Chem who is Ham, the Archon of Capricorn and Capricorn incarnate. Ham, the accursed one of the Christian Bible, moved to Egypt. As a Dragon God-King of the Line of Annunaki, the originators and Draconian Patrons of human kingship, Ham or Chem-Zoroaster—became Khem the first Sebekh. The Sebekh is the Crocodile (water/sea Dragon or Leviathan) God, who is the Patron of Kingship. He wears a solar (cf. Khem) disc upon his forehead suspended between two (goat) horns. Ham or Chem is Sobekh 1st; T'Ham'Pthis, the first Dragon king of Egypt to use the Sebekh title and thus proclaim his right to create kings, and was the first God King of the Egyptian Cult of Draco.

The Sobekh title may distinguish the grafted line of the immigrant Dragon kings of Sumeria from the indigenous Semitic, Nubian and other dynasties. Ham as Chem-Zoroaster and also as Khem and later Pan, son of Hermes, is closely linked to the concept of Aryan Dualism and its symbol—the entwined serpents, Mazda and Ahriman, light and dark.

Mazda is Ormuzd and Ahriman is Enlil or Jehovah. Ormuzd derives from the Indo-European Orm, a worm or Dragon and Masd, white or light, hence white worm (see Vampire mythology) or Dragon of Light. Ahriman is thus the Dragon of Darkness, hence the Satanic inversion "Good is Evil and Evil is Good". The entwined serpents or Dragons appear as the serpents of the caduceus of Hermes, who is father of Pan, the Goat-headed solar deity Khem. The caduceus is crowned with a solar winged-disc and the entwined serpents are reminiscent of the double-helix ribbons of the thyrsis wand of Dionysus, which is crowned by the pine cone, depicting the pineal gland. The symbols are variants of each other in a Hermetic sense.

Dionysus was the son of Zeus. The worship of Dionysus was brought from India by the Alexandrian Greeks. Zeus, his father, was known as the Indian or Aryan Dispater, which translates as Deus Pater or father god, also known as Enlil or Jehovah. If Hermes can be identified as a variant of Mithras, who was descended from the Aryan Zirvan, then Hermes is either an uncle or brother of Dionysus. Zirvan is Time. Saturn or Chronos is Old Father Time.

Therefore Zirvan and Saturn are identifiable. Consequently Mithras is Hermes, son of Chronos, who also fathered Zeus. Hermes and Zeus are brothers. If Zeus is Enlil, then Hermes is Enki, Samael, Masdoa (Mazda, i.e. Mazda is Mithras). Hermes is the father of Pan and Zeus is the father of Dionysus. Pan and Dionysus are always featured in the same retinue and, as Bacchus, Pan's rites duplicate those of his twin, Dionysus. The totem animals of Dionysus are the Panther (cf. Jesus ben Panther), the Goat and the wolf (Stregoica, werewolf, Mithraic totem, etc.). Other symbols include the basket with alchemical eggs and serpents. The Dionysic Rites were cannibalistic and Vampiric and echo the era of cannibalism and vampirism of the sons of the Nephilim (the era of Titans).

If Zirvan is the Titan Chronos, father of Zeus-Enlil, then Chronos is Anu, who is the son of Apsu or Uranus. The union between Hermes (Samael) and Aphrodite (Venus, as in Venus-Sheba-Lilith) included the nymph Salmacis with whom they enjoined much, as with Samael, Lilith and the blind serpent. Hermes is the uncle of Dionysus, who is the cousin of Pan.

The Baphomet

In Draconian Tradition (see Kenneth Grant) Baphomet is translated as Bapho Mitra or Father Mithras. Baphomet is also rendered as Head or Source of Wisdom. If Baphomet is rendered Father (or Source) Mithras, and Mithras is identified as Samael the Dragon, then one has the Source or Head Dragon, the origin of PenDragon.

Baphomet, the "Deity" of the Templars, was described as being both the Head of Wisdom, which has Celtic and Galatian origins, and the Sabbatical Goat. The Sabbatical Goat, in the form of the Templar glyph also used by the Cathars, the medieval Witches and later generally by satanists and left-hand path occultists, was more complex than the simple pentagram. Baphomet was pictured as a cross-legged figure (cf. Cernunnos and Krishna, both Lords of the Forests and identifiable with Herne the Hunter. He is Annwn and Odin, who led the Wild Hunt in search of "Fairy Women" (sic) with the head and legs of a goat, the scaly torso of a Dragon, the breasts of a woman and the phallus of a man.

Baphomet has Angel's Wings (Swan's feathers) and a torch between its horns. Its right arm is raised with index and forefinger extended. On the forearm is written the word Coagula. The fingers point to the new moon. Its left arm points down and to the side and the index and little finger are extended to form the horns of the goat. The fingers point to the old or black moon (Kali). On the left forearm is written the word Solve. Solve and Coagula are alchemical terms; spiritual death and resurrection played out in the perennial concept of Enthea.

On its forehead there is displayed a pentagram with its single point uppermost. In the simpler form, the goat's head traces the figure of the inverted pentagram and thus it is to be understood that one pentagram equals the other. Therefore, if the single-point pentagram represents the Goddess, then she and the Goat are one, as is represented by the combining of male and female sexual attributes in one symbol. Such a thorough union of the two sexes negates the individuality of both. On the magical level this again represents death (of the selves) through marriage of the two, leading to the alchemical, tantric concept of illumination. This occurs through hierogamy facilitated by the cubic jewel (Emerald of Venus) depicted in the inverted pentagram where the conjunction of the geometric lines with those of the crutch of the horns forms the "Jewel in the Crown of Lucifer", the cubic stone or Grail. Again, when reversed, the simpler pentagram represents the goddess.

The goat's chin becomes her head, its ears her arms, and its horns her legs. The Jewel, the emerald cubic stone, then becomes her vulva and womb. Baphomet reflects this idea with the conjoining of the goat head and upright pentagram and enlarges upon the idea by displaying a flame between the horns. The Flame is Womb Fire or Starfire, enlightenment through the fluid of the womb.

The sex and death idea, as we have discovered, belongs to Binah and the various attributes and symbols of that Sephira should be recollected in relation to the Baphomet symbol.

The wings of Baphomet are Swan's wings. This immediately speaks of the Swan Princes, Grail Princesses and Fairy Queens which symbolise the Dragon blood. Baphomet is a Nephilim. Its legs are the legs of Pan. Its head is the head of Khem, which conjoined to the serpent or Dragons torso representing Leviathan. This indicates the same as the Sabbatical Pentagram. The figure represents Ham or Chem or Khem-Zoroaster the Sebekh, Archon and incarnation of Capricorn, the goat-headed Dragon of the Sea.

Entwined around the phallus of Baphomet are the serpents of the type represented on the caduceus of Hermes. This also reinforces the Zirvan-Mithras-Ahriman identification. The Phallus as staff or Tree of Life is the Plantagenista in one sense which, in being capped by an egg, is the symbol of potential which qualifies the image. Conclusion: Baphomet is a type of Chem-Zoroaster who is the Quinotaur associated with Meroveus.

Baphomet and the Mendes pentagram are genealogical badges—early forms of heraldry—incorporating the symbolism of the blood rites. Note: We have shown the connection between Merovingians—Bees—Binah—Primordial Sea—Chaos—Tiamat—Dragon Queen. Therefore Merovingians = Dragons. The inverted pentagram and goat symbol is not Satanic, it is a dynastic marker. Satanism, as devil worship, is just Catholicism inverted.

The Picts

Whilst the Picts endured internal exile in Scotland, their distant cousins faired less well in England and Wales. Foreign encroachment had been intense in these countries and forestry had been decimated. Both populations north and south of the border were less technologically advanced and adaptable than the incomers, being essentially nomadic Priest Kings and not farmers. However the Picts in Scotland managed to survive longer than those on the rest of the island, who were forced to live in less and less space as time went on. Both cultures became even more insular because of their inability to cope with living outside the forests. Instead they retained their kinships and their culture separately from the outside world, venturing out to steal in order to supplement the dwindling resources in their own wooded kingdoms, or waylaying travellers who dared to trespass on their greenwood domains.

With the marriage of King Kenneth MacAlpin to Princess Uistnecc of the Picts in the 9th century, the Pictish and Scottish Kingdoms became united and many Lords and Princes of the Dalriada sought magical Pictish Princesses for themselves. In this manner, many Picts slowly became integrated within Scottish society and left their Forest Kingdoms forever to follow their Ladies and Lords. However not all succumbed to life outside the domain of the ancient woodland and a sufficient number remained to sustain both kingship and culture in the manner of their ancestors, against a new encroachment and a far more insidious threat—the rise of Roman Christianity.

By MacAlpin's era, the Catholic Church had enacted the Donation of Constantine (312 AD) for some centuries and had attempted to divest all but their own Client Royal Houses of the right of Kingship. By implementing policies of regicide and controlled marriage, the Church had attempted to breed out the pre-Carolingian royal bloodlines that stood for genuine kingship, and thus posed a potential threat to the stranglehold that the Church had gained over the monarchy.

By the medieval period a new weapon had emerged from the Vatican arsenal—the Inquisition. As the Grail and Pictish Royal and Noble Houses followed a separate spiritual path to that laid down in 325 AD at the Council of Nicaea, those houses and their retainers and supporters were subjected to several hundred years of persecution and terror. This was done ostensibly to purify the Christian Faith of heresy and rid the world of Witchcraft. In fact it was simply to thin out the opposition.

Pictish and Merovingian spiritual doctrines varied but were born from the same root tradition that Jesus followed, that being the Indo-Aryan Priest Caste, the Magi or Druids. This set of doctrines, so at variance with the Church's pretend-version of Jesus' teaching, was labelled Witchcraft and heresy. Countless people died as a result of believing in it and supporting the Royal and Noble Houses who were its hidden Priests and Priest Kings.

In Scotland and France many noble houses of Merovingian and Pictish descent were massacred and the Inquisition took on the proportions of a "holy" crusade, which often destroyed whole towns and villages. In England the Kings from William Rufus' time were far less inclined to indulge the Pope. The Angevin Houses were barely Christian themselves and had far more than "just a smattering" of both Danaan and Merovingian blood.

Consequently, up until the Tudor period the Witch craze in England was by comparison quite a sedate and subdued affair. Indeed the very "Fairy Kingships" that the Vatican were so scared of and were trying to eradicate, were actually recognised, lauded and supported by a succession of English monarchs. These included Richard I, Edward III, Henry VIII and Elizabeth I, despite the questionable provenance and claims of the two latter monarchs and their institution of illegal constitutional practices.

These ancient Kingships were ritually observed in the old families within which the right descended. The pre-Christian King in a late post-Christian setting was often called Robert or Robin Hood or Goodfellow. Often associated with Witchcraft, his realm, like his Fairy ancestors the Picts, was the Greenwood and his subjects were the pagan rustics who inhabited every district across the country. The stories of the coven meetings by dead of night in the forest deep or in the open moor are stories of the survival of a culture and its kingship. It precedes the coming of the Romans, the Saxons and the Church with its fraudulent and thus spurious form of Christian Monarchy.

Though two reasonably distinct but related lines, the Pictish and the Merovingian cultures amalgamated in Britain symbolically in the merging of the French and Scottish Arthurian legends and the Pictish tales of the Forest Lords and Ladies. A close study of the characters and some of the events in both traditions will reveal that not only are they similar to each other but they bare a striking resemblance to the story of Jesus who, in Celtic Christianity, is termed a Magus and Druid. This appears to be the problem as far as the Church was concerned.

Having broadcast the idea that Jesus, the rightful King, had no descendants, the way was left open for his "appointed" apostles, the Roman Bishops to assume the role of kingship. However, there still persisted the stubborn insistence in some families that they and not the Church were the rightful kings of the people by blood descent from Christ. In the matter of both Robin and Arthur, the Merovingians and the Picts, it was well known by Roman clerics that the line of Jesus and the line of the Tuatha de Danaan originated from the same Royal bloodline. They realised that all the time that line remained in existence, the Church was in danger of being toppled by a popular movement led by one of these dynasties.

Therefore the Church demonised Robin and pronounced the Grail heretical. Nevertheless, in the late medieval period in Scotland, England and France, the "Witches" still met and the Local Noble of the Blood Royal would preside as Robin Hood, Robin Goodfellow, Samael, L'Homme Noir or the "Devil". He was accompanied by his Queen and Priestess, the Diana or Marian. In Tudor England, Henry VIII reconstituted Priest-Kingship and his daughter, Elizabeth the "Fairy Queen", was excommunicated for refusing to allow the Catholics back into power. A case of right action, wrong actors.

The Stag of Windsor

Before Elizabeth was crowned by the Bishops, she underwent coronation by the people. Attending the ceremony were a host of "Wild Forest Dwellers" who had come to bless the new Queen. Later in her reign she attended a curious ceremony in the Forest of Windsor Great Park.

Seated before a pavilion in a clearing one spring morning, Queen Elizabeth, with her complicity and consent, presided over one of the most ancient Druidic and shamanic ceremonies in Eurasian culture. A ceremony that harked back to the time when much of Britain and the continent was covered by massive forests, namely the trial and accession of the King of the Caille Daouine, the Lord of the Forest.

The King of the Forest is the Stag of Nine Tines. In the lays of Robin Hood, Robin himself is revealed as the Green Stag and the Totem is repeatedly interwoven into the fabric of ancient northern Kingship. In pre-Christian and non-Christian Europe, to claim the Kingship of the vast Greenwood, the pretender was obliged to ride and kill whilst mounted, the great Stag of Nine Tines.

This task was possibly one of the most dangerous stunts anyone could pull. During the Spring Rut the Stag is vicious, belligerent and half mad with lust and territorial rage. Getting anywhere near him was a feat of courage in itself. However, to be rightly invested with the true kingship of the Forest Peoples, it was first necessary to depose the reigning monarch, the Great Stag.

On the spring morning in question one of Elizabeth's favourites, the Queen's Chamberlain, Edward de Vere, charged into the clearing mounted upon the great Stag of Windsor Forest. Its throat had been cut by the rider, and he and the Stag came to an abrupt halt at the Queen's feet. Edward de Vere was the premier Count of England and the senior Peer of the Realm. His lineage was far superior to that of Elizabeth, he descended from the House of Anjou, from Melusine and the ancient Pictish and Danaan Druid Kings of Gaul, Albany and Eire.

A necromancer, anti-Christian and libertine, Edward had contempt for the Tudors. He was a scholar under Dr John Dee and it is still insisted that Edward was the true William Shakespeare, whose work is teeming with stories of Elphame and Magic. Edward de Vere, Christopher Marlowe, Francis Bacon, Sir Walter Raleigh, Edmund Spenser, Edward Kelly and John Dee comprised the Secret Elizabethan Magical Cabal immortalised as the "School of Night" in the Bard's "Love's Labours Lost". Shakespeare's Oberon is Alberic, whose name literally means Elf King, whilst his Titania is Diana, whose Druidic, woad coloured Boar wears her crescent Moon upon its flank in the crest of the ancient family of Vere.

Three of Edward's recent ancestors had borne the name Alberic. The first of them in England had adopted also the falling star of Lucifer as a badge to denote, as Verily Anderson expresses it, the Vere's "near divinity" as descendants of the line of priest kingship that originated with the first Elf King—Samael or Lucifer.

What the Queen had attended and approved was the investiture of an ancient Forest King who, in her time, would have been the spiritual custodian of the hidden royal blood and the true cultural legacy of the British people.

For centuries the tales of Robin Hood had circulated around Britain. The ritual investiture of de Vere can be added to the corpus of that spiritual tradition which, apart from the obvious confusions between the ceremonial Forest Kings, the real Robin Hoods, and the plethora of common or garden murderers, villains and kidnappers, has thrived everywhere there has been a Grail family supported by the People, assuming their regional roles as the ancient Priest Kings and Priestess Princesses of the Dragon and the Greenwood.

Some one hundred and fifty years after Edward de Vere, a Scottish cousin of his was the hereditary chief of the 13 covens of Mid-Lothian. A Consort of the Queen of Elphame (a descendant of the early Pictish or "Fairy" Princesses), Major Thomas Weir, Laird of Kirkton and the infamous sorcerer of Edinburgh, had himself conducted the ancient rite of Druidic Kingship in the ceremony of Epona. Major Weir is Byron's Mannfred and is celebrated by Sir Walter Scott.

Professor Margaret Murray insists that he was, like his cousins and ancestors, a Priest King of the Elven Line of the Grail and the Dragon. In 1670 he and his sister were convicted of Witchcraft and burned at the stake. His trial records show that his conviction for being a Witch depended entirely upon whether or not he (and his sister) had been servants or consorts of the Fairies. They had, and they died for it. The Earl of Bothwell is said to have replaced him in 1690.

Attempts have often been made to identify "The Real Robin Hood". Numerous characters have been put forward as likely candidates and perhaps the nearest anyone has got to pinning him down was Professor Murray when she identified Robin Hood as a collection of composites from many regions and many times. At the heart of her theory is the assertion that Robin was a god figure that was at the centre of the cult of Witchcraft.

Indeed this is the case, as is her discovery that the Witches' god was represented at the Sabbats by one or other individual who, regardless of the regional or cultural variation of the period, invariably descended from a Grail or Dragon-Fairy family. The rituals of Witchcraft were varied and contained syntheses of Catharist and Templar Dualism, Druidism and Bacchanalian practices. The Dianic rites were observed by the Royal Covens, and generally the "religion" of Witchcraft more closely resembled Jesus' own doctrine than the Church itself.

This is borne out by the Druids' ready acceptance of Celtic Christianity, and the fact that Jesus' original, undoctored Gnostic teachings were founded on Essene Magian philosophy amalgamated with the mystical doctrines of Mithras and Dionysus. Alchemy, Cabala and Hermetics were the centre of Christ's philosophy. All the foregoing are components of that Eurasian "religion" we know as Druidism which, for the Indians is Hinduism and for the Persians is Zoroastrianism—and, in the West, eventually became our Celtic Christianity.

Robin Hood or Robert Hod or Od is Odin—the Blinded God "Samael". As Master of the Wild Hunt, he is Herne and Cernunnos, the Lord of the Forest. In Hinduism he is also the Lord of the Forest as Vishnu, in his incarnation as the Blue Boar. As Samael he is also Pan and Khem, Chem-Zoroaster and Mazda. The Son of Anu is a Dragon King of the Danaan. He is Herne—The Great Stag of Nine Tines—the King of the Ancient Eurasian Forests. Jesus played his part as evidenced by St. Augustine's letter to his disciple Ceretius in 400 AD. Augustine states that Jesus often sat cross-legged in the middle of a circle of his followers in the manner of Pan or the Templars' Baphomet, and he would play an accompaniment to their ring dances, invoking aloud the Ogdoad or Eight Great planetary Spirits of the Gnosis. English and European Woodcuts of the Reformation period show Pan or "Robin Goodfellow" engaged with his Witches in identical firelit, woodland frolics. If he were alive during the medieval period, Jesus Christ our Saviour would have been arraigned by the Inquisition and tried and burned at the Stake for both heresy and Witchcraft!

Chapter 15

Jesus Mac Art

The word Jesus used to describe his assembly was "Church". The word derives from "Circa", a Ring or Circle. In the Celtic Christian period, going to Church was called "Going to the Stones" or Stone Circles. Jesus was a Messiah or Dragon King. Those who followed him by blood descent, either through the Davidic Merovingian lines or through the Scythian descent of the Dragon Kings of Anu, both of which lines have a common origin and share many historical dynastic alliances, often assumed, as Jesus did, the role of the "Robin Hood".

Perhaps the name varied from country to country or from region to region but the identity was essentially the same, and the figures of the pageant of the Elven Kings of the Forest were perennial. Even Charlemagne, who wed an eastern Fairy Princess, belongs in the cycle of stories celebrating the continuity of the blood of the Dragon Queens and Grail Kings. His wedding to Frastrada was blessed by the appearance at the feast by a Dragon bearing in its mouth an Alchemist's Ring of Power, which it dropped into Charlemagne's chalice of blood red wine.

One might suggest that the Dragon Bloodline had forgiven the treachery of Charlemagne's fathers, and reconciled his House with the Merovingian Kings who had established it, by which they had effectively been betrayed as a result of the cunning wiles of the Roman Church. I doubt it though.

Charlemagne was a Merovingian caught at the back end of a dynastic reshuffle not unlike many other Merovingian dynastic reshuffles. Essentially his was fractionally the blood of the Grail and the Dragon, but the spirit of his house was slowly being twisted and condemned to servitude under a religion which claims him as being one of its greatest champions. Similarly it claimed that his predecessor, Constantine, took a timely baptism on his deathbed. It should be noted that history is written by the victors, and in retrospect the victors, from our point of view, have been the Church who rewrote history time and time again to suit their own ambitions.

Charlemagne belongs, if anywhere, to a variation of the Grail myth known as the Ring Cycle. Although Charlemagne is hailed as a hero of the Catholic faith he, like others who proceeded him, has what the Church might consider to be a dark undercurrent to his nature. On the surface he is a Christian emperor but even so, he accepts from a "Dragon" the gift of a Ring which, not unlike those of Solomon, was regarded by the Church as a symbol of Satan.

The Ring of Power, the Alchemist's Oroborus, was the figure of a Dragon or Serpent encurved into a circle and set in the act of biting its own tail. It was the symbol both of eternity and, as the symbol of primordial chaos, the Dragon Ring also represented Tiamat, the mother of Anu, the Nephilim and the Titans.

From these ancient Deific Rulers descended Lilith and Samael and the Race of Cain and Ham, the archenemies of the Church and, as they would have it, the archenemies of Man. The story of Charlemagne's Dragon Ring, rather than being allowed to stand unmolested, has become something of a morality tale. To remove the dark undercurrent and remove any doubt that Charlemagne was the Church's biggest supporter, the tale features a Merlin/Friar Tuck/Judas Priest figure called Bishop Turpin who, seeing that Charlemagne has become obsessed with the ring, steals it and throws it into a lake. This he does for Charlemagne's own good, you understand, and not in any way to:

a) pervert Charlemagne's attention from his true origins in order that he concentrate more on being a Christian, or

b) rob Charlemagne of a traditional Druidic source of power and divination, which were the functions of Solomon's Dragon Rings.

Of course not. Turpin was thinking solely of the good of his friend and acted entirely out of altruism for the Emperor. Having thrown the ring in a lake, the story twists upon itself again and recounts that Charlemagne was led, as if by spirits, to the very same lake, with which he became inexplicably obsessed to such a degree that he built a palace next to it.

If anything, the story illustrates that those of the Dragon Blood cannot deny their heritage, which eventually will find them, despite what they believe or where they are situated geographically or socially. Even if that heritage is "stolen" or discarded, it will still be there in the pool of the subconscious. Because it is genetic, once it is switched on it can never be completely switched off again, however much ridicule, disbelief or hostility it engenders from within or without.

The Church heard about Charlemagne's ring and stole it, but he never abandoned it or the heritage it represented, so the Church recounts that this Evil Ring obsessed him until the end of his days. Canines and feeding troughs come to mind. This story belongs to the Ring Cycle which inspired Tolkien, who unfortunately has inverted the Ring in much the same way as the Church did.

Tolkien's characters nevertheless are taken from the Dragon and Grail Families who, like Robin Hood, actually existed in one form or another. The Ring of Power, the Dragon and the Grail are exactly one and the same female symbol of sovereignty, nurture and subsequent transcendence, hence the never-ending circle of eternity and the joyous chaos of the unlabelled, unnamed and undefined that Tiamat really stands for.

Language creates structure, relatedness and psychological order which we think of as reality. The sequential nature of language and thought create time, but eternity is beyond time and consequently beyond thought. If eternity is beyond thought and its paranoid obsession with order, then eternity must be chaos.

The Ring equates with the well and the fountain deep within the maze hidden at the centre of the dark, mysterious forest. Guarded by a water nymph or Dragon Maiden, the flow of this fountain and the waters of this well bring union with the eternal, heal the divisions within the mind and bestow revelation. With a still mind the supplicant of the Maid feels the surge of power released and the gift of wisdom revealed.

At one with themselves and consequently with the Godhead and the source of all power, they understand themselves to be the centre and source of all things. In this revelation there is obtained absolute Sovereignty over selves, which itself becomes Sovereignty.

The Dragon that bestowed the ring on Charlemagne was Frastrada the Fairy. Like Tiamat, Lilith, Tamaris, Sheba, Diana, Arduin, Brigid, Lamia, Janet of Carterhaugh, Gwenhyfar, Pressina and Melusine, Frastrada was a Dragon Princess and a Grail Maiden. She is a Mary Magdalene and a Maid Marion.

Without these Queens and Princesses, none of the Kings associated with them throughout history would have been fit to reign. It is only she who can bestow the gift that brings sovereignty. As transcendence and creativity, it bestows blessing and fertility upon the kingdom through a wisdom and depth of vision that anticipates difficulty and initiates productivity through activity.

For any, apart from the King and Queen, it would appear totally uncausative. Through the ability to see situations several steps down the line, they are able to plan ahead and bring blessings upon the land and the people.

For this reason patriarchal religions hate women. Like little boys trying to be free of Mummy's apron strings, they deride the female for her authority. The Church is fully aware of the regal identity of the Dragon Kings and of the power of the Grail Princesses through whom and by whom those Kings reigned. For this reason the Inquisition was particularly directed against specific females.

Puffed up with male pride and misogyny, the Church fully knew and hated the fact that beneath the symbol of the Lamia lay the truth of a distinct neurological difference between not only Fairy women, but Fairy men as well. The Dragon Princesses produced a chemical that acted on their own physiology to produce a state of mental composure and grace that history symbolised as the Swan, not only because of their elegance, but also to denote the origin in the anatomy of that chemical.

The consequent state of grace produced by this chemical and the energy it afforded, uninhibited or wasted by any preoccupation with stress or inner conflict, appeared to make the female glow with an inner serenity and beauty that many people described as Fairy Fascination.

The state of peace that they enjoyed was, to an ordinary careworn observer, utterly alluring and charming, a quality to adore because in proximity to her the energy could be felt like soft electricity which had a calmative affect on the mind. As it slowed down and became still, it began to perceive the joy and sense of oneness that has no beginning, no cause and no ending but lies hidden behind the internal barriers, taboos, fears and attachments that we use all our mental energy to sustain in our minds. Usually this, when quite exhausted, has no energy to spare to see beyond the tired struggle with imposed illusions. In her company the observer would partake of her abundant morphic energy which could provide the observer with enough energy to see beyond and begin to understand that mortal care is unimportant. A mind thus stilled glimpses the eternal and this is one aspect of Hierogamy and the Love that is Death.

The chemical also has a physical affect when transferred to the observer. The same stillness occurs and produces psychotropic effects. The problem was, though, that the observer would have to have sufficient numbers of the correct axon membranes in the right type of synaptic receptors and an increased number of dendrites connecting the appropriate brain cells across both hemispheres. In other words the Dragon Princess had round pegs and Dragon Kings had lots of round holes, in contrast to non-Dragons, who seemed to have different shaped pegs and holes, and less of either.

The Church hated the fact that they couldn't use the "Magic" so they attempted to destroy it so that no one else could use it either. This they hoped would result in a level playing field where the glaring stupidity of their own monarchic clients wouldn't be noticed in comparison to the hopefully exterminated and thus unobservable wisdom of the true Fairy Kings.

It would also appear that the Church knew that the Fey, or Fairies, because they participated in the eternal spirit of the One, were themselves eternal, needing no forgiveness—for sins they transcended—and no priest to intercede for them to a god whose spirit they were at one with. The Fey knew salvation was chemical and physiological, being determined on the ability of the mind-brain to perceive the eternal mind of the Cosmos and join with it. With their inherited natural body chemistry they were predisposed towards the ability to negate the ego. They could see beyond time and tide and understand that their individual consciousnesses or spirits weren't individual or personal at all, but aspects of the one consciousness, which was eternal and did not require the salvational ministry of a Church that was run by the living dead.

Worst of all, the Dragon Queens and Kings, not being descended from Adam and Eve, completely bypassed the absolutely farcical doctrine of "Original Sin", the linchpin of the Church's contrived raison d'etre. Without Original Sin there could be no subsequent Sin and if there was no subsequent Sin there was no need for salvation. If there was no need for salvation for a people who could see beyond the contrived notions of good and evil and therefore could not be blackmailed into paying into the Church's spiritual protection racket, these people and their culture represented a threat to the profit margins of the prelates. The Church couldn't exploit what the Fey had and they feared what the Fey instilled in their client tribespeople and communities.

Therefore the Fey had to be eliminated in order for the Church to take over the communities and instil into them the kind of guilt and fear that encourages converts who can then be transformed into a pliant, captive consumer workforce. The Church recognised the problem and began a gradual process of demonisation, marginalisation, genocide and finally academic ridicule and incredulity.

Chapter 16

The Salmon of Wisdom

"The Maiden guards the fountain and the well and at the bottom of the well there lives the Salmon of Knowledge. Every month a nut drops from a tree that grows over the well and this blood red fruit is consumed by the Salmon."

The Druids who concocted these riddles were wise enough to know that Salmon didn't live in wells. If they'd meant "underground river", they would have said: "the Salmon of Knowledge occasionally happens to swim to exactly the right spot to catch a fruit that isn't even part of its normal diet. However, all the same, it will navigate thousands of miles just in order to flounder about in the dark, waiting under a bore-hole, for an alien and indigestible titbit". The Salmon of Stupidity?

Anyone who seeks a plausible answer to this riddle based on matter of fact, reasonable explanations has probably eaten a sizeable lunch portion of the very fish whose behaviour and habitat they are attempting to rationalise.

The Salmon of Knowledge therefore is not a fish. If one takes a whole salmon and cleanly slits its belly open and removes the lights, then spreads the reddish-pink flesh apart to form an oval shape, it is reminiscent of something or another, I'm sure. As the fresh meat bleeds under the knife, one also brings to mind the Blood Red Nut that the Salmon purportedly finds so irresistible. What is a nut? It is a seed, a beginning to new life, very much like an egg which, coloured red, is the object being held by a beautiful Mary Magdalene, whose pretty lips are slightly upcurved into a subtle, knowing smile which, it appears, is fully intended to taunt and infuriate!

By wisdom a Fish may become a Flower that begets a Flower.

The allegory of the well appears in the *Song of Solomon*, the *Annals of Irish History* and the *Story of the Winning of the Elven Lover—Tam Lin* (Thomas Lindsay), by Lady Janet of Carterhaugh.

It is fascinating that the Scythians and Jews have so many symbols and allegories in common with regard to the Holy Grail. The Scythian Gaels share with the Jews not only the symbol of the Well in the Garden or Forest with the Fountain, but also the Salmon which, in the Judeo-Christian tradition becomes the Christ, the Ichthys. By this means, Christ, his body and blood, shed for the remission of sins, becomes altogether a deeper allegory and his virgin birth finds echoes in the Lily of the Valley and the Rose of Sharon.

There is no doubt that Christ existed as a living being. However, he was a Dragon King of the Grail Bloodline and many of the stories associated with Christ are Rosicrucian and Alchemical. The salvation that he preached to his disciples was not obtained through faith, but knowledge or gnosis, and that knowledge is woven into the parables he told and the stories associated with him and with his close Royal cousins, the Sidhe of Ireland and Albany.

Indeed the Grail stories of the Gaels precede Christ by centuries and indicate that Christ was one amongst a long succession of Priest Kings whose teachings he too, in his turn, expounded. Jesus' teachings and the stories surrounding him did not come into being with his arrival into this life but were part of any already extant corpus of secret knowledge which had been held in common by the Holy and Royal families of Eurasia for millennia.

There are corresponding subtexts and symbols beneath the stories of Jesus' virgin birth, his life and death. Rather than being part of a lineal account of his unfolding qualities and exploits, they are references to the nature and quality of his, but more particularly, of his mother's blood and its dynamic. In this manner Christ himself becomes an allegory of the blood's qualities and potential.

a) If Christ is the Ichthys, related to the Salmon of Nechtan, then the blood of Christ shed for the remission of sins is the blood not of Jesus, but of the Messiah, the Messe or Dragon Kings, shed by the Salmon.

b) This Salmon lies at the bottom of a well which in the Gaelic and Frankish tales (cf. Melusine) is guarded by the Dragon Maiden. However, in the *Song of Solomon* it is the Maiden herself who is identified as "The Shunnamite", Sheba, the virgin child bride and sister of Solomon, who corresponds to both the Virgin Mary and Mary Magdalene in the New Testament.

c) The virgin birth of the son of God, "the seed of David" is symbolised by the Magdalene presenting the blood red egg. The egg is the son of God and the seed of David which, as the nut from the tree over the well, is consumed and retained within the salmon which represents the vulva that resides beneath the womb or well. "Christ" simply means anointed one and derives from Messe, the act of anointing a Dragon Queen or King with the fat of the Sobekh or Water Dragon (crocodile). By understanding the dual meaning of Ichthys we comprehend that Ichthys as both Christ (anointed-messe) and salmon (fish) means "anointed Vulva of the Dragon Princess". This means that her womb gives issue to the seed of god which is held in the virgin vulva (christ) which sheds its blood, and the seed, for the salvation of man. The body (ova) and blood (menses) of Christ (the sacred womb).

d) The anointed vulva can be found in the *Song of Solomon*. "My hands are on the lock of the door, my fingers drip with Myrrh"—Sheba. The act of anointing signifies sacredness and holiness, that someone or something is set aside for some sole Holy Purpose. The anointed Vulva/Womb that itself anoints is set aside for a higher purpose than mere procreation. It is the Holy Virgin Grail which contains the Blood of Christ, the Blood of the Messiahs or Dragon Kings and Queens. The Virgin Birth was not a child, but a seed of a child. Christ's (the Vulva's) sacrifice of its body and blood for the salvation of man was the "birth" or flowing forth of the spent ova in the menses which, in the Eucharist, is symbolised by the Bread and Wine. This, as we all know, must be consumed.

Chapter 17

The Little Nut Tree

The nut or seed which falls from the tree is properly the release of the chemical melatonin by the pineal gland. It overrides oestrogen and causes the "seed" to be discarded in the menstrual blood. This contains a naturally increased level of that chemical, which is what the story is really getting at. In the *Song of Solomon*, Sheba says that she will give Solomon the juice of her Pomegranate to drink. This is a symbol used repeatedly to represent the virgin female organs of which juice: Blood, is the red wine of the Pomegranate.

"I had a little nut tree,
nothing would it bear,
But a Silver Nutmeg
and a "Golden Pear",

The King of Spain's
daughter came to visit me,
and all for the sake
of my little nut tree".

Beneath the political allegory concerning the proposed marital alliance between Catharine of Aragon and Henry Tudor, there lies another alchemical message.

The Badge of Aragon is the Golden Pear or Pomegranate. On Card II of the Major Arcana of the Waite Tarot: The High Priestess, is a veil symbolising the virgin hymen. Printed on the veil are rows of pomegranates which in turn also symbolise the virgin vulva. The High Priestess is the guardian of wisdom and the "mysteries".

The palm fronds interspersing the pomegranates on the veil represent the palm trees that grow next to the pools in desert oases and equate with the nut tree in the story of the "Well of Nechtan". These palm trees lent their name to a species of Holy Virgin Princess who bestowed upon the King the right to rule. Their category was "Tamaris" and Jesus' daughter bore that name and title. In Sufism the Tree of Life is represented as a palm tree atop of which is perched a peacock. In the Welsh and Irish Tales the bird is an eagle, whilst in Hindu Tantra the bird is a Swan.

In the popular nursery song quoted, the nutmeg symbolises the pineal gland whose colour silver equates with the Moon and Diana, representing the virgin huntress's "moon" or menstrual blood. In Ephesus, Diana is depicted riding a panther. This means that the Panther clan carries her qualities—holy and therefore very special "Moon" blood. Jesus', and therefore, in anglicised form, Mary's family name was Ben Panther, or "sons of the Panther". In mythology this is interchangeable with the werewolf and was born by the Plantagenets as their family badge.

The nutmeg itself is known to be a powerful psychotropic drug. This has recently been synthesised as *MDMA* or Ecstasy. The story relates that the chemical discharged into the bloodstream by the pineal gland has psychotropic properties when processed via certain exercises relating to the Tree of Life.

The nut tree, the palm tree and most other fruiting trees can be said to represent the Tree of Life, but the sovereign of all these is the Apple of Avalon. If the well and the salmon symbolise the womb and the vagina, below which is the vulva, the tree growing next to the Well represents the lower and upper torso, the head and the arms of the Virgin female. The twigs and branches of the tree symbolise the veins and arteries of rich, Holy Royal Blood and the fruits of the tree represent the endocrinal glands that correspond to the Chakras in Tantrism, the Sephira in Cabala and the Nine Worlds in Viking mythology. The tree is Jacob's Ladder or the Ladder of Lights.

Chapter 18

The Rite of the Vampire

The tantric/hermetic, Royal Rite of the Vampire can never be predatory or sexual. It does not indicate any form of Freudian psychosis and, although it is an expression of True Love, this does not correspond to any mundane romantic expectations. Human love seems mostly needy, arising in response to a variety of chemical and emotional deficits. Rather than transforming the couple involved, it simply seems to reinforce old complexes and prejudices, being entered into in the hope of fulfilling preconceived expectations.

Starfire cannot be achieved by partial individuals seeking some form of socially conditioned notional completeness through the other person. Both individuals must have personal integrity in order to transcend the possibility of simply becoming each other's other half. The whole realm of Starfire in its varying manifestations should be entered into without preconceptions and without emotional inadequacy.

If there isn't a degree of prior individuation, then it does become just another variation on the theme of Freudian domination and the desire for personal power through the sexual victimisation of another person. In itself, Starfire is Death, the journey's end. Its symbolic expression is best appreciated in Waite's Two of Cups. It is a "Love which is not in Nature, but by which Nature is Sanctified". As the Rite of Quickening, it often happens at its greatest intensity when it is least expected to happen and the individual/s involved have no foreknowledge of it.

The endocrinal glands tend to be multi-functional, with more than just one gland being responsible for the production of a single hormone or neurotransmitter. The endocrinal system is fantastically complex and operates on a feedback loop of constantly changing levels of hormones, interacting and affecting each other in order to maintain a delicate balance.

It would require a separate book to attempt to give a full explanation of the Starfire Ritual in anatomical and physiological terms. Therefore, I shall restrict the discussion to those glands and organs directly associated with the psychosomatic Sephira system. This stimulates the production of the hormones most closely identified with Starfire, the Holy Grail and Vampire Lore. Firstly however it is worth defining the objectives of undertaking the Rite of the Vampire. These are:

1) To enhance intelligence

2) To promote longevity

Intelligence

Intelligence in cybernetic terms is defined as "The ability of an organism to exist and develop in symbiosis with its environment". The Rite of the Vampire was, in classical terms, a Royal prerogative which was undertaken on a regular basis with selected partners in order to promote within the reigning Queen or King a sequence of events leading to transcendent intelligence.

Originating in Scythian Royal Families, the Rite of the Vampire enabled the Queen to maintain and the King to obtain sovereignty, firstly over themselves, and secondly over the destiny which affected the people whom they served and guided. Whilst the Queen could reign independently, it was thought by the ancients that a King could not be a King without a Queen. In modern everyday terms this idea has a sound basis in the difference between male and female physiology, which difference in part is reflected in, and was balanced out by, the Rite of the Vampire.

In the ancient world the caste system defined the tasks of every individual within society. The Royal family was the nation's spirit, soul and mind, the warriors were its arms, the yeomen and artisans were its torso and its legs. Each caste performed its specific tasks and relied upon the other for direction, sustenance and defence. Each caste was considered as vital as the other in the task of maintaining the nation as a whole. Today the nations are being run by fools.

The task of the Royal Family was to guide and direct the efforts of the other castes. It could only do this efficiently if it was psychologically healthy and possessed of a considerable degree of wisdom and farsightedness. Its specific task was to foresee future problems and benefits and direct the nation accordingly.

To be able to exercise this amount of sovereign control over destiny, they first had to ensure sovereignty within themselves. This entailed adopting a practical, consistent method of integrating all the aspects of the psyche, by uniting and enhancing communication between the various areas of the brain contained within the general divisions of the left and right cerebral lobes. This task was not achieved by lengthy selves-analysis or psychotherapy, but simply by ingesting chemicals which would encourage a greater sense of union within selves. In this way a transcendent appreciation of the selves' union with the Mind of Godhead or the Universe came about. Thereby true sovereignty, the will of the One, could be integrated into the mind of the Royal seer and followed.

Within the mind are a host of barriers, many of which are caused by the brain's chemical and physical inability to communicate efficiently with itself. This causes a sense of confusion and isolation which encourages the spectrum of various forms to appear, from attachment to comforting delusions. Sovereignty over selves is attained by accepting the selves for what they are. In so doing the individual, dispensing with the energy-consuming need to erect and maintain defensive mental routines, allows the truth to prevail instead, without regret and without judgement. In this manner the mind becomes detached and observant.

The energy formally used to sustain defensive mechanisms and constellations of delusory complexes is freed from its shackles and can be used to enhance alertness and perception. In focused attention, there is discovered truth and this is the greatest manifestation of intelligence. Symbiosis is—above all else—harmony and harmony is transcendence. As a result of the Rite of the Vampire, Scythian culture itself was rooted in the love of truth and honour. The harmony they experienced within themselves as a result of their personal honesty affected their relationship with the natural world which they adored. Correspondingly they lived in harmony and symbiosis with the natural world. For the Scythian, who had an almost childlike love of life, dishonesty was the enemy of joy and the death of clarity.

In consequence it was said of the Scythian Royal caste that they hated usurers, merchants and tradesmen and abhorred the deceit of the marketplace. Above all, the Royal Scythian knew transcendent reality, and was able not only to read his or her own heart and mind, but those of other men. Therefore anyone attempting to lie to them or deceive them was proffering the greatest of insults and appeared to be turning the universe upside down and perverting the Harmony of the Natural Order of life itself.

In Gothic romance we have a particularly apposite example of the Scythian hatred of liars and cheats. It depicts the Scythian "Vampire" as living in terror of the Christian cross and holy water. Therefore we are fooled into believing that the Vampire was an evil denizen of Hell who cannot bear to look upon or come into contact with the greatest of all the symbols of virtue and righteousness. However the reverse is actually the case. Because of the intent of those who have stolen it, the Christian cross to a "Vampire" was the epitome of everything that is evil, malicious, selves-serving, deceitful, dishonest and corrupt. To the "Vampire", the Church consisted of individuals who were no better than racketeers and murderers. They were tradesmen and usurpers.

The Vampire's reaction to the cross was not holy terror but disgust and contempt. This was compounded by insult if the cross were wielded by a cleric, because to the Vampire the cross was also associated with the martyrdom of one of the Family. To use a Vampire family symbol to ward off a Vampire was the ultimate insult to the Vampire's intelligence. Likewise with holy water. In the medieval romances dire warnings are issued to those who would pour water upon the cubic stone of the Holy Grail.

Such an act would bring down thunder and lightning on the head of the transgressor. This symbolism indicates that the stone that pours forth the waters of life, namely the Grail Maiden, should not be baptised. Such a Christian act is an act of usurpation, which is viewed by the Dragon Bloodlines in much the same way as anyone else would view the person that writes graffiti on an historically significant building.

Christian clerics are usurpers and the act of sprinkling with holy water is taken as their arrogance and audacity in attempting to make their own, something they can never possess or use to further their own selfish, materialistic desires. The Vampire race did not live in fear of idolatrous trinkets, it viewed them with anger and contempt as a form of utter stupidity that insults the intellect.

To return to the central theme of the narrative, the achieving of internal union was a fairly straightforward and predictable event. This is because the Royal Scythians, the Vampire or Elven Kings and Queens originated from a bloodline that had specific physiological differences in comparison to other human species. Principally, as stated, they were in possession of a greater number of melatonin-sensitive synaptic receptors on both sides of the brain than ordinary human beings.

Secondly, they possessed also a greater number of axons uniting the right and left lobes of the brain via the corpus callosum. This allowed for an enhanced trans-lobal communication potential. Thirdly, both male and female "Vampires" had larger pineal glands than other people. In Vampire culture these assertions are reflected in the symbolism they used.

The synaptic and axonal connections via the corpus callosum were represented by the image of the Dove of the Holy Spirit descending, holding within its beak a paten which it intends to insert into a Grail Cup. This was a medieval Templar symbol. The wings of the Dove represent the axon branches of the limbic system of the left and right cerebrum, whilst the body of the Dove represents the corpus callosum which joins the two halves together.

Similarly, the Aryan symbol of the Swan displayed also takes the trouble to emphasise the same assertion but rather uses the Swan's head to distinguish the position of the pineal gland. Both birds are used to convey a sense of grace and serenity and the observer is encouraged to associate such states with the psychic condition of the Dragon Grail Bloodline, arising specifically from neurophysiological differences between that bloodline and the rest of humanity.

Differences in sensitivity to psychic or physical stimulus between the ancient Scythian Royal caste and other castes is emphasised in the West by the tale of *The Princess and the Pea*. This story has a variant in Hinduism which itself shares a common Aryan cultural root with the Scythians. Here the difference between a Brahmin and a Ksatriya attracts comment, and it becomes clear that a tendency towards heightened physical sensitivity distinguishes the Royal Priest from the Noble Warrior. One is quite clearly encouraged to associate caste difference with physical difference and conclude that caste was not a matter of social status but of physical and psychological function. The Priest was bred to be physically different to the Warrior.

The "Vampire" was born with a higher potential for perception, transcendence and intelligence. Although operating on a higher base line in these areas than other species, the Vampire race in their own perception of their everyday psychological and physiological condition, occupied a functional norm. They walked a tightrope between their own mundanity, which for others would be perceived as being transcendent, and an even higher state of being.

Because of the neurophysiological variations, achieving such a state would be quite a straightforward matter of ingesting certain neurotransmitters and hormones within the correct environmental conditions. Having so many more synapses and axons to accommodate these chemicals than other human beings, just a slight push could send them over the edge of their accepted reality and into another level of the universe.

A homeopathic dose would allow them to achieve critical mass, whilst in others, much larger doses would have no affect at all because there are not the number of axons connecting the two lobes anyway. A simple example of this odd phenomenon is that many devotees of various faiths follow gurus, attend seminars and retreats, or take drugs. Despite this, however, even after years of struggle, yearning and discipline, they get nowhere near attaining any state of mind that might be termed transcendent or intelligent according to the parameters defined herein.

Society encourages us to believe that we are all a homogenous mean, we are all built the same and we all share equal and similar attributes and potentials. The Church in particular is still very keen to push this particular piece of propaganda. This is, of course, blatantly untrue but those who are unaware of the physiological differences may strive for years in a state of utter perplexity, attempting to fulfil the desire to become enlightened.

Such perplexity is compounded when they meet others who make no attempt at all to achieve such a coveted state but simply live in it daily, having been born to it. Transcendence isn't a matter of getting a load of exercises right. It's a matter of being born with the kind of brain, endocrinal system and genetic memory that allows the mind to perceive such a state of being.

Being a Witch, magician, Vampire, Fairy or a Royal Dragon is not something that can be bestowed through rites of initiation or by adopting the pose. Such beings are of a different race, a race into which they are born. It is not a club that people can join and there are no human equivalents or substitutes. Even though the Church has attempted to usurp the status and power of these beings, the utter mess they have made of life on Earth just goes to prove my point.

They have usurped the positions formerly occupied by the transcendent. Lacking both the tools to perform the task and the innate desire to accept the "Oblige" which goes with the "Noblesse", they have stupidly and callously raped the planet and wiped out thousands of its precious species, bringing the world itself to the brink of disaster. The "Vampire" was bred, with man's collusion, to be man's natural overlord and was born with that transcendent potential which was an essential part of the employment requirement for Kings and Queens.

Longevity

This aspect of the Rite of the Vampire has two subtexts, the physical and the spiritual. The former, in social terms, was intended to establish a sense of continuity and consistency to the reign of a King or Queen. The latter is determined by the phenomenon of transcendent understanding. By performing the Rite of Starfire regularly, it was possible to extend the normal span of life up to about one third. Although the legend of the Vampire having eternal life can be said to be true, it does not relate to physical life. The Vampire is to all intents and purposes dead in one sense but far more alive than ordinary human beings in another.

There are two types of life. Both depend upon one's state of perception for their true appreciation. In Stoker's *Dracula* we are introduced to the idea that Dracula's image is not reflected in any mirror. Later on, towards the end of the tale the Count says to Mina Harker, "There is no life in this body". The former incident explains the latter statement.

It is expressed eloquently elsewhere: "Be dead to the old nature and alive to the new." Jesus taught that there were two types of life, one mundane and the other transcendent. The old nature, the old life, is lived in relation to its environment and the opinion of those around it. It is bound by taboo and morality and considers itself the only reality.

This is the ego, the individual, unregenerate personality. Being a component of the brain's function, it dies with the body. The ego or personality is a safety function, a minor form of selves-awareness that is formed by memory. In a sense, like memory, it is a quality of the past and in its functioning it relates all new experience to past memory in order to quantify the threat or potential of any newly experienced phenomena.

In so doing, it does not observe the new but makes of it the old, by comparing it to the nearest similar previous experience. Therefore as the ego is essentially memory, and memory is the past, and the past is dead and gone, so too is the human personality. Human beings are, to all intents and purposes, machines, and they are truly the living dead. The ego or personality, that is, all that human beings think of within themselves as being alive, is founded upon fear. During the process of quickening the transcending mind, fear begins to appreciate that it is beginning to disintegrate. It is dying.

As fear dies, the memory, which formerly prevented the perception from seeing anything new, suddenly sees all things anew. As memory is also the principal component of time, then what the perception also observes for the first time is the end of time: eternity. What is left after the mind dies is the eternal, the greater being, the spirit of the universe: life itself.

From that point onwards memory is founded not on fear but upon understanding. What lives from then onwards is the eternal perceiving itself through the senses of the Vampire. The former "personality" is dead. In terms that human beings would understand "There is no life in this body", that is, no fixed or immutable point of reference. This was why Dracula cast no reflection in the mirror. The face, the body, is what human beings think of when they affirm to themselves their selveshood. Being shaped by the personality, the body becomes the ego, the I.

The symbolic absence of a reflection is intended to assert that Dracula, and "Vampires" in general, are "dead to the old nature but alive to the new". This is the foundation upon which Jesus' entire message was built. It is only the Vampire that can truly say, with the voice of the eternal, "I AM THE TRUTH, THE WAY AND THE LIFE". For it is only in the blood of the Vampire that there can be found the secret of eternal life.

Did Vampires have eternal life? Well, yes they did. They were born Eternal in the sense that they were born to be transcendent and their Rites afforded them the ability to "yield" to the transcendent dynamic and perceive eternity. From that point on, time becomes less relevant and they never departed from the eternal now that is perceived whilst in this physical life.

Time is created by the mind, which is fear. Without fear there is no time. Whilst living in the physical body, Vampires perceive their mortal lives as immortal. So in the time it takes for a mortal to live out his natural life, the Vampire has already lived an eternity in the same space of years. When a Vampire body dies, the spirit lives on because it is the spirit of the eternal.

The greatest heresy of all for the Church is that it cannot ever achieve for itself or bestow upon others the ability to attain life after death. The greatest heresy is that humans die, whilst the Vampire and the Fairy live forever. The greatest lie that the Church has ever uttered is in trying to convince people that faith or transubstantiation in communion will grant eternal life.

Even if the blood in the Eucharist Chalice were the blood of Christ or the Virgin, it would avail Man nothing because he is not anatomically equipped to process the chemicals that allow the brain to see the eternal. Mortal man is equipped to live his allotted span and then die forever. Individual reincarnation of the personality is equally as spurious a lie which, like the Church's teachings concerning life after death, is propagated to induce behavioural conformity. However, there are still Grail Maidens on the Earth and the spirit of Kali has not yet completely passed into oblivion, despite the best efforts of the Church to breed her handmaidens out of existence.

We are all encouraged to conform. We have our expectations regulated accordingly. In particular, no one in the West is taught that there is a dynamic potential within human relationships which transcends the mundane desire to assuage loneliness or greed, to propagate the genes, replicate the selves or achieve selves-worth through sexuality. In consequence, those who have been taught that Dragons, Vampires, Witches, Fairies or Druidhes do not exist, and furthermore that all are sons of Adam and thus born equal in the sight of God, can be surprised by the startling effects on the soul of Starfire, as the Quickening.

A new reality manifests itself. The brain becomes sensitised to the chemical phenomena that accompany the revolution in perception and this new state becomes the norm, the base line. To maintain it, Starfire, as a ritual, must be continued. There is now a new physiological requirement that must be met that is beyond human understanding, because human beings are blessedly bereft of the dormant brain function that is now fully operational and has become addicted to *La Fontaine de Soif.*

It should be explained that Starfire does not necessarily have to be the consumption of blood in the first instance. As the Quickening it can sometimes occur in the Grail Bloodline spontaneously and unexpectedly. It can involve someone in a situation in which they become aware of a tremendous level of energy in a person they meet, and become close to. This energy field, in close proximity, does something to the subject's perceptions. There can be a feeling of tremendous stillness and peace and a cessation of desire. It is like Death.

The only way to explain it is to say that it appears to rewire the brain which then subconsciously expects a continuity of that selvessame stimulus. Without a regular fix there can be problems. It all sounds like the nonsense we read in Gothic novels, like some form of stereotypical motif that would-be Vampires would use to justify the idiocy of being seen in public with orthodontic augmentations.

However, *La Fontaine de Soif* does exist. The best way of understanding it is to think of the alcoholic who, before the first drink doesn't even know that s/he is an alcoholic. However, afterwards s/he needs that chemical fix regularly or their life goes to pieces. In alcoholism the chemical deficiency is, I believe, for a neurotransmitter called neuropeptide. In vampirism it is for melatonin, but that in itself is only one component. Prolactin, oxytocin, vassopresin and dopamine could also be implicated in the dependence.

A happy Dragon can go through life without any of this and without any of the Gothic overtones, just as long as they never meet another one of their bloodline. If they do though, there is a chance that they will discover a separate reality which they will find painful to lose.

When talking of Royal Vampirism, one should be aiming to associate the phrase with the evening scent of nightstock, with moonlight and starshine, and the song of the nightingale in the forest behind the rose-walk.

"In the centre of the chamomile lawn there stands a black marble plinth from beneath which trickles the waters of life, whose sparkling melody harmonises with the plaintive haunting song of the beautiful, Elven girl, the beloved who, leaning against the monolith, stares into the starlit western sky, as if surveying a vast abyss, a realm of infinite depth that no man could ever hope to see with human eyes".

She is the journey's end and the fulfilment of the Dragon nature. Royal vampirism is about devotion to the feminine and surrender to the goddess; it is about a love that sacrifices selves even unto death. It cannot be presented without the kind of romantic imagery whose symbolism transcends mortal love. Here we have a situation where the sidhe, in order to consummate his or her nature, must sacrifice that nature to the source of its consummation. The Dragon Maiden is not the victim and the Vampire is not the predator. Both consume and transform each other and ultimately the sidhe must die in the arms of the beloved.

The confusion between this imagery and that of the dentally gifted fashion victim is the confusion between royal and martial vampirism. This particular manifestation of the legend was real and there is no getting away from that. Like Royal Vampirism, it concerned itself with the assimilation of identities, but beyond that it was for adrenaline and thyroxine addicts. Originating in Scythian battle custom, warriors would drink the blood of fallen friend or foe alike in order to take upon themselves the valour and spirit of the dying warrior.

The more adrenaline and endorphins the victim or donor had in their bloodstream the better, because this provided fuel for the predators to continue the fray. It did not concern itself with high philosophy, transcendent love, intelligence or longevity and was itself in effect a short cut to the grave. A case of live hard, die young. Today athletes have been known to gradually extract their own blood, up to about two pints, and store it prior to events. Several hours before their performance they would re-inject the blood back into their systems, giving them a significant and very useful lift.

In stories such as le Fanu's *Carmilla*, Stoker's *Dracula* and lately the work of Warrington, the most significant component of the Vampire's personality is not the callousness or predation, but their adoration and love for the victim. The method of consummation, however, has been confused with that of the Scythian Warrior. Having said that, the stories themselves echo significantly the sentiments expressed in the world's first story of royal vampirism, the *Song of Songs*, to be given further consideration in relating and expanding upon the underlying theme in historical examples of the Royal Rite.

Starfire

Is Milis Fola Namhaid—Ach Is Milse Fuil Caraid

—Motto of the Dragon Court and the Dragon descent of the Royal House of Vere. Scythian-Gaelic, 5th-century AD

The Ritual of the Vampire

To prepare for this ritual, it took a subject six months to a year of consistent and methodical practice, undertaken daily, after dark. In the first few weeks of her retreat on the "Isle of Women" (Avalon) she would have been guided by an older companion, a Druidess or shamanka. The entire procedure was then summarised and condensed by using a series of Hermetic signatures or gestures as auto-suggestive prompts. The Rite was broken down into numbered steps. The maiden decided on the type of gesture or verbal command, or both, and then used these at the beginning of each step. After methodical practice these prompts automatically became associated with the steps by the subconscious which, on command, would initiate the dynamic associated with that particular verbal command or gesture or both.

The aim of the exercise was to encourage the female to increase the amount of melatonin in her bloodstream prior to or during menstruation. The exercise or its glyph commands were also repeated on the night of the rite itself in order to ensure the correct ionic polarity of the neurotransmitter being discharged either by the womb or the Graffenberg gland, which was stimulated manually to the point of orgasm and ejaculation.

A golden flute or pipe, inserted into the urethra prior to stimulation, was either held in the mouth to receive the discharged glandular fluid, or otherwise directed into a chalice. If blood was desired the Grail princess would position herself over the mouth of the reclining recipient and allow gravity to take its natural course, aided by oral stimulation and the resulting uterine contractions.

The preliminary exercise required attention and was only to be practiced at night. Likewise the fluids themselves were only collected at night because daylight to a large extent, prevents the manufacture of melatonin. To begin with, the princess and her Druidess chose a chamber without light. If the exercise were being practiced today, ideally the space chosen would be free of live electric cables or equipment, as electro-magnetic discharges affect the pineal gland, which is the command gland of the entire endocrinal system.

It was also vital that this exercise never be conducted in daylight. To do so would have resulted in the over production of seratonin which in certain respects can be very dangerous. Once the exercise had become part of the mental landscape, attention to such detail became less important. Relaxation and silence were however, very important in order to avoid distraction. The experience was extremely pleasant when done correctly, but it took work.

Modus Operandi

The energy centres lying idle within the morphic field of the body need a lot of encouragement to come out of that dormant state, and it requires a great deal of perseverance. Once they are established as a component of the conscious mind they will work on the physical centres that they correspond to. This produces sensations which, as they are the result of increased glandular function, cannot be confused with wishful thinking or autosuggestion.

Dragon Magic is the oldest magic in the world. Most other shamanic and ritual systems are corruptions of it. Being the earliest, it is also the simplest and most pure and arose at a time when religiosity and hocus pocus had yet to cripple man's mind. In Dragon Magic all phenomena are related primarily to the observer of the phenomena and the observer's perceptions thereto are determined by the condition of her or his hormonal balance.

Our entire understanding of and relationship with the universe is governed by our body chemistry. Aware of this, old Dragons compiled a series of exercises to which, of late, a vast amount of nonsense has been attached by people who probably refused to believe that it could be so simple. Magical ability is hereditary.

Undoubtedly a great many dubious individuals have set themselves up as authorities on Magic. Having tried it and having also failed miserably to achieve anything, they have deduced that the formulae were too simple and therefore must be something lacking. It would not occur to them that it was they, and not the discipline, that lacked the vital components. In an attempt to make simple, straightforward, workable Magic, over the centuries they and their underachieving successors have added to it layer upon layer of pointless, unnecessary junk.

Adenosine triphosphate is the fuel that fires up the body cells. The electrical discharge of these cells, along with the axonal discharge of the nerve channels which are comprised of these cells themselves, creates a morphic energy field around and within the body. Its shape is maintained as a stable continuum by the DNA blueprint which determines the body's form.

It was the naturally high strength of this field in the Fairy, emanating through pale, translucent skin and the quality of poise and transcendent, swanlike serenity that gave the Albe-gens; the Maidens of the Grail, the perceptible "glow" that earned them the Epithet "The Shining Ones". The Flame of Life burned brighter in them.

It is, however, possible to concentrate spheres of that energy in specific parts of the body at will. In this particular exercise the energy will be concentrated around specific glands within the endocrinal system. What happens then is that the cells of these glands will be fed more energy than is usual, causing them to work at an increased rate.

In Dragons it appears that a dormant facility for enabling energy to be manipulated in this way does exist in their genetic memories unlike the genetic memories of others. This means that they are more able than others to ignite these spheres of energy, which in Tantra are called wheels or Chakras and in Kabala are termed Sephira or Halos.

The exercise will prove initially fruitless to any newcomer because it seeks to make a warp in an energy field. This has, in the average individual, to all intents and purposes remained seated in a genetic armchair for aeons: it will have metaphorical stiff joints at first, and until perseverance has rendered it supple.

During the period devoted to practice, diet is important. Try to avoid anything that will encourage the production of free radicals and eat plenty of antioxidants like bananas, oranges, oats, tomatoes and so forth. The aim is to make the exercise as easy as possible and food that stresses the glands or works against them will have a deleterious effect on the health during this period. Eat plenty of garlic. It is an excellent antiseptic and blood cleanser.

The Preparation

Having selected a quiet dark space that is warm, familiar and comfortable, ensure yourselves a period of time free from all and any distraction whatsoever. The bedroom is ideal.

1) Loosen all clothing or disrobe, and lie flat on your back on the bed with your head cushioned at a low but comfortable angle. Place your arms by your side or upon the tops of your thighs with your elbows resting on the bed.

2) Starting with your feet, stretch your toes and tense the muscles in the ankles and then relax. Make a mental note of the sensation of tension and relaxation and repeat the tensing and relaxing exercises for the calves, thighs,

torso, neck, face and arms. Repeat this routine until you are familiar with the feeling of being relaxed and then concentrate your attention on all the muscles of the body to ensure they are loose and unknotted. Once you are certain that you are completely relaxed make the gesture or think the command word which you wish to be associated with this relaxed state.

3) In a completely relaxed state, exhale completely but comfortably and breathe in again, counting the seconds in your mind, until you are near capacity but not straining or in discomfort. Breathe from the abdominal area not the chest. Take the air in through the nose. Make a note of how many seconds it took to breathe in, then hold the breathe for two seconds and breathe out through the mouth gently and slowly, taking the same amount of time to empty the lungs as it took to nearly fill them. Once they are discharged, hold for two seconds and then breathe in again. Repeat this routine throughout the entire duration of the exercise. Adjusting the breathing to the frequency of the heartbeat helps a great deal. After a while you no longer have to count but simply breathe evenly in synchronisation with the heart. Continue to monitor your state of relaxation and adjust accordingly. After about ten minutes of relaxation and regular breathing you will feel the affects of the oxygen in the blood acting on the relaxed muscles of the body. You will begin to feel a pleasant buzzing in the head and a sense of weightlessness as if you are floating in mid air. When this happens, make the gesture or think the command word you wish to be associated with this stage. If you get infuriating itches, scratch them and start again. It always happens but as the exercise becomes more familiar, they subside.

At this stage a rhythmic pattern of breathing has been established which enables the mind to relax and attune itself to the brain's cycles. What is being attempted in the first few months is to establish a psychosomatic relationship between mind and body which is conducive to enabling the mind to exercise control over bodily systems which usually remain unconscious. By repeating the rhythmic patterns faithfully the brain begins to associate the exercise with relaxation and calm, which it will later habitually associate with the command prompts. When this happens, each command prompt will trigger the correct bodily response.

Having established the relaxation and breathing exercises successfully it is now time to begin the visualisation process of the exercise. The aim of visualisation is to assert control of the mind over the body. An example of this is that if you visualise in your mind the image of you eating a lemon, you will automatically begin to salivate. This is mind over matter. This process is involved in concentrating energy into the gland centres associated with the dormant Sephira in order to awaken them.

In the Rite of the Vampire there are five spheres which are utilised, corresponding to the brain and brain stem including the ventricals, the pineal gland, the pituitary gland, the hypothalamus, the thyroid and parathyroid glands in the throat, and the Graffenberg gland and or womb. Starting from the top they are the:

Name	**Location**	**Resonant**	**Colour**
Kether	Brain	Ti Ah Maat	White-Gold
Daath	Thyroid	Ah Nah Ouh	Mauve
Tiphareth	Thymus	Nin Kur Saag	Red
Yesod	Womb	Lih Lih Tou	Blue
Milathara	Graffenberg	Luh LuhAh	Green-Silver

4) As you lie with your eyes closed in a state of perfect relaxation begin to visualise the first sphere in the column—Kether. About five inches in diameter, this ball of white light should be envisaged as occupying the space within the cranium. Imagine looking at the sun on a misty spring morning and this will give you the exact image. Whilst visualising Kether, imagine that from its centre there is rolling a beautiful deep sonorous vibration similar to the haunting, unbelievably deep chanting of Tibetan Monks. As you are imaging the sphere glistening and glowing, and the three-syllable chant from the centre: TIR ARRH MAAT corresponds to the rhythm of your breathing out, you will begin to see in your eyes a white light. You will feel your head humming in a way different from that caused by the breathing exercise. When this sphere has established itself, imagine that from its centre a cylindrical channel of white light has emerged and travelled down to your throat. Doing this will direct the pineal and pituitary secretions to the thyroids.

5) Maintaining the Kether sphere and the rod of light, now imagine a glistening ball of the same size in mauve around the throat and lower skull. In the same manner as before, from its centre allow it to intone in your mind the chant AHH NAA OUU as one continuous sound. At this point, once it has become established, things get really interesting.

The thyroid gland starts to produce an excess of thyroxine 4, which the melatonin from the pineal converts into thyroxine 3—Rocket Fuel. Within a matter of seconds this has entered the bloodstream and united with every cell in the body. The feedback loop to the brain energises all the glands again and they in turn increase their output of hormones which increases the output and conversion of thyroxine 4, causing a snowball effect.

At this point you will have forgotten to breathe, visualise or chant. The thyroxine 3 has just united with the mitochondria to produce adenosine triphosphate, which is now causing every cell in the body to behave like a nuclear reactor. The weirdest sensation of all is caused by the boost of energy to the morphic field around the body. It begins to expand and appears to have just developed nerve endings on its outer perimeter which now feels like an egg-shaped aura encapsulating the entire body.

Whilst this is happening you feel bloated with energy like a balloon full of warm glowing water and most surprising of all is that you can actually see the cells glowing in your head. The discovery of an extra component to the human anatomy that you didn't previously know of or believe in can be a shock. Try not to forget the object of the exercise because it gets even better, especially for women. At this point remember to incorporate the command glyph or word.

6) After the initial surprise has worn off and the phenomenon has stabilised itself, resume the breathing pattern and check for muscular relaxation. Having restored the breathing pattern imagine that the "channel of light" has extended down from the mauve Daath sphere around the throat and come to rest behind the sternum bone of the rib cage. Here you should visualise a red-gold sphere the same size as the former two, scintillating and pulsing. From its centre, listen to its chant emanate. NING GURR SAARG. In all cases you should hear the chants, not in your head, but coming from the spheres. Direct the sound out as if it were coming from there. The thymus stores the T-cells which help fight infection and aid in the prevention of cellular damage. When the sphere has become stable and you can feel its warmth you will see in your mind that it is glowing without your wilful act of imagination. At this point think the command word or gesture associated with this stage.

7) Having accomplished this, imagine that the channel of white light is breaking from the Tifaret sphere and reaching down to the womb. Now visualise the womb being surrounded by a sphere of warm aquamarine light dappled like the moon reflected in water. The colour is vivid and opalescent. From the centre of the Sphere and the womb intone the chant LEER LEER TOO. As with all the spheres, remember that the chant begins at the peak point of the intake of breath and continues until exhalation is complete. It does not however break off abruptly at that point, but continues to resonate until you breathe in again. Make the chants flow. Surprise Number Two. After a while the womb will begin to react and the genital area will become sensate. As the visualisation and the chant continue and the sphere becomes stabilised, the feelings in the sex organs become more intense. Often this can result in spontaneous orgasm.

In the Rite, which is subdivided into two distinct sub routines, the firing up of the womb sphere causes various hormones to be deposited there in increased amounts, depending upon the stage within the menstrual cycle at which the exercise is performed. During the applicable point in menstrual discharge the blood will contain ATP (adenosine triphosphate) and thyroxine 3, which are collected for use as rejuvenants. In the second sub-routine, which is conducted mid-cycle, the content of the Graffenberg gland is harvested. This is thought to contain melatonin, vassopresin, dopamine, prolactin, retinol and oxytocin. The last two neurotransmitters will also be found in the menstrual blood. These are also present as a reaction to the Rite of the Vampire itself which, as one of the highest rites of Courtly Love, should be undertaken as an act of hierogamy or the union of the souls of the divine lovers. If this occurs then the brain of both the maiden and the Vampire will manufacture prolactin and oxytocin which will result in that feeling of intense bonding between the two so often recorded in Vampire lore. If it does not, the ritual is not being undertaken in the right spirit.

The two sub-routines within the Rite of the Vampire are entitled:

The Rite of the Grail — The Rose of Sharon — Blood

The Rite of the Cubic Stone — The Lily of the Valley — Water

(Sharon is Hebrew for Princess)

At the point where orgasm has subsided, if it does occur, remember to think the command or gesture. Rest and regain breathing and relaxation and return your attention to Kether.

8) At Kether, fire the sphere up again and resume the chant. Imagine in your mind's eye the layout of the brain and brain stem. From Kether, visualise the channel of light extending from the back of the brain, down through the spinal column to its base around the pelvis. From the pelvis direct the light to the bladder and urethra. When the channel is established to the urethra imagine that just behind the clitoris, under the pubic bone, following the duct of the urethra from the opening between the labia minora, there is a swelling. To help you locate this before commencing the exercise, it is best to feel just inside the vagina and up against the pubic bone. Located at that point of the urethra is the Graffenberg gland and at this point you should visualise it swelling and being engulfed in a light of lunar silver.

When this visualisation is established feel the vibration of the chant LO LO OUAH. This Sephira is a subdivision of Yesod. In western Kabala, Yesod covers the entire sexual region which, for the Rite of the Vampire, is too imprecise. By subdividing Yesod into two, Yesod and Milathara, concentration can be directed more effectively. Milathara is an Aryan variation found in Tantra. LO LO OUAH is the second part of the Yesod chant directed to the G region instead of being used for Yesod as a whole. At the point where the sphere of Milathara is established and experienced rather than willed, the G-gland will begin to become sensate and tingling. After a while it may also cause orgasm and discharge a clear fluid. The sensations accompanying this are utterly different from any other type of orgasm. In effect it is the female form of ejaculation. The possibility of this occurring whilst practising the exercises in preparation for the Rite depend of the visualisation capabilities of the subject. During the Rite the ejaculation is assisted manually anyway. If it does occur, allow the sensation to subside and think the command or gesture. Now reassess the state of the Sephira and channels, and enhance their respective intensities accordingly. Once they are all working at optimum level again, initiate the following process:

La Fontaine de Vie

The Red Egg

9) At this point the sensation of being egg-shaped will still be felt. The Fountain exercise is accomplished to ensure an evening out of the energies throughout the morphic field, which is then charged to sustain a field of negative ionisation. This field will then alter the polarity of the hormonal electrostatic charge which increases the hormonal impact and its affects on synaptic uptake following ingestion. Starting at the Kether sphere, visualise a fountain of brilliant, sparkling blue-gold water flowing from the top of the sphere down either side of the body to the outer perimeter of the morphic field and down to the lowest point of the field just beyond the feet. When it has reached the base of the egg, visualise its flow returning up the body, this time under the back and over the breast until the flow reaches and re-enters Kether. Repeat this exercise until a continuous outward and return flow has been established.

The hormones are now charged. After about five minutes, turn the water into warm, glowing blood. Red is the colour of energy discharging. As the object during the actual Rite itself is to expel the energy and donate the essence, the colour red tends to push matter away from the source of its nascence. This, in conjunction with the blood as a mystical symbol in itself, is the origin of the Icon of the Scarlet Woman and the Whore of Babylon, the Virgin Mother of Christ and the Maiden Magdalene.

In the Nine stages of the Nahash, the serpent of wisdom, the exercise is complete. In the Sacred Grove, the Maiden is now the Tree of Life* and the Tree of Knowledge and the serpent is entwined in her branches. The Sephira are the Apples of Avalon glowing under the leaves of her flesh. Her slender boughs are the myriad of vessels, arteries and nerve fibres through which flows the sweet sap of Holy Blood and the Waters of Life. In her topmost branches rests the white Dove of Peace, whilst at her feet the waters of the pool of eternal wisdom ripple with the eddying breath of her sacred scents.

Into the clearing, wandering in the Quest of life-giving waters, appears the Stag of Nine Tines, The Great Lord of the Forest.

The Green Stag

For the Vampire princess or prince the exercise is exactly the same in all points except that in the case of the male, he omits the Malathara sphere and the channel from the brain stem. In Magic, the use of colour and vibration

*Lilith's Stag Lord was Samael, the Dragon King. The Pictish variant of this is the Boar in the Orchard. The Blue Boar in the orchard consumes the apples of Avalon.

corresponds with known scientific fact concerning the qualities relating to the frequencies of light energy levels. For each colour there is its opposite and in the case of red, its optical correspondent is green. This can be ascertained by staring at a red coloured spot for about a minute. If one then looks at a white sheet of paper, the persistence of vision will make it seem as if a green spot has appeared on the sheet. The colour green is the true colour of the Vampire for this very reason. Whilst red is a positive, emitting colour, green is a negative absorbing colour which draws life into it. In consequence the Dragon princess or prince who is to act as supplicant to the Maiden should infuse their "morphic field" with green.

We have numerous examples of the Ancient Rites of the Elves and these were in many cases the Rites of the Vampire, both being of one and the same identity. The colour most associated with the Elves of the ancient forests was green. Similarly, the colour of the Stag of Nine Tines that drank from the Holy Grail was green, and that stag was the emblem of the Pictish Calle Daouine king and queen, the Oberon and Titania of Shakespeare. In medieval art, both the Stag and the Dragon were often depicted as being led on a golden chain by the Maiden. Thereby we are given to understand that the relationship between the Vampire and the virgin is one of female choice and male devotion.

It was only later with the advent of Catharism and the rise of the Dragon Court and its most famous prince, Dracula, that the colour black became associated with the archetypal Vampire. This arose because of the colour of the Cathar robe and the Dragon Court tradition of wearing Black on Fridays to honour the Cubic Stone and Venus.

Notwithstanding, the standard colours for the Dragon Court at other times were Hunter's green and blood red. Otherwise green was always associated with the Fairies and the Fairies were always associated with vampirism by the human population, who were encouraged to live in terror of their Otherworldly cousins, and exhorted never to wear the Elven Green, which was evil and unlucky.

The Time of the Season

Specific times during the cycle of ovulation were chosen to drink the Blood of Life and the Waters of Wisdom. As the constitution of every Dragon princess was different, the nights of the Rite varied for each one. Essentially two nights per lunar month were set aside for the alternate drinking of blood or water. The ideal time could be ascertained by counting a certain number of days from the discharge of the ova to mid-cycle. The calculation could not be written in stone as the human circadian cycle works to a rhythm that has a "day" of twenty-five hours. A time discrepancy occurs which adjusts itself regularly, but this causes fluctuations in the secretion of hormones. The body's day, beginning at 0001 hrs, finishes not at 2359 hrs. as the chronological day does, but at 0100 hrs., 25 hours later. As a result of this and other factors, female menstruation occurs within a plus or minus window which had to be anticipated.

The Temple of the Goddess

(See also Wild Hunt) The Rite of the Vampire was often conducted in a Forest or Sacred Garden. In Anjou, Melusine is said to have conducted the Rite in a maze garden in the midst of which stood her sacred fountain. The garden was situated in the forest of Verrieres-en-Forez which was an underwood populated by blackthorns and briars. The maze, conforming to classical Scythian design, would have been shaped like a spiral Swastika. In the centre stood a black marble cube. From beneath the plinth there flowed the gentle rippling stream, symbolic of the flow of the fountain from Melusine's own sacred being. The "Cubic Stone" and the "Fountain" symbolised the Graffenberg gland, the "Jewel in the Crown" of Lucifer, whilst the maze represented the "Spiral Dance of the Vortex". The direction one entered signified whether one was to give or to receive (see notes: Swastika). On another level the maze represented the "Quest for the Holy Grail", the end of being and thus the "Still Centre of the Universe", in which is to be found the truth of all truth. The spiral dance was a significant ritual feature of Witchcraft, whose practitioners provided the backbone of support for the ancient Elven families.

The Forez or thicket of blackthorn symbolised the forest of the mons veneris. A similar forest of thorns is to be found in the story of *Sleeping Beauty*. The blackthorn tree, the "Tree of Elphame", was thought to be ruled by Saturn, who was the angelic spirit of the Sephiroth of Binah, whose sacred flower was the lily of the valley. Binah represented "Understanding". Under-Standing is the act of giving way or yielding. It is passive perception. The act of yielding or bending to a greater intelligence was represented by the willow or wicker, from whence originated the word *Wicca* or Witch.

Binah was called the "Primordial Deep" which, also represented by Tiamat the great Dragon queen, was replicated in a multitude of sacred lakes and wells in Scythian myth which were said to be the gateways to the Otherworld. To drink from the waters of the sacred lakes, fountains or wells was to enter the Otherworld, Elphame, the source of Death and Rebirth. The symbolism of the Melusine's sacred garden is an extension of the Otherworldly sacredness of her own nature. It is an intimation of the magical qualities of her feminine sex and a hint of the promise of transcendence for all those who imbibe of her essences and the essences of those of her Fairy maiden kin and posterity.

Binah's sacred animal was the bee. This creature was used by the Merovingians as a totem dynastic badge which, in relation to the other glyphs associated with this sephiroth, recount the entire arcane wisdom of the Holy Grail and the Rite of the Vampire. Associated closely with Binah was the cypress. Used as an incense at both weddings and funerals, this tree symbolised Constancy or Transcendance (Death) through Divine Union (Marriage).

The message is straightforward. The Bee (Vampire) sucks the Nectar of the Lily (Grail Maiden), which act is an act of Union, resulting in Death, the Transcendence of Consciousness.

The Temple of the Goddess is the Maiden's vulva. Symbolically this is reproduced on a greater scale and becomes variously and euphemistically the Isle of Avalon, the Sacred Grove, the Garden of Love, the Rose Garden, the Hind in the Thicket, the Maze in the Forest and: La Fontaine de Soif dans le Jardin Sauvage. The end and beginning of all delights and all sorrows, this scented enclosure provides the stage within which is enacted the greatest of all mysteries: the Rite of the Vampire.

Chapter 19

La Fontaine de Soif

Intermingled, the warm, caressing summer evening scent of white Iris and Briar buffets against the heavier, closer perfume of apple and myrrh, of nutmeg and pomegranate.

Beneath Moonlight and Starshine, her hands tracing delicate arabesques, she sings softly in a tongue long forgotten, a haunting, breathless melody that embraces the night, harmonising with the sparkling plainsong of the soft cascading water, spilling from beneath the dark, unyielding plinth upon which she reclines.

The Shining One, his sister his bride; this Lord of yesterday holds close within his heart as she gazes deep into the stark abyss above the western sky. With childlike eyes as old as the Ancient of Days, she surveys with her infinite soul her sister, that eternal timeless realm, heedless of her lover's impatient foot falls upon the Chamomile swathe, amidst which her sacred monument stands rooted upon the earth.

Yielding the translucent flesh of her slender, glowing limbs to the hungry embrace of this ice black, unforgiving tomb; in her preoccupation, her stillness now feigns death's charade, causing the yearning approach of her lover to bridle, as he stands and meditates with wonder this moonbathed mystery, wherein soft pale skin and shimmering cubic stone entwined, become sculpted as one, in the eloquence of their radiant glory.

Countenancing such, what heart has he now that isn't bound about by Golden Chains and enslaved by the look of her? What has she left within him in that fleeting moment but a lonely chasm as cold as the bed upon which she lays and as hollow as the abyss upon which her Innocent Contemplation rests. His emptiness is filled with tears that can never quench his thirst for her.

In some middle distant glade, within the dark encroaching forest, a Turtle Dove breaks in upon his sweet agony with a spectral strain for some far off burnished love, echoing the pleas of his sundered eldritch soul. No murmured answer is rejoined, but the softly responding cadence of this lord's beloved bride, enshrined beneath the boundless canopy of heaven.

The dying refrain of her tender imprecation quickens his desire, as the incantation in its ceasing, summons him to his abeisance, to his heart's brief ease—and oblivion. To the Turtle the Phoenix replied:

"For my love, thy constancy;
For thy wine, my eternal soul".

Then raised she opens to him with Myrrh moistened fingers, and with one, heavy scented, dew dripp'd kiss, he drinks deep from the fountain of thirst and empties her cup of sorrows. With Myrrh moistened fingers she opens to him the door of a realm he now sees with her eyes. And trading longing for longing, in her tender arms he yields to her his promised soul, and dies.

If we define love as a prolonged and mutual attachment both sexual and spiritual between two people, we find that it is sometimes considered as primarily a European phenomenon. Romantic love in Europe appears to have been unknown prior to the appearance in late eleventh-century France of the troubadours and *trouvères*. That is not to say that attachments of this kind did not exist between individuals before that time, but that it was not accepted and formalised as a popular conception. For example, the emphasis in the Norse Sagas is almost entirely on heroic deeds and adventure. Heroines are formidable women who would not be guilty of lukewarm, feminine passions—they are admired for male qualities. This is in marked contrast to the essential erotic element of Provencal poetry of the following centuries.

The overwhelming emphasis on sexuality and sexual passion which is characteristic of the pagan literatures of Europe, particularly the Irish, is not evidence for the existence of romantic notions of love. For example, the picture that emerges from Celtic literature is of a society devoted to sexual pursuits but paying very little regard to the relationships between individuals. The incident in the *Feast of Bricriu* when the hero Cuchulain and his followers, who are being entertained by the King of Ulster, are offered fifty women each for their sexual needs—the number includes the Queen and her daughter—can be regarded as typical of Celtic ideas of love.

The essential refinement with which the troubadours cloaked adulterous love is indicative of the times. One of the most remarkable features of the rise of romantic love was that the same period was characterised by extremely barbaric, brutal and disgusting practices by both men and women. Sexuality might very well be the theme of magnificent poetry, but at the same time, to judge from contemporary poems and romances, the first thought of every knight on finding a Lady alone and unprotected was to commit violence against her.

There are numerous instances of this kind of behaviour both in prose and poetry. The *Lait de Graelent*, by Marie de France, tells how a gentle and perfect knight meets a damsel alone in the forest. He brutally assaults and rapes her. However he is forgiven, for underneath he is fundamentally courteous and honourable. The contradiction is quite extraordinary. It is seen again in the instructions given to the good knight Sir Perceval by his mother "...If thou, see a fair woman, pay thy court to her, whether she will or no; for thus wilt thou render thyself a better and more esteemed man than thou wast before." The argument is well put by Chretien de Troyes. A knight finding a damsel alone must offer her no harm but if another knight accompanies her, and he defeats him in combat the lady is his to do with as he wishes. The distinction is subtle but real. The adulation of fighting was on a level with love. No reasonable woman would refuse a conquering knight. To take her by force, as in Marie de France's poem, was really not quite the thing to do.

Different interpretations can be made of this early literature of romantic love. One view, which we are inclined to support, is that the essential lawlessness and brutality of the period was overlaid by a film of idealisation of the feminine which was at times acted out in reality, at other times grossly disregarded. Another is that the knights and troubadours (my note: of Provence and Flanders) constituted a kind of island of culture and gentility in a sea of (Norman and Catholic) barbarism—that in fact the two worlds were not connected. We find this difficult to accept in the face of the evidence.

Vernon Lee suggests in *Euphorion* a picture of a Provencal court. The court consists of all those with any pretensions to nobility from the greatest lord to the lowest page. These, as opposed to the brutal peasantry without, were united in their service to the wife of the great lord and her ladies.

The atmosphere is redolent of dedication and service; the realities of medieval life elsewhere—the burning and sacking of castles, the rape of women, the torture of peasants—are far removed. To pretend that there were not strong elements of graciousness, even spirituality, in some Provencal courts would be untrue, but at the same time to discount the barbaric elements both within the court and outside in the teeming world would be unrealistic.

It is true that Provence at the time enjoyed comparative peace compared with the rest of Europe. It is very probable that cessation from perpetual warfare and forays enabled the noble poets to develop and embellish this extraordinary manifestation of the human spirit. This would explain the transposing of an ordinary knight's service into service to a lady. Instead of preoccupation with war, the lord could now afford amatory adventures. It does not however explain the startling invention of the courts of love with their exacting interpretation of minute points of courtly behaviour in what seems direct imitation of scholastic theological disputes. Lovers were bound by the rules of "courtesia", patience and moderation—that is, restraint. The real problem is to discover the realities of the situation. In the literature there is a metaphysical and allegorical aspect together with an appreciation of the grossest sensuality. The precepts of behaviour we have quoted have to be set against the exacting fealty to one's lady demanded by the courts of love and exemplified in Chretien de Troye's *Lancelot.* (lines 5641 *et seq.*)

The obscenity of the earliest troubadours, Count William of Poitou, for example, is hard to believe. The vast majority of successors, such as Arnaud Daniel and Bertram de Born, are equally at pains to show that it is physical and not spiritual possession they desire. There is a very real contradiction here for in the *Lancelot* of de Troyes there are numerous references to abstractions such as love and reason on an altogether different plane from sensuality. There are many other examples. The blending of sensual love, service to womankind, allegory and ambition is a strange one. But whatever interpretation is used, the fact remains that the concept of Courtly Love invented by the troubadours in Provence was the starting point for all the subsequent European manifestations of romantic love.

My view, however, is that Courtly Love may not have been invented by the troubadours. The aggressive sexuality of William of Poitou and many of his contemporaries merely illustrates the point that the Church's noble and royal puppets had no notion of the courtly behaviour and exoteric elements. One might suggest that a progression towards decline and secularism in regard to the popular notion of Courtly Love was confirmed by people such as von Ragenau.

The exoteric view today seems to regard his following minnesang as truly defining the notion of Courtly Love.

I wish to be known my entire life as a master of one thing and one thing only; I seek the world's praise for this one skill: That no man can bear his suffering as beautifully as I. If a woman causes me pain to such an extent that I cannot remain silent night or day, I have such a gentle spirit that I'll accept her hate as a source of joy; And yet, alas, how deeply that discomforts me!

One might be inclined to the view that by the 14th century, when von Hagenau was writing, the Church had already begun to have a considerable influence on the concept. Some clerics, particularly the Anglo-Norman monk Fra. Orderic Vitalis, had previously roundly condemned Courtly Love for shifting the lord's or knight's attention from Mother Church and her holy wars. However it had quite probably begun to appreciate how the concept might be sanitised, twisted and manipulated to facilitate religious social control by exacerbating internal division and confusion within the individual.

As a consequence of and despite the influence of people such as von Eschenbach, the words of von Hagenau seem to have sealed the fate of Courtly Love for decades until the restoration of the fundamental raison d'e-tre of the concept. This came about in the esoteric publications of the meta-physical poets, in particular the works of Marlowe, Donne and Shakespeare. Shakespeare's poem from *The Passionate Pilgrim*, *The Phoenix and the Turtle* has, as its theme, the concept of "love and constancy". In itself as a euphemism, it would seem to underpin the spiritual rules of "courtesia". I quote, "...Leaving no posterity: twas not their infirmity. It was married chastity..."

The concept of an absolute monogomy or hierogamy, transcending sexu-ality, may be clearly perceived in this particular poem. The kabalistic refer-ence in the opening stanza is unmistakable and for these reasons, personal use was made of the Phoenix and turtle motifs in the *Prose Summary* of the Starfire modus operandi, *Rite of the Vampire*. One must make the observation that von Hagenau, despite being given ample opportunity not to do so, appears to have merely reiterated the popular view of Courtly Love as a source of lament prompted by unrequited love. Nothing could be further from the truth. Courtly Love is necessarily requited but often lost, and this, in a sense, is the source of the pain and longing: Le Soif, as *The Sundering* suggests.

The Sundering

For every bloodied rend
within that heart,
there was a silent tale
for which those lips had neither wit,
nor art.

And every tear he
shed, sullen eyed;
traced a shattered, ancient dream,
which in that dark despair and hopeless
silence died.

How could this be,
does grief end?
His soul desired much more
of her than man could know,
or manners condescend.

She loved him once
but that withdrawn,
Never could he love again
as life's hope from very life itself
was torn.

But is this the longing for the beloved, as it would appear to be in Keats' *La Belle Dame Sans Merci*, or for the condition she engenders and the vision of some "far away country" that can dissipate at her departure, or for both? It was fully intended that the sad anticipation of such a loss be intimated in the *Prose Summary*, along with the longings that accompany such encounters and relationships. This is because the literary evidence suggests that these unions, intended to be spiritual, inevitably come to an end, sometimes, but not always, disastrously and permanently. In the latter event, although the mythical cycles vary according to the personalities involved, it is because of the breaking of some taboo, or the misconstruing of the nature of the relationship and the spiritual dynamic, usually by the male.

In support of such a view we can quote the story of Arthur and Guinevere as well as that of Raymond and Melusine. Baring-Gould says, "...The framework of the myth is the story-radical corresponding with that of Lohengrin." The skeleton of the romance is this:

1. A human male falls in love with a Fairy female.

2. She consents to live with him on one condition.

3. He breaks the condition and loses her.

4. He either regains her or not....

In the *Prose Summary*, although being intentionally romantic by degrees, the main thrust of the piece is intended to convey the magical, initiatory purpose of the encounter. This is apparent in various concealed works on the subject, including the foregoing *Phoenix and the Turtle* and the *Song of Songs*, whose romantic element conveys in allegory, the ecstasy of hierogamical union through love.

Such unions appear to be temporary in nature and abide until the initiation intended by the mystical union is completed, or becomes completed through the pain experienced at the sundering, which is the method by which the Sumaire is awoken and the fontaine de soif is made apparent. The poem concerning the Cross of Lorraine and the Clear Fountain (from Baigent, Leigh and Lincoln: *Holy Blood, Holy Grail*) is significant in this regard. The physical manifestation of the object of longing, the Grail Maiden, seems naturally to re-enact the role of Ishtar within a cycle which happens spontaneously, as part of a recurring archetypal myth superimposed on real life. The response of the intimate should thus be that of the Tantric Brahmin to his lover Kali, whose blood sets him free, but necessarily "at the price of his mortal soul".

The imagery of love and loss, the Fairy Maiden, the garden and the fountain seem inextricably linked with the final stages of this process of introduction to a supernatural world of perception hidden from mortal eyes. This world, however, is one of blended pleasures and mixed blessings. Its beauty and pathos is far more evocatively, and therefore necessarily, conveyed within a prose style which attempts to describe, with the added components of imagery and emotion, the experiences of the subjects in their real life situations as they happened then and as they still happen now.

In this respect, by comparing the prose of von Hagenau with the dedication to Candida by Jack Parsons, former Grand Master of O.T.O., we would seem able to recapture the essential vision of the Dragon Maiden and the Garden of "Love". This is not intellectually in the words, but in the visions engendered by the spirit that prompted the pen. In this poem, *Narcissus*, one might gain a glimpse of the deeper alchemy beneath the "courtesia".

The work was first published as part of an alchemical compilation called *Songs for the Witch Woman* and later appeared in O.T.O's publication "Starfire". Candida enacted the role of Grail Maiden or Scarlet Woman. Again the cycle ended abruptly and in this case Parsons lost everything, including at the end of the process, his life, fulfilling, one might suggest, the requirement for the initiate to offer up to Kali or Ishtar his life blood on the burning ground or pyre of the Saints. Spiritual allegories sometimes become physical realities, especially if the magician has realised that the divisions between what is considered "spiritual" and what is conversely labelled "physical" are merely arbitrary and linguistic.

Narcissus

Drug me with drugs; slow acting, sensuous, sweet
Co-mingle Gin and Musk, Hashish and Amber,
Let me drink and breathe
and hear slow devious, music.

Until aroused to sub langorous moods,
Until I see Ochre and Mazarine
and Purple Emit lascivious sounds.

Then I shall go through dark and Gothic ruins,
Grey and Golden mist; down to a Forest Green,
With an Old Dream.

I shall go naked; and Magnolia and Oleander,
Datura and Jasmine,
Whose blossoms will open and vaginally flower,
In infinite time, for a relative hour,
Whose White subliminal flowers
will caress my breasts.

And I shall perform stately,
Phallic Arabesques,
In the Moonlight Pale and White.

Endocrinal dynamics

ATP (adenosyne triphosphate) is the fuel of life which in youth sustains an active, healthy body and mind. As the body ages the levels of melatonin drop and the body cells begin to slowly degenerate and become tired. In particular, the cells of the thymus which stores T-cells begin to atrophy and are replaced by fatty tissue. When this starts to happen the body's immune system slows down and finds it more difficult to shake off illnesses that in youth would not have warranted any attention at all. As the cells begin to atrophy and the mitochondria become frayed, it is less able to produce ATP and this itself weakens the cells further. It is thought that telomerase in menstrual blood is one of the major contributors to mitochondrial regeneration.

As the cells become weak and less able to maintain structural integrity, the ability of the mitachondria to convert thyroxine 3 efficiently is compromised. It begins instead to produce partial reactions resulting in the ATP being converted more and more into pyrophosphates and literally fossilises the body's cells. As the pineal gland begins to succumb to this process, it lays down calcium salts in the pineal body which results in the production of less melatonin.

With the production of less melatonin all the bodily functions suffer. However in this particular regard it means that there is less melatonin to react with the pituitary and thyroid glands which themselves have suffered a reduction in the amount of hormones they are capable of producing due to the affects of cellular atrophy. Less thyroxine 4 can be processed into thyroxine 3 because of the declining level of pineal output and the degenerating mitochondria produce less ATP, so the cycle of decline continues. The ageing process has begun.

Summary

The Grail comprises not only the Grail Maiden but a set of psychosomatic exercises which stimulate enhanced endocrinal function within her physiology. Furthermore, these exercises also polarise the general energy field around the body which in turn polarises the ions of the hormones required. In laboratory experiments on seratonin conducted in the USA, it has been demonstrated that the field should be positive, which correlates with what the Tantrics, Alchemists and Grail Knights already knew anyway. The recipient of the Grail Maiden's generosity similarly has to perfect the art of accomplishing this exercise efficiently. She or he engages in the rite in exactly the same manner as the Maiden until the fountain point. At this juncture the recipient's energy field should be charged negatively by using the reverse components to those being installed by the Maiden.

At the point where the Grail Maiden has successfully fired up her system and the recipient similarly has sensitised their constitution, the process of extraction takes place. In the case of the Rose of Diana this is achieved orally. However, in the case of the Lily of the Valley the beneficiary, like the Fisher King, sups from the Grail with a Golden Straw. Simply put, the Tantrics et al would insert a golden flute into the urethra and massage the internal area of the vagina just under the pubic bone. After a few minutes a swelling is detected. This is the engorging of the Graffenberg Gland which has, corresponding to it, a special little Chakra.

At the point of g-spot orgasm the fluid contained in the gland is discharged into the urethra and is sucked through the golden straw. As with the Rose of Diana, the Lily of the Valley is held sublingually for some time before swallowing. The reason for this is that the process of digestion reduces the intake of the required hormones, whereas sublingual ingestion is achieved directly through the blood vessels under the tongue.

This act is the physical aspect of Courtly Love. If intercourse were to take place, the psyche of the Grail Maiden would change. The same psychosomatic dynamics which allow her to affect the functioning of her endocrinal system would also radically affect subconsciously the levels of hormones she was capable of producing. In tandem with the reduction of melatonin in the bloodstream caused by an increase in body mass after puberty, sexual intercourse actually triggers the genes to start the ageing process and the reduction of hormonal output. The female body recognises vaginal penetration as a key to the maturing process.

This is Royal Vampirism on the physical level. Rather than being predatory, Royal Vampirism is actually founded upon intimacy and love. It offers spiritual depth and value in its celebration of the most private of female processes, ones with which other cultures insult and shame the female by claiming it to be unclean or taboo.

The legend of the homosexuality of the Templars is probably founded upon truth. On Lindon Hill in Lincoln there used to be a Templar Preceptory devoted to the Magdalene. In practice, so the local story goes, it was a Templar brothel. It is more than likely that the institution was a Solomonic Harem (harem means "Holy Place") devoted to the support of Virgin Maidens of the Grail. The Templars themselves probably did not indulge in penetrative intercourse with these girls but provided for their upkeep as Templar nuns whose task it was to perform the Rite of RTU, the first flow of the womb. To avoid intercourse with them the Templars relieved each other.

In the tradition of Courtly Love the interaction was described as non sexual and Platonic. The chosen maiden was not just considered to be the incarnation of the Goddess, she was the Goddess, and in the rites described, the devotion to her would have been considered to be worship. Here is an example of a form of union with the goddess Diana, where her essence is partaken of, but her flesh remains uncompromised. She gives birth to inspiration in her devotee and is the mother of their creative and transcendent perceptions, but like Mary the Ichthys, Diana remains the Virgin Queen of Heaven.

The original "Hierarchical Rule" of the Templars, founded by King Baldwin de Vere in 1100, admitted women and children.

Chapter 20

The Grail Maiden of History

The ideal Grail Maiden in classical times, generally speaking, was described by medieval and Renaissance writers as being between approximately 12 and 18 years old and of Royal Scythian Blood. Her hair would have been flaming red, her skin white, with an underlying hint of pale gold, like peach and cream. Her figure would have been slight, with understated gender development and her facial features would have been refined, framing large, penetrating eyes of blue or vivid green behind which would be suggested the vast abyss of eternity and infinite space.

The aura about her would have been physically felt as a charge, underlying which would have been detected an unselfconscious stillness, compassion and detachment from worldly cares. Above all she would have been a virgin for the duration of her attachment to the Queen or King as their Shunnamite or Twylleg.

Virginity

Females have larger pineal glands than males and even though they mature earlier than boys, girls with their larger pineal glands and smaller blood volume, usually tend to produce more melatonin and other hormones than boys. This continues throughout life and means that females certainly live longer and are more resilient than males.

As they grow up, both boys' and girls' pineal glands produce a constant unaltering amount of melatonin. From about the age of two years the pineal begins to function at its optimum level, and this doesn't increase as the child grows larger. When young, therefore, the child's bloodstream is rich with melatonin, but as the child grows in size the blood volume increases and the melatonin to blood ratio drops. When the serum level reaches its lowest point, this triggers the production of oestrogen in girls and testosterone in boys, which further inhibits the production of melatonin.

The reason there were no such things as Grail Youths is simply because the males do not produce as much melatonin as females, and the physical farming of the hormone would be problematical to say the least. However, even during puberty the female would produce a substantially larger amount of melatonin than the male, and because of the female constitution it would have been accessible by natural and non-aggressive means.

Although affecting the blood serum level of melatonin, the onset of puberty is the time when the physiological functions of the female permit the procurement of the hormones required. Between 12 and 17 there is a tight window of opportunity where the body hasn't fully grown and melatonin levels are not yet at their lowest point.

Additionally, as the chosen maiden was virgin, she had no experience of actual penetration and she couldn't fully anticipate what the experience felt like. Consequently the release of melatonin inhibiting hormones like oestrogen and adrenaline was likely to be less in an inexperienced virgin anticipating sexual penetration than it would be in a girl who fantasised about an experience she already knew and desired.

The desire level linked with the ability to visualise the act from experience was likely to stimulate the release of more oestrogen and adrenaline in the non virgin than it was in the virgin. In much the same fashion, a person in the anticipation of the consumption of their favourite dish is likely to release more saliva in their mouth than in the mouth of a person to whom that dish is merely described. Adrenaline in particular is a killer, which is why vampirism, which is supposed to be the harvesting of life-enhancing substances could not historically

a) involve any sexual context and

b) have been non-consensual

Both sex and fear cause the adrenal gland to work overtime, releasing adrenaline into the bloodstream. In the case of the Gothic approach, this would then enter the system of the Dragon and affect exactly the opposite result to that which was intended, namely longevity and transcendence. In any case, this had a subtle non-corporeal element which could have only been experienced with a female who entered “of her own free will” and who was prepared “to leave behind a little of the life and joy that she brought with her”, (Bram Stoker, *Dracula*). A willingness on the part of the female to act as a sustainer within a consensual interaction released all the right hormones and corresponding energies. Faced with force, the barriers would naturally have descended and the Grail would have become a Cup of Sorrows.

The effort in training an older female to perform the same rites efficiently would not have been compensated by the return obtained from her constitution, in comparison to a younger virgin female. In such a situation it would have been like preparing a table for a silver service banquet of five courses and ending up sitting there with a beef and tomato flavoured Pot Noodle. There would have been a discrepancy between effort invested and nutrition obtained, which in all species is against the natural law of the conservation of energy. This is why the Vampire's "victim" is always depicted in Gothic Romance as being a young female virgin.

Chapter 21

Witches, Dragons and Boggarts

In reading the following it should be remembered that the Druids, and the Scythians in general, loved putting double entendre and multiple layers of meaning within words and phrases, a linguistic practice which, in Hebrew, is mediated and facilitated by Numerology.

Flesh on Bones

In 14th-century Ireland, Dame Alice Kyteler was arraigned for Witchcraft. Amongst a number of charges she was accused of worshipping the Devil, a Witches' god named Robin Artisson. As an exercise in revision and expansion we will take another look at this name and develop further on the synthesis conducted in the last series of notes. The name Robin Artisson can translate as Robin, meaning "bright" or "shining fame" or "red-bright" and Artis-son, perhaps as the Artisan's son, giving either "The red-haired Shining One" or "The Fairy King, son of the Architect" (artisan-tekton-mason-smith). An earlier rendering might have been Artisson as Mac Art.

Let's deal firstly with Robin. This name, as bright or shining one, corresponds with Ahura Mazda, Lord of Light and Ormurd, which I mantain relates linguistically to the Serpent of Light from Orm, the root of Worm, a Dragon or serpent; and Mazdh, the Light.

This being the case, the "Architect" on one level would, in relation, be the Ancient of Days, who was Zirvan. In Monarchic Dualism, the three principles are Zirvan, Ahura Mazda, Ahrunan or: Space/Time-Increase-Decrease, whilst Ahriman is the Serpent of the Darkness. This philosophy approximates with the original Eurasian, proto-Zoroastrian tradition from which both Hinduism and Druidhism come.

We also know that pre-Nicaean Christianity had been closely associated with this root and included the triad comprising God-Satan-Jesus. In the following, the Witches' god, Robin Artisson or Robin Hood can be appreciated as being closely related to these triads. Jesus himself was thought to correspond with Mithras and Ahura Mazda and was also the son of an artisan. Directly descended from his line we also have Bera the Architect (Vera Mason!).

Robin Artisson is a variant of the British and Gallic Robin Hoods, and appears as the Witches' god in Ireland, as previously stated, who is interchangeable with the Gallic Basque god of the Witches, Janicot, who is also known in Britain as Little John. As we know Janicot is Jani-Gon or Janus-God, the two-headed or dualistic deity, which indicates clearly that the Witches were dualists, as were their cultic cousins, the pre-Nicaean Christians.

In England we have one of at least two triads. One consists of: Herne-Robin Hood-Little John, where perhaps, as I have suggested, Robin and John, in following ancient tradition, were either brothers or partners in an ancient Dragon family ritual—or one person—as were Jesus and Satan, variously and cosmically speaking, in some gnostic traditions.

In traditional English folklore, the father of Robin Goodfellow was Herne the Hunter. As Robin Goodfellow is identical to Puck, whose father was Oberon, then it follows that Herne the Hunter and Oberon are also the same person. In the tales concerning Robin Goodfellow, he was a flesh and blood character who lived with human parents. One night he felt the call of the wild and left home to wander the Greenwood, meet his real father, Oberon, and engage in various adventures with his own kind. One gets the impression that in some way, perhaps through unuttered longings, he was "called to the Dragon" or called to follow his true genetic nature which, prior to his departure, had been intimated to him in restless notions and strange dreams, but had been otherwise unknown. He is like the changeling or the Fairy orphan adopted by humans. In some senses the story of Jesus is the same, the humble son of the carpenter who is really the Son of God, a standard fairy tale motif which is repeated to this day.

Concerning the Boggart

C. S. Lewis called dwarves "The sons of Stone" whilst in Scandinavia these were the Trolls. Boggart may have had two spellings. The first and perhaps the older of the two was Boggard or Bog Ard, meaning the High God, who was the Dagdha. As the god-king of the Danaan, the Dagdha would have been the royal arch-Druid of the Tuadhe or nation. With regard to the other spelling, a reduction into two parts gives Bogg and Art.

The first means God and the second means Stone and hence, Godstone or God's Stone. In *Phallic Worship* by George Riley-Scott, one particular standing stone in Israel, said to be the God Stone and thought of as the habitation of the God was named Beth-El or the Bethel Stone, which is a Boggart. Alternatively the Boggart could mean God of the Stone, which easily renders itself as the God-King of the Lia Fail or the Cubic Stone, the Grail. Boggart, as the God's Stone; would be the Lia Fail.

As the Stone that fell to Earth, the jewel in Lucifer's Crown and so forth, the trail leads back to Robin Artisson. In which case, the anointed stone of the Beth-El and the Lia Fail, the cubic stone, would be female and not male. The female in question would be related to Astaroth, the forerunner of Sophia, wisdom or the Holy Spirit, to which the anointing oil of the Hebrews relates as the dew of the cup or Rosicrucis. Astaroth is Ishtar, who was a draconian relation of Lilith the Dragon queen, the ancestral grandmother of the Tuadha de Danaan.

A few Victorian amateur anthropologists, wishing to bring a breath of fresh air into the stuffy drawing rooms of the middle classes, made much of the fertility rituals and beliefs of ancient and primitive peoples. Given the social climate of the time, this intention was thoroughly laudable but, in their haste to attribute venal meanings to transcendent rituals and artefacts, they seem to have set in motion a movement devoted to missing the point.

One can imagine the relish with which some must have anticipated the opportunity afforded them. Here, it seemed, was a license to shock without let or hindrance, presenting itself under the guise of valuable scientific research. This notwithstanding, and despite the entertainment value, it must be said that any attempt to confront Victorian sensibilities proved in itself to have been rather pointless.

In many instances the work was either edited or suppressed by a society that was not only the most hypocritical and morally corrupt but also, behind closed doors, the most lascivious and sexually inventive in western history.

The work of these pioneers was ground breaking and in particular we remember Sir Richard Burton with respect. Even so, the foundations they laid seem to have been built upon later by others whose only thrust appears to have been in proving that everything they discovered that might be labelled primitive, was in consequence automatically associated with fertility.

Such a mentality was both an insult to simpler or earlier cultures and a serious hindrance to their understanding. It came to be thought that if one early culture was based on fertility worship at a certain period in history, then it followed that all cultures of that time were based on fertility worship. This approach didn't take into consideration the differences in outlook or perception that existed between castes living side by side. Nor did it appreciate the fact that environment and resources change from region to region which, as such, has significant ramifications on the social and spiritual development of a people.

Basically the thinking was, in blunt terms, that an early or primitive society must inevitably be thick, brutish and uneducated in comparison to the Christian, industrial culture of the historian, missionary or anthropologist. So it was thought that the primitive wouldn't have understood the process of conception or birth and would therefore have worshipped it as a magical act at every given opportunity, basing their entire spiritual belief system on fertility alone.

That kind of attitude was patronising, imperialist, arrogant and ignorant, born of the worst convictions of a society which itself had been and still is brutalised by its merchant classes and the greed of their ill-educated divines.

Anthropology in general, if one could call it that, arose as a discipline at a time when the Christian west was conquering the rest of the known world. No widespread or intrinsic desire to understand the culture or history of other races existed at that time because the prime motive in any study was to prove white Christian superiority prior to or during invasion, colonisation, conversion and exploitation. This meant that indigenous peoples were portrayed as ignorant, sex mad, cannibalistic savages, having ancestors who were also ignorant, sex mad, cannibalistic savages.

In the late twentieth century however, a swing towards a more liberal attitude has meant that societies are now being studied in greater depth and on their own terms. Nevertheless, to date, the hangover from our Victorian past means that some scholars still haven't quite got the picture. When confronted with an artifact or evidence of a ritual that appears to have a seemingly sexual context, they will often automatically label it accordingly and stick it in the pigeonhole marked “primitive fertility worship”.

A case in point is the Beth-El stone, which derives from a period in Hebraic antiquity when the Jews were polytheistic and worshipped the goddess. From a patriarchal Christian viewpoint, one that had swallowed the later Jewish concept of the one male god, the Beth-El Stone was thought to be, as previously mentioned, a phallic emblem associated with an early manifestation of Jehovah as Behemoth. One scholar, relating the Beth-El to Jehovah, further associated the two with a scripture which said “His rocks shall crash together”. The academic meant that God's Behemothic testicles banged together during the penetration and withdrawal of the Beth-El phallus, which accompanied God's numerous sex acts.

As Jehovah, via Zeus, became the northern Thor, one must assume that thunderstorms, euphemistically said to be the god banging away with his hammer, are in fact the result of his enthusiastic wedding tackle ricocheting against itself.

Whilst I am prepared to accept that this was a typical Jewish joke, and part of a colourful and imaginative folk culture of the time, I am hard pressed to accept it as part of the venal doctrine of a society which manifested itself during a phase of fertility worship.

People have not changed a great deal in thousands of years and humorous euphemisms were as much a part of everyday life then as they are now.

We are the greatest fools if we take these jokes seriously and then waste years of our lives on dour research in compiling so-called scholarly theses which soberly explain the finer points of a doctrine that probably originated as a humorous quip in the equivalent of a Jewish pub, and was thought funny enough to put down on clay, stone or papyrus.

On its own the Beth-El, as an anointed stone, is reminiscent of all the black monoliths that appeared in mediaeval literature and art as stones that were, of themselves, anointed or sometimes baptised, including the 15th-century picture "The Heart's search for Love".

There is no reason why any of them couldn't be a Boga Art, the Goddess' Stone. Their genital context, like that of the Sheelagh Na Gig, has nothing to do with sexual reproduction per se. Indeed, the black stones probably have a component of their iconography which is, in itself, a symbolic descendant of the Beth-El. This is because they are part of European Grail Lore which has part of its history immersed in the Hebrew culture, and further being associated with the Grail itself which is female and Tantric. This would then mean that it had absolutely nothing to do with the penis or its progenitive function, or indeed the reproductive functions of the female sex organs.

Both of these have been the subject of common knowledge amongst mankind for thousands of years, making it highly unlikely that every sexual symbol ever produced by so-called primitive or ignorant savages was solely manufactured for the fertility-cult market. With this and the foregoing in mind it is worth mentioning the ancient Hindu symbols of the Yoni or Vulva and the Lingam or Penis, as another example of simplistic over categorisation.

Originally the Lingam was not the phallus. The word Lingam relates to Lingua or speech and hence the tongue, so this means that the Tantric element of Hinduism and Buddhism relates primarily to the Beth-El and the Grail, and not to sex. When the Yoni was entered by the Lingam, it was an act of transcendence, not of copulation. The union intended was with the gods who resided in, or who could be joined with by imbibing, the blood of the womb.

It is entirely possible that Beth-El was once Beth-Elohim, meaning House of the Gods, rather than just the House of God. The House of the Gods, the place where a human being would find the gods and thus by implication attain transcendence, would be the womb. One would find the gods by drinking from the Grail, the Womb. "He who drinks in one draught will see God and the Magdalene".

The gods abided in the blood of the Sacred Womb, which is what the Beth-El would signify, along with all the later cubic stones. With Beth-Elohim we have Beth Lehem or Bethlehem, the Rath of the Womb of the Great Mother, which accords with Beth Seathan, a Rath or Tel which was a Repha'im temple of Nergal, the god of the Otherworld, built by the Scythians in Jordan.

The Otherworld is the House of the Gods and hence the Beth-El or Beth Lehem. If Jesus was born in a Beth Lehem, then he was born symbolically in the Otherworld and emerged from the womb of the Rath as a god-king.

The story of his being born in a stable which was a cave has a great deal to do with this symbolism, as caves and Raths were places of the dead. Like the Sidhe Mounds of Eire, they were doorways to Elphame or the Other or Underworld and here we have a link with Epona, Rhiannon and Slepnir, and with Robin as an equine deity and thus a Priest King.

Being born in a Beth-El, Jesus—the Christsonday god of the Witches—was Janus or Little John, the psychopomp, portal guardian and pontiff or bridge to the Otherworld. His priest kingship has much that is owed to this Scythian, Dragon symbolism. Here there is also a Mithraic link with the rite of the cave of the wolf (Jesus ben Panther, Son of the Eastern Werewolf) and a link with Apollo or the Sol Invicta.

Jesus would have been a son of the Beth-El, a Son of the Stone. According to Olga Friedenbourg, the Russian writer, these links, with the solar Mithras or Mazda, and hence Samael and the biblical Satan, are confirmed in his choice of an ass upon which to ride into Jerusalem. The ass is the Egyptian Set, who became Set-Typhon, or Sataniel-Lucifer the Enlightened and Enlightening One, identifying Jesus as the Buddha Siddharta of the Levant—A Boggart or Fairy.

Robin's Father

Oberon breaks down into Ober and ron. Here "Ober" can relate to uber meaning "over" or "high", and "ron" presents itself as being "reyn" or "regin". Regin relates to king, therefore Oberon means high or white king. Uber meaning Vampire, would render Oberon as "Vampire king", which, in this particular instance is not beyond the bounds of possibility; as Vampires, Witches and Fairies are all the same beings, and the following, taken from traditional sources, serves yet again to reinforce this.

In the case of Robin, the name might have presented some difficulties had it not been for the existence of intentional multiplicity. The name, coming from Robert, has a root—"Ro" which can be found in Celtic, but also in later

French and German, where the meanings expand collaterally. In German the root "Ro" can mean either "fame", as in Ro-bert, or "power" as in Rod-Erick.

As Robert was originally spelt Hrodebert it would seem that the root "Rod" is more appropriate than "Ro", which would render Robin or Robert, not as "bright-fame" but as "power-bright" or "might-right". In Gaelic, Roderick, spelt Roderigh (Rod-Righ) means "red-haired king" and has variants in the Welsh—Rydderch or Rhodri, and the Irish—Rhuardhri or Rory.

"Rod" as "red" in German would be "rot", and "Rod" as "power" could derive as it does elsewhere, from a Martian association between "red-blood-might". This would give us "strength derived from blood", this being either the possession of a certain bloodline or the ingestion of blood, as was the practice in the royal covens. Therefore if Hrode, as "Rod" or "ruddy", means "red" or "red-haired", in the particular case of Robin Hood/Artisson/Goodfellow (Puck-Boucca-Bolg), we have Robin or Robert as "Red-Bright" or the "red-haired bright (or shining) one". Consequently, as red was the Scythian king's hair colour and a Shining One was a Fairy, we would have Robin as the "red-haired Fairy-Dragon-Vampire-Witch king".

This is entirely appropriate to his legendary associations and cultic role, especially as we now know that he, as Robert de Vere, descended directly from Melusine des Scythes and had a father and grandfather both named Aubrey or Alberich, meaning Oberon, the High Fairy King. The "R" in Robin or Robert was quite often replaced by an "H" or "D". This gives the abbreviated "Rob" as Hob, as in Hob Goblin—a Fairy or Demon of the Mines (mounds etc.) and another name for Robin Goodfellow. Goblin comes from the German Kobelin, meaning a mine, cave or mound (Tepes) dwelling magician-smith (alchemist), and gives us another word—Cobalt, a metal which is silver in colour, resembling the colour of Odin's cloak.

Cobalt is highly magnetic and, as Cobalt 40, is also extremely radioactive, being used in the "Cobalt Bomb". Otherwise Cobalt is an essential part of the human and animal diet and can be found in spinach, cabbage, lettuce, watercress and liver. Cobalt was used in making coloured glass (alchemy) and was applied, as a coloured glaze, to ancient Chinese porcelain. Consequently, two pigments relevant here can be obtained from it:

1) green, Robin's and the Fairy's colour, and,

2) blue; with a range of hues including,

a) ultramarine (meaning "from beyond the sea", also obtained from Lapis Lazuli) and

b) sky blue, the colour of Odin's hood (OHO: Hood Hod, rel. to Hat) in his role as Sky or Ml Father, and

c) its darker shade Azure (the Persian “lazward”), one of the titles of Kali as “Kali-Azura”.

Chapter 22

Goblins, Pixies, Sprites and Gnomes

Hob Goblin is the name of one individual, rather than pertaining to a class of sprites. In Hob Goblin or Robert the Kobelin we have:

a) Robin-Smith of the Sidhe,

b) Robin the Magician,

c) Robin of the (eye patch and) Hood,

d) Robin the Alchemist.

Hereto, the name Robin may also pertain to the bright flame of the smithy's forge.

During the late 1600's to early 1700's, one could be hanged for wearing green. It was the Fairies' colour, as we know, and represented the amorality of nature which is unconscious of and beyond the stunted human, Christian notions of good and evil. By wearing green, a person was intimating that they were of faerie and, by blood, above the bondage of petty Christian morals, ideals and laws. This meant, more or less, that they had transcended and, as with nature and the Cosmos itself, were at one with God.

Robin Hood was an outlaw, not because he stole from the rich to give to the poor, but because firstly he was Fairy and thereby a Magus. He had transcended human perceptions and restrictions and because of this, he was by birth outside all human laws of existence anyway, as were all those of the Fairy race. The Cyclops of Greece, members of the Titanic, Fairy race of "giants" were also cave or Rath dwelling miner-smiths who forged thunderbolts (we are reminded of the properties of Cobalt-60) for Zeus (the Greek counterpart of Thor).

It is generally thought that their name derived, not from "one-eyed", but from "ring eyed" (cycle-ops), related to the practice of wearing cobalt blue woad bands or rings. Painted around the eyes, Graves reminds us that the rings of the Cyclops mimicked those of the sidhe of Eire.

It will be remembered that ultramarine and cobalt blue were, respectively, the colours of Vishnu and his brother/counterpart Shiva (Sidha). Nevertheless, the Cyclops were described also as "one-eyed". The one-eyed epithet is pertinent because of the smith's habit of wearing a patch to protect one eye from sparks. (The Fairy hood, as protective headgear, is also part of the alchemical/smithing tradition, and also pertains to the alchemist's hidden knowledge, kept "under his hat".)

This gave rise to the idea of the Cyclops being one-eyed giants. This one-eyed aspect in Elven lore also relates to the Irish Balor and his counterpart on one level; the Danish Odin. The names hobgoblin, sprite and gnome conjure up storybook images and memories of *A Midsummer Night's Dream*, and when we think of these characters we think of harmless, mischievous beings.

Although we have accused Shakespeare of perverting the true identity of the Fairy, it might be advisable to take a fresh look at his motives and bear in mind his own origins. He is guilty of diminution, as are the establishment—the Christian clerics and the academics—but there may be a sound motive behind his thinking.

The desire to belittle occurs in the first instance because of threat. It's as simple as that. To the process of the diminution of the Fairy by the establishment, we can also add the same process as practiced by the people themselves and, strangely enough when you look at it, the process of the diminution of the Fairy, by the Fairies themselves!

The Catholic establishment belittled the Fairy because the Dragon Blood posed a threat to that establishment's hold on government. This is easy to understand. It is more difficult to belittle them if Fairies were supposed to be harmless, friendly beings, or at worst just mischievous pranksters, which is what occurred between the late Dark Age to Reformation period, by the wider population of the period. The problem was that Fairies weren't just ethereal pygmies, nor were they just "almost ordinary folk", which is the picture we might tend to get from Murray's sympathetically understated description of them.

The true nature of the Fairy, one that has already been hinted at, can be found by studying the various names they were given over time, names which now conjure up images of garden ornaments and wispy elementals. In the past, however, they were epithets of terror. The last thing you would want in your little patch of suburban heaven is the original version of the Garden Gnome.

True enough, Fairies loved nature and greenery. They were, after all, the children of the Greenwood and descendants of the kings and queens who, at the dawn of history, laid out the Garden of Eden. So it seems appropriate that we have statues of them fishing in our goldfish ponds or sitting looking sternly at the lawn that should have been mown a week ago.

But the real thing itself was the very reason why the plastic version now holds court on patios across the length and breadth of Merrie England. The Gnome was, for man's more recent ancestors, a horrible creature and sometimes a very real threat to life. This is why it, along with all the other beings we think of as separate classes of Fairies, was reduced in stature by ordinary people.

What do we do if we are beset by problems that we can't get rid of? More often than not, we try to make light of them and ridicule them in order to make them smaller, thereby alleviating the fear in which we hold them. This was one of the reasons behind the diminution of Fairies by the peasants. Fairies, hard pressed by adverse conditions during the Church's burning times, and because of the relentless expansion of the human population into their territories, often continued old traditions out of a ritual context.

No doubt this occurred with a certain imperious callousness, considering the treatment they were then receiving at the hands of their former client peoples. It has been stated elsewhere that Elves did not steal human adults or children for ritual purposes and this stands true. Nevertheless during the medieval period cannibalism was endemic in the whole British population because of the disasters caused by war, plague and famine. It is warranted therefore that the Elves ate what they could, especially as they were additionally a people forced to the very margins of society.

It has become a tradition to put the little folk into classes or categories. However, if we look closely at the etymology and the origins of the words used to describe each type of Fairy, we will find that, rather than defining differences between various types of ethereal pygmy, the words or names describe the different attributes of only one type of being. Robin Goodfellow for instance is called Hobgoblin, which is another name for a Gnome, which we think of as a cute little fellow in a red cap. And indeed he or she probably was, to another Gnome. In fact the name "Redcap" associated with the fly Agaric or Fairy mushroom, was another epithet for the Gnome and the Pixy, which we know was the Pict-Sidhe.

Perhaps as time passed, the Fairy actually did became smaller in stature than ordinary people. However, as Murray points out, this was probably caused by the restriction in diet which, in turn, was caused by the increasing sparsity of resources available to them as a people, because of their having to go into hiding from the Church.

Nevertheless the Fairy, here described as the "Gnome", was once a being of considerable stature until he was forced into forest regions that could hardly support him and which were, even then, being populated and deforested by farmers wanting to clear the land to provide grazing for sheep and cattle.

In Tanzania, exactly the same process is now happening to the Hadza people. These nomadic tribesmen are the last true hunter-gatherers, they keep no livestock and depend entirely on their fantastic knowledge of the terrain to support themselves and their families. Their impact on the environment is minimal and sustainable. To all intents, they live in harmony with nature.

Today their range is diminishing even further because agriculturalists and pastoralists from the outside are coming into their lands, cutting down tree stock to provide overnight enclosures for their cattle, which they only use once before moving on, thereby overgrazing the entire territory. Because of this the Hadza population is dying out and over the last century their numbers have dwindled to no more than a thousand people. This was the fate of the Shining Ones and it is a story that has been repeated all over the world.

Chapter 23

The Wise Ones

So we have suggested that the Fairies, the "little people" in pre-Christian history times were Vampiric by necessity and inclination, and fed purely on the blood of their own kind for magical reasons. But later on, during the one and a half millennia following Christ's death, they were pushed into a corner. They also fed on human blood and the occurrences were frequent enough to become a major problem for incursive agriculturalists in the second millennium, who consequently held the "Gnome" in awe, as an object of fear. In order to cope with the danger of living in Fairy lands, the response of the invader was to belittle the beings, from once proud Kings to a race who eventually became dietarily disadvantaged fugitives of the forests, and finally into ethereal pygmies that were harmless.

As the Fairy populations in each region died out completely, the incomers were left with a memory of a small elusive folk who, as time passed, became smaller still in the mind's eye of those who, though responsible for their genocide would, nevertheless, rather forget them altogether. The words Gnome, Sprite and Goblin; like Fairy, Elf and Pixy therefore all refer to one race: the Scythians or Sidheans, and relate to various practices and ritual identities amongst this once ancient and noble people.

"Gnome" comes from the Greek and is related to the root "gno". From this same root we obtain our words gnosis and gnobilis or nobilis. Both these words relate to knowledge and wisdom, and point to an origin within the Aryan culture. Aryan also means wise, or "Race of the Wise", or "the Noble Race" in Sanskrit.

A "Gnome" is one of the race of the Wise Ones, the ancient king tribe of the Aryans or Scythians. They were the genetic guardians of a blood chemistry, of rituals and lore from which they derived a perceptual state of gnosis or transcendence. The Gnome is said to have been a creature of the mines and mounds, just like the hobgoblin.

This description, linked both to alchemy and smithing, is also associated with their ritual practice of living in specially prepared chambers in burial mounds, tombs and pyramids. This links the Gnome, as a priest-king figure, with the cult of Nergal and the Otherworld or underworld. For this very same reason the Fairy is also called the Sprite. This word is a reduction of the word Spirit and also has the same associations with the Scythian practice of regularly inhabiting tombs to obtain knowledge from the ancestors.

Gnome (also relating to "judge") as Nobilis gives us another familiar name for the Fairies—the Gentry or Noble ones. Gnome also refers to a canon or body of law and this is reminiscent of the role of the Pictish-"Pixy"-Druidic High-Kings as custodians of the Law and Culture of their peoples.

These Kings, the Brudes or Bruidhes, were the Judge-Poets and magicians whose expertise lay in spellcraft, rhetoric and satire. Their female counterparts were the Bruidhinas, Sirens, Morrigans and Melusines, the Raven women and Swan Maidens, female "Gnomes", Ban Sidhes—female Fairies—the custodians of wisdom and law, weavers of spells and Vampire princesses. This is exactly what Melusine d'Avalon was.

The "Red Cap" was not associated with the Gnome, Pixy, Sprite, or Goblin because of the colour of the mushrooms they were fond of sitting under. Nor was it solely from the later need for the consumption of human blood as a staple food. It was because they used to dye their hoods or their pointed, Phrygian headgear in menstrual blood which was consumed, along with its precious cargo of neurotransmitters, to facilitate wisdom.

As the cap covers the head, so symbolically the blood feeds the spirit, the soul and the intellect, situated in the pineal gland and the "Wings of the Swan" in the brain. The blood drinking rituals of the Gnome-Goblin-sprite and his or her habitual occupation of tombs, as god-kings or queens of the Otherworld, led to the notion of the Vampire as a bloodthirsty ghost.

Sprite, then, means Spirit-People, or people of the spiritual realms, those who have congress with the inhabitants and gods of the Otherworld. It also refers to the blood-drinking Scythian "Ghost-Warriors" who painted their bodies grey-blue to look like corpses when they entered naked upon the battlefield.

Sprite was a name given to Robin Goodfellow or Hood who was also known as Puck, meaning Boucca or Bolg, the God. Sprite therefore expands the meaning to include People of the Gods, which is entirely appropriate, as the Fairies, the Dragon Clan, were the descendants of the original gods of the earth.

Chapter 24

Elementals and Diminution

Given that the Fairies, according to Murray, were still around in Shakespeare's time (Edward de Vere?), it seems to me that at least one individual who is said to have been a member of the literary syndicate that produced *A Midsummer Night's Dream*, belittled the Fairies, his own race. It could be argued that this was in order to alleviate the persecution that was raging against them—persecution that carried on for nearly two hundred years after his death.

This individual used a form of diminution, turning Fairies into elementals, a type of anthropomorphisation, which in reverse is the same as the process of deification, turning the ancient priest-kings into the gods. Through this person's influence, the Fairies who traditionally wielded power derived from their understanding of the elemental forces in nature, became associated with those forces to the extent that they were thought to be the elements themselves. In doing this he instituted a situation in which the Fairies could side-step out of this world into another, taking them out of human history altogether and thus eventually out of harm's way.

It is possible that his patron, the self-styled "Faerie Queen" Elizabeth I, sympathised with and supported such a move. She was supposed to be marginally descended from Margaret of Anjou and this house claimed a supposed descent from Melusine, the High Queen of the Fairies of All Europe who were, like Elizabeth herself, the arch enemies of Catholicism.

Rob as Hob reinforces the Fairy element in the Robin Hood story as does Dob or Dobin. Odin's mount—the eight-legged Slepnir (a funeral byre) was similar to the Celtic Rhiannon and Epona. Like Robin's father, Herne or Oberon, who inhabited the underworld, the horse deities were also related to the Scythian death cult of Nergal. All three were white (Fairy) horses who carried the rider to the grave—the Otherworld, the realm of sovereignty and wisdom.

Related to this, the funeral byre in Pakistan which is carried by four men (eight legs), is called the Breghi Moru. Similarly Odin had a son called Breghi who can be related to Robin. Robin was said to be a gifted musician and Bereghi was a god of music who, like Orpheus, traversed the Underworld or Death.

The name often given to a horse was Dobbin and it is feasible that Robin Hood—son of Odin/Herne—was, as a Magus, a psychopomp associated with the Celtic realm of death, sovereignty and the horse deities. Robin Hood as Puck was related to the Irish "pooka" as well as the Boucca, from whence comes the Dutch "spook", meaning sprite or spirit, the Welsh "puca" and the Icelandic "piki".

The "peoka", was a shape-shifter which often took the form of animals, the horse being one of them. Likewise the Witches' god would often appear in animal form, regularly as a horse, often as a Stag, but also in a variety of shapes according to the tribal totem animal traditionally associated with the region or the clan of the officiate/god.

The Icelandic "piki" is close to "Pixy" or Pict-Sidhe, a painted Elf; meaning that piki-puck-boucca-bolg-god indicates the status of Robin Hood/Goodfellow/Artisson as a "Puck" or shapeshifting, shamanic, Pictish God-King or Priest-King. Puck is not a name therefore, but a title, related to bogey-man and boggart, a god-man, a Druid prince or priest king.

Included in the Dobbin epithet there is also a relation to the origins of Robin"s ancestors as mounted bowmen. We know from folklore that Robin was both a horseman and a gifted archer. We know from history that he was neither Norman nor Saxon, being of princely Flemish descent and an accomplished veteran cavalryman. We also know that the bow wasn't merely a yeoman's weapon and that the term yeoman was relative anyway. If one combines the two ideas, those of the archer and the cavalryman, one arrives at the origin of the Centaur and the Sagittarii.

The Centaurs were extraordinary mounted archers who were said to have fought at Troy, whilst in other accounts they were said to be, like the Scythians, rapists and pillagers. The amazing skill of the Thracian horse warrior, whose symbiosis with his mount seemed to make him a part of the horse itself, contributed to the development of the image of the Centaur as half man, half horse. It is likely that the Thracians and the Sarmatians, who wore fish scale armour, were originally related to the Zmei of Russia.

The Zmei were mounted, fish-scale or Dragon-scale armoured lords whom the people referred to as Dragons. Like the fabled Centaurs they were wise but brutal and, similar to the legend concerning the Cimmerians, they appeared at night. It is likely that they were descended from the same central European Scythian tribes that migrated to Britain to become the Picts and the Dalriada, or Horse Lords, from whom Robin Hood partly descends.

The Centaur Cheiron was, like all Centaurs, one assumes, the son of Cronos or Anu and the water Fairy Oceanid. This confirms that the Centaurs, the Sagitarii, were Dragon Lords. Cheiron kept a school for princes at Thessaly and was the tutor to Jason, Odysseus and Achilles.

The name Sagittarius can be broken into two separate words—Sagitta and Rius or Arius. From the root "Sag", though said to mean arrow from the Latin, are also derived the words Sagacious and Sage, both pertaining to wisdom. The last syllables Ri-us or Ari-us can mean either:

a) king or Rig with Latin male suffix "us", or

b) an arrow.

Sagittarii may then mean either "Wise Archers" or "Archer Lords". Either way it doesn't matter because both come down to the same thing. Related to Arya and the Noble or Wise Race of Kings, Lord is one of the order of the Nobilis or Wise Ones anyway. We are then back firmly in Scythian Dragon territory and the realm of the horse lords and the King Tribe, with its Gnomes, pixies, sprites, Fairies and boggarts.

As we have seen, Hrodebert was the original spelling for Robert and its affectionate diminutive Robin, which gave us Hob and Dob. Another affectionate diminutive of Robert is Robby which, as you might expect, also has an old variation which expands upon the story of the link between Robin Hood and his ancient cultic and equestrian roots. The abbreviation of Hrodebert is, as one would guess; Hrodin or Odin: The Lord of the Rings.

The Hobby Horse is a sight familiar to all who have attended the spring fairs and have enjoyed the sight of Morris Men or the Sweeps on surnmer outings to country public houses and village fetes in England. In earlier times, the Hobby Horse was a notorious character who accompanied the Coal Black Man, Jack-in-the-Green, Robin Hood and Maid Marion on the Maying, where he was noted for his lascivious behaviour in chasing and indecently assaulting young village girls as they paraded with the May Day throng.

Nevertheless, Charles Burland tells us that the Hobby Horse was a popular figure in those days, before political correctness had been thought up. Then, the only social workers for miles around were likely to have been called either Rosy or Mother Demdike.

The Hobby Horse and his antics have echoes in the Wild Hunt for Elf maidens at Samhain. Like Herne, Robin and the Witch princesses, or Odin and the Valkiries, the Vampire kings and queens, the Pictish and Scythian horsemen and horsewomen used to roam the forests in a ritual search of their Dragon princesses, whom they would ritually kidnap and feast upon. In this connection we have the Hobby Horse or Robin o' the Horse and the reinforcement of all the ancient connections between him and his Fairy cohorts in this world, and their longing to return to their Otherworld home—Elphame.

With regard to the Coal Black Man, some scholars have linked him with the Morris and both with some fertility ritual originating in Africa, based on the supposition that Morris was originally spelt Moorish. The Coal Black Man or the Sweep is a variant of Jack-in-the-Green. He is black because of the magical custom, like Santa Claus, of entering and exiting houses via the chimney which, when the house was a building similar to a Rath or a mound, also doubled up as the front door.

He is linked to the ancient chimney-climbing shaman, to the Witches who flew up chimneys to get to the Sabbat, all blacked up with soot and flying ointment based on goose grease. Thus the Witches' god, the Man-in-Black or Coal Black Man is Odin and St. Nicholas, the Horned God, always accompanied a'Maying by the mummer of the Dragon.

The Sweep therefore is also Jack or Herne, who is sometimes referred to as the Foliate Man or the Green Man, another name for Robin Goodfellow or Hood, the Sprite, Gnome or Pixy. He is the Witches' god, not from an exotic imported cult, but from the northern lands of Europe.

Chapter 25

Phrygians and Scythians

The Red Cap of the Gnome and the Pixy is the pointed cap associated with Witchcraft and shamanism. Examples of it can be found in Babylonian stone bas-relief depictions of the gods, in burial sites in Takla Makan and elsewhere in the Celtic world. In relation to the Gnome or Pixy, this headdress is of Phrygian origin, where it was once worn with the point folded towards the front of the head. A portrait of Liberty leading the French Revolution depicts her wearing this same Phrygian Cap.

The Phrygians migrated from Thrace, the original home of Dionysus, to lands adjacent to Galatia in central Anatolia around 500 BC. They were probably descended from the same stock as those earlier Scythians who migrated to Thrace from Ireland. Returning there they became the Fir Bolg and the Phrygians revered a Goddess Queen of the same Dragon Pantheon from which the Fir Boig of the Tuatha de Danaan were descended. This deity, Cybele, was a native of mountains and forests. Originally known to the Greeks as Rhea, the Titaness and mother of Zeus by Cronos, she can be identified as the Sumerian Antu, wife of Anu, from whence the Danaan derive their name—Tuadha d'Anu.

The Phrygians also worshipped Mithras who was the Persian god often identified with Mazda. Mithras is often depicted as slaying the "world bull", which represents what the gnostic dualists call the demi-urge, the subordinate creator and "Lord of this World". Cybele as Antu was the Mother of Enlil (who later became Zeus and Jehovah), whilst Mithras as Mazda was originally Enlil's brother Enki, and Enlil was Ahriman in the Persian dualist cult that revered Mithras who, like Herne, was associated with the Underworld and caves. Like Mithras, Herne is further linked both to the Stag and the Bull. Enki became Samael and here we enter the realm of the cult of the twin and the rivalry between the Light and Dark represented respectively by Mithras the bull slayer and the demi-urge, the bull itself symbol of Mazda-Mithras's brother, Enlil-Zeus-Jehovah.

In slaying the bull, Mithras is destroying the world of form and illusion created by the language we use to interpret the stimulus received by the human senses. In one sense human beings are the bull itself, and here we enter the true meaning of the Christian message. From the death of the bull is brought forth new life. From the death of the Christian believer is brought forth new life in the spirit of Christ.

This world of form hides the true nature of existence which is creativity, symbolised by the flowers that issue from the neck wound of the bull. Essentially Mithraism was a transcendent philosophy intended to get people to see beyond the semantic, material world—the "bull" of Enlil-Zeus-Jehovah, to the world of eternity beyond thought and beyond the form defined erroneously by language.

The bull features repeatedly in Druidic lore and was sacrificed regularly at the Nemetons, the major Druidic gatherings, which were held in Galatia, next door to Phrygia and in Ireland and Scotland. This sacrifice was the Mithraic sacrifice of human delusion, not the sacrifice of a god. The Druids didn't worship anyone and the bull was definitely no god. The Druids and consequently the Fairies, Vampires and Witches were dualist philosophers, not religious devotees. In history the deities (more properly "cosmic forces") have been reversed by various vested interests and in some variations of the dualist philosophy Enlil, Jehovah-Zeus the Appis Bull, was a symbol of the material world of nerve-endings. Hence it had the capacity to experience misery and suffering whilst Enki, the Dragon of Light or Satan, was the deliverer from pain, the Enlightener.

Traditionally Jesus was identified as the Sol Invicta or Mithras, the deliverer of mankind—the Enlightener: Lucifer or Satan. He guides the Magus in his quest to transform his perception of the material world in order that he may see that eternity and the realm of Elphame lie hidden just beneath the skin of our fears and opinions, the thoughts that make up our world of suffering. Similarly, the flowers lie hidden in the brutish body of the world bull. The philosophy of Dualism works on two levels, however, and whilst one relates to our perception of existence, the other relates to the interplay of those forces which make up the very life we so often perceive in error.

The Phrygian cap worn by Mithras, the badge of transcendence, was the same cap worn by all shamans since the Golden Age of the Titans, those Anunnaki (Anunnagi) ancestors of the Dragon Clans. From them emerged the Fairy Race of the ancient Dragon and Grail Blood—the Gnomes, Pixies and Sprites. It was once said that the Phrygian devotees of Mithras would soak themselves in the blood of sacrificed bulls. Anciently, the skull of the bull was used to symbolise the female organs.

The horns were often tipped with round golden balls and these and the horns themselves represented the ovaries and fallopian tubes which were joined to the cranium, which symbolised the womb, a symbolic connection between the brain and the uterus, or intelligence and menstrual blood.

The nasal passage and mouth of the bull represented the vagina. To be soaked in bull's blood, was to be soaked in the blood of the womb. The red cap of both the Phrygian and the Fairy therefore was originally coloured by the blood of wisdom. A garden Gnome will never look the same again.

Chapter 26

Tomb Dwellers

As predicted, the Ziggurat and the Pyramid are now academically confirmed as being symbolic, ritual mountains. Also as predicted, they are the monumental granddaughters of the sidhe hills: the Beth, the Tel, the Rath, the Kurgan and the Tepes, the ritual chambers. These are, in turn, also the symbolic caves in the mountains of the original Carpathian homeland of the Anunnaki where, like Cybele, the Dragon mothers once wandered amongst the forests.

These structures, like the caves themselves, were used to bury the dead. Adjacent to the main burial chamber was a sleeping chamber where members of the Clan would spend the night in order to obtain information from the ancestors in dreams. Here we have the origin of one of the Irish words for Vampire: Crechaire, meaning tomb, shrine, sepulchre. The Crechaire or Tomb Dweller was a Druidic, Fairy God-King or Queen who, as the mediator between this world and the Otherworld, would reside in the sleeping chamber of the Rath, next to the ancestors. The image of the Vampire as one who lives in tombs is therefore correct. Tomb dwelling was common amongst the Egyptians and Sumerians, and consequently we have another cultural Fairy link between these peoples and the Scythian Pict-Sidhes. Another reinforcing link also appears between the Vampire and the Smith, the Alchemist, the Magi, the Fairy or Titan, Robin Hood and Odin.

The shapeshifting Robin or Puck, shares this shamanic attribute with Merlin and with Odin/Hodi/Wolden, who also shares his knowledge of alchemy and forging, and his one-eyed attribute with the Cyclops. They were the

Titanic Fairy smiths who so closely resemble the Irish Sidhe and Balor of the Formorians, who were the formidable giants (often described as one-eyed), said to have been descendants of Ham.

In legend, part of the wave of Scythian migrants who settled in Eire decamped and fled for the Northern Isles of the World. This is obviously Scandinavia and it is interesting to note that on their return to Ireland they established their Fairy reign as the Tuatha de Danaan.

It seems probable therefore that the Danes and the Danaan are directly related. This would explain the link between Odin, later the "antecessor" god of the Scandinavian Witches, and Robin Hood or Hodin, Robin (Artis-son) being of Irish origin via the Picts.

It appears that Robin, buried in an Oak Tree, Odin hanging from an Ash Tree and Jesus nailed to the Rood or Holly Tree are culturally related to each other, as shamans and as Druidhes or Wallimen (men of the trees). This was a name of the Witches' god in the Viking isles of Orkney. In Britain, the Witches' god was often dressed as Odin and in the Orkneys it would be Odin who is Walliman or Ualla-man, a word related to Uilidian, the Irish Sacral Royal House of the Fir Bolg (Boucca/Puck/Robin), who settled in Scotland.

In Gundestrop in Denmark a cauldron was unearthed upon which was embossed the distinctly Celtic figure of Cemunnos or Heme, Lord of the Forests. He was wearing torcs [variants of the Ring] and sitting cross-legged, holding a serpent or Dragon in each hand, another Ualla-man and the father of Robin Hood. The cauldron is a common symbol in Celtic lands and always associated there with blood and the Grail. Similarly, the Gundestrop Cauldron is considered to have been a vessel for catching the blood of victims sacrificed to the Danish gods, Odin the Ring Lord being the father of them all. Sacred to Odin were the Raven and the Wolf. Similarly, the companions of Merlin at Hart Fell were the Raven, the Wolf and the Boar, being symbolically a Morgana (a Morrigan or Bruidnina), a Warrior and a Druid, who probably fled with Merlin following the battle in which his patron Gwenddolau was killed. The Wolf and the Raven are also connected to the cult of Mithras.

It is likely that Odin and Merlin, though not the same person, were closely linked as royal priests of Druidic castes. They performed similar invocational functions and shared similar attributes within a religious tradition that originated from the early Eurasian dualistic cult from whence arose the Druids, the Parsi, the Magi and the Brahmins. Odin was a Seer and Merlin means Seer. This being the case, then, the legendary relationship between Merlin and Arthur (and Lancelot) is the same as the relationship between Herne/Odin and Robin (and Little John).

Both, in a cultic sense, are late aspects of the Monarchic dualistic concept of the triad or trinity and the cult of the twin, which began with Arin-Enki-Enlil.

This has established a Dragon Culture whose symbolism, ritual practice and royal priesthood has lasted 7000 years and included Jesus as an apostolic successor of collateral blood descent.

The Danaan were sidhe or Fairies, which are Druidhes or Witches (derived from the Old English Wic/ca) and we know that these descriptions are aspects of one identity. Similarly the word Viking is derived from the word Wic, mistakenly thought to derive from Old Fresian—an inlet dweller. The word actually comes from the same Old English word as Witch does—*Wicca*, meaning to yield or bend, as the Christianised Saxons would have it—"to demons", which is a Greek word (daemons) and means gods or intelligences.

From this can be inferred that they obtained Otherworldly wisdom, as yielding or understanding—to "stand under" or "give way to". Therefore we can render Viking as Witch. In Celtic, Druidhe is also a Witch. This goes some way in explaining the close similarity between the Danish Odinic Nine World or Sphere system set against Yggdrasil; and the Druidic symbol of the Apple Tree. The Apple Tree bears the spherical fruits, the Chakras or Sephiroth, which is what the Viking Nine Worlds are. As the Danaan are Sidhe, so the Vikings also had their Siddhirs or weavers of dreams.

The Danish Vikings were generally an egalitarian people who operated a social system not unlike the Danaan of Ireland, who considered all of the blood to be equal. Both the Danaan and the Danes were Kings' tribes. The latter, in the 11th century, were invited to provide princes and rulers for a foreign land, such was their expertise in management and their love of order.

Hence the originally Danish, Svei Ruotsi Clan migrated to Novgarod and founded what is now known as the Russian empire. This occurred at the height of their power when, with an entire population of little more than 300,000 people, the Danes brought peace to the warring Slavs of Russia, settled in America and traded for gold, spices and silk as far away as the Indian Ocean.

Their markedly Celtic/Scythian artwork and jewellery is some of the finest in Europe and forges a link between them and their cousins, the Irish and Pictish Scots descendants of the original Danaan Clans. Whilst examples of ornate Viking masonry can be found in Constantinople, at home the Vikings tended to live in grass-covered halls often carved into hillsides. These are strongly reminiscent of the Raths or Sidhe Mounds of Ireland and Scotland, as are the prolific amount of stone circles one can find in Scandinavia. A Dragon people with Dragon ships, (cc Tiamat, the Sea Dragoness) the symbol is everywhere in Danish art. Their elite warriors, the Berserkers or Bare-Shirts, took Amanita Muscaria and fought naked in the same way as the Celtic warriors of the British Isles and Gaul, neither having any fear of death whatsoever.

Chapter 27

Steel Bras and Winged Hats

As the Valkirie maidens dispatched the Danish warriors to Valhalla, so also the Raven women of the battle field, the Morrigans of the Celts, dispensed release from this world to Celtic friend and foe alike. From Raven we obtain the word Ravenous, which is akin to the blood frenzy of the Morrigans or Morganas in the theatre of war as they drank the blood of the fallen. The Raven women, the Morganas, are the Baobhan Sidhe, the Vampire Fairies. Off the battlefield they become the Leannan Sidhe, beautiful Fairy maidens like the Countess of Salisbury (The Maid of Kent), who was called La Belle Dame Sans Merci and acted as the Queen of Fairies and Witches in England.

Those away from the field of bloodshed drank dry the life force of their human lovers. Along with the Ban Sidhe-Melusine, the serene and graceful ladies of the lake and guardians of the sacred Meres and secret fountains, are the legendary Swan Maidens, the Valkirie of the Danes.

The Priests of Odin were called the Godthi, which is pronounced Gothi. Perhaps Odin as Woden, the god of the forest dwelling Goths, is Woden the Wood Lord or Wolden or Wooden (Uailaman) and the Goths themselves were, like the Danaan, a tribe of Priest Kings. Where Godthi and Goth means "men of the god" or priests, so does Fir Bolg or Bog, and so again we have a clear etymological link between the Druids and the sacred priests of Odin.

It is feasible that from Denmark settlers moved south, taking the Valkiries (known in Ireland and Scotland as the Swan Maidens) and the Ravens of Odin with them. Odin, who has at least 30 other names, was originally a

Priest King named Waeldeg or Waldeg (Wald = wood, forest) who married the daughter of the Dalriadan king of Ireland, Cormac Mac Art. We are instantly reminded of Robin Artisson.

In ancient Irish, "Art" meant stone, which could refer to a mason (cf. Hiram Habiff and the Solomonic link) or to the Grail as the "Stone" that fell to Earth, the Lia Fail, the jewel from Satan's Crown, the *Lapsit Exillis*, the Cubic Stone of the Holy Vampire Grail. It might also refer to cobalt.

Odin was Lord of the Wild Hunt in which he was accompanied by his coven, the twelve Valkirie. In Celtic Britain the Wild Hunt part of the mythology of Windsor Great Park was led by Herne and his pack of red-eared, white (albe or Fairy) hounds. In Anderson's *Genealogy* there is a table of the kings of the Herulii. It is thought that this tribe of priests-magi were descended from the Danish Gothi of Odin and formed the link between the Goths and the Scandinavian Dan tribe. Herulii is composed, it would seem, of two words, Her and Ulii. Whilst Her is obviously Herr, meaning Lord, Ulii is reminiscent of Ualla and Walloon, which is the name of the Frisian people who occupy the region originally inhabited by the Herulii and the Chattoi (forest Panther) tribes. It appears then that the Herulii—as Her-Ulii, the sacred priests-magi, (the Druidhes, the "Men of the Trees", were also called magi), are the Lords of the Forest and relate directly to the Caledonian Picts, who were the Calle Daouine, the People of the Forest.

So it would appear that the Goths could be of Danaan descent via the Danes and the Herulii, giving a link between Odin and Balor/Herne/Merlin, meaning that the Gothi and the Druids are indeed cast from the same mould. If the Goths were the Godthi, sacred priest-kings of the Scythian Dragon, it would explain why the Merovingians formed alliances with Gothic princesses.

The Goths inhabited the vast, mysterious forests of central Europe where the tops of oak trees of some thirty feet in diameter formed a canopy of up to one hundred and fifty feet in height. This gave the impression, mimicked in Gothic architecture, that the observer was in the midst of a vast natural cathedral or many-pillared hall. Forests like this once spanned the length and breadth of the continent and its islands, including Ireland, Wales, Scotland and England.

It would be easy then to imagine that the Scythian tribes, though dispersed by various migrations into different regions in the north, would develop along similar cultural and spiritual lines that continued to Mica. They would control and emphasise the environmental conditions of the regions they chose to occupy, namely their natural and historical habitat, the great forests and the ancient greenwoods.

Chapter 28

In Forests Dark and Deep

In the German Rhineland, Wotan reigned as chief of the gods and Lord of the Wild Hunt. The Ring myth was prominent and the Swan Knights and Maidens were an intrinsic part of Gothic and Teutonic folklore. Wotan or Odin held court with his twelve Valkiries, making a Coven of thirteen priests of the old religion; and the Rhinemaidens and the Nixes, like the Melusines and the Morganas, abided as the guardians of Fairy fountains and forest rivers, brooks and meres. By understanding that these myths emerge from a common genetic and cultural source, which is manifest in these islands as well as on the mainland, we can greatly expand on our own appreciation of the finer details of the Dragon Tradition and the Fairy History in Britain.

In assessing numerous Irish, Welsh and Scottish legendary figures and events and comparing them with those on the continent, our aesthetic appreciation of the richness of our own Fairy culture is deepened in hue and in the clarity of its outlines.

In the depths of the vastness of the forest, Odin the Ring Lord and the twelve Valkyies reflected the myths of Robin Goodfellow and his twelve Witches. Odin's or Wotan's hall of heroes in that deep dark forest mimics the refuge of Robin and his valiant outlaws with their own Val-Halla or Wal-Halla, their own Hall of Trees, set deep in the heart of the Greenwood of Merrie England.

In a 12th-century manuscript, Odin is described as a trinity. Despite the possible Christian influence upon the writer, the god actually does appear to have been a late tripartite, composite figure. More likely, however, is that Odin, a Prince Priest representing a bipartite deity, had his own attributes added, by chroniclers or devotees, at a later date to form a trinity. In this sense, the actual name of the high priest incarnating the god or manipulating the creative force was eventually attributed to the god or force itself. Its name was then forgotten, if it had one in the first place.

In this way, behind Odin, Wotan, Herne, Jesus, Robin and a host of other gods, there may simply be one god or force with many aspects, represented by a different named or titled priest or priestess in different regions. In all other respects, the priests were all the same kind of people performing the same ritual function, arising from the same bifurcated cultural roots.

The first two aspects of Odin the "god" were Frey, who appeared during the early hunter-gatherer period, and Thor, who found popularity at a transitional period between pastoralism and agriculture—agriculture being something that the Celts were accomplished at but their overlords, the Danaan king tribe, the Scythian Fairies, could never master. Odin's particular areas of influence came to include the forces of sorcery and war, which might have reflected a move towards the raid or trade practices common amongst earlier Scythian and later Scandinavian peoples. Oddly enough, Odin, at one stage in his career, was also called upon as a god of mortal love, probably because of the Wild Hunt and the quasi-sexual practices within Royal Vampiric Ritual.

However, he is identified with Mercury, or Hermes in the Greek Pantheon, both of whom were messengers of the gods, as a guardian of portals and a psychopomp. Like Robin and St. Nicholas, they were also the patrons of thieves. Whilst the Nordic Taranis, Thor, is thought to compare with Zeus-Dispater or Jehovah, Frey is identified with Diana's brother, Apollo. Some confusion exists over who came first, Odin or Thor, with some commentators asserting that Thor was the son of Odin.

By studying his function and identity in other cultures, it is easy to see that Odin started out not as a god but as a priest-prince, performing exactly the same mediatory function as any other Scythian intermediary priest from whatever branch of the greater Dragon Tuadhe. As an aside, Tuadhe is pronounced Teetha or Tootha, meaning an Overtribe or nation. In this it is easy to see that the Dragon's Teeth, sown by Cadinus against Jason and the Argonauts, represented Scythian warriors of the Dragon Tuadhe or nation. In the fable *The Teeth*, a play on words, they were sown in the sand and rose up as skeletal soldiers, reminiscent of the grey-blue, blood-drinking ghost warriors of the Scythian north. In the mediatory sense, Odin's story is no different to that of Dracula or in fact Christ, who also acted as a priestly, human intercessor, only to become identified with the Cosmic force. His close associate, Prince Vlad IV, also became deified in popular folklore as the Prince of Darkness, Satan himself.

The Wild Hunt appears in Vampire lore and the association of the Valkiries with functions other than attending the fallen in battle, suggests that they were not necessarily Valkyria in the limited sense, but that they also had an earlier role in the mystical rituals of the northern tribes. The first syllable, Val, which scholars appear to associate with the Roman "Vallar", a wreath given to victors, may be an erroneous Latinisation. If that is the case, it would lead us back into the deep dark forest, because Val or Wal, in the language from which the word Valkirie originally comes, is related not to heroism, but to Wald or Wold.

In respect to the second part of the word—Kyrie—which seems related to the word Keuz—"to choose", we have a number of related themes associated with the given meaning. Of some of them, "pick", "select" and particularly "hunt" do not seem entirely inappropriate. The traditional task of the Valkiries, apparently, was to choose selected fallen warriors from the battlefield. It was taught later that they would conduct them to Valhalla where these heroes and Odin would feast together.

It should be remembered that an earlier manifestation of Odin was Frey and it has been suggested that Valhalla was once the Hall of Frey and his sisterbride, Freja. The specially selected warriors whom the Valkiries took to Valhalla were once intended, so it is said in older traditions, to become repast for this particular Goddess, who fed on their souls. "We would be delighted to have you for dinner" might not have necessarily been an invitation to accept hospitality.

We will remember that in Celtic battles the Morrigans administered the coup de grace. They dispatched the fallen by drinking their blood and decapitating them. If we completely Latinise the word Valkirie we obtain Val, meaning victor, and Kyrie, which is related to mercy. This combined meaning forms the basis of the idea behind the coup de grace. We may further recollect that the purpose behind this was based on the idea that the spirit of a person whose body had been thus mutilated was bound to this plane of existence. Doubtless the Morganas gave these heads to their tribal chieftains who had also drunk blood and hunted for heads themselves, which they had then, as Tacitus attests, either nailed to the lintels and posts of their own Valhalla's, or had kept lovingly preserved in display chests.

By doing this, they added the spirit and strength of the fallen warrior to their own, both via the blood consumed on the field of conflict and by later consuming the soul from the head. These corrupted late practices fall into the category of martial vampirism, whichever way you dress it up. There is nothing to suggest that the Valkiries played any different a part in Nordic or Gothic lore than the Morganas did in Celtic tradition. It seems highly likely that Valhalla was a forest temple, though originally little different to a Scythian chieftain's hall.

Close to the Grecian Lamia was the figure of the Dragon-tailed woman Medusa, whose hair was a mass of writhing serpents. Both presaging

Melusine, the serpentine Lamia gave her name to a class of female Vampire in Romania, whilst the Medusa's hair was reminiscent of the wild flailing Elf locks or dreadlocks of the Morganas or Morrigans. From a short way off these looked like a head of slithering snakes as, in a frenzy of lust, the Morganas or Valkiries bled the dying and took their heads to the Halls of Feasting. Here the souls of the fallen, imprisoned in their skulls, were kept to feed the body and spirit of the early God-King Frey, whose priest was once Odin, and the Goddess Queen Freja, whose priestesses were once the Valkiries.

The activities of the Valkiries were not just restricted to the battlefield. In the Wild Hunt, accompanying Odin, they would hunt for their own kind, Elf Women, to feed on. In so doing, they fed the god and goddess they incarnated. The Wild Hunt is similar to the Dyonisia of Greece and the Bacchanalia of Rome.

Thus the Val-Kyrie was a northern Bacchante, a Forest Hunter, and Odin was the Bacchus or Dionysus, the Forest Lord of the North. This practice however, wouldn't necessarily be murderous, but would have comprised the corpus of the tradition of Royal Vampirism. It formed the basis of later Witch tradition in the noble covens of Britain, where Herne and Robin conducted the Wild Hunt themselves with the Witches, with joyous hearts and mirthful songs.

At this kind of Sabbat, records of which exist from 17th-century Scottish accounts, the Noble Witches fed their Lord on their own blood. It must be suspected that this ritual is a leftover from a time when both the Valkiries and the Morganas fulfilled the same function, by filling themselves with blood. After the Wild Hunt or the battle perhaps they took it back with them, so to speak, to where its spirit and vitality was let from their own veins to feed the Odin, the god-king in Valhalla, the Temple of the Greenwood and the Forest Groves.

Odin was later known as the "Sky Father" and is reminiscent of Anu, whilst Thor identifies with Enlil, and Frey shares similarities with Enki. Here we have a late and perhaps confused dualistic triad which, comprised of two figures and a mediator, compares with the original pattern that first set the trend for the whole Dragon Tradition. By looking at the various triads through history, it is possible to construct an apostolic succession of mythic gods-incarnate (High Priest-Kings) with a close descent.

Chapter 29

Dualism and Christianity

The Figures: Anu, Kether, Brahma = Mediation, Balance.

Zirvan, Chronos, Lucifer, Odin, Merlin, Oberon, Herne,
Arawn, Jehovah, Ra, Isaac, Joseph, Aubrey = Space-time, Potential.

The Figures: Enki, Ormuzd, Prometheus, Jesus, Frey, Arthur, Robin,
Pwyll, Chokmah, Vishnu, Christ, Osiris, Esau
Robert = Light, Kinesis, Expansion, Expression, Fire, Heat, Yes.

The Figures: Enlil, Ahriman, Zeus, Jehovah, Thor, Lancelot,
Little John, Friar Tuck, Hafdan, Binah, Shiva, Satan, Set, Jacob,
James, John = Dark, Stasis, Contraction, Definition, Ice, Cold, No.

In the tradition associated with all of the foregoing examples, bar one, the figures represent complimentary forces that work together to produce the manifestation of Life. There being no such process as destruction, the apparently opposed forces work both in conflict and in harmony to produce change. In both are elements of the other, represented in the yin and yang symbol.

In the objective observation of these processes of expansion and contraction we see movement and define this as Space-Time, a phenomenon which arises from the dynamic interplay of forces, but also provides the setting or potential for their relationship to each other. In the mediatory sense, both forces emanate from the one potential or balancing force, whilst the extent of the activity of either force is determined by the mass or extent of the potential itself.

Ultimately the forces are impersonal and beyond moral hypothesis. This being the case, in order to make them understandable and accessible, numerous esoteric philosophical expressions have been publicised in exoteric forms that were intended to enable people to get to grips with a few of the profound ideas being expressed.

Invariably, the people, over the course of history, have responded by turning these ideas into "gods" and, instead of trying to understand them, have anthropomorphised them and elected priests, whom they also later deified, to assist in their worship. Buddhism is an ideal example of this process. The Buddha Siddinarta, a Royal Brahmin, stated emphatically that there were no gods, only forces, so people turned Buddha into a god and worshipped him instead.

In the case of Dualism, and in this last example, that of Catholic Christianity, the people have relatively recently decided, aided and abetted by unscrupulous Christian priests, that the two opposing forces of Light and Dark must be either good or evil. This is because of the way humans are, or rather the way the priests would like us to see ourselves. Having had the forces anthropomorphised, it seems inconceivable that they could exist without some moral imperative and hence some kind of motive or raison d'etre.

The moral quality of either force seems governed by the consensus of religiously guided popular preference reinforced by propaganda. Similarly, the expansion potential of either force in Christianity is governed not by natural law, but by the projected personal ambition or desire of the body of believers. This is invariably for ease and security.

However, this is not how the universe works. Therefore, the priests have modified people's expectations by turning the forces of darkness into the arch-enemies of the forces of light. This means that people cannot always expect to live in prosperity because nasty old Satan, the enemy of all that is Good and Godly, is forever trying to upset the boat.

In turn, the priests have assured the righteously expectant that the God of Light, Jehovah, is ultimately all-powerful and will defeat evil in the end. Let's assume that good and evil existed as morally motivated forces. This would mean that as soon as the force of containment and definition, the dark force of so-called evil, is finally vanquished by the Great and Good God of Light, the entire universe as we know it would expand and express itself without either limit or definition.

Indeed if "God" were more powerful than "Satan" this would happen anyway and we would simply vanish in a puff of indefinability. From the point of view of a religion based on motivation, in this case Fear, there is no point in saying that the forces are balanced because balance implies that there is ideologically nothing to fight for.

If both forces define parameters and are in balance, both are essential to the maintenance of life. If this is the case, neither can be sinful. Without sin, you don't have a hook into the people or a big stick to beat them with.

The essential elements in the success of late Christianity, as a way for a lazy minority to take control of a majority and their material resources with the least amount of effort, are fear and confusion. In a sense the way was already paved for ecclesiastical exploitation because sadly, the majority of people are also either inherently lazy themselves or neurochemically inept and will not, or cannot, think for themselves.

This is generally the case—otherwise there wouldn't be any politicians.

Understandably, most people just want to get on with their immediate lives and attend to the upkeep of their comfort zones. The most they expect from religion, if anything, is to be assured that things can't or won't get any worse.

They welcome leaders, religious or otherwise, as a way of shifting the decision-making process onto someone else. Arising from their ranks in about 300 AD there emerged, in response, an equally inept and slothful group of freeloaders who saw an opportunity to get as much out of life as they could, for the least amount of personal effort. They were able to achieve this by virtue of the inbuilt incapacity or lethargy endemic within the population as a whole.

They were secure in the knowledge that the majority of people were not interested enough to figure out that they, the self-appointed divines, were tricking them. Therefore these early Christian priests modified the philosophy of Dualism to render it imbalanced. They introduced the Gentile population to the concepts of Mortal Sin, the Prince of Ultimate Evil and the surety of eternal suffering and damnation. It is quite possible that many of them actually came to believe this themselves. This created a gap in the market, a gap characterised by new fears. Surprisingly enough, the parvenu priesthood of the nascent, exoteric form of the Christian faith had the power to assuage, at a price. This example of exoteric Dualism with conscious, motivated forces, in the form of gods as anthropomorphisations of universal principles, owes its emergence to the same inherent laziness, indifference or incapacity of mind which is responsible for the decline of factual ancient history into the realm of myth.

Writing in 300 BC, Euhermerus pointed out that the ancient gods and goddesses were originally great men and women of renown who had undergone the process of deification. This is shorthand for the process whereby a people forget their original goals and the finer detail of the stories from their past. The process, in which whole chunks of heritage are disregarded for one reason or another and have to be best-guessed by later generations, is called myth-making.

The ancient gods and goddesses were flesh and blood beings and the word "god" had altogether different connotations than those that it has now. In those ancient times the "gods", essentially the priest-kings and priestess-queens of the people, were responsible for a variety of functions, not least that of being the shepherds and teachers of their client tribes. In this capacity the "gods" performed plays or rituals in which they were expected to be the incarnate representatives of the forces they depicted in the rites they enacted for the edification or blessing of the people.

The passage of time and the absence of a standard of oral teaching ensured that right up to the last millennium the Druids still didn't worship "gods". Because of this, many other races came to believe that the priest-kings and priestess queens who incarnated the universal forces were in fact those forces themselves.

The net result of this process of forgetfulness was that the impersonal forces of the Cosmos and the elemental animistic, pantheistic forces of client tribes took on the everyday characteristics of the priest-kings and priestess-queens. They in turn became deified and secondarily associated with lower, animistic elementals because they had become identified with the forces they represented in a ritual context. This would have tended to occur amongst the laity, particularly where these forces or elementals were perceived in relation to the priesthood as a result of the use of phytological, hallucinogenic drugs during ceremonies, for example.

The ancient gnostic, Hermetic philosophy of Dualism has generally become identified with the slightly later Cult of the Twin, precisely because of this mythic process. At the same time, the Fairy kings and queens have become associated with the dryads, sylphs and undines commonly associated with drug-induced states and vice versa.

The primal dual forces of increase and decrease became confused with two ancient brothers, Enki and Enlil. One was a genial and amicable fellow who favoured man, whilst the other detested human beings altogether. Both were God-Kings of the sort hereto described.

The friendly, helpful one—Enki, by a process of human projection, became associated with the force of increase and "Good" as one would expect, given human nature. However, the other, Enlil, became hated and feared, ultimately to be likened to the force of decrease and "Evil". Whilst the family and descendants of the two brothers remained aware of the fact that these two boys were not Cosmic Forces in themselves, other tribes and their descendants, on the other hand, developed, and continued with, and embellished upon the anthropomorphisation.

These two brothers had a domestic squabble one day and as a consequence of this, several thousand years later, the Cosmos is described as being divided into two conflicting sections, one "Good" and one "Evil", according to one's tastes and expectations. Early on, the two brothers had attracted two factions, each one demonising the other.

The stronger, or, it might be said, the more fearful faction won the day and the so-called "Evil" brother, by this time a Cosmic Force, had been cast in the role of the God of Light. The other, however, who had originally been the nice and helpful one, became, in the minds of millions, the epitome of moral destitution and desolation.

The faction that thought Enki was a decent fellow were known as gnostics and some of them believed he was a transcendent God. The factions that called Enki Satan and cast his misanthropic brother in the role of the transcendent God Jehovah, the God of Light, were known as Jews and Catholics. The faction that knew Enki was an ancestor of theirs and not a god were called Druids and Witches, whilst the faction that knew that Enki's descendant Jesus was an ancestor of theirs and wasn't a god either, were called Celtic Christians, Cathars, Albigensians and Witches.

Typical also of human nature, other than going after the main chance and the easy option, is to dislike being in error or backing the wrong horse. People want to be associated with winners and in pursuit of this aim it became necessary for one of these lately superannuated characters to become the stronger, ultimately victorious one. They also wanted scapegoats.

The only people who seemed particularly bothered by this were the Jews and later the orthodox Christians, with their deliberately imbalanced interpretation of early Christian doctrine. By a twist of fate, the doctrinal perversion gained imperial sanction, for political expediency as much as anything else. Its somewhat pedestrian, grossly manipulative and opportunistic view of life became widely adopted, aided greatly by fire, the sword, threats of torture—and torture and death itself.

Railing against such a view were the Manicheans, the Arians, the Nestorians and numerous other pre-Nicaean Christians. For them, Jesus, like Enki, with whom they identified, was not a god. Nor was he the son of God. In the fullness of time, however, this inconvenient opposition was dealt with in the manner to which we have become accustomed, as far as the Catholics are concerned.

As a result, the legacy of their religious ambition has left us with a lopsided form of monarchic Dualism where Jehovah is God, Jesus is the Light. The reversed Satan or Enki, rather than being the essential facility of restraint, is instead the quintessential manifestation of absolute evil.

In Christianity there can be no reconciliation and no compromise. The cult of Joy from Death has become the cult of the Fear of Death. Satan, the weaker enemy of all that is "Good", will finally be crushed and obliterated at the end of time. The earlier forms of Dualism, some represented in the other foregoing examples, even though sometimes they might have confused the issue and gone in for a bit of deification, generally understood Cosmic reciprocity and unity. For them each aspect of the Cosmos was related and reconciled with the other, forming an eternal and infinite whole.

Christianity however, stands alone in demanding that mankind believe in two unequal, bitter enemies who are neither part of each other nor work together or compliment each other. Supposedly therefore, as "God" is separate from His creation, so also is He separate from the Dark Side for whose creation, by their Christian logic, He is ultimately responsible for, since He is the superior being.

Not only is such an attitude cowardly and irresponsible, God's minions deflect any blame for "evil" from their Master to another unattached, intentionally wicked entity and to those people who are weak enough to succumb to its temptations. Furthermore, this attitude creates a religious mentality that is riddled with fear, bitterness and multiplicity. The truly sinister aspect of this whole situation however, is that the irresponsible and cowardly, divisive and paranoid, self-hating spirit of corruption which rests at the heart of Christianity, does so with the express intention of its hierarchy, who are further committed to ensure that it remain there permanently. Without it, people cannot be controlled and without social control, the Catholic priesthood loses its access to unlimited wealth.

In Mithras we have an example of symbolic conflict in Dualism which intends that in the destruction of one principle by another, the two may be united and together transcend. The same dynamic is found in the story of Morgan le Fay and Holger Dansk. The whole point about Dualism on the personal level is not one of exacerbating strife or perpetuating violence, as it is in post-Nicaean Christianity, but of healing it and going beyond the very elements of human perception that cause it in the first place. In this respect the Dualism of the Draconian Fairy culture and all its collateral branches demonstrates a far earlier origin than that of modern, imbalanced, post-imperial Christian Dualism. In tracing a line of blood descent for the Fairy race, we also trace a line of apostolic succession for its original Magean, dualist prince-priesthood, a line with many collateral family branches.

Chapter 30

Morrigan and Morgana

The following is partly a collection of etymologies based on the themes that suggest themselves in association to ritual identities. These two names are the same, one being a reduction of the other. The name Morgan is said to mean "sea bright" in Welsh, but the Morrigan or Morgana is Irish Scots. Accepting this, the following origins for the names are offered.

1) Morrigan: broken down into three syllables, Mor-Rig-An

a) Mor: this word in Gaelic means Mountain, Hill, Rath, Barrow, Creachaire, High.

b) Rig: this only translates to Righ, meaning Royal or King or Queen.

c) An: as in Anu. However, as Gan or gang, we have "going".

Consequently, we have Morrigan as:

Mori—a "Fate" or Fairy and High Queen of Anu, or Queen of the High Way, as in Queen of Heaven or the Sky, or even, if a Latinisation of Mor has appeared as Mori meaning death—Queen of Death's way, meaning perhaps Queen of the Otherworid.

When reduced to Morgana we have Mor-Rig-Anu, High Queen of Anu. With both spellings, either way we have a High Queen of the Dragon. Whereas with the Welsh Morgan, we might have Morgana as the Sea Dragoness.

Finally, though, the construction would comprise of two linguistic roots, the Welsh and the Scotic. We could have the Welsh Mor as *bright* or *shining* or *sun*, and Gan as Gang meaning *to go*, *path*, *way*. This would give the epithet "The Shining Path", the road to Elphame, as in "Morgana is the path to Elphame" or as in "The Fairy Way, Route or Path".

In whatever sense, they all combine, because the Shining Path is the sun-dappled bow wave of the Swan Barque, sailing across the Mere to Avalon at sunset, carrying Morgana the Dragon Queen of the Waters. Hence Morgana as Sea-Bright.

Chapter 31

Takla Makan

With regard to the Mummies of the Takla Makan, although the shamanka's headdress was shown to be the conical hat of the Witches, the headgear of the Tocharians in general was the conical hat with the rounded end which, when bent forward, becomes the Phrygian Cap. This cap is also shown in relation to the Scythians on a bas-relief stone carving of them presenting gifts to the Persian emperor. The Tocharians have been in Takla Makan since 1200 BC. Academics believe they came from the Steppes of Greater Scythia, forming part of an easterly and westerly migration of the Scythian Peoples.

This is the movement of the Danaan nation at that period, part of which ended up in Ireland and eventually Scotland, where they became the Picts. It is even more feasible to suggest therefore that Tocharian "A" script is closely related to Pictish, and hence Fairy. It is now thought that the Scythians of Takla Makan came from Thrace. This would mean that they had much in common with the Scythian Fir Bolg. It also means, if this is the case, that both languages are indeed Arshi Kantu, Arya-Sidhe Canto, or Aryan Sidhean Chant, and are the magical-religious singing languages both of the Buddhist priests and shamanic priestesses of the Tocharians, and of the Pictish and Irish Druids.

A cursory look at the written script reveals close similarities between written Tocharian and carved Pictish. It is now thought that the Tocharians were semi-nomadic, mounted bowmen who operated the same raid or trade policy as their Pictish cousins in northern Europe.

Living on the edges of Takla Makan, they occupied the mountains and rich upland pastures to the north of the desert region. In this they are identical to the Scythian bands so often confused with the Celts in Britain and Eke. They are also probably the ancestral cousins of the tattooed Scythian Chieftain, found buried in permafrost a few miles north in lower Siberia.

PART THREE

Chapter 32

Additional Fairy Lore

Though a similar reference can be found in Yeat's *Celtic Twilight*, I found this reference in an old Irish Fairytale called the *Potato Supper*. "Some folk say that the Little People, the Fairies, were once angels that were cast out of Heaven for their sins". In the same work there is also a reference to the shining path to Elphame.

In a small children's book by Robin May called *Hallowe'en,* there are two references of particular interest. The first states that it was once believed that however unlucky the Fairies could be in human affairs, it was even more disastrous if the land lost its Fairies altogether.

I feel sure that this is a folk memory which harkens back to the time when the fertility of the land relied upon the presence of the Fairy Queen or King and their contact with the wisdom of the Otherworld. Its Sovereignty meant that her or his management of the land, and her or his guidance of the people in its proper husbanding, was essential for the survival of the nation. This was despite the occasional costs which, in any event, have been largely exaggerated and added to later stories of predation under adverse circumstances.

The Apple Trees of Avalon

The second reference reiterates previous notes, from another angle on the Apple symbolism. May states that apples were once thought to be a link between men and the gods. What this obviously means is that they facilitated a link between the two, which means that apples had some psychotropic effect. Naturally they do not, if they are ordinary apples.

In Cornwall, Hallowe'en or Sanihain is called Allan Day and the apples involved in the holiday ritual there are called Allan Apples. To eat them brings good luck, apparently, which is a watered-down version of the idea that when one ate an Allan Apple, one would see the gods. Allan is an abbreviated form of Avalon and so the lucky apples—the ones that forge the ethereal link and facilitate transcendence—are the Apples of Avalon.

Avalon, the Isle of Apples, is the Isle of the Swan Maidens, the priestesses who, like Lilith, are the Apple Trees themselves, whose endocrinal fruit brings wisdom and vision. The foregoing reinforces the assertion that Druidism is Tantric as well as dualistic and that Druids were men "Of the (Apple) Tree".

Zen and the Wild Hunt

Several games which are associated with both Hallowe'en and apples are particularly interesting. They have ancient roots in ceremonial Druidic and Witch pageants which had a teaching role to play within the Samhain festivals.

The first, Apple Ducking, where one attempts to catch apples, floating on water, with one's teeth, links two Fairy symbols—the apple of Avalon and the mere or lake in which the Fairy isle is situated. The apples bobbing in the water represent Avalon itself. To gain wisdom from the fruit of Avalon, one must first be immersed in the water and thereby enter Elphame in order to win the coveted prize.

The second game involved eating an apple whilst balancing, legs astride, on a seesaw, in the middle of which, between one's legs, there was placed a lighted candle. The trick was to make both ends of the seesaw balance at the same height from the ground. The meaning of this is discovered firstly in the pentagram of the Goat of Mendes where the candle, stuck between its horns, represents illumination from the womb of the goddess.

Secondly, this illuminating wisdom, facilitated by the reinforcing symbol of the participant eating the apple and thus obtaining the enlightening fluids of the womb, sustains balance within the individual, represented by the balance of the seesaw. In perfect balance, positive and negative forces cancel each other out and produce an equilibrium, which is both everything, and nothing, stillness, the Nix or Zero. The seesaw, like the Zero, is another principal symbol in Zen Buddhism. Enlightenment exists in balance and the candle, at the pivotal point, also suggests this teaching.

The third game involves taking an Allan Apple to bed on the night of Hallowe'en. One places it under one's pillow in order to dream of an event or of some knowledge one wishes to be appraised of. The apple is a symbol of the Otherworld. The act of taking it to bed and placing it under the pillow is a substitute for the ancient practice of sleeping in the tomb chamber or later, of sleeping in a graveyard overnight in order to obtain knowledge from the ancestors.

It is interesting to note the amount of lovers' games that are attached to Sainhain, a time when all hell was supposed to break loose. Previously I said that Odin was often called upon out of context as a god of love. It appears that the Starfire hypothesis is correct because two Hallowe'en divinatory games in particular relate the symbols of transcendent wisdom to the cause of love.

In the first game, which is played at night by either sex, the performer eats an apple and brushes his or her hair whilst looking in a mirror. The image which, it is said, appears in the glass is supposed to be that of one's future lover or spouse. Firstly, the apple represents Fairy wisdom obtained by eating the fruit of the glands. Secondly, mirrors, like meres or lakes are doorways to Elphame, the land which is the reversed, mirror image of this world. Thirdly, the comb or brush is a symbol of the mermaid and royalty.

The code translates as an invocation. By brushing the hair one mimics, and thereby invokes within one's self, the godform of the mermaid or merman, the Fairy inhabitant of the mirror world of the sacred lake within which lies the Isle of Avalon, the Otherworld.

This corrupted act identifies one with the Dragon Blood. The act of eating an apple shows the ritual intention of knowing, by looking into the Otherworld behind the mirror, the identity of who will either eat of one's fruit or give of their fruit in a Starfire ritual—not out of mortal love, but of transcendent hierogamy. The person one sees in the mirror is the person with whom one will be united in the *Love that is Death*. Alternatively, the ritual can serve as a spell to draw that person near. This is achieved by sending a message through the mirror and through the subtle energy of the matrix underlying all form, which is Elphame. By invoking the person in the mirror, one implies that the person desired will not be human, which would be no good, but of Fairy or Dragon Blood themselves.

The act of staring into the mirror is a method whereby the conscious mind can be persuaded to concentrate whilst the subconscious mind projects the image of the prospective alchemical lover into the glass. As such it mixes sympathetic magic, which is basic Hermetics, with scrying. Pools of ink, black mirrors, the still surface of lakes or ponds have all been used for this type of scrying, which is in itself a form of hypnosis intended to bypass the conscious mind. This indicates that the doorway to the Otherworld is, in fact, the subconscious mind itself. Plenty of archaic symbolism speaks to that effect, including the tenets of Dualism on the personal or microcosmic level.

Hazel and Hearthfire

In previous notes I have covered the symbolism of the hazelnut in some depth. In relation to Hallowe'en, a game exists wherein an individual, wishing to know whether they will unite with another successfully or not, throws two hazelnuts into the hearth. If they burn to ashes, the marriage or affair will be thought of as doomed to die. No esoteric overtones need apply here.

The symbol of the hazelnut comes from the tale of the *Well of Nechtan*, and its Salmon of Knowledge, and the symbol itself is corrupted. Perhaps some sympathetic magical component survives, but it serves nothing to belabour the point.

It is interesting to note, however, that another fruit associated with the Rosicrucis and the act of Starfire has been linked to mortal love. This further confirms that originally in the hierogamical act there was parasexual physical contact, an act "of love", as an intrinsic part of the alchemical process, of which this game is but a dim folk memory.

Although these games were once an intrinsic part of Hallowe'en, especially in the last century, they started out as Druidical and Witchcraft practices. Consequently in their purer, older form, they are part of Fairy tradition as magical rituals conducted long ago by the Fairies themselves.

Traditionally, Hallowe'en is the time when the gates of hell or the Otherworld are thrown open and the Fairies, Witches and ghosts walk the earth creating mayhem. However, this tale arose because Hallowe'en was the beginning of the lean time of winter and to the Fairies, whose ancient Scythian ancestors were traditionally used to raiding, it was the time to stock up for the cold months ahead.

This is the basis for the identification of Samhain as Mischief Night, which has been carried forward to the present day by both the Guisers and the Trick or Treaters. In their respective times, they have dressed up as demons, Witches and sprites to knock on people's doors and demand food or gifts. The Fairy would have taken this night as one of the last shopping opportunities before the snows set in, and would have created havoc by raiding the surrounding countryside for food and goods.

This, then, was the time of the Wild Hunt for consumer durables and comestibles, as well as for Elf women, whose serum levels at that dark time of year, would have been naturally high. It will be remembered that from the Dark Ages onwards, much of their lands had been cleared and therefore, they were a dwindling, persecuted and beleaguered people who found it increasingly difficult to support themselves on fewer and fewer resources.

It is no wonder then that stories have come down to us today of the times when the very demons of hell would visit torment on a terrified mankind. It seems a just, inevitable and unavoidable retribution for man's treachery and betrayal of an ancient, beautiful and mystical people. Without them, man has lost his wisdom and sense of balance, and has raped the Earth to his own doom.

The Sword of Durandel

The sword of Roland de Vere, who was born around 809 AD, was called Durandel. An earlier spelling of this curious name, from the Oxford Dictionary of English Literature, is Durindana.

The word Dwarf appears in Old Norse as "dvergr" (Dva-Righ), with no apparent etymology. The closest word to it in English is Dwale, which, in Danish is spelt "dvale"—a soporific drink made from deadly nightshade or belladonna, an ingredient of the Witches' flying ointment.

Tolkien took names for his dwarves from the Icelandic *Prose Edda*. These names included Dwalin or Dvale, the shamanic flying potion, and Durin, who was creator of the nordic Dwarves. Durin is perhaps Dva-Rign, implying Death's King or the King of the Otherworld, which seems appropriate in relation to the Scythian cult of Nergal, etc. Dwar appears in Transylvania as the god Thor of the (smith's) hammer. Dwalin was the Elf-Smith who forged the head of Odin's spear, Gungnir, perhaps with meteor iron.

The word Dwarf has nothing to do with midgets. Like the Troll—whose name simply means migrant wanderer—the Dwarf has become an underground-dwelling spirit of diminutive proportions, when once they were probably, like the trolls, of "giants" size. We must appreciate such a term in the same way as we would think of Titans as being gigantic or "great" men of renown. The dwarves represent an early class of Danish god.

The Dwarfs were miners and smiths and, as such, are identical to the cyclopses, Titans and kobolds. Therefore, they are human-sized Elven alchemist-smiths. Their habit of drinking dwale to contact the Otherworld gave them the name Dwarfs. In every respect they are of normal height or perhaps taller, and the same as Robin Hood, Robin Artisson, the Sprite, the Pict-Sidhe, the Red Cap, the Boggart, the Troll and so on. They are the "sons of stone" and the children of Anu. They are the Elf Lords of the Scythians. The "Dwarf" is just another branch or "ritual characteristic" of the Scythian Tuadhe. In relation to the Danes, the Dwarfs were like the Fir Bolg of Scandinavia, representing an earlier wave of Danaan migration.

Durin d'Ana is probably the original spelling of the name of Roland's sword, meaning perhaps Elf-Father of Anu. The alternative spelling, Durandel, likewise could mean:

Durin Dail (Lord Durin)—Lord-father of the Elves. This, during the European "Age of Heroism" seems an entirely appropriate name for the sword of an Elven Prince and a Brudhe-Bard of the Druids, who was a son of Melusine. (Michael Hunter)

This confirms him, as it says in the Vere charts, as the weapon's "custodian", as it is likely to have been passed down to him as the sword of a hero. This is similar to the sword Gram, which was given by Regin to Sigurd, who killed Regin's brother, the Dragon Lord Fafnir. Hence we have Roland as "Keeper of the Sword of the Durin Dail", the Durin d'Anu or Elf Father.

As the sword of the Elf Father, this reinforces the Durandel's heroic identification with Gram, the weapon Odin thrust into the Oak Bransock. Charlemagne, Roland's uncle, had a sword named Joyeuse which was forged by the pagan god Wayland or Volund the Smith. It is not unreasonable to assert that Roland's sword was probably forged by his ancestral forebear, the alchemist and Druid, Kai ap Emrys. Therefore Durandel was made by a type of Andvari, the Elf King who lived in the original Scandinavian "Mirkwood" who was the final keeper of Andvarinaut, the Draupnir Ring of Midgard (or Tolkein's "Middle Earth"), which he kept hidden in a pool adjacent to that forest. Roland appears in *Lord of the Rings* as Boromir, whose sword and horn are smashed at the last stand against the Orcs on Amon Hen, Boromir's Roncevalles.

In defence of Charlemagne, he is, as David Day points out, a supposedly Christian king with a Pagan Ring and Magical Sword. His capital is founded on the Mere in which, like the Andvarinaut, that ring rests at the centre of his kingdom. Like so many other kings during the Christian period, Charlemagne's throne is positioned under the Damoclesian sword of the Catholic Church.

If one reads his letter to Pope Leo III, written in 796, one can see, as the commentary suggests, that Charlemagne was no fool. He appears to have anticipated the continued rise of the Church and its desire to interfere with and ultimately control the secular world. It is very possible that in this respect, he was aware that the Church had sponsored the counterfeiting, in his kingdom, of the *Donation of Constantine*. His response was to assert that it was the king's job to defend the Church from pagan hordes (by which he really meant protect his kingdom), whilst it was the Pope's job to pray for the success of the king. In a sense, in his words, he reduces the rank of the Pope to that of a glorified "canting cleric".

The letter goes on to engineer a psychological scenario in which the Pope accepts Charlemagne's authority and control over the Church, rather than that of the Church over Charlemagne. He asserts that he never agreed to be emperor and would have avoided the Basilica of St. Peter's that day if he had known that the Pope had intended to exceed his authority by crowning Charlemagne. His genteel diplomacy was necessarily addressed to an institution that had sponsored the murder of Charlemagne's ancestor Clovis. (Ehler and Morral, *Church and State through the Centuries*, p.12)

Roland's descendant, Alberich I, is supposedly named after the Dwarf of the German hero cycles. However, a curious passage appears in David Day's *Tolkein's Ring*:

"In many German Hero Cycles, the most persistent character in the ring quest tradition is the guardian of the ring and the treasure. This is the Dwarf known as Andvari in the Norse tales and Alberich in the German legends. Although capable of being tamed, he is usually a sinister figure; however in late romances his appearance and powers often change. He often lends help to other heroes under alternative names: Alferich, Laurin and Elbeghast. Increasingly this character supplied all the supernatural elements in German romance: Dwarf; wizard, Elf, smith, guardian and god. By the sixteenth and seventeenth centuries, he is entirely transformed. In Britain he becomes Auberon, and by Shakespeare's time he is the remarkable Oberon, the King of the Fairies. In this role in *A Midsummer Night's Dream*, he is said to be the radiant god of love, and the Immortal son of Julius Caesar and Morgan La Fay".

All herein, concerning midget miners and the like, supports the evidence that Dwarfs, Elves, Fairies, Pixies, Witches, Dragons, Vampires, Druidhes, magi, gods, Gnomes, Sprites, pucks, pouccas are all the same species. They have been variously caught or observed, at different times and in different places, in the commissioning of one or other weird or nauseous act after which they are then named, and for which they then become remembered for all time!

a) Andvari is Andurin or Durin.

b) Alferich is Elf King.

c) Laurin is C12H2402, a crystalline substance obtained from the berries of the bay tree or *laurus nobilis*. Compounds derived from it include *lauric aldehyde*, ether and chloroform. The bay tree, the elder and the yew comprise the sacred grove of sleep in Ogham. Laurin, like Dwale and Dwarf is a name that derives from yet another way that the Pixies got intoxicated. Laurin is also "the tunnel" or labyrinth.

In Tolkien's world, Lorien was a Lord or Vala (see previously mentioned book) called Irmo and Lothlorien. In *The Lord of the Rings* there was the garden of Lorien, or the land of Elphame. Tolkien's description of Lothlorien is identical to numerous descriptions of the state of being variously named Union with Godhead, Samadhi and the Kingdom of Heaven.

The reader is strongly advised to read Cohen and Phipps' *The Common Experience* (Rider and Co. London) in relation to this concept. Lothlorien is a place, as is Elphame, that can only be seen in a special state of being. The whole universe is Lothlorien or Drakenberg* —the Kingdom of the Elves—

*Drakenberg is the legally recognised name of the Nation State of the Dragon Peoples. Drakenberg was officially recognised in 1997 by one Western Government. The Dragons wanted to see whether they could get their old enemies to recognise the Kingdom of the Elves, they having spent 1000 years attempting to eradicate all trace of it from the public consciousness. The exercise was successful and Drakenberg—the Dragon Sovereignty (Lothlorien, if you like)—exists with all the powers of an incorporeal state of peoples as defined by the United Nations. Essentially therefore, being an Elf or a Dragon is a recognised nationality! This was a serious political move undertaken for serious environmental and social reasons.

one just has to see it for what it is. Lothlorien translates into English as the Loth or Lot of Laurin, "The Sorrow of Laurin". Laurin is the Kingdom of the Elves, the Labyrinth: the Gateway to Heaven, Atman or Kether. The Sorrow of Laurin is the sorrow of a place departed from. The whole world is becoming grey as the living death of consumerism takes hold across the planet. The wolves really are at the borders and soon Laurin will be gone forever. Hidden under a gigantic pile of discarded Macdonald's cartons, Coke cans and reams of printer paper from former trees, covered in corporate consumer nonsense.

Richard Dufton has contributed some research he did on the subject of the Holy Mountain. Before the Black Sea flood, the water level was obviously a lot lower than it is now. Richard Dufton has maintained, having studied the soundings, that in the centre of the Black Sea there was an elevated piece of land. This, he asserts, must be the original home of the Ogdoad, the eight gods of the Ubaid who attempted to restore this little bit of high heaven on earth after the deluge, but failed and scattered with their tribes to the four winds. In Tolkein's Akkabaleth, the sundering of the Elves follows a major flood and in their wanderings across the Earth they take with them the biblical deluge story and the memory of their sacred mountain home. This first post diluvial migration marked the beginning of the Elven calendar, which counts the days after the flood that removed them from their Sacred Home. In 2004 the date stands at 7068.

Additionally it is also of interest to note that the "Bay of Belfalas" in Tolkien's "Middle Earth" appears to have an identical contour to a bay on the eastern shore of the Caspian Sea. Essentially this region is "Middle Earth" in geographical terms we would understand. Whilst I would not for one moment use Tolkien's work as an "academic source", it is worth pointing out again that Tolkien borrowed a lot from myth and history. Although he denied an allegorical component in his work, it does nevertheless plot the fortunes of the Elven families, simply because of the material he used. In some works, I believe, his Third Age was said to correspond with the period of earth's history corresponding to roughly 10,000 BC.

It is usual to think of this time as being highly primitive and entirely dissimilar to anything Tolkien described in *The Lord of the Rings*. However, we should take a fresh look at our own history and disregard the old school indoctrination we received that discounted anything as being historically significant or culturally evolved before the time of the Greeks and Romans. We will then discover that the new archaeological evidence would point to there being a fantastic level of social, cultural, spiritual and industrial civilisation in Eurasian history as far back as 22,000 years BC.

Richard Ridgley's recent work in dismissing the myth of primitive ancestry is truly inspiring in this respect, and gives birth in the mind's eye to a world of incredible antiquity which, nevertheless, is far closer to ours than we could have ever previously envisaged. Tolkien's Third Age could have sat as comfortably in 22,000 BC as it was said to have done in 10,000 BC. Although we cannot use Tolkien as a scholarly resource, we should remember that the human mind has an imagination. Tolkien's work, because it is not too far off the mark and uses aspects of lore that exist in human history, does stimulate the mind to imagine what things were like so long ago.

This is no bad thing if objectivity is exercised, because if we dismiss imagination and vision as fantasy, we dismiss a tremendous creative faculty. The imagination unlocks doors to racial and genetic memory, and a wealth of information that we might call anticipatory, inasmuch as it seems to appear out of the blue. Einstein is said to have used creative imagination to assist in formulating the Theory of Relativity and without imagination and reverie, Kekule would never have discovered the indole ring. Chemistry as we know it would never have existed.

d) Elbeghast is white ghost or Elf Spirit, giving us Sprite, or Puck or Robin.

e) Shakespeare's Oberon was Aubrey de Vere. Thus Aubrey and Alberich were Dragon Ring Lords, as was Robert the third earl, who was Robin Hood. Robin's father was Oberon, Oberon's father and mother were Caesar and Morgan La Fey. In real life Robert's father was Aubrey, who's father and grandfather were Alberic. This is how Alberich became Auberon who became Oberon, father of Robin or Puck. Alberic de Vere's ancestors included Melusine's great great grandmother; Morgan La Fey and Julius Caesar's family!

Edward de Vere seems to have "been" William Shakespeare, and as such he seems to have written *A Midsummer Night's Dream* as a genealogy of his family! As the ancestry Edward gave for Robin, also known as Puck, also known as Pan (the Witches' god) is accurate in the play, it seems fair to assert that Melusine was directly descended from Morgana. Therefore the marriage between Morgana and Julius Caesar in *A Midsummer Night's Dream* is the marriage together, in reality, of the bloodlines of Morgana and Julius, both in the union of Melusine and Raymond, and in the union of Elinus and Pressina.

This makes sense. Having such an accurate knowledge of his family history makes it even likelier that Edward's Stag Ride was intended to assert his dynastic descent, just as *A Midsummer Night's Dream* did. The star therefore that alighted on the lance of Alberich I was indeed the falling star, Lucifer's emerald, the Lia Fail, the cubic stone of the Grail. This made the Robin Hood of England identical to the Robin Artisson of Ireland, as Art's Son or Mac Art, son of the Lia Fail. It also confirms Robin Artisson, like Jesus, as son of the tekton or craftsman. The legendary Alberich was a smith-tekton. Perhaps the star on the lance tip of Alberic de Vere also symbolised its forging from star iron, like Odin's Gungnir.

f) Oberon as the god of love directly corresponds with Odin as a god of love, and both connect with Herne and the parasexuality of the Wild Hunt. Oberon is Andvari in the Danish cycle, the possessor of a Ring of red gold called Andvarinaut—"The Web of Andvari". This ring of red-gold itself made gold, a bio-alchemical allusion to wisdom through the possessing and the imbibing of royal blood. The Ring symbolised the "rose" of the Swan or Dragon Maiden, whilst the web was the interwoven mass of blood vessels of her body, symbolised by the branches of the Tree of Life. A similar symbol is the Ring as a pool nestling at the foot of Yggdrasil, like Nechtan's Well.

In this way the Dragon Ring becomes the Holy Grail, and the Cross and the Circle unite as one. Odin possessed an identical ring called Draupnir, "The Dripper of Gold", which gave him power over the Nine Worlds, the nine spheres that are the sephiroth of Yggdrasil, making Odin, Andvari and Oberon or Alberic, Lords of The Rings. In the *Volundarkvitha* of Iceland, Volund, or Wayland the Smith married a Valkirie who appeared to him as a Swan Maiden. To keep her, he stole her Swan guise which, after nine years, she found hidden. Making her escape, she leaves Volund a Magic Ring which, after a series of adventures, is the one that ends up in Alberich's lands.

Swan Maidens

In Germany these are identified as the Nixes or Mere Maids, thus Melusine and the Ladies of the Lake. To confirm them as the Valkiries, we have the foregoing example. Also we have the Valkirie habit of hanging the heads of the fallen nobility (not rank and file warriors) from their horses' harnesses in very early depictions of them recently discovered, which appear exactly like the Morganas or Morrigans, the Swan Maidens or Ladies of the Lake.

Brunhilde, Sigebert's wife, was a Valkirie. At some point in her adventures she ends up enclosed in a ring of fire by Odin. This brings us to the Phoenix. The Phoenix is the Raven, the Morrigan of the Scythians and the national emblem of the Danish Vikings. This black bird became the double-headed eagle of the empire, but began in Tartaria or Transylvania as the two-headed Raven or Phoenix.

The Phoenix

Ravens and the Corvidae (corpse-watchers) family in general like nothing more than to sit and fumigate themselves over a smoking fire. Often, as history attests, they will take burning brands back to the nest which inevitably bursts into flames itself. The Raven rising from the flames gave rise to the legend of the Phoenix, whose sun-dappled plumage, like the Raven's, is red-gold and rainbow-hued.

The Raven as a badge of the Scythians became associated with Phineas Farsidhe and in consequence was named after him. If we think of Phineas' clan as being both the root and head of the Tuadha d'Anu, as well as its most wise, then the double-headed Raven or Phoenix would be the senior totem of the Danaan. It makes sense then, that in terms of explaining the levels of wisdom, a serpent eating a serpent became a Dragon, and a Dragon eating a Dragon became a Phoenix.

The Phoenix rising from the ashes reborn as a symbol of youth and eternal life is related to the Morrigan's and the Danaan Chieftain's habit of sustaining youth and wisdom by drinking noble blood, like Odin (Samael-Hearne-Oberon-Alberich-Wotan) and Freja (Lilith-Venus-Diana-Titania) and the Valkiries or Morganas. Shakespeare links the Phoenix and the Turtle as does Hebrew magical literature, which links both with the serpent N'H'sh and the Qlipphoth of the Kabala. In essence the Raven or Phoenix consumes the blood of the turtle-Dove, symbol of the Holy Spirit, Sophia, Venus-Lilith (the falling star or Lia Fail), Magdalene and the San Graal.

The Raven as a symbol of death is counterbalanced through the Phoenix as a symbol of life. In a sense this reinforces the Life through Death philosophy of the Nergal cult of the Scythians. The Morganas and Valkiries are the Angels of Death in their black, Raven feather cloaks. In their Swan Feather cloaks, however, they become the Repha'im, the Angels of Light, the Swan Maidens and fountain Fairies whose blood gives life and wisdom.

In the story of Volund, as in many others, men often win Swan Maiden wives by acts of deception and theft. The common scenario is the descent of the maidens to some private mere where they divest themselves of their Swan's skins and bathe naked, as humans, in the secret pool. The peeping tom, having fallen madly in love and desirous of taking one of these women to wife, steals her skin which prevents her from leaving the mortal realm. The truth behind the myth is that the Swan skin is in fact a ritual garment, a cloak or mantle of office upon which is laid a heavy geis.

It is the raiment of a Bruidhina (Vruidhina or Veruidhina—a truth or law speaker), a Repha'im, and as significant then in social terms as would be the authority implied within a royal staff or seal ring. The wearer would have been invested with all the power implicit within the Swan Cloak, as a shaman, a priest, princess or king, and a member of the Tuadhe of the supreme overlords.

To lose one would indeed bind the maiden or knight to "this world" until she or he recovered it. To have one stolen, with the possible implication that it might be worn by someone outside one's own caste, would have been a reversal of all that was understood to be governed by the natural laws of the cosmos. It would have represented a reversal of the naturally ordained social structure of the time. To have one stolen and possibly worn by a thief would be an abomination.

The very essence of the identity of the Valkiries, Morganas and the Bruidhinas was that they were Oath-Keepers and Truth-Speakers. Valkirie is related, like Valhalla, to the Goddess of Truth—Var, and to Va or Vere, the Oath, the Truth and Verte, the Green.

To these Ladies of the Green, the Law of Nature was the Law of Truth, as the words Var and Ver suggest. To have someone posing as a Swan maiden or knight, in effect to be lying in the very act of wearing a Swan Cloak, was a loathsome impertinence to a race that loathed liars. It would bring a curse upon the wearer and the owner. The unfortunate princess would be bound to tarry until the cloak was recovered. To return without it would have been unthinkable and could have exacted extreme penalties.

If we look at the role of the angels in biblical myth they are originally derived from the Nephilim and later the Repha'im. In popular art these beautiful, almost asexual, angelic figures are shown with Swans' wings. The Repha'im, whose cult was founded in Idumaea and the region around Scythopolis, were ancient Dragon Queens and Kings who, so it was thought, had passed into the Otherworld, from whence they emerged from time to time, to aid or judge in the affairs of mankind.

In fact they were the mound-dwelling Fairy royalty whose practices included living in tombs and Beth Seathans or Sacred Mounds which, like all temples in classical pagan belief, were thought to be the dwelling places of the gods. Historians state that the early believers thought that the "gods" (inhabiting carved images) lived in the statuary.

This may have been the case later on, but originally the gods were the royal priestesses and priests themselves. Acting originally as the ambassadors of the Anunnaki, the Nephilim and later the Repha'im, they were the police of the ancient world. The Swan Cloak, representing the height of the wisdom of the Dragon, was the symbol of their authority. Like an angel's wings, it denoted that they soared above the common realm of mortal understanding and concern.

If we think of them as starting out in history as a kind of royal-blooded police force, then one might equate the loss of the Swan Cloak with the loss by a modern police officer of his or her warrant card and uniform. The social havoc a police impersonator can wreak is considerable. The Druidic Repha'im were much more than modern police officers, they were judges and lawgivers as well, and had the power of life and death over all men. Thus the loss of a shamanic cloak was a disaster.

Loosely speaking then, we can think of the Raven Cloak as the Blood-Hunting or War Cloak of the Angel of Death, and the Swan Cloak as the Blood-Giving or Peace Cloak. The Swan Guise is often associated with the Fairies' appearance as a boon or help to mankind, as in the case of Lohengrin. Similarly, the Swan Guise is often associated with Love as well, as is the case with Caer and Oenghus and Volund. So we can consider the Swan Cloak as the mantle of the Elven Lord or lady in their role as the giver of wisdom, the giver of sacred blood and life, and the Divine Lover.

Leprechauns

The word is said to come from the old Irish luchorpan, lu=small + corp=body. However, as we know, the Irish leprechauns or Sidhe were the

Danaan, and these were full-sized people. Old Irish would have been spoken at the time when the Danaan were still around, if only as a remnant. St. Patrick was the guardian of a Danaan Princess and her descendants are recorded as witnessing the Battle of Clontarf. Therefore Irish people would have known that leprechauns were not small. The leprechauns are most commonly depicted wearing green—Robin Hood or Artisson's colour. In the case of leprechaun the lepre stands for lepra, meaning scaled, as in leprosy, rendering leprechaun as "scaly-bodied", not small-bodied.

This is explained by the fact that the Zmei or Dragon lords, the Sarmations, Cimmerians and the Dacians (who had a winged serpent or Dragon cult going back to the post-migrational Ubaid culture of Transylvania in 3000 BC), as well as the later Danes, all wore fish-scale armour.

It is also possible that as Dragon Lords they would have worn serpentine or draconian helmet-masks, not too dissimilar to the animal-masked helmets of the Roman gladiators and the masked helmets of the Greek Warriors. This may account for the Ubaid pottery figurine's snake-like looks and the descriptions of the Anunnaki as having "serpentine" faces. Additionally, certain cults wore snake masks.

The Sumaire of Ireland are the serpent Vampires. The scaled skin of the serpent or Dragon is the armour of the Leprechaun who is thus the Sumaire, as is Robin Artisson and hence Robin Hood. The same may be said of the fountain Fairies who appeared as Dragon women. It is likely that they were similar in function to the Danish shield maidens, dressed in the scale armour peculiar to their race. Contemporary descriptions from Russia have the scales made of bull's horn or bone fillets which would give the impression that it was reptilian skin, and not a suit of armour. It is possible that if the Fairy maidens didn't wear scaled armour, they wore a ceremonial outfit constructed along similar lines, but far lighter and more functional. In such ritual regalia, they and their ancestors, both Samael and Lilith, would have looked like serpents.

In the image of Samael and Lilith in Eden, there is an intimation of the later image of Odin and Freja in the Forest Hall of Valhalla. Where God was a physical presence in the Garden, Samael and Lilith were like its spirit, resting in the Tree. Similarly this spiritual presence in the Forest is echoed in one of Odin's epithets—"The wind in the trees". (*The Spirit in Valhalla*)

As a type of paradise, Valhalla, the hall of 390 doors (30 x 13 blood moons), represents Eden or Avalon, and in Freja of the Apples, we have a contemporary variation of Morgana of the Isle of Apples and a later version of Lilith of the Apple Tree of Wisdom.

In very early versions of Norse myth it is only the Noble Dead that end up in Odin's Forest Hall. Once there, he and Freja split this human booty 50-50. We could imagine the Valkiries, of which Freja seems to be a High Queen (like Morgana), to be like Shepherdesses and Grim Reapers of the blood and souls of mortals, and this brings us back to a theme in earlier notes.

The image of the Shepherd Kings of Kish suffers from association with the fluffy bunny image of gentle Jesus, meek and mild as the kind, compassionate shepherd and teacher of his flock. In not a few instances, the Dragon blood has treated humankind with imperious indifference as a separate species, below its own on the food chain. I ask myself again, in the light of more recent data, what shepherds do for a living? We know that the Shepherd Kings of Kish were Transylvanian Dragons and thus of the Scythian Blood Royal. Consequently they were predators and in the totem guises of werewolf and panther, they preyed on human beings for food.

Yggdrasil is "the steed of Ygg". Whilst a "steed" is a mode of transport, a method of getting to the Otherworld in this case, Ygg is Odin who obtained the runes from the stone tablet that lay next to the pool at the base of the Tree. The stone tablet is the Cubic Stone, the womb, within which is the blood, within which is all wisdom. The Stone is the Uterus, the Utterer of whispered secrets, the Runa.

Like the Fisher King and Jesus, Odin was pierced in his side by a lance and hanged from the tree. After nine days and nights, the holy completion of the Scythian mystical three and the number of the Dragon, Odin obtained the Runes or whispered secrets, which were revealed to him by the Elves who made them.

The whispered secrets are the province of Odin as the (whispering) wind in the grove and, as the ancient letters of the Birch forests of Carpathia and Scythia, are the property of those who first carved them, the Scythians or Sidineans. As a Forest Script, Runic is an Elven language of the Trees and a variation of Ogharn, which was discovered by Ogma or Ogg or Ygg or Odin, who is the later invocational priest of the Danaan God-King Ogmios, who first invented them.

In the sense that Yggdrasil is the same as the apple tree on the microcosmic level, then Odin's partner in Valhalla—Freja (Iduna) of the apples—is both Yggdrasll and Andvarinaut. Her apples, like those of the ladies of Avalon, who are also themselves the Apple Trees of the Sacred Orchard, are the endocrinal centres or Chakras of her sacred body. She is then the steed of Ygg and corresponds symbolically to Slepnir and to the role of Rhiannon in the *Mabinogian*, and Epona as the white mare who carries the rider to the Otherworld, the grave or womb. Here is contained all wisdom and is where Odin, the breeze, whispers gently through the branches of the trees in the sacred grove.

The Breeze is the biblical Sophia or Holy Spirit, signified by the Greek Pneuma or Breath of God. The branches of the Trees of Life are the blood vessels of the bodies of the Freja, the Valkries, and Morgana and the Swan

Princesses. The symbol denotes that the spirit of sovereignty is carried in the blood of the Queens of Hell. The deified Odin, the Ogmios or spirit of wisdom then, is the spirit of absolute kingship. He is the fully realised being—the priest-king who has mastery over the Nine Worlds, which represent also the various divisions of experience and energy within the individual being.

The Carolingian Ring Myth

In the story of Holger Dansk or Ogier the Dane and his meeting, at a vast age, with Morgan la Fey and his restoration by her, we have a variation of Ogier as Odin (Og or Ygg) and Morgana as Iduna-Freja of the Apples. Holger Dansk was one of Roland de Vere's brother knights in the Court of Charlemagne. Holger, like Roland, was one of the great Paladins or Counts Palatine of the Franks, celebrated in the *Chansons de Geste* and hailed as the greatest warrior of all the Danes. He is still a national hero of Denmark.

Ogier has obviously become a composite figure like Robin and Alberich. He could not have been so incredibly old when he met Morgan la Fey because Morgan was born 200 or so years before Ogier. She was the great great grandmother of Maelasanu, Roland's mother, and so if Ogier had met her, it would be she who would have been of a great age. In this case it is possible that he has inherited the attributes of another historical figure:

Waeldeg, the Odin or Odin priest-king or Royal Godthi who married the daughter of Cormac Mac Art in 300 AD. If Waeldeg the Odin or Ogg had met Morgana, a descendant relation of Cormac's, then indeed Ogg or Ogier would have been of a great age indeed. It appears to me that Holger or Ogier was, like Waeldeg, an Odinic Goddil and the legend attributed to one Odin priest, as history has shown in other cases, can become the legend attributed to all Odinic priests.

Often they become the actual God. The finer details are not important and neither are the discrepancies. The story relates that, at a great age Ogier the Dane set sail on one last adventure before returning home from Jerusalem. He travelled to an island on which stood a castle built of lodestone.

As he sailed nearer, all the iron on his ship was ripped away and the ship itself was wrecked. Making his way to shore he entered the castle, which was lit by a magical light, and went to the central court. There he discovered a great serpent guarding a tree at the centre of the court garden. Resting in the shade beneath the tree was the most beautiful woman he had ever seen, and on her hand was a gold ring.

Ogier slew the serpent and went to the woman, who was none other than Morgan la Fey. She gave him the ring from her finger and he was magically restored to youth, health, vitality and life immortal. Morgan and Ogier then sail off to the land of the immortals, which is Tir Na Nog. The island with the castle is a common image which is repeated in the castle of Loreli on the

Rhine, whose maiden is a fatal siren who lures sailors to their doom and wrecks their ships on the rocks.

This motif has numerous variations in the cycle of stories concerning Sirens and Mermaids. The island itself is a form of Avalon and the garden, the Garden of Love, is repeated in the medieval story of the maze of Melusine. At the centre of the garden or maze is the source of life and love, either a tree or fountain pool, guarded by a maiden. This story works on two levels, Inner and Outer, singularly and relatedly.

The first level is psychodynamic and the second level is psychobiological. The first level is identical to *Beauty and the Beast* and *Sleeping Beauty*. Morgan's castle is the mind-brain of Ogier. It is magnetic and attracts all experience, learning, opinion, fear, hatred, attachment and prejudice, which create a huge serpent, much like the Mithraic bull. The serpent, like the bull, is Ahriman, the serpent of darkness or human ego-consciousness. It is the unregenerate experiencer and judge, the critical censor.

The garden is the right brain and the suppressed side of consciousness. Morgan is the Anima in Jungian terms; the Tree is the symbol which joins Morgana, the anima, to the second level of the allegory. She is the Tree. An Apple Tree and an Yggdrasil, the method by which Ogier or Odin gains access to Elphame.

On this level, the ring symbolises the gaining of consciousness of the eternal, the new bond forged between the left and right brain and the subsequent integration of the whole being, leading to the voyage to the perception of the eternal. On the first level, the aim of the alchemical rite is outlined and the steps to transcendence are mapped out. Arriving at the island is answering the inner call for transcendence.

Ogier's slaying of the serpent with yet another Magical Sword, which he named Courtain, is like slaying the Mithraic Bull. It is the obviating and neutralising of the ego. Taking the ring is joining the left and right brain, and travelling to Tir Na Nog is gaining enlightenment: Zero, the One Ring that rules them all.

In the tales of Loreli and the other mermaid or siren stories, in answering the call of the mermaids that leads to doom, one does not experience the doom of death, but the doom of the ego and the rebirth of the whole being into the light.

On the second level the Tree and the Ring are aspects of Morgan herself. In taking the ring, the Aridvarinaut, one takes from the essence of the priestess whose vitality spreads through the branches of her tree. The ring is also the spout at the base of Melusine's cubic stone, it also symbolises the union that occurs with her as hierogamy and the perception of the eternal.

The ring as the Orobourus is Mazda, the serpent of life and light which, when accepted and symbolically worn, returns the slain serpent of darkness to life and to a new relationship with the serpent of light. In this sense Ogier was Ahriman, the left brain, and Morgan was Masda, the right brain and, joined in hierogamy, they become the twin serpents entwined around the tree which they both also become.

This symbol is emphasised in the Baphomet of the Templars and Witches and in the caduceus of the Swan's winged disc and the serpents. It is the symbol of the single soul transcended and of twin souls joined in divine union, all at the same time.

In *Sleeping Beauty* the hero has to find his way through a thicket which is the confused tangle of thoughts, fears, attachments and so on which hides the castle in which the maiden, or right-brain Anima sleeps. When he reaches her and kisses her, this is his acceptance of her, and this is his desire to be *united* with the other aspect of himself.

The kiss, the acceptance, brings her and the entire castle to life. In other words, the suppressed element of his consciousness is reawakened and integrated into the individual who becomes a whole being and transcends. *Beauty and the Beast*, *Theseus and the Minotaur*, and *The Frog Prince* are variations of this acceptance theme which, however, can work when the characters in the stories are in fact real people enacting the roles.

In this case one states that the Anima is externalised as a Grail Princess, and union with her causes union with the internal Anima. This is a central characteristic of the second level, where "Beauty" is a real person with real psychodynamic power and real psychobiological essence. The tantric union with such a person does lead to transcendence and a glimpse of Tir na Nog. Both partners entwine in spirit to become the caduceus. By becoming one being, they negate the dynamic within each other and become still. This stillness is the Nix or Nil point where the minds are silent and observing "what is", not the internal dialogue of what they think "should be".

The story of Ogier and Morgan appears to be the joining together of two seemingly separate racial traditions, the Danish and the Danaan, which are, in fact, related both by blood and by philosophy, both being in essence from the exact same Scythian root. The tremendous advantage here is that we can assess the earlier Danaan culture and synthesise elements of it from the later variant expressed in Danish Viking culture, thereby enriching our view of the Fairy race as a whole.

With so many Magic Rings, Swords and Fairy Maidens attached to Charlemagne's Court, it becomes difficult to accept the historical view of his devout Christianity. He seemed to surround himself with and elevate people with whom the Church was at odds, and to whom he supposedly was an avowed enemy. Increasingly I see Charlemagne's Christianity, like

Constantine's before him, as being a political convenience and not a heartfelt belief.

The Dragon Myth

A legend exists stating that a couple of miles from Bamburgh Castle, there once lived a serpent which occupied a cave in a magic mountain. Beyond the cave there was a raised stone, out of which had been carved a large bowl-like receptacle. On occasion the local people filled this bowl with cow's milk, as a voluntary gift-offering to the serpent. (Deike Rich and Ean Begg, *On the Trail of Merlin*, Aquarian Press, 1991)

The serpent is reminiscent of the story of Melusine. The tale is significant, in light of the fact that the legends concerning her say that she walled up her father in a cave near there, fled to a place called Avalon, and then decamped for France. Perhaps the serpent was a folk memory not of her, but of her father who was, despite the legends, not a "mortal" but a Sidhean of Druidic Royal Blood, of the Ver Boig House of Ulidian.

The folk story of the Dragon in the Cave is universal. The scenario runs as follows. A Dragon takes up residence in a cave near human habitations and begins to terrorise the countryside. In order to bring an end to the killing and destruction, the rural inhabitants appeal to the Dragon for mercy and leniency. Negotiations are undertaken between humans and the Dragon and a compromise is reached. If the villagers regularly select a virgin female as a sacrifice, offering the same at selected intervals for the Dragon's sustenance, the Dragon agrees to spare the others. The virgin is to be tied to a stake at the mouth of the cave and left there for the monster to collect. When he is peckish, he emerges from his cavern and eats her whole. This is the story that has come down to us.

The truth behind it conveniently excludes the rest of the bargain. In exchange for ritual food, the "Dragon", a Scythian Priest King or Priestess Queen probably accompanied by his or her entourage of Druids and Warriors would, in exchange for a regular supply of fresh, readily available royal virgin blood, undertake to settle permanently in the region. This Dragon Clan, the custodians of sovereignty and fertility, wise seers and indomitable, terrifying warriors, would elect to protect their clients and organise more efficiently their social structures and industries in exchange for material support and Starfire. The legend of the hoard of gold, which the Dragon uses as a bed, is as alchemical in origin as the tales relating to the Dragon and the virgin.

Pure gold, as well as "red gold" or virgin's menstruus, was used to enhance consciousness. The Dragon is not a Dragon without her or his magical vision and transcendent being. Therefore, in alchemical Dragon tradition, the symbol of the Dragon sleeping on a hoard of gold signifies that the dynamic of the Dragon identity "rests" upon the foundation of blood and gold ingestion. The Dragon is the ultimate guardian and *fons et origio* of the Sacred Wisdom.

Often these Dragons were sought out and especially invited to take on the overseership of other tribes, who provided them with gold, food, provisions and virgin menstrual blood, which was drunk to enhance the Dragons' magical performance and longevity. The Virgins rarely died, except perhaps from a surfeit of what the outsider might think of as amorous attention.

That Elinus, the King of Dalriafa, was given gift offerings voluntarily, perhaps by a grateful clientele, tends to suggest that the "Dragon in the Cave" story has been twisted from being a common social arrangement into a terrifying bogey story. In any event we can say with certainty that Elinus wasn't a mortal, but a Dragon of the Elven Blood.

Chapter 33

Clerical Connivance

The Scythians or Sidheans instituted Pharaonic marriage in order to prevent the dilution of the Titanic, Royal Elven Blood. As an insular group in Eire and the far northern reaches of Britain, it is therefore highly unlikely that they would have habitually married out of their race in Gille Sidhean's time, either from choice or by necessity. And the frequency with which it occurs in the story of his family is fast becoming suspiciously habitual. Therefore the stories of mortals marrying Fairy Princesses have to be questioned, because the motives for suggesting that such alliances took place as regularly as medieval chroniclers claim, might not be prompted entirely by the desire to record historical or legendary events faithfully.

In the received story of Elinus or Gille Sidhean, he is the mortal, whilst his betrothed is the Elf. They first met at a fountain, of which his future spouse, the Fairy Princess Bruidhina or Pressina, was said to be the guardian. Their daughter Melusine also married a mortal who encountered her at another Fairy fountain over a thousand miles away from where her parents reigned. This is a bit of an unlikely coincidence, isn't it?

Two elements emerge from this story.

a) The Fairy females both married mortals.

b) The mortals just happened to chance upon the Fairies at magical, and therefore one would assume secret, fountains.

The Church hated Fairies because they carried the only true, royal Dragon blood and thus the sovereign rights to kingship that, earlier in history, these petty peddlers coveted so much. However, in the subsequent position of power that the Church held in the medieval period, they could direct myth-mongers to write exactly the sort of "history" that served the Church's purposes best, on pain of death. Conversely, those who voluntarily took up the Church's cause were often rewarded handsomely for their complicity. This happened regardless of whether they were the chroniclers who fabricated the Church's image of sanctified authority, ubiquity and omnipotence, or the churls with ecclesiastically enhanced, fraudulent family histories, who were raised from the bourgeoisie and promoted as the grateful, slavish puppet kings and false nobility of the Church state.

It is interesting to note that despite the fact that the Church has condemned outright the Dragon blood and its culture, it still recognised that only through that blood and culture could kingship be retained. Such a recognition is borne out by their fraudulent *Donation of Constantine* that we examined previously. The Church claimed that the Emperor Constantine had given it the right to crown kings and institute governments across Eurasia. Constantine was a direct descendant of the British PenDragon Kings, themselves of Danaan origin from the Scythian Dragon King Tribe. Their choice of fraudulent donor clearly indicates that the Church itself actually admitted that only descendants of the Dragon culture were rightfully permitted to exercise such powers and bestow such dignities.

In the case of Elinus in the first principal;

a) above—as the only true royal blood is Elven, the Pressina-Melusine story was doctored to make the two male partners mortal and therefore, quite frankly, commoners.

In the first instance, this would make Melusine appear to be only half Fairy and, as the Church thought, only half royal in the eyes of the people. That the Elven blood was of Titan origin and the Titans bore Mere Maids such as Melusine as full blooded Titans, instead of half Fairy, half mortal, has escaped the modern commentators who have used literary sources doctored by the Roman Church. The symbol of the woman with a human torso and the tail of a fish or Dragon has lately been assumed by writers to mean that the figure has human attributes. The earliest myths would contradict such a view.

The Church deliberately propagated these myths and consciously intended to lead audiences to these conclusions. They put forward that this falsely attributed human element to the Fairy nature of the Mermaids meant that, as these individuals had human blood, and thus the blood of Eve in their veins, they were no better than anyone else. Therefore they were culpable for original sin, capable of mortal sin and thus consigned to damnation, unless administered a salvation that could only be sanctioned by, or more importantly derived from obedience to, the Holy Mother Church, just like anyone else.

If this failed, they could always turn the people against their rightful Dragon queens and kings by claiming that they were half-human monsters, beyond the Christian pale and thus evil emissaries of Satan, to be feared and vilified. By degrees and in turns, the Church has used all these tactics. On the point of Original Sin, this was Eve's disobedience to "God". As the Elven blood was descended from Lilith, who was not "guilty" of Original Sin, all Dragons and Fairies and their descendants to this day were and are sinless and had and have no need for salvation. This has been something of an irritant to the pious Popes.

In the second instance Melusine, Bruithina the Younger or Bruithina Maelasanu, is questionably recorded as marrying, like her mother, yet another mortal—rendering the royal blood that subsequently flows through her descendants' veins appear to be of no significance at all. Such diluted blood would thus present no threat. Otherwise it might have derailed the Church's materially motivated financial ambitions. It would act as an inspiration to a downtrodden populace by contrasting its preternatural wisdom and ethos of service against the miserable example of the Church's intellectual paucity, spiritual vacuity and insatiable greed.

Such a propagandist tactic has been used by the Church in numerous instances. Beyond this they took practical steps to annihilate these, their sovereign rivals and spiritual enemies, by falsely claiming jurisdiction over the choice of so-called "noble" and "Royal" marriage partners, insisting that such marriages be sanctioned and licensed by the Pope. In this way they could pressurise the true nobility into marrying the Church's burgeoning bourgeoisie and encourage these bourgeois, lately elevated puppets, to marry each other. In this way they attempted to breed the Dragon blood out of Europe, replacing it with a parvenu class of false, tradesman nobility, selecting their sycophants from within the ranks of the tinkers and merchants. Any Dragon or Grail families they couldn't intimidate, pay off or breed out, they either murdered, discredited, genealogically disinherited, ridiculed or wiped out of the history books altogether.

In the case of the second principle in;

b) above, the women, Pressina and Melusine, were in fact the fountains themselves, as evidenced by the medieval depiction of Melusine's fountain issuing from a Cubic Stone.

In any event two identical chance meetings, separated by time and geography, but occurring in exactly the same circumstances are not likely. We are led therefore to the conclusion that the fountain scenario is quite probably an Elven, Royal "courtship" ritual. As these women were themselves the fountains, like Sheba in the *Song of Solomon*, we are led to the further conclusion that the courtship ritual was bound up within the Starfire cycle. This was a magical Fairy rite so secret that no human would have been permitted to attend anyway, making the idea that either man was "mortal" untenable.

Throughout history and in any of its forms, Starfire was reserved for Queens and Kings alone, and the only true Queens and Kings are those of the Fairy, Dragon blood.

To have met the women "at the fountain" was to have engaged in the most intimate and profound magical intercourse with them, forbidden to those outside the holy race. The reference to the fountains indicates that both the couples were involved in a special form of alchemical relationship which was common before marriage amongst the Dragon royalty. Therefore, they all knew each other intimately prior to wedding. It could have started when, as girls, both Pressina and her daughter in their turns were serving as "fountains" or Grail Maidens, and lasted until the time when they were physiologically in their marriageable prime, as Dragon Queens, capable of bearing children without too many complications.

Considering these points and the fact that Gille Sidhean, Pressina's husband, and Raymond, Melusine's husband, and also both the women themselves, all had comparable Vere descent, it is quite clear that the men were related to their spouses, by blood, race or name. In the case of Gille Sidhean as stated, his descent was from King Erc of the 4th-century Ulidian house of the Ver Bolg of Ulster and Strathclyde, Druids whose tribal badge was the Blue Boar.

Likewise, Raymond de Verrieres, or Ver-en-Forez, Lord of Pictavia and Anjou, also had the Druidic Blue Boar as his family badge. Furthermore, Pictavia was founded by Melusine's maternal forefathers, the Ver Kings of the Danaan remnant. Therefore the assertion as fact that the House of Vere, the First Royal House of Anjou, was of the pure Elven, Royal Dragon Blood appears inescapable. This was much to the annoyance of the Church and its chroniclers. They appear to have attempted to eclipse the pure origins and thus the genuine sovereign status of the Royal House of Vere by various means, as they did with many other Royal Dragon families of the Sang Real and the San Graal. For the Dragon and the Grail, for the Vere it is of some considerable importance that we maintain our Royal status and assert our Elven, Dragon origins.

Otherwise, to allow the Church or the Church-backed establishment, retrospectively or contemporarily, to continue to suppress or marginalise our singular royal heritage or to ridicule our ancient magical legacy, is to conspire in the victory of all their lies. It would declare as acceptable the last thousand seven hundred years of hypocrisy, greed and terrorism and sanction, by our silence, the inhuman oppression of generations of defenceless, disenfranchised human beings. In so doing, we share their ecclesiastical guilt and capitulate to their murderous, immoral, megalomaniacal ambition, perhaps for even more years to come; accepting the defeat of truth, wisdom, kindness, social equity and personal responsibility.

The Dragons have asserted and had popularly accepted the historical sovereign Dragon identity, its rights and its magical, Elven, genealogical legacy.

In this way they have provided another small nail in the establishment's coffin, one more small example of how the Church-state and the establishment have committed fraud, even genocide, to protect their historical interests. The authorities have twisted or concealed the truth concerning many issues for centuries, in order to control information. By this strategy, to this day, they still continue to exercise significant subconscious control over the minds of the public, over a population which formerly they have oppressed for centuries, a people over whom they have no sovereign authority and no divine sanction or innate, moral right to rule.

Chapter 34

Dreamcast

The Scythian-Goidelic roots Bri, Bre and Bru are found in connection with the concepts of dreams, judgement, poetry and spellcraft.

1) I suggest there is a link to the Welsh word Bre-uddwyd, related to the process of dreaming as in *Breuddwyd Rhonabwy*. In *wyd* we have the root wid, which, like wit in Saxon, means "to know", and *Breudd* or *Bridhe* means dream. *Breuddwyd* might translate out as "the dream of", but it doesn't actually mean that. The strict interpretation of *Breuddwyd* is "Dream to Know" meaning;

a) to discover knowledge through dreams and;

b) to interpret that knowledge through seership.

Both these functions are within the remit of the Bruidhe, the Druid-King who judges the signs and who interprets the secret Law, Brehon or Logos of the Cosmos, which invariably manifests itself through dreams.

These are the symbolic language of the intuitive faculties of the so-called right brain. Uncluttered by the paranoid obsession with materialistic logic and the need to rationalise everything according to an arbitrary set of received principals, it is itself in open congress with the cosmic mind, which "remembers" the future as well as the past. The right brain is not so governed by sequential, rational linear thought. As this is what creates time, being free of it to a much greater degree, the right brain is itself free of the chronological definitions of past, present and future and the strictures upon seership that these contrived notions impose. Underneath time is the desire for order, under which is the desire for predictability, under which is the desire for security, under which is the desire to be free of the absolute and ever-present grip of the fear of the unknown and discontinuity.

The observation of the passage of thoughts, running one behind the other in a sequential linear pattern, is a conditioned reflex that creates time. In this manner, time is simply the regulated passage of thought or memories and assumptions which have been related to units of measurement conceived of by minds that think in this linear fashion. Without linear thought there would be no linear time. However we are taught to respond to our environment in a sequential fashion. As we develop as children, these responses get hard-wired into the neuronal pathways in the brain to become fixed and habitual. Psychobiologically the brain is trained to think in terms of past, present and future and actually produces chemical signals at regular intervals in order to maintain the illusion.

Some time ago scientists believed that one of the principal chemicals involved in this process was serotonin. It was thought that it acted like a jailer, opening and closing neural circuit doorways or pathways in order to regulate the stimuli entering the brain through the senses, thereby creating a form of sequential order. In any event the learning process is bipartite and involves both socio-psychological, as well as chemical stimulus. One could argue that as the hardwiring process continues, the brain itself learns to release hormones sequentially in response to the demands of the social environment. Whether or not this is the case, both the notion of time and the subsequent inability to perceive the present-future are subjective rather than objective phenomena.

By using various means, the Bruidhe could rewire her or his brain to make it receptive to impressions usually edited by a normal mind. Anyone who has children will have noticed that teaching one about the concept of chronological time is generally quite a difficult task. Children of a certain age have no concept of time at all. This is sufficient evidence upon which to argue that time is not a natural, intrinsic law of the universe, but an acquired response to outside demands. Jesus himself taught that one could enter the "kingdom of heaven" whilst still here on earth. This kingdom is eternity and it lies beyond death in life, i.e. the cessation of thought.

The ego is thought and thought is time, so once the ego is nailed to the cross, time stops and eternity begins. It's as simple as that. Unless ye become as little children ye shall not enter the kingdom of heaven. Similarly, the realm of Elphame is described as a "place" where seven years can be seven minutes, and seven minutes can be seven years; a place of infinite beauty and delight that describes Jesus' kingdom of heaven (transcendent consciousness) with greater succinctness than the Bible ever does.

The Uni-Verse, the One Perfect Phrase, has already been uttered—it is spherical, complete and here now. It is not unfolding or progressing anywhere. It is not achieving anything. It is just all at once. Everything it is or can be is happening, all at once, now. We don't see its completeness because we think of ourselves as being incomplete and having constantly to achieve, which in reality we don't.

This is just an external pressure put upon us by those who wish us to continue to produce and consume, and from childhood this is how we learn to see the universe. We learn fear from a brutal society and develop our defence strategies accordingly and in subordination to wills stronger than our own. We sequence events according to our desire for our own form of secure order and familiarity. In so doing we block out everything we don't have words for in order to prevent ourselves from curling up into a tight ball in a dark room and screaming in terror.

In response to this conditioning, when we are asleep and relatively relaxed, the mind has the ability to perceive in other ways. In order to compensate for our torturing it into perceiving life solely in a manner which is contrary both to its nature and the way in which the universe is formed and manifests itself naturally, it can produce what we think of as prophetic dreams.

These are memories of a different kind of perception whose language is different, because the observational skills that the mind utilises in sleep are at variance with those we normally use to create the illusion of a waking reality governed by time and necessity. Such dreams are not prophetic at all. However, they are simply the result of the off-duty mind perceiving its environment in a calmer, more complete and singular manner.

2) Bre-hon; from whence is derived "The Brehon Laws" from old Irish-Brithemain—A Judge. The Brehons were an old Druidic order which existed in the pre-Christian period. Another related word is *Bretha*, which means Law and suggests *Brude* as *Bruidhe*, *Bruidhainn* or *Bruidhne* (*Cruithne*) and *Bruidhina*, as law makers and law givers, Druidic judges and keepers of the Veritas or Oath—Truth.

In the name Vere there are many varying definitions. This does not necessarily mean that only one is correct. The Druids had a deep love of language which they considered sacred, reminiscent of the vibrations or "words" of power that created and sustained life. According to Dr. Anne Ross they delighted in the double entendre and the word Vere is particularly interesting in this connection, as it has at least six related meanings which fall naturally within the class of definitions related to magic, kingship and Druidism.

c) *Brichtu* is an Irish word for the chanted spell or rhyme. On the Chamalieres tablet found in Puy de Dome near the Loire, *Brichtu* appears as *Bricti* in a sixty word written spell or curse.

This particular practice was often the remit of the bards whose praise poetry was the upside of the satire curse. Relating Bri: versical power words, with Bre; words of Law, gives us the origin of poetic justice, where the judge poet delivers the law and the sentence against law breakers in rhyming verse with such power as to be able to kill the listener. Here we have the origin of the *Song of the Siren* or Mermaid, and the Mantra of Hinduism.

The essential element of such judgement magic was that the words constructing the poem or spell, as we call it, would, like the word Vere, be able to succinctly, eloquently and completely encapsulate and encircle the intention of the Druid or Druidess. This would be suggested within the meaning of words. These would be formed within a carol or round which, like the mantra, is a cyclic or circular-structured chant, the shape of which suggests irrevocable completeness. Better still, the rare poetical chant is structured in 3D, like a sphere—the most succinct and eloquent shape in existence. The first and last building block of such a mental power structure is the Och or "YES", the affirmative expression of absolute Truth and Will: the Ver.

The key to creating such an all-encapsulating vessel for the conducting of power is to ensure that the words used make the intention absolutely and perfectly succinct without waste or unnecessary embellishment.

Examples of this level of truth and the psychological power it has to strip away self deceit still exist today. The bardic practice of creating satire chants that could kill is based on judgement as assessment of the character, and the ability to strike right at the heart of delusion and pretence. Satire is probably not the word academics should use here because it doesn't convey the weight of such an ability.

Having smashed through the protective barriers of the persona, the bard could then implant a seed message within the victim's subconscious that would autosuggestively produce any required effect. Hence the tales that the bards could maim or destroy with their words. The chant was delivered by the bard in the posture of the Crane. He would stand on one leg, with the foot of the other resting on his knee to form an upside down 4, similar to the posture of the Hanged Man of the Waite Tarot. With one arm outstretched and one eye closed he would deliver his curse. This ritual posture was called Corrguinecht, referring to the Crane or "Crane-Wounding". It is exactly the same posture once used by Australian aboriginal shamans for "pointing the bone" or "singing the death". In short, this is sophisticated hypnosis, using similar but more sophisticated resonant pitches that seem to pass beyond the inner ear and sound within the inside of the skull of the recipient. Certain metal healing spheres, which have become popular in the last ten or so years, if skilfully constructed, can appear to emit their chime—not from the ball itself but from inside the head of the listener. This makes it appear as if the mind is the source of origin of the sounds. Hence the *Song of the Sirens*.

Consequently Sirens, Harpies or Mermaids could lure men to their deaths and mantras could create miracles. The added dimension of resonance is also pertinent here when willing the occurrence of desired events. The spell or chant constructed in the same way as the judgement poem impresses itself here, not on the mind of the listener, but on the subconscious of the singer, and suggests an inevitability to the event or phenomena desired. In a sense, the repetitive cyclic or spherical nature of the spell acts as a garter or womb in which the intention is held and sustained. The repetitive, cyclical rhyming nature of the chant impresses itself on the mind and continues to express the will of the singer without the singer having to be conscious of the act of spelling. At the same time, the resonant pitch chosen is selected to match the frequency level of the objective article. Added to this is the concept of will and visualisation.

It is possible to influence humans or human related events by pitching the resonance at theta, which is below the conscious delta wavelength, and use this as a carrier wave within which is mixed the visualised desire of the practitioner. This is not magic. This is quantum physics. The dynamic of the will aspect of it has been verified by the Princeton University Engineering Department and other reputable institutes researching dream telepathy and remote autosuggestion. The entire process involves subtle levels of energy and frequency. All so-called magic using subconscious sustaining devices, even the "Witches' Bottles", is based on this principle.

In the construction of the verse element, within which is retained and conveyed the intent, the spellcaster must bring to the surface such accuracy and truth that no artifice could stand against it. The chant must be constructed in such a way as to express and encapsulate that essence of conceptual and wilful beauty, balance and order that the Greeks called Xocmoc, the complete sphere. The concept enjoys the validity of being an absolute truth and hence a reality. It draws wilful energy from the mind and becomes sustained there as an absolute conviction, or, as Jung would describe it, a semi-autonomous complex. In the mind of the victim it becomes the desired destructive obsession, whilst in the mind of the spellcaster seeking a result elsewhere, it becomes a sub-routine—geared to making what is external conform to the pattern of the unbending, internal will.

d) Bruidhne, Bruidhe (King Brude), Bruidhina (Pressina). The Bru or Bri element in these names confirms the Druidic origin of the Picts and of Brude and his daughter Pressina. Bruidhe and Bruidhina, father and daughter, can be seen as Druid and Druidess of the rank of Judges and Spellcasters whose roles, with their obligations and powers, were passed on to Maelasanu. As a Fee, d'Avalon Maelasanu was a Morgana or Morrigan, a descendant of the black robed Druidesses who, according to Tacitus, cast spells against the armies of Suetonius Paulinus on Anglesey in 61 AD. We can say with confidence that these priestesses were the Black Ravens, the Morrigans who swept across the fields of battle despatching the fallen.

These Morganas and Maelasanu after them were the Poetess-Judges who wielded the power of the Sirens or Mermaids with whom Mealasanu was identified so closely. The Brude King or Druid King was the custodian of tradition, and this too must have been one of Maelasanu's natural duties as a Druidess. It would seem appropriate to think of her not simply as Maelasanu, but as the "Bruidhina Maelasanu", the Druid-Princess and Siren Queen. Tradition states that Maelasanu was the niece of Morgana La Fey. It is obvious that this relationship is confused because of the sister-wife arrangement shared between Morgana and Arthur. It is also clear therefore that King Brude himself married a sister of Tortolina and that that sister was Pressina's mother. After all, Morgana herself was a "Bruidhina" and a Fee d'Avalon, and the similarities between her and Maelasanu are striking. As a maiden of the Grail, Maelasanu corresponds to the Page of Cups and the sign of the Swastika is attributed to her by Joseph Maxwell. Writing in the last century, he confirms to be representative of sexually derived energy. In other words, Starfire. In the French Tarot, Maxwell describes the Page holding a Grail from which emerges the Swastika or, as we know it, the vortex, which either emits or draws life energy. This echoes the layout of Maelasanu's maze garden as the Swastika and the symbol of the procession being drawn into the vortex or Sumaire, or her energy being projected from it as it exudes from her Fairy fountain.

e) The role of the Druid as seer or prophet, the interpreter of the future through dreams, can be related to Brude, Bruidhina and Bruidhina Maelasanu, as well as Morgana, through the word Breuddwyd, pronounced Brith or Bridhe-wyd. Here in the realm of dreams we have a clear connection between the Fey and the High Druid castes. The Weaver of Dreams, the Sithann, is the weaver of fate or Fey, and this role fell solely to the Druids and the Bruidhe caste therein.

The Morgana or Morrigan, the black-cloaked Druidess, had as her totem the Raven. In Kabala, this bird, as stated further on, was related to N'h'sh the serpent, as a divinatory being, i.e. an interpreter of dreams. Furthermore, the Raven itself was also identified with the white Dove. In a similar way to the Swan, it represents the brain and pineal gland, the Grail and the transference of Starfire from the brain to the womb, as in the glyph of the Dove descending from heaven with the paten, which it is depicted as depositing in the chalice. Consequently, we have a direct connection between the Morgana, Magdalene and Maelasanu, with the interchangeable symbols of the Raven, the Dove and the Swan (Caduceus of Hermes), which all relate to the N'h'sh or serpent of wisdom: the Dragon. Therefore, as stated before, the Fairy identity lies within the Pictish Druidic Kingly line. The same applies to the Vampire, as the supreme manifestation of the Vere-Tighema or ultimate overlord, the Witch and the Dragon, the Elven Queen and the water nymph, siren and mermaid, all of which are the Sumaire, the vortex of the grail.

Another bird sacred to the Druids was the wren. In the Druidic tradition of the double entendre, Druid as dryw actually means wren. So it follows that the Druids identified themselves, in one sense, with this tiny bird. Why?

One of the offshoots of the bardic order were called the Parasites, a name which might well have been applicable to the entire Scythian race. This Vampire race was parasitical and, like the wren, it was very small in comparison to the client tribes that it fed from. Like the Aryan tribe that it has been identified with, the Scythian overlordship constituted by ratio, a minute percentage of the overall population to which the arbitrary term "Celtic" has been attached. The great Aryan migrations of 1800 BC were great migrations of whole tribes, which included the tiny Aryan Tuadhe. In reality, neither the Scythians nor their Aryan parent culture were assimilationists and hence they always kept their numbers small and more or less pure-blooded. Compared to other cultures, the Scythians were consequently likened in size to a wren compared to a golden eagle, and this is the story of how the Druids adopted the wren as one of their symbols. It also explains their vampiristic nature and relationship to their client cultures.

Nisse as a shortened version of the Fairy Nicol, Nicholas, Nick (Nix). (source: *European Mythology*, J. Simpson). Nix is German and it is a name associated with water Elves. In German it also means zero, nil, nothing. One's memory is drawn back to:

a) Dracula's mirror and consequently to;

b) the "grail quest", for the absence of ego or, in Zen Buddhist terms, the still point of Zero—the Eternal Now—wherein lies all and nothing.

Samael, as Mazda "the Light", could only be perceived in just such a nil state of ego annulment. As Satan or Old Nick he is therefore the Axle of "Hamlet's Mill", the still, unturning centre point of the hub of the great cosmos, the nil point, the end of the journey, the pilgrim's destination, the sum of all things men seek, which is nothing.

Samael's identification as Mazda—the Light—is equal to Jesus' being identified in Revelations as the Bright and Morning Star or Venus-Lucifer. Jesus is Satan and Satan is the Still Point, the ultimate goal of all pilgrims.

"Come unto me all ye who are weary, and I will give you rest."

The Lamb of God also wears Lucifer's horns. Subsequent to the seeker's unravelling of this inversion of Samael or "Satan" by the Jews and the Catholics, there may be discovered therein the central teachings and tenets of tile Onosis of the Cathars and Templars.

In Languedoc the Albigensians (albe = Elven + gens=blood: albegensian=Elven blood) revered the Ankh Cross of the Inner Dragon Court, upon which was suspended the crucified Christ-Serpent. The Ankh symbolises eternal youth and is replicated in the Cross of Venus which, as the Star of the Morning, represents Lucifer. In this way the true identity of Jesus and his antecedents can hardly be mistaken. It would seem peculiar therefore, if he were not one of the Witches' Gods.

An example of this cross can be viewed at the Musee de Carcassonne. A similar cross of the 3rd century AD, a drawing of which is now in the

Staatliche Museum of Berlin, shows the crucifixion of Orpheus-Bacchus. The vertical beam of the cross is surmounted by the upturned New Crescent Moon, which symbolises the virgin womb of the goddess Diana. Formed into an arch above the scene are the seven stars of the Pleiades.

Whilst Orpheus, Bacchus and Jesus were all crucified as saviour god figures, Jesus and Bacchus additionally share the sigil of the IHS or In Hoc Signo Vinces. They are both, like Bacchus' Greek counterpart, Dionysus, associated with the vine, wine and blood ritual. The identification of Jesus as Lucifer replicates the role of Samael-Prometheus as the earlier benefactor-saviour of man before Christ. Jesus' clan name was ben Panther and this animal, the African version of the werewolf, was sacred to both Bacchus and Great Diana of Ephesus. IHS was attributed to Bacchus long before it was appropriated by the early Christians. Emblazoned onto Grail chalices, In Hoc Signo Vinces: "By This Sign Prevail" pertains not to wine, as the supposed component of Bacchus' ecstatic mysteries, but blood, which was consumed as the elixir of life and the doorway to eternal wisdom.

It is evident that the followers of Jesus, the early Christians, and the Bacchantes and Maenads of Bacchus and Dionysus, all drank blood as part of their ritual. This was a common feature of mystery cults across Eurasia, including Mithraism, whose devotees, like the Masai tribesmen of Kenya today, drank the blood of living bulls.

However, in the two latter instances, the Bacchanalia and Dionysia, the rites are reported as being particularly savage and also cannibalistic. This corresponds to reports of the Vampiric and flesh eating practices or the more primitive manifestations within the lower orders of the Witches and Fairies of Britain and France. In Scotland, the blood rituals were called the "Teind of Hell" and replicate the stories of the Vampires of Transylvania, one of whose initiatory grades, the Stregoi or Werewolf, lent its name to the followers of Diana in Italy, the Stregas or Witches.

The Teind of Hell, the sacrifice of a sacred individual by members of the Fairy-Witch tribe, was accomplished in stages. The first stage was strangulation with a ligature, the infamous Silken Points or Witches' Garter. In later times the body was said to have been burned and the ashes scattered. What happened between garrotting and burning remained a mystery and the purpose of the rite has always been held to be motivated by a desire to promote fertility. However this was not always the case and some light might be shed on the mystery concerning both the rite and its reason by looking at a similar, but earlier series of sacrifices which have come to light in recent history—the bog or pool people.

In earlier times, from the pre-Christian Iron Age up until roughly the fifth century AD, the "victims" in these types of sacrifice were strangled and the blood was let from a wound made at the side of or across the throat. The intact body was then placed either in a mere or peat bog, in contrast to being cremated, as in later mediaeval examples of this process. Of particular interest is the case of Lindow Man in Cheshire.

This individual was strangled and his throat was slit. A wound, made by a dagger or similar instrument, was found on the top of his skull. There appears to be a similar process in the killing and disposal of the other bog bodies that have been found across Europe. Firstly the garrotting was not fatal strangulation. This being the case, the theories of some forensic experts concerning Lindow Man, that the ligature made no scar and was therefore nothing more than a necklace, cannot be sustained.

The garrotte was not meant to kill, but to render the victims insensible. Secondly, the victims' "live" blood was then drained off and drunk. In all Vampire tales it will be noted that "dead" blood is held to be useless. Thirdly, at death, an aperture was made in the top of the skull—quite specifically a type of trepanned hole. Through this the spirit could leave the body and travel as an intercessor to the Otherworld via the Fairy portal, symbolised by the watery grave, the Mere or bog in which, fourthly, the corpses were interred. That the bodies were left intact seems to be a fair indication that the victim's souls were not meant to act as portal guardians. The practice of trepanning was common amongst the Egyptians and their later descendants the Merovingians. They both have a Dragon ancestry shared with the Druids who were, it is generally agreed, often the most likely victims and perpetrators of the bog killings. These were ritual precursors to the Teind of Hell sacrifices of the Witches, their descendants.

The drinking of the blood, practiced in Mithraism, early Christianity, Bacchic and Dionysic worship, was the Act of Eucharist. It took on the powers and characteristics of the divine victims whose sacrifice had a dual role. That is, it enabled them to go beyond and communicate to the god-ancestors on behalf of the Clan, and it provided their blood as spiritual sustenance and fortitude for the priests left behind. In battle, Scythian Warriors practiced similar rites and an old saying of theirs goes, "The blood of an enemy is sweet, but sweeter still the blood of a friend".

Like the collecting of severed heads as trophies, supposedly by the Celts, the practice of drinking the blood of the fallen in battle was intended by the practitioners to add to their own strength. In the case of head-hunting, the body of the fallen protagonist thus mutilated would trap the soul in the head and its virility in the mortal realm, where it was enslaved by the living warrior to increase his own might. The Celts, like the Greeks, and later Descartes, believed that the soul resided in the head. In this head hunting tradition, one can firmly place the Valkirie and the Morrigan or Morganas. Both are related to the Swan Maidens of the Mere and are "Ladies of the Lake", and thus Mermaids. The Valkirie were said to take the souls of the fallen heroes to Valhalla. It is by looking at the Scythian Morrigan however, that the method of dispatch used by their Nordic cousins, the Valkirie shield maidens, can be ascertained.

The Morganas were the goddesses of the battlefield and were likened to the Ravens. The Raven is another bird sacred both to Odin and Lilith in the Qliphothic Kabala, next to the owl and the Dove (Magdalene). It is a carrion bird that feeds on the fallen and was invariably to be found at the scenes of battle, feeding from the dead and dying. It is highly likely that the Morganas, the Ladies of the Lake who took Arthur off to Avalon, swept across the battlefields of their day, dressed in black, drinking the blood of the fallen. Thereby, like Odin's Valkiries, despatching them to the Otherworld or Tir Na Nog, the "Celtic" Valhalla. The Morganas, of which Melusine was one, were the daughters of Lilith. They were the Druidesses and Mermaid guardians of the Avalons, the sacred groves on the Fairy Island Mounds in the midst of the Swan Lakes that, for the Celts and their overlords the Scythians, were the doorways to eternity.

Mithraism or Mazdaism, named after Mazda or Enki-Samael, was, like other mystery religions which came before and after it, an ancient derivation of the original Aryan-Scythian philosophy which originated with the Anunnaki. Its blood rituals, along with those others presently under discussion here, were a decadent form of the Vampirism practiced by those first Dragon Gods of Sumeria. The original form of their rites became corrupted, but were reconstituted as Alchemy—and later as Courtly Love and Royal Witchcraft in the first millennium AD, whilst the more primitive forms persisted in tandem across Europe. All, however, at one point or another, suffered the disapprobation of the Catholic Church.

Chapter 35

The Ladder of Lights

During the medieval period, it is said that the Jewish Divines appear to have formulated the glyph of the Tree of Life to elucidate upon the teachings of the Kabala. The actual tree, however, is far more ancient. Later western occultists became enamoured of the Kabala and the Tree of Life and inserted their own quasi-Christian symbolism into the system. Whether either the Jewish mystics or the Christian Occultists are aware of it or not, the Tree of Life, which seems to have been copied from much earlier non-Hebrew sources, appears to be as much a genealogical chart as it is a magical glyph.

And it is by understanding it as a family tree that the truly magical elements it conceals can be more fully appreciated. Each sphere or Sephiroth on the Tree is essentially a theurgic dynamic. These forces or gods bear the names of the original Elohim, the Dragon Kings and Queens of the Anunnaki. The position of each sphere on the Tree corresponds with the relationships enjoyed by each of the gods with each other, so the spheres represent husbands, mothers, fathers, brides, sons and daughters.

In the Christian Occult Kabala, the eighth Sephiroth, Tiphareth, is thought to represent Christ and the Cubic Stone. This, the philosopher's elixir, the Lapsit Exellis or Fallen Star would, if such it be, serve to reinforce the identity of the Christ with Lucifer. However, the Cubic Stone is a component of the Grail. The Grail is a chalice, a female symbol, as is Venus, the Bright and Morning Star, who is Lucifer. Here there would seem to be a confusion of gender-related symbols, but there isn't. In an earlier essay it was suggested that Christos meant not the man, but the anointing. Earlier versions of the

Chrism or Christos were called the semen of God, the divine pneuma, the Logos or Holy Spirit. George Riley-Scott has suggested in *Phallic Worship* that this enlivened the mind of the anointed one, thus bringing enlightenment or "salvation". See Scott's comments on the Bethel Stone. It would, however, be more correct to call this Chrism the semenal fluid of the Goddess rather than that of God, as the Holy Spirit is traditionally female, being Astarte or Sophia, meaning wisdom.

The saving body and blood of Christ, the anointing of the Christos of Astarte or Sophia, thus becomes recognised as being the ovum and menstruus of the Goddess. At the beginning of the first millennium, she was represented by Mary Magdalene, the Scarlet Woman, who some say was the Priestess of Ishtar or Venus. If the Tree is taken as a genealogical chart then Tiphareth occupies a position mid way between Geburah (Samael Enki) and Chesed (Jehovah Enlil). In Anunnaki tradition, this place on the family tree would be occupied by the Dragon Queen, Nin Kursag. She was wife to both Enki and Enlil and the grandmother of Ishtar or Venus, who is represented on the Tree by Netsach, positioned in exactly the same place on the Tree, as Ishtar is on the chart. Essentially, therefore, Nin Kursag, called the Lady of Life, was the First or Great Venus, wife of Enki Samael or Lucifer, hence the association between the two.

One of her responsibilities was to feed the Dragon Kings with her blood and water, both of which together comprise the prima materiae of alchemy, the "Christos", in order to expand their consciousnesses and increase their life spans. This exactly replicates the phenomenon attributed to the Grail and the Cubic Stone. Magdalene, similarly, is suspected of having performed the same function. Like Nin Kursag, her predecessor and her goddess, she also provided her womb, in her proper season. This served as the vessel within which, in Nin Kursag's case, was carried the forefather of the subsequent Dragon Kings and from whom, in Mary's turn, Jesus' children were descended as scions of the root and branch of the Dragon Tree, the Planta Genista of the Anunnaki.

In some depictions of the Kabalistic Tree of Life we can seen entwined within its branches a Dragon or serpent. Said by some to represent the wisdom of "God" descending from Kether to Malkuth, rather it suggests that the Dragon Blood of the great mother touches and infuses all the Sephira which symbolise the Dragon Goddess-Queens and God-Kings, whose family tree it is. That serpent is Tiamat, the "Tree Mother" whose realm is Tir Na Nog.

The secondary function of the Kabalistic Tree of Life is to enshrine the secret wisdom that made the Dragons what they were. The utilisation of the Grail system which gave them their power relied upon the charting of the endocrinal system, the enhancing of hormonal output and the collection of the Christos. This information can be found in what is called the Middle Pillar of the Tree of Life, and the position of the Gods in relation to each other therein, doubles up as the position of the glands within the human body.

Chapter 36

Hearts and Flowers

Tiphareth can be understood as both Christ and Female at the same time if one regards the situation in the foregoing manner. To this may be incorporated the essay findings regarding Ichthys, the Fish, and the Salmon of Knowledge as the Christos or Menstruus emanating from the Vulva or Cubic Stone of the Goddess or the Scarlet Woman, represented by that Fish. The earliest manifestation of this tradition amongst the Dragon Goddesses of the Anunnaki serves as the origin of true vampirism as an act, not of Freudian sexual violence or perversion, but of necessity, love and nurturance.

Royal Vampirism has been horribly corrupted at various times. However, one might say that Solomon and Jesus, and the Royal Covens whose blood fed the Fairy Kings right up to and beyond the time of the Reformation, adhered the most closely to the original Draconian concept. They assisted in their own way in the maintenance and furtherance of proper alchemy and the concept of Courtly Love. Indeed it can be said that various exoteric aspects of this Vampire tradition emerged in its royal form, principally through the poetic works of the troubadours. They originally wrote and performed in the Occitan language of Provence, and contributed greatly to the birth of the Age of Romance and the seemingly fundamental change in some men's idealised views of women and the function and conduct of male-female interactions.

However, the key components of the philosophy seem to have been omitted or suppressed. It could be argued that women's fortunes have not been improved by our culture adopting only the trace elements of a tradition that, with its essential ingredients missing, has had only limited success. The concept of romantic love, with its original purpose perverted and its magical content removed, has been the ruin of countless lives. Human nature has regularly failed to acquit itself against the reality of human expectation. This has resulted in domestic violence and misery and in the annulment of marriages inspired by a concept of romantic love that never was intended to have anything to do with mundane human bonding, mating or propagation. It certainly had nothing to do with the idealised foundation upon which couples outside the Dragon tradition expectantly and inadvisably build such breeding arrangements.

Courtly Love Romance and everyday romance are two entirely different concepts, and it is not realistic to expect everyone to live up to what, in Dragon terms, is an achievable reality, but which, in human terms, is no more than a somewhat disappointing, market-driven and unattainable ideal. Courtly Love was a feeding arrangement intended to result, not in marriage on the mundane level, but in hierogamy and transcendence on the highest of all levels of organic experience.

The efficacy of such successful alliances relied both upon the genetic origin and age of the female. In these terms alone, these qualifications in themselves were sufficient to have excluded the majority of the female population of Europe. The remainder who were biologically suitable and ritually adept only served a few short years as an alchemical or divine lover before their blood chemistry altered. They then moved on to form dynastic alliances where the central concern was not "Romance" or "True Love", but the purity of the Dragon Blood and the well-being of the Dragon offspring.

As a consequence, and contrary to our present mores and social expectations, Romantic or Courtly Love and the unrealistic illusion of romantic monogamy were diametrically opposed to each other. The efficacy of the former would eventually decline if it were expected that such could continuously and permanently function in tandem with the biochemical shortcomings related to the built-in obsolescence innate within the latter. The two were simply mutually exclusive concepts. However, formerly the Church and latterly, burgeoning market forces, have conditioned us to expect that we and the entire population should "Fall In Love" and marry for such love. In reality the majority haven't got a clue what "love" really is, beyond the imposition of their projections on another.

If love is understood to be the emotional manifestation accompanying a socially acceptable interactive norm which expresses or satisfies people's domestic or erotic expectations, then love is just a collection of egocentric illusions underpinned by self-deception and self-interest. It is wrapped in the pretty packaging of self-sacrifice and altruism, because people have never been taught the philosophy underlying the principal of Courtly or True Romantic Love. In any case, they are psychobiologically incapable of ever attaining it. Consequently they are unaware that true love is the destruction of the self through another, not the fulfilment of the self through another.

Love is Death, not acquisition. Love is the end of desire, not the object of its own continuous gratification.

Singularly, Courtly Love may be described as the hormonally driven hunger to extract organo-chemical compounds from the Grail Maiden for ingestion. It is not the hormonally driven, somewhat cynical desire on the part of the male to inject unwanted genetic waste material into her for entertainment. The fundamental difference between Courtly Love and domestic congress is one of hormonal imperative. One activity is driven by an entirely different set of hormones than the other. Unlike the urge to frequently nominally replicate, Courtly Love or Royal Vampirism is most certainly not inspired or driven by testosterone or oestrogen. The litmus test for detecting the presence of the Dragon genome and those aforementioned propensities within themselves now, is to make a mental check as to whether or not one has often felt previously an urgent and recurrent inclination to eat the chicken without actually stuffing it.

If this is indeed the case, then you may congratulate yourself on having discovered an entirely new vessel of potential, sailing under the hitherto unknown flag of the Dragon in sacred waters you would otherwise never have guessed existed. Vampires' mothers always taught their children not to play with their food. That way it keeps better and lasts longer. Upon this principal is founded the basis of Courtly Love, a singular exercise in self discipline for the male or female Dragon beneficiary, providing hours of gratuitous, pleasurable diversion for the female Dragon benefactress.

The end result of this ritually structured arrangement is a transcendent dynamic principal which leads to the experience of or continued abidance within Truth, or True Love, if you wish to call it that. This has nothing to do with the genetic imperative, buying matching curtains and soft furnishings or getting another set of keys cut.

Chapter 37

Sexual Communication Amongst Animals and Humans

What are pheromones?

Pheromones are naturally secreted chemicals you can smell in the odour produced through the sweat glands of the body. In mammals, pheromones play an important role in the establishment of their territories: the marking activities of priests and dogs; the use of incense, and urinating against trees and lampposts are well-known examples. In a mouse the sexual and territorial marking functions come together when the female ovulates [produces an egg] after smelling a male.

Some primates, like the baboon, secrete pheromones during their receptivity to sex. In man the functions of pheromones are not totally clear, but we do know that smell plays a role in our attraction to a member of the opposite sex. However, today's propensity for covering our bodies with unnatural odours, like perfumes and deodorants, has probably led to a decline in our sensitivity and receptivity to these more natural odours.

Whatever it is that attracts us originally to a particular member of the opposite sex, one thing is certain. That is, that there are some chemical hormones we produce that have their role when we are playing the mating game.

The Function of the Relevant Hormones in Human Beings and the advantages and pitfalls of sexual communication:

Across a crowded room

1) When you are first attracted to someone, the principal sensory stimulus is usually visual. In this particular instance, perhaps in a social context, the eye sends messages along the nerve endings to the brain and the brain releases two hormones, vasopressin and dopamine, which begin to act during the phase of heightened attention, in order to assess the object's suitability as a potential mate. If the object continues to attract one, and advances are reciprocated, another hormone is released. This chemical, serotonin or 5-hydroxytriptamine, one of the amine group of stimulants similar to amphetamine, begins to produce a feeling of euphoria and excitement. By a process of association, this feeling becomes related to the immediacy of the object of desire as the interaction develops.

If the couple are mutually attracted and begin to take each other's advances seriously, the brain releases two other hormones, oxytocin and prolactin. These act on the mind to produce a feeling of bonding which, in anticipation of or during subsequent encounters, grows stronger, along with the sense of centredness or focus and euphoria felt in the presence of the other person, produced by the accompanying vassopresin, dopamine and Serotonin respectively. The whole process is called psychosomatic, inasmuch as the chemicals produced act on the brain and stimulate various emotional and intellectual responses in the mind. In tandem with the release of these hormones, when the subjects first enter physical proximity, traces of pheromone will be released to stimulate a heightened level of secretion of the other hormones in order to increase the overall effect of attraction.

And so to bed...

Two powerful hormones are also released by the sex organs during this whole process. They are oestrogen in the female and testosterone in the male. Prolactin is predominantly a female hormone which is secreted in breast milk. When prolaction is released in the male, he is also likely to release traces of Oestrogen, whilst the female will release traces of Testosterone.

The reason why members of the opposite sex produce hormones not readily associated with their gender is that testosterone in the female enables her to judge the masculine qualities in her prospective sexual partner, whilst the same happens with oestrogen in the male. The preliminary chemical phases completed, the sexual hormones will stimulate the desire to copulate and sexual intercourse takes place. After the sex act, the levels of hormones plummet and remain low for hours, sometimes for a day or so, until the brain chemicals resume a heightened level again and stimulate the couple to copulate again. This whole process is reactive and based almost entirely on conditioned responses stimulated by a variety of chemicals working together to act upon the central nervous system and the mind. The process is mediated and modified by personal inclinations and social conditioning. In our society, until very recently, encounters between males and females for purely sexual purposes of recreation or fun were discouraged. The initial feelings produced by the neurotransmitters were described by moralists as the process of "falling in love".

Fantasy Feelings

The guardians of the nation's moral welfare ascribed a spiritual and romantic quality to this. It was an illusory and unrealistic dimension, in which the establishment encouraged people to disassociate with and separate from the procreative act. This delusion was promulgated more for political and social reasons rather than from any altruistic desire to educate, enlighten or prevent the transmission of sexually transmitted diseases. One wasn't supposed to copulate unless one was married to or had "fallen in love" with one's prospective sexual partner. It seems odd to say that one mustn't engage in the fulfilment of one hormonal process unless the other had first taken place. The feelings associated with falling in love are focus, bonding and, most importantly from a psychobiological point of view—elation. All of these derive from purely chemical reactions and have nothing to do with real Love whatsoever. If they did, people wouldn't fall out of love as often as they do. The flowery moralistic attitude which encourages people to have such unrealistic notions about the purely natural processes we all undergo creates expectations about the potential of human relationships which are pure fantasy.

During a relationship, the brain slowly reduces the levels of the "falling in love" hormones. Because of this some people find that their relationships become mediocre and boring. They often blame this on the other person, which is also unrealistic and sometimes quite unfair. The reason that the relationship has lost that "buzz" is that the serotonin levels have dropped. For this reason many people constantly seek new people with whom to fall in love. In truth, they aren't in love with the person at all, but rather with the "drug rush" and the "chemical high" that human encounters so often afford. In reality it is advisable to know the truth and to take a long look at a subject that is so often misunderstood and often poorly and incompetently covered in national education. Because of the consequent ignorance and romantic idealism being fostered, it can cause much personal misery and social chaos.

England Expects Every Man to Do his Duty

Society has trained people to harbour unworkable moral ideals about human nature. It encourages them to attempt to adhere, and expect their fellow humans to adhere, to standards of behaviour that are frankly dishonest and unreasonable. Subsequently people's expectations in a variety of social interactions with their fellows, including bonding and mating, are full of deceit and hypocrisy. The projections of a fashionable moral ideal can change confusingly from decade to decade. If people were trained to be themselves, then society and social interactions would be a lot healthier and more enjoyable, leading to far less disillusionment and bitterness on an individual and national scale.

Beyond the Fantasy

Honesty produces natural centredness and clarity. In such a mental condition it is possible to perceive a transcendent quality in life which many have called True Love. It has nothing to do with sexual attraction or acquisition. It is in no other way dependent upon or relative to human behaviour or experience. This quality, when on occasion it becomes the foundation of human interactions, goes beyond the merely sexual or emotional to produce a state of communication and compassion that sexuality, with all the greed, self-deceit and cruelty that often accompanies it, can never understand or provide.

When entering into a relationship it would be a lot more honest for one to build its foundations on something far more substantial and meaningful than a sense of sexual or romantic, chemically-derived titillation. It would then stand a far greater chance of being successful.

The Cathars are known to have proscribed against any form of intercourse which would result in fecundity. The exoteric reason they gave for this was that procreation produced more matter and that matter caused pain and suffering. The real reason was that they favoured alchemical, non-procreative relationships for the very same reason the Holy Bible feverishly rails against them with its "Sin of Onan", "increasing one's tent pegs" and so forth. Jehovah encouraged copulation because it bred more terrified slaves. The Catholics hated alchemical marriages because they liberated the mind from slavery and didn't produce any more brainless, but brainwashed, cash machines. The Vatican's proscription against contraception is simply a recruitment-through-breeding programme. Never mind overpopulation, environmental catastrophe or social deprivation. As long as the fat foodboys* have enough catamites, whores, cigarettes and alcohol by each successively bred batch of tithe-paying morons, they and their multi-denominational scions can sit back and the whole planet can implode for all they care.

*Foodboys was a term of derision and contempt used by Yugoslav soldiers on all sides during the Bosnian conflict to describe their politicians. The "foodboys" sat back at home behind the lines cashing the welfare cheques from the World Bank and spending the money on luxury residences, flashy cars and fast women, or vice versa. In the meantime, everybody else was enduring a living hell. Politicians, priests—what's the difference?

Chapter 38

A Rose by Any Other Name?

The Church's insistence on differentiating between Paganism and Christianity is absurd. Many so-called modern *Wiccans*, unaware of its higher purpose, think of "their religion" as being pre-Christian and pagan. Witchcraft was viewed by the Inquisition as being heresy. However, a belief can only be heretical if it is at variance with that which is viewed as being its orthodox parent doctrine.

Witchcraft could not be heretical unless it was considered to be a Christian religion in the first place. Even though Witchcraft can be said to be pre-Christian in origin, its contributory cult, Jesus' form of Christianity, is also pre-Christian in origin. This makes a nonsense of the arguments on all sides, as well as the partisan labels used variously by Wiccans and sensationalists alike to define, contrastingly, Witchcraft as a pagan religion compared with Christianity.

In Roman Catholic terms, Jesus would have been labelled a Witch and his cult a heresy against the true faith of mother Church. If he had timed his second coming to coincide with the medieval period, he would have been burnt at the stake by the Inquisition. However, in true primal Christian terms and in comparison to Jesus' original teachings, Roman Christianity and all its collaterals and splinter groups, including modern so-called "born-again Christians" are themselves wicked idolatries and evil heresies. Jesus warned of false prophets. All we have had for over 1600 years is false prophets and wolves in sheeps' clothing. It has been said that Jehovah roams across the face of the Earth like a lion, seeking whomever he may devour.

The Witches of the Basque worshipped a God called Jauna or Janicot. De Lancre regarded this as a diminutive, which he said meant Petit Jean—which was the name applied by the Witches of the Basses Pyrenees to Christ.

With regard to *Hamlet's Mill*, Witches would often meet in windmills. In magical terms these structures sympathetically represented, on the microcosmic level, the Great, Ever-Turning Mill of the Cosmos, so anything done by a Witch in a windmill, it was believed, would be replicated magically in the greater universe.

1) Petit Jean translates into English as Little John, a companion of Robin Hood. It is possible that Robin and Little John were aspects of the one character, repeating the Jesus-Lucifer composite. It does not appear that these two aspects were conflicting, but rather that the early devotees were at pains to convey the idea that Jesus and Lucifer were the same person, and that Jehovah, if he figured at all, would have been the dark aspect.

2) Jauna is Janus, and Janicot is Janus-God, the two-faced guardian of portals. Being two-faced, Janus is similar to the gods of Mazdaism and Gnostic Dualism, which represent the forces of light and dark, of "God" and "Satan". It is significant that Jesus is worshipped by Witches, and that some Witch names for their "devil" and his followers are associated with Jesus, such as Christsonday, or Christ-son-Dei, Christ son of God. One is reminded of Columba's assertion—"Jesus, Mo Drui, Mac Dei". Quite often Witches took for themselves the name "Christian", or picked Witch names directly from biblical sources.

It becomes increasingly difficult to dismiss the idea that an early, homogenous, Levantine type of Witchcraft was the original form of Christianity, originating from the same mystical Eurasian root philosophy that gave birth to Druidism in Anatolia and the north-west, and Hinduism and Mazdaism in the east. In this case, the Dualism of Jesus-Lucifer is not the reconciling of opposites in Janus. Rather, in that guise, he is the identification of the Witches' god as the Pontiff or bridge, like the Druidic Blue Boar of the Irish Chronicles, but with faces looking both ways. Jesus is a guide to souls travelling to Faery. This Son of Solomon is an Elvish Lord who straddles the space between the worlds and conversely, like Hermes, he is also the messenger of the Gods to Man. It is worth noting that both Hermes and St. Nicholas are the patrons of thieves. One thief in particular, Prometheus, comes to mind. He stole fire from the gods to give to man. Prometheus is Samael or Old Nick. Robin is also known as the "Prince of Thieves".

Chapter 39

Jesus and Robin

Robin could be seen, in one sense, to have symbolically robbed the gold "of privileged, initiated wisdom", hoarded by the wealthy, and given it freely to the poor. Conversely, the wealthy who were entertained by Robin paid dearly for the privilege of gaining such wisdom.

"He who would keep his life shall lose it, but he who would lose his life shall gain the whole world."

The rich merchant gave up his entire fortune to purchase one Pearl of Great Price—Transcendent Wisdom. In this sense the adage "It is easier for a camel to pass through the eye of a needle than for a rich man to enter the kingdom of Heaven" is also applicable. The riches of this world keep the mind fixed on the cares and pleasures of this world. In order to perceive the "Otherworld", the transcendent reality, it is necessary to focus one's attention on matters far removed from the pleasures of the senses. In this sense, the pleasure of Robin's Feast would cost a man dearly, for his feast was that of the spirit. In order to taste its delights, a man must give up everything that ties him to his own world. Several stories concerning Robin tell of his hospitality and also that those he often entertained were often persuaded to part with everything they had in exchange for the board and entertainment they received. Considering Robin's Ritual identity the symbolism appears pertinent.

In northern Europe, the ancient Nick or Neck held such sway amongst the people that the Church was forced to adopt and canonise him as St. Nicholas.

In Cornwall, St. Nicholas still retains his horns. Being much older than Nicholas of Myra, it is far more likely that this horned St. Nicholas is the model for Father Christmas. The traditions linked to him are distinctly northern European and related to Hearne and Odin. In Professor Margaret Murray's work on the Witch cult and the Witches' god, the Deity whom the Church called the Devil or Satan was known in Sweden as the (Witches') antecessor or ancestor. This also suggests that in Sweden the Witches were related by blood to their "Devil", either their Fairy Master or Mistress. They were also related to the Devil's Elven ancestors.

In Britain he was known as Puck (Boucca or Bog/Bolg meaning God) and Robin Hood or Goodfellow. Murray cites at least ten references for the God being named Robin, whilst in Orkney be was known intriguingly as "Walliman", which means, one assumes, Wood Lord, another rendering of Robin's title and of the title of Hearne/Cernunnos/Vishnu. The Druidhe were also known as the men/women of the Trees (or Tree), which is another variation of the Wood Lords or Lords of the Forest, the Calle Daouine. Bearing this in mind it is feasible that Witchcraft was an underground continuation of Druidism in decline, as indeed Murray has suggested.

In Britain the God or Goddess was a man of the Fairy race, of flesh and blood. Nevertheless he, or sometimes she, was worshipped still as deity. Perhaps like Jesus, they became, as Avatars or living representations, the sons or daughters of the great Goddess-God of the Vast Cosmos. Significantly, the Witches' "goddess", Diana, was one of the four classical Titanias or Titanesses, the other three were Circe the Witch, Pyrrha and Latona. The Titanias, and hence Diana, were all Queens of Elphame. The Swedish name "Ancestor" seems appropriate here, especially as Witchcraft is seen by Murray as a Fairy "religion". In ancient Fairy tradition the Elves themselves were the gods, the Ubaid or Anunnaki (Anunnagi), who were later and elsewhere revered as the Titans, the Gods of the Aryan Hindu pantheon, the Pharaohs, the Gods of Israel, the Tuatha de Danaan and the Catholic Saints.

Murray says that she believes Witchcraft to be the leftovers of the religion of the Fairy race of the Neolithic period. The word Neolithic automatically makes us think of the word primitive and it conjures up images of cave men and wooden clubs. The Ages—Neolithic, Iron or Bronze could easily run concurrently according to the wealth or dearth of resources of any region that any particular population inhabited. Whilst Britain was in its Bronze Age, other regions had been using iron for centuries. The point has been made that we tend to judge a period or Age by its artefacts and come to the mistaken conclusion that a race was primitive simply because we rarely tend to find less durable goods than stone or metal.

Settled agricultural populations in the temperate zone have more free time to develop technologies than migrant pastoral communities or peoples inhabiting more hostile environments. However, civilisations can and do go into decline. Highly developed settled communities have been known to become low technology migrants because of local disasters or because the type of agriculture they were using did not work in the long term, or because resources dried up. Someone once said that civilisation is only three inches deep, that being a common depth of usable topsoil. Migrant communities would be forced to use the materials available to them in the new homelands in which they resettled. If the only land available was infertile or sparse in mineral resources, the most advanced communities of the time could plummet back down the developmental ladder, possibly becoming "Neolithic" again.

Witchcraft, rather than originating as a cave man's religion, was the decadent survival of a highly evolved Eurasian philosophy. It migrated to Britain and later absorbed the accretions of numerous settlers and invaders including the Danes, who seem to have held out against Christianity for far longer than the Anglo Saxons.

It is highly likely that what we think of as Witchcraft was not in fact an indigenous Neolithic British religion but was imported by the Picts as their "Fairy Religion"—Druidism. This was devastated by the Romans and later, in its varying corrupted forms, took on other influences as the centuries passed. It is recorded that up until the Reformation period, Witches still practiced the Pictish Scythian custom of whole body tattooing, of which the so-called "Witches' mark" was a minor but nevertheless culturally associated manifestation. The mark was originally a wound opened to let blood, which was consumed by the "Devil". The wound was then pigmented with soot or woad and acted as a sign of the sacrifice made by the Witch on her initiation, thereby marking her as one of the Witches' clan. Royal Covens did not use this practice. This marking practice has also been discovered on the Italian Ice Mummy named Oetzi. He was covered in marks that corresponded to the meridian points in acupuncture. The meridian map is related to and incorporates the outer columns on the Kabalistic Tree of Life, thereby lending further support to the academic assertion that acupuncture was learnt by the Chinese, not invented by them. Oetzi's body was over 5000 years old.

One particular influence, the Danish or Nordic, has given us historically, in some regions of Britain, a Witches' god who wears a grey cloak and blue hood or mantle. The choice of colours indicates that the god figure here is the archetypal "Lord Of The Rings", Odin or Hooden. The hood is specifically associated with Fairies, as it is with Robin Hood, his Pictish-Gallic double or counterpart. The Fairy Hood can be found associated with the Haxi Hood game. This was originally a sort of football played with a decapitated, hooded head, a sacrifice intended to make a portal guardian—and also with the remains of the sacrificial victim we know as Tollund Man, who was excavated in Scandinavia, Odin's old stomping ground.

Where the God appears otherwise in the shape of an animal, this tends to indicate that in Britain, a Pictish tribal totem was being revered in much the same way as the Scandinavian Witches' "ancestor" (antecessor) would be.

The animal shape assumed by the local "Devil" represented the heraldic badge of the Royal tribe from which the "god" originated (amongst the Fairy race).

Pictish tribes used different animal totems as tribal arms or badges and these changed according to the status or function of the tribe—as Druids, smiths, warriors and so on. The grades within the hierarchy of tribes within a Tuadha were also denoted by animal symbols, such as the Dragon, Eagle, Bull, Boar, Wolf, Goat, Stag, Horse, Salmon and so on. Depending on the country or region, there were variations in the type of animals depicted by the resident tribes. Originally the totem system might well have followed an initiatory grade, or caste system, similar to that manifested respectively in Mithraism or Mazdaism, and Hinduism, all of which originate from the same Indo-European root culture, the early proto-Aryan Scythians. Likewise, the grades may well have been originally associated with the seven Chakras or Sephira.

Certainly in Transylvania, the earliest known homeland of the Dragon Kings, the Vampire comes in various grades, including the Dragon, Bird, Boar and Wolf—an Odinic totem animal. Similarly, Vishnu in the Hindu pantheon follows a similar series of earthly manifestations in animal form including the Blue Boar, indicating an ancient link between all these cultural icons and concepts. Consequently, the local Witches' god representative may well have dressed as the animal formerly associated with the tribe of his ancestral origins, or of the tribe associated with the region within which the Witches lived.

Chapter 40

Santa Claus

As Old Nick, Jesus and Robin are therefore variants of St. Nicholas, who was the Celtic Hearne, the Lord of the Forest (Brahma-Vishnu-Shiva/Sidha), Odin the blinded (late composite version of Anu/Samael), and the Finnish shamanic wanderer, who travelled on a Sled drawn by Reindeer. It is pertinent to remind oneself at this point of the Pict-Sidhes, and of Amanita Muscaria. In the bleak of midwinter which, as a season, could have magically represented the wasteland of the Grail, he would come down from on high (slip down the chimney pole [descend the magic tree] of the snowdrift covered, half-hidden tepes) and leave gifts (fruit and food) for the occupants.

This in a sense, may symbolise the god giving succour to his beleaguered devotees, pilgrims on the journey of life, who were symbolically seeking guidance, sustenance and direction in the wasteland. His teachings helped to keep them resolute in winter's "dark night of the soul" and give them wisdom to continue the journey up the Tree. The fruit traditionally given at Christmas symbolised the Sephira and their wisdom, which both Odin/Samael/Lucifer and Jesus had obtained by hanging from a sacrificial Tree. One is also reminded of Moses and the Israelites in the desert wasteland, and Moses' brazen serpent held up on a "tree" or Tepes (a pole), as a symbol of healing.

In this connection I have heard it said that the custom of hanging baubles from the Christmas Tree was symbolic of the semen of the God who was represented by that tree. It is conceivable, but more probable is the idea that the baubles represent the Sephira and the tree, in its esoteric sense, is a Goddess.

Here one is further reminded of the figure of Samael as the serpent entwined around Lilith, his Tree. In connection with Moses' serpent staff as a healing symbol, the serpent is again Samael. He is a precursor to the Fisher King, who is healed by the Grail, i.e. the Woman who, as the Cup, is also the Tree or Staff around which he, Samael, the Serpent Fisher King, is entwined and healed.

One recollects the shaman's journey back up the magical tree. In Runic, Tree is spelt Tir and is represented by an upturned spear-like glyph reminiscent of the Tepes or Dragon Pole (Sarkany) found in Sidhe Mounds. We should look at Tir Na Nog, the "Land of Youth", to see if the word Tir in Gaelic has a conceptual relationship with tree and house. Although mistakes have been made with regard to the academic understanding of the origins of Gaelic ideas and words, the "Land of Youth" is associated with the "Tree of Ogmios"—Tir Na Nog.

Oghma is a Danaan God who, like Odin, is credited with discovering a magical script associated with the Otherworld. In Odin's case, this was Runic and was attained through death on the Tree Yggdrasil. In Oghma's case, the script he obtained has been called the language of the trees. Formulated in about 400 AD as a written script based on Latin, it originated with continental Druids as a system of magical symbols in about 500 BC. Of further interest is the connection between the words *Og* and *Och*, as in *Och Aye* and *Occitan*, the language of Provence. It is distinguished by its use of the word *Och* for yes, in place of *Oui* in the French. *Og* or *Och*—yes—are affirmatives or assertives, these words being the primary foundation of the positive state of mind and the will underlying all magic, the state of mind that allows and accepts; and thereby learns wisdom.

Och is the Oath positively asserted, and for the Druids the Oath was truth. Allowing a synthesis between these concepts we might further discover a Tree of Youth or Tree of Life, and a Land of Youth attained by ascending that Tree. Perhaps we might also discover that Tia Mat or Tir Mater, is the Mother Tree or Tree Mother. She was the original womb of the Fairy race and the first Lady of the Forest, the first Grail Princess who was both the tree and the fountain of magical wisdom—Ogham, and the "Source" or "Land of Eternal Youth"—Tir Na Nog. Perhaps also, ascending the Tree could be seen as a sacrifice of self as returning to the Mother, to the womb of the Otherworld—Tir Na Nog—and thus to death, the ultimate truth. Nothing.

This sacrifice, death on a "Tree", is symbolic of the total submission to the female which is found in Courtly Love. She is the Tree, as we have seen in other essays, and as such is the implement by which the Priest King is "destroyed", and thus healed. The total submission however, is ultimately to the Nix or nothingness, which her nature affords and her soul reflects. She is the Egyptian Nuit, the boundless abyss of infinite space beyond time. Her fruits sustain and nurture the Cernunnos or Odin, the Priest-King-Magician who, in turn, nurtures and sustains his supplicants and followers. Similarly,

Jesus (Moses' Brazen Serpent) descended from his Rood Tree and was thus "resurrected". He gave gifts of the fruits of its (Her or Death's) wisdom when in transcendence. He preached to his disciples.

In these tales, where Jesus, Robin and Odin, or Hearne, as the original Santa Claus, gave gifts to the poor and needy, the essential elements of Magician-Priest-Kingship are manifest. It was the King's duty to sustain and guide the people. He could only do this through sacrificing his ego to the Nix, and by uniting with it to perceive the transcendent wisdom. He could only do that by "hanging from a tree", by "riding Epona or Slepnir to the Otherworld". Thus a king could only be a king if he had a queen.

Father Christmas is Merlin et al after all, and therefore the so-called dyslexic devil worshipper who "sold his soul to Santa" was also not so stupid. In earlier depictions he also represents Old Father Time, Saturn or Chronos, the father of the Titans. In this guise he is Iapetus or Anu. Merlin and Odin were the inspiration for Tolkein's wizard Gandalf or Gand-Aelf, meaning "Grey Elf Sorcerer" in Norse. Odin wore a dark blue hood (Robin!) and a grey mantle. Hence Tolkein's Gandalf the Grey, and Od-in or Hood-en. Robin or Robert means Bright Flame, which appears to be linked more or less to Lucifer. Here we return to the concept of the Wild Hunt. Chronos ate his kin (his children). Hearne (Oberon/ Alberich) or Odin was Master of the Wild Hunt for Elf women (also his kin) whom he also "ate". In France one name for the Devil, the God of the Witches, was Albirin—which obviously is Oberon, king of Elves.

The French had a separate, Frankish, Robin Hood and Maid Marian (see J. Hunt) who were probably derived from a common early Gallic cultic root.

It is from this tradition, one might assert, that Robert III inherited his role as the Robin Hood-en, or Odin, The Hooded Wanderer.

One can see Raymond and Melusine echoed in Robin and Marian even though the latter fit variously the Jesus and Magdalene, Arthur and Guinevere cycle more easily. Robin and Arthur have a number of identical Celtic adventures. This does not apply to Raymond, but five elements seem to bind their cycles together.

1) Raymond kills Aymeri, Mordred kills Arthur. (Chronos cycle)

2) Guinevere deserts Arthur, Melusine deserts Raymond. (Lohengrin cycle)

3) Jesus and Robin are both betrayed and killed. (Priest King cycle)

4) Robin and Arthur are betrayed by women. (The Abbess and Morgana)

5) Melusine betrays and also kills her father.

It is arguable that these tales were enshrined in Druidic lore in the first place, because in reality they happened all too often. At least they happened often enough, perhaps, for the Druids to recognise that these events followed archetypal and repetitive, psychologically ingrained patterns, like treadmills. Some of them needed addressing and avoiding, for the good of the kingdom and the people.

Addenda

1) In a delightful little children's book entitled *Hamish aud the Fairy Gifts*, by a Scot named Moira Miller, I noticed a repetition of the red hair business:

A couple has a red-haired son, newly born, and the grandmother wants to take precautions against his possible abduction by the Sidhe because he has hair which is "The Kings' Colour", the very thing they (the Sidhe) prize most". Precautions are ignored by the couple and they notice one morning that their child's eyes have changed from blue to green, though he still has hair of the Kings' Colour. The child is of course a changeling.

What is interesting is her comment about the child's hair being the colour of kingship. Again we have an assertion, found often before and elsewhere, in a story obviously derived from Scottish folk sources—that Sidhe hair is red and their eye colour is green, with the added element that this is also the pigmentation of Kings. Therefore, if Red is the Fairy colour and also the Royal colour, the two are the same. Here we go back to red-haired Lilith and the Anunnaki, who are the original source of kingship. One will notice in the medieval pictorial ensemble of "Melusine by the fountain" that she too has red-gold hair. In a variant of one of her tales related by Baring-Gould, her first son (Milo) has one red eye and one green, as opposed to blue in the other story we began with. In Serbia, red hair is the mark of the Vampire.

2) From: *Frozen Tombs of the Scythians*, by M. I. Artamonov: Scientific American, page 238. All the corpses had had their heads partly or entirely shaved but before their burial, hair had been attached artificially to the heads of the women and beards to the faces of the men.

3) From: *Research on Lilith*. Page 13, under Zohar 1 :54b-55a, a quote from R. Yitzhaq. "Female spirits come and play with him (man) and get hot [C] from him and thereafter bear [those demons] which are called the Plagues of Mankind. And they turn into likenesses of men but have no hair on their head." (Patai 81: 471)

This is directly related to the Liliths and their brothers, the Lilin, who are those from the North. Lilith is the alien crown, the northern queen. (Patai 81:453) One is reminded of the habit of the Egyptian Priests who also shaved their heads. However, in this case I believe that it refers specifically to the Scythians.

The reader might recall some excerpts from Dr. Miranda Green's compilation, *The Celtic World.* In this work it suggests that in Celtic Europe, corpses were sometimes dismembered in order to prevent the soul of the departed from passing over to Tir Na Nog, the Otherworld. This explains the thinking behind the concept of Portal Guardians and therefore, the reason why Dracula's headless body was buried under the entrance of the Chapel, etc. It also explains why the Scythian corpses had their hair glued back on, post mortem.

Although certain of the castes would perhaps have shaved their heads during life, perhaps leaving a plaited pony tail at the crown, in the style adopted by the Chinese, would have been considered incomplete if some attempt at replacing the hair had not been undertaken. Being incomplete, they would have been tied to the this world, unable to make the transition from death to rebirth. This belief possibly originates from a root Indo-Aryan belief that is also shared by the Hindus. During the Raj period in India, the greatest punishment that could be inflicted upon a Hindu was to be strapped to the muzzle of a cannon and have the limbs and vitals blown to kingdom come. Presumably, it would have been impossible to completely reconstitute the shattered-and-splattered remains of the recidivist.

We are aware of the tradition of Ring Hoards, Oath Rings and Rings of Power, and their symbolic role in the Dragon Myth as a version of the Grail in tales ranging as far and wide as Mesopotamia, Tibet, Scandinavia, tribal Africa (The Naga people) and Japan. The ring in Zen is Zero, the Eternal Now, the Gateway to Elphame and so on. We also know that Charlemagne was given a magical ring by a Dragon on the occasion of his "magical" wedding to an unknown eastern Fairy Princess called Frastrada. As Oroborous, the Dragon *is* the Ring.

Charlemagne's ring eventually found its way into a mere, thanks to Bishop Turpin. Water is the female element, and therefore all Fairy Maidens are types of Melusine. It could be argued that the involvement of the Dragon suggests that this marriage was also an alchemical wedding or hierogamy, in the tradition of Courtly Love. Here yet again is the basic story of sovereignty. It is achieved through transcendence, via the union of the king to a Mere Maid, a "portal guardian" who allows the King participation in the Otherworld or Eternity which, in this story, as in the story of Odin and his sovereignty of the nine worlds, is symbolised by the Ring. The Ring of Power is necessarily the Ring of Love, because that Love bestows Transcendence or Wisdom, the proper exercising of which, affords power.

Chapter 41

The Dragon Sovereignty

The ring as a symbol of kingship originated with Enki (Samael) or Satan, as the Church would have us call him. Samael was the earlier name for Prometheus and Loki, whom the Zeus prototype vowed would remain chained to the White Mountain forever. After some time Zeus regretted his vow and wished to release Prometheus, but was bound by his word not to do so. At last a compromise was reached and Zeus tore the chains which bound Prometheus. From one link of adamantine he forged a ring and set upon it a stone cut from the mountain. In this way he was able to keep his word, that his old adversary would forever be bound to the mountain, but afforded at the same time his release.

The mythical conflict between the Grecian Zeus and Prometheus originated in Scythia. There the two gods were named Enki (Samael) and Enlil (Jehovah). The war between them arose firstly as a dispute over seniority. They were the sons of one father, Anu. Enki was the younger son of Anu's senior wife, Antu. Enlil was the elder of the two sons but was born to Anu's second or junior wife, Ki. In Anunnaki culture the female was the source of sovereignty and by rights Enki or Samael (Satan) was therefore the rightful heir to his father, Anu, King of the Anunnaki or gods. Enlil disputed this claim and furthermore resented Enki's patronage and assistance of mankind, whom Enlil (Jehovah-Zeus) hated and wished constantly to destroy.

This story is repeated in the Greek tale of Zeus' hatred of mankind and the war for supremacy and control of man waged between the elder gods, the Titans, led by Prometheus, and the younger gods, the Olympians, led by Zeus.

It is repeated again in the tale of the war between Satan and Jehovah. In all these stories, it is the son of the elder queen who is the rightful heir, and this is Enki-Samael-Prometheus-Satan, the friend, saviour and supporter of mankind.

Enlil or Zeus-Jehovah further objected to the idea of investing in man the right to kingship and self rule, as this was, by tradition, the sole prerequisite of the Anunnaki alone. A compromise was reached in the Dragon Council, and it was decided that an Anunnaki queen would incubate a human ovum fertilised by Enki or Samael-Satan. The resulting child would be the first king or queen of the race of men, being mostly Anunnaki. Several attempts were made at producing a suitable child by adopting varying permutations of the Anunnaki-human interaction. Samael inseminated an Eljo woman, resulting in the birth of Adam, the first prototype of mortal kingship.

The second experiment was between Enki-Samael and Eve, his daughter. The child they produced was called Cain, who was mated to Lilith Luluwa, the pure-bred Anunnaki daughter of Lilith the Beautiful and Samael. To Lilith Luluwa, Cain and their sacred offspring was given, via Nm Kursag, the Tiara of Dragon (not mortal) Kingship from the hand of their father Enki-Samael, the rightful overlord of the Gods, whilst Adam and his children were still considered by Enlil to be serfs. However, upon them the usurping Enlil conveyed his own kingship without the authority of the Council of the Dragon Gods, the Anunnaki. This he did in an attempt to gain support from humanity for his illegitimate claim to leadership of the Council.

In a later rendering of the story of the origin of kingship, which accompanies the story of the war between the rightful gods, the Titans, and their younger rivals, it is said that rings became the symbol of kingship. They were apparently worn in memory of Prometheus, from whom all true kings were descended. These rings of alchemical or magical priest-kingship are specifically Dragon Rings, which are symbolised by the alchemical Oroborous, the Serpent or Dragon eating its own tail, the 0 or Zero.

Prometheus the Titan is the "elder god". He is Enki, later called Satan. Therefore the two stories, originating from a common source, attest to the idea that the holy, Draconian, Otherworldly origin of the blood of kings ultimately derives from Satan or Samael-Enki, and Lilith. It does not come from their rival, the usurper Jehovah-Zeus or Enlil, and the race of Adam from whom is derived the origin of the later Tinker Kings, the false monarchies that are based, not on service and transcendent wisdom, but on worldly greed, tyranny, trade and usury.

The bloodline of Lilith and Samael, the pure royal blood of true kingship descended, therefore, from Transylvania and Mesopotamia, through the Sobekh queens of Egypt who, after the Anunnaki, established the first Royal Dragon Court. From that point it devolved down to the Tuatha de Danaan of Eire and their descendants, the Pictish, Dragon, Fairy princesses of the Holy Grail, whose families colonised Caledonia and Anjou.

Such was the strength and purity of this ancient bloodline, that it was never forcefully assimilated, interbred or conquered. Through the Tuatha de Danaan and their daughters and sons, the Pictish Dragon queens and kings, the Elven ladies and lords of the British Isles, the Royal Dragon blood devolved to the ancient Vere-Bruidhe, the priest-kings of the Calle Daouine in 400 BC. This lineage descended through the centuries to the arch-Druidic, Pictish Priestess-Queen Bruidhina who married King Gille Sidhean of Albany, an eighth-century descendant of the Druidic, sacral house of the Ulidian of the Ver Bolg. Taking her Elven entourage—her Royal Dragon Court—with her, their daughter, the Fairy Princess Maelasanu de Scythes or Sidhe, the second niece-granddaughter of Morgan la Fey, moved from Scotland to France. There she married another Vere, the Frankish prince of Gallic Pictavia, Raymond de Forez, through whom she continued, in the early eighth century, the first Royal House of Vere of Anjou or Anschau, meaning “mystical revelation”.

Their eldest son, Prince Maelus or Milo de Vere, Duke of Angers, became the second Prince-Comte of Anjou, after his father. From him the ancient Royal Dragon blood, the mystical lineage of Vere of the first royal house of Anjou, continued to descend for another 1300 years to the present day, in an unbroken, single named, senior dynastic line of Royal Dragon princesses and princes. In the 19th century, Baron Thomas Macauley wrote of them that they were the most ancient, most noble and most prestigious family in Britain, and indeed in Europe as a whole.

In Jewelled Torrents fell the Midyear's light as playfully into the eagerly awaiting mere, it Swirled below the mountain ridge.

Dark then the waters layin that shaded forest pool Which concealed forever the mournful Mystery, lying beneath its bridge.

To the Northern Star; the Yearning currents cascaded forth, to Wed the crystal leaded tumult Of the Druid Healer's Flow.

Embracing, these Undines wandered the Summer's Lands, below the bridge Of the Ford's High Cross, Behind the Boar's wide brow.

The Dragon's Power; the ancient Sovereignty of an Ancient Fairy King laid there, hatefully torn From his heart; ere Broken.

A Maiden Fair and Fey, The Dragon Queen must be, Who astride Rhiannon rides in Quest for Love's Last Token.

Appendix 1

The Biological Basis of Elitism and "Divine Right" Rule

by Tracy R. Twyman

Originally published in *Paranoia* magazine

On October 28th, 1998, a number of newspapers across the country ran an Associated Press article entitled "Presidential Hopefuls Share Blue Blood Lines." The article, based on information put forth by Burke's Peerage, claims that every single President of the United States has had a notable amount of royal European ancestry, and in each Presidential race, the one with the most royal genes is the one who wins—every single time. This tendency has been noted in supposedly Democratic European politics as well, prompting some to charge that a global conspiracy exists to keep power within the hands of a specific gene pool. This charge is not entirely baseless, and many books have been written tracing modern aristocratic bloodlines back to the royal houses of Israel, Egypt, Sumer, and beyond. The charge is further supported by the fact that many of the supposed conspirators proudly boast about the ancient origins of their ancestry. The traditional explanation for why power is passed down through the ages by blood has been the mystical Divine Right of Kings. This dates back to the 17th century and states that a king is created by God, and therefore kingly authority resides in the blood irrespective of anything else. Many have claimed that there is a genetic characteristic carried in the blood itself which makes this so. But what would it be? Is there a legitimate physiological reason behind the Divine Right of Kings?

Fields of the Nephilim

The all-important element of the Divine Right is that it comes from God, or alternatively, "the gods". And who were these gods? Authors such as Zecharia Sitchin, Sir Laurence Gardner and Nicholas de Vere are authoritatively convinced that kingship was created by an advanced race of beings called the Annunaki, also called the Nephilim in the Old Testament. They reportedly civilized the human race and interbred with a portion of it to create the kingly caste which until this day has maintained control over the Earth. These celestial creatures have been variously identified with Dragons, Elves, Fairies, Gnomes, Leprechauns, Sprites, Nymphs, Pixies, Angels, Demons, Devils, Witches, Giants, Vampires, Werewolves, and just about every mythical being you can imagine.

Some, like Gardner and Sitchin, claim that they come from another planet. Others say that they're from the Hollow Earth. Some, like David Icke, say that they are humans inhabited by the spirits of multidimensional reptiles, capable of shapeshifting into reptile form at any time. Still others claim that they were humanoid, but more than human, with pale white skin. The human hybrid offspring that they created as the Royal/Priestly caste was, according to most, the Aryans, who usually had red hair with green eyes—in stark contrast to the traditional Hitlerian vision.

Nicholas de Vere, the leader of an organization called the Dragon Court which claims to represent this royal Aryan caste, writes, "the depiction of the Aryan (Scythian) as a tall, ruddy-complexioned blonde racist yeoman-farmer-warrior-god has no basis in truth." He further suggests that the "yeoman-farmer" Celtic, Gaulish and Pictish tribes which we now think of as Aryan were actually of a different race, but had hired the extra-human Aryans to be their leaders.

These Aryans were also the masterminds behind the Indian, Hittite, Greek, Egyptian, Hebrew, Sumerian and Pre-Sumerian Ubaid civilizations. Some believe that their descendants can be found amongst the segment of the population with the RH Negative blood type, roughly 5% of the Earth's population, most of them Europeans. These people are often born with an extra vertebrate, have a lower than normal body temperature, and can rarely mate with one another successfully, suggesting that they may indeed be a hybrid species. Conspiracy enthusiast Arizona Wilder takes it a step further saying, "The Aryan bloodline is alien to this planet... There are 13 bloodlines from this kind of stock (the Merovingians being one), and all of them have to a greater or lesser degree the capacity to play host to the Shape Changer reptiles." The other 12 families have been identified as Astor, Bundy, Collins, Dupont, Freeman, Kennedy, Li, Onassis, Reynolds, Rockefeller, Rothschild, Russell, and Van Duyn, with the rest—the European royal families—being categorized as "Merovingian." These are the people referred to by the fanatic group the Sons of Jared when they "pledge an implacable war against the descendants of the Watchers, who as notorious pharaohs, kings and dictators, have throughout history dominated mankind... like super-gangsters, a celestial Mafia ruling the world." *The Book of Enoch* says that the sons of the Nefilim are destined to "afflict, oppress, destroy, attack, do battle and work destruction on the earth."

Nicholas de Vere, himself a prince of the "Dragon blood", sees it quite differently. He sees them as the rightful shepherds of the human flock. "The Fairies were tuned to a higher frequency of perception and activity generally. In the past, therefore, because the Fairies were, for millennia, physiologically bred and exhaustively trained to operate at a higher level than men, humans often invited them to become social navigators... A Dragon was one who saw clearly, and the clarity of vision engendered was always classically associated with wisdom, which itself produces power...."

The Annunaki and their quasi-human offspring are attributed with remarkable traits. They lived for thousands of years, were capable of levitation, dimension-hopping, clairvoyance, and a million other magical powers, all a product of applied eugenics. "Selective unions gave the race the opportunity to breed outstanding magicians whose gift of natural perception and understanding: and whose ability to access the "Otherworld", helped to produce and guide brilliant kings who ruled with elegant aplomb. The ability to perform magic was carried in the blood" and "the Elves were relied upon by their client races to be able to see things and perform feats that these client races couldn't."

Laurence Gardner, himself a former member of the Dragon Court, concurs. "In short, these people were bred to be leaders of mankind, and they were both mentally and physically maintained in the highward state." But what property did they inherit in the blood which makes this possible? Those who have written on this subject are nearly unanimous about the fact that the answer is endocrinology. Says de Vere, "hormonal levels [are] influenced by genetic inheritance and hormones [affect] the individual's perceptions, psychological unicameralism and the subsequent ability to transcend and perceive the intricacies of the cosmos. Elven blood [is] rich in these substances."

Starfire Bloodfests
"The best blood is of the moon, monthly..."
Aleister Crowley, The Book of the Law.

The beneficial effects of the hormone melatonin have been part of the health supplement scene for some time. High melatonin production is known to be synonymous with a high immune system, a low cancer risk, long life, energy, stamina, and according to many, enhanced spiritual awareness. Perhaps it is fitting then that this hormone is secreted by the pineal gland, a mysterious little item long believed by mystics to be the "Seat of the Soul", "the Third Eye", and the organ through which psychic powers are exercised. In fact it actually functions as an organ of sight in some reptiles, and it still seems to possess some sensitivity to light in higher mammals, as melatonin production increases when the person is exposed to darkness. Thus melatonin means "night worker." Writes Laurence Gardner, "High melatonin production thereby increases the facility for receiving and transmitting high-frequency cosmic and local broadcasts, and leads to a greater state of cosmic awareness—a state simply of "knowing." In this regard, it is interesting to note that the Pineal Third Eye has been found to contain very fine granular particles, rather like the crystals in a wireless receiving set." Many magical rites and meditation techniques are aimed at gaining control of this organ and the fluid it produces, the live melatonin. Rumor has it that the members of the super-secret society Skull & Bones, to which both George Bush Sr. and George W. Bush belong, engage in a ceremony called "The Obscene Rite". This involves the consumption of the live pineal gland of a human or animal sacrifice in order to get the fresh secretions. Supplements bought over the counter are ineffective because, as Gardner explains, "their inherent secretions are obtained from the desiccated glands of dead animals and they lack the truly important elements which only exist in live human glandular manufacture."

But the Aryan overlords who ruled over mankind in ancient days had a simpler way of acquiring this fluid. Their ancestor-gods, the Annunaki, had endocrine systems that produced large amounts of this and other beneficial substances. Therefore they drank it straight from the source: the menstrual blood and vaginal fluids of the goddesses themselves. This they referred to, lovingly, as "Starfire" and drank in a ritual ceremony called the Black Mass, after which the Catholic Mass is said to have been modeled. Later, as direct contact with the Annunaki ceased, the fluids were collected from sacred priestesses referred to as "Scarlet Women", or "Grail Maidens." You may recognize the Scarlet Woman as the Whore of Revelations, as well as the title which Aleister Crowley gave to all of his sex magick partners. "These sacred, royal princesses,", writes de Vere, "virgins of High Birth and Pure Blood, at an optimum age would be chosen to act as feeding females". Their essences contained such valuable substances as, "oxytocin, prolactin, melatonin, seratonin, adenosine triphosphate, dopamine, telomerase, and retinol." There is another important ingredient in the mix here. De Vere explains that, "many think that only men have semen when in fact women also have it." And so a Starfire ritual involves the use of a golden straw. "Such a device would have been inserted into the virgin's urethra to the depth of about one inch, whilst the partner in the rite inserted his or her finger into the vagina and massaged the "roof of the mouth" or uppermost wall of the cannel nearest the opening of the vagina, behind the public bone. After a few conducive moments perhaps, orgasm would occur and the fluid from the gland would discharge itself through the straw, either into the waiting mouth of the recipient, or onto a "grail platter" or dish held next to the vulva." Keen readers will recognize this as being identical to a sex magick ritual advocated by Aleister Crowley for members of his "Order of Oriental Templars" (OTO). The only difference is that his rite also involved the use of male semen which was called the "Red Tincture" or "coagulated blood", while the female fluids were called "Gluten" or "The White Tincture." Together they made "The Elixir of Life", and in alchemy blood and semen are the primae materia or first matter of the Great Work. "This is the true Key to Magick", writes Crowley. "That is, by the right use of this secret, man may impose his Will on Nature herself."

Monatomic Gold: The Substitute

But according to de Vere and others, ingesting the fluids of mundane women has only a slight effect, certainly not enough to maintain the members of a Royal Dragon family in the manner to which they are accustomed. And after a few thousand years, the genetic purity of their Grail maidens began to deteriorate, so the Starfire lost its potency. This reportedly began around 1960 BC and is equated with the time that an edict was handed down to Noah by God demanding that the consumption of all blood cease immediately. (*Genesis 9:4*) Thus, a substitute had to be found, and so the alchemical process was created, as a means of artificially creating the Elixir of Life, the Philosopher's Stone, also known as "potable gold." This is achieved using a black powder known as occultum, the universal solvent which has the power to transmute metals. When placed against gold it converted it into a white powder which could be ingested. It is said to cause nothing less than immortality, as it sets off a self-correcting mechanism in one's DNA that lasts for thousands of years. It also bestows the enhanced melatonin production and magical powers associated with Starfire, including clairvoyance, dimension-hopping and flying capabilities. It is believed that this "white gold" is the same as the "shew-bread" and "manna from Heaven" mentioned in the Old Testament.

Today, there are those who publicly proclaim knowledge of the Philosopher's Stone. A man named David Hudson claims to have created a technique for manufacturing this white gold, which he's pattented as ORME (Orbitally Rearranged Monatomic Elements.) Ormus is a name associated with the Holy Grail, and so readers may not be surprised to learn that Hudson himself is related to the Merovingian Grail family, through Claude de Guise. Basically, the powder is created by putting gold into a higher atomic state through a series of intense heating and cooling sessions, during which it loses and gains weight radically, as though portions of the mass were being transferred into another dimension. David Hudson continues about the magical quantum properties of his white gold:

These M-state elements have been observed to exhibit superconductivity, superfluidity, Josephson tunneling and magnetic levitation... They may enhance energy flow in the microtubules inside every living cell. Ingesting M-state gold has different effects on the body than the effects of ingesting metallic gold. At 2 mg. it totally has gotten rid of Karposi Sarcomas in AIDS patients. Within 2 hours, their white blood cell count goes from 2500 to 6500. ... Stage 4 cancer patients have taken it orally, and after 45 days have no cancer left anyplace in the body. It's been used on Lou Gehrig's disease, it's been used on MS, it's been used on MD, it's been used on arthritis. It literally corrects the DNA.

Sympathy for the Devil

All of this puts a nice, friendly face on the whole thing, a secret power held only by an elite caste of Aryans who use it to lord themselves over the rest of the human population. And there are those who would say that the "substitute" white gold never did away with the original practice of blood-drinking as a method for obtaining the substances needed.

David Icke and his associate, Arizona Wilder, have campaigned the globe to inform its citizens with Chicken Little-like hysteria that most of its financiers, politicians and aristocrats are actually under the control of Reptilian beings from another dimension, who are inhabiting their bodies. "To hold their human form, these entities need to drink human (mammalian) blood and access the energy it contains to maintain their DNA codes in their "human" expression. If they don't, they manifest their reptilian codes and we would all see what they really look like." Icke believes that most of this blood is obtained in human sacrifice rituals engaged in by the Satanic Illuminati. "From what I understand from former "insiders", the blood (energy) of babies and small children is the most effective for this, as are blond-haired, blue-eyed people. Hence these are the ones overwhelmingly used in sacrifice, as are red-haired people also." His compatriot, Arizona Wilder goes into a bit more detail when she writes, "They have a hypnotic gaze which fixes the victim—in a trance of terror—which promotes secretion of the pineal gland—at that point, they cannot hold human form any longer and begin to shapeshift in anticipation of supper."

Wilder claims to have witnessed Laurence Gardner drinking blood and shapeshifting during a sacrifice at Montauk, New York. Wilder also claims to have seen a number of others who were transformed during similar blood-fests, including, "...Bush and his two sons, Albright, Kissinger, Reagan and Nancy, J. Rockefeller, Ford, Carter and LB Johnson, the Queen Mother, Queen Elizabeth II, Princess Margaret, Charles, Tony Blair, Prince Philip, and Zecharia Sitchin." She acknowledges that Starfire rituals go on as well. "In the underground vaults of his castle in the Alsace Region of France, green glowing fluorescent rocks turn stored menstrual blood black to be used at that special ritual. All members of the British House apparently have jewel-encrusted goblets with which to drink the blood from the symbolic female grail and a symbolic dagger to give it a bit of a stir. Some Spencers were at these rituals, but Diana would not attend... the smell of Diana's periods would have caused Charles to shapeshift—especially whilst sleeping, because the reptiles cannot retain their human form without concentration." This may shed new light on Prince Charles' reported desire to become a tampon.

Aware of these charges, Nicholas de Vere has tried to clear the record. He has acknowledged that vampirism does take place at his Dragon Court rituals, but maintains that they only drink the blood of their own family members, who participate willingly. "You cannot take the essences by force, they are only given in love", writes de Vere. "Otherwise their systems will react by producing chemicals during one's assault upon them that will completely knock out the chemicals traditionally required." He claims that vampirism was originally the purview of a few noble families who practiced it in order to maintain their powers. "The most famous stories", writes de Vere, "those of Dracula, Bathory and de Rais, support this conclusion." He and Gardner enthusiastically embrace Dracula as one of their own. "This Sacred Prince, a Hermetic scholar and initiate, a student of magic, a Magus, Witch Lord and Dragon Prince, counterbalanced the bloodlust of his forebears with a refined knowledge and advanced practice of Grail procedure", writes De Vere. Dracula was a member of Sigismund's Dragon Court in Hungary, and therefore of the Grail blood. He also attended a Hermetic academy called the Austrian School of Solomon. "The orthodox establishment's fear of Dracula," writes Gardner, "was not his treatment of enemies but his in-depth knowledge of alchemy, kingship and the ancient Starfire customs." As for the claim that they use these rituals to conjure up Dragon ancestors from another dimension, de Vere calmly admits that this is the case, and that the participants have their bodies taken over by these spirits, who "rise from the dead to take possession of the Witch's soul." He further explains that, "Any spirit, including the archangels, conjured by the Witch or magician was actually the ancestor of the Witch. ...It was carried in the Witch's blood which, the purer it was through the unbroken descent from the Dragons, the stronger would be the return from the ancestors within. In other words, they brought together and spoke or gesticulated a series of mnemonics that would trigger off pre-contrived, imprinted states of consciousness that acted as doorways into deeper seats of consciousness."

The charge of Satanism is not entirely refuted either, but de Vere proffers that they are not worshipping Satan so much as honoring one of their forefathers whom they stick right in the family tree along with Jesus, David and the rest. "The Sabbatical Goat of the Black Mass was Chem-Zoroaster,", he writes, "one of the early ancestors of the ancient Dragon Families," and, "Satan was also called by the Witches "Christ, son Dei". ...Jesus' heredity and the descent of the Druidic dynasties...was devilish, because the descent of both bloodlines was from the Sumerian Enki who was the Akkadian Samael, the Roman Lucifer, and thus the Catholic Satan." But the Dragon Court members make no apology for this, because, "To any intelligent person, to any true seer, concepts like white or black magic or good and evil are irrational, childish nonsense; both in terms of logic and actual fact."

Every Elf For Himself
"This is our Law, and the Law of the Strong."
—Crowley, ibid.

To the charges of "conspiring to take over the world", the Dragons deny that they give two licks what the rest of humanity does with itself. Their primary concern is, according to de Vere, "the restoration of their own Tribes, their own Nation and their own Homelands.... the foundation of their own distinct society...re-introducing their old social structures and values." This results in "The Grail Code", a system of Egalitarian, Chivalric ethics that governs how Dragons treat other members of their race. However, "it is not the code that efficiently orders the behaviour of the Dragon families in their dealings with those not of the Grail blood." They acknowledge and defend their own elitist attitudes towards mankind, whom they regard as, according to de Vere, "thoroughly stupid and dim-witted, with a clear indication that this condition is genetically inherited." Whereas in contrast, "The Elves were naturally transcendent of spirit and their queens and kings were insulated from the common round of nuisances and petty concerns by minds which were bred for deeper matters." Despite their hatred of humanity, they will kindly agree to be the guardians of our governments again (if they aren't secretly doing so already), should the population choose to accept them, and offer them the thrones of the Earth, which de Vere and friends indicate are rightfully theirs anyway. They are just waiting for mankind to realize it again.

Whether we choose to or not, we will have to deal with the fact that these "Elves" seem to be in possession of a material that bestows long life as well as fantastic physical, mental, and spiritual powers. This gives them a distinct advantage which they are clearly attempting to hold over us, while they allow our populations to wallow in disease, death, and spiritual degradation. As an excuse, de Vere and Gardner state that the Starfire and white gold are only effective for those already of the Dragon blood anyway, because the rest of the people, "won't have the right blood serum or the right connections in their cerebral lobes." De Vere denies the claims of most people who believe themselves to be of this bloodline. "Some people argue that because of the outbreeding of the old families, there must be millions of people "of the Fairy blood" living today: but such a statement flies in the face of accepted fact of history. The genuine old royal families rarely outbred at all, whilst the later, fake parvenu, tinker nobility whom people now confuse with them often did."

So that leaves little hope for Joe Sixpack of ever obtaining the fruits of this magnificent "Philosopher's Stone", which "gives youth to the old" and is described as, "The summation of the heart's desire." But if such a substance were available to the public, how much would it cost? Would it be obtainable by everyone, or only the rich and privileged? What if it could be administered for free in the water supply, or was available in tablet form at your local pharmacy, covered by your health insurance policy? What would happen to our already exploding population?

Appendix 2

The Phoenix and the Turtle

By William Shakespeare

Le the bird of loudest lay
On the sole Arabian tree
Herald sad and trumpet be,
To whose sound chaste wings obey.

But thou shrieking harbinger,
Foul precurrer of the fiend,
Augur of the fever's end,
To this troop come thou not near.

From this session interdict
Every fowl of tyrant wing,
Save the eagle, feather'd king;
Keep the obsequy so strict.

Let the priest in surplice white,
That defunctive music can,
Be the death-divining Swan,
Lest the requiem lack his right.

And thou treble-dated crow,
That thy sable gender mak'st
With the breath thou giv'st and tak'st,
'Mongst our mourners shalt thou go.

Here the anthem doth commence:
Love and constancy is dead;
Phoenix and the Turtle fled
In a mutual flame from hence.

So they lov'd, as love in twain
Had the essence but in one;
Two distincts, division none:
Number there in love was slain.

Hearts remote, yet not asunder;
Distance and no space was seen
'Twixt this Turtle and his queen:
But in them it were a wonder.

So between them love did shine
That the Turtle saw his right
Flaming in the Phoenix' sight:
Either was the other's mine.

Property was thus appalled
That the self was not the same;
Single nature's double name
Neither two nor one was called.

Reason, in itiself confounded,
Saw division grow together,
To themselves yet either neither,
Simple were so well compounded;

That it cried, "How true a twain
Seemeth this concordant one!
Love has reason, reason none,
If what parts can so remain."

Whereupon it made this threne
To the Phoenix and the Dove,
Co-supremes and stars of love,
As chorus to their tragic scene:

THRENOS

Beauty, truth, and rarity,
Grace in all simplicity,
Here enclos'd in cinders lie.

Death is now the Phoenix' nest,
And the Turtle's loyal breast
To eternity doth rest,

Leaving no posterity:
'Twas not their infirmity,
It was married chastity.

Truth may seem but cannot be;
Beauty brag but 'tis not she;
Truth and beauty buried be.

To this urn let those repair
That are either true or fair;
For these dead birds sigh a prayer.

Appendix Three
Descent to the Royal House of Vere of Anjou

DESCENT TO THE ROYAL HOUSE OF VERE OF ANJOU
ELVEN DYNASTY OF THE BLUE BOAR AND THE DRAGON

"The longest and most illustrious line of nobles that England has seen"
History of England - Baron Thomas Babington Macaulay (1800-59) - *Burke's Peerage*

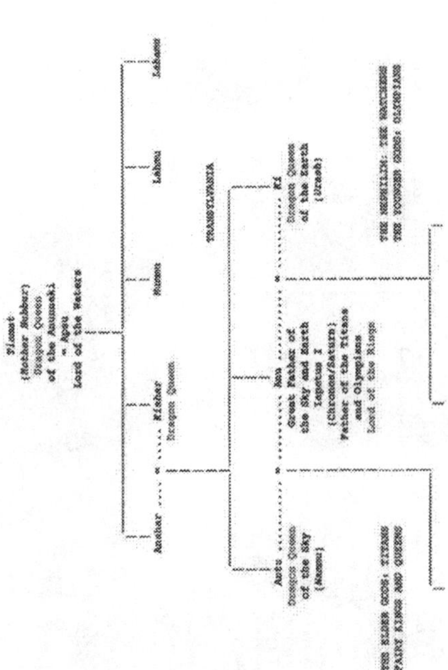

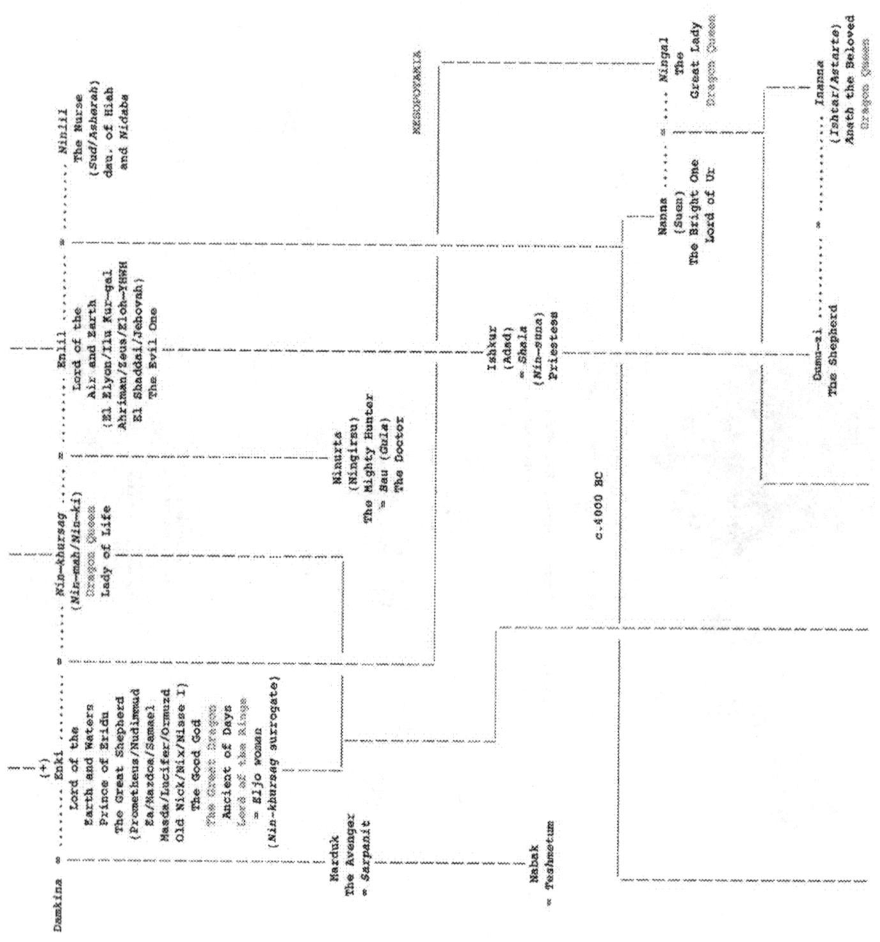
Damkina = ... Enki .... = ... Nin-khursag ..... = ... Enlil .... = ... Ninlil
(+)
Lord of the
Earth and Waters
Prince of Eridu
The Great Shepherd
(Prometheus/Nudimmud
Ea/Mazdoa/Samael
Masda/Lucifer/Ormuzd
Old Nick/Nix/Nisse I)
The Good God
The Great Dragon
Ancient of Days
Lord of the Rings
= Eljo woman
(Nin-khursag surrogate)
(Nin-mah/Nin-ki)
Dragon Queen
Lady of Life
Lord of the
Air and Earth
(El Elyon/Ilu Kur-gal
Ahriman/Zeus/Eloh-YHWH
El Shaddai/Jehovah)
The Evil One
The Nurse
(Sud/Asherah)
dau. of Hiah
and Nidaba
Marduk
The Avenger
= Sarpanit
Ninurta
(Ningirsu)
The Mighty Hunter
= Sau (Gula)
The Doctor
MESOPOTAMIA
Ishkur
(Adad)
= Shala
(Nin-suna)
Priestess
Nabak
= Teshmetum
c.4000 BC
Nanna ...... = ... Ningal
(Suen)
The Bright One
Lord of Ur
The
Great Lady
Dragon Queen
Dumu-zi .... = ... Inanna
The Shepherd
(Ishtar/Astarte)
Anath the Beloved
Dragon Queen

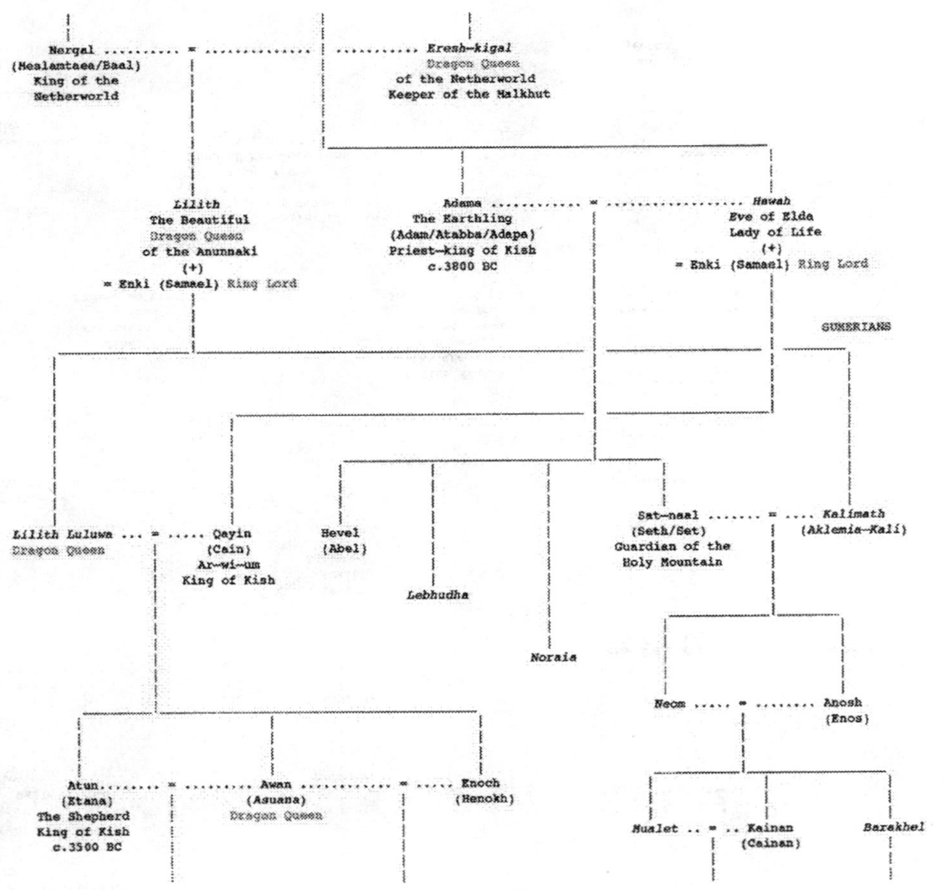

Nergal .... = ...
(Meslamtaea/Baal)
King of the
Netherworld
.... *Eresh-kigal*
Dragon Queen
of the Netherworld
Keeper of the Malkhut
Lilith
The Beautiful
Dragon Queen
of the Anunnaki
(+)
= Enki (Samael) Ring Lord
Adama .... = ... *Hawah*
The Earthling
(Adam/Atabba/Adapa)
Priest-king of Kish
c.3800 BC
Eve of Elda
Lady of Life
(+)
= Enki (Samael) Ring Lord
SUMERIANS
Lilith Luluwa ... = ... Qayin
Dragon Queen
(Cain)
Ar-wi-um
King of Kish
Hevel
(Abel)
Lebhudha
Noraia
Sat-naal .... = ... *Kalimath*
(Seth/Set)
Guardian of the
Holy Mountain
(Aklemia-Kali)
Neom ..... = ... Anosh
(Enos)
Atun........ = ... Awan .... = ... Enoch
(Etana)
The Shepherd
King of Kish
c.3500 BC
(Asuana)
Dragon Queen
(Henokh)
Mualet .. = .. Kainan
(Cainan)
Barakhel

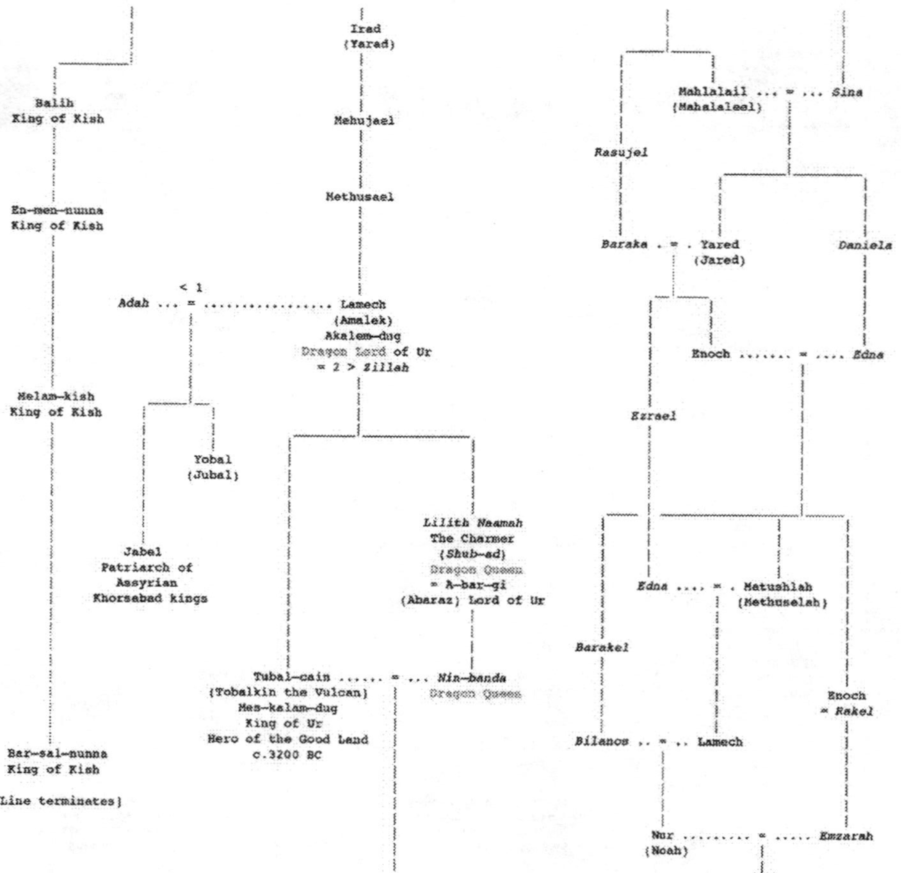

Irad
(Yarad)
Mehujael
Methusael
Balih
King of Kish
En-men-nunna
King of Kish
Melam-kish
King of Kish
Bar-sal-nunna
King of Kish
[Line terminates]
< 1
Adah ... = ... Lamech
(Amalek)
Akalem-dug
Dragon Lord of Ur
= 2 > Zillah
Yobal
(Jubal)
Jabel
Patriarch of
Assyrian
Khorsabad kings
Lilith Naamah
The Charmer
(Shub-ad)
Dragon Queen
= A-bar-gi
(Abaraz) Lord of Ur
Tubal-cain ...... = ... Nin-banda
Dragon Queen
(Tobalkin the Vulcan)
Mes-kalam-dug
King of Ur
Hero of the Good Land
c.3200 BC
Mahlalail ... = ... Sina
(Mahalaleel)
Rasujel
Baraka . = . Yared
(Jared)
Daniela
Enoch .... = ... Edna
Ezrael
Edna .... = . Matushlah
(Methuselah)
Barakel
Enoch
= Rakel
Bilanos .. = .. Lamech
Nur .... = ... Emzarah
(Noah)

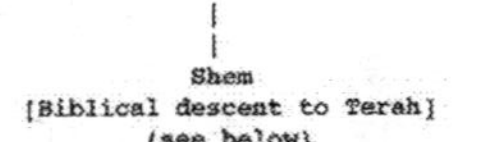
Shem
[Biblical descent to Terah]
(see below)

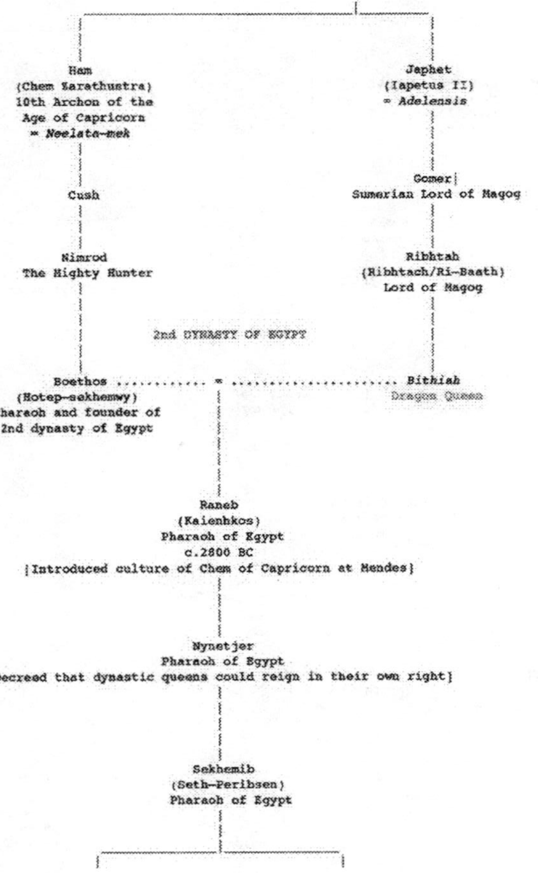
Ham
(Chem Zarathustra)
10th Archon of the
Age of Capricorn
= *Neelata-mek*
Cush
Nimrod
The Mighty Hunter
Japhet
(Iapetus II)
= *Adelensis*
Gomer
Sumerian Lord of Magog
Ribhtah
(Ribhtach/Ri-Baath)
Lord of Magog
2nd DYNASTY OF EGYPT
Boethos .... = ... *Bithiah*
(Hotep-sekhemwy)
Pharaoh and founder of
2nd dynasty of Egypt
Dragon Queen
Raneb
(Kaienhkos)
Pharaoh of Egypt
c.2800 BC
[Introduced culture of Chem of Capricorn at Mendes]
Nynetjer
Pharaoh of Egypt
[Decreed that dynastic queens could reign in their own right]
Sekhemib
(Seth-Peribsen)
Pharaoh of Egypt

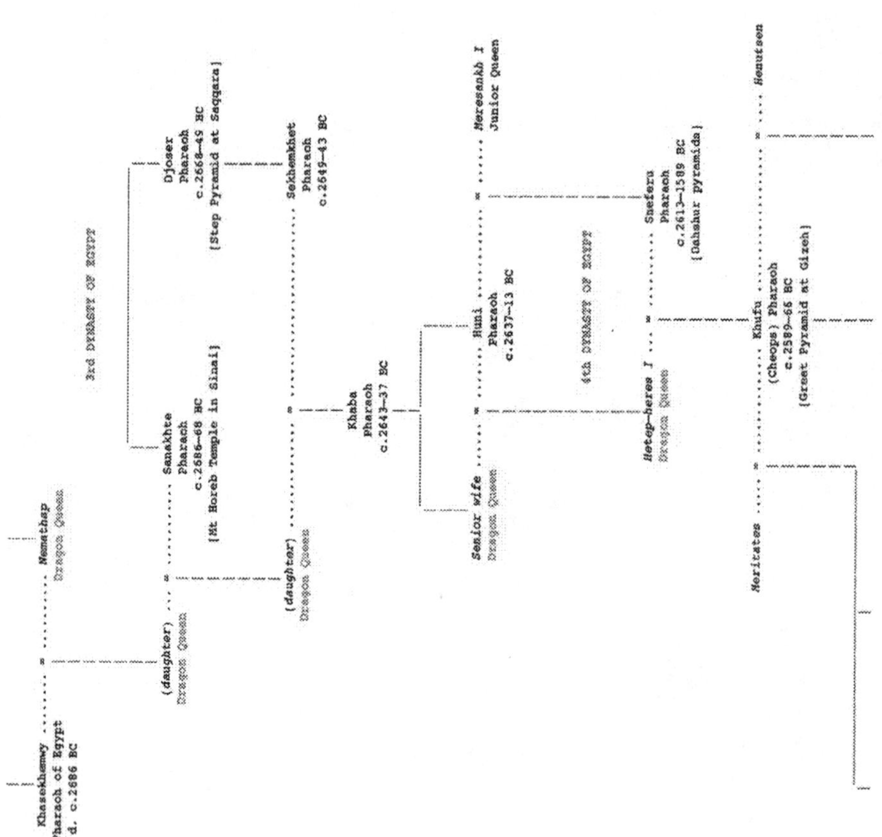
Khasekhemwy .... = ... *Nemathap*
Pharaoh of Egypt
d. c.2686 BC
Dragon Queen
3rd DYNASTY OF EGYPT
(*daughter*) ... = ... Sanakhte
Dragon Queen
Pharaoh
c.2686–68 BC
[Mt Horeb Temple in Sinai]
Djoser
Pharaoh
c.2668–49 BC
[Step Pyramid at Saqqara]
(*daughter*) .... = ... Sekhemkhet
Dragon Queen
Pharaoh
c.2649–43 BC
Khaba
Pharaoh
c.2643–37 BC
Senior wife ...... = ... Huni .... = ... *Meresankh I*
Dragon Queen
Pharaoh
c.2637–13 BC
Junior Queen
4th DYNASTY OF EGYPT
Hetep-heres I ... = ... Snefern
Dragon Queen
Pharaoh
c.2613–1589 BC
[Dahshur pyramids]
Meritates ..... = ... Khufu .... = ... *Henutsen*
(Cheops) Pharaoh
c.2589–66 BC
[Great Pyramid at Gizeh]

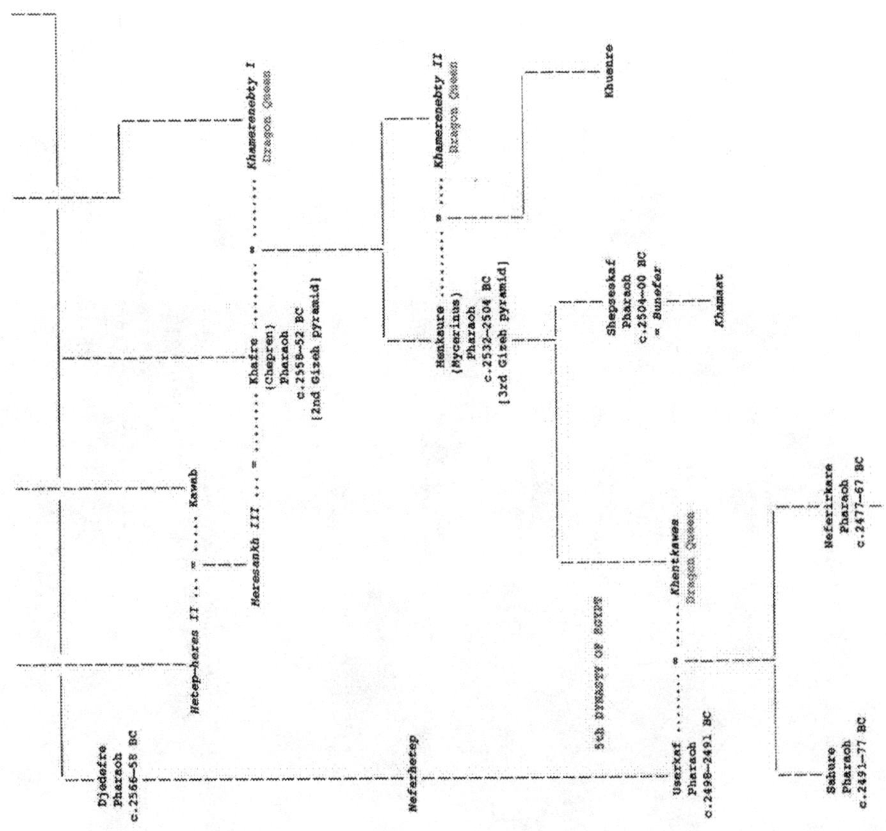
Djedefre
Pharaoh
c.2566–58 BC
Hetep-heres II ... = ... Kawab
Meresankh III ... = ... Khafre .... = ... Khamerenebty I
Dragon Queen
(Chepren)
Pharaoh
c.2558–52 BC
[2nd Gizeh pyramid]
Menkaure .... = ... Khamerenebty II
Dragon Queen
(Mycerinus)
Pharaoh
c.2532–2504 BC
[3rd Gizeh pyramid]
Khuenre
Shepseskaf
Pharaoh
c.2504–00 BC
= Bunefer
Khamaat
Neferhetep
5th DYNASTY OF EGYPT
Userkaf .... = ... Khentkawes
Dragon Queen
Pharaoh
c.2498–2491 BC
Neferirkare
Pharaoh
c.2477–67 BC
Sahure
Pharaoh
c.2491–77 BC

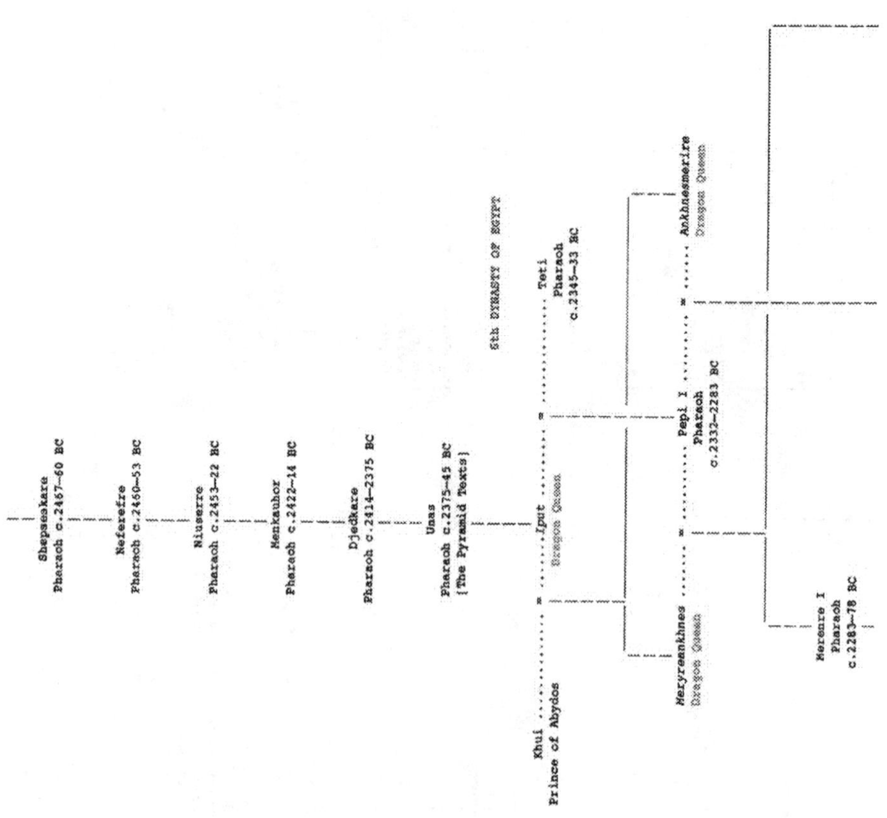
Shepseskare
Pharaoh c.2467–60 BC
Neferefre
Pharaoh c.2460–53 BC
Niuserre
Pharaoh c.2453–22 BC
Menkauhor
Pharaoh c.2422–14 BC
Djedkare
Pharaoh c.2414–2375 BC
Unas
Pharaoh c.2375–45 BC
(The Pyramid Texts)
6th DYNASTY OF EGYPT
Khui
Prince of Abydos
Iput
Dragon Queen
Teti
Pharaoh
c.2345–33 BC
Meryreankhnes
Dragon Queen
Pepi I
Pharaoh
c.2332–2283 BC
Ankhnesmerire
Dragon Queen
Merenre I
Pharaoh
c.2283–78 BC

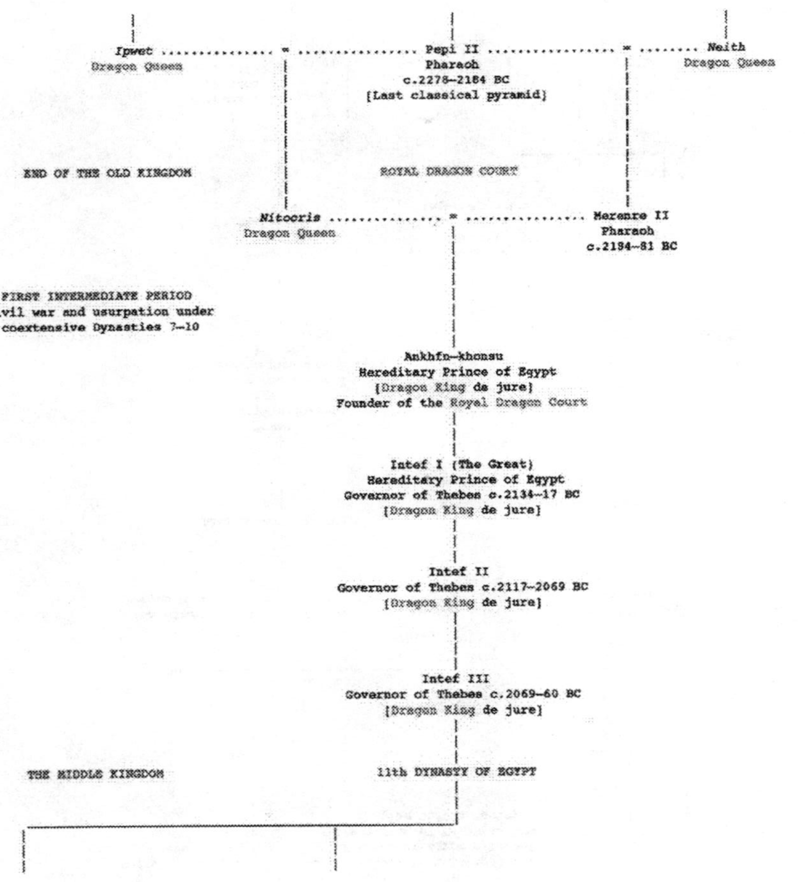
Ipwet
Dragon Queen
Pepi II
Pharaoh
c.2278–2184 BC
[Last classical pyramid]
Neith
Dragon Queen
END OF THE OLD KINGDOM
ROYAL DRAGON COURT
Nitocris
Dragon Queen
Merenre II
Pharaoh
c.2184–81 BC
FIRST INTERMEDIATE PERIOD
Civil war and usurpation under
coextensive Dynasties 7–10
Ankhfn–khonsu
Hereditary Prince of Egypt
[Dragon King de jure]
Founder of the Royal Dragon Court
Intef I (The Great)
Hereditary Prince of Egypt
Governor of Thebes c.2134–17 BC
[Dragon King de jure]
Intef II
Governor of Thebes c.2117–2069 BC
[Dragon King de jure]
Intef III
Governor of Thebes c.2069–60 BC
[Dragon King de jure]
THE MIDDLE KINGDOM
11th DYNASTY OF EGYPT

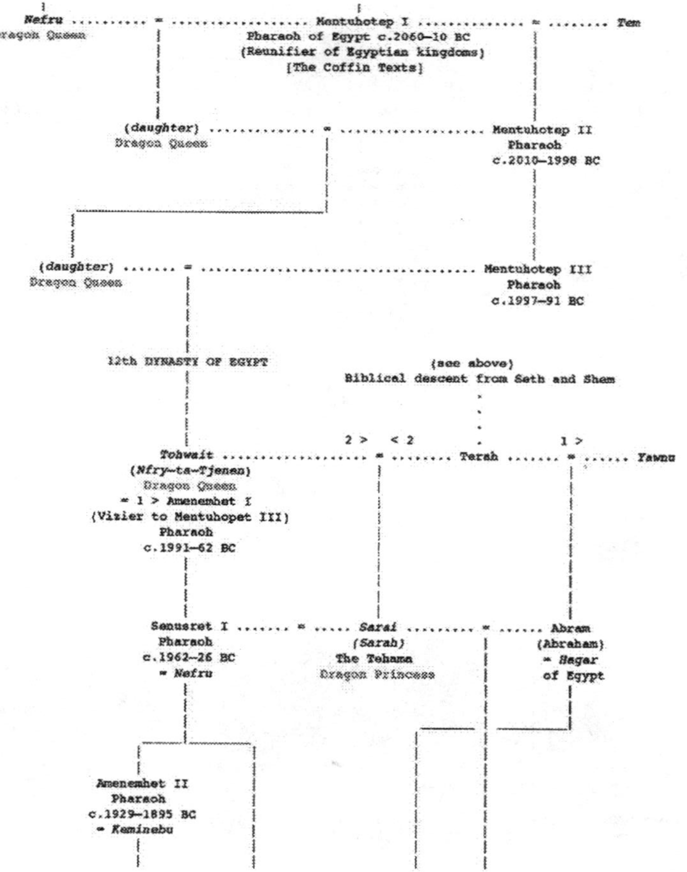
Nefru
Dragon Queen
Mentuhotep I
Pharaoh of Egypt c.2060–10 BC
(Reunifier of Egyptian kingdoms)
[The Coffin Texts]
Tem
(daughter)
Dragon Queen
Mentuhotep II
Pharaoh
c.2010–1998 BC
(daughter)
Dragon Queen
Mentuhotep III
Pharaoh
c.1997–91 BC
12th DYNASTY OF EGYPT
(see above)
Biblical descent from Seth and Shem
2 > < 2
1 >
Tohwait
(Nfry-ta-Tjenen)
Dragon Queen
= 1 > Amenemhet I
(Vizier to Mentuhopet III)
Pharaoh
c.1991–62 BC
Terah
Yawnu
Senusret I
Pharaoh
c.1962–26 BC
= Nefru
Sarai
(Sarah)
The Tehama
Dragon Princess
Abram
(Abraham)
= Hagar
of Egypt
Amenemhet II
Pharaoh
c.1929–1895 BC
= Keminebu

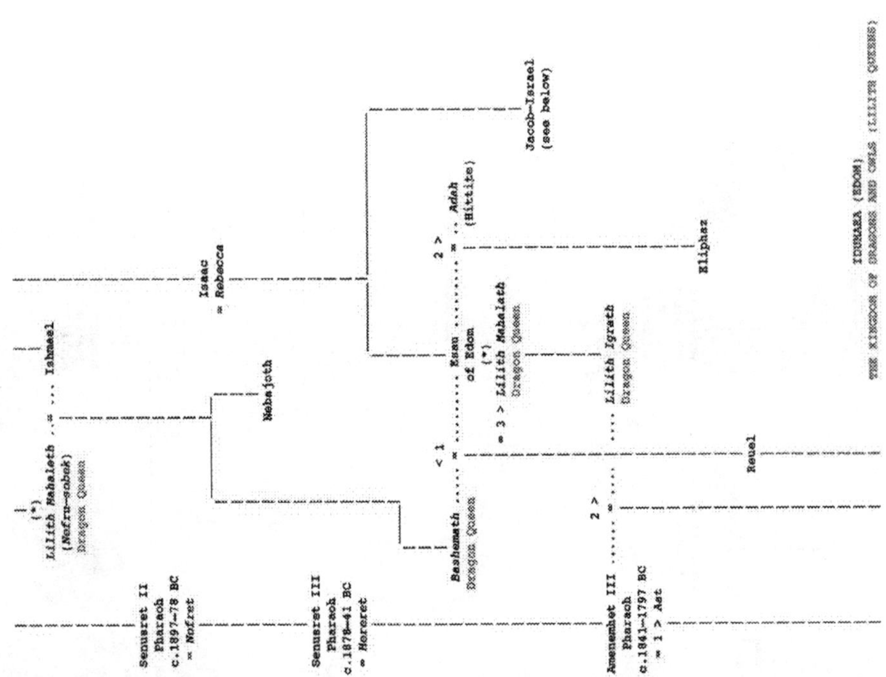
(*)
Lilith Mahaleth
(Nefru-sobek)
Dragon Queen
Ishmael
Isaac
= Rebecca
Nebajoth
Jacob-Israel
(see below)
Senusret II
Pharaoh
c.1897-78 BC
= Nofret
Senusret III
Pharaoh
c.1878-41 BC
= Mereret
Basemath
Dragon Queen
< 1
Esau
of Edom
(*)
2 >
Adah
(Hittite)
= 3 > Lilith Mahalath
Dragon Queen
Eliphaz
Lilith Igrath
Dragon Queen
2 >
Reuel
Amenemhet III
Pharaoh
c.1841-1797 BC
= 1 > Ast
IDUMAEA (EDOM)
THE KINGDOM OF DRAGONS AND OWLS (LILITH QUEENS)

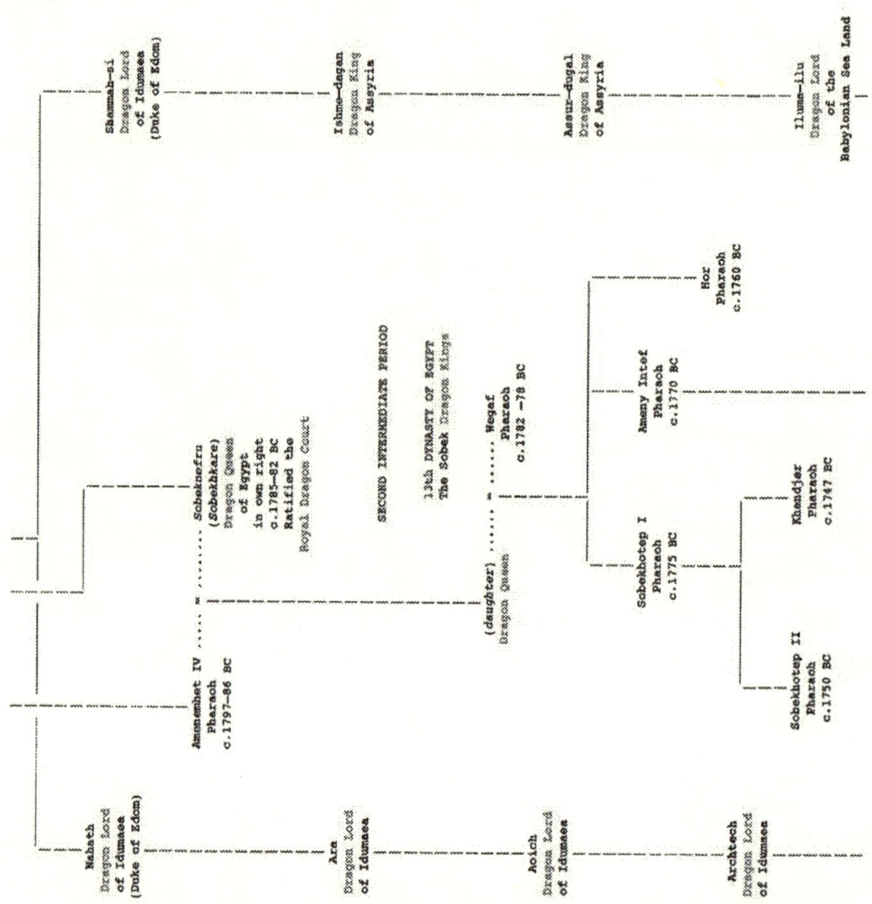
Shemmah-si
Dragon Lord
of Idumaea
(Duke of Edom)
Ishme-dagan
Dragon King
of Assyria
Assur-dugal
Dragon King
of Assyria
Ilumu-ilu
Dragon Lord
of the
Babylonian Sea Land
Hor
Pharaoh
c.1760 BC
Ameny Intef
Pharaoh
c.1770 BC
SECOND INTERMEDIATE PERIOD
13th DYNASTY OF EGYPT
The Sobek Dragon Kings
Wegaf
Pharaoh
c.1782 –78 BC
Sobeknefru
(Sobekhkare)
Dragon Queen
of Egypt
in own right
c.1785–82 BC
Ratified the
Royal Dragon Court
Khendjer
Pharaoh
c.1747 BC
Sobekhotep I
Pharaoh
c.1775 BC
(daughter)
Dragon Queen
Sobekhotep II
Pharaoh
c.1750 BC
Amenemhet IV
Pharaoh
c.1797–86 BC
Nahath
Dragon Lord
of Idumaea
(Duke of Edom)
Ara
Dragon Lord
of Idumaea
Aoich
Dragon Lord
of Idumaea
Archtech
Dragon Lord
of Idumaea

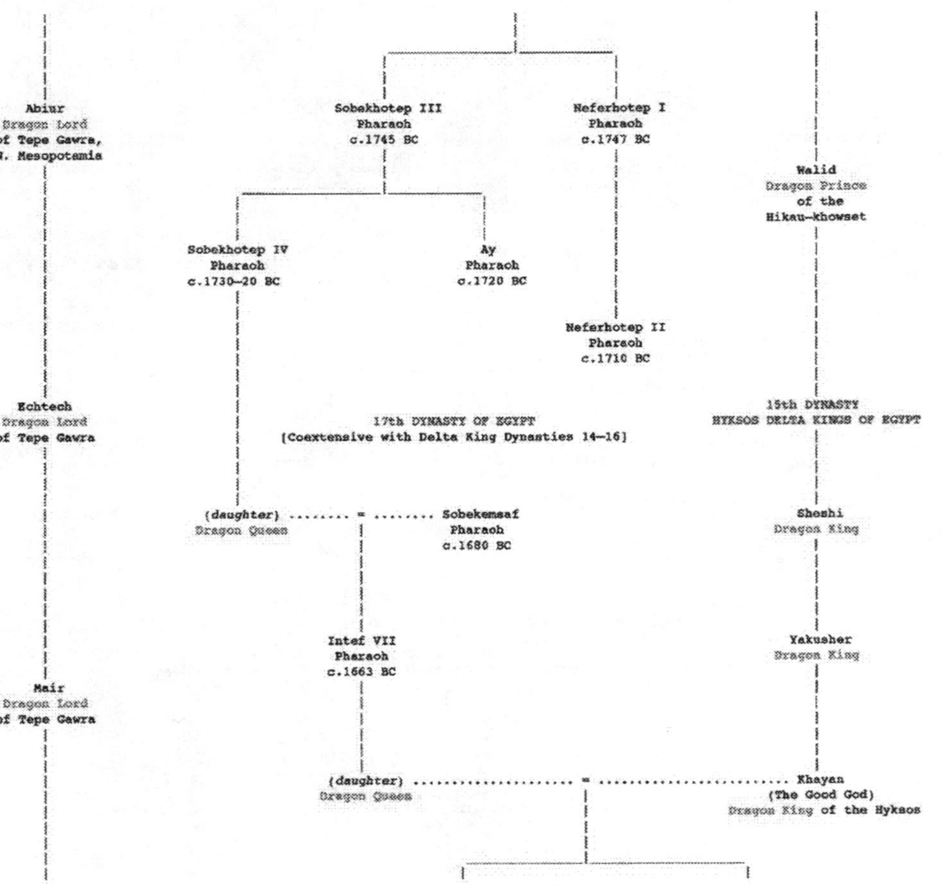
Abiur
Dragon Lord
of Tepe Gawra,
N. Mesopotamia
Sobekhotep III
Pharaoh
c.1745 BC
Neferhotep I
Pharaoh
c.1747 BC
Walid
Dragon Prince
of the
Hikau-khowset
Sobekhotep IV
Pharaoh
c.1730–20 BC
Ay
Pharaoh
c.1720 BC
Neferhotep II
Pharaoh
c.1710 BC
Echtech
Dragon Lord
of Tepe Gawra
17th DYNASTY OF EGYPT
(Coextensive with Delta King Dynasties 14–16)
15th DYNASTY
HYKSOS DELTA KINGS OF EGYPT
(*daughter*) .... = ... Sobekemsaf
Dragon Queen
Pharaoh
c.1680 BC
Sheshi
Dragon King
Intef VII
Pharaoh
c.1663 BC
Yakusher
Dragon King
Mair
Dragon Lord
of Tepe Gawra
(*daughter*) .... = ... Khayan
Dragon Queen
(The Good God)
Dragon King of the Hyksos

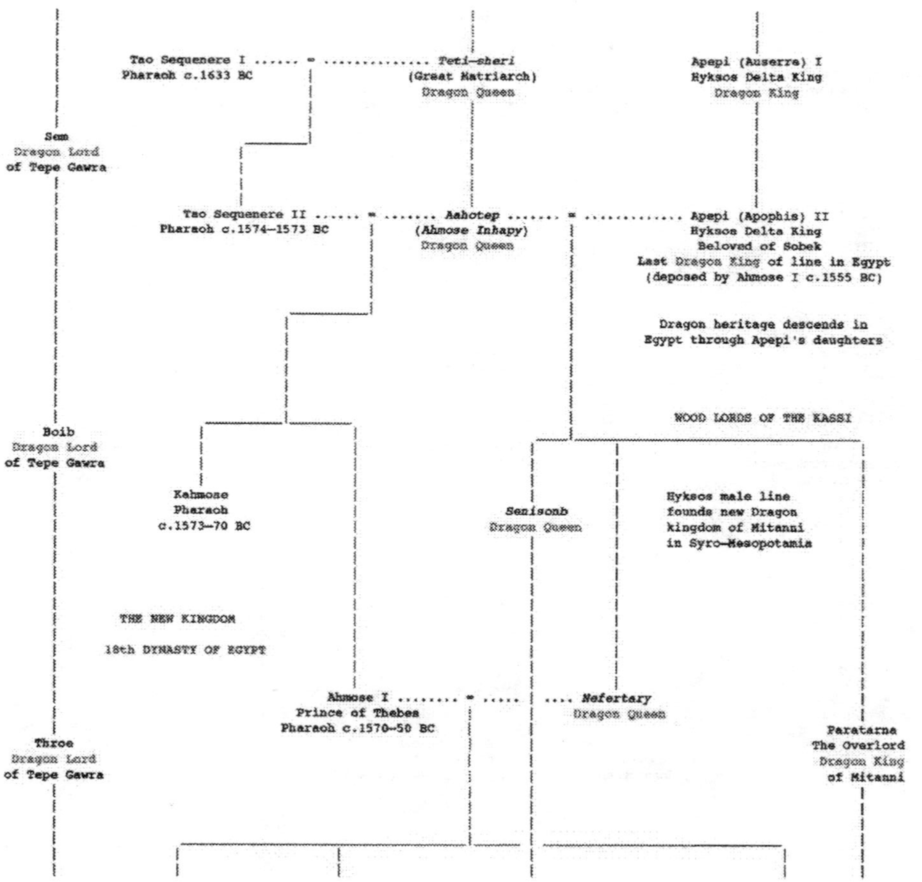
Tao Sequenere I ...... = ... Teti-sheri
Pharaoh c.1633 BC
(Great Matriarch)
Dragon Queen
Apepi (Auserra) I
Hyksos Delta King
Dragon King
Sem
Dragon Lord
of Tepe Gawra
Tao Sequenere II ...... = ... Aahotep .... = ... Apepi (Apophis) II
Pharaoh c.1574–1573 BC
(Ahmose Inhapy)
Dragon Queen
Hyksos Delta King
Beloved of Sobek
Last Dragon King of line in Egypt
(deposed by Ahmose I c.1555 BC)
Dragon heritage descends in
Egypt through Apepi's daughters
WOOD LORDS OF THE KASSI
Boib
Dragon Lord
of Tepe Gawra
Kahmose
Pharaoh
c.1573–70 BC
Senisonb
Dragon Queen
Hyksos male line
founds new Dragon
kingdom of Mitanni
in Syro-Mesopotamia
THE NEW KINGDOM
18th DYNASTY OF EGYPT
Ahmose I .... = ... Nefertary
Prince of Thebes
Pharaoh c.1570–50 BC
Dragon Queen
Throe
Dragon Lord
of Tepe Gawra
Paratarna
The Overlord
Dragon King
of Mitanni

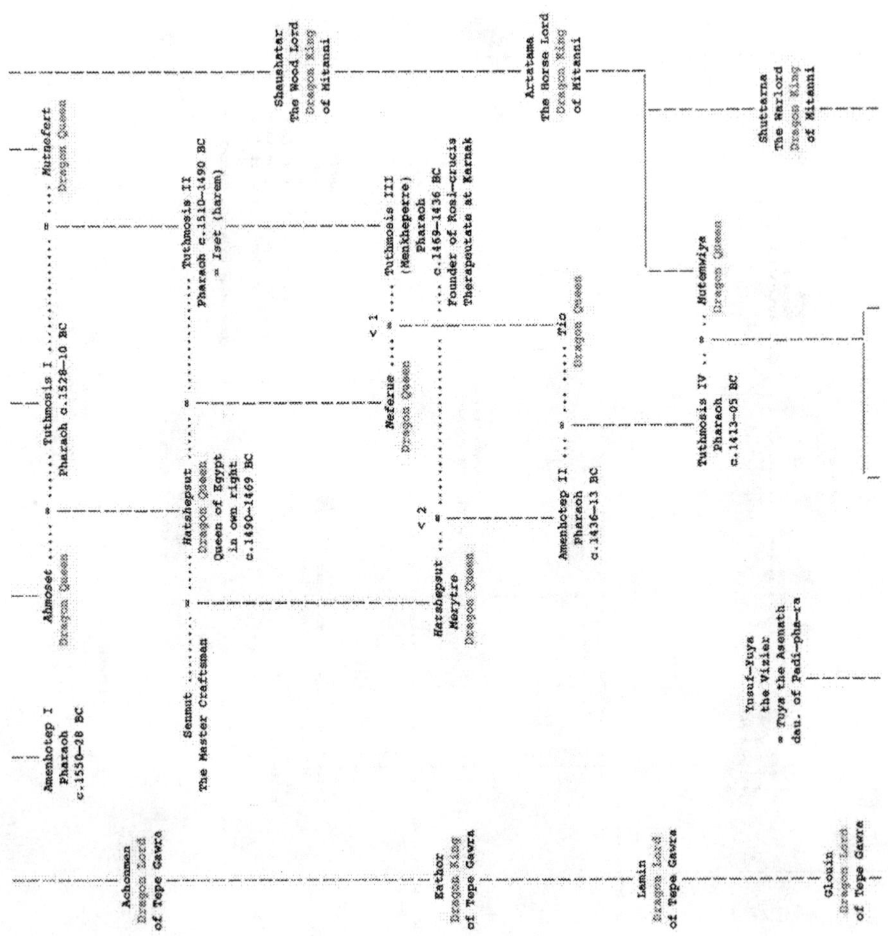
Amenhotep I
Pharaoh
c.1550–28 BC
Ahmoset ..... = ... Tuthmosis I .... = ... Mutnefert
Dragon Queen
Pharaoh c.1528–10 BC
Dragon Queen
Senmut .... = ... Hatshepsut ...... = ... Tuthmosis II
The Master Craftsman
Dragon Queen
Queen of Egypt
in own right
c.1490–1469 BC
Pharaoh c.1510–1490 BC
= Iset (harem)
< 2
< 1
Hatshepsut ... = ... Tuthmosis III
Merytre
Dragon Queen
Neferue ..... = ... Tuthmosis III
Dragon Queen
(Menkheperre)
Pharaoh
c.1469–1436 BC
Founder of Rosi-crucis
Therapeutate at Karnak
Amenhotep II ... = ... Tio
Pharaoh
c.1436–13 BC
Dragon Queen
Tuthmosis IV .. = .. Mutemwiya
Pharaoh
c.1413–05 BC
Dragon Queen
Yusuf-Yuya
the Vizier
= Tuya the Asenath
dau. of Padi-pha-ra
Shaushatar
The Wood Lord
Dragon King
of Mitanni
Artatama
The Horse Lord
Dragon King
of Mitanni
Shuttarna
The Warlord
Dragon King
of Mitanni
Achoman
Dragon Lord
of Tepe Gawra
Kathor
Dragon King
of Tepe Gawra
Lamin
Dragon Lord
of Tepe Gawra
Glouin
Dragon Lord
of Tepe Gawra

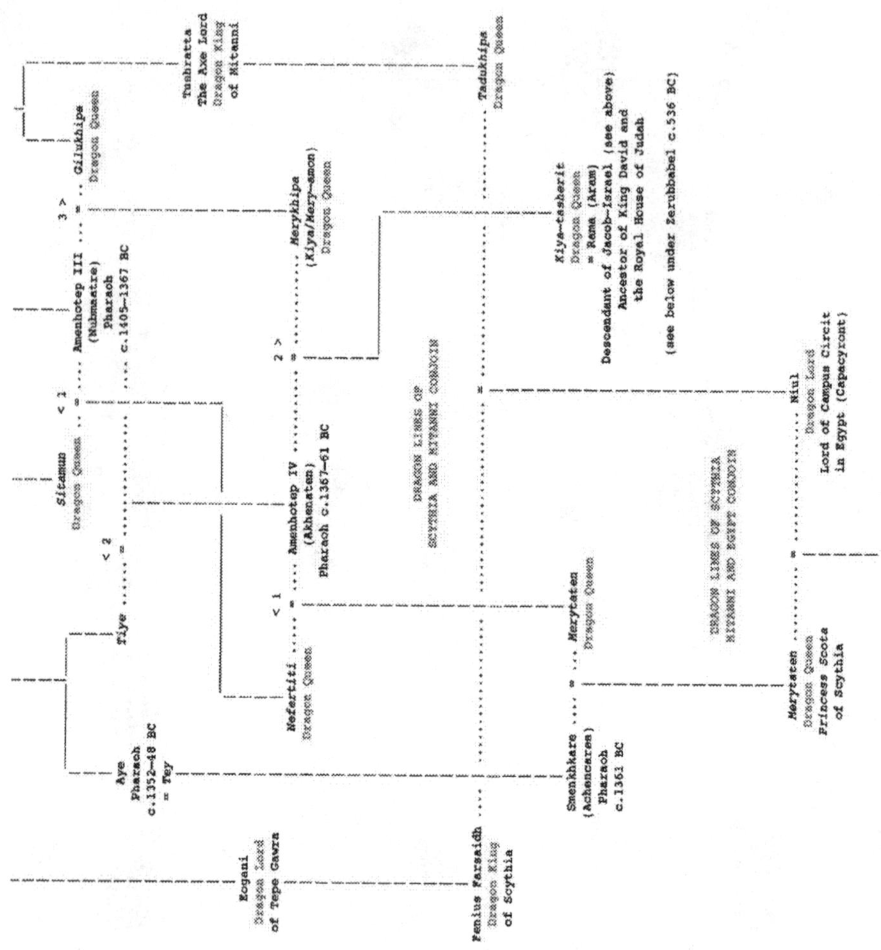

Tushratta
The Axe Lord
Dragon King
of Mitanni
Gilukhipa
Dragon Queen
Amenhotep III
(Nubmaatre)
Pharaoh
c.1405–1367 BC
Sitamun
Dragon Queen
Tiye
Aye
Pharaoh
c.1352–48 BC
= Tey
Kogani
Dragon Lord
of Tepe Gawra
Merykhipa
(Kiya/Mery-amon)
Dragon Queen
Amenhotep IV
(Akhenaten)
Pharaoh c.1367–61 BC
Nefertiti
Dragon Queen
Tadukhipa
Dragon Queen
Kiya-tasherit
Dragon Queen
= Rama (Aram)
Descendant of Jacob-Israel (see above)
Ancestor of King David and
the Royal House of Judah
(see below under Zerubbabel c.536 BC)
DRAGON LINES OF
SCYTHIA AND MITANNI CONJOIN
Merytaten
Dragon Queen
Smenkhkare
(Achencares)
Pharaoh
c.1361 BC
Fenius Farsaidh
Dragon King
of Scythia
Niul
Dragon Lord
Lord of Campus Circit
in Egypt (Capacyront)
DRAGON LINES OF SCYTHIA
MITANNI AND EGYPT CONJOIN
Merytaten
Dragon Queen
Princess Scota
of Scythia

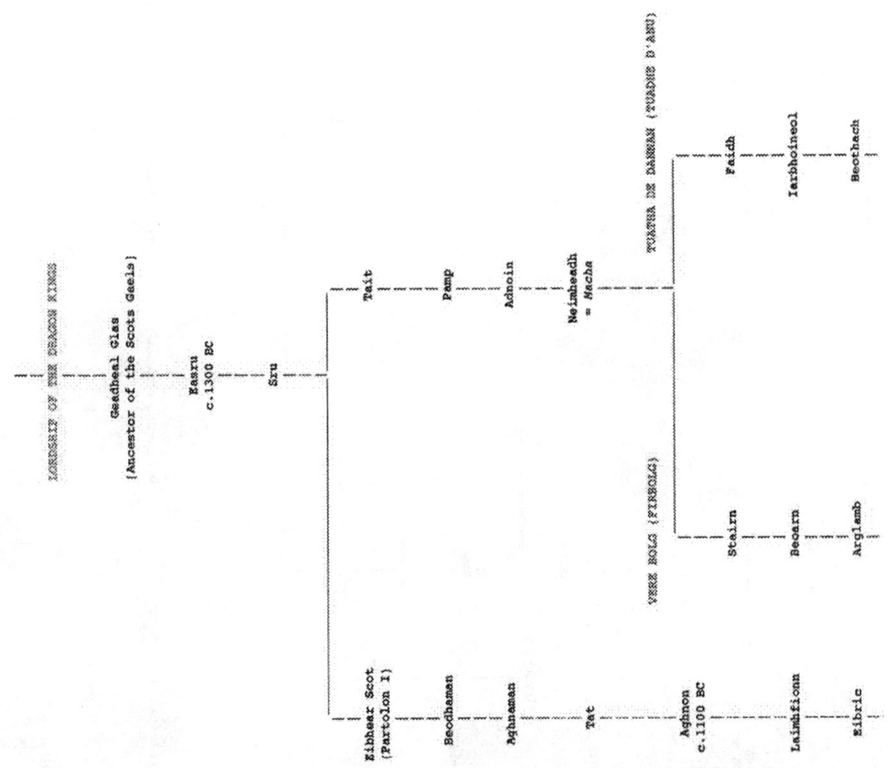
LORDSHIP OF THE DRAGON KINGS
Geadheal Glas
(Ancestor of the Scots Gaels)
Kasru
c.1300 BC
Sru
Eibhear Scot
(Partolon I)
Beodhaman
Aghnaman
Tat
Aghnon
c.1100 BC
Laimhfionn
Eibric
Tait
Pamp
Adnoin
Neimheadh
= Macha
FERE BOLG (FIRBOLG)
Stairn
Beoarn
Arglamb
TUATHA DE DANNAN (TUADHE D'ANU)
Faidh
Iarbhoineol
Beothach

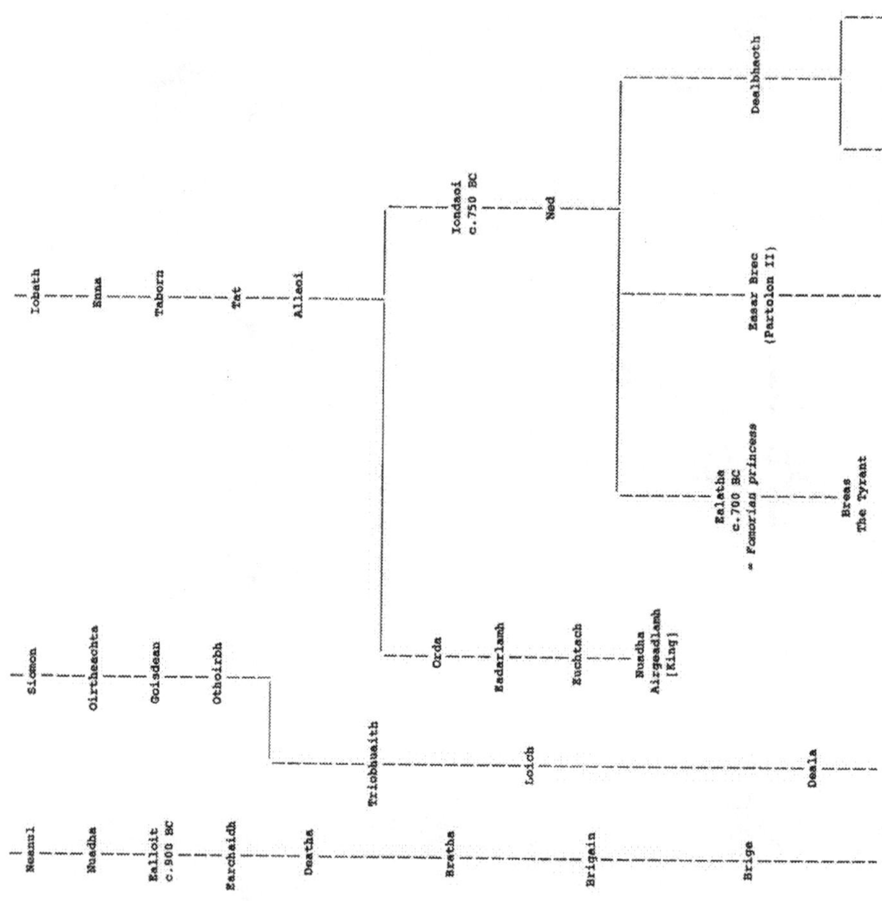
Iobath
Enna
Taborn
Tat
Allaoi
Iondaoi
c.750 BC
Ned
Dealbhaoth
Esar Brec
(Partolon II)
Ealatha
c.700 BC
= Fomorian princess
Breas
The Tyrant
Orda
Eadarlamh
Euchtach
Nuadha
Airgeadlamh
[King]
Sioman
Oirthaochta
Goisdean
Othoirbh
Triobhuaith
Loich
Deala
Neanul
Nuadha
Ealloit
c.900 BC
Earchaidh
Deatha
Bratha
Brigain
Brige

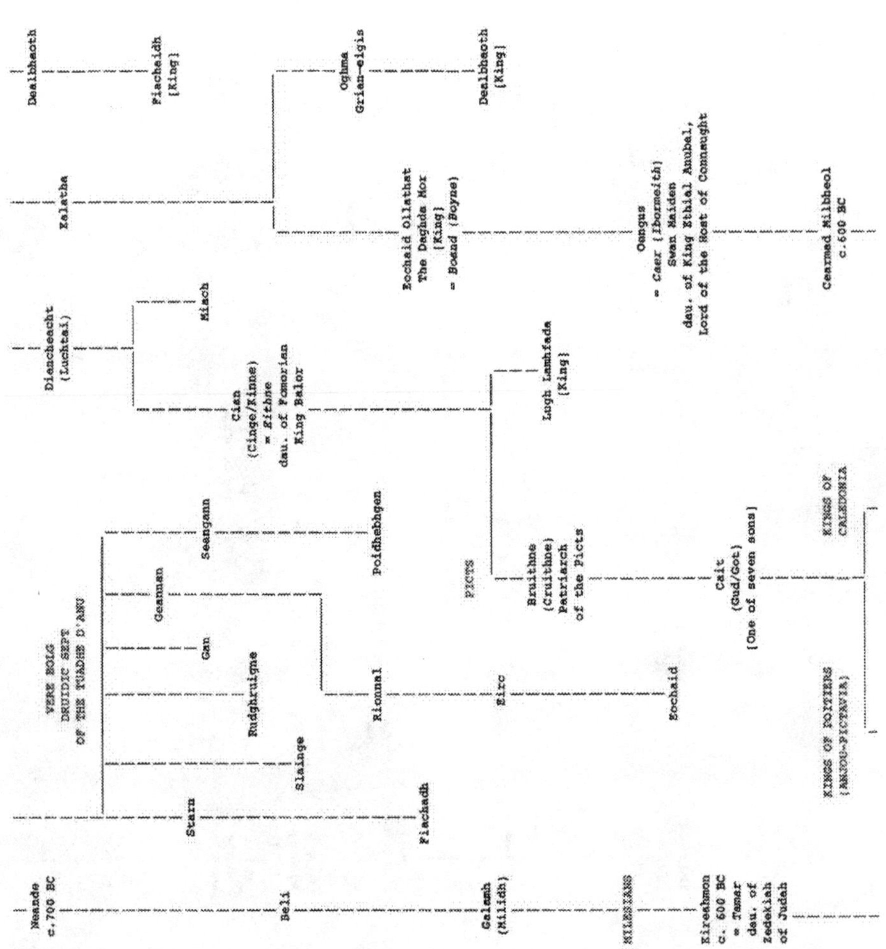
Neande
c.700 BC
Beli
Galamh
(Milidh)
MILESIANS
Kireahmon
c. 600 BC
= Tamar
dau. of
Zedekiah
of Judah
Starn
Fiachadh
Slainge
Rudghruigne
Gan
Geannan
Seangann
Poidhebhgen
VERE BOLG
DRUIDIC SEPT
OF THE TUADHE D'ANU
Rionnal
Eirc
Eochaid
PICTS
Bruithne
(Cruithne)
Patriarch
of the Picts
Cait
(Gud/Got)
(One of seven sons)
KINGS OF POITIERS
(ANJOU-PICTAVIA)
KINGS OF
CALEDONIA
Diancheacht
(Luchtai)
Miach
Cian
(Cinge/Kinne)
= Ethne
dau. of Fomorian
King Balor
Lugh Lamhfada
[King]
Ealatha
Eochaid Ollathat
The Daghda Mor
[King]
= Boand (Boyne)
Oengus
= Caer (Ibormeith)
Swan Maiden
dau. of King Ethial Anubal,
Lord of the Host of Connaught
Cearmad Milbheol
c.600 BC
Dealbhaoth
Fiachaidh
[King]
Oghma
Grian-eigis
Dealbhaoth
[King]

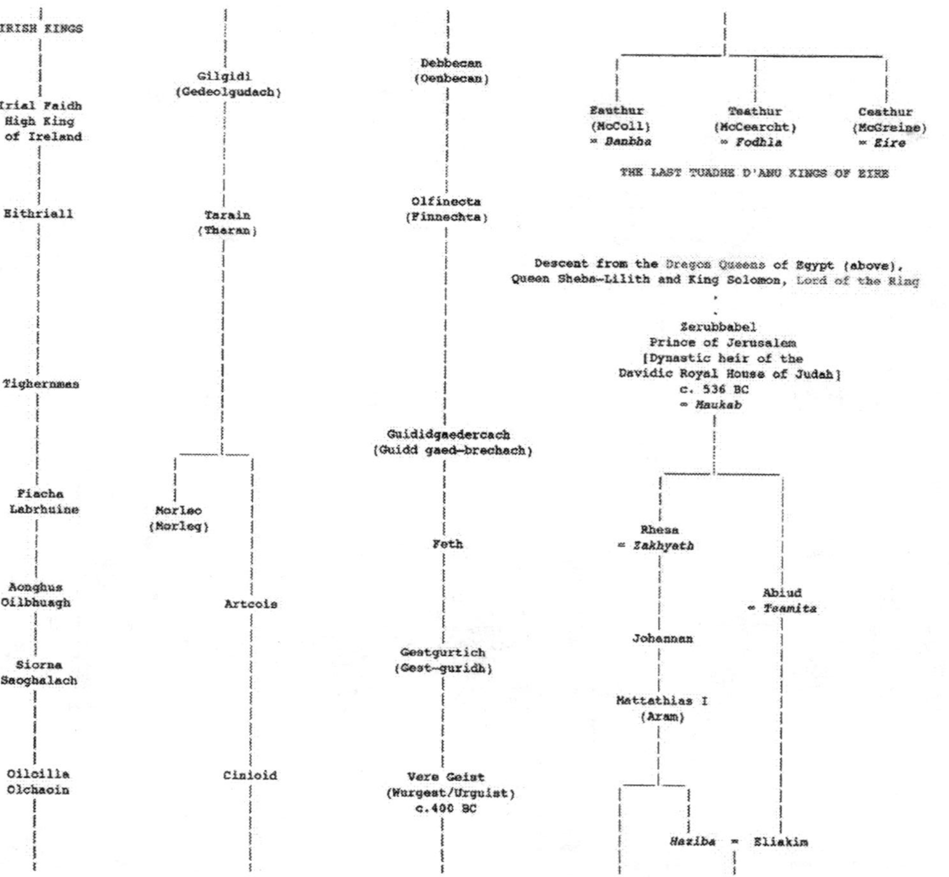
IRISH KINGS
Irial Faidh
High King
of Ireland
Eithriall
Tighernmas
Fiacha
Labrhuine
Aonghus
Oilbhuagh
Siorna
Saoghalach
Oilcilla
Olchaoin
Gilgidi
(Gedeolgudach)
Tarain
(Tharan)
Morleo
(Morleg)
Artcois
Cinioid
Debbecan
(Oenbecan)
Olfinecta
(Finnechta)
Guididgaedercach
(Guidd gaed-brechach)
Feth
Gestgurtich
(Gest-guridh)
Vere Geist
(Wurgest/Urguist)
c.400 BC
Eauthur
(McColl)
= Banbha
Teathur
(McCearcht)
= Fodhla
Ceathur
(McGreine)
= Eire
THE LAST TUADHE D'ANU KINGS OF EIRE
Descent from the Dragon Queens of Egypt (above),
Queen Sheba-Lilith and King Solomon, Lord of the Ring
Zerubbabel
Prince of Jerusalem
[Dynastic heir of the
Davidic Royal House of Judah]
c. 536 BC
= Maukab
Rhesa
= Zakhyath
Abiud
= Tsamita
Johannan
Mattathias I
(Aram)
Haziba = Eliakim

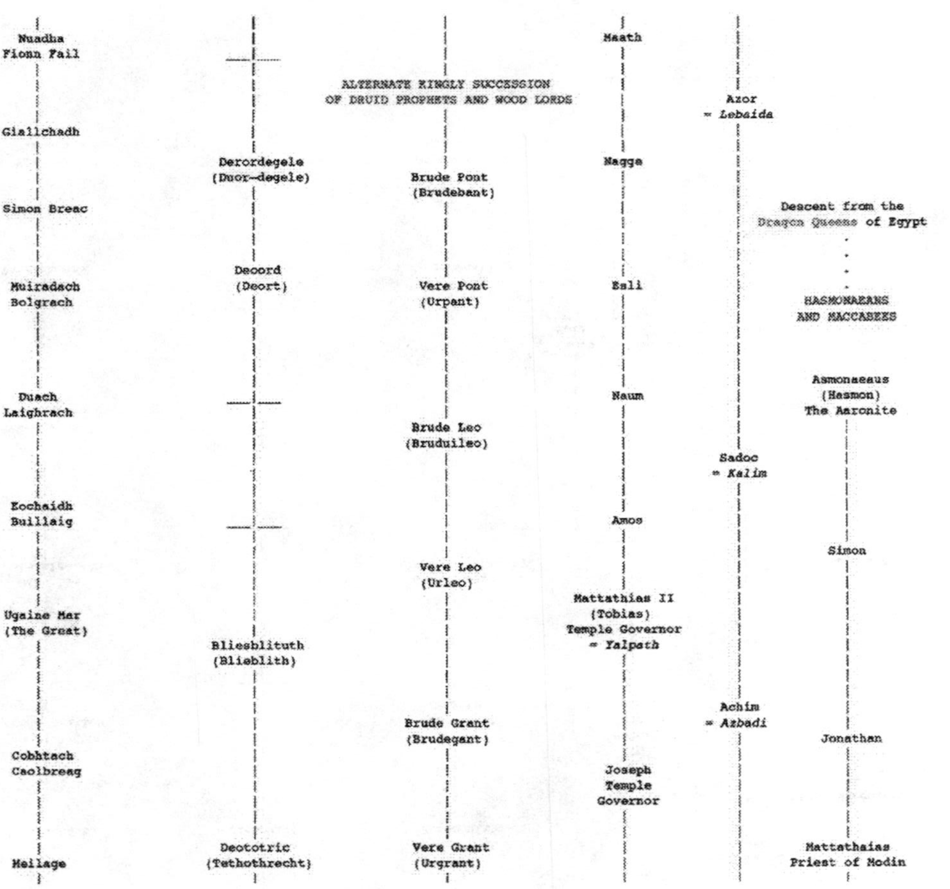
Nuadha
Fionn Fail
Giallchadh
Simon Breac
Muiradach
Bolgrach
Duach
Laighrach
Eochaidh
Buillaig
Ugaine Mar
(The Great)
Cobhtach
Caolbreag
Meilage
Derordegele
(Duor-degele)
Deoord
(Deort)
Bliesblituth
(Blieblith)
Deototric
(Tethothrecht)
ALTERNATE KINGLY SUCCESSION
OF DRUID PROPHETS AND WOOD LORDS
Brude Pont
(Brudebant)
Vere Pont
(Urpant)
Brude Leo
(Bruduileo)
Vere Leo
(Urleo)
Brude Grant
(Brudegant)
Vere Grant
(Urgrant)
Maath
Magge
Esli
Naum
Amos
Mattathias II
(Tobias)
Temple Governor
= Yalpath
Joseph
Temple
Governor
Azor
= Lebaida
Sadoc
= Kalim
Achim
= Azbadi
Descent from the
Dragon Queens of Egypt
HASMONAEANS
AND MACCABEES
Asmonaeaus
(Hasmon)
The Aaronite
Simon
Jonathan
Mattathaias
Priest of Modin

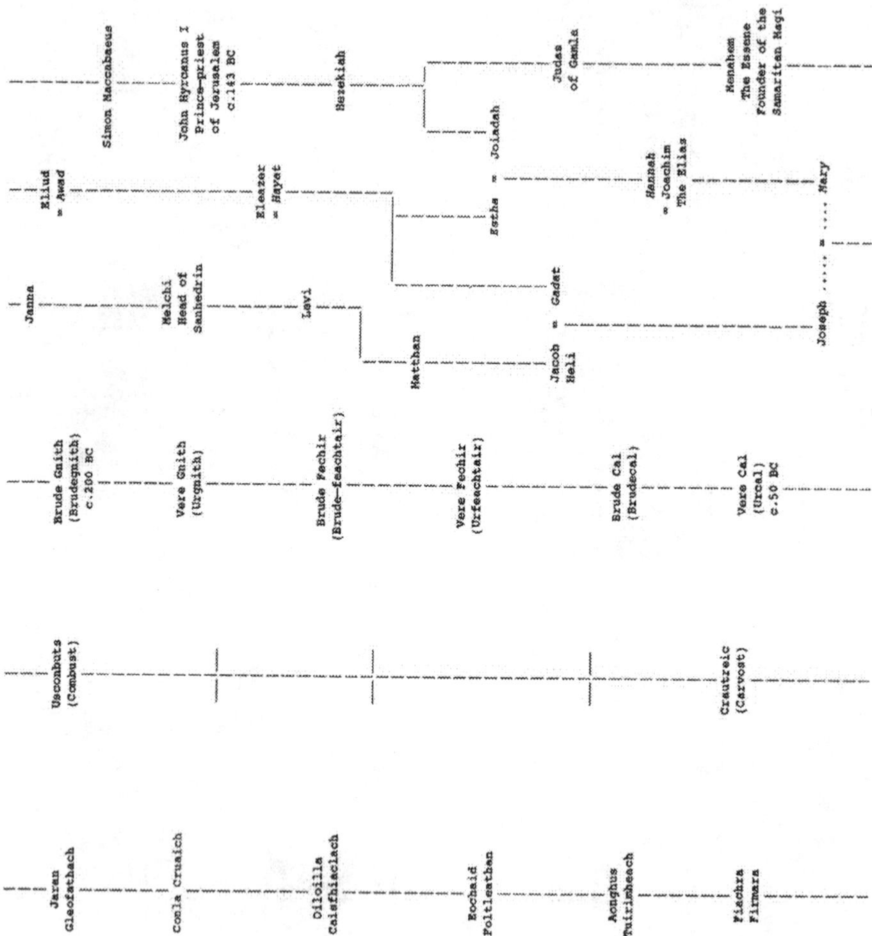

Simon Maccabaeus
John Hyrcanus I
Prince-priest
of Jerusalem
c.143 BC
Hezekiah
Judas
of Gamla
Menahem
The Essene
Founder of the
Samaritan Magi
Joiadah
Eliud
= Awad
Eleazer
= Hayat
Estha
Hannah
= Joachim
The Elias
Mary
Janna
Melchi
Head of
Sanhedrin
Levi
Matthan
Gadat
Jacob
Heli
Joseph
Brude Gnith
(Brudegnith)
c.200 BC
Vere Gnith
(Urgnith)
Brude Fechir
(Brude-Eeachtair)
Vere Fechir
(Urfeachtair)
Brude Cal
(Brudecal)
Vere Cal
(Urcal)
c.50 BC
Usconbuts
(Combust)
Crautreic
(Carvost)
Jaran
Gleofathach
Conla Cruaich
Oiloilla
Caisfhiaclach
Eochaid
Foltleathan
Aonghus
Tuirimheach
Fiachra
Firmara

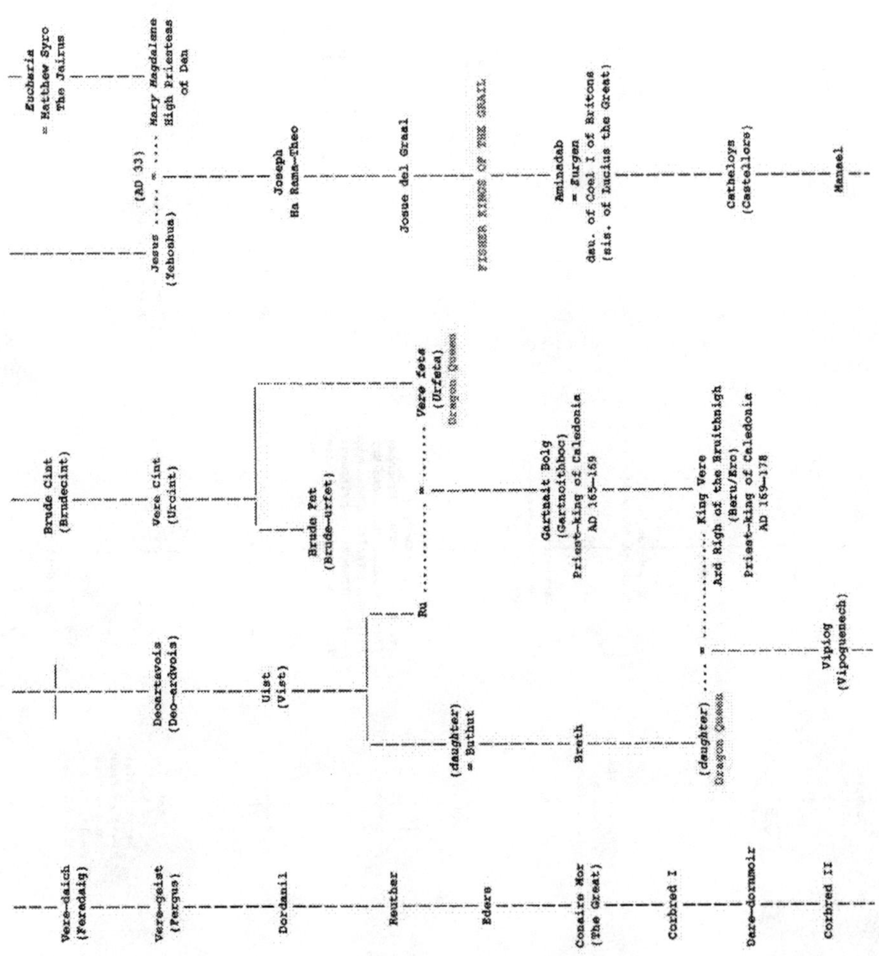
Vere-daich
(Feradaig)
Vere-geist
(Fergus)
Dordanil
Reuther
Eders
Conaire Mor
(The Great)
Corbred I
Dare-dornmoir
Corbred II
Deoartavois
(Deo-ardvois)
Uist
(Vist)
(daughter)
= Buthut
Breth
(daughter)
Dragon Queen
Vipiog
(Vipoguenech)
Brude Cint
(Brudecint)
Vere Cint
(Urcint)
Brude Fet
(Brude-urfet)
Ru
Vere feta
(Urfeta)
Dragon Queen
Gartnait Bolg
(Gartnoithboc)
Priest-king of Caledonia
AD 165–169
King Vere
Ard Righ of the Bruithnigh
(Beru/Erc)
Priest-king of Caledonia
AD 169–178
Eucharia
= Matthew Syro
The Jairus
(AD 33)
Jesus
(Yehoshua)
Mary Magdalene
High Priestess
of Dan
Joseph
Ha Rama-Theo
Josue del Graal
FISHER KINGS OF THE GRAIL
Aminadab
= Eurgen
dau. of Coel I of Britons
(sis. of Lucius the Great)
Catheloys
(Castellors)
Manael

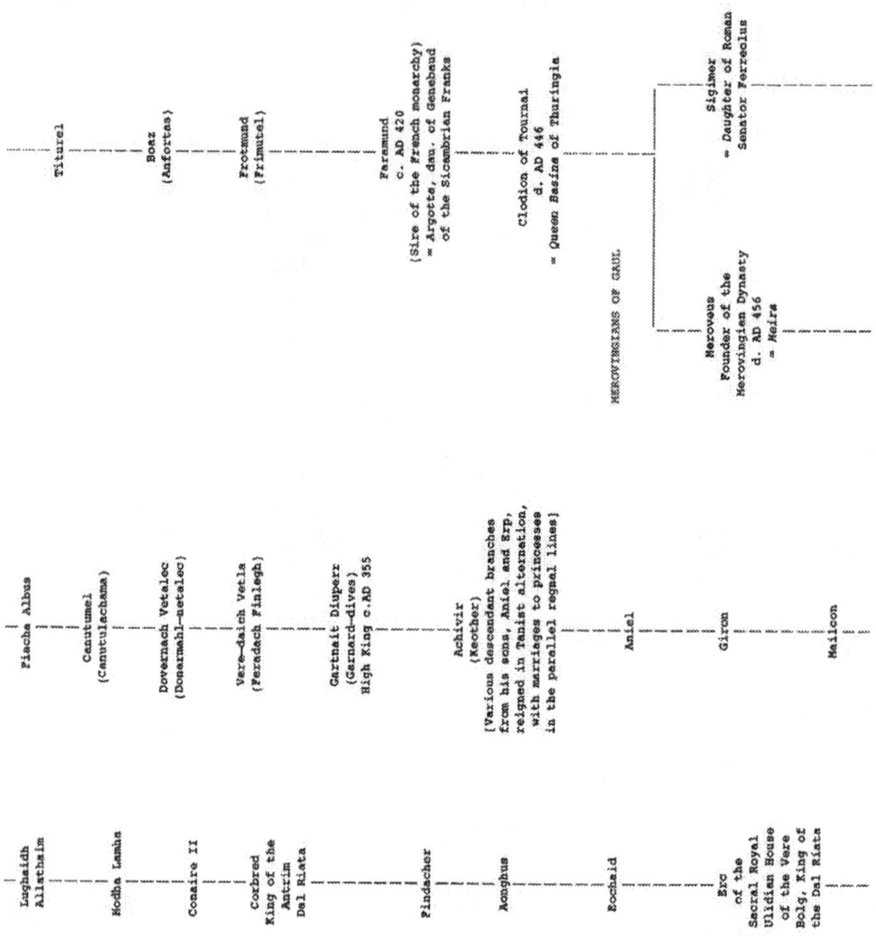
Titurel
Boaz
(Anfortas)
Frotmund
(Frimutel)
Faramund
c. AD 420
(Sire of the French monarchy)
= Argotta, dau. of Genebaud
of the Sicambrian Franks
Clodion of Tournai
d. AD 446
= Queen Basina of Thuringia
MEROVINGIANS OF GAUL
Meroveus
Founder of the
Merovingian Dynasty
d. AD 456
= Meira
Sigimer
= Daughter of Roman
Senator Ferreolus
Fiacha Albus
Canutumel
(Canutulachama)
Dovernach Vetalec
(Donermahl-metalec)
Vere-daich Vetla
(Feradach Finlegh)
Gartnait Diuperr
(Garnard-dives)
High King c.AD 355
Achivir
(Keother)
(Various descendant branches
from his sons, Aniel and Erp,
reigned in Tanist alternation,
with marriages to princesses
in the parallel regal lines)
Aniel
Giron
Mailcon
Lughaidh
Allathaim
Modha Lamha
Conaire II
Corbred
King of the
Antrim
Dal Riata
Findacher
Aonghus
Eochaid
Erc
of the
Secral Royal
Uldian House
of the Vere
Bolg, King of
the Dal Riata

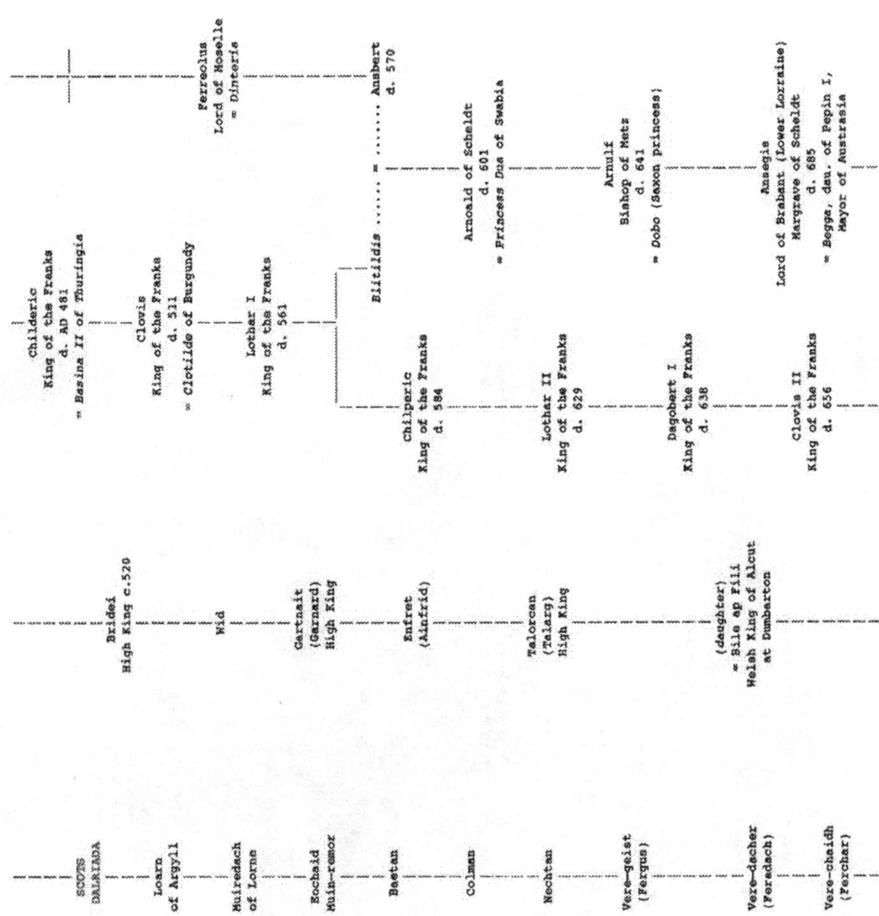
SCOTS
DALRIADA
Loarn
of Argyll
Muiredach
of Lorne
Eochaid
Muin-remor
Baetan
Colman
Nechtan
Vere-geist
(Fergus)
Vere-dacher
(Feradach)
Vere-chaidh
(Ferchar)
Bridei
High King c.520
Wid
Gartnait
(Garnard)
High King
Enfret
(Ainfrid)
Talorcan
(Talarg)
High King
(daughter)
= Bile ap Fili
Welsh King of Alcut
at Dumbarton
Childeric
King of the Franks
d. AD 481
= *Basina II of Thuringia*
Clovis
King of the Franks
d. 511
= *Clotilde* of Burgundy
Lothar I
King of the Franks
d. 561
Chilperic
King of the Franks
d. 584
Lothar II
King of the Franks
d. 629
Dagobert I
King of the Franks
d. 638
Clovis II
King of the Franks
d. 656
Ferreolus
Lord of Moselle
= *Dinteria*
Blitildis ...... = ... Ansbert
d. 570
Arnoald of Scheldt
d. 601
= *Princess Dua* of Swabia
Arnulf
Bishop of Metz
d. 641
= *Dobo* (Saxon princess)
Ansegis
Lord of Brabant (Lower Lorraine)
Margrave of Scheldt
d. 685
= *Begga*, dau. of Pepin I,
Mayor of Austrasia

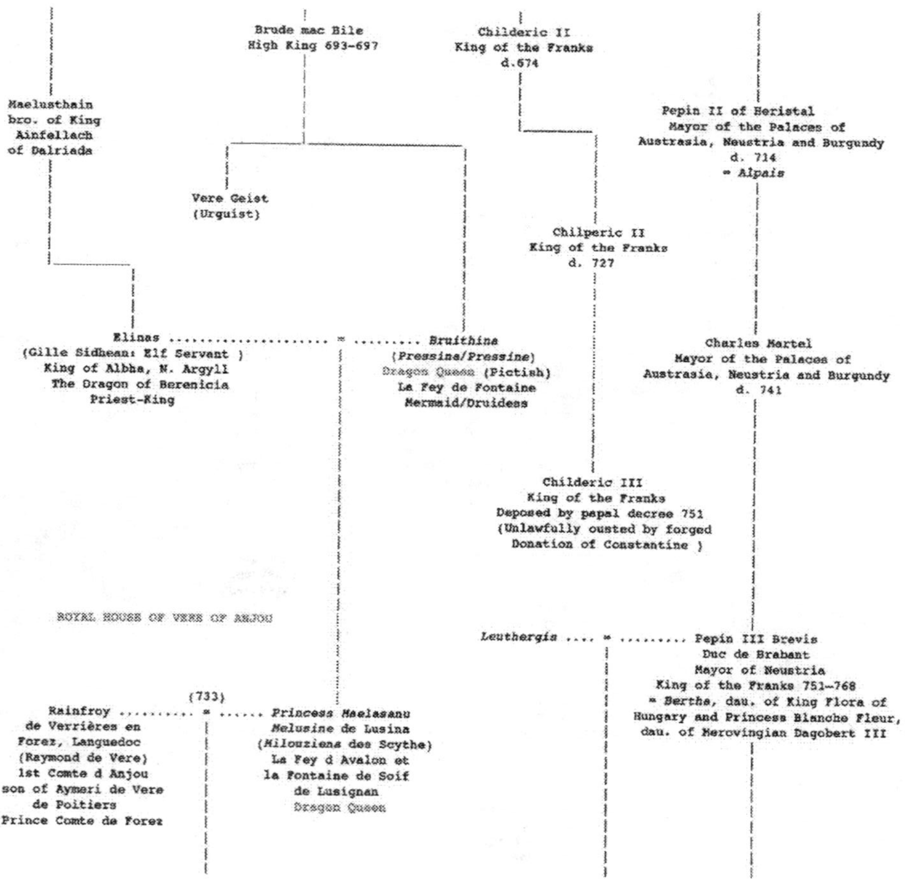
Maelusthain
bro. of King
Ainfellach
of Dalriada
Brude mac Bile
High King 693-697
Childeric II
King of the Franks
d.674
Pepin II of Heristal
Mayor of the Palaces of
Austrasia, Neustria and Burgundy
d. 714
= Alpais
Vere Geist
(Urguist)
Chilperic II
King of the Franks
d. 727
Elinas .... = ... Bruithine
(Gille Sidhean: Elf Servant)
King of Albha, N. Argyll
The Dragon of Berenicia
Priest-King
(Pressina/Pressine)
Dragon Queen (Pictish)
La Fey de Fontaine
Mermaid/Druidess
Charles Martel
Mayor of the Palaces of
Austrasia, Neustria and Burgundy
d. 741
Childeric III
King of the Franks
Deposed by papal decree 751
(Unlawfully ousted by forged
Donation of Constantine)
ROYAL HOUSE OF VERE OF ANJOU
Leuthergis .... = ... Pepin III Brevis
Duc de Brabant
Mayor of Neustria
King of the Franks 751-768
= Berthe, dau. of King Flora of
Hungary and Princess Blanche Fleur,
dau. of Merovingian Dagobert III
(733)
Rainfroy .... = ... Princess Maelasanu
de Verrières en
Forez, Languedoc
(Raymond de Vere)
1st Comte d Anjou
son of Aymeri de Vere
de Poitiers
Prince Comte de Forez
Melusine de Lusina
(Milouziena des Scythe)
La Fey d Avalon et
la Fontaine de Soif
de Lusignan
Dragon Queen

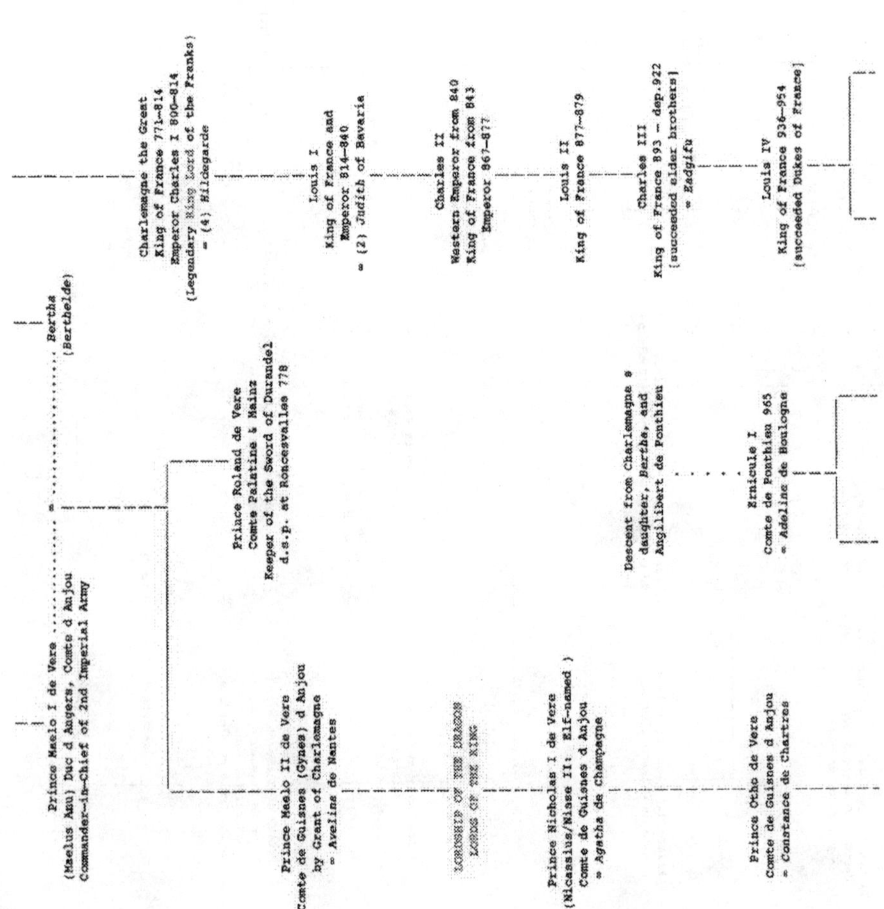
Prince Maelo I de Vere
(Maelus Anu) Duc d Angers, Comte d Anjou
Commander-in-Chief of 2nd Imperial Army
=
Bertha
(*Berthelde*)
Charlemagne the Great
King of France 771–814
Emperor Charles I 800–814
(Legendary King Lord of the Franks)
= (4) *Hildegarde*
Prince Roland de Vere
Comte Palatine & Mainz
Keeper of the Sword of Durandel
d.s.p. at Roncesvalles 778
Prince Maelo II de Vere
Comte de Guisnes (Gynes) d Anjou
by Grant of Charlemagne
= *Avelina* de Nantes
Louis I
King of France and
Emperor 814–840
= (2) *Judith* of Bavaria
LORDSHIP OF THE DRAGON
LORDS OF THE KING
Charles II
Western Emperor from 840
King of France from 843
Emperor 867–877
Prince Nicholas I de Vere
(Nicassius/Nisse II: Elf-named)
Comte de Guisnes d Anjou
= *Agatha* de Champagne
Louis II
King of France 877–879
Descent from Charlemagne s
daughter, *Bertha*, and
Angilibert de Ponthieu
Charles III
King of France 893 – dep.922
(succeeded elder brothers)
= *Eadgifu*
Prince Otho de Vere
Comte de Guisnes d Anjou
= *Constance* de Chartres
Ernicule I
Comte de Ponthieu 965
= *Adeline* de Boulogne
Louis IV
King of France 936–954
(succeeded Dukes of France)

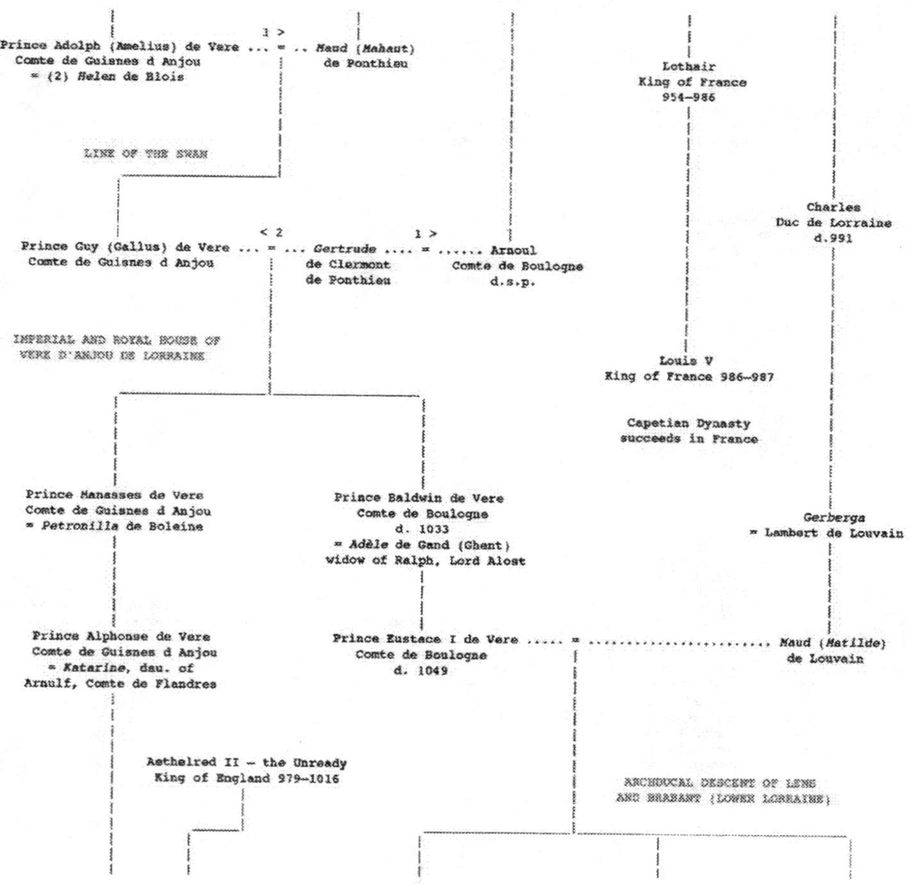
Prince Adolph (Amelius) de Vere ... = .. Maud (Mahaut) de Ponthieu
Comte de Guisnes d Anjou
= (2) Helen de Blois
1 >
LINE OF THE SWAN
Lothair
King of France
954–986
Charles
Duc de Lorraine
d.991
Prince Guy (Gallus) de Vere ... = ... Gertrude .... = ... Arnoul
< 2
1 >
Comte de Guisnes d Anjou
de Clermont
de Ponthieu
Comte de Boulogne
d.s.p.
IMPERIAL AND ROYAL HOUSE OF
VERE D'ANJOU DE LORRAINE
Louis V
King of France 986–987
Capetian Dynasty
succeeds in France
Prince Manasses de Vere
Comte de Guisnes d Anjou
= Petronilla de Boleine
Prince Baldwin de Vere
Comte de Boulogne
d. 1033
= Adèle de Gand (Ghent)
widow of Ralph, Lord Alost
Gerberga
= Lambert de Louvain
Prince Alphonse de Vere
Comte de Guisnes d Anjou
= Katarine, dau. of
Arnulf, Comte de Flandres
Prince Eustace I de Vere ..... = ... Maud (Matilde) de Louvain
Comte de Boulogne
d. 1049
Aethelred II – the Unready
King of England 979–1016
ARCHDUCAL DESCENT OF LENS
AND BRABANT (LOWER LORRAINE)

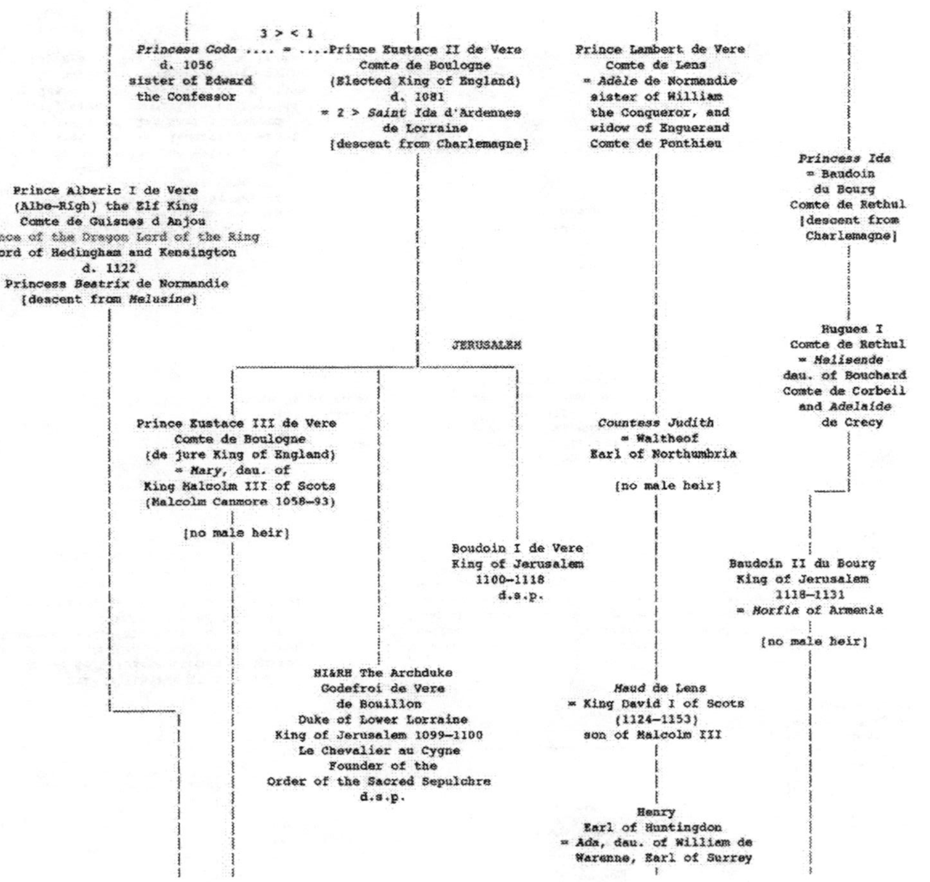
3 > < 1
Princess Goda .... = ...Prince Eustace II de Vere
Princess Goda
d. 1056
sister of Edward
the Confessor
Prince Eustace II de Vere
Comte de Boulogne
(Elected King of England)
d. 1081
= 2 > Saint Ida d'Ardennes
de Lorraine
[descent from Charlemagne]
Prince Lambert de Vere
Comte de Lens
= Adèle de Normandie
sister of William
the Conqueror, and
widow of Enguerand
Comte de Ponthieu
Princess Ida
= Baudoin
du Bourg
Comte de Rethul
[descent from
Charlemagne]
Prince Alberic I de Vere
(Albe-Righ) the Elf King
Comte de Guisnes d Anjou
Prince of the Dragon Lord of the Ring
Lord of Hedingham and Kensington
d. 1122
= Princess Beatrix de Normandie
[descent from Melusine]
JERUSALEM
Hugues I
Comte de Rethul
= Melisende
dau. of Bouchard
Comte de Corbeil
and Adelaide
de Crecy
Prince Eustace III de Vere
Comte de Boulogne
(de jure King of England)
= Mary, dau. of
King Malcolm III of Scots
(Malcolm Canmore 1058–93)
[no male heir]
Countess Judith
= Waltheof
Earl of Northumbria
[no male heir]
Boudoin I de Vere
King of Jerusalem
1100–1118
d.s.p.
Baudoin II du Bourg
King of Jerusalem
1118–1131
= Morfia of Armenia
[no male heir]
HI&RH The Archduke
Godefroi de Vere
de Bouillon
Duke of Lower Lorraine
King of Jerusalem 1099–1100
Le Chevalier au Cygne
Founder of the
Order of the Sacred Sepulchre
d.s.p.
Maud de Lens
= King David I of Scots
(1124–1153)
son of Malcolm III
Henry
Earl of Huntingdon
= Ada, dau. of William de
Warenne, Earl of Surrey

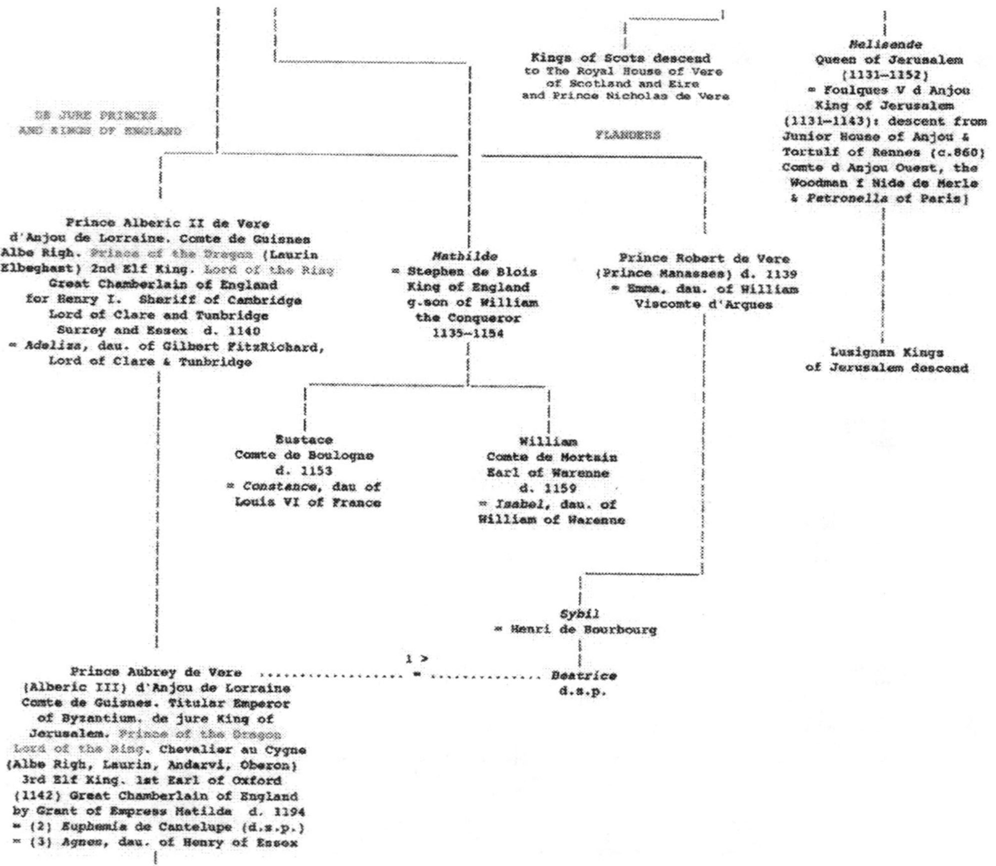

DE JURE PRINCES
AND KINGS OF ENGLAND
Kings of Scots descend
to The Royal House of Vere
of Scotland and Eire
and Prince Nicholas de Vere
FLANDERS
Melisende
Queen of Jerusalem
(1131–1152)
= Foulques V d Anjou
King of Jerusalem
(1131–1143): descent from
Junior House of Anjou &
Tortulf of Rennes (c.860)
Comte d Anjou Ouest, the
Woodman f Nide de Merle
& Petronella of Paris)
Prince Alberic II de Vere
d'Anjou de Lorraine. Comte de Guisnes
Albe Righ. Prince of the Dragon (Laurin
Elbeghast) 2nd Elf King. Lord of the Ring
Great Chamberlain of England
for Henry I. Sheriff of Cambridge
Lord of Clare and Tunbridge
Surrey and Essex d. 1140
= Adeliza, dau. of Gilbert FitzRichard,
Lord of Clare & Tunbridge
Mathilde
= Stephen de Blois
King of England
g.son of William
the Conqueror
1135–1154
Prince Robert de Vere
(Prince Manasses) d. 1139
= Emma, dau. of William
Viscomte d'Arques
Lusignan Kings
of Jerusalem descend
Eustace
Comte de Boulogne
d. 1153
= Constance, dau of
Louis VI of France
William
Comte de Mortain
Earl of Warenne
d. 1159
= Isabel, dau. of
William of Warenne
Sybil
= Henri de Bourbourg
1 >
=
Prince Aubrey de Vere
(Alberic III) d'Anjou de Lorraine
Comte de Guisnes. Titular Emperor
of Byzantium. de jure King of
Jerusalem. Prince of the Dragon
Lord of the Ring. Chevalier au Cygne
(Albe Righ, Laurin, Andarvi, Oberon)
3rd Elf King. 1st Earl of Oxford
(1142) Great Chamberlain of England
by Grant of Empress Matilda d. 1194
= (2) Euphemia de Cantelupe (d.s.p.)
= (3) Agnes, dau. of Henry of Essex
Beatrice
d.s.p.

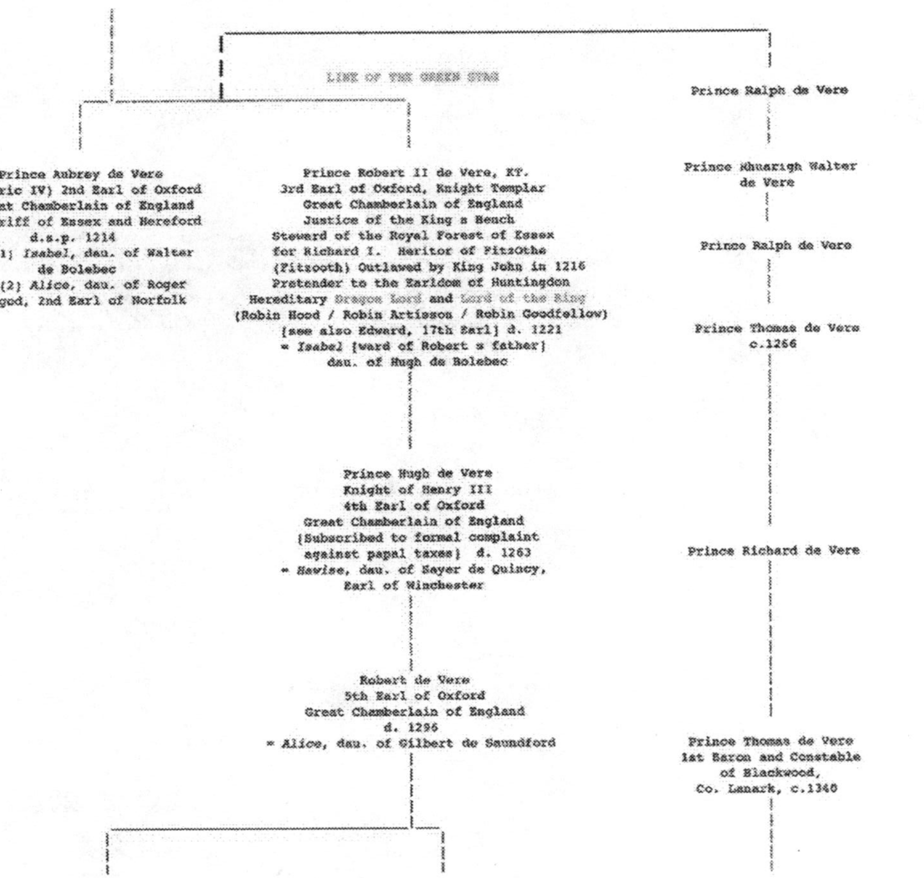
LINE OF THE GREEN STAR
Prince Aubrey de Vere
(Alberic IV) 2nd Earl of Oxford
Great Chamberlain of England
Sheriff of Essex and Hereford
d.s.p. 1214
= (1) Isabel, dau. of Walter
de Bolebec
= (2) Alice, dau. of Roger
Bugod, 2nd Earl of Norfolk
Prince Robert II de Vere, KT.
3rd Earl of Oxford, Knight Templar
Great Chamberlain of England
Justice of the King s Bench
Steward of the Royal Forest of Essex
for Richard I. Heritor of FitzOthe
(Fitzooth) Outlawed by King John in 1216
Pretender to the Earldom of Huntingdon
Hereditary Dragon Lord and Lord of the Ring
(Robin Hood / Robin Artisson / Robin Goodfellow)
[see also Edward, 17th Earl] d. 1221
= Isabel [ward of Robert s father]
dau. of Hugh de Bolebec
Prince Hugh de Vere
Knight of Henry III
4th Earl of Oxford
Great Chamberlain of England
(Subscribed to formal complaint
against papal taxes) d. 1263
= Hawise, dau. of Sayer de Quincy,
Earl of Winchester
Robert de Vere
5th Earl of Oxford
Great Chamberlain of England
d. 1296
= Alice, dau. of Gilbert de Saundford
Prince Ralph de Vere
Prince Khuarigh Walter
de Vere
Prince Ralph de Vere
Prince Thomas de Vere
c.1266
Prince Richard de Vere
Prince Thomas de Vere
1st Baron and Constable
of Blackwood,
Co. Lanark, c.1340

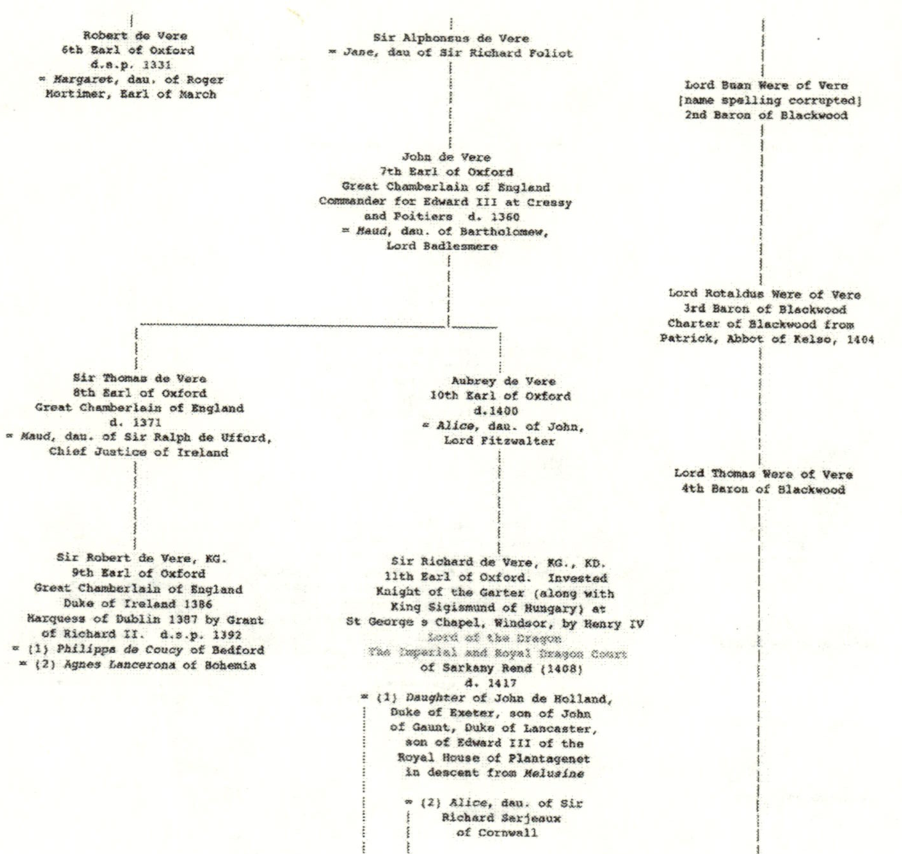
Robert de Vere
6th Earl of Oxford
d.s.p. 1331
= Margaret, dau. of Roger
Mortimer, Earl of March
Sir Alphonsus de Vere
= Jane, dau of Sir Richard Foliot
Lord Buan Were of Vere
[name spelling corrupted]
2nd Baron of Blackwood
John de Vere
7th Earl of Oxford
Great Chamberlain of England
Commander for Edward III at Cressy
and Poitiers d. 1360
= Maud, dau. of Bartholomew,
Lord Badlesmere
Lord Rotaldus Were of Vere
3rd Baron of Blackwood
Charter of Blackwood from
Patrick, Abbot of Kelso, 1404
Sir Thomas de Vere
8th Earl of Oxford
Great Chamberlain of England
d. 1371
= Maud, dau. of Sir Ralph de Ufford,
Chief Justice of Ireland
Aubrey de Vere
10th Earl of Oxford
d.1400
= Alice, dau. of John,
Lord Fitzwalter
Lord Thomas Were of Vere
4th Baron of Blackwood
Sir Robert de Vere, KG.
9th Earl of Oxford
Great Chamberlain of England
Duke of Ireland 1386
Marquess of Dublin 1387 by Grant
of Richard II. d.s.p. 1392
= (1) Philippa de Coucy of Bedford
= (2) Agnes Lancerona of Bohemia
Sir Richard de Vere, KG., KD.
11th Earl of Oxford. Invested
Knight of the Garter (along with
King Sigismund of Hungary) at
St George s Chapel, Windsor, by Henry IV
Lord of the Dragon
The Imperial and Royal Dragon Court
of Sarkany Rend (1408)
d. 1417
= (1) Daughter of John de Holland,
Duke of Exeter, son of John
of Gaunt, Duke of Lancaster,
son of Edward III of the
Royal House of Plantagenet
in descent from Melusine
= (2) Alice, dau. of Sir
Richard Sarjeaux
of Cornwall

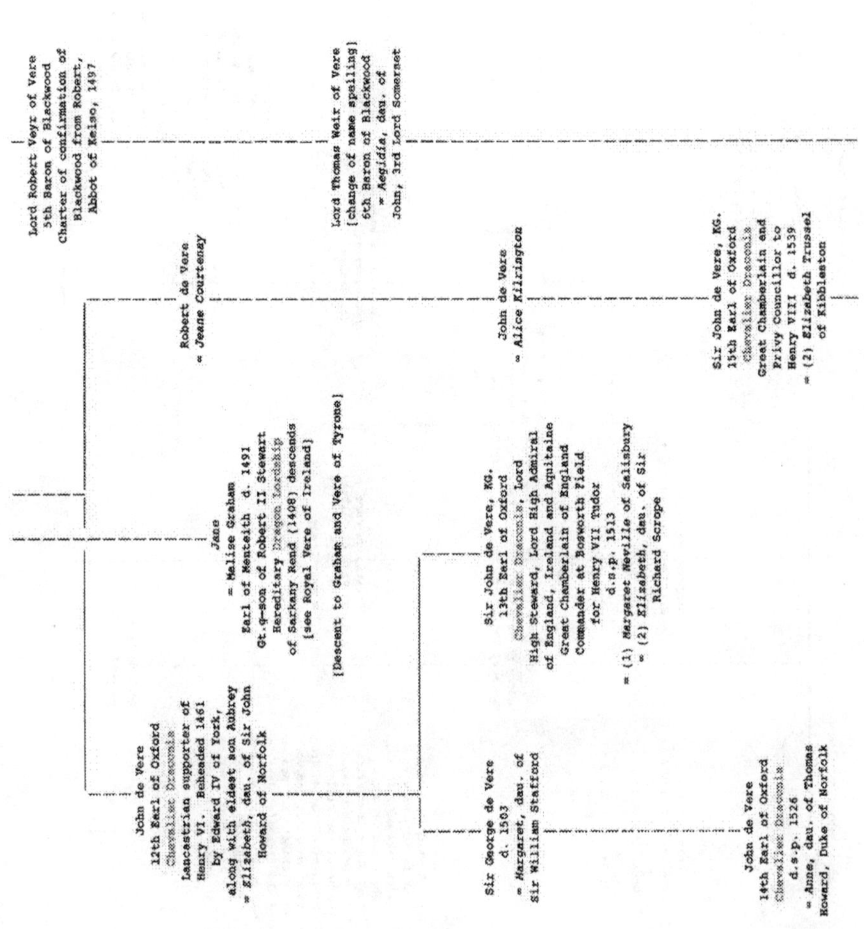
Lord Robert Veyr of Vere
5th Baron of Blackwood
Charter of confirmation of
Blackwood from Robert,
Abbot of Kelso, 1497
John de Vere
12th Earl of Oxford
Chevalier Draconis
Lancastrian supporter of
Henry VI. Beheaded 1461
by Edward IV of York,
along with eldest son Aubrey
= Elizabeth, dau. of Sir John
Howard of Norfolk
Jane
= Malise Graham
Earl of Menteith d. 1491
Gt.g-son of Robert II Stewart
Hereditary Dragon Lordship
of Sarkany Rend (1408) descends
[see Royal Vere of Ireland]
[Descent to Graham and Vere of Tyrone]
Robert de Vere
= Jeane Courtenay
Lord Thomas Weir of Vere
[change of name spelling]
6th Baron of Blackwood
= Aegidia, dau. of
John, 3rd Lord Somerset
Sir George de Vere
d. 1503
= Margaret, dau. of
Sir William Stafford
Sir John de Vere, KG.
13th Earl of Oxford
Chevalier Draconis, Lord
High Steward, Lord High Admiral
of England, Ireland and Aquitaine
Great Chamberlain of England
Commander at Bosworth Field
for Henry VII Tudor
d.s.p. 1513
= (1) Margaret Neville of Salisbury
= (2) Elizabeth, dau. of Sir
Richard Scrope
John de Vere
= Alice Kilrington
John de Vere
14th Earl of Oxford
Chevalier Draconis
d.s.p. 1526
= Anne, dau. of Thomas
Howard, Duke of Norfolk
Sir John de Vere, KG.
15th Earl of Oxford
Chevalier Draconis
Great Chamberlain and
Privy Councillor to
Henry VIII d. 1539
= (2) Elizabeth Trussel
of Kibbleston

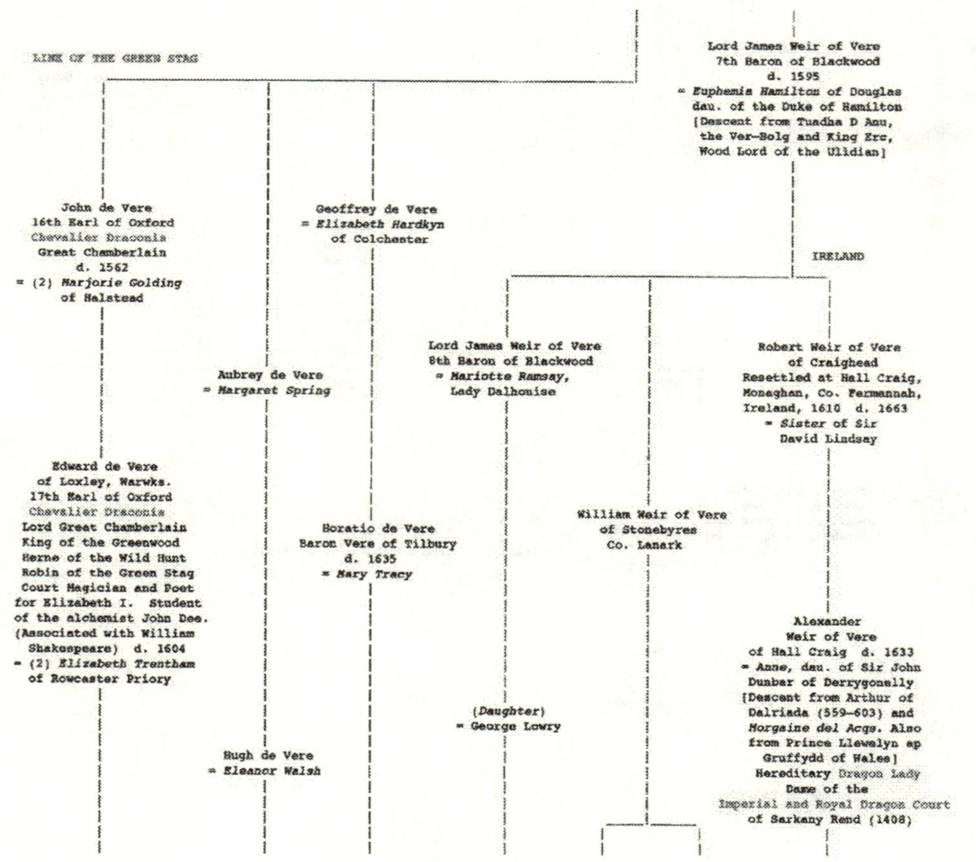
LINE OF THE GREEN STAG
Lord James Weir of Vere
7th Baron of Blackwood
d. 1595
= Euphemia Hamilton of Douglas
dau. of the Duke of Hamilton
[Descent from Tuadha D Anu,
the Ver-Bolg and King Erc,
Wood Lord of the Ulidian]
IRELAND
John de Vere
16th Earl of Oxford
Chevalier Draconis
Great Chamberlain
d. 1562
= (2) Marjorie Golding
of Halstead
Geoffrey de Vere
= Elizabeth Hardkyn
of Colchester
Aubrey de Vere
= Margaret Spring
Lord James Weir of Vere
8th Baron of Blackwood
= Mariotte Ramsay,
Lady Dalhouise
Robert Weir of Vere
of Craighead
Resettled at Hall Craig,
Monaghan, Co. Fermannah,
Ireland, 1610 d. 1663
= Sister of Sir
David Lindsay
Edward de Vere
of Loxley, Warwks.
17th Earl of Oxford
Chevalier Draconis
Lord Great Chamberlain
King of the Greenwood
Herne of the Wild Hunt
Robin of the Green Stag
Court Magician and Poet
for Elizabeth I. Student
of the alchemist John Dee.
(Associated with William
Shakespeare) d. 1604
= (2) Elizabeth Trentham
of Rowcaster Priory
Horatio de Vere
Baron Vere of Tilbury
d. 1635
= Mary Tracy
William Weir of Vere
of Stonebyres
Co. Lanark
Alexander
Weir of Vere
of Hall Craig d. 1633
= Anne, dau. of Sir John
Dunbar of Derrygonelly
[Descent from Arthur of
Dalriada (559-603) and
Morgaine del Acqs. Also
from Prince Llewelyn ap
Gruffydd of Wales]
Hereditary Dragon Lady
Dame of the
Imperial and Royal Dragon Court
of Sarkany Rend (1408)
(Daughter)
= George Lowry
Hugh de Vere
= Eleanor Walsh

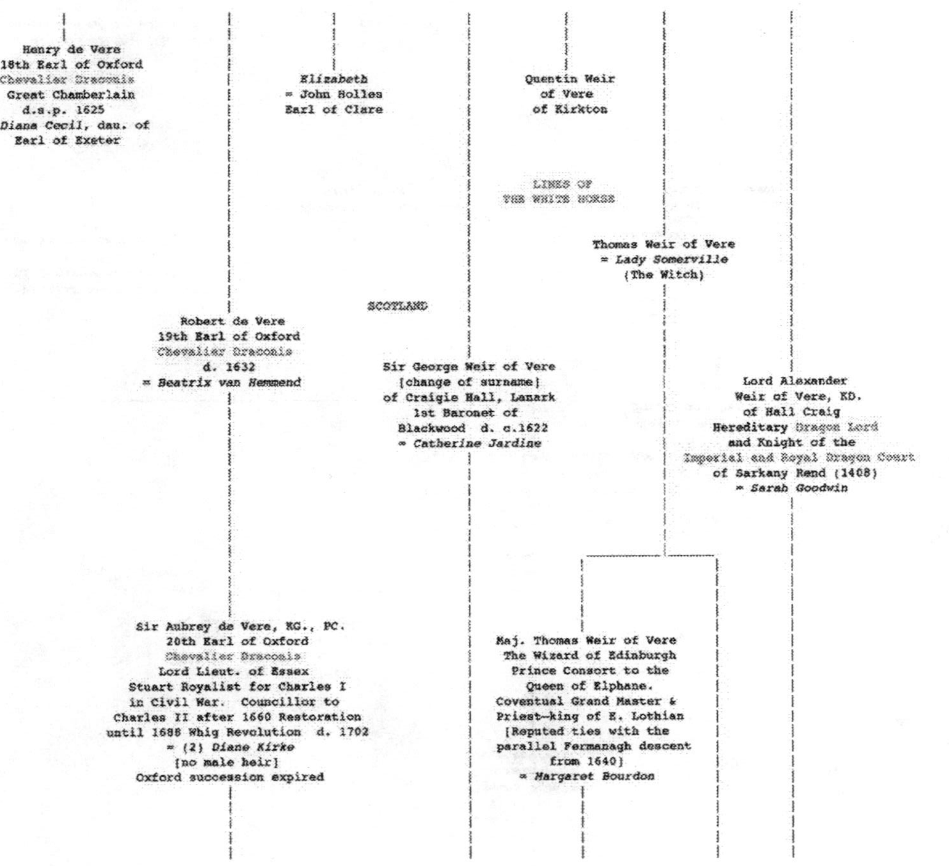
Henry de Vere
18th Earl of Oxford
Chevalier Draconis
Great Chamberlain
d.s.p. 1625
= Diana Cecil, dau. of
Earl of Exeter
Elizabeth
= John Holles
Earl of Clare
Quentin Weir
of Vere
of Kirkton
LINES OF
THE WHITE HORSE
Thomas Weir of Vere
= Lady Somerville
(The Witch)
SCOTLAND
Robert de Vere
19th Earl of Oxford
Chevalier Draconis
d. 1632
= Beatrix van Hemmend
Sir George Weir of Vere
[change of surname]
of Craigie Hall, Lanark
1st Baronet of
Blackwood d. c.1622
= Catherine Jardine
Lord Alexander
Weir of Vere, KD.
of Hall Craig
Hereditary Dragon Lord
and Knight of the
Imperial and Royal Dragon Court
of Sarkany Rend (1408)
= Sarah Goodwin
Sir Aubrey de Vere, KG., PC.
20th Earl of Oxford
Chevalier Draconis
Lord Lieut. of Essex
Stuart Royalist for Charles I
in Civil War. Councillor to
Charles II after 1660 Restoration
until 1688 Whig Revolution d. 1702
= (2) Diane Kirke
[no male heir]
Oxford succession expired
Maj. Thomas Weir of Vere
The Wizard of Edinburgh
Prince Consort to the
Queen of Elphane.
Coventual Grand Master &
Priest-king of E. Lothian
[Reputed ties with the
parallel Fermanagh descent
from 1640]
= Margaret Bourdon

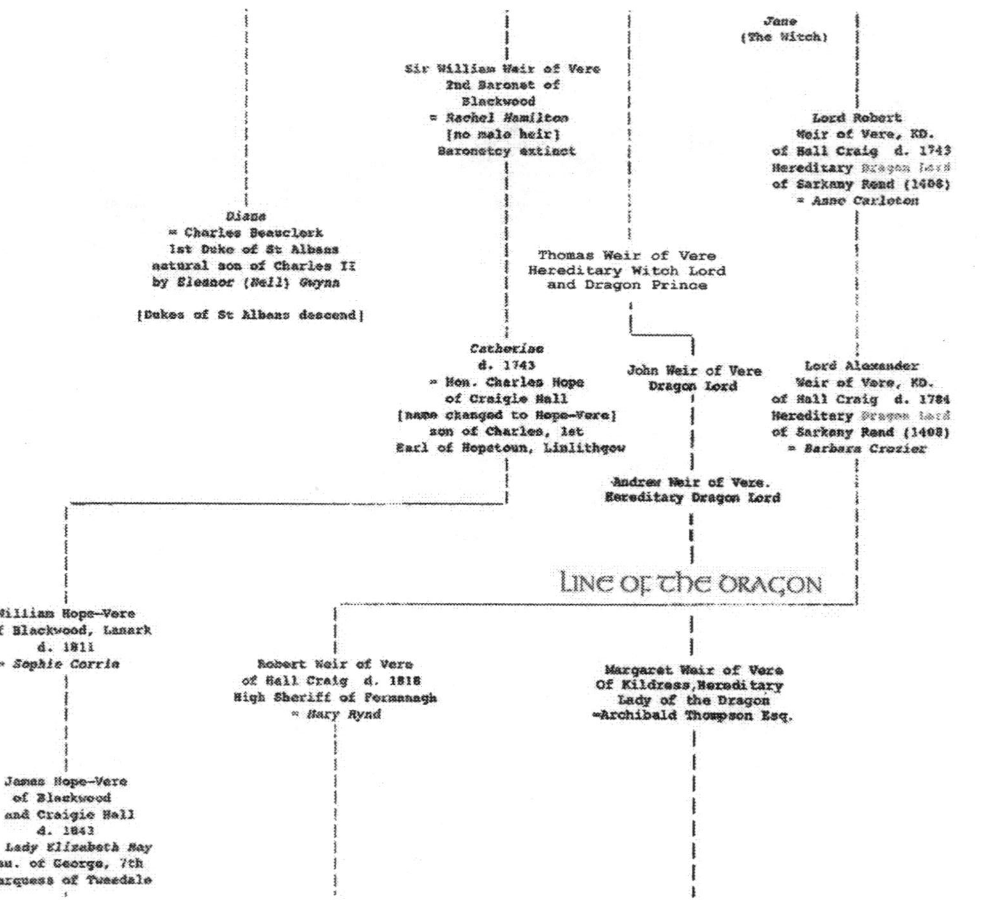
Jane
(The Witch)
Lord Robert
Weir of Vere, KD.
of Hall Craig d. 1743
Hereditary Dragon Lord
of Sarkany Rend (1408)
= Anne Carleton
Sir William Weir of Vere
2nd Baronet of
Blackwood
= Rachel Hamilton
[no male heir]
Baronetcy extinct
Diana
= Charles Beauclerk
1st Duke of St Albans
natural son of Charles II
by Eleanor (Nell) Gwynn
[Dukes of St Albans descend]
Thomas Weir of Vere
Hereditary Witch Lord
and Dragon Prince
Catherine
d. 1743
= Hon. Charles Hope
of Craigie Hall
[name changed to Hope-Vere]
son of Charles, 1st
Earl of Hopetoun, Linlithgow
John Weir of Vere
Dragon Lord
Lord Alexander
Weir of Vere, KD.
of Hall Craig d. 1784
Hereditary Dragon Lord
of Sarkany Rend (1408)
= Barbara Crozier
Andrew Weir of Vere.
Hereditary Dragon Lord
LINE OF THE DRAGON
William Hope-Vere
of Blackwood, Lanark
d. 1811
= Sophie Corrie
Robert Weir of Vere
of Hall Craig d. 1818
High Sheriff of Fermanagh
= Mary Rynd
Margaret Weir of Vere
Of Kildress, Hereditary
Lady of the Dragon
=Archibald Thompson Esq.
James Hope-Vere
of Blackwood
and Craigie Hall
d. 1843
= Lady Elizabeth Hay
dau. of George, 7th
Marquess of Tweedale

Bri. William Hope–Vere
of Blackwood
and Craigie Hall
d. 1872
= *Lady Mary Boyle*
dau. of Viscount
Dungarvan, and sister
of Earl of Cork

James Hope–Vere
of Blackwood
and Craigie Hall
d. 1933
= (2) *Countess Marie*
Elizabeth Francoise
dau. of Auguste
Guillemin, and g–dau.
of Duc de Montebello

Descent from Royal
Collison of Norfolk...

Ralph Hope–Vere, O.B.E.
of Blackwood
[2nd son] d. 1959
= *Esme Crabbe*
of Duncow

John Weir of Vere
= *Caroline Chomley*
of Belcamp, Co Dublin

Rev. John Weir of Vere
1825–1896
[Hall Craig vacated]
= *Clara Sadler*

Octavius Weir of Vere
1870–1934
= *Flora Collison*

Terence Collison Weir of Vere
b. 1898
= *Rosamund*, dau. of Major
William Gibson of Roserea

Archibald Weir of Vere, KD.
b. 1792
Hereditary Dragon Lord
of Sarkany Rend (1408)
= *Rachel Stewart*

Robert Weir of Vere, KD.
1828–1880
Hereditary Dragon Lord
of Sarkany Rend (1408)
= *Sarah Graham* of Tyrone

John Weir of Vere, KD.
1854–1925
Hereditary Dragon Lord
of Sarkany Rend (1408)
= *Mary Logan* of Stranraer

Thomas Weir of Vere, KD.
1880–1954
Hereditary Dragon Lord
of Sarkany Rend (1408)
= *Anne Grant McDonnell*
of Inverness

Extracted from the archives of the Royal House of Vere

Appendix 4

Structure of Dragon Court and Dragon Society

Sovereign
Nicholas de Vere

Chancellor	**Grand Master**	**Dragon King of Arms**
Martin Lunn	Renee Drakenberg	Michael Hunter

The Dragon Society
Prince Grand Master
Martin Lunn

Membership

FLYING SERPENTS AND DRAGONS: The Story of Mankind's Reptilian Past, by R.A. Boulay. A highly original work that deals a shattering blow to all our preconceived notions about our past and human origins. Worldwide legends refer to giant flying lizards and dragons that came to this planet and founded the ancient civilizations of Mesopotamia, Egypt, India and China. Who were these reptilian creatures? What was the real reason for man's creation? Why did Adam lose his chance at immortality in the Garden of Eden? Who were the Nefilim who descended from heaven and mated with human women? Why did the serpent take such a bum rap in history? Why didn't Adam and Eve wear clothes? What were the "crystals" or "stones" that the gods fought over? Why did the ancient Sumerians call their major gods USHUMGAL, which means literally "great fiery, flying serpent?" What was the role of the gigantic stone platform at Baalbek? What were the "boats of heaven" in ancient Egypt and the "sky chariots" of the Bible? **BT-388 • ISBN 1-885395-38-8 • 276 pages • 6 x 9 • perfect bound • illustrated • $19.95**

ANCIENT SYMBOL WORSHIP: The Influence of the Phallic Idea in the Religions of Antiquity, by Hodder M. Westropp and C. Staniland Wake. Sex worship has been practiced by cultures throughout the world for thousands of years. This book explores the origins of phallic worship, its influence on the religions of antiquity, serpent symbolism, the tree of knowledge, the "fall of man," and sun-god worship in antiquity. This work contains important knowledge that would otherwise not be known today. **BT-484 • ISBN 1-58509-048-4 • 120 pages • 6 x 9 • perfect bound • illustrated • $12.95**

HIGHLIGHTS OF TEMPLAR HISTORY: Includes the Knights Templar Constitution and Abbrev-iated By-Laws, by William Moseley Brown. The Knights Templar is a secret society that has existed for many centuries. Few books have been written about them from an insiders point of view. This book was originally released by the Grand Encampment of Knights Templar, United States of America, after seven years of historical research by an assigned committee. The author, Brown, was a member of that committee and their purpose was to provide Templars with an accurate history of their organization. It was for members only and much of the information is not found elsewhere. We've also added, from another source, their Constitution and Abbreviated By-Laws, as a service for potential members or for those who desire a better knowledge of the inner workings of the Templars. These two works, combined together, will hopefully shed new light on an interesting and sometimes mysterious organization. **BT-304 • ISBN 1-58509-230-4 • 136 pages • 6 X 9 • $13.95**

CPSIA information can be obtained
at www.ICGtesting.com
Printed in the USA
BVHW051932161122
652107BV00001B/68

9 781585 091317